For Geraldine Watkins
With love

Foreword

It is not often that an author gets the opportunity to revise a published novel, though most of us would probably like to be given the chance to reconsider work written years before. Such good fortune came to me when Granada wanted to reprint the trilogy of books we are now calling *The Enchantress Saga*, previously published by Macdonald/Futura under my other pseudonym of Katherine Yorke.

Katherine Yorke is not defunct, but she now largely writes modern novels. On the other hand Nicola Thorne, who used mostly to write modern novels, now tends to write historical ones. Thus *The Enchantress Saga* fitted very well into this growing list of long historical novels of which *The Daughters of the House* was the first.

The story of Analee the gypsy who becomes a marchioness, an intimate of the Royal families of France and England, has always been one of my favourite creations, and I was delighted when Granada asked me to look at it again and possibly revise it for a one volume edition. It has no 'message'; it is not very profound but it is, I think, full of fun, adventure, intrigue, and, because I have a passion for historical accuracy, I always try my very best to ensure that the historical people and occasions presented in my books are as accurate as I can make them. Thus in addition to a host of fictional characters we also meet Bonnie Prince Charlie, Louis XV and the Pompadour, George II of England, various members of his court and the sad Princess of Wales, Augusta, whose husband's death deprived her of the chance of ever becoming Queen of England.

The books have been revised, cut – I think to their benefit – and are offered here in one volume, for the enjoyment, I hope, of all my readers.

Nicola Thorne

Contents

BOOK I

The Enchantress
1744–1746

Author's Note

In the eighteenth century, when this book is set, many places in what we now call the English Lake District had different names, or the spelling was different. I have used modern names throughout so that the areas in which the action takes place may be more familiar to the modern reader.

In the spelling of the various gypsy words I have used the translation by Charles Duff of Jean-Paul Clébert's classic book *The Gypsies* (London 1963). I am also indebted to this book as well as E. B. Trigg's *Gypsy Demons and Divinities* (London, 1975) for much of my information about the gypsy people.

I consulted many books on the English Lake District and the Rebellion of 1745, but I am especially grateful to David Daiches whose *Charles Edward Stewart: the life and times of Bonnie Prince Charlie* (London, 1973) was constantly by my side.

N.T.

1

Where she came from no one knew; no one asked; few cared. In the huge roving community of drovers, pedlars, tinkers, whores, gypsies, pick-pockets, horse thieves and honest traders that descended on the Cumbrian town of Appleby for the June Fair in the year 1744 she was scarcely noticed.

But some there were who did notice her and ask themselves questions. The men who followed her progress through the town – surreptitiously, if their wives were watching, or with open admiration if they were not – could not help but appreciate her beauty beneath the pallor; the graceful dignity with which she walked, even though her feet were bare; the proud tilt of her head, the fierce defiance in the eyes of one who has learned to protect herself.

The women, those who noticed her, pitied her for her air of extreme weariness, her slow tired pace, the sloped shoulders, the tattered clothes she wore and the picture of poverty and loneliness that she presented.

Everyone came to the June Fair in Appleby; everyone that is who had to do with horses, cattle, sheep or chickens or who had farm produce or home-made goods to sell. Those who wanted to buy or exchange came, and those who wanted to hire servants or be themselves hired for the farms or great houses. They came in vast numbers from across the border with Scotland; they came from all parts of Cumberland and Westmorland; some even came from as far south as Preston or as far east as York.

But few came from the real south. It was a long way. Even by horse or carriage it was a journey of many days. On foot it would take weeks. And those who did notice or speak to the girl agreed on one thing: she came from the south; she was not one of them. But she said few words as she walked with her bundle in her hand, stopping occasionally to admire some glass beads or metal jewel-work displayed on many of the stalls in the market place, her fine eyes glinting as though in imagination she could see herself adorned in such finery. Or her fingers would tentatively feel the satins and silks, the brocades and soft cloth, her face alight at the vision of herself such richness conjured up.

But no one tried to sell her anything because it was so obvious she could not pay; and the men smiled and winked at her or made some coarse gesture, or promised her a bauble or a yard of cloth for a certain favour she might give them, while the women told her to be off so that she should not spoil the view of those who could afford to buy.

Finally, as though instinctively seeking home, she came to the tents that stood a little apart from the town where the gypsy folk set up their camp . . . those wanderers of the road who spent the year going from one fair to the next. The tents and carts clustered around smoking fires, and in the late afternoon the enticing odour of wood smoke and roasting meat filled the air.

The town of Appleby lay in the broad valley between the range of Pennine mountains in the east and the hills of lakeland to the west. She had followed the jagged line of the Pennines in her journey north knowing that they led from Derbyshire to the Cheviot Hills that formed the border with Scotland; that they would lead her away from all that she was fleeing from, the hateful memories and painful regrets of her past life.

Boroughgate, the steep main street of Appleby, led to the huge red stone castle built in the time of the Normans. At the bottom a bridge crossed the river Eden and, asking her way, the girl had trudged wearily up the bank towards the gypsies' field. Ahead of her, almost obscured in the hazy mist of late afternoon, were the Pennines which had guided her and knowing they were still near, in sight, comforted her. They seemed to offer both a consolation and a way of escape if she needed it. But now she was hungry and tired and at last she stopped by a fire on which stood a huge iron cauldron, and her nostrils twitched as though she were already eating the savoury fare.

'Eh the lass is hungry; give her sommat t'eat.'

The family sitting round the fire, huge bowls on their laps, looked up at the words of the speaker, first at him and then at the hungry girl.

'Wilt eat lass?' the big man said, moving up as though to make a place for her.

The girl smiled with the timorousness of one who is not frequently offered kindness.

'Aye, if it pleases you.'

'Margaret, give her a bowl and some of this good stew. Lass sit thee down.'

Everyone wriggled to make way for her and crossly the woman got up and ladled into the bowl a measure of stew, muttering bad-temperedly to herself.

'More, Margaret, more,' the man said authoritatively. 'This one looks as though she's not eaten for days.'

Yes, she was very thin, he noticed, and hollow-eyed as though she hadn't slept much either; but the meagreness of her clothes seemed to emphasize the contours of her young body, the firm swell of her fine young breasts. His eyes gleamed appreciatively – for Brewster Driver was not primarily an altruist and it is doubtful whether a less well endowed girl would have been offered as much as a bone.

The girl saw his expression – it was one she often saw in men – but she was not in a position to make conditions so she sat down next to him, smiling her thanks.

'You're very kind; very kind,' she said, taking the bowl from the woman and hungrily stuffing great chunks of mutton into her mouth. The man watched her.

'And from the south I reckon?'

'Aye,' between mouthfuls.

''Tis a long journey.'

'A very long one.'

The man continued to look at her and saw how she wolfed her food and didn't stop eating until it was all gone. Then she wiped the bowl clean with her fingers and licked them carefully one by one. Brewster Driver laughed.

'Giver her some more Margaret, she's famished!'

'Nay,' the girl said quickly. 'I've had enough, thank you.'

She could see that the careworn wife was not best pleased at having to feed a stranger with scarce victuals, and she knew how women disliked her anyway, particularly when the lecherous look in their husbands' eyes was clear for anyone to see.

'Now some ale,' Brewster said. 'Alan, give her some porter.'

A tall youth, like the man in looks only beardless, got up and poured ale from an earthenware jug into a pot which he handed to the girl as reluctantly as his mother had ladled the food.

'Thirsty too, I see,' Brewster said.

'Yes,' she wiped her mouth on her arm and handed back the pot. 'Thank you, thank you very much.'

The girl glanced round at the faces gazing at her sullenly. She had the picture quite clear in her mind; it was so familiar. The lecherous, ill-tempered, heavy drinking father who burdened his wife with too many children and never made enough money to feed them. They all resented her; the children because she had eaten some of their food and the wife because she knew that all he wanted was to bed her.

Brewster got up, a huge man in shirt and breeches, the latter secured at the waist by a broad leather belt. From his pocket he drew a long clay pipe into which he carefully pressed tobacco from a leather pouch which hung on his belt. He lit the pipe with a spill taken from the fire and gazed thoughtfully at the girl through the smoke issuing from his mouth.

'How do they call thee lass?'

'I am called Analee.'

'Gypsy stock, like us?'

'Aye.'

'Not that I'd have thought otherwise with thy dark hair and black eyes . . .'

Margaret, thin faced and haggard of body, made an exclamation of annoyance and got to her feet clattering the dishes.

'Black eyes indeed!' she muttered.

'Now Margaret,' roared Brewster in a voice that instantly cowed his wife. 'Let us have none of thy jealous spite. This girl is young enough to be my daughter. See here Analee,' he pointed proudly around the fire, 'there you see my fine sons Alan, Roger and John and my daughter Nelly who will be about your age, eighteen she is; and my Jane who is thirteen, and the little ones playing over yonder, Peter, Agnes and Toby. Driver's the name.'

He gazed fondly at his brood, momentarily the family man pleased with his achievment.

'You're very kind, Mr Driver, to share your food . . .'

'And wi' so many mouths to feed an' all,' grumbled Margaret; but Analee thought, or imagined, that the young-old face of the wife had grown softer, the voice less harsh. Maybe she resented at first the generous impulses of her husband, or the reason for them, but relented after a while.

Analee, invigorated by the rest and the food, got agilely to her feet.

'I must go . . .'

'Whither lass?' Brewster's eyes were speculative. Analee avoided them.

'I must go on, from one place to the next.'

'And how dost live?'

'By a little of this, a little of that,' she replied flinging back her head and gazing at him with that look which was meant to be defiance, but which men found so attractive. 'On kindness such as yours in the big towns, from berries and nuts in the woods through which I pass; from the clear water in the streams. And then when I can I work. I can gut a rabbit or hare, aye and trap them too, wring a chicken's neck or spear a fish. I can cook them, and also clean and scrub and make baskets of wicker, I can . . .'

'Cans't ride a horse?'

'Aye, very well. I was brought up on the back of a horse.' Brewster's eyes glinted. 'Maybe I can give you some work.'

'Here?'

Analee had a familiar feeling as to what the work would entail, and yet his tone was businesslike.

'Aye. Appleby is famous for its horse fair; everyone comes to buy and exchange. A few days work with food and a pallet on the floor. Eh?' Brewster was looking at her hard, calloused feet; between the toes brown, congealed blood. 'Not so much wear on your feet, maybe. What say?'

Analee followed his gaze and looked at her feet – as brown as leather and almost as hard from walking. She pushed her hair back from her forehead and gave a deep sigh.

'But where are your horses?'

'Ah,' Brewster said with a cunning look, lowering his voice, 'we have to find them.'

It was not the first night that Brent Delamain had kept watch by the side of his dying grandfather. Since he had been so hastily summoned home from Cambridge he had taken turns with his mother, his sister and his elder brother to see the old man through the night.

But Sir Francis Delamain was stubborn, a fighter. He had been long in the world and he was reluctant to leave it. His still bright blue eyes gazed unseeingly at the wall, but his chest rose rhythmically though his breathing was harsh.

A solitary candle guttered in its holder as Brent sat staring at the old man and pondering his own future. The death of his grandfather would make a vast different to his life, all their lives. George was the heir. George who had been groomed since childhood to succeed to the vast Delamain estates. George, the good one, the sober, clever, industrious one, the obedient one . . . whereas Brent. Well, everyone thought that Brent was a disappointment.

Brent's stay at Cambridge was considered to be a passing visit. All the Delamain sons went to Cambridge, it was a tradition. But how long they stayed depended on their scholastic ability, and everyone knew that Brent had none.

Brent had a fine record as a boxer, a rider, a hunter and a fighter. But where did that get a man? Especially a younger son who seemed to have no aptitude for anything except chasing women and killing foxes, and losing money he hadn't got at cards. It was even rumoured that Brent had fought a duel because there was a long thin scar on his cheek which he swore he had got merely fencing.

Sir Francis Delamain who had increased the family fortune, already considerable when he inherited it, three-fold by his thrift, financial acumen and industry, had no time at all for Brent. His charm may have worked on a lot of people, but it didn't impress his grandfather. Old Sir Francis was a canny northerner, and he couldn't abide to see people idle or wasting money. Brent showed no interest in the land, except for hunting over it, or the army or navy in which his grandfather would gladly have purchased him a commission. He had no appreciation of how to acquire money, or even how to keep what little he was given. He had certainly no aptitude for the study of the classics or history. What was to become of Brent, no one knew.

Now George, his brother . . . why there was a fine fellow of a man. Keen, industrious, a good scholar and what was more, he had given up the great chances he had to shine in London, in politics or the university, to help his grandfather run his estates. And what a success he had made of that! How quickly he had mastered the arts of animal husbandry, forestry, and estate management.

No, George was like his grandfather, a true Delamain, and Brent was too like his father Guy, another reckless ne'er do well who had carelessly thrown his life away for the Stuart cause, leaving Francis to care for his wife and children and bear the shame, into the bargain, of having a son who was disloyal to the lawful government of England.

Brent knew all this and more as he gazed at the withered face of a man he had respected and feared but never loved. When he was dead George would have all. Though he did not fear him, Brent neither liked nor respected his brother. Where would Brent fit in when his grandfather finally breathed his last? Nowhere.

The candle flickered and went out. Brent cursed and got to his feet. It was a cold night for June and he went to shut the window that he had opened to try and get rid of the stench of death, before finding a tinder to relight the candle. From the window of his grandfather's room he looked down on the courtyard, across the outbuildings with the stables and the bakehouse, onto the meadows stretching as far as the river which gleamed like a ribbon of silver in the moonlight.

The whole of the Delamain estate, or what he could see of it from here, was bathed in clear, golden light and Brent thought how beautiful it was, how dear to him, and how much he would miss it when, as was inevitable after his grandfather's death, he would have to go. For George had made it clear that he thought it was time he got married, and that when he did his family would have to make room for the huge number of new Delamains that he intended to breed. Mother was to go to the dower house in the grounds with their sister Emma; the middle brother Tom was a monk at Douai and safely out of the way, and Brent . . . well it was time he found gainful employment, anyway, George made clear, and now was no concern of his.

Suddenly Brent stiffened, seeing a movement by the trees which began the Forest of Delamain at the end of the water meadow, the great forest – one of few in a mainly agricultural area – that stretched almost as far as Penrith on one side and Appleby on the other. Maybe it was the moon playing tricks, the shadow of a branch waving in the breeze. Brent peered out again, just to be sure. No, he had been right – it was a distinct, stealthy human movement; not a movement of the horses in the paddock there . . . and suddenly it was joined by another. There were two! There were at least two people in the meadow by the river, maybe more. By the height of the moon Brent knew it to be well after midnight, and all the castle servants long in their beds.

Brent opened the door and ran silently along the stone corridor to his mother's room. Always alert, as anxious for her son and their future as well as he, she rose as soon as the door opened and hurriedly put on her robe.

'Your grandfather?' she called abruptly.

'No, mother, he is still alive; nothing further ails him. But hurry. I want you by his side. I have seen strange movements by the river.'

'Movements!' his mother grasped his arm – the arm of this dearest, most favourite son.

'Horse thieves, mother, if you ask me. They're from the fair at Appleby I doubt not. I told George that he should lock his new yearlings up and not have them loose in the field, but of course George knows everything and I nothing. First rouse the servants for me, mother, and George and I will hasten down before they escape with all the stock.'

'Oh, Brent . . .' eyes full of love followed him. So gentle and gallant and like his father; so warm and passionate, such a good friend. If only Brent had been born first instead of George . . . 'Take care,' she didn't want to let him go, 'they might have weapons.'

'Mother, I'll take care; that's one thing I can do. Even George says that.' And he kissed her lightly on the cheek, squeezed her arm and sped down the steps of the great majestic staircase that led into the long gallery. The moonlight was bright enough to show the way, though Brent could have found it blindfold in this beloved place. Every inch of Delamain Castle was dear and familiar to him.

He strode through the kitchens, the cockroaches scurrying away from him on the stone floor, and let himself through an outhouse into the yard where he paused and listened, his nose sniffing the air for the scent of disturbance. Brent was a countryman and knew you could smell danger before you could see it. But no, the air told him nothing. Had it, after all, been merely shadows?

Quickly he ran across the yard to the stables. Ah, yes. Here he did sense danger; he could hear the sounds of restlessness within, a few snorts and whinnies. But it would not be the thoroughbreds, the hunting mares, that the thieves would be after. It would be the young yearlings in the field, half-tamed, unshown, unknown.

Brent listened for sounds from the castle that George and the servants had stirred; but there was nothing. He would have to act himself. He grasped a stout staff that stood against a shed and opened the door of the stall of his own stallion Marcus, who had brought him home only the week before. He made a gentle familiar noise so that Marcus should recognize him and not alert the thieves on this still night. There was no time for a bridle but Brent was an expert rider and, clasping the horse's mane, sprung lightly on its back and gently urged it forward into the yard. He turned towards the field and, jumping over the gate, thundered across it.

Then it was as though hell had erupted. Simultaneously from the house came cries and the sound of many feet, whereas from the edge of the forest shadows materialized into running people, and riderless horses tethered together or single were driven into the direction of the far gate which was open. The running figures sprang onto the horses and urged them at a gallop across the field.

Pandemonium reigned. Some horses threatened to trip over the rest and the leader, who was near the gate, was cutting the riderless horses loose and urging the others to do the same.

'Break loose! Break loose!'

But already several were beyond the gate, having cut loose already. The released horses shot back towards Brent and he had to avoid cannoning into them himself.

'Hurry!' shouted Brent over his shoulder, but already he knew it to be too late and cursed when he saw the useless gaggle of servants rush into the field waving staves and sticks.

A fierce hatred of the horse-thieves possessed Brent and he dug his heels into Marcus's flanks. Although it was not his property they had been after, it was certainly not theirs.

Now all the riders were away, and Brent after them, but the riderless horses still tethered together got in his way. He pulled Marcus to a halt, dismounted and tried to seize the rope that hung from the neck of the leader of a riderless group when suddenly a mounted figure swept up to him and tried to snatch the rein from his hand. Helpless as he was, and disadvantaged, being on the ground, Brent caught at the wrist that had snatched the rope from him and held it in a vice-like grip, hearing a sharp exclamation of pain.

He looked down in amazement at the slender wrist he was holding, then up at the rider. He saw bright eyes gazing fiercely at him, a full, firm mouth that grimaced in pain and a beardless chin tilted in the moonlight.

A boy! A mere boy. The voice had given him away if not the narrow wrist and unshaven face. Well he'd have a mere lad off his horse in a trice and he'd beat him soundly before handing him over to the magistrate, who no doubt would eventually hang him. Brent tried to spring on to the horse behind the lad but in the effort loosened his grasp on the wrist and, with the cunning of an expert horseman, the boy sharply backed his horse, causing Brent to lose hold completely and fall flat on his face.

With a laugh the boy grabbed hold of the two horses tethered together and sped off.

Now Brent was furious. To be worsted by a mere lad, a beardless youth scarce fifteen, or maybe younger since his voice was still unbroken. He grabbed hold of Marcus, sprang onto his back and kicked him into full gallop after the disappearing thief who had not only taken the horse he was on, but had had the nerve to steal two more as well, despite being pursued!

The path through the forest taken by the thieves – leading towards Appleby as Brent had suspected it would – was tortuous and narrow. It was familiar to him from boyhood ramblings, but he guessed that the riders in front of him were gypsies and no one rode as gypsies rode, especially when they were stealing other people's horses. A grudging admiration for them rose in his breast. And to employ a boy into the bargain – what nerve!

Suddenly Brent saw his quarry in front of him; he was being held back by the two other horses he was leading. Looking back and seeing his pursuer, the boy let the tethered horses go and they halted abruptly causing Brent to falter. As he turned aside to avoid a collision Marcus at the same time stumbled on a gnarled bough in the undergrowth and Brent, without a bridle or saddle, went over his horse's head and fell heavily to the ground. In front of him, the rider hearing the cry and the commotion of horses whinnying turned and paused. When he saw what had happened he kicked his horse and sped towards the fallen man.

Brent lay on his face, winded and heaving, but aware that he was not hurt. He was also aware that the rider was coming back and as the horse trotted gently up to him made no move. The rider paused for a while and then dismounted, coming stealthily towards Brent. Brent saw the feet then the legs of the rider's harsh leather boots, waited until they were a few inches from his face and then, drawing a deep breath, he gave a mighty lurch and dragged the

24

boy thief to the ground sitting astride him so that this time there would be no escape.

The boy gasped and struggled but Brent had his wrist between his knees and his hands on the boy's shoulders.

'Now my young rogue, I've got you,' Brent cried banging his head on the ground. 'They hang horse thieves, you know, no matter how young.'

The boy gave a cry and struggled, arching himself, and Brent's hands moved downwards to pinion him more firmly by the chest. But instead of a bony boyish frame such as he expected, his hands encountered twin mounds of firm flesh such as Brent had never felt on a male body, but many times on that of a woman. With an exclamation he drew his hands away still sitting astride, and pulled off the cap that the 'boy' had worn on his head.

'My God. 'Tis a woman!'

He was so amazed that he continued to sit where he was gazing at the defiant face that looked up at him, the dark luxurious hair that now, loosed from its cap, spread on the ground. That firm small mouth, that tilted beardless chin pointing aggressively at him belonged to no youth but a full grown, beautiful – nay voluptuous even, he thought, aware of her curved hips beneath him – woman.

'A woman horse thief,' Brent continued as if talking to himself. 'I do not believe it.'

The woman stopped struggling and decided on another tactic having seen the look on his face, so clear in the moonlight. And a handsome, noble face it was too – certainly the master of the house, no servant he, no clod-hopping menial sent to catch them.

'Sir,' she said. 'I beg you will let me go or I will be horse-whipped.'

'Or you will be hanged you mean,' Brent said beginning to smile at such audacity. 'Horse-whipped will be mild compared to what they do to thieves in Carlisle. You are a thief, are you not? Woman or no? A common thief.'

Analee – for it was she – knew men well enough to realize when a threat was real and when it was not. And this fine lord, this nobleman whose graceful body was sitting astride hers in the sort of position that, despite the gravity of the circumstances, could not help but give rise to idle fancies – this gentleman with his light bantering tone surely didn't mean what he said.

'I am not a common thief sir, but a woman reduced to what I do

25

through harsh circumstances. I beg you to free me for if they know I am caught I shall be given no more work. *Please* sir. We are to leave here soon; we shall not trouble you again.'

'But be free to steal from others, eh?'

Brent was reminded how much he had hated the thieves but a short time ago; how willingly he would have given a mature common gypsy man to the sheriff to be hanged.

He stared at the girl and saw her teeth gleam in the light of the moon that streamed through the trees. He was aware of her body under his, a soft pliant body with a narrow waist, full hips and legs spread just that little bit enticingly apart. He was aware that she had stopped struggling and the look on her face was no longer defiant – it was warm and inviting, coquettish.

The moment passed. Her thighs were encased in breeches, her body in a thick jerkin.

'I cannot make love to a lad,' he laughed and reluctantly released his sure hold on his captive, pulling her to her feet with him.

She was tall and her body was still close to his. He was aware of her round full breasts beneath her leather jerkin, even though they'd been flattened and tied with some sort of cloth to make her look more like a boy. And indeed in her man's garb with her long black hair and her sinuous gypsy body, her dark flashing eyes looking so challengingly at him, he thought she looked even more desirable than she would dressed as a woman, or indeed dressed in nothing at all.

They stood for a moment – aware of each other but not speaking. There was a tantalizing body smell about her, a fresh smell as though she either washed or soaked herself in a compound of herbs and exotic spices. It was a lingering alluring smell that made him want her even more.

'I will let you go if I can see you again,' he said, 'if I could meet you on proper terms.'

'*Terms* sir?'

'I would not take advantage of a woman like this – you know what I mean.'

'Oh I can see you *are* a gentleman,' Analee said mockingly. 'I'll warrant the first one I ever met.'

Of course she was crude, Brent thought, what else could he expect of a gypsy? Her voice was from the south. It was not as uncultured as he might have expected; but whichever way she spoke troubled him not. She excited him.

'I will see you again,' he murmured, his voice shaking. 'I will, I must.'

He grasped her hand, but Analee shook her head, regretfully, and backed away.

'Why not?' He followed her, still holding her hand.

'Not now. Not here. They might come back.'

'When then, where?'

She continued to walk backwards and he followed her, looking for the chance to pinion her against a tree and seize her in his arms. As though aware of his intention Analee stepped back carefully, enjoying the game, her mouth beginning to show an enticing smile.

She was such a coquette! He reached out to grasp her, but she eluded him.

'Take care lest you fall again, sir. This time I might *not* help you to get up.'

Analee knew she had to deceive him, get away from him . . . alas. Alas because he was so handsome, with his blond aquiline looks, his strong young supple body. It was not hard to imagine the ecstacy their union would bring. But she had to resist him, this *gadjo* with the strong, clever face, the suspicion of a sardonic smile, blue eyes set deeply on either side of a straight, broad nose. His thick curly hair was so very fair that it appeared almost silver in the moonlight, and a lock of it fell over his forehead enhancing the virile, dramatic quality of his appeal – someone, she felt, who was masterful and sure as a lover, yet tender and gentle as well.

With a last rueful glance she turned and sprang agilely on to the horse that stood docilely where she had left him.

'We cannot meet,' she said looking at him, observing the desperation of his stance as though he would spring onto her.

'But you said . . .'

'I like you well enough, sir. I like you very well. Were circumstances other than what they are I would with pleasure . . .'

Analee sprang on her horse and set its head up river.

'Why?' Brent cried. '*Why* can't we meet? I will not betray you. I want only to see you dressed as a woman, yes, to hold you again in my arms . . .'

'Some things are possible,' Analee said sadly, 'some things are not. You and I are not of the same ilk. There would be no point in our meeting again. It would only bring disaster. Besides, where could we meet?'

'There are *taverns*,' Brent cried furiously, angry with himself for letting such a chance go. 'I only ask to see you again, then . . .'

'Then when you tire of me you might remember the magistrate, my lord.' Analee said, glancing back, 'As you observed, I am but a common horse thief.'

And she kicked the horse's flank and rode off through the forest.

'Women,' snarled Brewster Driver, as soon as he saw her emerge from the trees, 'incapable of doing a thing right. Where the devil have you been? I feared you were taken. They'd hang you.'

'Aye, I know,' Analee said, thinking how near to the truth he had got. 'I waited in the shadows until they gave up.'

'And the horses?'

'I had to let them go. They held me back. Anyway I got this fine one,' and she gestured towards the mount she was riding.

'Aye,' Brewster said grudgingly, 'we didn't do too bad. The boys have gone ahead. Well, we have taken eight horses between us and saved our skins.'

'Just,' Analee grunted, thinking if he knew he'd flay her!

'They're good horses,' Brewster turned towards the town. 'Belong to Sir Francis Delamain, one of the most notable breeders in the country.'

Analee thought of her handsome captor, her would-be seducer, of the light in his fascinating blue eyes. Sir Francis Delamain! She felt regret, but knew she had had no other choice. No time, no chance for adventure here. Besides they were moving on as soon as the horses were sold.

'Won't his horses be recognized?'

'Not with a lick of paint here, a touch of varnish there,' Brewster smiled. 'We'll get rid of them by first light, which it nearly is now by God, and we'll pay you and you can be off.'

'Off?' Analee cried, 'may I not move with you?'

'Oh no girl,' he looked at her slyly. She was a fine strapping girl and a good trouper, wonderful horsewoman too. Any other qualities he'd not been able to find out about; she was too agile, not unfriendly, just quick off the mark. But the children liked her, and even Margaret had got used to her. She cooked and cleaned and had made herself useful. 'No. We don't need thee.'

'You do. Tonight without me you would have had four horses instead of eight. 'Twas I enabled you to make off while I kept them looking for me. I can be the decoy.'

'Ah . . .' Brewster's eyes grew thoughtful. She wanted to stay, that was a good sign and yes, she was useful. 'Maybe you could be more . . . accommodating,' he said, 'if I allowed you to stay. Not so quick to be off, if you know what I mean.'

Brewster's eyes were always watching her; she could sense that he was for ever looking for an opportunity to be alone with her. Thankfully it was almost impossible to find such a moment, living in a close community with eight children and a watchful wife hardly ever out of sight. At night Analee shared a tent with the women. On the whole Analee thought she was safe; safe enough now to give Brewster one of her flirtatious smiles – a hint of a promise she didn't mean to keep.

'I'll have to see about that,' she said, 'but then if I'm to go it's out of the question, isn't it?'

'Well you can stay,' Brewster said, excited by the bold look she'd given him, 'for a while. We'll move on to Carlisle, steal a few more nags.' Brewster looked anxiously up at the sky, 'Come let us make haste, 'tis nearly dawn.'

Analee fell into line behind Brewster; she was tired and dejected, now that the excitement was over. What sort of life would she have, stealing horses, always trying to be one step ahead of Brewster, to be out of reach of his roving hands? But she'd wanted money and shelter, a rest from walking and wandering as she had been now for a year ever since . . . well that didn't bear thinking about. Even now she couldn't think about it. That was why she'd gone back when the man pursuing her had fallen, just to be sure she wasn't leaving someone else half dead or wounded, needing help. But to have seen him again . . . no, a risk she could never have taken. Men, being what they were, turned nasty when spurned.

And she was now a horse thief, a criminal, not merely a travelling gypsy girl. One who lived by singing and dancing, eating berries or begging food, and sometimes getting pleasure in a dry ditch or a sheltered corner of a field from a wandering gypsy lad picked up on the way, who helped her just for a time to forget the memory of the love she had lost.

2

Brent Delamain and his brother George, accompanied by a single manservant, rode out from the huge gates of Delamain Castle later that morning, well after the sun had risen. George was full of righteous indignation, a determination to see those villains hanged and his horses restored. He sat pompously on his horse and fulminated about the lawlessness of the society in which they lived.

But Brent cared little about restoring the horses or capturing the thieves. He knew something that his brother did not . . . that one was a woman. There had been something so extraordinary about that midnight encounter that he could still hardly believe it had happened. Was it a dream to find such a beautiful girl wearing men's clothes? To know without any doubt that they were destined to meet.

No, it had felt real enough. Brent knew he must find her again; to taste once more the excitement that he lacked now and craved – an adventure with a beautiful woman, and a horse thief at that!

But she was no ordinary thief, no ordinary gypsy, of that Brent felt sure. He had had many casual encounters with beautiful women – albeit none so romantic as in a forest glade in full moonlight – and sometimes pleasure had followed and sometimes it hadn't. But whether he lay with them or not they were usually quickly forgotten, appreciated but unremembered. Some called him the will o' the wisp of love, a man whose affections were incapable of real depth or emotion.

But this was a woman he wanted desperately to know, an unusual woman . . . one he would not forget. He had scarcely slept a wink all night thinking about her. He was determined to find her.

Had his brother known what sensuous thoughts were passing through Brent's mind, he would have exploded even more. But the brothers, so dissimilar even to look at, didn't share confidences. Their inner reactions to the task ahead typified the eldest and youngest of the Delamain brothers, as different as nature could make them – George dark and thickset with a dour complacent countenance, as though he had known from an early age the importance of his place in life and intended to prevent anyone else from usurping it. This particularly applied to his younger brother, tall, fair like his mother from the noble Allonby family, and with a charm and ease of manner and a fascination for women that George so conspicuously lacked.

After an hour's ride they were at the outskirts of the town within sight of the castle on the hill, flag flying boldly, and George grimaced with distaste.

'How I detest fairs! The scum of the county gather here! A chance for whoring and dissipation and all manner of evil-doing.'

'And commerce, brother,' Brent said solemnly. 'I believe you do not disapprove of that?'

'Indeed I do not. Some of my cattle and sheep are this very day to be sold and a stronger breed of Herdwick purchased in order to try and survive our savage winters. Yes, and I want to see for myself some new equipment about which I have heard for ploughing the land. But the rest of the fair . . . bah!'

'Let us split up then, brother. You to see about your business and I after the horse thieves!'

'Ah, *you'll* have no luck,' George retorted. 'If I know you you will be dissipating yourself in the tavern and among the women. You'd not recognize the nags if you saw 'em. What is to become of you, Brent, I know not. Idle and stupid!'

Brent's face darkened at these unjust and unfair remarks. Even though he knew they were partly inspired by jealousy, he also knew that his clever and astute brother had the power not only to wound emotionally, but to inflict real physical hardship on him and his mother and sister after his grandfather died. Suppressing a retort he said,

'Shall we part then?'

'Aye, and see you bring the thieves back with you!' George called back contemptuously, summoning his servant and urging his horse up Boroughgate, which was away from the main body of the fair.

Once George had gone Brent's good spirits returned. Possessing a happy and ebullient nature he was seldom depressed for long. And oh! it was such a perfect day for a fair! The smells and sounds of the market seemed to beckon to him. Tethering his horse to a post, he strolled along the streets by the river, savouring the jostle about him, the frenzied enjoyment of life. Stalls lined the streets selling all manner of goods – fine carpentry, jewellery, woollen cloth, silks, ribbons, shoes and gloves made in Carlisle. The food stalls groaned with cheeses, loaves of fresh baked bread, gingerbread, jams, quinces, jars of furmety, newly churned butter. And the clothes and colours – everyone decked in their best; corpulent merchants and owners of land with their smiling, satisfied-looking wives parading on their arms.

Everyone tried to stop him, sell him something, but Brent walked on smiling and bowing when occasionally he saw someone he knew.

'Tell your fortune, sir, tell your fortune!'

Brent shook his head and was about to pass by the gypsy who sat on a stool by the side of the road dressed in traditional gypsy garb – long skirt and embroidered blouse, scarf tied about her head, gold rings in her ears. Her black eyes gazed boldly up at Brent, reminding him of those other gypsy eyes and on impulse he stopped and extended a palm for her inspection. The gypsy grasped his hand and studied it eagerly.

'Ah, a wealthy man, I see, a lord without a doubt.' The smooth well kept hand was a certain indication of quality, and so was the cut of his cloth and the high polish on his boots. 'And a long and happy future for you, my lord, with a beautiful fair wife and many children to grace your lordship's hearth and . . .' she glanced up at him to see how he was taking these unremarkable deductions, 'other happiness too besides, my lord, for I think you do like the company of ladies . . .'

Brent smiled.

'Aye, I do that. Tell me . . .' he gave her a silver shilling and leaned forward. 'Do you know a gypsy girl who works with horses? Very striking, a beautiful lass she is.'

The woman looked startled.

'You ask me for a *gypsy* girl who works with 'orses? 'Tis like looking for a starling in a field of birds when the hay is being cut. *All* gypsy girls have to do wi' 'orses one way and another . . .'

'But this is a *very* attractive girl, a clever rider. Unusual I would say . . .'

'Ah,' a cunning look came over the fortune teller's face, 'you would not be from the magistrate would you, my lord?'

'Oh no, nothing like that!'

'But you is talking of *stealing* 'orses, isn't you my lord?'

'No, no, leave it then. Here is another shilling for your trouble.'

Brent smiled again and strode off. After all it had been most unlikely that the first gypsy he met would know his mysterious woman. On the other hand he'd heard they were a close community.

'Wait my lord, wait!'

The call came from behind him and as he glanced over his shoulder, the gypsy woman was waving to him. Brent hurried back, his spirits rising.

'Yes?'

The gypsy leaned confidentially towards him.

'*If* my lord could part with a sovereign I think he would find what I have to say not unhelpful.' Calmly she extended a grimy palm towards him. Brent took a gold sovereign from his waistcoat pocket and placed it in the middle of her hand watching her fingers curl greedily over it.

'Well?'

'They *say*,' she leaned over closer, 'that Brewster Driver had a girl working for him. No one knows where she came from or why, but she is very comely and good on horseback. I ain't seen her myself; but those who have say she is southern and gives herself airs, though what she is doing with Brewster Driver, God knows.'

'She is his *woman*?' Brent cried with horror.

The gypsy gave a lewd cackle.

'Well, I'm not saying she is and I'm not saying she isn't. Brewster Driver is a law to himself; but he does have a wife and goodness knows how many children and . . .'

'Where do I find Brewster Driver?' Brent said sharply.

'By the 'orses in the field up yonder my lord across the river. He is a big man – very strong, very short tempered. Be careful you do not pick a quarrel with him, my lord, if you value your pretty face. A *very* pretty face, my lord, it is. One the ladies love I'll warrant.'

Brent, bestowing his charming smile, briefly thanked the woman and went swiftly over the bridge and up towards the field where a few horses stood chafing and whinnying, some being led off the field, some on to it. Prospective buyers poked their flanks and looked into their mouths, or watched them being paraded in a ring. Brent gazed about him with dismay. There was such a clamour, combined with the smell of hay and dung, that he knew not which way to turn.

'Looking for a 'orse, sir? Fine gelding?'

A small ferrety man holding a tired looking horse by a thin piece of rope was gazing hopefully up at Brent.

'Do you know Brewster Driver?'

The man looked crafty; Brent proffered a shilling. The man bit it and put it in his pocket.

'I do know him, but he is not here.'

Brent's heart sank. 'Then where can I find him?'

'They say he's gone.'

'Gone *where*?'

'The next place, sir, the next place. We gypsies move on. Maybe Newcastle, maybe Penrith; but you can see how few nags there are left sir. The fair is nearly over . . .'

Brent turned away biting his lips with disappointment. Of course Brewster would have disposed of his stolen horses as quickly as he could and got out.

'You could try the camp sir. Maybe he is still there. Up yonder past the cattle pens.' The man pointed to where Brent could see gypsy tents in a field. But there was an air of bustle, and many small carts piled high with goods and children were already on the move. The roads in northern England were bad and the gypsies travelled mainly on foot or by horse, steadying the narrow carts which contained their tents and other worldly possessions. He threw the man another shilling and ran towards the gypsy settlement.

Those who were left gazed with interest at this tall elegant gentleman, with the fair hair curling over his ears and fine clothes, looking about him. It was very seldom you saw such a person coming among gypsies.

Brent stared at the faces gazing impassively at him, dark, canny gypsy faces. An invisible implacable wall separated them from him. What was he doing searching for a strange gypsy girl anyway. What would he do when he found her? For the first time the ludicrousness of the situation struck Brent – what a wild, madcap thing for him to do! This was why his brother George thought him such a fool. If he knew about it he would say how like Brent it was, running after a woman he'd lusted for as he'd straddled her body on the forest floor in the moonlight. How like Brent to put the needs of the flesh before anything else – his inheritance, his grandfather's death, his very existence in this uncertain world. Brent turned away back towards the town.

'Are you looking for someone, sir?'

A tiny dark-haired creature gazed up at him out of great brown solemn eyes set in an elfin face. He was no more than ten or eleven years old.

Brent smiled at him kindly. 'Do you know Brewster Driver, lad?'

The boy nodded. 'Everyone knows Brewster Driver, sir.'

'And is he here?'

Brent's heart beat faster again; the boy was pointing. Brent followed the direction of his finger.

'Where, boy? Where?'

'That was where his tent was, sir, there in that spot. They loaded the horses and moved out early this morning.'

Brent's eyes fixed on a long empty space between two other tents whose occupants were on the point of moving too. Brewster Driver had gone.

Analee walked alongside the cart as the small procession made its slow way along the road from Appleby to Penrith, some thirteen miles distant. The small children ran after the riders in front, and Brewster Driver strode at the head of the horse that pulled the cart. His elder sons rode on the horses they had kept from a previous night's forage to Delamain Castle.

To one side of them was a river and far away in the distance the dim outline of lakeland hills; but immediately to the east were the Pennines over which Analee had come. Sometimes a low bank of cumulus cloud made the mountain range seem very high, and at others the sky was clear and the ridge of purple-topped hills, some of them still capped with snow, was so clear that even the sheep grazing on them could be seen.

They had camped overnight by the side of the River Eamont which wove its way towards Penrith, sometimes narrow and sometimes broad. Nearby was the huge redstone castle of Brougham, surrounded by a moat and heavily fortified. The gypsies took care to keep well out of sight of the castle and its inhabitants, caring little for the thought of the dungeons which lay below the water level.

The second day on the road dawned fine and warm and Brewster Driver and his family set off early, while the birds were chirruping their early morning songs, to creep past the castle before the owner and his guards were awake. Sometimes wandering gypsies disappeared altogether, captured by some robber baron who slaughtered the men, raped the women and turned the children into slaves . . . or so the fearful stories told around camp fires went.

Analee felt light at heart and a little song came spontaneously to her lips. The flat, green valley through which they walked was interspersed with hillocks and copses. Well cultivated fields were watered by little streams which ran from the high ground to feed the Eamont.

The sun came up and warmed her back bringing her a feeling of luxury and ease. Suddenly, in imagination she was no longer a gypsy, but a grand lady surrounded by servants, adorned in silks and wearing fine jewels . . . Analee shook herself; for a moment it had seemed like a vision. It was the thought of the nobleman, the beautiful *gadjo* who would gladly have taken her in the forest. But what then? Would he have carried her off to his home, set her up in style? Why, no! He would have cast her aside, or at least . . .

Suddenly Brewster halted and pointed into the distance with his crop where, on the outskirts of a forest, was a large pile with crenallated battlements, gothic spires and a square Norman tower. Surrounding it were lawns and paddocks, a church and various small cottages and outbuildings such as belonged to a great house.

'See, the village of Delamain and its castle! Minus a horse or two, and seeking us doubtless!'

Brewster gave a harsh laugh and Analee felt her flesh grow cold and her heart miss a beat.

'Ah, but we've put them off the scent,' Brewster continued, resuming his walk. 'They'll have gone off to Appleby looking for us, and see, yonder lies Penrith.'

Brewster pointed ahead and in the distance Analee saw a town perched on a forested hill; they were entering wooded country.

No, he would have given her to the magistrate, the tall stranger with the bold eyes. Analee tossed her head and decided to put him forever out of her mind.

Though but twenty, in her short life Analee had lived through experiences not known to some in a whole lifetime. She glanced at Nelly walking beside her, Brewster's eldest daughter with whom she had found an affinity. Nelly was a pale, almost ethereal looking girl, taller than average, and with an air of delicacy and sensitivity about her lacking in the rest of his brood.

Nelly was a dreamer, forever gazing into some imaginary world seen only by herself. Compared to sturdy Jane who was only thirteen, Nelly was considered useless by her mother and father alike, having no aptitude for cooking and cleaning and mending on the one hand, or horse riding on the other. Nelly said little, but Analee was aware of an unspoken sympathy between them from the way Nelly's great sorrowful eyes followed her about.

Nelly had stopped with her father, and stood, her head on one side, her eyes fastened hungrily on Delamain Castle which looked like some fairy palace in the haze of noon.

'Imagine living some place like that,' Nelly said as the procession moved on. 'Even being a servant there would be a paradise. Imagine, enough to eat, a comfortable place to sleep, clean dry clothes to put on. I would settle for such an existence.'

'Aye, 'tis very different from our own,' Analee agreed, looking again at Nelly, noting her pale tired face – the girl looked almost sickly – her eyes great dark circles as though she slept badly.

Analee, so used to a roving life, never thought of anything different. She could have slept on a bough hanging over a lake such was her adaptability; she could curl up under a hedgerow with only the stars for light, her bundle for a pillow and her cloak for warmth and slumber until the birdsong which lulled her to sleep awakened her again. Analee was used to a completely natural life and, because of it, enjoyed a rude health which she took entirely for granted. The pale countenance and thin body of the girl beside her awakened her curiosity as much as her sympathy.

In the weeks she had spent with the Driver family Anale had experienced her first period of stability for over a year. Until then a ruthless need to move on, to escape from bad memories, had kept her permanently mobile. But in time memories fade and motion, obsessive motion, defeats its own purpose. Analee had become aware of such an exhaustion that when she did bed down with the Drivers she realized she was at the end of her tether. Now, after two weeks of good regular meals and sleep under cover, she felt strong, vibrant and healthy, in contrast to the pitiful figure beside her who sometimes awoke her at night on the palliasse they shared in a corner of the tent with her pitiful weeping. But when she gently questioned her during the day Nelly shook her head and said she did not know what Analee meant.

Her reverie was interrupted by a shout from Brewster who halted at the head of his horse. Analee could see a cluster of tents and carts in a field to the right, sheltering below the hill upon which lay tiny Penrith. They had reached another resting place. What would Brewster have for her here? More horse thefts? More sidling glances and groping hands? More hot passionate breathing on the back of her neck?

Analee knew she could not stay long with Brewster and his family or she would commit murder. Her situation was too precariously balanced between trying to placate and please Brewster by her petty acts of pilfering and trying to keep his bulky, clumsy, repulsive body off hers.

'Thank God we have somewhere to settle for a few days,' Nelly said, 'how I hate this life on the road.'

'Have you ever talked to your father about it? Maybe he would not mind if you went into service in some great house.'

'You think I can talk to my father about *anything*?' Nelly said with unaccustomed spirit in her voice. 'You think he ever listens to *me*?'

No. Brewster never listened to anyone except sometimes his sons if they shouted very hard. It was Brewster's loud voice and masterful presence that dominated the family, that cowed his pathetic wife and silenced his children, even the gambolling of the very little ones. Analee could imagine the difficulty Nelly would have trying to convince her father that she found her way of life unsatisfactory.

'Then you must run away.'

Nelly gave a tired smile, a mirthless chuckle escaping almost unbidden from her throat.

'You think I can run away so easily? He has tied me to him for good.'

'But how? How can he do that?'

Nelly's glance was enigmatic, cynical and worldly-wise. Analee was shocked to see an expression of such despair and disenchantment. Further enquiries were hindered by more shouting from

Brewster, who led them into the field where the familiar arc of tents and carts proclaimed yet another gypsy site.

Analee went forward with the kind of delighted anticipation she always felt when she saw her own kind gathered together. Saw the rough familiar faces of gypsy folk, heard the Romany language, smelt the wood fires and the odour of food cooking. Yes, she did belong to them; she was one of them. She helped unload the cart while Brewster and his sons, with many a foul curse, were untethering the horses. Margaret got out the food they had caught or stolen and Jane, the little housewife, started to scamper around with pots and pans, while the smaller ones ran off to gather kindling and the older boys prepared to light the fire and erect the sleeping tents, one for the men and one for the women.

Analee had her place in this familiar bustle and set to with a will. She was hungry. On their journey that day they had caught several rabbits and a few pigeons. Analee's task was to skin and pluck them while Jane cut up onions and the elder boys were sent with pitchers to draw water from the well. As soon as it was lit Nelly sat by the fire gazing into the flames, huddled over it as though to draw warmth and life from its fierce, crackling heat. Once or twice as he passed her Brewster gave her a savage kick accompanied by curses, but she appeared not to heed him and simply shifted in the direction he had kicked her.

'I don't understand what ails our Nelly,' her mother grumbled, her face streaked with sweat and charcoal as she placed the pot over the flames, 'she is worse than usual.'

'Do you think she may be sick?' Analee enquired softly, helping Margaret correct the angle of the sloping pot.

'*Sick*?' said Margaret wonderingly as though she didn't know the meaning of the word.

'She is so pale and listless; her eyes are ringed so darkly. Her shoulders are so thin.'

'Aye, she is not a healthy girl. Never has been. It was her chest last winter. We thought to leave her in a poorhouse but none would take her as we are Romany people and do not belong to a town or village. Sometimes I wonder she did not die of the cold last winter as many of our folk did.'

Analee shuddered. She remembered the cold of the previous winter too and thought of her own thin weak body, scarcely recovered from her ordeal, tramping through the snow, looking for food and shelter and every time despairing to find it. Each day she thought might be her last.

But the winter seemed a long time ago today as she looked at the sun setting over the majestic lakeland hills in the west, nearer to them now, casting its final beams in a splendid gesture of farewell. Her spirits and her hopes rose at such a magnificent sight and then, in the twilight, she joined the others around the fire to partake of rabbit and pigeon, bread and a flask of ale the youngsters had managed to steal while passing through a village on their way. The young ones were always sent off to do the petty pilfering. Brewster thought it good training for them and watched with admiration their tiny, wiry little bodies scampering craftily through the throng, to disappear and then reappear with booty skilfully hidden under their rags. Peter at seven was a particularly adept thief and Agnes at five was catching up with him.

But Nelly, Nelly had never been a good thief; showed no aptitude for it at all; had been clumsy and awkward and looked to be heading for the gallows even as a tiny child, until Margaret persuaded him not to send her any more. It might have been a good thing if she had swung, Brewster thought savagely, looking at her creased apathetic face through the flames, all the trouble she'd caused.

The chattering good-natured calls of her own folk seemed to Analee like music as she sat by the fire in the darkness, her belly feeling replete with the good fare. Her chin was propped on her knees as she stared at the dancing flames, which seemed to form and reform until they appeared to make a face – a handsome, noble face, eyes gleaming, mouth slightly curved. Analee shook herself and sat up. The picture of the man in the forest haunted her almost every night, driving out memories she thought she would never forget. She got up to collect the bowls – all licked clean except Nelly's, which had hardly been touched. Analee was aware of little Toby's eyes staring greedily into it and with a smile she quickly gave it to him and watched how his skilful thieving little hands, adept at concealment, hastily conveyed the succulent morsels of pigeon and rabbit to his mouth until, in a trice, the platter was empty and Analee proceeded on her way to the water bucket that stood by the women's tent.

Suddenly the air seemed momentarily still and she lifted her head as the clear silver tones of a flute rang out with such urgency and sweetness that she felt her blood chill because of the memories that took her back so long ago. Then the soft, subtle brush of the tambourine joined in gentle accompaniment to the flute, a haunting vibrant gypsy dance, that made Analee's toes start to tap and her body sway involuntarily to the sound of music.

She looked up and saw the faces around the many fires in the camp and observed how everyone had fallen silent as if in appreciation of the sweet harmony of the music. Then suddenly a fiddle came to life and the music changed to a merry jog that quickly had youths and maids on their feet while the older ones sat and clapped in time to the music.

Analee impulsively dropped her pots and leapt into the circle formed by the dancers. Now the musicians came from out of the shadows and she saw that the man who played the flute so sublimely was a cripple and leaned on a crutch, while the fiddler was a robust hearty Romany lad and the tambourine was played by a girl about the same age as herself. They stood near the Driver tent and, because of the closeness of the music, Brewster's sons Alan, Roger and John joined in, clapping their hands, tapping their feet and swirling with the gathering throng. Then with a roar Brewster got up and energetically mingled with the dancers until the only ones remaining were Margaret, even her sallow face transformed by a smile, and Nelly, who gazed apathetically in front of her seeming neither to hear nor see.

But Analee observed none of this. It was a long time since she had danced, since she had even wanted to. She had wondered if the sound of music would ever stir her again. As she whirled, clasping first this hand and then that, the sweating happy gypsy faces passing by her in kaleidoscopic confusion, from the throng of bodies came one that caught her in his arms and threw her in the air then, as she landed, she found her feet stamping time in harmony with a young gypsy lad. Their bodies twirled and bent and spun and jumped until Analee suddenly realized they were dancing on their own, lit by the flames of fifty fires, the circle of watchers panting and clapping, beating time to the music.

Analee felt possessed as she danced, inspired to surpass herself by the agility and grace of her partner. She was unaware of the roaring, shouting and clapping, hearing only the haunting melody as the beat quickened and the stamping grew louder as she and her partner reached the climax of the dance. Then, as he whirled her finally into the air and she sank to the ground, the music stopped and she was aware of smiling faces, laughing and shouting and furiously clapping hands.

Analee remained in a low curtsey, aware of her beating heart, the agonizing shortness of breath. The youth still held hard onto her hand and then he drew her to her feet and bowed, smiling, his face very close to hers, his even white teeth caught brilliantly by the flames. He even brushed her face with his lips and drew her body close to him as the music started again, and the couples who had retired to leave the floor to Analee and her partner, began to dance, this time to the slower rhythm of a love song.

'How art thou called?' the young man whispered into her ear. She was aware of his warm breath, the beginnings of a beard on his face, his hard supple male body drawing her even closer to him.

'I am called Analee. And thou?'

'Randal. I haven't seen thee before.'

Analee smiled and her body began swaying to the rhythm again as Randal put his arm around her waist and led her into the throng of dancers.

Suddenly a rough hand seized her and drew her almost to the ground, a sharp painful grasp of her shoulder that made her wince from pain. Randal was pushed roughly away and Analee found herself pressed hard against the gross form and overhanging belly of Brewster. She could feel his hot breath on her cheeks bearing the rank, stale smell of ale and onions.

'So we have a dancer have we? An acquisition I daresay more useful than a horse thief.'

'What do you mean?' Analee said furiously, trying with all her might to strain away from his powerful grasp.

'There are taverns are there not? Gypsy dancers are much sought after in taverns, ale houses, the castles of the nobility. Aye, we could put thee to good use.'

Analee tried to shake herself free from Brewster and beat vainly on his thick arms with her clenched fist but he only laughed and drew her closer to him, knowing that in the press of bodies under the cover of dark no one would notice them.

'What am I that I am to be put to good use?' Analee shouted. 'Some kind of animal?'

'Aye, a bitch,' Brewster said his eyes glinting lustfully, 'or a mare to be put in foal.' And suddenly his wide fleshy mouth came down hard on hers. He gripped one of her breasts in his huge hand and squeezed it so tightly that she would have cried out had she not been breathless and choking with the moist pressure of his mouth against hers, his tongue vainly seeking entrance between her clenched teeth.

Analee suddenly lashed out with her knee, catching him full in the crotch and Brewster, roaring with pain, released her and nearly fell to the ground. Analee felt a hand on her arm and she was being dragged through the throng to the cover of the darkened tents. She was still panting and gasping as she leaned against the side of a van. Her mouth and her breast ached and the front of her dress was torn. She wiped her mouth on her arm and gently kneaded her bruised breast.

'Is he thy husband?'

In the dark she could see little, but she knew from the outline of the body made familiar by the rapture of their dancing that her saviour was Randal.

'My *husband*! God forbid. Nay, I lodge with his family.'

'But the way he took you! I thought he had a right.'

'He would have the right. Tell me Randal do you have a tent here where I can hide?'

'Nay, I sleep rough with my brothers and sister. They are the musicians, I the dancer. We pass from camp to camp, town to town, making a little money here and there.'

'Oh.'

Analee felt downcast; her hopes had been high; but here, on reflection, was an opportunity, of a kind, to take to the road again.

'May I come with thee?'

'With us?' Randal's expression went from doubt to pleasure. 'You want to be with us?'

'I have to get away from him.'

'Then he *is* your husband.'

'No, he is *not* I tell you! I promise we are not wed; but he does desire me and after tonight I think he will have me, his passions inflamed by the dance and drink. I am not safe.'

'Then come with us. We can leave at first light. We have a cart and some belongings, for my brother cannot walk. He is a cripple.'

'Aye, I saw it. I am sorry. I too have belongings. Look, after everyone has gone to sleep I will creep back and collect them, then

I can join you at once. Brewster will be too addled by ale to stir before the sun is well up.'

'Away then. I'll take thee to our cart.'

'You are sure your brothers and sister won't mind?'

'Nay. My sister will be glad of company, and to have another dancer – why, we could do a good turn.'

Analee laughed suddenly, delighted by the prospect. To be on the road again, but not on her own, was an attractive proposition for one who had grown used to company, who needed friends to ease her solitude.

'Quick, show me where your cart is. I think the dancers are growing tired.'

'Oh, it will be an hour or two yet. Come.'

Stumbling through the dark after Randal, Analee wondered how she could say goodbye to Nelly, the one member of the Driver family for whom she had formed any affection. There was something about the forsaken, forlorn girl that moved her deeply. She would miss Nelly and she knew Nelly would miss her.

After a while, on the very outskirts of the camp, they came to a solitary cart with a roof of sorts and a horse standing nearby. Analee looked back and saw that the dancers were indeed thinning and beyond them she could see the outline of Brewster's tents.

'I will go now while there are still fires burning and I can find my way,' she whispered. 'Do not leave without me.'

'Never fear. Take care. Shall I come with thee?'

'No, no.'

Analee sped away in the darkness, careful to keep to the periphery of the camp. Sometimes her face loomed up in the light of the camp fires and she was recognized as the inspired dancer. People called out to her and wished her well. Then the music stopped and the remaining dancers came straggling back to their tents. Analee imagined the musicians packing up, their surprise at learning she would soon join them.

When she neared Brewster's tents she crept on her knees, keeping below the level of firelight. It was as she thought. Alan was stamping on the embers and there was no one else to be seen. It was unusual for the Driver family to be up much after sunset. Soon there were just a few embers glowing and Alan disappeared through the flap of the men's tent to join his father and brothers. Analee waited until all was still and then she silently entered the women's tent.

Inside it was pitch dark. Margaret was lightly snoring as she sometimes did and this gave Analee her bearings to the far corner where she shared a palliasse with Nelly. She stepped gently over the bodies of Jane and little Agnes and then got on her knees, her hands feeling in front of her for her small bundle of things which she always kept ready, as though permanently poised for flight.

Suddenly a hand clasped hers and she nearly cried out with fright but stifled the sound.

'Analee! Is that you?'

'Yes.'

'Thank God. Father is very angry with you.'

'I know.'

'He says he will horsewhip you in the morn and that you won't be able to sit down for days.'

'Did he say why?'

Nelly was silent. 'No, but I can guess. We can all guess; we saw him go after you in the dance.'

'Well he'll not horsewhip me or see me again. Nelly, I'm going to leave. I have come for my things and to say goodbye to you.'

'Oh, Analee,' the frail hand clasped her arm again and Analee heard her weeping softly.

'Nelly, I can't stay, don't you see? You know what your father is like. He'll . . .'

'Aye, you must go. I know what he is like; what he wants.'

Nelly's sobs were quieter and she took Analee's hand and drew it down on to her body so that it rested on her belly. Startled by the action Analee let her hand trace the roundness of Nelly's belly which she found swollen and hard. It did not yield as she pressed it.

'Nelly! Are you with child?'

'Yes.'

'*That's* what ails thee! Why did I never notice?'

'I am not too far gone; it is easy to conceal.'

Suddenly an awful thought struck Analee and then she knew the reason for Nelly's action in placing her hand on her swollen belly.

'It is . . . oh Nelly!'

'Aye, my father. He has been doing it regularly since I became a maid. My only care is that he will soon start on Jane.'

'Oh, Nelly. How you must hate him!'

'Well, it is not unusual you know among country folk such as us, or so I understand. My mother hates it, but what can she do? He used to lie with her in the tent, but then he started beating her until she could take no more. Now he catches us when he can, and others. Oh, I knew he wanted you Analee, all along.'

Although Analee was a gypsy girl and knew that fathers did impregnate their daughters, and sometimes sons their mothers, she still thought it a disgusting unnatural custom. To think of the foul Brewster having carnal relations with this sweet, fragile girl filled her with nausea.

'How can I help you, Nelly?'

'You can do nothing. I can see how it is with you and you have more spirit than me, Analee, more courage. I feel my life is over in a way. I care for no one and nothing. I cared for you though. You have been my friend. Oh, I wish I could come with you!'

'Then *come!*'

'No, I dare not. I have not the strength to travel by road and he will kill me. He will find me and kill me, I know that. Maybe we shall meet again – I hope so. I wish I knew more about you now; that we'd talked more. Somehow I didn't think you would be going so soon . . . I should have known.'

Analee leaned towards Nelly in the dark and kissed her cheek. She felt such love and pity for the poor girl that she would have taken her with her; but on the other hand she knew Nelly was right. Brewster, enraged, would find her and when he did he would probably do what she said – kill her.

'Nelly, I know we shall see each other again. I am travelling with the musicians. Yes! The man I danced with, Randal, those are his brothers and sister. So I shall make a living dancing after all. We shall meet again, Nelly, I'm sure of it.'

She kissed her and pressed the thin hand. Then she crept stealthily from the tent, all the possessions she had in the world wrapped in a small bundle.

And by the time dawn lit the slumbering camp the dancers were on the road.

3

'Go forth, oh Christian soul, from this world . . .'

A single candle burning by the bedside of the dying man cast upon the stone walls the sepulchral shadows of those who were gathered around his bedside.

Sir Francis Delamain, so long near death, had suffered a fatal seizure and the life slowly ebbed from his body as the priest uttered the majestic words urging the Christian soul on its long voyage from this life. It was a solemn group that surrounded the bedside of old Delamain, a solemn and divided group. There were those who thought he should be ushered from the world by a priest of the old religion – Brent thought so, and his mother, Susan, thought so. She was a member of the Allonby family, staunch Catholics, who had been steadily dispossessed of their lands and titles over the years for their faith. His young sister Emma thought so too as she fearfully gazed at her grandfather whose face and closed eyes already looked like an image carved from a tombstone.

But the heir, George Delamain, who stood some distance from the body of his family as though to emphasize his separateness from them, listened with satisfaction to the awesome words delivered in good strong English and not the devilish Latin tongue of popery. The eldest Delamain had always been on the side of the establishment, and George was no exception. The eldest Delamain had sided with King Henry against the Pope; with Queen Elizabeth against Mary Stuart, and with Cromwell against the Royalists, then when the tide turned, welcomed Charles II back to the throne. Delamain loyalty doubled about again when James II was sent into exile and the Prince of Orange and his wife Mary, James' daughter, were invited to take the throne of England. It had supported the Hanoverian Succession in 1714 and had helped fight against the Pretender, Prince James, in 1715.

And so the Delamain lands and properties flourished while the Allonby family, always on the side of opposition, had lost power and worldly wealth.

'In the name of angels and archangels . . .'

Brent was aware of George standing apart – his proud firm stance proclaiming that he was within a heartbeat of being the head of the Delamain family. George seemed already to have assumed the mantle of authority and responsibility bequeathed to him by his dying grandfather as though, in parting, the old man had assured the line of continuity by the survival of his eldest grandson. Had Guy Delamain been here in his place, Brent thought, how very different things would have been.

Brent had no recollection of his handsome, brave father who had died when he was seven, worn out by illness, misery and poverty – the lot of an exile. But the stories told by his mother built a vivid picture in his mind; stories which enthralled Brent and Emma and Tom, but to which George always turned a deaf ear, stepping aside, determined not to listen, in order to preserve his own fixed idea of his father as an outlaw.

From a very early age George had shown himself in every way to be a complete member of the Delamain establishment. He had abhorred the memory of his father, disliked his mother, despised his brothers, tolerated his only sister and developed a firm – no one could tell if it was sincere or not – affection for his grandfather.

Now George was to come into his own – the inheritance for which he had striven for so long; the vast possessions and great acres of the Delamain estate.

'*In the name of Seraphim and Cherubim . . .*'

The candle nearly died, then the flame leapt in the air, blown to gigantic proportions by the keen wind which whistled through a door gently opened and quietly shut. The shadows on the wall rose and shrank with the flame and then they were joined by a fifth shadow which stood by the door as the family turned to see who had entered.

'Tom!' Brent could scarcely keep his voice to a whisper and, leaving his mother and sister, went rapidly to his brother's side. Tom smiled in greeting, but put a finger to his lips and listened attentively, or appeared to, his head bowed in silent prayer as the voice of the clergyman droned on.

The old man's hands which had occasionally plucked the coverlet of his bed were now still, his face waxen, his cheeks sunk. His pulse had stopped, nothing stirred. Long before the exhortation was finished Sir Francis Delamain had joined that company to which he had been called. He was dead.

When the voice ceased no one spoke, cried or uttered a word. If anyone grieved for the old man they did not show it; not even George showed it. He stood staring at the dead countenance and then as the minister removed his stole and closed his book, George, Sir George, turned to him and bowed. Only Tom remained, with lowered head, his lips still moving. Tom in his own way, in the Latin of the old faith, was bidding the soul of Sir Francis Delamain prepare itself for its meeting with its maker.

George opened the door and announced to the servants assembled outside that his grandfather was dead. They bowed or curtseyed, acknowledging his succession, and then they entered one by one and stood or knelt by the master few had loved but whom they had served for so many years. One or two of the women, overcome by the solemnity of the occasion, even wept.

Tom raised his head, inclined it again in the direction of his grandfather and then went up to his mother and kissed her. She embraced him, leaning her head for a moment on his shoulder and then she groped for his hand and allowed him to lead her from the chamber. Brent and Emma followed while George remained until the last of the servants had paid their respects.

When the last one left George closed the door and went up to his grandfather's bed. He gazed for a long time at the immobile body, his face showing, by the spasms that passed over it, more expression than for many hours.

In so far as he was capable of the finer emotions that uplift the human spirit George had loved the old man. They had been two of a kind – unimaginative, unemotional, thrifty, hardworking, respectful towards lawful authority. Both cherished a long-held goal; the aggrandizement of the Delamain estates, the glory and enhancement of the name Delamain.

The old man had spent too much time in Cumberland, not enough circulating in the court and business circles in London. George Delamain intended to make good this omission – he would work doubly hard, at home and at court. He was determined that before many years were out the King would ennoble his family with a barony and to this end he would spend any amount of money, devote any amount of time. George meant to establish a great baronial family, a power not only in the county but in the land.

'You have served the family well, old man,' he said in a whisper.

'Be sure I will extend the fruits of your stewardship until the name Delamain rings through the length and breadth of the land.'

George took the still, dead hand and lifted it to his lips. Then he placed it on the old man's breast and raised his own hand in a gesture of farewell before snuffing the candle and striding purposefully from the room to claim his inheritance.

In the privacy of her own chamber alone with her children, Susan Delamain broke down at last, having maintained so impassive, so serene a face during the long agonizing hours of the old man's death. This was all changed by the arrival of Tom, whom she hadn't seen since she made her furtive journey to France for his solemn profession as a monk of St Benedict seven years before, in 1737. She had pretended to be visiting her home, her brother John and his children at Furness Grange in Cumberland, but a desperate voyage from Whitehaven to France had followed and two treasured days with her son until the Church had claimed him forever.

Now she gazed at the tall lean figure of Tom, his ascetic countenance, the hollow eyes. Why, he looked like a saint already, though his hair was long and untonsured and he wore the clothes of a sober merchant, a man perhaps of small property, and not those of a priest.

'Tom, oh, Tom.' He held her in his arms, his head resting on hers, his eyes gazing at his brother Brent and sister Emma who stood behind her.

'There, mother. There, it is all right. No need for tears. I am safe and well or is it . . .' He stood away from her and looked into her eyes, 'or is it my grandfather you weep for?'

'Oh, Tom! How can I mourn that evil old man? No, it is you for whom I weep. My second born whom I have not seen since you foresook the life of man for that of God. Oh, Tom, how has it been with you? You look tired and weary; has the life been too hard for you?'

Tom's face was transformed by a boyish smile.

'Why, no mother! I am weary because I have been travelling for a week, ever since I heard the news that grandfather was not expected to last the month. But I am very happy, both as a monk and . . .'

'Yes?'

His expression grew secretive and he glanced at his mother as though wondering how much he could tell her in front of Brent and Emma. Of his mother's devotion to the old Faith and the Stuarts he had no doubt; but what had the years done to his younger brother and sister? He knew quite well what they had done to George.

'Is it something you would not have Brent and Emma hear?' His mother saw the direction of his eyes.

'Well . . .'

Brent, who had also been delighted to see his brother, looked puzzled. What news could Tom have for his mother's ears only? What secret that was unfit for him and Emma?

'If you would rather . . . we will leave the room, Tom,' Brent said beckoning to Emma who clung to the side of the brother she hardly knew, but about whom so much was said, as though she could not bear to leave him. She looked dismayed as Brent gestured to her.

Tom sensed the solidarity that bound his brother and sister to his mother; they were united; as one. Surely his secret would be safe with them?

'It is just that . . . I have been in Rome.'

Brent was the first to react and stepped forward.

'Rome, brother? You are no longer a monk of Douai?'

'Oh, yes. You know that a Benedictine monk joins a particular community, not just the Order of St Benedict. My allegiance is to Douai. However, I was sent by my superiors on a mission of the utmost importance at the request of the King . . .'

'The King!'

'His Majesty James III of England,' Tom said solemnly, watching the reaction on the faces of his listeners to his words. The expressions, at first puzzled then fearful, suddenly became transformed with understanding, even joy, and Susan went over to clasp Tom's arm.

'Oh, Tom. The King! You are serving the true King of England?'

'I have that honour, mother. You do not disapprove?'

'Disapprove? Oh, Tom never fear. We are loyal servants of the same King – Brent and Emma here, and I. All my family too of course, John and Stewart with the exception of . . .'

Susan bowed her head.

'I know, mother,' Tom said gently. 'You do not need to say more. George. I know well how he feels about our sovereign Lord, King James.'

'He has allegiance, like his grandfather, only to King George. He even announces that he will spend more time in London at the Hanoverian court in order to further his ambitions.'

'And I am sure he will be successful, mother! The Hanoverian Elector needs all the supporters he can get. People are restless, now that Walpole has gone and England is at war on the Continent. They are tired of the German influence at court, the licentiousness of the Hanoverian Prince and his mistresses.'

'By "prince" you refer to the King I presume?' Brent ventured.

'We never acknowledge the Hanoverians as kings of England; they are Electors of Hanover, Princes of Germany. But rightful kings of England? Never. Anyway, to resume my story. I was sent to Rome as Chaplain to Prince Charles Edward. I am a contemporary of his and the names Delamain and Allonby are well known and loved by the Stuarts. Of course I was loath to give up my monastic life, but my superior is a staunch supporter of the Stuarts and he has hopes that, with their Restoration, the Benedictines will be allowed to return to England and re-establish their houses there. Then I will become a proper monk again. So much does the father Abbot have this as his prayer that he was determined to have me further the cause by proximity to the rightful house.

'Thus I went to Rome just at the time the French were defeated by a force commanded by George II at Dettingen and the spirits of the Stuarts were low. However, since then the French prime minister, Cardinal Fleury, has died and been succeeded by Cardinal de Tencin who is very sympathetic to the Stuart cause, despite the disinterest of the French King Louis XV. The cardinal was once helped by His Majesty King James and is now anxious to be of assistance to the Jacobites.

'So, in January this year, His Royal Highness, Prince Charles Edward, journeyed to Paris and since then he has been actively engaged in preparations for the conquest of England.'

'Aye, we heard of it,' Brent said dispiritedly. 'How in February this year a French fleet under Marshal Saxe embarked from Dunkirk only to be dashed to pieces by a storm in the Channel.'

'I was there,' Tom said, his grave tones echoing Brent's. 'We were on the same ship as the Marshal and succeeded in returning safely to port. It was a bitter blow. The French seemed to lose interest after that and Marshal Saxe was sent to Flanders. His Royal Highness was for sailing to Scotland alone in a fishing boat, but we dissuaded him. He even wanted to serve with the French troops against the English, but we said what folly that would be! It would disgust the English that the rightful heir to the throne was taking arms against them.

'It was Murray of Broughton, who arrived in France last week to find out the truth for himself, who informed me of grandfather's illness. John Murray is one of His Majesty's most ardent supporters in Scotland and, on learning that I was to come to Delamain to see my grandfather, he bade me appraise the strength of support for the King here and in northern parts of England.'

'Among the Catholics and the old nobility support is strong,' Susan said, 'but our merchant classes have grown too satisfied and rich under the Hanoverians. They do not yearn for the old way of life as we do. You will find very small support here.'

'Why, brother,' Brent said, his eyes gleaming with excitement. 'Let us *engender* support. Let us whip it up. If we have a small active number surely support will grow? We have connections from here to the border. Oh, Tom, is it really possible His Majesty will land in England?'

'Not His Majesty yet I fear,' Tom said smiling. 'He is an old man and he looks to his son to capture England in his name. No, it is Prince Charles Edward, scarce twenty-four years of age and as handsome, as upright and as fearless a man as ever you could wish to see – he already saw fighting at 14 years of age – whom we shall welcome to these shores, and before very long, I'll warrant you. He kicks his heels in Paris and will do anything to board ship for England; though his advisers would have him land first in Scotland where support is greatest – some of the Scottish clans having been long persecuted by the Hanoverians because of their devotion to the Stuarts. From the north the Prince will journey with an army to join up with supporters in the south and the Elector will be packed back to Hanover where he belongs, you mark my words.'

'May it please God,' his mother said, bowing her head. 'But Tom, you know how it goes with George? If word of this were to come to his ears you would be dragged off to prison in Carlisle, brother or not. What you do must be very secret.'

'It cannot be done from here, mother,' Brent said. 'This is no longer our home; we are unwelcome here. George said that the moment grandfather died you and Emma would be banished to the dower house and I must be about my way . . .'

'And where to, pray?' Tom demanded, his eyes narrowing. 'Are you not a gentleman? Does he expect you to work like some artisan?'

'I think he would have me in the Hanoverian army or the navy. George thinks I am good for nothing, Tom, and it is partly true, I must confess. I lack direction, I . . .'

'What is it you want to do Brent?' Tom said softly, his eyes betraying warm affection for his brother.

'Why, nothing better than to serve the King. Do you think I may?'

'Come to France?'

'Why not? With you? When you go back. Let me come with you Tom. Oh, please.'

Tom paused and looked at his mother, his face doubtful. He knew how much she had suffered already. Her life had been one long martyrdom to the Stuart cause, first husband and brother, now maybe her two sons. But Susan's head was proudly raised and her eyes shining.

'I know of nothing that would make me more proud, Brent my son. I know how restless you have been; how you have kicked your heels and wanted for direction. In the service of the King your talents can find a home, and then when he comes to his own country he will reward you by ousting your brother and bestowing on you the lands that should rightfully have gone to your father – Delamain, village *and* Castle.'

Her voice rang out proudly and Tom felt his eyes moisten. His mother was like the woman in the Bible extolled in Proverbs: 'She hath put out her hand to the strong things; and her fingers have taken hold of the spindle . . . Her children rose up and called her blessed; her husband, and he praised her.'

Tom clasped his mother's hands and held them to him. 'Mother, you will be on your own . . .'

'I . . . I will be with her,' Emma cried. 'I will take care of mother, while you and Brent bring back the King to England.'

Tom looked at his sister, grown so comely, so tall since he last saw her. She was a maid ready for marriage, for adorning the house of some great noble. But what future did eighteen-year-old

Emma have? What future did any of them have unless the Stuarts were restored to the throne of England?

'You are a noble girl indeed,' Tom said, kissing her. 'I know you will look after mother and she you. We shall not be far away and we shall see you are both protected. Scotland and the south of England are well taken care of. It is here in Cumberland and Westmorland that we seek support for our cause.'

The silence at dinner the following day was uneasy. Apart from the stealthy movement of the servants, their soft murmurings as they served, no one spoke. At the head of the table George sat wrapped in thought. Next to him his mother kept her face expressionless. Brent and Tom applied themselves to what was on their plates. Emma hardly ate at all.

It had been a difficult day, getting the old man laid out and ready for burial. Taking his body to the vaulted Delamain church that stood in the grounds with the family tomb among the gravestones, listening to the prayers intoned over it. Tom, Brent and George took it in turns to stand guard with the male servants. People came and went, some to pay their respects, others on business.

Now the Delamain family was alone, restless in its solitude. After the last course had been served George motioned to the servants to leave and, as the heavy doors closed behind them, apprehension seemed to hang heavy in the air.

At last George, who had appeared to be warring with some inner turmoil, lifted his head, took a draught of wine and leaned over the table.

'Let us not mince words. Tom you are not welcome here. Brother you may be, but you have turned aside from your family to an alien cause, a foreign faith. You have forfeited the name of Delamain and I am glad you are known only as Father Anselm. Once grandfather is in his tomb you must go, Tom. I do not want the authorities to hear of your presence among us. They know it already, but there is a reason. Once grandfather is buried that will have gone. I do not want you another night in the castle after tomorrow, the day of his burial.'

Tom seemed about to reply, but observed the caution in his mother's eyes and he bowed his head in acknowledgement biting his lip. George then turned to Brent.

'Brent, for other reasons you too are not welcome here. You are idle and good for nothing. You do no honour to our family name. You are twenty-one, without fortune or prospects. I cannot keep you. I refuse to. You are to go for the army or navy or find some other suitable occupation as befits a gentleman. I have no room for you on my estates.'

Brent too seemed about to speak but on seeing his mother's eyes upon him held his peace.

'Mother, the dower house is being prepared for you and Emma. I have told you I wish to marry and to this end I want the castle prepared for my bride. Of course I will not marry until a suitable period has elapsed after grandfather's death.'

'Have you anyone in mind George?' His mother enquired with a trace of mockery in her voice. It was not lost on her son who replied with asperity.

'There are many women in London, mother, who would consider it an honour to have me ask for their hand. I do not anticipate any difficulty. Indeed I am much sought after as a dinner guest and to accompany young ladies to fashionable balls. You may expect an announcement quite soon.'

George nodded and sipped his wine, the fingers of his left hand drumming the table.

'But all of you know why I am so anxious to be rid of you. You have always in your hearts adhered to the old faith, the Stuart cause. You are a danger and a hindrance to my advancement. Your family, mother, has brought shame on the Delamain name. I do not care to be tarred with your brush. Would that the Allonbys, one and all, were safely over the water with their beloved Pretender. Tom, you openly espouse the old faith and, Brent and Emma . . . I know well you are with mother rather than with grandfather or me. I want to be rid of you, once and for all. I cannot wait to start a new life.'

Brent rose to his feet and crossed to where his brother sat.

'Gladly, George, will we absent ourselves from our home. For it is our home whatever you may say. Even grandfather let us know that, however much he deplored the fact of father's exile. You have abused that sense of hospitality that has always been a mark of our family name.

'As for Tom and I, we shall go, and willingly. As soon as grandfather's remains are laid to rest we shall take ourselves to people who do value and respect us, the Allonbys whom you so despise. We shall not lodge a night longer than necessary in a place where we are so unwelcome.'

'Good,' George said with satisfaction. 'And when the militia come to disperse what is left of the Allonbys, God grant they take you off too and fling you in some loathsome dungeon where you are best forgotten . . .'

'George!'

His mother rose to her feet, eyes blazing.

'I am still your mother, though God knows I sometimes wish I were not, for you disgrace me and the memory of your father. It is you who have caused this rift in our family, brought us to shame. You with your greed and your petty spite, George. I will stay in the dower for that is my right; but I will have as little to do with you as I can and Emma likewise. For if you cut us off we scorn you too. In your own family, George, you have this day made implacable enemies. Be it on your head, my son.'

George faltered and looked at his mother as though wondering if he should retract his words. He seemed to be once more the victim of warring forces as he stared at his mother and sister, his brothers whom he had just dipossessed.

But George Delamain – Sir George Delamain – had trained himself to eschew emotion from an early age. If momentarily he regretted the force of his words he quickly overcame such a sign of weakness and, without glancing backwards, strode purposefully out of the room leaving the great doors open behind him. His heavy footsteps echoed along the stone corridors as his family, still shocked at the abruptness of his words, gazed at each other wondering what the future would bring.

4

Analee felt instantly at home with the warm-hearted troupe of brothers and sister, Selinda, who welcomed her to their ranks. Selinda, who played the tambourine, was the most reserved, as her brother explained to them what had happened as they came back, exhausted from hours of playing. Each carried a large bag of coins which clinked satisfactorily together, indicating that there would be enough to eat for several days to come. Randal spoke hurriedly to them, bidding them pack up and be ready to start before dawn. By the time Analee had rejoined them they were all asleep curled up in the shadows of the cart, all except Randal who advised her to get as much rest as she could.

Now they were on their second day away from the gypsy camp wandering around the countryside near Penrith.

'There we may bide the winter,' Randal said, 'for when the snow and the winds come 'tis no place to be wandering on the roads.'

'There is not enough work for us to bide there all winter,' Hamo the fiddler said, ''tis best we go up to Carlisle and stop there.'

Hamo and Randal took turns leading the horse, and the girls walked by their side. Benjamin, the cripple, rode in the cart, entertaining them with his flute. Benjamin was like the runt of the litter compared with his tall strapping brothers – lean, wiry men with jet black hair and dark brown eyes. Selinda resembled her brothers, being dark and slim but of medium height. Her skin was whiter than theirs and there was an air of fragility about her, unusual in one who spent her time on the road. She had none of the sturdy robustness of Analee who swung along, easily keeping up with the men. From time to time they would halt to give Selinda time to rest or travel for a while with Benjamin in the cramped cart.

Benjamin was short, having suffered damage at birth and one of his legs was completely bent at the knee so that he had to hobble on his stick. He had a thin, emaciated frame and his arms and legs looked as though they would snap if any pressure were applied to them. His cheeks were hollow and his hair was sparse, unlike the thick thatches of his brothers, the luxurious raven locks of his sister. But the size and quality of his eyes, their luminosity as they blazed with amusement or affection, made Benjamin's face almost beautiful. His skin had the transparency of fine porcelain and his mouth betrayed a sweetness of disposition as though he found himself permanently at peace with the world; in love with life.

Thus it was a gay troupe that Analee found she had joined as they walked briskly along chattering and laughing. Yet once on the road they were busy. There were rabbits to snare, hedges to explore for berries and ditches for hedgehogs, the odd fat pigeon to stalk, pounce upon and kill. There were herbs and grasses to gather to flavour their soups – mushrooms, nettles and wild garlic. Occasionally a lone fowl or chicken wandering on the road was seized and its neck wrung before it was plucked and roasted on a stick over a fire, its belly filled with rosemary and garlic.

At nightfall they sought the shelter of a wood or rocks and Randal and Hamo would make a fire while Selinda and Analee cooked whatever they had gathered during the day. Sometimes they had caught a hedgehog and then they made the favourite gypsy dish of *hotchi-witchi* by wrapping it in leaves and baking it in earth. They would take the prickles out with their fingers and divide the succulent flesh before cramming it into their mouths. More often than not, however, it was a rabbit or pigeon, or sometimes it was no meat at all but a soup made from berries and herbs in the gypsy way.

The other thing they did to pass their time on the road was to tell stories, and here Benjamin the dreamer excelled. They would gather around the little cart in which he rode and listen as he told tales about gypsy lore, or invented new ones himself about those far off days when the gypsies had come from the east and dispersed all over Europe. There were so many legends about the Romany folk handed down from generation to generation that no one knew whether they were true or false. The true ones were embellished in the telling and the false ones came, in time, to be regarded as true.

They skirted the town of Penrith and its surrounding hamlets and villages, moving all the time across that flat plain to the hills that proclaimed Ullswater and the range of lakes, valleys and mountains that stretched to the sea. At times hills appeared out of a haze, as though floating on cloud, and then they reminded Analee of some enchanted land such as she had heard her grandmother talk of in her far-off childhood. When the sun rose or set behind the hills and the sky was streaked with reds, purples and many shades of gold, Analee would be spellbound by the sheer beauty of it and yearn to be among the peaks, clambering along the narrow passes, roaming through the bracken and short wiry grass or sleeping in some sheltering cave.

At the head of Lake Ullswater they played in the tavern of the tiny village of Pooley and the next morning Analee crept out of the tent she shared with Selinda just as dawn was breaking. She stood by the side of the lake which, it seemed to her, was so large it must lead to the sea for it disappeared out of sight hidden behind the high fells on one side and the thick woods on the other.

There were one or two tiny islands on the lake, and the calm water with scarcely a ripple disturbing its surface was so enticing that impulsively Analee stepped into it wading out until it was almost up to her knees. She held up her skirts and nearly cried at the bitter cold of the water which came from high in the ice-bound hills.

All that day the troupe wandered along by the side of the lake with its wooded bays and rocky inlets, through the tiny villages nestling on its shores and across the broad valley of Patterdale with truly gigantic peaks towering on either side. One or two remote farmhouses were tucked in the folds of the steep fells upon which the hardy Herdwick sheep incredibly found purchase with their nimble feet.

The valley seemed to be the limit of their journey and when they came to the small lake at the end of it they bathed their weary feet and gazed upwards seeking a way out. Although beautiful and fertile, it was an empty desolate place with no more hamlets with taverns to play in.

A crofter, passing the time of day with this curious group, told them that there was a bridle path over the mountains to Ambleside and Windermere but he shook his head at the pony and cart and the sight of the cripple and the pale weary girl. Selinda tired easily and sat on a stone shivering, her arms pressed to her chest for warmth.

'Them mountains terrify me,' she said. 'If you go on, I go back.'

'Aye and me too,' Benjy said, remembering the crofter's piteous glance. 'You cannot get the cart over there and I cannot go without it.'

Analee held her hand over her eyes and looked towards the

massive mountain range which hemmed them in. They didn't terrify her; they thrilled her. Were she alone she would take off along that narrow winding path that soon disappeared out of sight among the jutting crags. It was a ravaged, harsh wilderness with the individual alone among the elements.

'We could perish in the mountains and none be the wiser,' Hamo whined, and Analee looked at him with contempt; there was a soft side to Hamo and, more than anyone else, he was always grumbling and complaining about the lack of comfort.

Randal was whittling at a stick, frowning, indecisive for once. She knew he wanted to go on, and yet he was aware of the drawbacks. He glanced at her as though to say why did they not venture on alone and leave the others? She knew what was in his mind, had been for some time. All that prevented him was the presence of his brothers and sister.

He didn't displease her; on a cold night she would rather have his body hugging hers than poor Selinda whose thin frame brought no warmth. But she liked things as they were; the dancing, the adventure. If they made love she would have to leave, for she never stayed with casual lovers for more than a night or two. If she wanted to ease the yearning of the flesh she saw nothing wrong with it; but her affections could not be engaged. Her heart was ice-bound like the mountains. It was not to be taken, certainly not by Randal Buckland.

'We best turn back,' Analee said. 'We have not eaten well for days, Randal, and Selinda grows even thinner.'

Analee looked at her with pity; yes, a puny, delicate girl with large eyes black-rimmed with fatigue. She was ill-suited for the road, for the harsh life they led.

Randal threw his stick into the bushes and took the reins of the pony, circling the cart so that it faced the way they had come. Analee didn't know why, but the gesture filled her with foreboding and she glanced behind her at the massive wall of rock they were forsaking as though there were something about it that would protect her. Somehow she felt there was some symbolic meaning in the act of turning back, that it was the wrong thing for her to do. She wondered if she should abandon them and go on, press on ever towards the sea?

Randal was looking at her. He smiled and held out a hand beckoning her on.

So they turned their backs on the heart of lakeland, and returned the way they had come towards the flat countryside lying between Ullswater and Penrith. Their spirits rose as they found more nourishing food to eat, sometimes given them by crofters or a kindly farmer's wife.

In many ways it was an idyllic life in that fine hot summer. Sometimes they would stop in a village and Hamo would get out his fiddle and Benjy his flute, and Analee and Randal would link arms and begin the measured steps of a saraband, Analee accompanying herself on the castanets and Selinda throwing her tambourine high over her head. At the end of an hour or two when the whole village had gathered and some were beginning to drift away, Benjamin would limp around with a bag attached to a stick, going one way and Selinda going the other so that the whole circle of onlookers was encouraged to give a coin or two. Then they would buy food in the village and that night they would eat well.

Thus they made their way back to Penrith the town perched on a hill, so high that from parts of it you could see into Scotland. The great castle in the centre towered over the narrow streets and houses, which clustered together so that in some places they almost seemed to lean over and touch one another.

As soon as she came into a town Analee was aware of a constriction that made her long to be away from it again. She hated the feel of cobbles beneath her bare feet, the noise and shouts of those who thronged the streets going about their business. Selinda seemed aware of her fear and moved closer to her.

'We know several of the tavern keepers here and always do a good trade. Sometimes we are asked to one of the great houses in the area. Twice we have played and danced at Lowther Castle, but at night we go to a field outside the town to make our camp. Do not fear.'

Analee smiled and grasped Selinda's hand. 'I do not fear; but I hate towns. Would we could always keep to the open road.'

Selinda glanced at her companion about whom she was curious because she said so little about herself. With the gypsy's respect for an individual's privacy neither Selinda nor her brothers would have dreamt of questioning Analee. They knew she was not from the north like them. Like them she spoke in the *Romani* tongue, but her accent was not theirs. At first they had thought she was foreign; she was so tall and her skin was of an olive cast like their brother and sister gypsies they occasionally met from Italy or Spain. But at night as they sat around their fires Analee just listened while they spoke of their experiences or joined with them as they quietly sang the gypsy lullabys which were universal.

They stopped outside a busy hostelry and Randal went inside, emerging after a time with the tavern keeper who knew them and welcomed them. He looked with open admiration at the lithe form of Analee, noting with approval her brightly coloured gypsy skirt, her loosely tied bodice with her big firm breasts carelessly exposed in the gypsy fashion. Yes, he thought, she would put his customers on fire. Now that she was more rested, her skin had burnt to a deep olive brown with exposure to the fine weather, and the sun had given her black hair a lustrous sparkle.

The innkeeper grunted and nodded towards her with satisfaction.

'A relation?' he queried.

'We are all brothers and sisters,' Randal replied, his brown eyes flashing a little with jealousy as he saw the looks the innkeeper was giving Analee. Almost from the moment he had seen her coming to him in the light of the many fires that night in the camp, Randal had felt that here was the woman for him, the promised one, the *tomnimi*. Because he and his brothers and sister had moved outside the formal tribal structure, and as no one knew where Analee had come from or to which tribe she belonged, an elaborate courtship was not necessary. However, strict customs governed gypsy life and these were inbred enough in Randal for him to want to adhere to them.

But he was always close to Analee, helping her, trying to show his feelings by his presence. However, not by so much as a glance or a smile did she indicate whether he had succeeded or not.

But the way the *gadjo* innkeeper had looked at Analee enraged Randal, the way he'd ogled her breasts which, like a true gypsy she did not try to conceal. The important parts of a gypsy woman to keep concealed were her midriff, her thighs and her legs and, in accordance with custom, Analee kept these very well hidden indeed by her long skirt and the several petticoats she wore underneath.

Analee became aware of the tension as the innkeeper's red face, after staring at her bosom, peered into hers. It had happened to her too often for her to be affected by it. But what surprised her was the way Randal's face grew dark and his chest heaved; for a moment she thought he would strike the innkeeper. And then she understood. Randal wanted her.

But before she had time to weigh these implications, the innkeeper stepped aside and, in a gesture of benevolence, motioned them into the inn where there was a roar as soon as they were seen and a space on the rush and sawdust strewn floor was made for them.

Hamo had seen his brother's wrath and was disturbed by it too. But he put his fiddle to his chin and started a merry gypsy zorongo. Benjamin lifted the flute to his mouth and Selinda shook the tambourine above her head while Analee, impatiently clicking her castanets, her head raised expectantly, her body taut, her feet tapping time, waited for the cue to enter. Then as Randal, excited as much by the sight of her preparing to dance as by the music nodded to her, his eyes gleaming, she lifted the edge of her skirt, her other hand curled on her hip and made the zarandeo, or swirling movement of the skirt, that preceded the dance. Then his hands on his hips, Randal came in from the other side and, their bodies so close together that at times they almost touched, they went through the intricate movements of the dance.

Such was the atmosphere, the appreciation of the crowd that all, musicians and dancers, gave inspired performances. But perhaps it was Randal who worked the hardest because he was trying, through the proximity of his body, the messages sent from his eyes, to tell Analee how he felt about her – how much he resented the armorous glances of the *gadjé* who leered at her flying breasts, trying to catch a sight of her legs as the skirts whirled and twirled about her lissom form. And then when each dance finished they would crowd around her, trying to touch her with their hands, offering her drink and food.

Selinda, at the edge of the crowd, was aware of the charged atmosphere, a feeling that had been absent from their previous performances since Analee had joined them. For the first time, she felt apprehensive and wished that they and Analee had never met. Somehow she felt she would bring an unwelcome change to their fortunes. Randal had admired women before, may have loved some of them, but he had never quite reacted as he did with Analee so that he seemed hardly able to bear her to be out of his sight. His temper had not improved either since she had come among them. He was short and snappish with them and everywhere Analee went his eyes followed her.

Selinda sighed as her body swayed and her knuckles tapped the tambourine or she shook it above her head in a long trill. She knew that compared to Analee she was an unformed slip of a girl. She was neither as tall as Analee nor as well built; she lacked her swaying hips, the full bust and the luxuriant black hair that fell over her shoulders. And Analee's eyes . . . by any standards they were beautiful as they either flashed boldly or were modestly concealed by lowered lids while her thick lashes curled up even more enticingly, if that were possible, on her cheeks.

Of the many gypsy beauties Selinda had seen, none were quite like Analee; she certainly far eclipsed her, Selinda, and she had been told many times she was beautiful. For the first time in her gentle life Selinda realized she was jealous – jealous of another woman's beauty, and afraid of what she might do to the close-knit family with whom she roamed the northern parts of England.

Suddenly Selinda saw a tall, well-dressed man step out from the back of the tavern and join those who pressed forwards eagerly, scarcely able to restrain themselves, in the front row of the crowd. But, unlike the heaving lascivious men whose tongues had lolled out and whose foreheads perspired as their lustful eyes followed the leaping shimmering body of Analee he merely stood, his pot of ale in his hand, and gazed at her thoughtfully, his face unsmiling. There was something about the intensity of the look that intrigued Selinda and made her feel sure that Analee and the graceful young man with a fine broadcloth jacket and breeches and a crisp white cravat, had met before.

Then the music stopped again and, as the crowd once more pressed towards Analee, the man, who stood a head taller than the tallest man there, gave an imperious gesture with his hand and stepped forward. Analee, who had been about to turn and seek refuge with the musicians, stopped in her tracks and gazed into the face of the blond stranger.

'So we meet again.' The man's eyes bored into hers, but he was not smiling. Analee's heart gave a lurch and she stepped back.

'I know you not, sir.'

'I think you must remember if I remind you . . .' he glanced round, his expression now roguish, and put his mouth to her ear. 'The first female horse thief I ever encountered.'

Analee felt her face redden under her dark tan despite the heat. She had recognized him immediately; the unforgettable sight of his young vibrant face lit by the bright moonlight peering into hers as he straddled her body.

'My lord, I . . .'

'Don't disturb yourself. I shall not betray you. I want to talk to you!'

'But my lord I'm dancing. I cannot!'

'After. Meet me outside. I'll wait for you.'

There was a commanding note in his voice and Analee found she was impressed, despite her dislike of authority. Her mind in a whirl she turned to join her companions. What bad luck! But what did he want, this young nobleman? Surely not to betray her, *now*? No, she knew what he wanted. She could feel the press of his body as his thighs imprisoned her, the urgency of desire that he had transmitted to her in that forest glade transfigured in the shadows cast by the moonlight.

And then his face had come out of the crowd, so different from the coarse, brutal, lecherous faces that leered at her, seeming strangely evil and cruel in the light of the glittering candles. His had been aloof, unsmiling; but as he had looked down at her she noticed the tenderness in his eyes, the hint of a smile on his curved aquiline lips.

Randal had seen it too. As he came up to them the joy, the ecstasy of the dance, had vanished from his face and she saw it was sullen and suspicious.

'Who was it?' he whispered. 'What did *he* want with thee?'

'Like all the rest I suppose,' Analee said nonchalantly, gratefully accepting a jug of ale from a serving maid and putting it thirstily to her lips.

'I thought you knew him?'

'Me? Did you see the cut of his clothes, the elegant way he walked? *I* should know a nobleman like that? I'd be lucky indeed!'

Randal looked at her doubtfully. He was sure she was lying, but her face turned to his was so innocent and beguiling. Randal's heart flooded with love for Analee at that moment and he knew that he must have her; an overwhelming desire for her possessed him. Yet he knew she didn't return his feelings; her attitude to him was just the same as towards the others. He would have to find a *drabarni*, a herb woman, to make him a love potion with which to win Analee.

The crowd of drinkers started calling for music and dancing again, but Randal and his companions were tired. Analee had been on her feet, twirling and swirling, for over three hours. It was getting late and they had to find a camp for the night. Analee wondered how she could get away from her companions to meet the lord – because meet him she knew she must. In him, from the beginning, she had felt an unusual challenge; someone with the power to hold her, to make her cease her wandering.

Analee had suspected Randal's feelings for her; he made them so obvious, poor youth, as he hovered around her. She could feel him following her everywhere with his eyes. But she had known many men like Randal, many gypsy lads with whom she had lain for a night or maybe two before going on her way. If she was to stay with Randal and his troupe of musicians she could not allow herself to become involved with him. If she did she would have to leave, and as for a wedding, why, it was out of the question.

Analee glanced round the crowded tavern and could see no sign of the nobleman. Then she saw that Randal and Hamo were engaged in a harangue with the tavern keeper, doubtless about payment. Most tavern keepers kept a proportion of what the gypsies took – some of them demanded as much as half, and it was best to keep in with them or else you would not be welcome again, either to the tavern or maybe even the town. There were still those who would harry and persecute the gypsies, as happened in parts of Europe. She had heard that in places like Spain, at the sound of the *tocsin* the local population of a town set about hunting the gypsies like animals; they were even rewarded for each gypsy they captured.

Analee slipped outside and went round to the back of the inn. The sun was sinking. Horses were tethered to the posts and grooms went back and forth saddling one here, unsaddling another there where the owner had come for a night's rest or entertainment. Analee looked round and then, feeling conspicuous in her dress, knowing how she stood out among all these men, turned to go back inside again when a hand gently grasped her shoulder and she could feel warm breath on her cheek.

She turned around and looked up at him. He was now dressed in a travelling cloak, a tall hat on his head. He looked even more elegant and awe-inspiring.

'Sir, what is it you would have with me? I am but a wandering gypsy, not fit for the likes of you, milord.'

'I sought you the day after we met in the forest and you were gone,' Brent said, smiling down at her. 'I felt we were destined to meet again, but my grandfather died and I could not come and look for you. Now I am bound for Keswick with my brother, and chance has let me find you again. What is your name?'

'Analee, my lord.'

'I am not a lord, Analee, merely a gentleman – Brent Delamain by name. My brother is now Sir George Delamain and, having come into possession of the great Delamain estates, has sent me packing.'

'*Packing*, my lord. You?'

Brent laughed bitterly. 'Aye. But my brother Tom has come from France and we journey to our cousins who will give us food and shelter. Analee, I may go to France with Tom, my brother. How can I see you? How can we meet?'

He came close to her and looked into her eyes. Unlike other men, other *gadjé*, the non-gypsies, he was not groping and fumbling for her bosom as soon as he had the opportunity. Although he was tall she did not feel dwarfed, as she too was tall.

'I am on the road,' Analee said, 'with the musicians you saw. We earn a living dancing and singing . . .'

'Then dance and sing for my cousins! Analee, that is a capital plan. They dwell near Keswick . . .'

'But sir, we are bound for Carlisle. To go to Keswick is to turn back. We have just come from Lakeland – 'tis too remote, there are too few people, the nights are too cold. The troupe does not wish to go to Keswick. I cannot do that.'

'Then come by yourself, Analee. What happened to the people you were stealing horses with?'

'Oh, I left them in our last camp. I cared not for the father of the family I was with. But here, with these people I have a nomad life which I like and money, so that we can eat well and occasionally buy materials for new clothes.'

There were footsteps behind them and Tom appeared, also caped and hatted like Brent.

'Brent what ails thee? Why . . .' Tom's eyes opened wide in wonder to see his brother in such intimate conversation with the wild gypsy dancer. Even though he was a monk and dedicated to celibacy, Tom was still a man; and both as a man and a monk he had admired the grace of the gyspy dancer, felt the power of her supple sensuous body as she had danced before him, her hands high in the air, her skirts whirling about her body, her bare feet moving so fast over the floor that at times he could barely see them.

'Tom, this is Analee. We have met before. Analee, my brother Tom Delamain.'

Analee dropped a small curtsey as Tom bowed his head. She felt shy in the presence of this stern-looking stranger; like Brent, yet not like him – there was distance about him, something forbidding.

'Brent, we must go. We shall never be there before dark.'

Brent glanced at the sky.

'Tom, it is already getting dark! Let us stay here for the night in the tavern. We cannot risk the horses over the paths to Keswick. 'Tis too far Tom,' he pleaded. Tom smiled and glanced at the gypsy. It was an hour or so to darkness yet. Still, Brent was right. They had tarried too long in Penrith. Tom felt awkward in the presence of the girl.

'Brent, I'll go and seek rooms for the night. They may be hard to find if it is market day, as I think it is.'

'You go in, Tom, and I'll join you.'

Tom smiled at Analee and inclined his head, while she gave a brief bob.

'Analee! Come sup with us! Surely you will not say no?'

'But my friends . . .'

'They will sup with us, too. Say yes.'

'Oh, I know not . . .'

Analee couldn't remember when she had last eaten indoors. The thought of the succulent roast pig, barons of beef and fowl that she had seen in the dining room tempted her . . . Surely Randal would not mind, for once . . . But what then?

'Well . . . I will sup with you, though if my friends will or no I can't say. But . . .'

'Yes . . . ?'

Brent moved nearer to her, wanting so much to take her into his arms; but he knew that now he could not. This strange wild girl had an effect on him he'd never known before.

'When will we meet again, Analee, is that what you wanted to say?'

'Yes,' she whispered.

'We shall find a way,' Brent said, '*I* shall find a way.'

All during the meal Randal was aware of the glances between Brent and Analee even though they did not sit together, but gazed at each other across the table. For the Buckland family it was a new and strange experience to sit on a chair and have your food put on a platter before you on a table. Randal was at first suspicious of the food and asked a servant what they were eating so as to be sure it was not horse or cat or dog, food abhorred by gypsies. Brent laughed uproariously at the very idea and patted Randal on the arm assuring him that it was bullock and pig and fine fresh chicken.

Tom didn't laugh. He knew well the strict customs of the gypsies. He had come across many of them in his journeys through France and Italy. His monastery had often sheltered them as they fled from persecution. What worried him was the fact that his brother clearly had designs on this gypsy girl.

It seemed that where love was concerned Brent had a reckless foolish streak in him. Tom could see it now, and grieve for it.

Tom had the cripple on one side of him and the shy young girl on the other. A very different type she was from the bold Analee who, aware of her charms, flaunted them in front of his ena-moured brother – surely her bodice was too far down, even allowing for lack of gypsy modesty? To gypsies the breasts were purely functional, for the purposes of rearing children, not for alluring men. Yet Analee would know how the *gadjé*, the non-gypsies, reacted to that portion of the female anatomy. But she was a beautiful woman, Tom thought – there was a proud, almost aristocratic tilt to her head, a disdain in her eyes that he had seen in noblewomen far, far better born. Was she perhaps half-gypsy? The daughter of a gypsy woman and a nobleman, or the other way round? If the sin had been known the gypsy parent would have been an outcast from the tribe, particularly if it was the mother. Any gypsy having anything to do with the excluded member would have been polluted, *marimé*. No, it was fanciful, Tom decided; he had seen her dancing. That magic, that special skill, came from a pure bred gypsy, little doubt of that.

Still, she was a puzzle. She was different from the troupe she was with, that was clear. She was taller and spoke good clear English. Her fingers were long and thin, and there was an air of breeding about her that was certainly at variance with the Romany life – the hard life of the road. Only her calloused feet and her tanned complexion betrayed that.

Tom saw Randal's dark glances as he listened to the prattle of Benjamin, the engaging little cripple, or tried to induce the shy Selinda, who kept her eyes on her plate, to say a few words.

Brent and Analee didn't need to speak – their eyes did that for them. Brent found it difficult to stop looking at her, although as the host he was aware of his duties. He was also trying to seek a way of seeing more of her. But how could he? He was bound for Keswick and then France. He was dedicating his life to the service of the King. What place did a wandering gypsy girl have in that?

The genial landlord appeared at the table, honoured to have served their lordships but indicating that the hour was growing late.

Tom got up, looking at Brent who rose reluctantly, his heart heavy. If only he could think of a way. He walked with his guests to the door aware of Randal just behind his shoulder, Analee a little in front of him.

'Will you stay at least as my guests for the night at the inn?' Brent said desperately.

'No thank you, my lord,' Hamo replied. 'We have found a place just beyond the town up by the forest. We gypsies do not like to sleep under a roof. It is foreign to our natures.'

Brent nodded, keenly aware of Analee's receding back. Soon he would see her no more. Outside the moon had risen, as round and as bright as on the night they had first met. Analee was looking at it too. Randal and Hamo paused to bid farewell to Tom and thank him and Analee, looking up at Brent, whispered.

'Our camp is in the forest up the hill.'

'We can meet . . . ?' Brent could hardly believe his ears.

'When they are asleep. Say within two hours . . . I will stay on the edge of the wood looking for you. Take care not to get lost. You will see the cart and the horse in the field nearby.'

Without another word she walked swiftly away from him and waited for her companions in the shadow of the inn. Then, after farewells were said, they turned and walked out of sight.

Brent and Tom watched them go, Brent's heart still thudding from the excitement of the unexpected initiative.

'I see you were fascinated, Brent,' Tom said cautiously.

'She is a fine woman,' Brent said, then frankly to his brother, 'Tom, we have met before. I am very taken by her.'

'Oh, folly,' Tom said aghast, 'but Brent, 'tis absurd.'

'I know it is absurd. But it is a fact. I am taken by Analee the gypsy girl and I think . . . I think she is not indifferent to me.'

'But what can you do? She is a nomad, a wanderer . . .'

'Do you not detect something about her, brother, that is not like a gypsy? She has breeding and refinement such as the shy young lass with her has not. Analee is not true gypsy if you ask me.'

''Tis odd you should say that . . .'

'Then you feel it?'

'There is . . . *something*. Has she said aught to you?'

'No. We have hardly spoken. But I will find out.'

'How? We leave on the morrow. By next week we shall be in France. Brent, you must not let this passion, this folly, hinder you from serving the King. It is not the time for indulgence.'

Brent gazed at his brother, that good man, that ascetic monk. How could he understand the awakening of desire, the burning of the flesh? Tom had put this aside from him, but Brent could not. However much he tried, the thought of Analee, the desire for her, obsessed him. How it would work out he did not know. He turned away from his brother, his head bowed.

'Nothing will hinder me from serving the King, Tom.' Brent stretched and yawned. 'Right now I'm for my bed.' Tom smiled to himself with relief. At least Brent had got his priorities right. For a moment Tom had thought he was going after the girl. He clasped his brother round the shoulder as they climbed to their respective chambers and bade each other goodnight.

Brent felt his skin tingling with excitement. The town below was bathed in moonlight and above it lay the thick forest. Brent went up the steep slope of the main street and on the outskirts of the town, following the brief directions given to him by Analee, saw the field and the wood beyond. In the clear light he could see in the distance the cart and the horse grazing beside it. Suddenly a shadow appeared from the tree and Brent walked quickly towards it.

It was Analee. The moonlight was behind her, nearly obscured by the tops of the trees, but it seemed to make a halo round her head so that she looked of almost ethereal beauty. Brent gasped and the blood pounded in his throat; his chest felt tight and constricted. As he drew near her she put a finger to her lips and, turning, disappeared quickly into the trees. He followed her, terrified of losing her because she wore a big black cloak, and was guided by the path of light made by the moon glinting through the trees.

When they were in the heart of the wood, surrounded by trees, she stopped and turned to him. He saw they stood on a smooth green sward about the size of a bed and beyond that everything was dark. It was so magical that Brent felt he must be possessed by some sort of gypsy spell and he drew her towards him pressing his face into her hair, murmuring into her ears.

Analee was trembling and as her mouth sought Brent's he clasped her round the waist. The cloak she was wearing slipped from her shoulders exposing her beautiful rounded breasts, the nipples erect like tiny rose-buds.

As they kissed the rest of the cloak fell to the floor revealing that she was naked underneath. With a cry Brent held her away from him and gazed at her vibrant body shimmering in the moonlight. Leaning forward, he kissed her. His hands moved from her breasts to the small of her back and, still locked in a deep embrace, they slid gently backwards until they they rested on the soft grass.

Eventually they lay facing each other, the intimate parts of their bodies still in contact, their mouths almost touching, their eyes open, gazing at each other.

'I love you,' Brent whispered.

Analee, her eyes smiling, said nothing.

'Ever since that moonlit night when we met, when I merely felt the outline of your lovely body, I have wanted this. I have thought of nothing else.'

Analee touched his lips with her finger pressing them together.

'Do not say it. It is not love.'

'It *is* love. For me it is.'

His heart grew cold at the thought that, for her, it was not so. Was this just some ritual at which she was particularly adept?

'Love grows with time,' Analee whispered. 'This is passion. It is good of itself. It needs no other commitment.'

'I am committed,' Brent said, 'to you.'

Analee stared beyond him to the sky, dark blue velvet above the trees.

'Sir, you know it is not possible. I am a wandering gypsy . . . you a nobleman. I must go one way, you another. I . . .'

'I have nowhere to go. No home. Analee, let us go together. I am free. Come with me!'

Analee's face twitched with amusement; the sadness had gone. 'And what will your brother say?'

'My brother? He will be going to France. I can stay here with my cousins. I can serve the King *here*. Analee –'

Analee suddenly gazed sharply over Brent's head, her eyes filling with horror. He saw how, petrified, she was about to speak and turned quickly to try and see what it was that had so terrified her. But the blow fell too soon, and the darkness when it came was sharp and sudden. The moonlight was extinguished completely.

5

The cart jogged along the narrow road that wove through the flat
country between Penrith and Carlisle. The mountains of Lakeland
receded into the distance the further north they got and soft
undulating hills had replaced the high Pennine range.

Analee lay in the back of the car, Benjy humped up beside her.
There was now no room for Selinda, so the troupe of formerly gay
musicians had to make frequent stops so that she could rest. No
longer gay . . . indeed it was a melancholy group that strode
silently beside the lurching cart and the tired old horse.

All Analee could see as she lay on the floor of the cart was the
lowering sky, for it had begun to rain and nothing protected her
from the soft insistent drizzle. Her feet had been loosely bound so
that she could not leap over the side and run away; those who had
seen her dance had no doubt as to her ability to perform this feat.
They had let her hands free and she used them to pillow her head
against the rough planks of the cart.

Sometimes she sat up and propped herself against the side,
straining to see the peaks of Lakeland now well to the south; but
they were scarcely etched in the mist and even as she looked they
disappeared altogether. There was no hope for her, no comfort or
solace; no beauty around her, no bright skies or singing birds. She
closed her eyes as she once again recalled the awful events of that
night. She had seen Randal coming. He must have been skulking
in the woods, watching her and Brent making love. Indeed, he had
confessed that it was that sight which had driven him to such
madness, made him pick up the huge stone and crash it down on
Brent's head. Whether he was dead or not Analee had no means
of knowing. It had been nearly dawn, and immediately Randal had
ordered his family to pack up. Within half an hour they had left the
field and the still figure lying face down, the back of his head a
tangled mat of blood and hair.

Randal had gone about his business very deliberately, saying
nothing, giving no explanations – his brothers and sister meekly
obeying him. Analee, too shocked to react let alone protest, was

bound hand and foot and tossed in the cart like a trussed sheep. No one thought to explain anything to her or say a word, no one asked what had happened. Randal had thrown her cloak at her in the forest and until nightfall when they stopped this was all she wore. Selinda had quietly and unquestioningly packed her few things – her brightly coloured skirt, her petticoats and her stiff white bodice with the black lacing up the front.

They knew something terrible had happened; but no one asked what.

Analee was used to this taciturnity – the instinctive obedience of the gypsy to the head of the family. They would not question Randal's motives or his right. He was the head of the family and that was enough. Even Analee fatalistically thought he had a right to behave as he had. He had wanted her, had been prepared to court her in true gypsy fashion and then he had caught her making love in a forest glade to a non-gypsy, a *gadjo*. In some gypsy tribes a maid would have had her head shaved, be an outcast and forced to wear a headscarf knotted under the chin, rather than at the nape of the neck as was the custom, so that everyone would know of her sin.

Before her own downfall, her own exclusion from her tribe, Analee had seen – sometimes, not often, because although the gypsy code of sexual ethics was strict, it varied from tribe to tribe – wrongdoers punished in this way. More often she had seen on her wanderings old gypsy women without an ear, or a nose, or an eye missing – mutilations carried out for transgressions committed in their youth. Men of course got off much more lightly; but didn't men anywhere?

Even though Analee was free, belonged to no tribe and conformed to no custom, she accepted Randal's right to behave as he had. Now he was claiming the ancient gypsy right to marriage by abduction. He was taking her bound to the gypsy camp where he came from, to the *phuri-dai*, the head woman, or to the chief of the tribe who would offer them the bread and salt which were the traditional elements of gypsy marriage.

Randal had explained it to her on the night after her abduction. Until then he had said nothing at all. After the meal he had motioned to the others to leave him and Analee alone and then he had squatted on his haunches, stirring the embers of the fire with a long stick while Analee, hands free but feet firmly bound, sat helplessly before him.

'You knew I wanted you, Analee. I had never wanted a woman like you . . .'

Analee said nothing at first, her eyes smouldering like the embers of the fire. She wanted Randal to know with what contempt she regarded him and what he had done. But he just squatted there stirring the burning wood, his dark, lean face reflective.

'So you take me by force . . .'

'It is the only way. The *phuri-dai* will have to marry us because I have captured you for my bride. If the *phuri-dai* knows you have lain with a *gadjo* your head will be shaved, maybe your nose cut off.'

Analee shuddered. Randal she might one day be able to get rid of; but a lost nose or an ear or an eye could never be recovered.

'You know I will not be happy with you Randal. Why don't you let me go? I have been free for so long, on my own. I belong to no tribe . . .'

'You do now,' Randal said firmly. 'You belong to me. I have captured you.'

With that he got up and stamped out the fire, then went to join the others. Analee had lain down where she was and tried to sleep, aware of the family coming back and bedding down for the night, of the watchful eyes of Randal or Hamo gazing at her every time the bonds cramped and she woke.

The cart rolled on and Randal and Hamo steadied it on either side, taking care to see that Benjy was alright, but having no regard for her at all. She was a chattel, a piece of merchandise tied with string. Even Benjy gazed at her with contempt and Selinda avoided her altogether. She had laid with a *gadjo* – she had committed a grave sin. They knew it, somehow they knew it.

On the third day they came to the camp outside the old town of Carlisle not far from the Scottish border. This was where the Buckland family had its roots. In so far as they had a home this was their home. Those too old to travel lived here permanently and the young ones came and went.

In the distance, as they approached the camp, Analee could see the smoke rising from the many fires, the tents and one or two wooden huts that gave the nomadic camp an air of permanence. Usually when Analee saw a gypsy settlement she felt a sense of belonging, of homecoming – a rest from her wearisome wandering, a reminder of former, happier days. But now she looked at it with terror. What would happen? Would Randal, full of vengeance, report her misdeeds? She would be taken before the *kriss*, an assembly of the elders who meted out justice, and without a doubt she would be punished. No, at best all she could hope for was marriage to a man she didn't love, who had killed her lover, or at least maimed him.

Brent. How often had Analee thought of Brent during that slow tedious journey along the narrow road. They had been attracted from the beginning, and it was fitting that they had come together in the moonlight, in a forest like they had first met.

She had known that it was meant she and Brent should make love and in her heart, even now when it seemed hopeless, she had a feeling she would see him again and that it would happen again. How this would be achieved she knew not. It was the power of her gypsy's second sight, a gift she knew she possessed. She had known that she would wander and then there would be a time of great difficulty, a dark cloud in her life. Then she would be happy again. All this she knew, but how and why were veiled from her.

This was the time of the dark cloud. How long would it last?

As Randal and Hamo led the cart into the camp, ragged children ran towards them, hands were raised in greeting. Some called out. One or two looked curiously into the cart. Randal neither smiled nor responded to greetings but, with his face set, led the horse to the large tent that stood in the centre of the field. Outside a swarm of children played happily and women bustled backwards and forwards between tents and fires preparing the midday meal. The men were busy mending pots and pans, or grooming beyond recognition for resale horses they had either stolen or bought very cheaply. Outside the large tent an old woman sat puffing a clay pipe and beside her sat a man younger than her by many years, but old just the same. Randal left the cart where it was before the tent and with Hamo went over to speak to the couple sitting outside. The old woman's toothless mouth cracked in a joyful grin and her hands reached up to clasp and embrace him. Then they listened carefully while he pointed to the cart where Analee sat alone. Benjy had been helped down by his brother and was now hobbling towards the large tent where he was also greeted and embraced. Then the old man got stiffly to his feet and leaning on a stick walked slowly with Randal over to the cart.

He gazed at Analee, saying nothing, then he chuckled. 'You have captured yourself a fine bride, son. Well . . . does she consent?'

He spoke in *romani* and Analee caught the nuance in his voice. Randal didn't reply but looked at her. Analee thought of the face without a nose, the hideous one-eyed crones . . . She nodded.

'Good.'

The man seemed satisfied and Randal's face relaxed. He smiled at Analee and helped her out of the cart. She stood cramped on her tired legs, unable to move and Randal picked her up and carried her over to the big tent placing her roughly on the ground in front of the tent, almost throwing her in fact.

'This is Rebecca . . . the *phuri-dai*,' he said motioning to the old woman. 'This is Lancelot her son. My father Rander Buckland was married to Lancelot's daughter's sister-in-law. We are all Buck-lands and all related. Lancelot is the head man of the tribe.'

Analee nodded that she had understood and tried to sit up. Her legs were stiff. The old woman was looking at her enigmatically – not unsympathetically, but in a way Analee didn't completely understand.

'Untie her, Randal,' Lancelot said. 'You have her consent.'

'Oh, she has consented?' the old woman said in a voice firm despite her years.

'She nodded,' Lancelot said, 'when I asked her if she consented.'

'You must hear her say it,' Rebecca said. 'Then we have her bond and can untie her feet.'

'Do you consent to be the bride of Randal Buckland who has claimed this right by capture?' Lancelot intoned solemnly. Again Randal looked at Analee, his face impassive, his chin tilted, his stance proud. It made him feel a man to have captured Analee, like a gypsy brigand of old. Even though he had tied her up and had given her no chance she was still his by right of capture. Forced capture. She was reluctant, Randal knew. How she must hate him. Her eyes burned with resentment and her nostrils flared like a horse that refuses to be broken in. He had seen that stubborn refusal before in the eyes of an untamed horse; but he tamed them in the end. Oh yes, he did; and then it was sweet to see how meekly they submitted – as Analee would to him. In his mind's eye he could see her body glistening in the moonlight responding to the demands of the *gadjo*, giving willingly of herself.

His eyes grew bright with desire at the memory of the sight – which mentally he had dwelt on many times. Analee was a fitting prize to capture – stubborn, untamed, but – oh – what booty for the man who lay with her.

'You must say it, woman. Say the words,' Lancelot said. Analee looked at Randal, at Hamo, at Benjy . . . they all gazed stonily at her. Even Selinda showed no pity . . . She had sinned with a *gadjo*. If the tribe knew she would have her hair cut off, at least, perhaps worse . . . Analee saw the look in their eyes, the unified hostility and knew they would all condemn her. She fingered her nose . . . 'I consent,' she said.

All those who had gathered around to witness the strange ceremony clapped and shouted. The expression in Randal's eyes and that of his family changed from suspicion and hostility to relief, even to gladness. She had submitted. There would be no more trouble from Analee now.

'Let us have the bread and salt at once,' Randal said, bending to untie Analee's legs, 'and we can be wed.' Rebecca looked surprised.

'You wish it so? You do not wish a proper gypsy wedding with dancing and feasting?'

'We can feast later,' Randal said laughing, chafing Analee's ankles to make the blood run through. 'Now that I have this prize I do not want her to escape me again!'

Analee, astounded, gazed at Randal. How could this man force her into a marriage when he had hardly spoken a civil word to her in days? Randal who had been so kind before, so adoring, seemed to hate her . . . but he wanted her, she knew that. He had seen her make love in the moonlight; goodness knows how long he had watched, maybe he'd seen everything. He'd been inflamed. Randal wanted her as Brent had. All men were the same. Well it might as well be got over. There was an inevitablity about it. Marriage to Randal would not be forever; she knew that. Her second sight had told her that this was just a dark cloud, a bad time. One day the cloud would pass and the sun would shine again . . . and Analee, the wandering gypsy, would be free.

The gypsies in the camp were excited by the unexpected news of a wedding and immediately ceased the tasks in which they were engaged to run to the tent of the *phuri-dai* who would perform the marriage. Most of them had seen Randal and his family come in with the cart, and many had seen Analee unceremoniously taken out from it, her feet bound, and dumped on the ground in front of Rebecca.

It was a long time since there had been a marriage by capture in the camp. What they did not know was whether the captured bride was willing or unwilling. If she were willing it meant that she and her *tomnimi*, her betrothed, had met secretly, had been denied permission to marry by her father. The man had thus made a show of forcing her, but in fact she had gone willingly to stay a while with him and consummate their union. Now the marriage would consecrate this physical union that had already occurred, and then the bride and groom would return to the girl's father and a reconciliation would take place. But if the bride were reluctant, if she had been forced against her will, then after the wedding the bridegroom would do his best to woo her, to win her love – for true love was an essential element in gypsy lore. He would go to the *cohani*, the sorceress, and obtain from her spells to win the heart of his captured bride.

Now, as they hurried to the tent looking forward to the feasting and dancing that would take place later in the day, the tribe did not know what was the case with the bride that Randal Buckland had brought home tethered in a cart.

Although Lancelot was the leader of the tribe, the undisputed head was his mother Rebecca, the *phuri-dai*. She did not know how old she was, but some thought over a hundred years of age. She, his mother, knew how old Lancelot was and he was nearly eighty. She was said to be able to remember as far back as the Civil War and the execution of the King and that was nearly a hundred years ago.

Rebecca had held dominance over the Buckland tribe gathered outside Carlisle for so many years that there were few who did not remember her as *phuri-dai*, even the very old ones. In her youth she had been a great beauty, something of a *cohani* herself, a weaver of magic spells, a fortune-teller of reknown. She had been married three times, all to members of her own tribe – maybe more, she couldn't remember – and she had fifteen children, at least; she couldn't be quite sure of that now.

Everyone in the tribe was related to her one way or another and as she waited, a new rug around her shoulders for the ceremony she was about to perform, her old eyes still bright, still piercing, noted where everyone was and what they were doing.

Rebecca, in her long life, had seen many enforced marriages – and knew every variation of betrothal and marriage within gypsy lore. She had seen willing brides and reluctant brides, passionate brides and those whose feelings towards their husbands were cold. On the whole gypsies wanted warm romantic love to bless the marriages but, being human, Rebecca knew you could not always have what you wanted.

Randal's bride, she had known from the moment her wise old eyes saw her tossed on the ground, was very reluctant, very unwilling. Randal may perhaps have done better to have thought again; but she knew what Randal was – headstrong, a law unto himself. He had wanted this woman and he had captured her. God knew from where. She looked foreign; she was so tall that Rebecca felt she could not possibly have hailed from these parts where the women were medium or small in height. Maybe not even from England. She had a glowing olive skin and dangerous-looking dark eyes. She was a beauty alright; but she would give Randal a bad time if she wanted to.

Soon he would come to her or to Reyora, the *cohani*, and ask for spells to bind his bride to him. Rebecca slowly shook her head. Even strong spells would be difficult to tame that one, she thought.

Standing quietly by the tent Analee too was watching the preparations, noting how everyone put down what they were doing and hurried to where the old *phuri-dai* was sitting. And the *phuri-dai*, she saw, was watching her – an old, old wise-looking woman, and shaking her head.

She thought she saw sympathy in those knowing old eyes, friendliness and, for the first time for days, Analee lifted her head and smiled. Rebecca seemed to nod her head as though she understood, and then she turned to take the bowl of salt and the large piece of bread offered her by a young boy of the tribe, one of her great-grandsons she thought.

Suddenly the babel of noise stopped at a signal from Lancelot and everyone was quiet; nothing moved except the tops of the trees, beside the field, which rustled gently in the breeze. Autumn was in the air; one or two of the leaves were falling already. Winter came early in these parts. Rebecca nodded at Randal who stepped over from where he had been standing with his brothers and sister and held out his hand to Analee. Analee stared at him, her face a stubborn mask.

'You have consented,' Randal murmured menacingly under his breath and slowly she put out a hand and took his. Then he led her before the *phuri-dai* where they both knelt, hands clasped.

Rebecca leaned forward, her bent arthritic hands carefully breaking into two halves the large piece of freshly baked bread. Then from the bowl held by the boy she took salt and, sprinkling it on to each of the two pieces, gave one first to Randal then one to Analee. At the same time she murmured according to custom, 'When you are tired of this bread and this salt you will be tired of each other.'

Analee took the bread and gazed at it for a long time, then at a nudge from Randal she gave her piece to him and took his.

'Eat,' Rebecca commanded and she watched over them as they consumed the bread and salt.

Then she took a pitcher handed to her by Lancelot and poured over the heads of the kneeling couple grains of wheat that had been freshly gathered in the harvest. When she had finished and the newly married couple, the yellow grains spilling all over their dark hair and bright clothes, still knelt before her she gave the pitcher to Lancelot who dashed it to the ground, keeping the handle for himself. Then the boy who had helped to officiate in the ceremony carefully picked up the broken pieces, gave one each to the bride and groom and handed the rest to Randal's family and those who, nearest the couple, eagerly reached out for these good luck symbols.

It was over. A babble of voices broke out and Randal helped his bride to her feet, dusting the grains off his clothes, shaking his black curly hair. He smiled at Analee but she looked coldly past him at the *phuri-dai* because she had sensed that the wise old woman knew she was married against her will.

Then a man stepped forward and held up his hands. This was Sacki the son of Lancelot, grandson of Rebecca and father of young Gilderoy who had helped his great-grandmother with the ceremony. Most of Lancelot's sons were now dispersed over the kingdom, but Sacki had remained in the camp to help control tribal order. As a boy he had been forced into the army and had the lower part of his leg shot off at Malplaquet when Marlborough and Prince Eugene defeated the French in one of the wars of the

Spanish Succession – though little did Sacki Buckland, a boy of 14, know what the war was about or who was in command. He was lucky to come home alive. The gypsies, being considered the lowest of the low even in the scum of the army, were not deemed fit to treat and were normally left to die where they fell. It was only because the leg was clean shot off and one of his fellow gypsies had applied a tourniquet to staunch the blood that Sacki had lived at all. In fact his life had surely been saved by the brotherhood of gypsies who had spirited him away from the army and nursed him in France until, on a makeshift wooden stump, he was fit to return home.

Sacki had a loud firm voice which seemed to make up for his physical disability and everyone stopped talking and listened to him.

'Now that we have Randal and his bride married according to our law we shall gather in the afternoon for feasting and dancing. So hasten to your tents and make preparations.'

The throng cheered and smiled and, breaking up, some gathered round Randal and shook his hand or clasped his shoulder. Few took notice of Analee – the men because it was not allowed to ogle a new bride and the women because they knew that, to have been married in such a fashion and so quickly, she had offended against gypsy honour – she had lain with Randal and could not be a virgin. She was *marimé*, unclean, a woman to be scorned and pitied even among themselves. So they moved away looking at her over their backs and one or two made signs to her that meant they despised her.

Analee saw the dark glances and knew the reason for them. She knew how much the gypsy women enjoyed a conventional wedding where everything was agreed beforehand, the bride known and preferably a member of the tribe. They would enjoy preparing her for days, making her clothes and gradually building up to the climax which was the wedding ceremony and the feast. But the focus of interest, above all, was the physical union of the man and woman which took place during the feast in a tent set aside for the purpose.

The ceremony of the *dichlo*, the official deflowering of the bride, was an essential part of the gypsy marriage ritual and it was enjoyed the more by those who had undergone the humiliation of it rather than by those for whom it was yet to come. At a sign from the new husband four matrons would go into the tent to inspect the newly deflowered bride, and emerge bearing a white silk handkerchief soaked in her vaginal blood which they would take round for the inspection of the members of the tribe gathered outside.

Analee thought the ceremony of the *dichlo* was disgusting and degrading and she did not regret that on her wedding day it would not be performed, even if the women slunk away pretending to despise her because she was *marimé*, unclean. They thought she and Randal already had carnal knowledge of each other. What would they have thought if it was revealed that her most recent experience with a man was with a *gadjo*, a non-gypsy – and scarcely a week before at that!

Analee suddenly recalled to mind Brent and the way he had lain. He must have been dead or mortally wounded. How long ago it all seemed, how trivial life was for events of such importance to be over and others to happen so quickly. Within a week she had made love to a *gadjo* and married a full-blooded gypsy, a member of a tribe.

So be it. She would bide with him as long as was necessary; she would be a wife to him because she had promised; she had eaten the salt and the broken bread and seen the pitcher smashed to smithereens. In gypsy symbolism this meant she was bound to respect him for as many years as the vase had been reduced to pieces. Seven pieces she'd counted – seven years. Was it possible that she could live with a man who had forcibly wed her for seven long years?

For the rest of the day the camp resounded to laughter and the sounds of voices raised in song. A wedding was a good thing and even a reluctant bride – and she clearly had been, anyone could see that by the way she never looked at her husband all during the ceremony – better than no bride at all. Randal was popular and they wished he had found someone who obviously loved him. But beautiful as his bride was she was foreign-looking and proud. The women could see that the men secretly admired her and they despised her the more that she had given herself easily, that she was no virgin, *marimé*. Pah! Well maybe the *cohani* would give Randal a potion and his bride would fall madly in love with him. It had happened.

The *phuri-dai* took the newly wedded pair into her tent and they drank ale or herbal teas. The men gathered on one side and the women on the other. No one talked to Analee; few even looked at her.

Then the curtain over the tent parted and a woman came in and everyone momentarily stopped talking. The woman looked at Randal and then, for a long time, letting her gaze linger, at Analee. Then she went over to talk to Rebecca. Analee knew without doubt that this was the *cohani* – she could tell by the way that her eyes turned up like those of a bird and the peculiar intensity of her gaze as she stared at Analee; also by the way everyone stepped respectfully aside for her to pass.

The *cohani* could exercise magic for good or ill; she could tell fortunes, weave spells and provide potions. She could cure and she could kill. Every tribe had a *cohani* – someone who from girlhood had developed special skills, learning the craft, often from their mothers or a near relative.

Some said that, while still in her childhood, a demon had penetrated her as she slept and when the girl awoke she was aware of her special powers and that she was *cohani*.

In her youth many had considered Analee to be *cohani* – they had sworn she had magical powers and, in fact, she knew that she had the gift of second sight and that sometimes things which she said would happen, did. But she knew she was not a real *cohani* – she knew a lot about herbs and spells having learned about them from her grandmother. She had the gypsy's respect for the influence of the *cohani* and especially for her prowess when she was also *drabarni*, a woman skilled in the medicinal use of herbs. In some tribes one woman was both *cohani* and *drabarni*; in others they were different – the *cohani* was primarily concerned with black magic and with evil, the *drabarni* with good.

Reyora the *cohani* was a great-granddaughter of Rebecca and she had learned many of her powers from her great-grandmother and assumed her mantle when Rebecca grew too old. She was the daughter of Rebecca's grandson Spartus and she had married her first cousin Wester Buckland, the son of Rebecca's granddaughter Zia.

Everyone had known from her early childhood that Reyora had *cohani* powers like her great-grandmother. She had known so much about potions and spells and had saved a new-born baby from death merely by incantation. People came to fear Reyora because she could exercise her gifts both for good and ill; they took care not to cross her path.

When Reyora married it was well known she had chosen Wester Buckland and that he wanted to marry someone else. He was even *tomnani*, betrothed, and then his beautiful bride-to-be, a big strong healthy girl, suddenly sickened for no apparent reason and died. Reyora had been asked to help her, but she would do nothing and even Rebecca, who was *cohani* until a very advanced age, would not interfere.

Wester was terror-stricken when his *tomnani* died so young, so unexpectedly, and he immediately took Reyora for his bride, as she wished, however reluctantly. Reyora was not beautiful, not good-looking even by gypsy standards; but she was not ugly like many *cohani* – she was arresting, with her slanted eyes and the quiet determined way she had of moving like a bird of prey about to strike its victim. Reyora was now thirty-three.

As soon as she entered the tent and looked at Analee Reyora knew she was not in love with Randal, that she had not wished to marry him and that she bore a grudge against him and his tribe. Reyora had four sons and no daughter which was a disappointment to her because she would have liked the *cohani* powers to have continued in her branch of the family. Try as she had to weave the right spell she had been unsuccessful in bringing a daughter to herself and Wester.

After talking to Rebecca and greeting her relations and Randal, Reyora walked slowly over to Analee and smiled at her, the first person, the first woman to show her kindness apart from Rebecca, since she had come to the camp.

'What is your name?' Reyora said softly, seeing the fear and the despair in Analee's eyes.

'Analee.'

'I am the *cohani*.'

'I know.'

Reyora smiled a mysterious smile, aware that her powers had been instantly recognized by someone who, Reyora sensed, had some *cohani* gifts herself.

'I am called Reyora. Rebecca is my great-grandmother. Were you ever *cohani*, *drabarni*?' she added casually.

Analee shook her head.

'Your mother?'

Analee's eyes were veiled. She didn't intend to reveal her past to anyone, let alone the *cohani*. But she knew the *cohani* could divine much that she couldn't see. Analee felt already that Reyora knew all about her.

'I have some *cohani* powers. I have been able sometimes to predict the future; but herbs, and spells . . . no.'

Reyora noticed that Analee lingered on the word 'spells'. She knew Randal would be looking for a spell to make her love him.

'I hope you will be happy with the tribe now you are among us,' Reyora whispered, 'and that you will count us among your friends. Even though you came unwillingly, and I know how unwillingly, we here are now your family to love and help you.'

Analee didn't reply, and Reyora could tell from the smouldering look in her dark eyes that she would do all she could to resist the love spells, all the magic, all the incantations that she could perform.

From outside came the sound of the flute and, looking around, Analee saw that none of the musicians were present. They had gone to play at the wedding feast. Randal came up to her and, smiling at her, took her hand.

'Will you dance at our wedding?'

Analee stared at him, her gaze meeting his.

'You have accepted,' Randal murmured. 'We are wed.'

Analee tilted her head, her feet tapped time to the music, her body swayed and she allowed him to lead her out of the tent.

Outside, the field had been transformed in a few hours into a spectacle of colour and gaiety. Streamers and banners had been hung from the tents and mats spread on the ground for the food. A pig was slowly being turned over a huge fire, its succulent smells reminding Analee that she had not eaten properly for a week. The hedgehogs were being wrapped in clay and laid in the red hot ashes under the slowly turning pig. On another spit a sheep was roasting and on yet another a young heifer. The smell of baking bread mingled with that of roasting meats, and cakes, sweetmeats and jellies were also being prepared.

The young men had taken a cart into Carlisle and now came back with flagons of ale and some wine for the chiefs at the wedding. The children, half naked, were running about playing with their dogs or hoops and wrestling with one another in the grass.

Looking at the scene Analee felt grow in her an approximation of happiness that she had not expected. Here she was with her own people, accepted into a tribe again, a member of the Buckland family. She belonged; she was Randal's wife and related to Rebecca the *phuri-dai*, head of the tribe. She could, if she liked, settle to a life of ease bearing children for Randal and establishing herself as one of the matriarchs of the tribe, a power, a force.

Unless she wanted to she need never go on the road again, wandering from town to town, eating berries, making out with men like Randal to sleep with, or being chased by others less pleasant like Brewster Driver. Yet, unlike the others who had been content with a night or two, Randal had wanted her forever. He had cared enough to take her by force, despite seeing her in the arms of a *gadjo*. Why, he might have killed them both on the spot. Analee's eyes sidled to the face of her bridegroom who was now presenting her to the gathered tribe, who called out and clapped. He was a handsome man, no doubt; tall and well built despite the slight wiry frame of a dancer. There was a savagery in his eyes, a pride in his mien that she had not noticed before as he followed her about, trying to please her in order to gain her attention.

Capturing a bride, taking her by force, had transformed Randal; given him stature. She thought if he had behaved like this before she might have been more interested; might have been indifferent to the advances of Brent Delamain. Now he firmly gripped her hand and led her into the circle made by the tribe and Benjy struck up a theme on his flute and Hamo on the violin and Selinda raised her tambourine into the air. At a signal Randal lifted his arms above his head and slowly circled his bride, his eyes flashing, his belly thrust forward in a primitive erotic gesture. For this was an ancient dance, the *alborea*, which had been brought all the way from Spain, a dance full of meaning and significance and much performed at weddings.

As he circled her, his hips undulating, his fingers clicking and his chin tilted proudly and aggressively forwards, his eyes never leaving hers, Analee felt rising within her an unexpected surge of excitement, even of desire such as she had never dreamt she would feel about Randal.

He was, after all, a good-looking man, a gypsy like herself, a romany, a wanderer, above all a dancer – a superb, excellent dancer who understood the rhythms and cadences of the gypsy dances which they performed so well together. In time with the music Randal stopped suddenly and then Analee slowly began her part of the intricate courtship dance, first stepping slowly and deliberately, then raising her hands above her head, her breasts thrust forward, her hips swaying as she gently circled her partner. Their eyes never left each other's and, as she revolved he turned on his axis and slowly smiles broke on their faces in mutual accord and their teeth gleamed. As though sensing that her hostility was breaking the crowd warmed to the magic of the dance and began to tap and clap and sway to the rhythm of the music.

Then the pace of the dance increased, sweat pouring from Hamo's brow as he frantically bowed the strings of the fiddle, his fingers appearing to have magical properties of their own. Analee and Randal were now stamping their feet together, their torsos almost touching, each with a hand nonchalantly on a hip, the other raised above the head, Analee clicking her castanets, Randal his fingers. Their bodies moved together and parted, their hips gyrated and, because it was a wedding dance, it seemed to anticipate the act of love intended to cement the ceremonial vows they had just made.

But, as the rhythm increased and the blood pounded in their temples and their bodies grew fevered and hot it was instinct that spoke, not thought or words, not memory of violence committed or love lost.

Randal and Analee danced until their feet were bleeding and their bodies ached. They danced while the bold sun sank low in the sky and the moon timidly appeared over the horizon, so that at one point night and day merged as their bodies fused in the dance. Then, at last, in front of one of the myriad fires they sank exhausted to the ground and ate pork and beef and the delicacies which were offered to them.

For a long time after they were replete they sat staring into the flames, not speaking, watching the other dancers, the other musicians who had taken over, their own bodies limp with weariness.

Then quietly and without being noticed, when the merriment was at its height, at a gesture from Randal they got up and silently stole away towards the tent that had been prepared for them.

* * *

At dawn some gypsies were still dancing and feasting and fires still flared to meet the rays of the rising sun. Inside the nuptial tent Analee lay on her back aware of the light glimmering through the curtained entrance, of the man asleep beside her, of his heavy regular breathing.

Randal had thrown himself on the palliasse prepared for both of them, too exhausted to stir or say a word, to make any attempt to take her. And Analee had lain throughout most of the night thinking, reviewing her life, trying to see into the future, trying to decide what would happen, what would be best for her to do.

Randal was her husband now; he had captured her, but not won her. It would take a long time to win her heart; but her body he could have as many others had. As Brent Delamain had. But if she did see Brent again, ever, it would not be for a long long time. Analee meanwhile had her life to lead, a life difficult enough without moaning over the thoughts of a great love that might have been. Or might not. He had looked for her, yes, and wanted her; but so had many men. So did Randal. He had wanted her enough to capture her; make her his bride by force.

As the sunlight filtered through the tent flap, Analee looked at his face, softened in the half light, dark with his beard, the hairs on his chest still matted with sweat. He looked very handsome as he slept, manly and virile, his dark hair tumbling over his brow. Suddenly he groaned and turned over so that he lay on his belly with his head facing hers. Looking at him she could see his eyes were wide open, staring at her, at the mound her breasts made, at the sweat trickling between them on to her own flat stomach. It was very hot inside the tent; they were both panting a little.

Randal put a hand on her thigh which was exposed to him as she had moved back the coverlets because of the heat. She felt a tremor, but she did not resist him.

As he raised himself, for a moment she saw his dark intense face, his brow glistening with sweat, leaning over her. His eyes were a strange colour, a reflection of herself, and then his mouth pressed hard down upon hers and she could feel his even white teeth against hers, and she bared her mouth with a savagery which equalled his. Then they began twisting and turning as though playing out once again the slow preparatory rhythm of the wedding dance.

When they awoke it was because the curtain had parted to let in the light and old Rebecca stood there, a bowl in her hands, her old face cracked in a smile of satisfaction. Randal was still lying on Analee, his head resting on her breast, her legs crossed over his as though still to imprison him.

The old woman gazed at the naked bodies covered with sweat, glistening, and she smelt the air with satisfaction. She still thought it was a wonderful sight to see two nubile, fertile bodies coupling, easy with replete desire. She had noticed the change in the dance, saw how well suited they were, and the sight in front of her pleased her the more.

There would be no need of spells now.

She put the bowl of scented herbal tea beside them and silently withdrew, closing the curtain behind her.

Randal had seen the old woman and the satisfaction on her face, and now gazed at the face of his half sleeping bride. Now she was his. He had taken her many times and he would again. And how well she received him! She was a fine creature, an earthbound human being and now his; his seed inside her, the mother-to-be of his children. He had conquered Analee as a stud conquers a fractious mare; he had tamed her and moulded her to his desire. She opened her eyes and saw his gaze, understood it, and his lips brushed hers.

'Well?' Randal said, the first words, almost, they had spoken since they had been married.

Analee smiled lazily back.

'Well?'

'We are wed then.'

'Truly it seems. Well and truly.' She glanced at their bodies and smiled.

'I will be a good husband to you, Analee. I know I took you by force; but I felt there was no other way. I . . .' He looked uncertainly at Analee and she turned her gaze from his. 'The gadjo,' he said at last, his voice bitter.

'I know. What you did was wrong.'

'I was beside myself. To see you with him . . . and I wanted you so much.'

'I know. Don't speak of it. It is finished and over. You captured me and I accepted it and now, well we are wed . . . and we are right well bedded.'

'Aye, thoroughly,' Randal said with satisfaction, and he took her to himself again while outside the noon sun climbed higher and higher into the heavens.

6

In medieval times much of Lakeland belonged to the great monastic foundations established mainly in the twelfth and thirteenth centuries. One of the greatest, founded in 1127 by Stephen, Count of Boulogne, nephew of the reigning monarch, Henry I, was Furness Abbey. Here in a sheltered valley overshadowed by steep cliffs of red sandstone and surrounded by green woods, the Cistercian foundation had for 400 years acquired and controlled lands and possessions that amounted almost to a kingdom. The Abbots were nearly as mighty as the marcher lords who wielded such power from the reign of William Rufus onwards.

The Abbeys controlled wool and pastures, sheep and cattle and they built earthern dikes that wound across the moors and pasturelands as boundaries to show the limits of their properties. In 1209 the monks of Furness bought the greater part of Borrowdale from the heiress to the Barony of Allerdale, Alice de Rumelli. The boundaries of the property reached from the Head of Derwentwater to the Sty Head Pass. Most of this land was used for the grazing of sheep and cattle, but to the west the Forest of Copeland arose from the Buttermere fells and was kept as a deer reserve.

Grange-in-Borrowdale was one of the chief monastic settlements of that beautiful valley. The name 'grange' meant a farm belonging to a monastery and from the Borrowdale settlement the monks ran their estate, 'grangia nostra de Boroudale.'

The monastic lands were broken up at the time of the Dissolution and parcelled among the local nobility or gentry. Some were acquired by right of tenure by the yeoman farmers – 'statesmen' as they were called, who formed the backbone of the population in northern England. But now in the first half of the eighteenth century a new class was developing, thanks to the opening of trade routes; new inventions that were improving industrial techniques, and the prosperity brought about by years of peace under the first Hanoverians and their able Prime Minister, Robert Walpole. The rich yeoman farmer now might also dabble in business, become an ironmaster, a forgemaster or a dealer in wool. The pack-horses plied between the coastal ports of Cumberland and the hinter regions of Lakeland where the sturdy Herdwick sheep gave of their wool and the mines yielded their rich ores – iron, copper, lead, plumbago and tungsten.

The Allonbys were part of the old nobility, part of the Lakeland heritage that went back to the Conquest, yet they had not acquired the new skills of making money by commerce. Maybe the intrinsic awareness of their class held them back; the knowledge of the statesmen they had sent to Parliament in London, the soldiers and sailors to the wars, the monks to the abbeys and the scholars to the universities.

Several members of their family had been monks of the Cistercian Order at Furness and two of them abbots. Now, stripped of their lands and great possessions by successive monarchs and rulers bent on vengeance, all the Allonbys had left was their lovely house, Furness Grange, which stood on a tree-covered promontory jutting into Lake Derwentwater.

The promontory was known as Catsclaw because it sprang out from the steep smooth slope of Catbells mountain which swept downwards to the lake. And indeed the jagged rocks and stones of the peninsula did resemble those of some massive predatory cat and the spiky coniferous trees its fur. Rising from the trees Furness Grange, largely an Elizabethan construction, was build of warm, pink sandstone – maybe quarried from the hills surrounding Furness Abbey or, at the Dissolution, the abbey itself – with black crossbeams and narrow mullioned windows.

But the most spectacular thing about the Grange was its view of the lake and the surrounding fells and mountains covered with heather, bracken or green woods. Occasionally there were stark, grey, rocky crags whose sharp teeth rose unevenly above the lake like those of some monstrous giant.

In the mornings when it was fine a mist rose from the still waters of the lake, and when it cleared the rosy tops of the hills and mountains could be seen in all directions from massive Skiddaw at one end to, at the other, towering Castle Crag which almost blocked the narrow opening known as the Jaws of Borrowdale. Opposite were the wooded precipice of Walla Crag and the sharp tongue of Friar Craig, above which the rough, rocky ridge of

Glaramara could just be seen, topping the hills on the east side of Borrowdale.

Every morning Brent Delamain, from his bed by the window on the first floor of the Grange, could look out on the peaceful scene. The hardy permanence of the rocky crags, the calm immutable serenity of the lake not only consoled him for his misfortune, but seemed to give him strength so that every day he felt a little better.

After being found in the copse near Penrith by a farmer on his way to milk his cows in a nearby field, Brent was taken to the town mortuary where he was left for dead. The surgeon found no pulse and no breath and he was put on an icy slab, the blood on his head already congealed into a sharp black rock-like substance. It was thought that he had been the victim of some jealous husband for he had been found naked, his fine clothes neatly folded nearby. From those it was deduced he was a gentleman who had seduced the wife of a farmer or some person of lowly station.

It was the mortuary attendant who recognized Brent and probably saved him from death. He had once been a servant with the Delamain family, moving to Penrith on his marriage to the daughter of a shopkeeper. Even the blood and dirt could not disguise that noble brow, that fine aquiline face. Out of respect for his late master the attendant, Norbert, covered his naked body with warm blankets and set out to seek someone who might know what Brent Delamain was doing in Penrith. It was but a short step to the hostelry where Tom was staying, already having alerted the town authorities about his brother's disappearance.

For the rest of his short life Tom Delamain thought that God had intervened to save his brother. The form had indeed seemed lifeless as Tom bent to inspect it and then knelt to say in Latin the prayers for the dead. As he gazed through his tears on the still waxen face of his brother he saw colour slowly steal into the white lips and, imperceptibly, a small pulse began to beat at his neck.

Quickly the surgeon was called and Brent was removed to the tavern and placed in a warm bed and everything that could be done to bring him to life was done. But although Brent breathed and his pulse grew stronger he did not recover consciousness and remained in that state for nearly a week. In that time his cousins, John and Stewart Allonby rode over from Furness Grange and a coach was hired which, under their escort, went very slowly along the narrow road to Keswick. There the coach was abandoned and the rest of the journey was made across the lake by water to the landing stage at Catspaw.

It was a sad arrival for Tom who had not seen his Allonby cousins for years. He felt closer to this other branch of the family than to the Delamains because their loyalty to the Stuart cause was legendary abroad, in those places where exiles waited and plotted. He had a fierce, proud love of the Allonbys and what they had endured, still endured, for the rightful king and the old faith.

How different was the arrival on this cold day in September of the year 1744 from the one he had planned. True Brent was there, but unconscious and, some thought, unlikely to recover. There was a sadness about the house for days as those around prayed and waited for a sign of change.

But Brent was a young, vigorous man and whether it was the result of all the prayers offered up for him or the skill of the doctors who were called from as far away as Preston and Carlisle to attend him, or his own robust constitution, none knew. But one day, as Tom sat beside his bed, saying his Office, he looked up and suddenly saw Brent's blue eyes, a little faded because they had been shielded from the light for so long, gazing at him with the uncertainty and confusion of a new-born baby. They were unable to focus properly, and they scarcely seemed to recognize Tom. Brent found difficulty in talking and could not move his limbs and for the first few days it was hard to tell whether his recovery was to be desired or whether it were better he had died; whether he would be a normal human being, or a lifelong invalid.

But gradually Brent started to recover; his eyes cleared and remained fixed when he looked upon a person. He started to form words that made sense and his limbs began to move. Then one day, as Mary Allonby was sitting by his bed reading, he looked at her with a clarity that was startling and smiled.

After that his recovery was swift. There was no impairment to the brain or the limbs, as far as the doctors could tell. He would make a complete recovery; he would live to father children, if God wished it, and serve the King. And then, knowing all was well, Tom set out one morning and, accompanied by Stewart, made his way to Whitehaven where he took a ship for France. He could delay no more.

* * *

Every morning Brent was a little better, but he loved to lie in his bed looking out on the lake watching the mist break and, if it was fine, the sun rise above the purple slopes of Skiddaw. He could feel the blood flowing strongly in his limbs and he would twitch each muscle to be sure it still worked. Then he would turn and look towards the door with anticipation, waiting for his cousin Mary to bring him his breakfast.

Mary Allonby, fair-haired and oval faced, petite, very like his mother, her aunt, had become indispensable to Brent. Like a good angel she was to be observed sitting quietly by his side, reading to him, or keeping a companionable silence if he did not feel like it or wished to sleep. At first she had fed him, preparing his food herself, making it delicate and tempting for the invalid and spooning it gently through his cracked parted lips.

She was the first thing he saw in the morning and the last thing at night as she gave him the gentle smile he had come so much to love, kissed his brow and blew out the candle. He would watch her close the door, the soft light in the corridor outside gradually receding, leaving him in darkness and he would think of her moving quietly along the corridor, her braided hair gleaming in the glow of the candle she carried in her hand, the soft fabric of her dress swirling around her slim figure.

Four weeks after he had been found and left for dead Brent Delamain gazed with anticipation at the door, waiting for it to open and Mary to come in with her tray. Today he would get up and dress and go for a walk; just a short one, as far as the lake. Usually he dressed for part of the day or sometimes he didn't dress at all, but stayed in his nightshirt with a warm shawl about his shoulders, a rug over his knees as he sat by the window.

But today he felt so well and vigorous. Why, he could run up Catbells and down again. He wanted to be well to go and join Tom in France, prepare the way for the conquest by the King. There was a tap at the door and Mary came in with the tray in her hand. Brent stretched his arms over his head in an expansive gesture.

'Mary, I feel so well today. I could walk over Honister. I could . . .'

'Brent, Brent,' Mary laughed, placing the tray with fresh rolls, Cumberland butter and hot coffee on a table by the bed. 'Mr Lorrimer said only *short* distances first. He has been a good doctor, done you well and you must abide by what he says.'

Brent shrugged and turned to butter his rolls. 'Maybe you're right. The Allonby common sense my mother always called it. We'll go to the lake and throw stones. What say, Mary?'

Mary smiled shyly, looking into his face, so thrilled he was recovered, and that she had helped in some small way to bring it about. Mary Allonby had always been half in love with her handsome cousin, who was four years her senior, but he had never seemed aware of her, in that way, behaving towards her like a brother, fond, chiding, but never at all loving. Mary, a gently nurtured country girl, was well aware of Brent's reputation with women. That he ran after women in London and at Cambridge and they ran even faster after him. That the women with whom he associated were never nice, well brought up ladies like Mary, but the sort who frequented taverns or were to be found on the boards of theatres or, worse, who sold their favours for money or gain.

Mary could never believe it of her handsome, fastidious cousin, that he could associate with women of this kind. Why, to his very finger-tips he was the epitome of an English gentleman with his proud, erect carriage, his lean aristocratic face, his easy manners, his soldierly bearing on a horse. But Mary had known some of the young women in whom his mother had tried in vain to interest her son – and they had all said the same thing with a woeful shaking of the head; Brent was not interested.

Even the reason Brent was here in this sorry state was supposed to be due to a woman, though no one knew for sure. Tom had breathed the awful truth to John, and John had told Stewart and Stewart had whispered it to her – Brent had been found in a forest without his clothes on; not robbed, for his clothes and wallet were nearby. It all looked as though Brent was up to his old tricks again, but this time with more serious consequences. It had nearly killed him.

Was this why she had detected a change in his attitude towards her? She was sure his glances were becoming loving rather than friendly, his touch amorous rather than brotherly. Had he realized at last that this sort of woman was no good for him, got him into trouble, nearly killed him? Mary didn't know. All she did know was that the late September days were golden with happiness, and rich with promise. For her hope was that the cousin whom she had loved for so long was returning this love.

Brent was aware he had met death, maybe lingered in its

shadows. He seemed to have emerged from a long dark passage in which mists had swirled and fearsome odours prevailed. Thus to open his eyes on scenes of such natural beauty as Derwentwater in the autumn; and such feminine physical beauty as his gentle cousin Mary doing her needlepoint beside him, was enough to make him fall passionately in love with life all over again. Maybe for the first time really to value being alive.

He had never really looked at Mary properly before, appreciated the grace of her long, white throat, the depths of her clear blue, almost violet eyes, the soft swell of her young virginal bosom. Her dull-gold hair was braided around her head and little wisps which had escaped the pins fell engagingly about her forehead. When she was near him her face was always transformed by a soft smile and when she looked at him it seemed to deepen into something very special.

Gradually Brent came to be used to Mary beside him, quietly reading or sewing. They would look over the lake together and their eyes would meet and he would think it must always be thus; he and Mary Allonby were made for each other.

But what of the future? Brent's heart grew cold at the thought of the war that would ensue in his wake if Prince Charles should ever land in this country; of what it would do to his and Mary's tranquil life together. But he knew it was his duty; honour before love, and as he grew stronger and the days shortened into October he knew he would soon have to sail to France and keep his promise to join Tom.

Brent ate quickly as Mary moved about the room straightening the books; freshening the flowers with bunches of autumn leaves she had brought with her. She was happy just to be in the same room as Brent, to have him near her. Would it could be so always.

Brent finished his breakfast with a clatter of cup on saucer, wiped his lips on the napkin and swung one leg out of bed. Mary looked quickly away because his nightshirt had ridden up and one long, brown, hairy leg had a great tuft of even darker hair at the top.

'Mary, send up James to shave and dress me and we shall walk to the lake. I feel better than ever today! Come, get your shawl and wait for me in the hall.'

'But Brent, I have a lot of mending to do. I promised myself that today . . .'

'Pah! Today you will leave the mending and the darning and walk with your cousin. We will not have many such fine days before the winter sets in.'

It was true. Winter could come with awful suddenness in Lakeland, fine skies one moment became grey and heavy with snow the next. Besides, her eyes sparkled at the thought of a whole hour with Brent; maybe two.

'All right. I'll send up James with hot water and make my excuses to my brother as to why I cannot housekeep for him today.'

Because of the burden of taxes and fines they had had to pay over the years the Allonbys were considered poor by some standards. They had relatively few servants, and John and Stewart put in a full day in the fields or supervising such small possessions as they had left and which could still be worked, mainly forest and pastureland. Mary was the housekeeper since her elder sister Sarah had married a prosperous merchant from Cockermouth and moved away from home.

Not given to her were the amusements, diversions and follies of other well brought up young women of her class. From an early stage she had learned to make do with the solitary comforts of home and life at the Grange. Her mother had died years before and there had been a sick father to nurse, brothers to care for, servants to feed and a house to run. At the age when young ladies of the nobility and gentry were going to balls and parties or decking themselves with fine clothes, Mary was getting up at four in the morning, working all day and falling exhausted into bed at dusk. Although only eighteen she was already old in knowledge, and the harsh experience of a life where one didn't hope but simply existed, knowing that the following day would not be much better than the one just over.

But now her cousin Brent had come, and her life had been transformed just by nursing him and seeing the expression of fondness and gratitude with which he greeted her turn, she thought, into something more profound.

'Aye, you'll not housekeep today. Maybe bring some ham and bread and a bottle of ale and we'll sup by the lakeside!'

Mary fled down the stairs as Brent started to remove his nightshirt, apparently unaware of the unseemliness of it in her presence. He was so natural he was like a young animal, she thought, both liking and fearing what she'd seen. She had washed him as he lay almost naked many times when he was half conscious; but somehow there was something different about the sick body compared to the healthy one. As he'd stood there his nightshirt half on and half off, turned in profile away from her, the sight inspired in her an awareness of a sensation that hitherto she had known little about. This young male cousin was an awesome as well as a desirable creature.

Brother John was passing through the hall as Mary flew excitedly down the broad staircase. Despite his cares he stopped and a gentle smile illumined his tired face at the sight of her animated features.

'Where art thou off to, lass? Escaping from thy cousin?'

'Oh no, John! He is feeling so well he wants me to go for a walk with him, take a picnic. May I John?'

'Of course, lass. I can't recall when you had a day off last, seeing to your household duties and nursing Brent as well. 'Tis well deserved. Fetch some pie and ale from the kitchen and make a day of it.'

'Oh, John, may I? That's just what Brent suggested.'

'Did he? Good. But take care he does not go too far; he is not well yet.'

'Of course I won't; I'll see he doesn't tire himself.'

Mary threw her brother a smile and was about to dash into the kitchen when John gently clasped her arm and gazed at her gravely.

'Take care, Mary. Don't let him play with your emotions. You know that Brent . . .'

'Oh, I know, John! Of course I won't!'

'But I see you looking a lot at him lately, in that fashion, and him, too . . .'

So John had seen it. Then it was true. Her cheeks flamed, and she put her hands to them, both to attempt to disguise the colour from her brother and to cool them.

'Much as I love Brent, when it comes to women,' John said gravely, 'he is a philanderer. You know how he was found . . .'

Mary's eyes grew solemn.

'But would he philander with *me*, John? I am not the sort of woman . . .'

'You are a *very* pretty girl, Mary. Alas, because of our solitary life there are not enough about to tell you so, but any man would be inflamed by you if he was in his right mind. Imagine the effect on someone who had become enfeebled by illness. But when Brent is recovered, and 'twill be soon, he will be off to France, Mary. Do not let him trifle with you here.'

'Be sure he will not, John. He is not like that, really.'

'Take care, my little sister.'

Impulsively, John Allonby, a man older than his thirty years, whom misfortune and worry and the loss of a beloved wife in childbirth had prematurely aged, bent towards his baby sister and kissed her softly on the cheek.

The woods that surrounded the house on Catspaw stretched along the length of the lake towards Keswick. At times they thickened, and at times there was a clearing either in the midst of the wood or by the side of the lake. It was this fine timber that helped keep the Allonbys out of the debtor's prison, and it was Stewart who was the expert woodsman, who knew when to cut and when to plant and when to trim back.

The larks sang that fine October forenoon as Brent walking slowly and still with a slight limp because his left leg had not quite recovered its full use, and Mary a little ahead of him, paused and looked about for a green sward on which to sit and eat their picnic. Brent pointed to a place where the trees fell back from the lakeside and a grassy stretch reached down into the water protected from view of anyone, other than a boat on the lake, by a hillock. Mary, the hood of her cloak falling backwards from her head, had been gathering fircones for the fires that needed to burn so brightly in the large cold house in wintertime, and on her arm she had a large basket, half full. Brent had carried the warm bread and large ham pie in another basket and when they stopped he took out the flagon of ale and put it in the water to cool.

It was quite warm so he removed his greatcoat and laid it on the grass for them to sit upon. Underneath he wore the jacket and breeches of good broadcloth that had been found by him on the night of his attack, and a fine linen shirt, that Mary had freshly laundered for him with her own hands, open at the neck.

Mary's cloak slid to her feet and Brent took that and placed it alongside his, aware as he did of her neat ankle just visible beneath a dress of locally woven cloth that was of a becoming blue, particularly complementary to Mary's colouring. Brent's heart beat a little faster at the sight of the ankle, and his mind was a confusion of thoughts and desires and of women remembered long ago.

What puzzled Brent was that he could remember none more recently than Joan Shuttleton, a whore he'd taken up with during his last days in Cambridge. He'd met her in London and taken her with him to live openly as his mistress, which was one of the reasons that his brother had summoned him home even before it was clear that grandfather's last seizure would kill him.

Even the memory of Joan Shuttleton was hazy, as though that part of him had somehow become involved in his injury. He could remember very clearly his family and events and the death of his grandfather and the arrival of brother Tom; but the women who had formed part of so many of his amorous adventures were unclear in his mind, and particularly the one whom Tom had sworn was responsible for the state in which he had been found.

Tom had been quite blunt in describing to Brent the circumstances. How, even after many hours lying in the forest and on a slab in the mortuary, the traces of lovemaking were still evident about his body, quite apart from the fact that he had been found naked.

It was hushed up of course, Tom said. Norbert knew the family, and the doctor was bound by his medical oath not to tell. But Tom had no doubt his brother had an assignation in the forest with the gypsy he had met that night in the tavern and of whom there was no sign, of her or her troupe of travelling musicians, afterwards.

Gypsy? Brent's face crinkled again as his eyes moved from the well-turned ankle of his gently nurtured cousin towards the lake. Gypsy? Brent had no recollection of a gypsy dancing in the tavern as Tom had said, flaunting herself before him. He had apparently told Tom they had met before. Brent closed his eyes and tried to reform half remembered impressions in his mind. But no . . .

'Brent are you all right?' Mary had seen the spasm as his eyes closed and bent anxiously forward.

'Yes, yes dear cousin. It is the light on the lake. What a splendid day we have here. Look how old Walla Crag dips into the water yonder, and Skiddaw, is it not a picture? First thing this morning you could not see it for mist. Here, come sit by me,' he looked up and reached out a hand and saw that Mary was gazing at him timorously, not offering him her hand, her eyes almost fearful.

'Why, Mary, don't be afraid. I shall not harm thee!' He laughed and her eyes met his and she saw all the strength and gentleness in them, not the fearful animal young male she'd caught a glimpse of in the morning and of whom, as he'd looked up at her and stretched out his hand, she'd instantly been reminded. After all, she was a grown woman. Her mother had been wed at her age. It was quite common hereabouts even at 16 or 17; some were no longer maids but matrons at 15. That she had been protected was due to the presence of her brothers and lack of close female company. Sarah was almost as old as John and they had never been intimate. Certainly Sarah had never confided in her about womanly things, never told her her thoughts on her approaching marriage to Ambrose Rigg.

Mary had grown up in an all-male household for so long, except for a few women servants and none of them close. Unlike richer friends of hers she had no maid, no old nanny to enlighten her about the things between men and women. All she knew, Mary surmised, and when she saw it as exactly and as explicitly as she had seen Brent that morning, boldly outlined against the window, she'd been frightened and disturbed.

And now here he was turning to her smiling, patting the ground beside him. Was her whole world about to change? Take on new meaning?

They ate hungrily; the fresh air and short walk had restored Brent's appetite and Mary's face glowed with pleasure as she saw him making short work of the pie, the freshly baked bread and the strong ale he had fished out of the lake.

'It is so good to see you well again, Brent.'

'And good to be well, cousin. I think Old Man Death thought he had me, but I thwarted him!'

'Don't speak like that. You are but a young man. 'Twas an unfortunate accident . . .'

Mary faltered, thinking of what Stewart had told her. She looked at Brent from under lowered lids.

'Accident? You think it was an accident? I know not how I came to be there nor does anyone else. Ah, I see you looking at me Mary. You have heard that they said it was the fault of a woman. Well . . .' Brent shrugged, ''tis the first time being with a woman was such a dangerous thing.'

He laughed and she saw the expression in his eyes change as he looked at her and moved closer. It became bolder. Her mouth went very dry and her heart started to beat quickly in her chest. As he moved closer his arm stole about her waist and she could feel his hot breath on her cheek. 'Women are not so dangerous are they, Mary?' he murmured, his big hand pressing her slim waist.

'I think it is *men* who are dangerous,' she managed to whisper, aware of his hand, his presence, his warmth, 'or so I heard tell.'

'And you heard it of me, I'll warrant. Well, I'll not deny I love women. Ever since I was a young boy I was chasing the maids. I have had some of my best moments in a woman's arms – every man will say the same if he is honest, and yet . . .' He moved away from her, his arm resting now on the ground.

'I am not a womanizer, Mary. I am looking for someone perfect to whom to give my love. I know what people say about me, that I am idle, no good. But I have a good sword arm, a steady seat on a horse. I can box and run, and fight . . .'

'Fight?' Mary looked up at him startled.

'I mean fight in battle, Mary. 'Tis true I never have; but . . . Mary, can you keep a secret?'

'You know I can.'

'Then this is why Tom was here; not just to see grandfather. Tom is . . . you are sure you won't tell?'

Mary looked at him enigmatically, her eyes steady. Her heart had ceased its hammering.

'I know why Tom was here. While you were so ill upstairs Tom and John and Stewart spent many hours talking – about the King. That is what you were going to say?'

Brent sat back, resting his weight on the palms of his hands, and looked across the lake. The sun had risen high over the opposite hills whose brown and purple reflections shimmered in the clear water, so that they seemed to form one very steep continuous range. The thick, wooded slopes of Lodore led up to Ashness Fell whose jagged rocky outline formed the horizon against the clear, blue sky. If he looked to the left he saw the spires and roofs of the little town of Keswick diminished by the huge Skiddaw range which towered protectively over it. To his right the lake narrowed and Castle Crag and King's How loomed up on either side of the Derwent River as it meandered past Grange into Borrowdale.

The islands, too, reflected in the water so that the fir trees seemed to point up to the sky and down to the depths at the same time. From where he sat he could see St Herbert's island and Rampsholme, and up towards Keswick, shadowed by Friar's Crag, the home of the Earls of Derwentwater, firm supporters of the Stuart monarchs. It was from here that one had gone to fight for King James in 1715; from here that his brave wife, fleeing by night up by Walla Crag, had tried to save his life by selling the family jewels in London – all in vain.

The exquisite poetry and magic of the scene vied with the practical reality of the fate of Lord Derwentwater. One who had died for the man for whom Brent was prepared to sacrifice his life: King James III of England – languishing in Rome and exile.

'Yes, about the King, Mary. I should have known you would know. And how do you feel about it?'

'Why of course I am for it, Brent! My family, as you know, have always been staunch supporters of the Stuarts. I am with them heart and soul.'

'Even to death?'

Brent gazed at her and she solemnly met his eyes. She felt then a bond with him that was stronger than death and wondered if he felt it, too. It was not just a desire for him as a man, a husband, a lover; but a feeling of union with him as a person, a fusion of their lives. What did it matter that Brent went with women of ill repute, that he was considered idle – though she had never considered him such? He was half Allonby, her first cousin, and the same blood flowed in their veins, the same obsession for a cause – the Restoration of the Stuarts, as nearly one hundred years ago another Stuart, Charles II, had been restored to his rightful throne after many years in exile. It could happen again. It would.

'Even to death, Brent; my brothers', and mine and,' she paused and her voice trembled, 'even yours.'

Brent drew her to him and his arm encircled her once more. His cheek for the first time touched hers and he whispered into her ear.

'The Cause is my life, Mary. My salvation. I will be a man and a warrior and show those who despise me that I am as bold as they are. My brother mocked me because I had no money and no occupation, no calling, he said. Now I have! I am going to France to be with Prince Charles, to fight for him unto death.'

'Oh, Brent!' Mary turned to him and threw herself into his waiting arms, pressing her face against his chest. Huge tears rolled down her cheeks, wetting the fine lawn of his shirt. 'Brent, do not die! I cannot bear it. Do not speak like this, I beg of you.'

'There, there.' Brent patted her back and pressed her closer to him, sensing her womanly smells, her soft clinging body. He wanted her violently, to take her on the ground where they were now and make her sweet girl's body his, see it yield its secrets for the very first time to any man – and how many women had done *that* for him? Precious few, if any. Certainly no one had done it as Mary would because he knew so well, had known for a long time, that she loved him, that she would do his bidding, even now. He held back her face and removed the tears with his fingers. Then he kissed the wet path they had made from her eyes to her mouth very gently like the pecking of a bird. Her head was held back and her eyes were closed as his mouth came very softly down on hers in a kiss that was tender at first, but became more passionate as he felt her response, saw her open her eyes and look at him, saw the longing in them, the desire matching his.

He pressed her back on the grass and lay beside her, his mouth still fast on hers as he slipped a hand through her bodice to feel the soft young breasts beneath. She didn't stop him, but moaned as though the action pleased her. Surprised that she had not resisted, and excited by her passion and his own headstrong needs he grew bolder and unlaced her bodice and exposed the breasts completely. He gasped with wonder as he saw how soft and yet voluptuous they were, how the tender pink nipples, like plump raspberries, grew erect, either from the sudden exposure to the cold air or from her own desire. He knew not which as he bent his head and caressed them gently with his tongue, first one and then the other.

Mary, awakened for the first time, had never believed that such physical pleasure was possible. She didn't resist or even mind as he felt beneath her bodice and then unlaced it. As his mouth left hers to caress her exposed bosom she opened her eyes to gaze tenderly at him, so proud of her gentle lover, that he wanted her and had treated her with such delicacy. She would have given herself completely to Brent then if he had asked it of her. She wanted to. She was not afraid and felt in her loins the need to merge with him. And there was a moment as he looked at her breasts and she gazed at him that it could have happened. She was aware of her nudity, and the sight of being so gazed upon by a man, seemed to inflame her own desire. But suddenly Brent drew her bodice close again and then lying down beside her, panting a little, took her head into the crook of his arm and kissed her hair.

'Not now, Mary. I could never forgive myself.'

'I am willing.'

'I know; but I want you and your family to know that I am an honourable man, not a rogue who will even seduce his young cousin. I know what they say about me . . .'

'They *love* you, Brent.'

'I know, but they still think I am a rogue. I want to win you, Mary. Show them I am worthy to be your husband.'

He could feel her stiffen in his arms and he turned her face and saw the expression in her eyes, the tears that lurked in the corners. 'That is, if you will have me, Mary?'

'*I* have you! Oh, Brent, can you mean it? What can I give you? I am a simple country girl, completely unused to the ways of the world, inexperienced. How can I be a fit wife for you?'

'Then neither of us thinks we are worthy of the other. Capital! 'Tis a good start.' Brent broke the charged atmosphere by sitting upright and slapping his knees with laughter. ''Tis the oddest proposal I have heard.'

'Did you make many?' Mary said slyly, echoing his mood.

'Not of this kind. Not honest proposals. In fact,' Brent looked mildly astonished at his own admission. 'I have never asked the hand of a woman before.'

The laughter went out of his eyes and he looked at her again, noting how her hair stirred in the soft breeze that came from the lake, saw the grave look in her eyes, the sweet dimple of her upturned mouth. She looked a picture of English womanhood at its best in her soft blue dress enhanced by the wonderful background of the lakeland scene. At that moment Brent Delamain who had never hitherto doubted himself, his prowess or his abilities as a lover did wonder if he was fit for her, good enough for her. Could he possibly deserve such a creature?

The look in her eyes told him that whether he deserved her or not she was his. He bent towards her again, sliding his hands once more under that bodice still enticingly unlaced, cupped the small breasts in his big hands and drew Mary towards him, seeing her parted mouth and feeling beneath his palms the warmth of her skin, the pounding of her heart.

As they kissed the breeze from the lake grew stronger and a cloud obscured the sun. Mary trembled and Brent, unsure whether it was from fear or cold, broke from her, solicitously covering her with her cloak. He drew her up to her feet and held her for a long time in both his arms to warm her, until they turned to go back together to the house.

7

Susan Delamain and her daughter, Emma, were among the first to come over at the news that Brent and Mary intended to be married. In all her wildest dreams Susan had never dared hope that her tempestuous wild rogue of a son would be taken by his cousin's delicate beauty. She loved her niece almost as much as her own daughter and had tried to take the place of a mother to her in the years since Sarah Allonby had died.

Susan was glad to get away from Delamain Castle and the cramped dower house where she had lived since the death of Sir Francis. Her eldest son had immediately left for London; but even his welcome absence did not quite compensate for the loneliness and unease she felt without Brent. And there had been the terrible suffering while he was ill, and her inability to travel to his side because Emma had developed a fever that the doctor feared might be the pox and, although it was not, she had taken a long time to recover.

Brent went in the boat over to Keswick to welcome his mother, leaving Mary to supervise the preparations for the feast that was to solemnize the betrothal that night. Sister Sarah – named after her mother – and her husband Ambrose Rigg were also due to arrive with their young son Henry and the baby Elia just six months old.

It was the longest trip Brent had made since his recovery and he was glad of the presence of Stewart because he still felt nervous, in case he should falter on his left leg which was still lame. Each day, accompanied by Mary, he walked a little further but nearly always they stood at the spot where he had asked her to marry him, first awakened her woman's desire, and they embraced all over again.

Brent and Stewart waited by the Moot Hall in the old market place for the coach to arrive from Penrith. It would be put up in the town while they made the journey across the lake. There was still no proper road, or one big enough for a coach and four, from Keswick to Catspaw. Transport was either by horse or boat and the latter was both the fastest and the prettiest way.

Although it was only two months since he had parted from his mother, in the interval he had nearly died, his sister had been ill, and it seemed an eternity to Brent as he anxiously paced up and down waiting for the coach to appear. Stewart laughed at his impatience.

'Why, Brent, you would think you had not seen your mother for years.'

'It seems like it Stewart. Think what has happened. I have nearly died and I have got myself a bride.'

Stewart, nearest in age to Mary and close to her, like her too to look at with his clear deep blue eyes and very curly blond hair, grew suddenly solemn and the laughter abruptly ceased. Brent knew why. Stewart thought he was a philanderer and unfit for his sister. Neither of the brothers had been very enthusiastic at the news, but Stewart the least. Stewart had been taciturn and had not offered Brent his congratulations. Brent wanted very much to convert his cousin whom he so much admired, to have his approval. Stewart was a solid countryman, an expert in wood and tree felling. He was close to the soil and his values were good earthy ones. He smiled seldom and, like his brother John, seemed bent with the cares of the last years.

Fortune had rarely smiled on the Allonbys since anyone could remember. John's wife had died with her baby after an agonizing birth and soon after that their father, stricken with grief at John's bereavement, so like his own. His wife had died giving birth to Mary. The brothers toiled and hoped for better times, praying that the Stuarts would one day return, restore their lands and recompense them for their losses. It was their only hope. That and, maybe, a good match for Mary. And now Mary had decided to throw her heart at her cousin, a man they loved but whose attitude to life was so unlike theirs, so casual and reckless. For the last thing they had wanted when Tom had brought the stricken Brent with him was to have him end up betrothed to Mary.

'You like it not, Stewart, do you?' Brent said quietly. Stewart shrugged and looked away.

'I like you well enough, Brent, you know that. But as a husband for Mary . . .'

'I have no fortune.'

'Oh, it is not that . . . well, not only that. It is . . .' Stewart avoided his cousin's eye and banged his hands against his thigh.

'You think I am not steadfast?'

'Well, Brent, up to now . . .'

'True, I have used women ill, Stewart – or they me, I know not quite which. I have played with them, and dallied with them. But Mary I love truly. As I have no woman before . . .'

'Brent, you hardly know her . . .'

'Hardly *know* Mary! Of course I know her. I have known her since she was born!'

'Yes, but as a wife . . . I mean you did not think of Mary like that before.'

'She was young.'

'She has been a maid for many years now; but you never looked at her before, Brent, as other than a friend.'

'Is it so wrong that I learnt to love her?' Brent said defensively.

'No, of course not. But in such a short time, and most of that you have been ill . . .'

'And not in my right mind, is that what you want to say?' Brent said harshly, now stopping his pacing and staring at his cousin.

'I don't say not in your right mind, of course not, but emotionally. Mary has nursed you and you have become dependent on her. I say you should wait . . . to be sure, Brent.'

The pleading look in Stewart's eyes moved Brent as no words had done. He was well aware of the misfortune that had dogged the Allonbys; of the suffering of the brothers and the concern for their youngest sister. The only one who had done anything was Sarah, and it was doubtful if she was really happy with the pug-faced, pompous Ambrose Rigg. She had married beneath her and she had married for money, for security and possessions and all the things she had been without for so many years. And now she had a fine house and her own coach, and a personal maid and a nursemaid; but whether or not she was happy no one knew. Sarah was a woman who kept her own counsel. In many ways she was more a Delamain than an Allonby, shrewd and calculating, like George.

Brent's thoughts were distracted by the thudding of horses' hooves, and the coach with the Delamain arms blazoned on the doors swept into sight. His heart filled with joy at the thought of seeing his mother and, as the coach stopped and the groom jumped down, Brent bounded ahead before him to open the door for his mother and sister. When Susan saw him she remained in her seat and Brent saw that tears were cascading down her face as she reached out her arms for him. He leapt into the coach and sat beside her, folding her in his arms, hugging her to reassure her all was well. Beside her mother Emma stared at Brent, her great brown eyes filled with tears. She looked pale and thin. Thank God it had not been the pox, but she had been very ill.

'I am here, mother, all is well.'

'Oh, Brent, they told me you were dying and I thought I would never see you again. God is good, God is good.'

'God *is* good, mother. But for my left leg which moves a trifle slower than its fellow I am in good health, and in love mother! The best tonic for recovery.'

Susan gave her son a wry look and offered him her hand. 'Of that I am not so certain. Help me out, Brent, and take care with Emma. She is delicate, too.'

Outside the carriage Stewart bowed and kissed his aunt's hand and then gallantly that of his little cousin, a year younger than Mary and her equal in good, though very different, looks. Emma was dark like the Delamains, brown hair, brown skin and eyes that were an enticing tawny colour like those of a wild bird. Even her recent ill health had not dimmed her beauty and Stewart, who had been smitten since she was fourteen, once again felt his heart turn over.

But Emma, unaware of these emotions, and certainly not reciprocating them, smiled at her cousin and pecked him on the cheek in sisterly fashion. Emma liked exciting young men like Anthony Webber or Lord Borfield, whom her brother occasionally entertained to dinner or invited to escort her to balls. They danced well and spoke entertainingly and made bold glances as she partnered them in the quadrille. Stolid cousin Stewart was too silent, too clod-hopping to attract such a one as Emma Delamain. The trouble was he knew it, but he continued to hope and his devoted gaze followed her as she tripped out of the carriage and instructed the maid she and her mother shared to unpack her things, and help the boatman load them into the boat.

It was a merry party that took to the boat for the short journey to Catspaw. Brent sat in the stern with his mother while Emma tried to draw the taciturn Stewart into a conversation on the prow. She was vexed at having to come to Furness Grange which she considered the most boring of backwoods, and her earnest cousins the Allonbys were very hard going. But her mother had insisted it was good for her health and as Emma hoped to persuade George to give a season for her in London, the restoration of the colour to her cheeks was essential.

Besides, Emma was intrigued at the speed with which Brent had declared himself for Mary and wanted to know what was behind it. The quiet and serene Mary was the last person Emma would have expected her dashing, wilful brother to be attracted to. She knew all about the sort of things he got up to – the servants who had to leave suddenly, to say nothing of the story about the mysterious gypsy who apparently nearly caused his death. Mary Allonby of all people . . . Emma was agog with interest.

'You also think I am not fit for Mary, mother?' Brent enquired as the noise from the oars and the prattling of Emma on the prow drowned his voice.

'Of course I think you are fit, Brent. In every way a desirable husband. But for *Mary*, Brent? She is so quiet and docile, so serious. The last person I would have supposed you to be attracted to.'

'She is an angel mother. Sitting by my bedside . . .'

'That is what I was afraid of,' Susan said, pursing her lips in the Allonby fashion of being sensible. 'I wish I could have come to nurse you. You grew dependent on her, saw her in another light. Brent, is it wise? Shouldn't you wait?'

That was the second time someone had said the same thing to him in an hour, Brent thought, the excitement suddenly draining away. He felt tired and uncertain. Of course they were related, his mother and Stewart; both sober and careful Allonbys. But they had both asked him to wait – until he was sure. Was he being fair to Mary?

'The future is so uncertain, mother. We thought we should have some happiness before . . .'

'In case there is war?'

Brent nodded.

'I might die, like Uncle Robert . . .'

Susan's eyes flew shut in a spasm of grief for the premature death of her gallant brother on the scaffold beside Lord Derwentwater in 1716 – a young man so full of charm and promise. Now to think of her son, not unlike Robert in looks and temperament. She wrung her hands in an involuntary gesture of despair and looked over the lake, her eyes scanning the high peaks crowned by

Glaramara that crowded together at the end of Borrowdale and stretched as far as the eye could see. How different, how serene the mountains were from a distance than when you were close to them or cowering under them, attempting to climb them as she had when a girl, with her father and boisterous brothers.

Happy days of her childhood in the red house on the lake surrounded by the protective fells and woods. It had seemed to pass too quickly, and to give place to uncertainty and anxiety as she reached womanhood and had waited for the war to come, dreading what it would do to her brothers and to her husband Guy.

Only they had been wed, they had some years of happiness together. Was it right to deny Brent and Mary? Was it right to deny *Mary* the happiness for, in her lonely solitary life away from civilization, she scarcely met any young men at all, let alone suitable ones? She could see Brent's attraction for Mary quite clearly; but Mary for Brent . . . it was as she had feared, an infatuation based on need and, being Brent, it would not last once the need was past. They were very different people.

'I know not what to say for the best,' Susan clasped Brent's hand and squeezed it. 'I would not deny you or her. But Brent what if there is no war, if the Prince does not come? He has tried to come often before you know.'

'He will come, mother. This time it is sure. In a year we shall have the Stuarts again on the throne.'

'Oh would it could be. How different everything might be. But I cannot bear to think of what is going to happen until then. Oh look, Furness Grange, and there is Mary on the jetty with John.' She clasped Brent's hand again and turned to him, her eyes shining.

'For you I *will* be happy Brent. We may have so little time.'

There had not been such a feast at Furness Grange since anyone could remember. There had been little enough to feast about and few resources with which to do it. But the family reunion as well as the betrothal of Brent and Mary was considered sufficient reason, and extra servants had been engaged from the neighbouring hamlets to prepare the succulent food and serve it.

The long dining table was set with silver marked with the Allonby crest, crystal goblets stood by each place setting and white linen napkins. The feast was already spread on the sideboard as Brent sat down, on the right of his cousin Mary, and he wondered how much they had sacrificed to prepare this repast for them – a great baron of beef, sides of ham, chickens, pies and crispy newly baked bread.

While they dined and the servants moved around the talk was kept to generalities about the weather, the state of the soil, the quality of grazing land and the bad winters they were having and which had taken off so many souls in recent years.

Brent knew that they had to talk with care because of the presence of Ambrose Rigg, that worthy merchant from Cockermouth who gave Sarah fifteen years and already had a paunch and the heavy-jowled look that comes from excessive fondness for food and drink and the good things of life. But it was not his appearance that worried the Allonbys, but his politics. It was men such as Rigg who ensured the survival of the Hanoverians, who had benefited by years of peace since George I came so wrongfully to the throne. Rigg's ancestors had been serfs, then 'statesmen', yeoman farmers. Ambrose himself had broken away, gone to Whitehaven as a youth and slowly built up a fortune from very humble beginnings first as a sailor then as a ship owner and merchant.

But no amount of money could make up to Ambrose for his lack of breeding, his coarse ways and uncivilized manners. He had looked for a wife to remedy these defects and had found one in the impoverished Allonby family from whom he bought wood to build boats and houses. The history of the Allonby family was well known, how they had once been among the greatest in the county, but how foolish political involvements had reduced them almost to penury. But nothing could take away a good lineage and fine manners and Sarah Allonby, already well over twenty when he met her and looking for a husband, and a fortune, was just what he needed.

There was no question of love on either side, or even of much respect, at least on Sarah's. Ambrose was nearly forty, an uncouth old bachelor who picked his nose and scratched his behind in company. His face was already purple and his eyes had the rheumy look of the drinker; but as he began to come increasingly over to Furness Grange on his fine horse accompanied by a groom, she knew the reason was not to buy more wood from her brothers, though he did, but to court her.

Then he had invited the family to his new house in Cockermouth, built in extensive grounds with two floors and outbuildings. He had taken them to Whitehaven to inspect his ships and his warehouses and then, while they were still gawping at the scale of his wealth and possessions, he offered for Sarah's hand. Although her brothers were aghast she had known what to expect and promptly accepted. Not only would she no longer be an old maid, she would be a wealthy woman, too. What did Ambrose's origins, looks and disgusting manners matter?

Over the years they had been married Sarah had improved both his manners and his appearance. He was still paunchy and florid but he did not drink so much; his clothes were well cut and of good cloth, and he no longer broke wind at the table. He had also sired two exceptionally beautiful children and although Sarah found the process of the siring disgusting, she was willing to put up with almost anything to achieve the status in life she now enjoyed. Let Ambrose get her with as many children as he wanted; she was able, and the more she had the more secure was her station in life, the more certain her hold on his possessions and wealth for her progeny.

Susan thought that night, as she looked at her niece from across the table, that you could see from the set of Sarah's mouth that she had sold herself for money. The mouth was turned permanently downwards as though in a sneer and there was a hard calculating look in her eyes. She had never been a beauty, but had looked well enough and she had had the robust good sense and cheerfulness of the Allonbys. But now Sarah looked every inch a Rigg – the wife of a rich Hanoverian merchant of low origins but great ambition.

Sarah was as much taken aback by her sister's betrothal as anyone, but at the dinner table she saw quite clearly the reason. Mary was infatuated by Brent's animal charm – he had nothing else, no money, no prospects. Well Ambrose would not provide for him, that was for sure. Nor a dowry for Mary either. He bought enough wood and produce from her brothers that he did not need and, besides, his own family would increase and his duty lay with them.

'Now then,' Ambrose was saying, his face florid with the abundance of good claret he had drunk. 'This war in Europe is doing us no good. 'Twas a mistake to embark on it in the first place. What care we who reigns in Austria? Get out of it. Let us have the peace good Walpole brought us in his day.'

'If we have foreign kings they will concern themselves with

foreign parts,' John said, clearing his throat. 'We need English kings on the throne.'

Brent looked at his cousin with alarm, but Ambrose frowned and tapped his goblet on the table.

'I do not have any love for the Germans,' he said, 'as you know John, but I have no love for the Stuarts either if I follow your meaning. I would favour the sort of government this country had under Cromwell. I would do away with kings and such wasteful nonsense and have a good honest republic.'

Sarah smiled at her husband, not fondly, but as one cynically amused. The only thing that mattered to Ambrose was the amount of money that he could amass in the shortest possible time. Politics or who reigned in London were of not the slightest interest.

'My husband thinks that his coffers would swell greater with a man of business at the head of government,' she said. 'Isn't that true Ambrose?'

'Aye, 'tis,' Ambrose nodded. 'No frippery, no nonsense, mistresses and the like, such as I hear they have at court. A good man of business.'

'Some say,' John said slowly, looking at his brother-in-law, 'that the war is good for certain business.'

'Oh?' Ambrose looked interested as though he might have missed something.

'Illicit brandy, tobacco, silks from France.'

Ambrose's frank, shrewd expression which he had when discussing business grew guarded. Although it was well known that the smuggling trade thrived through successful respectable business-men like himself, it was still unlawful, punishable by confiscation of property, fines and imprisonment. It disturbed him to think that John, in whom he did not confide, might have heard something of his activities in this connection. Many of his ships ran a profitable line in smuggled goods through the large entrepôt depot on the Isle of Man, plying from Roscoff and Nantes in France and Port Rush in Ireland.

'I know naught of illegal business,' Ambrose said blandly. 'I am a good honest merchant and I pay my duties and taxes. Now, wife, it is late; we should make an early start in the morning . . .'

John was quite used to Ambrose's habit of assuming he was the head of the household at the Grange. He did everything but sit at the head of the table, calling for food when his platter was empty and wine when he needed it. Now he had announced that the dinner was over and it was time for bed.

It was late; the candles had grown low in the sconces and some had even been replaced by the servants. Mary and Brent had said very little, preferring to excite each other by sly amorous glances, or the quick clasp of hands under the table.

But Ambrose had been looking surreptitiously at Brent throughout the dinner, noticing that he was a fine strong man, broad shouldered though slim hipped. A fast mover. Without a home too, Ambrose had heard; a wastrel, kicked out by his brother. He did not look a wastrel, though, to Ambrose who had only met him a couple of times in his life whereas his brother George he knew quite well. They did business together and he knew that George despised him because he was of yeoman class, ill-mannered and self-made. George Delamain had always made it very clear how he felt about Ambrose Rigg: he would take his money or his goods but he would not sup or dine with him, or invite him to his castle – Sarah or no Sarah Allonby for a wife.

Ambrose was a man who nursed grudges. He was conscious of his origins and ashamed of them. His ancestors had been serfs for generations, serving the needs of the Allonbys and Delamains and such folk. Nothing was guaranteed to inspire greater enmity in Ambrose than to be patronized and snubbed by such as George Delamain, now Sir George, and the like. He had, therefore, looked at young Brent with interest; there would be no love here between the brothers. What a good way to pay George back for the humiliations he heaped on Ambrose – he had once made him wait outside the kitchen door when he called in person for payment, Ambrose not being a man to extend credit for too long.

'Aye,' John said, echoing Ambrose, ''tis late. But let us drink to the health of Brent and Mary.' John got up and took his glass and the rest of the assembly joined him. 'Brent and Mary . . . Brent and Mary, health, happiness.'

Brent stood up and made a graceful, short little speech of thanks on behalf of himself and his betrothed and then everybody clapped and, at the signal from John, the servants appeared and drew back the chairs.

Ambrose went over and stood with his back to the fire getting out his pipe and filling it with fragrant American tobacco newly smuggled via Nantes.

120

'A word with you, Master Brent.'

Brent was passing, his arm through Mary's, and stopped as Ambrose called to him. He bowed to Mary who continued with her sister into the drawing-room, and went over to where the tall broad merchant stood with a proprietorial air puffing his pipe as if he owned the place.

'Yes, sir?' Brent said, respectful of the years between him and his cousin's husband.

'Now lad, what do you do with yourself?'

'Well . . .' Brent faltered. He had done nothing and it was hard to say what he was about to do, especially to someone as much of the Establishment as Ambrose Rigg.

'Turned out of the castle, I hear.'

'In a manner of speaking, yes sir.'

'What are you going to do then?'

Ambrose spewed smoke right into Brent's face and gazed at him, chin slightly tilted, his hands behind his back.

'I thought of going to . . . abroad.'

'Ah, to seek work?'

'Yes.'

'The colonies maybe, America . . .'

'Yes, yes you could say that.'

'But you don't have anywhere in mind?'

'I thought . . . the West Indies,' Brent improvised.

'You have connections there, of course?'

'No, sir.' Brent began to realize he was sounding like an idiot. This man was trying to find out if he was suitable for his sister-in-law and clearly the answer would be no, at this rate. 'I mean to try and find my own way, sir,' he said, raising his head and meeting the level gaze of Ambrose.

'"Twill be difficult with a wife.'

'Oh, Mary will stay here. I have . . . today given her brothers and my mother a promise not to marry her until I am able to support her.'

Brent still choked at the thought of the solemn family conference that had taken place in the library just before dinner and made him so silent during it. As yet Mary knew nothing about it, which was just as well.

'Ah . . . pity.' Ambrose tapped out his pipe on the chimney piece and belched, looking quickly around to be sure his wife had

121

not observed him. 'Look here, young Delamain . . . I hardly know you but I like what I see. A capable strong lad with a good pair of shoulders, and a good head . . . Cambridge I hear? Oh don't worry, not much of a scholar I know, but neither am I and I've done well enough. How would you like to be taken into employment by me?'

Brent wondered if his ears were deceiving him. To work for Ambrose? Doing what? Keeping accounts? The idea was horrifying.

'Oh sir, 'tis kind of you but I have set my heart on abroad . . .'

'You'll get there soon enough, boy. I'll put you on one of my ships. Learn to be a captain, a master mariner maybe. Learn all the business; be my right hand if you're good. My son is far too young and will take a long time to catch up wi' me. You're about the right age.'

Brent's senses reeled from the impact of what Ambrose was saying. Here he was about to embark for France on adventure and he was being offered a job as a merchant! The bile in his throat nearly choked him. But he knew Ambrose was far too important to offend out of hand – the Allonbys depended a good deal on business with him and, besides, there was Sarah, a sour piece and going sourer, but an Allonby all the same.

'Sir, you make me a very generous offer. May I have time to think about it?'

Ambrose's clap on his shoulder nearly sent Brent staggering. He was a powerful man, almost as tall as Brent and twice as large, though most of it was fat.

'Think on't lad, do. Not too long, mind. Talk it over with Mary. A few months in each part of the business, at sea, the warehouses and so on and then maybe a nice house in Whitehaven to bring the bride home to. You'll have a secure future within a year, Brent. I don't give a penny for your chances in the Indies or seeing Mary again before five years are out. Besides, are you not lame?'

Ambrose looked curiously at Brent's left leg which even now was hurting Brent through standing too long.

'Only temporarily, Mr Rigg. It was injured in an accident.'

'But they take time to heal, boy. I heard about the "accident" too which makes me think you should hasten to the altar before she fetches you another one and despatches you for good!'

Ambrose leaned back roaring with laughter, his red face puce with merriment, his eyes watering. Here was a lad of spirit! A seducer of every woman he came upon apparently, and bold to boot. Brent's face was nearly as red as his.

''Twas not like that . . .'

'Oh, I know you can't remember. Knocked cold. No lad, wi' your hot blood you need a good woman and a steady job. Take my advice. There will be plenty of time for dalliance when you are wedded and your wife bedded with an infant or two.' A roguish look came into his eyes, 'I can show you in time one or two places in Whitehaven, and not just for sailors of the rough type either; but well kept, nice girls . . . don't worry, when you are settled there is no need to become a dull fellow!'

Ambrose winked broadly and roared with laughter again and Brent began to understand why the perpetually sour look had transformed Sarah's once not unpleasing face. 'There now, come and see me in a day or two. Talk it over with your family. 'Tis a fair offer.'

Brent slept badly that night, tossing and turning in his bed. The thought of working for Rigg was abhorrent to him, yet one thing did trouble him and continued to do so. He *was* lame; his leg seemed the one part of him which refused to get completely better. If he walked or stood too long it hurt, not just a mild pain but an agony that precluded long hours marching, for the time being anyway.

Also there was Mary. She expected to marry him almost at once. She wanted to and so did he; but tomorrow he was going to have to tell her of his promise to John and his mother after that fearful family scene when they had both accused him of being a philanderer – too easy with women. The only way to show his sincerity was to wait, to prove to himself and them, and, above all, Mary that he was a man of honour, someone who kept his word, capable of giving and receiving true love.

They were immune to his arguments about the war, the question of losing his life. Who knew when the war would come? The Prince might stay in France forever, for all they knew. No, a year.

Brent gave a promise for a year. Now he would have to tell Mary.

Brent arose with the dawn, and, dressing quickly, went to look for his eldest cousin who was always about at that hour doing his accounts or walking in the grounds. He found John in his study hunched over his ledgers, the room still lit by candles because the dawn light outside had scarcely penetrated the thick mullioned windows.

John looked surprised as Brent came in and rubbed his hands.

''Tis cold. The winter will come early. Could you not sleep, Brent?'

'No.'

'I thought as much. I know how keen you are to wed and I know why. But you owe it to Mary . . .'

'It is not that only,' Brent sat down, legs apart, hands on the arms of his chair and gazed at his cousin. 'Ambrose wants me to work for him. He wants an answer, not today but soon.'

'Work for Ambrose?' John said, echoing Brent's own sense of amazement. 'Doing what?'

'Learning the business, being his right hand.'

'But you don't want to do it, do you?'

'No.'

'Then say no and that's it. Say it today before he goes,' John cocked an ear. 'I think I hear them stirring now. See, 'tis dawn.' John blew out the candle and gazed at his cousin in the half light.

'John, I have been thinking a lot during the night; plans tossed about in my head like a bobbin on water. My leg is much worse than I admit . . .'

He saw a sceptical look come over John's face.

'Oh? I thought it was mended.'

'Well not quite. It gets very painful if I walk far. Well that is a factor about going to France. If I become a fugitive I shall have much walking to do. How can I serve the Prince . . .'

He left the sentence unfinished noting the steady unfriendly gaze of his cousin.

'Aye. 'Tis as I thought. You do not wish to join your brother because, as always Brent, you put your heart first. You want Mary and by God you will do anything to have her – even renege upon your duty . . .'

Brent rose from the chair his face white with fury. 'John, how can you say such a thing! You think I am a renegade? I tell you I'll not touch your sister whether I go to France or no. I'll not see her or have ought to do wi' her, just to *prove* to you that I am not what you think, a craven rogue. Whether I go to France or whether I stay in England I will *not* abide a moment more at Furness. You have worked me up right proper, John.'

And before his astounded cousin could say a word or intervene Brent stormed out of the room and took the stairs two at a time to where Ambrose was just emerging from his bedroom door fastening his cravat.

'Why Brent, you're abroad early lad!'

'I'll work for you,' Brent said. 'I'll come with you today, if you'll have me. I can start at once.'

Ambrose's taciturn morning face broke into a grin. He put out an arm and drew Brent into the bedroom where Sarah was putting the finishing touches to her toilet.

'Excuse us, my dear,' Ambrose said, observing that his wife was fully dressed and decent. 'But Brent and I have business to discuss.'

'I have the children to see to,' Sarah said shortly and gathering up her shawl and putting it over her shoulders against the chill morning, left the room.

'Now, Brent,' Ambrose said turning to the light so that he could see his face, 'you've reached a decision overnight?'

'I have.'

'Why do you look angry then? You look as though you were in some sort of temper.'

'Well . . . I told John and he . . .'

'Thinks you're too good for me. All the Allonbys do, lad, aye *and* the Delamains . . .' Ambrose reached out and patted Brent's shoulder. 'I am well used to their contempt; but I could buy and sell them all, you know, maybe even your brother although I do not take his property into account. No I'm used to the scorn of the Allonbys – John and Stewart – I know what they think. But they take my money right enough and they tolerate me because I am wed to their sister. Oh, not worthy of it, I know . . . don't think she doesn't make me feel that too, rather she tries but I take no notice. An Allonby woman in bed is like all the rest, I find; and once you've lain with a woman that's all you need to know about her . . . as I don't need to tell *you* lad!' Ambrose gave him the same obscene wink as the previous night. 'Oh no, what they say don't worry me . . .'

Brent felt he should defend his cousin but didn't know how. To tell him what John had said was to betray the cause. He bowed his head in shame at his inability to tell the truth.

'No, it was not like that exactly, Mr Rigg. John thinks I stay here to be with Mary. That is why I want to come with you today, to get right away.'

'Oh good. Capital. Pack your bags boy and you can come with us. Sarah and the children go with the maid to Keswick and back by coach, the way they came. I have to be in Cockermouth by dinnertime and it is hard riding over the hills. Be off now.' He took Brent to the door and shook his hand, well satisfied that the day had started so well.

Brent hurried to his room and began to put together his possessions. The mist from the lake was gradually being dispersed by a wintry sun whose weak beams played across the floor of his room. Brent suddenly stopped and looked about him. He had come to love this room; it was his home. How could he have known this time yesterday as he waited for Mary to enter with his breakfast, and the brief kiss she allowed to go with it, that today he would be gone?

Everyone told him he was too quick off the mark, too sharp tempered. He'd hardly given John a chance . . . but what chance had John given *him*? Accusing him of philandering, of reneging, of pretending hurt, or forsaking the cause, all for a maid.

His wounded pride made him angry again and he hurriedly crammed his things into a small leather bag that stood in the corner. Then he cast a final look round and strode to the door which, just as he reached it, burst open and Mary flew in, her face ashen.

'Brent, Brent what is this? You are going? What is Ambrose saying?'

She hurled herself into his arms and, putting down his bag he folded them about her and hugged her to him, caressing her hair with his lips. Suddenly he felt too uncertain, too broken-hearted to speak. He felt a rare idyll was coming to an end. She leaned away from him and looked into his eyes.

'Is it true?'

He nodded.

'*Why*, Brent?'

'I have to prove myself . . . for you.'

Mary broke away and stood back, a finger pointing incredulously towards herself.

'For me?'

126

Brent observed how pale she was, how her thin frame trembled and his heart went out to her in pity, and remorse. But he was still too angry, too stung with John's remark. He drew Mary to him and kissed her hungrily, pressing her body roughly against his until he felt her shudder with pain and try and draw away. Brent roughly let her go.

'Ask your brother! He has taunted me this morning and I have had enough Mary. I have sworn not to see you or to have aught to do with you until *they* think I am worthy. Ask *them*!'

The look of anguish she gave him told him she did not understand – the reason for his sudden departure, his brutal and passionless embrace. He felt tears of frustration and rage sting his eyes as he ran down the stairs, aware that she was not following him.

He did not see Mary again. As he quickly broke his fast and said his farewells she remained upstairs. John did not try to make him change his mind, did not know what to say, but shook his hand and wished him well. His mother, so lately reunited with him, only sorrowed to see him set off so quickly again; but she knew the reason. Had she not herself helped to contribute to it? She kissed him sadly, her eyes half filled with unshed tears.

'Go well, my son. Thank God you are recovered. You know where I am when you need me and, Brent,' she looked gravely into his eyes, 'I *do* trust you. I know you will do what is right and that in time you will think that what we did was right.'

Brent turned from his mother, kissed his sister, still half asleep, shook the hands of his silent cousins and mounted a horse lent to him by Stewart. Then with Ambrose Rigg panting on his horse behind him he set off along the narrow track that led over Catbells, across the Newlands Valley, and up over tree-covered Whinlatter to the prosperous little town of Cockermouth.

8

Analee lay in the dark next to Randal. She was cold and she pressed up against his body to draw the warmth from it. Randal stirred and sighed in his sleep; she was conscious of his buttocks against her stomach, her breasts against his lean hard back.

It was two months since Randal had bound her hand and foot and tossed her in the cart, taken her off and married her. Two months and the weather had turned from a warm and mellow September into a bitter November. But more than that, Analee had turned from a free wandering gypsy into a settled married woman who cooked for Randal, kept the tent clean and chatted endlessly with the other women of the tribe while the men squatted together mending pots and pans, smoking and drinking beer.

At night she and Randal came together and made love but, apart from that, apart from knowing that she was his woman and he was her man, they had very little knowledge of each other; they had very little to say. It had not been like that with her last real love, the reason for her wandering – they had talked the day and night round, yearning continually for each other's company, the touching and the hearing of sounds.

Analee knew it was not usual for women and men to want to be together so much, to have so much to say to each other. She had observed enough around her, experienced it in her own life, to know that the sexes were very different. Except for making love, or dancing, they kept apart even in the camp. She and the women chatted and gossiped; the men talked in low tones about what they were doing. Men and women had really nothing in common at all, except for this one thing – the need to communicate with each other bodily in order to breed.

And that was what worried Analee this bitter November night as she lay awake pressed against Randal. She knew she was with child. It had happened to her before and it was happening again; she knew the signs – the absence twice of her woman's monthly time when, in some tribes, women were considered unclean, *marimé*, and had to go into a separate tent and sleep apart from their menfolk until it was over. In addition her breasts pained her and she felt tired and listless.

Analee didn't want a child. She was already feeling constricted living here in this camp with the chattering women and the swarms of children who ran around their feet every day. The thought of a baby and then another, until she was fat with heavy pendulous breasts and a perpetually tired and harassed expression . . . it didn't suit her at all. Analee already wanted to be off on her travels. The compulsion she'd had ever since the tragedy was with her again: to be tied to Randal as his wife and the mother of his child, children . . . she shuddered. She couldn't take to the road when she had children. She would be trapped.

Besides, Analee, because she had second sight, because she was experienced in these women's things as well, knew this child was not Randal's. She knew the cycle of the woman and that when she had lain with Brent she had been fertile.

Brent Delamain was the father of her child. Even if she had not known the physical signs; she knew in her gypsy's heart it was so. She with child by a *gadjo*, not by her husband, and the child might have blond hair, a white skin and an aquiline aristocratic face – just like Brent Delamain and not like Randal Buckland at all.

Analee felt heavy-hearted as she lay in the dark waiting for the glimmer of dawn to appear through the entrance to the tent. She thought with tenderness of the beautiful *gadjo*, of their two meetings in the moonlight forests – one to meet and one to make love. That was all. Oh, but she had danced for him. When she had seen him in the tavern standing looking at her darkly from the shadows, it was for him *alone* she had danced, flaunting her body and offering herself to him as only she, Analee, knew how.

Randal stirred and he whispered into her ear that he loved her and she smiled. He wanted to hear her say she loved him; but although she said many things to him she never told him that.

'I want us to have a child, Analee,' he whispered, there in the dawn, knowing how many times he had put his seed deep inside her, knowing every time that he was aware of his urgent need to create. 'I want many children. Maybe move away and start our own tribe.'

Analee was silent. She felt pity and sorrow for Randal knowing that what he wanted so much was inside her, but it was not his. She couldn't tell him. She would have to see Reyora the *cohani* and do something about it.

'It is not Randal's child,' Analee said, deep inside the *cohani*'s tent.

Reyora nodded as though she'd known already. She looked very wise, squatting on her haunches with her shawl round her head half obscuring her face. On every finger she had rings, and on her bare ankles Analee could see the glow of gold bands. She'd sought out the *cohani* after the noonday meal when Randal had gone off with the men to look for hedgehogs and pigeons. The women would think she was asking the *cohani* for a spell, maybe to make her fertile. They would not know the reason.

But Reyora had been waiting for Analee to come to her; she had not known why, but she had known it would be Analee and not Randal who would come. Everyone could see that after the wedding they had been happy and could not wait to go to their tent at night. They would creep away from the fire even before it was dark.

'It is the child of a *gadjo*,' Reyora said after a pause. 'A blond, handsome *gadjo*. Maybe a lord?'

Analee looked at her, marvelling at the skill of the *cohani* who could tell not only the past but the future as well.

'You see I cannot have the child of a *gadjo*, Randal would kill me if he knew. If the child is dark as we are, then . . . but I will not know until it is born.'

Reyora nodded again. She was often asked for potions or philtres to abort gypsy women, usually when they were with child before marriage or when they had too many. Such was her skill that she did it for the *gadjo* women too, and often would depart for Carlisle in answer to an urgent summons carrying with her her bag of herbs and ointments.

'If you do it now, early, he will never know,' Analee said, 'and then we can have his child.'

Reyora looked enigmatic and, for a moment, Analee thought she was going to tell her to clear out, to expose her before the whole camp. She had lain with a *gadjo* and then married a gypsy. But Reyora was merely looking at her, swaying backwards and forwards on her hips, her face leaning sideways on her hand.

'You are not full gypsy are you Analee? You are *didakai* – half gypsy?'

'You have known all the time?'

'Pretty well,' Reyora said, swaying. 'There was so much about you that I did not understand. You look like a full blooded gypsy and behave like one, but I know.'

'My father was not a gypsy,' Analee said slowly, quietly, fearing that anyone should hear. 'That is all I know for my mother died when I was born. Her mother brought me up and all she would say was that my father was a *gadjo*, but that as he was dark like my mother no one could tell. It was said I was her child, my grandmother's, because otherwise my mother would have been cast out from the tribe. My mother was only sixteen when I was born. That is all I can tell you.'

'And now you have a child by a *gadjo*,' Reyora smiled softly. 'Was it someone casual you met, or do you love him? That was why you were so reluctant to wed Randal.'

Reyora nodded, rocking back and forwards slowly. It was all making sense now.

'I knew him hardly at all; we met in an extraordinary way. But we had affinity; it was like love.'

'Then the child was conceived in love, that is good.'

'But I don't want the child . . .'

Analee looked with bewilderment at the *cohani*. Surely she realized that?

'You are sure?'

'I don't know where the *gadjo* is, or even if he is alive. Randal injured him when he saw us together. I cannot have his child. I know nothing about him.'

Reyora got up and went to the corner of her tent. She took a taper from a box and went outside to light it from the fire that burned in front of the tent. Then she came back and, lighting the candle, put it on a box beside the palliasse on the floor.

'Come and lie here,' she said to Analee, and she busied herself with a box that stood by the palliasse.

Analee felt frightened but she did as she was bid. She lay on the straw and watched the *cohani* taking powders from different boxes and mixing them in a bowl. Then she spat into the bowl and said some sort of incantation over it and left it in front of the candle.

131

She took a jar from some vessels by the box and brought it over to Analee.

'I want you to make urine in this for the spell,' she said passing her the jug. Analee obeyed her knowing quite well the power of urine in gypsy magic. It was sometimes used for weddings when the man and the woman urinated into the same bowl, and the produce was mixed with brandy and earth and used in the ceremony. Diseases of the lung, it was said, were often cured by drinking urine and it could heal skin and eye diseases. Some women even washed their faces in it to have good skin.

Reyora took the jar and bade her lie down again. She poured a little of the warm liquid into the bowl and added some more powder until she had a paste.

Then she took it to Analee and told her to spit into it and the paste became runny like thick syrup. Reyora brought cushions over to the straw and put them under Analee's buttocks.

'Now roll up your skirt,' she said, 'and make yourself as high on the cushions as you can.'

Analee did as she was told while Reyora removed her rings and washed her hands in water. Then she knelt by Analee and put her hand gently between her legs smiling encouragingly to still her terror and telling her to relax. But Analee's heart beat fast and the groping caused her pain and made her uncomfortable. She could tell by the slow delicate way that Reyora probed and her solemn expression that she was very experienced, that she knew what she was doing.

When Reyora had finished she bade Analee rest.

'You are already big,' she said, 'have you had a child before?'

Analee was silent wondering what to say. She felt hot and uncomfortable and there was a little pain inside her.

'It is not like the womb of a woman who has not given birth,' Reyora said turning to her, 'it is soft and slack like a womb that has already been stretched in childbirth.'

'I did have a child,' Analee said. 'It died.'

'Ah.'

Reyora nodded, as if in understanding and knelt down again. Then she told Analee to be as she had before, and stirring the ointment in the bowl with a wooden spoon she gently, slowly poured it between Analee's legs. Analee felt it fiery and burning inside her and cried in pain; but Reyora went on relentlessly, holding Analee with one hand while she poured with the other until all the liquid was gone or had spilt over onto Analee's stomach. Then she held her firm looking at her, while Analee sobbed with the pain and she bit her hand to hold back the screams.

Suddenly the burning stopped and Analee felt calm. She looked at Reyora and took her hand out of her mouth. The hand was covered with the marks of her teeth, where she had bit deeply.

Reyora removed the cushions and gently wiped Analee's belly with a cloth, then she pulled down her skirts and covered her with a rug.

'Now you will feel tired for a while,' she said. 'Rest.'

'When will it work?'

'*If* it works,' Reyora said, 'it will be within two days.'

'And if it doesn't?'

'Then you will have a child.' Reyora turned to her blandly and smiled. 'That is the strongest philtre I have. But you are a hardy woman, Analee, good and strong for child-bearing, and it will be difficult to dislodge.'

Analee felt her eyes closing with drowsiness; as she went off to sleep Reyora was kneeling beside her, smiling and stroking her face.

That night as she lay against Randal pressing again for warmth, Analee felt a searing pain in her belly. She cried out and bent up her legs to try and ease it; then she felt something sticky and wet come out from between her legs. She started to sweat and, putting her hand there, knew it was blood. The philtre had worked. She felt both relief and dismay; a curious emotion she had not expected – not the dismay. Then the pain started again, only twice as bad and she called out to Randal to help her. Randal turned and clasped her.

'What is it, Analee?'

'I have a terrible pain in my belly.'

'But what is it?'

'I . . .' Analee nearly screamed with the pain and thrust her legs up to her chin. Randal jumped off the palliasse, and hastily putting on his breeches flew out of the tent without another word.

Within minutes he had returned with a candle and Reyora who had her little bag of ointments in her hand. She looked at Analee stretched out, and covered her top part. Kneeling down she put her hand again between her legs to examine her.

Randal hovered anxiously by, the candle guttering in his hand as the thin wind blew around the tent. Reyora finally completed her examination and sat back on her heels, her hand on Analee's belly.

'Have you had any movement in the belly? Any cramps?' she asked. Analee shook her head.

'I just get the waves of pain . . . you think?' She looked at Reyora, her expression a compound of fear and hope. 'The blood . . . ?'

Reyora looked onto the palliasse.

'There was only a little blood, there is none now.'

'Blood . . .' Randal said stepping forward, 'she is injured?'

'She is with child,' Reyora said shortly, 'maybe losing it. It is hard to tell.'

Randal gave a cry that nearly put out the candle and knelt beside Analee.

'Oh, Analee, a child. Do not lose our child.'

Reyora looked away and Analee pursed her mouth grimly through the pain. Her eyes caught those of Reyora.

'Is there anything else you can do?' she said. Reyora knew Analee was asking her to do more to remove the baby. She shook her head.

'I can relieve the pain in your belly, but inside . . . I can do nothing.'

She opened her bag and took an ointment that smelt strongly of dung which she massaged on Analee's aching stomach. The strong firm hands went back and forwards and slowly Analee began to feel a delicious relief, a calm that swept away the pain and left her free. Randal grasped her hand and cradled her head in his arms. 'Do not lose our child, Analee. Reyora, stay with her . . .' Reyora nodded soothingly and went on rubbing up and down, from side to side. Then she crooned a little song and Analee's eyes drooped and her head lolled against Randal's arm.

Two hours later the dawn came and still Analee slept while Randal held her head and, from time to time, clasped her in his arms. Reyora sat watching them, occasionally swaying back on her haunches, getting fresh ointments and soothing the flat brown belly.

Analee sighed and opened her eyes. She stared at Randal and looked at her stomach and then questioningly at Reyora.

Reyora smiled and shook her head, ceased the rubbing and drew the covers back over Analee's naked thighs and legs. Then she got up and looked down at her and Randal. 'You will be all right now. There will be no more pain. You will have the child. It is ordained.'

Analee didn't know whether she was happy or sad and pressed her head into Randal's arm, so that he should not observe such confusion.

On a cold January morning in the year 1745 Sir George Delamain set out from his newly acquired house in Essex Street for the long drive to his northern home. Sir George was pleased with his visit to the capital. Not only had he acquired a home which was well fitted to the important station he intended to assume in life from now on, but he had made an inroad in Whig politics by dint of skilful social climbing. He had made the acquaintance of the Prime Minister, The Duke of Newcastle, and had almost got for himself a bride.

Almost. Sir George Delamain had been introduced a year before to Lord Dacre who had immediately selected him as a fitting escort for his daughter Henrietta who, although plain, had much to commend her for marriage: she was an heiress. Her mother, Constance Dacre was, like Henrietta, an only child and had brought with her all the wealth of her family, the Farthingales, on her marriage to the third baron Dacre.

The Dacres had an estate on the borders of Lancashire and Lord Dacre and old Sir Francis Delamain had been acquaintances, but George and Henrietta had never met until George was asked to deliver a message to Lord Dacre in London some months before his grandfather's death.

In George Delamain Lord Dacre saw a marriageable proposition for his plump, gawkish daughter. The Delamains, Dacre knew, did not lack wealth or possessions and they had the acquisitive instinct – that is, they always wanted more than they had already. It was a well known Delamain trait. Henrietta, married to George, would be free from the adventurers who courted her solely for her prospects, aimless good-for-nothings with nothing but the sort of dashing good looks which appealed so much to someone as ill favoured by fortune as poor Henrietta Dacre.

In his way George Delamain too would be a fortune hunter, but

Henrietta would have as much to gain: a husband with an old family background, large estates and plenty of ambition. Lord Dacre knew of George's singular wish for a barony; he felt he could help George in every way.

It was he who had introduced George to the Prime Minister and leading figures in Whig politics, who had given balls and soirées at which George was an honoured guest. Above all, it was he who had warned George about the danger of a Jacobite rebellion; the effect it would have on their fortunes, possible confiscation both of the Delamain and Dacre estates if the Stuarts were restored to the throne. London was full of rumours of a Jacobite invasion. The Earl of Traquair known to be sympathetic to the Stuart cause had been in London that very winter sniffing out the support among suspected Jacobites. There was intelligence of his activities, and the fact that he had gone to France to see Prince Charles to bring – who knew what tidings?

The Delamain connection with the Stuarts was well known; above all their close relationship with those traitors the Allonby family – Robert Allonby who had been beheaded on Tower Hill and Guy Delamain, his brother-in-law, who had died in exile in France. George was perpetually anxious to shed this painful association with the Stuart cause. He thus became more pro-Hanoverian than the King himself, and did everything to make his own antipathy towards the Stuarts clear to all concerned. Had he not expelled his brother Brent, and his more notorious brother Tom, from the house the instant his grandfather died? Had he not hastened to London to establish a house, ingratiate himself with the Hanoverian politicians, with the court itself? No one was more anxious to stamp out any trace of Jacobitism than George Delamain and he was thus regarded, perched as he was at a strategic point in the north of England, as an important recruit by those who intended to preserve the Hanoverian Succession at any cost.

Looking out of the windows as his coach rumbled mile upon dreary mile northwards, George had plenty of time for reflection, for planning the future. There were frequent stops to change horses, and five nights were spent in inns on the way as the roads got worse and more narrow and the journey more tedious.

Yes, he was well pleased with his visit – Dacre had become not only a prospective father-in-law, but a good friend. He was a powerful man. He would help to remould George's image from that of a farming squire to a land-owner and politician of importance. The part George did not altogether like was the role that had been urged upon him of spy. Even he, a man of few scruples, did not relish having to ingratiate himself with his Allonby cousins to try and discover what was afoot in France. But he had promised not only Dacre but the small circle of serious-minded men, men of power and political importance, who had gathered at Dacre's house in Covent Garden to discuss the importance of the visit of the Earl of Traquair and the threat of Jacobite invasion.

George, they had pointed out, was a pivot – through no fault of his own he had access to traitorous elements. Why, by getting the information they sought he could not only pay a lasting service to his country but, who knows, maybe elevate himself to the peerage at the same time?

Baron Delamain – *The* Baron Delamain – George rolled the name round his tongue. It suited him well . . . Baron Delamain in the county of Cumberland, and Baroness Delamain . . . George felt a little less easy when he reflected on the charms, or rather lack of them, in his intended bride. He made no bones about it either to himself or Dacre – it was a marriage of convenience. It suited Dacre and himself that he should take Henrietta for a bride: what the girl herself thought about it was of no concern to either of them.

She would breed well, George reflected. She had ample girth, too much in fact, and good broad hips. The trouble was there was a history of only children in her family, and girls at that . . . but still, the woman was merely the vessel, it was the man who decided the nature and sex of the progeny, and everyone knew Delamain men were good breeders, breeders of sons.

Yes, it was time he had a son, got rid of the menace of the whippet Brent taking over the title and estates should anything happen to him. Pity he had recovered from the injury that his folly had inflicted upon him . . . hit over the head by a gypsy! Even George, who seldom laughed, smirked at the thought. Thank goodness no one in London knew, or could ever possibly find out, about *that* peculiar piece of idiocy.

The coach rumbled northwards and no one, neither Allonby, nor Delamain nor even the Buckland gypsies in their camp near Carlisle knew what a momentous year 1745 was to be for them, and how fundamentally the fortunes of so many concerned were to change.

9

From the distance Brent Delamain could see the outline of the slate cliffs that meant Maughold Peninsula and journey's end – or nearly journey's end. From the beginning he had proved a good sailor. 'A natural affinity with the sea,' Ambrose had proclaimed proudly when Brent was the only man still on his legs after a particularly severe voyage from Port Rush. But this comparatively short journey from Whitehaven in Cumberland to the Isle of Man had provided seas such as Brent had never before seen or wanted to again.

Once again he was the only man on his legs and, because the hold was almost empty, the boat had rolled about until at one stage he had thought it would turn turtle, and that would be the end of them.

Now the waters were calmer and the sailors started to stagger up from below, all except the master who had drunk himself into a stupor through sheer fear and was out cold in his bunk. Brent had just been down to see. He would have to bring the ship into the cove himself with the help of the mate, a dour fellow called Quiggan.

The ship rounded Maughold Head and then turned inland following the rugged coast to the harbour at the north end of Laxey Bay. Brent was grateful that it was wide and shallow because he had only been a sailor for three months and his knowledge of navigation was elementary.

They tied up at the jetty at Laxey and, leaving the master in his berth, Brent made for the narrow main street of the town which lay in the shadow of Snaefell, the highest mountain in the Isle of Man.

Brent had been glad to take to the sea and get away from the watchful eye of Sarah Rigg with whom he lodged in Cockermouth. He had proved an adept apprentice and pupil and had soon justified Ambrose's confidence that the man was no idler but possessed of a good brain as well as a hardy body.

Indeed, a curious and unexpected friendship had grown

between Brent and his employer, who proved not only fair and hardworking but curiously honest in his rough-necked kind of way. Brent had discovered how much in awe of his wife Ambrose really was; how he resented his humble ancestry, his lack of manners and how he looked to Sarah to turn him into a gentleman.

It was too late to turn Ambrose Rigg into a gentleman, Brent knew that. As he listened to his outpourings over the port when Sarah had gone to bed, he tried to persuade him that the things Ambrose considered important were not – that using a napkin and developing fine airs were of far less consequence than charity, kindness and honesty and the sort of diligence and business acumen that Ambrose so successfully displayed.

Brent envied him these things and he told him so and, as Ambrose listened to this young lad, his eyes were opened and he developed a sense of self-respect for his own innate attributes that were God-given and not acquired.

Consequently Sarah Rigg, seeing how affected her husband was by his association with Brent, how less respectful towards herself, was eager to have him out of the house and gladly concurred when it was suggested that Brent should leave clerking in the warehouse and take to the sea.

Brent went to sea at a very bad time – mid-February, a month of storms and gales; but he found his sea legs quickly and also a sense of survival. He learned rudimentary navigation and the storing of ballast, and how to stow the sails with the maximum of speed when the storm winds blew up.

He had survived a battering three month's apprenticeship. Now it was May and the seas were calmer. The trees and hedgerows were abud with new life in the lanes of Cumberland and the Isle of Man, and he felt a lightening of the heart as he climbed up the steep main street of Laxey. His object was to see to the new cargo for Whitehaven of lead and copper ore, products of the mines at Dhoon north of Lazey, the purpose of this trip. At other times he put into the creeks nearer Maughold and Bradda Head to take off zinc and galena. In return he brought timber and wool and food, for the Isle of Man was very dependent on the mainland of England from which it had been ruled since 1300, the Dukes of Athol having recently taken over from the Stanleys who had been Lords of Man for three hundred years.

It was a fine clear day, a breeze blew in from the sea and Brent came to the house of John Collister, a ship's merchant and chandler with whom he had had commerce before and who was one of Ambrose's agents on the island.

John Collister, a bluff handsome man of fifty and an ex-sailor who had acquired a wooden leg in the wars against France, was waiting for Brent, sitting at a table piled with bills and ledgers. He got up as Brent came in and called for his daughter Harriet to fetch some ale.

Harriet, wearing her best bonnet and apron was pleased to answer her father's summons: she always had a glad eye for Brent Delamain whenever he came to Laxey – but he only gave her the most casual of glances, polite but nothing more. Not that Brent was unaware of Harriet's charms or her obvious intention of bestowing them on him, freely, for the asking. She made it quite clear by the way she flounced in and out or lingered by the door gazing slyly up at him. Once she had even followed him on some pretext or the other; but all to no avail. Since he had wrenched himself from Mary Allonby, Brent was a different man. He was determined to make a fresh image for himself from that of a philanderer and idler: to work hard and preserve his virtue in order to be worthy of Mary.

For a man of Brent's disposition the work was no hardship, but the maintenance of chastity was, especially with Ambrose forever suggesting a visit to the local bawdy house and making it clear that he frequented the place often himself.

'Art a puritan lad?' Ambrose would chide suggesting he had expected better. But it was the only complaint he had against Brent, so he decided to keep a wise counsel, say no more and continue to visit the bawdy house by himself.

Brent and Mary had made up for the force of the separation by an exchange of letters. He had written, on reflection, to explain his behaviour to her and asked her to show the letter to her brothers as a sign of his good intentions. After a short interval Mary had replied indicating her acceptance of the situation and her happiness at the sacrifice Brent was prepared to make to woo her.

From then on they corresponded chastely every week, but they never met. Brent had imposed on himself this condition: their next meeting would be to wed.

He well knew the meaning of Harriet Collister's glances as she brought in ale and oat cakes. He smiled at her in his detached friendly fashion, willing enough to exchange the time of day with her, but John seemed anxious for her departure and waved her away. His face was serious as he poured out the ale from the jug into a tankard of thick pewter and pushed it over to Brent.

'Good voyage?'

'A devil for the time of year. We were very light and bobbed about like a cork.'

'And Dinward?'

'Drunk.'

John nodded. Dinward was the master and seldom sober, good sea or bad.

'Ambrose should get rid of him. He is a menace and a threat.'

'He is a good sailor when sober, and I am learning fast.'

'So I hear.'

John got up and, with his tankard in his hand, hobbled over to the window looking through the thick panes which gave on to the harbour. He turned and glanced at Brent as though to say something and then turned away again. Brent knew the signs of restlessness.

'You have aught to say to me John and cannot?'

John turned round, quaffing his ale from his tankard so that a line of fine white froth remained on his upper lip.

'I know not where to begin.'

'John, if it is your daughter, I am promised . . .'

John gave a hearty laugh and wiped his lip on the sleeve of his coat.

'Oh, you observe how she hankers after you. No, I told her she had no hope there, a nobleman . . .'

''Tis not *that*! I am promised to my cousin. Harriet is a fine lass.'

'Aye, aye and she'll get wed soon enough; but it is not of Harriet I speak. Brent . . .' John sat down heavily and put his large hand squarely on his good knee. 'I wonder which way you are?'

'Which way . . .' Brent looked at John in bewilderment.

'Because if I speak out of turn I am undone.'

Collister stared at Brent as though willing him to understand what he was saying, and then Brent did understand. It came to him suddenly and clearly.

'Which way . . . politically?'

'Aye, aye.' Collister sat back with a sigh of relief; now he had no need to fear compromising himself.

'You are only asking me for one reason, John. There is much unrest abroad, much talk of revolt. You are asking me if I am for the Stuarts?'

'Aye.' John gazed at him, mouth half open, eyes glinting.

'Of course I am for the Stuarts; you know our family.'

'I know they are divided, that much I heard. That one of your brothers is a popish priest and the other a Whig baronet. It was through the priest that news came of you . . .'

'From Tom? You have heard from Tom?' Brent jumped up, his face glowing. 'I have tried so hard to contact Tom since I came to Whitehaven; but he has gone aground.'

'Not gone aground. He is with the Prince, but the Prince is now surrounded by many men. Most wish him well; but some harm. He has to be careful. It is hard to tell who the traitors are – disaffected Irish soldiers, men of all descriptions and every nationality you can think of surround him. Not all honest men. But now . . .' John leaned forward his eyes gleaming, 'the Prince has made up his mind to sail.'

'For England?'

'For *Scotland*. The recent defeat at Fontenoy by Marshal Saxe of the combined British and Hanoverian force under the command of the Duke of Cumberland has determined the Prince that the time is ripe. He is preparing to sail this very instant.'

'But surely it is *folly*?'

'Aye, folly and a grand one at that. All Scotland will flock to such a brave Prince and then all England, too. You will see, in a few months the Stuarts will be again on the throne.'

'Then how do you know, what part do you . . . will the Prince land *here*?'

'Nay, in the north of Scotland where all is prepared. But men close to Murray of Broughton, one of the Prince's right hand men, have been in touch with contacts of mine in Scotland and Cumberland. We are to get as many provisions for the Prince as we can from France and Ireland and America, muskets and cannon and gunshot and swords – and smuggle them into England.'

Now the light dawned. Brent stood up and refilled his tankard.

'And you want me to help?'

'Can you?'

'Can I not!' Brent shouted. 'John Collister, I was born to live for this day. You have made a man of me. I was sworn to serve the King and the Prince, but I had an injury that has affected my leg. But for it I would have gone to France with my brother, been by his side and that of Prince Charles this very instance. But I could not go and Tom, perforce, left without me. He left no message and nowhere to find him. Then Ambrose offered me work and he is well known for his Hanoverian sympathies, though sometimes I wonder . . .'

'Oh, he is Hanoverian all right,' John said grimly. 'Make no mistake about it. That is why he must never know of what is afoot, that we are using his ships to smuggle arms into England.'

'Then how shall we do it?'

'Easily. You know Fleswick Bay close by St Bees?'

Brent nodded.

'We will have a boat waiting to rendezvous with you; a small craft capable of travelling over shallow water. You will get the Captain drunk, put out the anchor and it will all be done. Then you proceed to Whitehaven with your ore.'

'A smuggler!' Brent exclaimed excitedly. 'An arms smuggler.'

'And a price on your head if you are caught.'

'My family have already died for the Stuarts.'

'I know. I heard. But I had to be sure.'

'Oh, John, you can be sure of me.' Brent went over to the older man and clasped his shoulder. Then they solemnly shook hands and downed the rest of their ale. 'Now tell me how it is to happen.'

'I have the goods here in my barn,' John said leaning towards Brent and lowering his voice. 'We will load the ore this afternoon and the arms tonight. Then you set out with the morning tide.'

'But Dinward. He will be sober by then.'

'He will be sober to see the ore loaded on board. Then the hatches will be closed and he will be taken to the town by one of my men.'

'And sloshed with ale.'

'Precisely, while we load the ship with arms. By first light if he is sober he will not know what he carries in his ship. You should approach Fleswick at nightfall tomorrow. That will be the difficult time; so you must ply Dinward with enough drink to ensure a good slumber and tie him up in his cabin. Our men will rendezvous at midnight.'

'But if Dinward wakes? He has a good head.'

John looked at him, his face grim. 'Then you must kill him.'

Brent stared for a long while at the old mariner. It was the first time that the prospect of death as a part of the forthcoming battle had become a reality. He had talked about it often enough with gallantry and without any real understanding. He had made it romantic in connection with Mary Allonby. But now it might mean a blade through the back in the small hours of the morning and the dumping of a weighted body out at sea. Now it was reality.

'Could you *kill*, Brent?'

Brent considered before answering.

'In cold blood I cannot think of it; but we are engaged in war . . . I have considered it often enough. I could do it.'

'Good. Dinward would be not such a bad thing to start on. He is a good-for-nothing rogue and I believe he has no family so you would not be leaving a widow and orphans.'

'Let us hope it does not come to that,' Brent said. 'But what of the crew?'

'They are stupid men, also fond of drink. Quiggan the mate is fond of money and him we can bribe. He will help you.'

'Good then give me the details – who I am to meet and how.'

Later that night Brent stood on the deck smoking a pipe. The great crags rose up towards Snaefell which looked as though it was snow-capped in the white light of the moon. It had been a bad night for loading dangerous goods; too bright and too mild, too many people strolling on the quayside. But now it was done and Brent leaned over the side of the ship gazing into the clear water, hoping for a calm run on his first mission as a servant, albeit a humble one, of the true King.

And indeed at first all went well. Dinward was brought aboard drunk and slept all night; but at dawn he was wide awake, alert and on deck. The trouble with Dinward was that he got drunk easily but he recovered very quickly. Brent could see that a problem would occur in twelve hours time as they anchored off Fleswick Bay.

But problems occurred before that. The promise of good weather did not hold and it was a rough voyage. Instead of drinking, Dinward stayed on deck eagle-eyed, directing the passage of the boat through the high waves that pounded from the west.

After a stormy voyage the seas still pounded against the ship but, before dark, the welcome coast of Cumberland came into sight, first as a thin line on the horizon. Then, as the boat got nearer, Brent could see in the distance the mountains of Lakeland topped by great Scafell rising from the flat coastal stretch. He thought of Mary so near and yet so far, whom he could not see. She would be getting the supper now or reading a book by candlelight, or gazing into the twilight as night began to fall upon beautiful Lake Derwentwater.

The nearer they got to the coast the calmer grew the seas and Brent went down to the galley to eat, a scratch meal at sea consisting of chunks of bread and salted beef and pots of warm ale. The five crew members, who included the mate Quiggan and the master Dinward, sat around already well into their food. Brent was glad to see that Dinward was also well into the whisky, of which he kept a private store. Dinward looked on suspiciously as Brent sat beside him, steadying himself against the rolling sea.

'Ye're a lot on deck this voyage.'

''Tis to keep away the sickness,' Brent said. ''Tis too stale for me down here.'

'"Too stale for me",' Dinward mimicked Brent's voice. 'Oh dearie me.' The crew tittered.

There was no love lost between Brent and Dinward. Dinward objected to the fact that Brent was somehow in the place of his master, Ambrose Rigg. He felt he was being spied upon. He resented his breeding and what he thought of as his fancy manners. Brent was no swearing seafaring man but, because he was the captain and in charge, Dinward did all he could to make it hard for Brent, to make him do the basic unpleasant tasks at sea and teach him as little as possible.

But Brent wasn't slighted. Although he didn't like Dinward he knew what was behind his treatment of him, the reason for the dislike. He did as he was told and said little. Now as Dinward went on taunting him Brent doggedly ate his food and drank his ale, grimacing because it was sour.

Quiggan the mate munched solidly not looking at Brent. He had been easily bought having little liking for Dinward. He, too, knew about the cargo, only he thought it was silk and tobacco. It was his job to get Dinward drunk. It was also up to him to suggest the ship should halt before Whitehaven.

'Best anchor over night, Dinward. Stop the rolling. Too rough to approach Whitehaven.'

Dinward gazed at him calmly but drained his whisky straight from the bottle, one rheumy eye on his mate.

'Aye. Drop anchor by St Bees. We can have a good night's sleep.'

Brent's heart leapt. Dinward was playing into his hands! But he made no movement or comment apart from glancing at Quiggan who had started to sing. The fact that they were going to anchor made the company relax and everyone, except Brent, got down to drinking in earnest.

Brent was on watch and after he had eaten went up on deck again. It was a cloudy night, no stars and no moon. He looked towards the shore but could see nothing. After a while Quiggan joined him.

'That was well done,' Brent said. 'Fleswick is just past St Bees Head.'

'I don't like it somehow,' Quiggan said, and Brent could see him scowling in the light of the lantern that hung from the mast.

'Why not?'

'That he suggested St Bees. Don't it seem weird to you?'

'No. Should it?'

'Fleswick nearby is known for smuggling. Why should Dinward suggest it?'

A cold finger of fear momentarily touched Brent's heart, and he looked in the gloom towards Quiggan.

'You think he knows?'

'I just think it odd, is all. He's well into his second bottle of the hard stuff, but I still don't like it,' Quiggan said, stamping his feet in the cold air. 'I don't like any of it. Best abandon it if you ask me. It was done in too much of a hurry.'

'But we can't! We'll have the customs on to us in Whitehaven. They know well what is afoot in France. They'll open the hatches and that will be that.'

'Overboard then?'

'All those guns and gunpowder?' Brent whispered hoarsely. 'Are you mad? They are badly needed, and the money for such is not easy to find. We'll have to chance it. Go below and see they all get drunk. We can manage ourselves.'

Kelly at the wheel shouted. 'St Bees sir!'

Quiggan called Brent and they ran together to the fo'c's'le to let down the big anchor. As it slid into the water the boat shuddered and stopped but it was still tossing like a cork on the sea.

'Bad light for smuggling,' Quiggan said quietly.

'Shh. We do not rendezvous until midnight.'

'They won't make it in a small boat in this weather.'

Brent looked anxiously down at the swirling sea.

'Can't we get further in?' he asked Quiggan.

'Too dangerous,' Quiggan said, 'too shallow. Best drop it all overboard if you ask me and get a good night's sleep.'

Brent turned angrily away and began to regret accepting Collister's mission so easily. It *was* badly and hastily planned. He had been too enthusiastic and too thoughtless. He hadn't even begun to wonder, as he did now, if it was a trap. It was difficult to trust Quiggan and what did he know of Collister, after all?

After a while Brent went below and found the entire crew including Quiggan singing and drinking hard. He couldn't bear the noise and the stench and went on deck again. He had on a heavy seaman's cloak which he clutched around him for warmth. His eyes peered into the darkness towards Fleswick looking for the light that was to be the signal.

Brent leaned over the bulwark and gazed into the sea. They were just round the Head from St Bees, within sight of Fleswick Bay. He could see the phosphorescent white foam on the crest of the waves. To his relief the sea was growing calmer, the wind was dropping and in the sky he could discern a few stars. He realized that from below deck all was quiet and he stepped to the top of the ladder that led into the galley. Dinward had rolled off his bunk and lay snoring on the floor; beside him the remains of a bottle of whisky soaked into the floor. Two of the crew were drunk but still awake and Quiggin sat in a corner, apparently half asleep. Brent, satisfied with the scene, signalled to Quiggan who lurched unsteadily to his feet and came across, staring up at Brent.

'Quickly,' Brent whispered sharply, 'I calculate 'tis near midnight.'

Quiggan appeared to have difficulty in focusing his eyes and Brent cursed him for being a drunkard like the others.

'You will not get the rest of your pay!' Brent hissed. The thought of money seemed to make an impact on Quiggan who began to shin up the ladder. At the top he shivered in the wind and shook his head.

'I still don't like it.'

'Come on man, open the hatches.'

'Have you seen a light?'

'Not yet, but the light will be the sign that they are ready. Quick.'

They unfastened the hatches and Brent leaned down to make sure the cases they had loaded aboard were still intact. Then when the canvas was loose he went to the port side of the ship which lay parallel to the shore. There was still no sign of a light and he started to despair. They would not come; the cases *would* have to be dumped into the sea.

Suddenly Quiggan grasped his arm and pointed. To Brent's astonishment a light came not from the coast as he had expected but from the sea, close to them.

''Tis a boat,' Quiggan said.

And there it was, bouncing below on the choppy waves. Brent leaned over the side and flashed his own storm lantern, heartened to see an answering wave.

'Quick,' he cried, 'they will not be able to lie alongside of us for long in this sea.' Running to the nearside hatch, he cast back the tarpaulin and heaved up the first case, staggering with it to the side of the ship. Just as he came to the bulwark the boat drew alongside and faces peered up at him in the darkness. One man, standing up and balancing in the boat addressed Brent.

'I'm Macdonald. Do you have it all?'

'Aye.' Brent said, and began to lower the case which Macdonald caught with the help of another man and stowed in the boat.

'Quickly,' Brent called behind him to Quiggan, 'the boat is swaying horribly.'

Quiggan was slow. Brent cursed and ran to the hold expecting to pass him on the way.

But of the mate there was no sign. He'd probably fallen down drunk. Brent would have to get one of the Scotsmen to help him if they were to despatch this lot. He grabbed another case and, staggering to the rail with it, dropped it over calling out:

'I think my helper is too drunk. One of you will have to come aboard.'

In the gloom Macdonald gave a broad smile and grasped the

side, about to heave himself aboard. But suddenly his eyes glanced beyond Brent and, before he could call out, Brent felt sharp steel in the small of his back.

'Caught you red-handed,' Dinward said in a flat sober voice. 'You bastard.'

'Quick, get away,' Brent called and, seeing the confusion on Macdonald's face, cried out again, 'as far as you can. Get away.'

Macdonald jumped back into the boat and, carrying only two of the score or more cases of guns that were aboard the *Lizzie*, they grabbed their oars and made off into the darkness. The point of Dinward's knife dug deeper and Brent winced.

'Get below, you scoundrel. Think to trick the master, would you? Think I didn't know what you were up to? Think you could *trust* Quiggan? Came to me as soon as you talked to him. He knows better'n to trick me.'

He shoved the point of his knife again into Brent's back and Brent stumbled down the ladder into the galley. The drunken sailors gaped at him but said nothing. Dinward shoved Brent forward into his small cabin screened from the galley with a curtain. There Quiggan sat dejectedly on a stool.

'You traitor,' Brent spat at him, and at that Dinward's knife cut into his flesh and he knew he had drawn blood.

'He's no traitor, only doing his duty to the master, Mr Rigg. You think we don't know a good job when we see one? Years we've worked for Mr Rigg and a fancy upstart like you thinks you can bribe us with gold.'

Quiggan hung his head avoiding Brent's eyes.

'What is it you've got there? Silks is it? Tobacco? Well Mr Rigg will see. We'll leave it all for him when we dock tomorrow. Best he should know what sort of man he's grooming for his successor.'

'Take care of the customs,' Brent said shortly knowing that further words were useless.

'Oh, we'll take care of them all right. Mr Rigg *always* takes care of the customs.'

He laughed and Quiggan sniggered. Suddenly Brent remembered what he'd heard about Rigg. That much of his fortune came from smuggling. Only as yet he had seen no evidence of it himself – nothing in the ledgers, nothing in the warehouses, nothing on the *Lizzie* which plied backwards and forwards with the minerals, wood and wool. Yet he had only been on the *Lizzie* – Rigg had more ships and a small fleet of fishing wherries as well.

'Tie him up!' Dinward snarled and Quiggan moved towards Brent.

'There is no need, I'd not get far,' Brent said.

'Tie him up!' Dinward roared and Brent felt the sharp cutting edge of a rope round his wrists. Then Quiggan shoved him roughly on the floor and bound his ankles. Like that Brent remained until dawn when the *Lizzie* raised anchor and set sail for Whitehaven harbour.

'Guns is it?' Ambrose Rigg said, gazing down at Brent from what seemed a great height. 'For whom I wonder?'

Brent was stiff and his back ached. His blood had run down onto the floor, but it had only been a flesh wound and had soon congealed. The boat had tossed all night and what with that and the stench of drink and sweat Brent had felt sick. He had not slept and at first light the *Lizzie* had made a rapid run into Whitehaven harbour. As usual Ambrose Rigg had been on the jetty to welcome back one of his ships. It was this attention to detail that made Rigg such a good businessman. He met them and saw them off; even the fishing boats that plied along the coast.

Brent had heard Rigg's steps on the deck, listened to voices, knew that the tarpaulins were being drawn back and the contraband inspected.

Then Rigg's huge bulk had come carefully down the ladder, and he'd stood for some time gazing at Brent lying trussed like a hen in the corner.

Brent didn't reply to his question but lay looking up sullenly at his master, his thoughts too jumbled and fragmented to control. At his first task he had failed; let everyone down – betrayed Collister and, probably, Macdonald. He would bring shame on the Delamains, on the Allonbys. For this he would be hanged. All he wanted now was for death to come soon.

The only thing that surprised Brent was the expression on Rigg's face. He had expected harshness and hatred, maybe a kick in the ribs. But Rigg looked thoughtful. He stroked his whiskers and scratched his head, tipping his hat back on his head. He even seemed to have a smile of sorts on his lips.

It was very strange.

'No answer? Untie him.' Rigg motioned to Dinward who was grinning with self-satisfaction and hastened to do his master's bidding, undoing the heavy sailor's knots that had bound Brent.

Brent sat up and rubbed his wrists, his ankles. Then he tenderly felt his back, the congealed blood, the torn shirt. He got unsteadily to his feet and stared at Rigg. To his astonishment Rigg winked then, turning round, said slowly to Dinward and Quiggan.

'One word of this gets round and your bodies will be fished unrecognized out of the sea. I'm warning you.'

He held a fist under Dinward's nose and both he and Quiggan cringed.

'You have done what you thought was right. 'Tis all I can say at the moment. Come to my office after you've unloaded, and take care those cases are well out of the way.'

'Aye, sir.' Dinward touched his cap and Quiggan backed away looking at Brent with bewilderment.

Brent, bewildered himself but giving no sign of it, assumed an air of injured innocence, glared at Dinward and Quiggan and ordered the latter to fetch his cloak and be quick about it. Quiggan and Dinward stared at each other in amazement and, giving them a surly look, Brent followed his unexpected saviour up the ladder. On deck he saw that the tarpaulin was over the hatches again, neatly battened down, and there wasn't a custom's man in sight.

Rigg didn't speak but walked quickly down the gang-plank to the jetty and Brent, wrapped in his cloak against the morning chill, followed him to Rigg's office, which overlooked the harbour, and indeed the *Lizzie* as she lay at her moorings, and was soon reached over the cobbles of the narrow quayside. On the ground floor Rigg had his warehouse, and the office was reached by means of a back staircase.

Brent had spent many hours crouched on a stool by the window transferring figures from one ledger to another. Now there was no sign of the clerk who had taken his place. A fire burned in the grate, flames leaping up the chimney and on either side were great leather armchairs in one of which Rigg ensconced himself after removing his coat and pouring two glasses of brandy. One he offered to Brent, the other he nursed in his large calloused hand – the hand of a man who had made his way up by dint of sweat and his own hard work. He still hadn't spoken, and Brent found the experience unnerving. Now as he stood uncertainly grasping the balloon of brandy, Rigg pointed to the chair opposite him and smiled.

'Sit lad. Warm yourself. 'Tis no way to spend the night on a floor bound hand and foot, is it now?' Rigg gave a short explosion of laughter and his red face creased like that of a squealing new born infant.

'I understand you not,' Brent said at last. 'What . . . ?'

'What am I doing, eh? Condoning smuggling, eh? Guns, eh?'

'You *knew* about it?' Brent began incredulously, and stopped as Rigg shook his head.

'No, no. I knew nothing. At first I thought it might be silk or brandy, tea or tobacco but one glance and I saw the gleam of metal . . .' Rigg paused and looked severe. 'Nay, that is very serious indeed. For brandy and tea you could spend years in gaol, but for guns you could swing. You knew that?'

Brent nodded.

'You're a brave lad. Foolish maybe?'

'It is for . . .'

'Oh, I know what it's *for*,' Rigg said abruptly. 'I am not married into the Allonby family for naught you know. It is for the Stuarts; they say the unrest in France will bring the Pretender back to this country. Everyone is expecting it. Am I not right?'

'Are *you* for the King?' Brent began hopefully.

'I tell you I'm not for any king!' Rigg banged a large hand on his silk-covered knee. 'I thought I made that clear. I'm for business and making money and peace and prosperity. I'll have no trafficking wi' politics.'

'So why don't you mind? I can't understand you.' Brent put the glass to his lips and took a draught of brandy. It was so smooth and fiery that it caught in his throat and made him choke. Then suddenly Brent understood. He lowered the glass and looked at the amber liquid glowing at its base; the pungent, exquisite aroma of the finest French brandy assailed his nostrils. Contraband.

He looked up at Rigg, and a slight smile hovered on his lips.

'You're beginning to understand,' Rigg said, also smiling and saluting Brent with his glass.

'Fine brandy,' Brent said.

'The best, and the silk of my breeches . . .' Rigg plucked at his knee and smoothed the arm of his finely cut coat. Then he took up his pipe and reached his arm out for the tin of tobacco that stood on the table by the side of his chair. He contentedly began stuffing it into his pipe and glanced over at Brent.

'All smuggled?'

'You never knew? Oh, I can see you didn't. I took care you should not find out until I knew you better – to see whether you were with me or against me.'

'You needed me for smuggling?' Brent said with astonishment. 'Not business?'

'Smuggling *is* business ain't it? It is the best part of my business. I keep one or two clean ships like the *Lizzie* with clean crews who know not of my other enterprises. Dinward and Quiggan are simpletons. I can only employ bright men on my smuggling ventures.'

'Did you set out to trap me then?'

'Not at all. I know naught of gun-running, nor want to neither. Very dangerous *that*. You will tell me how you got air of it. No, Brent. I need a good bright lad to help me expand my smuggling enterprises. I needed *you*; but I had to get to know you better first. I could see you were not like your brother George. *Sir* George, by God . . .' Rigg threw back his head and laughed with irony. 'He will fancy himself now. All set to marry into the Dacre family I hear tell.'

'Really?' Brent said without much interest. 'I didn't know that.'

Rigg leaned forward. 'Well, *I* know Lord Dacre is a committed Hanoverian. I have done business with his brother the Honourable Timothy, and I know just how committed Lord Dacre is to King George and his descendants.

'So, what did I know about *you*? I knew you were a rebel, a womanizer, that you didn't fit in. I saw you were a fine, tall lad, athletic and brave. I saw the love of adventure in your eyes, and I knew you had courage. "Aye," I thought, "he's for me. But can I trust him?" So I gave myself a year to find out. But you've beaten me to it, Brent. Only six months gone and already I see you have a smuggler's heart.'

He got up and gave Brent that friendly shove on the back which, for Rigg, was a term of endearment. He refilled his glass and poured one for Brent. But Brent was struggling, his mind bewildered.

'You mistake me Mr Rigg, sir. I am a patriot, not a common smuggler. I do this for the Cause, not for gain.'

153

'Ah,' Rigg sat down again and nodded, his chin on his chest, his eyes on Brent, 'a patriot, I see. A *criminal*, my lad, it is if the authorities come to hear of it. I suppose it all depends from which vantage point you observe it. Now *I* see my business activities as a man of business, for gain. I see the taxes imposed by Sir Robert Walpole and his ilk, may they rot in hell, as against my interests. First it was tea, coffee and chocolate, then a year or two later tobacco and wine. The Tories could do nothing against the government. So what happened? A lot of honest businessmen decided to take the law into their own hands, myself among them. The stuff was run into the Isle of Man or Ireland where taxes were paid so we did not offend against those countries; but then we brought it here where *no* tax is paid and honest men can make a profit.'

'That's why you've got no truck with politics.' Brent smiled at the virtuous indignation shown by Ambrose Rigg, whose face grew redder as he recounted the iniquities of the government.

'Aye. Tax us out of existence. But wars? No, I don't want wars. We've had enough, if you ask me. I want peace and stability and prosperity.'

There was a silence and, as a log fell smouldering into the grate, Brent stirred it with his boot.

'I am beginning to understand, sir.'

'Good.'

Ambrose got up and stood with his back to the fire, his hand beneath the tails of his coat. First of all he looked at the ceiling, then he looked at Brent.

'I don't like saying this, but I have got a hold over you young Delamain. Aye, and you've got one over me an' all. I've spilt the beans. I'm a smuggler and you're a smuggler. If you betray me to the authorities, then I'll betray you . . .'

'I will *not* betray you sir! I would rather clear out and go to France where my business may be legitimate.'

Rigg's face clouded and he cleared his throat, looking darkly at Brent.

'Oh no, young man. You're not getting out of this one so easy. I *need* you. I *like* you. You're not clearing out to France and spilling your blood in a wasted cause; not yet. I'll make a bargain with you.' Rigg drew himself up and stretched a forefinger towards Brent, shaking it vigorously as he spoke. 'You aid me and I'll aid you. You join my smuggling fleet, organizing and assisting, planning and helping to control it, and I'll turn a blind eye to your gun smuggling. I'll not actively assist you, but I'll not hinder you either. As long as you work well for me I'll not enquire what else goes into the holds of my ships, and I'll see you're troubled neither by the customs nor any of my men. That's a promise.'

Brent sprang out of his chair, his face alight. He only thought of the help he could give to the Cause, the amount that could be smuggled in with the extensive fleet owned by Rigg. And no questions asked! Why it was a fantastic, unlooked for, unhoped for, opportunity. He thrust out his hand towards Rigg who took it and ceremoniously pumped it up and down.

'I see we have a bargain,' he said. 'A true partnership is based on mutual need. You and I need each other Mr Delamain.'

10

Now that spring had come Analee only looked forward to the time of her delivery. She was big and the baby was heavy, kicking inside her, making it difficult for her to move easily, to sleep at nights. She would lie on her back, her hands on her belly, gazing up at the roof of the tent, Randal snoring or breathing heavily beside her, and her thoughts were full of dread for the future.

She still didn't want this child, Brent's child or Randal's or any other. She wanted the child that had given one cry and died as it was born, its first cry in the world its last. She could still hear the tiny cry and see the small limp lifeless form attached to her by the cord. The child had been too thin to survive, it had been born too soon – for Analee had been cold and hungry and full of grief, and it had been a bitter winter. An old woman, a *gadjo*, had looked after her as she'd lain in a barn giving birth to the baby who died so soon; an old woman who worked on the farm and felt sorry for her. The woman had held her hand and wiped her dry mouth, and then she'd cut the cord and tied it, severing the lifeless child from its mother.

She'd given it to one of her sons to bury, as though it had been an animal, and Analee had been forced on her way.

Now this brought all those memories back and although she tried to be happy and wanted to be, she could not. She had nothing to say against Randal; he was a good man, though limited and set in his ways. Now that they no longer danced or made love he seemed to have lost his love for her; he was no longer as tender as he had been and soon she would be put in a tent by herself, away from the others, to await the baby's birth. For a woman in labour was *marimé*, unclean, and the husband could not be with her or else he would be contaminated too.

There was so much in Analee that would not conform, that had lived for such a long time away from the formal gypsy tribe, that she resented this treatment still meted out by the gypsies to women. She would often sit near the labour tent when other gypsy women were giving birth and listen to their cries, and then imagine that soon it would be her turn. Some of the women cared, but most of them did not. They had endured it and expected others to do the same. When you were very near your time the *cohani* came and assisted the new baby into the world. But even then the father didn't come near for days. Both mother and baby were *marimé* until the child had been baptized by immersion in water and thus made itself and its mother clean.

Analee could see how Randal accepted the customs of his tribe. He neither knew nor cared that she feared to be alone and needed him, because it reminded her of the time she had lain alone in an evil-smelling barn and had given birth to the child who had died with its first cry.

But she knew already that the tent was being prepared for her and that very soon she would be moved into it. She would not be allowed to come out, and there she would be on her own or occasionally with the *cohani* or Rebecca.

In the long months of her pregnancy Analee had come to realize that she could never be a true member of the Buckland tribe. She no more belonged here than she had anywhere else. She was a nomad, born to wander. The thought of the baby, of a life with Randal, was stifling and the way Randal had so quickly adapted himself to being a husband, had become just like any other gypsy of the Buckland tribe who squatted for hours smoking or chewing tobacco and mending pots and pans brought from Carlisle. His sister and brothers had soon gone off to make music without him and he no longer sang or danced as he used to. He was content to let his wife become as other wives, to sit with the women and cook and mend. Soon he would expect Analee to be just like them, with a baby in her arms and another in her belly. He had told her so. It was her duty.

He no longer seemed to remember the glory of their love-making, or the magic of the dance. He gazed at her dully because she was just a wife, an object, and it was her duty to look after him and bear children.

Randal turned in his sleep and Analee moved away from him. Though they no longer made love she didn't even want him to touch her. Already he was beginning to think of her as unclean. He showed it by the way he looked at her.

Analee wondered why Randal had changed from a lover into a husband so quickly. Was it because of the baby or had he tired of her beauty and her charms? Reyora had become a friend to Analee who tried to ask her the reason for this, but Reyora would smile and shrug and say it was the way with men. They quickly tired. Randal would want her again. He would be tender with her again after the baby, only then they would be kept awake by its screams. It would never be quite the same again as it had been after they had married. It could not be. It was not the way with men and women.

Reyora saw that Analee didn't understand. She was not true gypsy; she was romantic. Sometimes Reyora, who could see certain things but not everything, wondered what would become of Analee.

One beautiful June day Reyora beckoned to Analee after the noonday meal and bade her come over to her tent. Analee had been walking restlessly around the camp in the morning, too uncomfortable to remain sitting and had even followed a footpath towards Carlisle until fear drove her back. She was heavy and tired and to be near her own people was important.

The smell of the hedgerows in early summer, the wisps of pale clouds in the sky, the thick burgeoning leaves, the spring of the grass underfoot, made her yearn to shoulder her bundle and steal away – to make for the sea or to go deep into the mountains and regain her true freedom.

Reyora told Analee to lie down and, placing a hand on her belly, prodded it gently. Then she put her ear to it, resting her cheek on the bulky flesh. 'It will be soon,' she leaned back and pulled down Analee's skirts. 'You must go to the birth tent.'

She looked at Analee's face, her own expression enigmatic.

'I'm frightened,' Analee said, 'I don't want to be on my own.'

'I will be near you,' Reyora said tersely, 'though I have other things to do, people to take care of, my own family to see to. It is the custom that our women are with their mothers when they give birth. As you have no mother, or mother-in-law, you must be on your own.'

'Please,' Analee begged, 'don't leave me on my own.'

'If you were a true gypsy woman you would not speak thus,' Reyora said contemptuously, 'that is the trouble with you *didakais*, especially with you Analee. I have observed how you dream and wander away. You are more like a *gadjo* in spirit than a gypsy.'

'That is not true!' Analee said spiritedly, getting to her feet with difficulty and smoothing her skirt over her swollen belly. 'I have the heart and the looks and the blood of a gypsy! But I cannot abide this life. It is like death to sit around all day chewing nuts and gossiping about nothing with the women. The men live their lives and we live ours.'

'That is the way it is,' Reyora said smoothly, her eyes flashing. 'You must go now to the birth tent and wait there. You must do as a gypsy woman does. Get your things and do not let your husband near you; you are very close to your time.'

Analee walked slowly from the tent across the field to the one she shared with Randal. In the distance the birth tent looked forbidding. Then she thought of the pain and terror she would have to endure alone. She wished even now she could leave and have her baby in some remote field or barn as she had the last time; but she was too afraid. The baby would die and there would be no one to cut the cord.

When she got into her tent Randal was sitting on the floor mending a shoe. He gazed at her with indifference as she came in and made no attempt to move or let her past.

'I must go to the birth tent,' Analee said. 'It is nearly time.'

'Then get thee gone,' Randal said. 'It is an evil time and you must not come near me until you're clean again. Be quick.'

'Will you at least help me?' Analee said, because it was hard to bend and get her possessions from the floor.

Randal's answer was to get up and look at her. There was no love there, or desire or even pity.

'You are on your own now Analee, as you have always wanted to be. There is no place for a man in childbirth, you know it is our custom.'

Analee stood and looked at him, panting slightly because it was so hot in the tent. Was this gaunt unbending man really the tender lover, the passionate wooer who had made love to her so many times a night when they were first married?

'I am still Analee, Randal,' she said quietly, 'the woman you loved. I have not become something else, something disgusting.'

Randal looked at his toes, a blush on his handsome face.

'You are not as other women, Analee, you know that. Everyone says you are different, not of our people. You do not behave as the othe women, your ways are alien.'

'You *brought* me here,' Analee said bitterly getting awkwardly to her knees to gather together her things, 'by force. You forced me to become your bride.'

'It was the heat of the moment,' Randal said still not looking at her. 'It was madness in me. I didn't know you, like you really are. You are not happy, not settled, not a true gypsy woman. But,' he moved closer to her, only not too close unless he touched her and became *marimé*, 'you are my wife Analee, wedded according to gypsy law. You are the mother of my child and it is you who must change, must become obedient and docile. Rebecca says that having a child will calm you, make you want to wander less. Then we will have another, and another, and then Analee, you will become a true Buckland gypsy, one of the tribe. That is what I intend. To do that you must learn the hard way, and go now to the tent and have your child.'

Analee knew it was useless to say more to this man who had become a stranger. Now that there was no lovemaking there was no bond, nothing. To him she was a possession, a vessel for childbearing; it was her business to cook and clean and be obedient.

Without another word, no endearment, no caress, not even a glance of sympathy or compassion Randal Buckland turned on his heels and left the tent. Analee gave in at last and, lying on the ground, her head pressed to the earth, gave vent to a spasm of sobbing such as she had never done before in her life.

After a while she grew quieter and lay there listening. There were sounds outside, shouts and the noise of horses. She crawled on her knees to the entrance to the tent and looked out, the canvas framing her face. What she saw astonished her. Brewster Driver and all his family were arguing with Rebecca and Lancelot, pointing to a figure who lay on the ground and then gesticulating, arms raised to the heavens. Yes there he was and Nelly and all the children gathered round; but the person on the ground was his wife Margaret; she was pale and still.

Analee didn't want to see Brewster Driver now, but she had no option. She had to pass by him to get to the birth tent and already she felt a cramp in the lower part of her belly, a dull ache across the back. She got slowly to her feet and tied her things, her few things, in a bundle. Then she crept out of the tent hoping to avoid being seen.

160

But she was unlucky. For as she came out there was a stillness and she realized that everyone had seen her, had been waiting for her. It was an event to give birth, envied by the ones who hadn't, pitied by the ones who had. They all knew, too, that Analee was different, reluctant, an odd gypsy. It was even noised abroad that she was *didakai*, no real gypsy at all, and Randal Buckland had made a mistake marrying her. Normally the pregnant woman was led by her mother; there were murmurings and a few sympathetic glances as she made her way to the birth tent. But this time Analee was alone. Most of the looks she got were hostile.

The stillness on that hot day in June was unnerving. Analee was aware of the flies buzzing around, of the horses flicking their tails in the heat. Then suddenly someone cried out and came running over to her.

'Analee!' an arm was thrown round her neck and she felt hot tears on her cheeks. But the tears didn't come from her, they came from Nelly Driver, thin and sallow, ill-looking but with her face shining with joy. 'Oh, Analee it *is* you. It *is* you. Analee?'

She stood back and looked at the large misshapen form before her. Analee attempted a weak smile.

'Of course.'

'And . . .' Nelly's eyes fell to her belly, so heavy that Analee had to support it with an arm.

'I am with child, as you see, about to give birth.'

'You are wed?' Nelly exclaimed with astonishment as though not particularly expecting an affirmative.

'Yes to Randal Buckland,' Analee said boldly so that all could hear. 'He abducted me. I was a bride by capture shortly after I left you last summer. Nelly I must go to the tent, my pains are starting. What ails your mother?'

Everyone had begun talking again and the shouting and gesticulating went on outside Rebecca's tent.

'She has a fever; she has been sick for weeks. Father wants to rest here; but they said it is no common gypsy camp but only for the Buckland tribe. Father is talking to them about the gypsy traditions of hospitality.'

Nelly's eyes lit up in a wry smile.

'And the baby, Nelly. Yours?'

'It was born dead. I don't think it ever had a chance. 'Twas as well . . . Analee, you are all right?'

A fierce pain shot across Analee's abdomen and she nearly fell. She clutched Nelly's arm.

'Could you see me . . . there.'

'Of course.'

While the women of the Buckland tribe idly watched, Nelly Driver helped Analee over to the tent and came inside with her. She assisted her on to the palliasse and loosened her clothes to make her comfortable.

'I will stay with you, Analee.'

'No, you must not. It is not allowed,' Analee said weakly, but Nelly saw how her eyes pleaded with fear, contradicting the firmness of her voice.

'But you have no mother. Does your husband have a mother?'

'No. The *cohani* will come from time to time. She is a good sort. Go to see to your own mother. She needs you.'

Nelly got up and looked around fearfully. 'It is so dark here, so lonely.'

Analee was about to reply when the pain came again, sharper this time. She cried out and grasped Nelly's hand holding it tight until the spasm had passed. Then the curtains of the tent parted and Reyora came in, glancing at Nelly and motioning towards the entrance.

'Go. Your mother can stay until she is better. I will come and see her after I have attended to Analee. I see you know each other?'

Nelly nodded. 'Analee was a good friend to me when I needed someone. May I not stay with her?'

Reyora shook her head and knelt down by Analee producing a long sharp knife.

'You know the custom. She is a good strong girl. She will be all right on her own.'

'She is afraid.'

Reyora looked at Nelly and sneered.

'I think you are no true gypsy either.'

As Nelly left Reyora leaned towards Analee with the knife and, not knowing what to expect, Analee shrank back afraid. Reyora grasped the knot of the loose tie of the belt at Analee's waist and cut it; then the knots of the laces of her bodice. She hacked at each one until the bodice fell loosely open.

'There,' Reyora said getting to her feet. ''Tis the custom to cut all knots on the clothes, as a symbol of cutting the umbilicus. It is sympathetic magic.' Then she cut the skirt from top to bottom and opened it exposing Analee's belly and thighs completely. Before she could protest at the destruction of her lovely skirt, bought in the happy days with money earned from dancing, Analee felt the pain again, stronger this time. It went round in a tight circle from her navel to her back. She arched her back compulsively and bit her knuckles to stop herself screaming.

Reyora leaned down and felt her belly which was now a seething rippling mass. She knelt beside her and massaged it gently, with her long supple fingers. The pain went and Analee gazed gratefully at her.

'Do not leave me alone.'

Reyora said nothing but continued with the soothing massage, right over the belly, between the legs, across the back, easing and helping. Every time there was a pain it did not last so long. But suddenly Reyora got up, leaned over and gave Analee a piece of cloth. 'Bite on this if the pain is too bad. I must go.' Then she left the tent, drawing back the curtain so that it was quite dark inside.

Analee sweated now in fear and pain, her breath grew shorter and her whole body seemed alive with one long agony. The pain went, but never for long and never completely. It was dark in the tent but outside she knew it was day; soon it would be dark outside as well, pitch dark. Then inside the tent it would be black. Analee wished Reyora had left her knife so that she could plunge it in her breast and kill herself.

But somehow she survived; even when the night fell and it was so black she could not see the rest of her body. Then suddenly when she had almost despaired there was a soft voice, a hand pressed hers.

'Analee, I have come back to you. I can't leave you by yourself. I care not what the *cohani* says. I know what it's like when I had my own baby, and my mother and sisters were there. I waited for nightfall so that no one could see.'

Analee pressed her hand and, drawing the thin face down to hers, kissed it.

'You will be my friend forever, Nelly.'

'I have brought water and some bread. How *can* they leave you like this?'

'It is the custom,' Analee smiled bitterly in the dark. 'Also they don't like me. Randal captured me and they have never accepted me. Even Reyora, who is not as bad as the rest, wants to let me suffer, tame me and teach me a lesson.'

'She is kind. She was very good with my mother – gave her a potion that immediately brought the colour to her cheeks.'

'She is limited by what she is and who she is and where she is. She – '

The pain stabbed again, this time ten times worse across the small of Analee's back. She twisted and would have screamed but for the rag Reyora had left her, now wet with her saliva. The pain in the back was so bad that it seemed to consume her entire body, and her stomach felt hot as though there was a fire inside it.

This continued through the night, and the misery of the long hours was only relieved by the presence of Nelly who comforted her with soothing words, and assuaged the pain by rubbing her belly and back with a cloth soaked in water and then moistening her lips.

At dawn the curtain parted and Reyora entered again. She stood for a long time gazing down at the tormented face and twisted body of Analee. Then she knelt and prodded her abdomen with her hands, and felt gently inside. Her face looked worried. She ignored Nelly.

'The pain, it is all in my back,' Analee gasped.

'The baby has turned,' Reyora said shortly, 'the head is the wrong way. It will be a long labour. The waters should have broken. I will fetch the *phuri-dai*.' She got up and went quickly to the entrance.

'What does she mean?' Nelly whispered.

'I am going to die.'

'No you are not!'

'I cannot bear the pain any more. The baby has turned: it is trapped.'

Analee arched again and this time the spasm was unbearable. She screamed aloud, forgetting about the rag. She knew the scream would be heard by the whole camp and the women would be glad that she suffered so, and maybe Randal would be glad because it would teach her a lesson and tame her.

'I cannot bear it . . .' she gasped and the curtains parted again and Reyora came in, followed by old Rebecca.

They both stood for a long time looking at Analee watching her twist about, trying to stifle her screams.

'I am dying,' she called to them, pleading to them to help.

Rebecca shook her head and held aloft a round object between her forefinger and thumb, which, in the dim light, Analee could see was an egg.

Reyora looked at Rebecca and nodded. Muttering an incantation in *romani* Rebecca dropped the egg so that it fell on the ground between Analee's legs.

> Anro, anro hin olkes
> Te e pera hin obles
> Ara cavo sastovestes
> Devla, devla, tut akharel

(The egg, the egg is round . . . all is round . . . little child come in health . . . God, God, is calling you.)

Reyora scooped up the broken yolk of the egg and rubbed it against Analee's thighs, up over the heaving belly.

'It is a spell, an incantation,' she said, 'to help with the birth when it is slow. See, you will soon be better.'

She leaned over Analee, staring into her dark pain-filled eyes, the eyelids heavy and drooping with weariness. 'It will be soon,' she whispered.

Suddenly Analee felt a rush of liquid between her legs and cried out again, thinking it was blood. She was dying. Reyora saw it too and smiled, nodding her head with satisfaction.

'The gypsy spell has worked; the waters have broken. Soon, soon now, the baby will come.'

Analee looked into those dark mysterious eyes and suddenly the pain went and she felt at peace. Reyora gripped her hand and with the other massaged gently the belly round and round. Then Analee felt a sharp tugging, a feeling that she must push and she grasped Nelly with one hand and Reyora with the other and pushed.

Suddenly her whole body arched convulsively and the final push left her feeling empty and free, and then there was a long wail and then another and another.

Analee jerked up her head as Reyora knelt upright, her hands clasping a pair of crumpled bloody tiny legs. She smiled broadly and laid the baby on Analee's abdomen. Then she skilfully cut the cord with the knife and tied it.

Analee gazed at the baby lying on her belly crying lustily. Nelly had reached over and was wiping it gently with a cloth, removing the blood and the yellow sticky protective covering. Analee looked at the baby and suddenly the crying ceased and her new born infant opened a pair of eyes that seemed to look straight into the eyes of its mother – a beautiful, large, perfectly formed blue-eyed baby girl with a thatch of bright golden hair.

Reyora took the baby from Analee and gave her to Nelly. Then she called for hot water, and one of the boys brought a bucket and left it outside the tent, running quickly away again unless he should be tainted by the birth.

Nelly gently washed the baby all over, noting its beautiful white skin and blue eyes, its fair hair and rather imperious face even at this early stage. It was the loveliest baby Nelly had ever seen, and so sturdy and well formed with chubby dimpled limbs. No wonder Analee had had trouble in bearing her.

While Nelly washed the baby and wrapped it in swaddles Reyora delivered the afterbirth, which she put in a bowl to keep because the afterbirth was very useful for unguents and lotions. Dried out in the sun and ground to powder it helped infertile women to conceive and made impotent men virile.

She bathed Analee all over and rubbed her with a sweet-smelling balsam made from pine and essence of roses. She covered her with a blanket and left her to sleep. Then she sat for a long time by her side gazing alternately at Analee then at her baby, her face very thoughtful.

Nelly was perplexed by Reyora. She knew enough about *cohani* to know that they were usually very brusque and always in a hurry. Why did Reyora linger, now that the birth had been accomplished? She crooned over the baby in her arms. Like her mother the baby slept.

After a long time Reyora sighed and held out her arms for the baby. She looked at her, tenderly tracing her finger over her perfectly chiselled features, noting the deep cleft of the mouth and the long straight nose and the determined chin.

'It is not the child of a gypsy,' she said at last.

'No?' Nelly was puzzled. Never having seen Analee's husband she did not know what the *cohani* meant.

'It is the child of a *gadjo*!'

'A *gadjo*!' Nelly was appalled.

'A blond, handsome, aristocratic *gadjo*. A lord.'

'A *lord*!'

'It is not Randal's child. Randal is Analee's husband. I thought if the child were dark it would pass for his child, but it won't. Like Analee, Randal is very dark and swarthy; so is all his family. All the Bucklands are dark; there is not a fair one among them.'

'Maybe in Analee's family . . . ?' Nelly said helpfully, beginning to understand.

'No. She is olive skinned. Besides, Randal knows about the *gadjo*. He saw them lying together. It is why he married her. Oh, don't look like that, child!' Reyora said impatiently, noting Nelly's uncomprehending expression. 'I don't know why he did it. The way men behave is past my understanding. He thinks the child is his now, but when he sees her he will remember the *gadjo* and he will know. He will be very angry.'

'What will he do?'

Reyora shrugged. 'Maybe kill it, or them both. He will be forgiven by the *kriss* because of his rage and grief.'

'Oh no,' Nelly looked at the beautiful baby in Reyora's arms thinking of her own puny little dead one buried now under some stone on the wayside – unwanted, unlamented.

Reyora clasped the baby closer and sighed. A plan was forming in her mind whose seed had been there ever since she knew that Analee had conceived by the *gadjo*. It could be done and only she, the *cohani* could do it. The only chance the plan had to succeed lay in the gypsy laws of *marimé*: that a mother and child were unclean because of the birth, until baptism had driven away the evil spirits.

The father would not come near the tent for days, maybe a week. He would not know the child was blue-eyed and blonde. Only Rebecca would see the child apart from herself and Nelly, and Rebecca was very close to Reyora; she knew her longing for a daughter. How she had tried and how she had failed. Reyora knew that only she could save this child; only she could give it respectability, make it acceptable to the tribe. Otherwise it was as good as dead or, at the very best, an outcast.

Reyora closed her eyes because she too was tired, and she hugged the beautiful baby girl very closely to her bosom, wanting it, cherishing it.

Rebecca came in that night as Analee, rested and recovered, was preparing to feed her baby for the first time. Attended by the devoted Nelly and the experienced Reyora she was trying to ease the large engorged nipple into the baby's mouth; but she was clumsy and the baby kept turning its head away and crying.

Reyora showed Analee how to nurse the baby pressed to her stomach, so that the bellies of mother and child touched, and to cradle the head in one hand while offering her the breast with the other.

Analee experienced a surge of joy at the feel of the baby's mouth at her breast, the fact that milk was flowing from herself to her child, and she pressed her closer and put her face against the soft little head.

Yes, she was Brent Delamain's child. There was no possible doubt about that. It made her remember the night she and Brent had lain in the forest; she could see in imagination the moonlight and feel the breeze on their bare flesh. It had been good and beautiful and the baby was lovely . . . a love child. She smiled at Reyora over the baby's head and she saw that Reyora knew what she was thinking.

Then Rebecca came in and she knew, too. She stared for a long time at the baby, contrasting its very white skin with the olive skin of the mother, the full brown breasts and the big splayed nipples the colour of russet crab apples.

Reyora had said nothing to her but now Rebecca knew. She said nothing to Analee, but beckoned to Reyora and, talking quietly together, they left the birth tent and walked slowly over to Reyora's where they spent a long time together.

Reyora waited for almost a week before she told Analee about her plan. Randal was becoming anxious to see his child and the preparations were being made for the gypsy baptism. The baby and Analee would be immersed deep in the waters of the river that flowed nearby, and then all the objects used for the confinement would be burnt, all her clothes and dishes and bowls, and Analee and her child would be judged fit to be admitted to gypsy society.

Even Reyora who was not a hard woman but not a soft one either, didn't know how she was going to say what she had to to Analee. She saw the delight Analee had in her baby; how she fondled her and dallied with her. With what care she washed and nursed her and the intense pleasure she had in feeding her, watching the milk froth up at the mouth, forming little bubbles when the baby had had enough.

Analee thought she had never known such happiness as she had that week, seeing her sturdy well-formed baby girl, noting how easily it fed, how contentedly it slept, what a happy loving child it was. She held her to her last thing at night and, when she opened her eyes in the morning, she was the first thing Analee saw.

It was a gypsy custom that the mother gave the baby a secret name, that was not known to anyone, even the father. In her heart Analee called the baby Morella, because that had been the secret name of her own mother. Whatever name the baby was eventually given, only Analee would know the real name, the name given to deceive the spirits, Morella.

Nelly helped her all week; her mother was recovering well with the potions prescribed by Reyora. Her only fear was that they would be tolerated only for as long as her mother was ill. Brewster was not popular with the men of the Buckland tribe; he was forever after their women.

A week after the birth Nelly knew that they would soon have to leave. Margaret was walking, and Brewster had begun to make preparations to go north to Scotland.

She broke the news to Analee, interrupting at a time when Analee was playing with the baby, tickling it under the arms and in the groin and making it reach out its hands towards her as though it wanted more. Its large blue eyes were unfocused, but Morella seemed to know her mother, even to smile for her, though this was scarcely considered possible.

'We have to leave next week.'

Nelly stood at the entrance to the tent and Analee looked up sharply. Her expression changed from one who had come from a fairytale, delightful world into the real harsh one.

Nelly thought how beautiful Analee looked with her shining olive skin, sweating now in the heat. Her face was no longer haggard with pain, but rested and rounded with contentment and fulfilment and the good food she had been eating. Her hair which fell about her shoulders shone and the clear eyes sparkled with good humour and the love of motherhood.

Nelly, undeveloped, emaciated with spotty skin and mousy hair, venerated Analee. She thought she loved her in so far as it was possible for a woman to love another. She wanted to reach out and touch her breasts, and let her hands run over her silky supple skin.

But now she had to leave. She choked with emotion as she looked at Analee.

'To the border, to Scotland. We all have to go.'

'Can't you stay? Just you?'

'No. They don't like us here. The boys have been run out of the town for stealing and Lancelot says they give the camp a bad name. Father is always drunk and abusive and they say he is after the Buckland women. He is lazy, too.'

'But just *you*. You can stay with me.'

'I cannot. Oh, Analee . . .'

Nelly threw herself against Analee who clasped her, stroking her thin hair and letting her hands run gently over the plain pockmarked face. She felt that Nelly, too, was like a child who needed her as much as Morella did. Nelly was trembling, and then she turned her face to Analee and wept, letting the tears flow unchecked.

Analee felt the hot tears against her skin and knew how much Nelly loved her, but like a mother. Nelly had never known a real mother's love. Margaret Driver had always been too harassed by a thousand cares to love or pay any attention to this plain unappealing delicate girl who though a maid and, briefly, even a mother, was unformed and immature.

Reyora saw them like this. Noted how Nelly clung to Analee. She entered quietly and drew the curtain shut behind her. Analee looked over Nelly's head towards Reyora and smiled at a woman she had come very much to respect and admire. Reyora had compassion. Of few women she knew could Analee say that.

Reyora sat beside Analee placing between them a dish of sweetmeats she had brought from the town. She looked at Nelly and wondered if she should ask her to leave, then thought better of it. Analee would need some support.

Briefly Reyora played with the baby, tickling its tummy and seeing it dimple, then she smiled at Analee and took her hand.

Analee was surprised at the gesture, and stared at Reyora, answering the pressure of Reyora's hand with her own.

'It has been a happy time, Analee, with the baby.'

'Oh yes!'

She looked closely at Reyora's face and saw how solemn it was. Her heart began to beat quickly and she put a hand to her breast.

'Why did you say it like that?'

'I have been thinking, Analee, about all this, not only since the baby was born, but long before. What if it should be blue eyed and golden haired and fair skinned?'

'And . . .' Analee began to understand.

'What would happen when Randal saw the baby?'

Analee sighed and let her hand fall from Reyora's. A weight seemed to press on her heart.

'I know. It must happen soon. He sent a message with Nelly that he was preparing the baptism.'

'When Randal sees the baby he will not let her be baptized. He will kill her.'

Analee's hand flew to her face, her mouth felt dry; her heart started to pound and she thought she would faint.

'What are you saying?'

'You know Randal Buckland, or rather you should. You have been married to him for nine months. He is a proud stubborn man; a real gypsy. He will know this child is not his and he will not want her.'

'But they would not let him kill her!'

'They might not be able to stop him. They might not even try. You know his temper; his passion. Imagine his outrage, his humiliation at knowing it is the *gadjo*'s child? That you were carrying it all the time he made love to you? Maybe he will kill you, too.'

Now Nelly, listening to everything from the corner, cried out:

'Oh, *cohani*, do not let this happen to Analee and her baby.'

Reyora looked at Nelly and then at Analee. It was difficult to put into words what she was thinking.

'Analee, you must go, leave the camp, Analee – tonight. I will take the baby. I will bring her up as my own and once I, the *cohani*, have said as much, no one will dare touch her. She will be special and apart.'

Analee felt an involuntary spasm shake her body and suddenly she was looking into a great void. There was just darkness in front of her eyes, emptiness. Somehow she had known it would happen. Such joy was not meant. She had tried to get rid of the baby which she now wanted more than anything on earth – and God was punishing her.

This was the vengeance of God and Reyora knew it – a blonde, blue-eyed baby when it could just as easily have taken after her and been dark.

But this had been intended from time immemorial. Analee knew that. She was never meant to be happy, to have a lover or a husband who was tender to her and stayed with her, to have a baby of her own or to belong. She was meant to wander until she died; to roam over the face of the earth, over the mountains and across the valleys just like her people always had. Harried on from one place to another; never allowed to rest.

Some said it was because the gypsies had offended God, had blasphemed Christ, that they were doomed thus. And she, Analee, without a name, was one of these.

The darkness disappeared and the faces of Nelly and Reyora became clear again, tender, unsmiling, concerned. The baby Morella gurgled and smiled and reached out for its mother.

'One more time,' Reyora said, 'then you must prepare to go. You must go under cover of dark and take the road to the west, over the mountains. You are stronger now, but you must not weary yourself. Rest well.'

'And the baby . . . ?' Analee could not bring herself to look at the child she was leaving.

'I will be her mother. I will look after her well. She will be very special.'

'I have called her Morella,' Analee said brokenly, 'after my mother. It is her secret name.'

'I will remember it,' Reyora said, 'and you will know that she will be safe with me; but make a new life for yourself Analee. Try and find the *gadjo* – make a new life with him. He loved you and you loved him. You are not a full gypsy and you will never settle with a tribe. You will not adapt to our ways. I think you were meant for other things, Analee. But start afresh with the *gadjo*. Do not come back to take your daughter. That is all I ask you. I will not allow it. From the moment you leave this place, she is mine. Do you promise that? For her sake, her safety?'

Analee could not bear to look at Reyora. She knew she was helping her, was doing it for her sake, but it was a hard, bitter bargain.

'It is that or her death,' Reyora said. 'You must understand and make me a promise.'

'I promise,' Analee said and then she lay with her head on the ground near to her baby and wept.

After a while she grew calmer and she sat up and bared her

172

breasts. Very gently she gave her baby the nipple and pressed her close knowing that it was for the last time.

There was little to do once it was dark. Just the familiar bundle to make up and a new skirt from Reyora to replace the one that had been cut in two before the birth. In the light of the candle, Analee waited for the signal from Reyora that all was clear. Morella slept in her crib and she tried not to look at her again. Instead Analee started slowly around the tent which had been her home for over a week – a place where she had known great pain and great joy, great hope and now great sorrow. She was off again into the world, with a bundle and no more, no more than she'd had when she'd come to the Buckland camp – but this time she was leaving a husband and a baby behind.

Nelly helped her get ready and then sat with her trying to support her with her presence, saying nothing.

'I could have taken her with me,' Analee said at last gazing desperately at Nelly.

'Nay; think of the harm she would come to.'

'Yes.' The scraping for food and berries, the scratching for a living, the cruelty and curses of people she met on the road. Morella would have no chance on the road. Here she would be protected; groomed to be a *cohani*, to succeed the powerful Reyora. Marry well, be a full member of the Buckland tribe.

Suddenly Nelly rose and came to kneel before Analee. She brought her hand up to her lips and kissed it. 'Let *me* come with you, Analee!'

Analee stared at her, gazing at the hand holding hers as though it were some kind of amulet.

'No, no Nelly. What chance would *you* have on the road?'

'What chance have I got now? I hate my father and he hates me. He leaves me alone since I had the baby, but who knows how long that will last? I cannot bear it. Please let me come with you. I will look after you, be your friend.'

Analee gazed tenderly on the poor thin young girl, so like a child herself; who stayed by her and helped her. Maybe they did need each other – she Analee as much as Analee needed her. Why not?

'You will have to come as you are.'

'Who cares? I have nothing of my own anyway. Oh, Analee – may I come?'

173

Analee gazed at her baby and then at Nelly. She knew which one she'd rather leave behind, but she had no choice. She smiled at Nelly and nodded.

When Reyora came to say all was quiet Analee didn't dare glance back at her baby for fear she would break down. She grasped Nelly's hand and stole out of the tent, across the sleeping camp towards the path that led to the town.

It was a half moon and there was enough light for them to pause and glance back to where Reyora stood like a sentinel outside the tent, one arm firmly cradling the sleeping baby. Then she raised her other hand in a gesture of blessing and farewell.

11

Brent watched the longboat make for the shore in the faint light of dawn. It was cold even for late September and in the far distance beyond the fells the mountain peaks of Cumberland were white-capped. All around the coast the land was flat, broken only by the copses of thickly covered trees with here or there a solitary farm or cottage.

Brent stood on the deck of the small fishing wherry of which he was the sole crew. The captain was Matthew Clucas, a Manx-man, an ex-pugilist and a supporter of the Stuarts. Ambrose Rigg had kept to his bargain and Brent had kept to his. After that memorable day in May when the two men had confronted each other in Rigg's office there had been no going back.

In order to deceive Dinward and Quiggan, Rigg had appeared to be disciplining Brent for his misdeeds by transferring him to the fishing fleet as a deckhand. There was no dirtier, smellier or harder work than as a deckhand on one of the small fishing wherries which, on account of their size, were tossed about on the sea like flotsam in a storm.

It had given Dinward a good laugh to think of the fastidious Mr Delamain getting in the catch on a wherry, and every time he saw him he grinned and made an obscene gesture with his fingers.

But the plan had worked; the small fishing boats needed a small crew, sometimes only two or three at the most. Brent only caught a token catch which went on top of the cases and barrels he smuggled in from the Isle of Man, and two men were enough.

Matthew Clucas was a friend of John Collister and even had a mind to make Harriet Collister his wife, if she would have him. But the bold Harriet was hoping for better things than a former boxer with a hard square jaw, a broken nose and blunt manners.

Clucas and Brent had got on from the start. Brent never shirked hard work or long hours and his diligence as well as his devotion to the cause were infectious. He had no airs or fuss about him, but slept on the deck among the nets, ate his food out of a tin and became an expert at scaling and gutting the fish when time was against them.

Brent wiped a wet hand across his forehead with satisfaction as he turned and prepared to swab the deck. He felt hungry and thirsty, but rewarded. It was good to be alive. Now the dawn, once begun, came very quickly over the mountains in the east and the calm still sea, which could be so treacherous in its many moods, shimmered in the pale morning sun, a light haze drifting over it. 'Come, Matthew. Let us make for Whitehaven. I am half starved.'

Matthew smiled and gazed with affection at the man with whom in only three short months he had shared so many adventures. They plied continually between the creeks and bays of the Isle of Man and the coast of Cumberland. Sometimes they went north to Scotland, but Brent had developed a route that was considered safer, whereby the guns were landed in one of the many small bays of Cumberland and ferried across the steep mountains on pack horses. Then there were depots all over the north – at Carlisle, Penrith, Lancaster, taking the route followed by the Prince's father, King James, in 1715. Many thought the rebellion then had failed for lack of arms; for lack of depots and storage. This time it was going to be very different. Brent had rapidly become acquainted with the hard core of Jacobite sympathizers in the north-west, those who were prepared, as he was, to risk all, to lose all.

Only this time they would not. They were going to win. The Prince had landed in Scotland in July accompanied by only seven men. All the promises made by the French to provide arms and men had been broken. But such was his calm, his presence, his determination, his sheer magnetism that all Scotland was flocking to him. The faithful were rewarded, the waverers converted. He had raised his standard in August at Glenfinnan, proclaiming himself Regent in the name of his father King James III, and before it a body of 1400 Highlanders had assembled. Even from the beginning he had won small skirmishes against Hanoverian forces taken by surprise, and his progress south had been one of triumph.

Brent heard all this through the Scottish connections who ran arms to the border from the coast. Across the north of England and Scotland there was a line of information that stretched to the Prince and back down again. And the tales that were told of the Prince – of his gallantry, determination and wisdom for one so young. Of the way he had with the ladies and how he could melt the heart of the strictest Jacobite dowager. Now he had come as far as Perth and, according to the latest information received by Brent, was about to take Edinburgh.

The tide of enthusiasm that had swept Scotland had now crossed the border and was rolling remorselessly on as far as London. Some said the government was in disarray, others said it was not and that several large armies had been despatched north. Where they went would determine the Prince's strategy. Either he would come south by Newcastle, or he would come via Carlisle as his father had done in '15.

Brent, who wished so much to see the Prince, hoped it would be Carlisle; but above all Brent wanted to be in at the fighting. He was not content just to smuggle arms.

The quay at Whitehaven was already lined with wherries putting in their catch or going out. Brent could discern, as always, the broad figure of Ambrose Rigg and waved to him. Rigg was on the deck of another of his boats, a genuine fishing smack groaning with herring and mackerel. Only about half of his fleet actively smuggled, it was the understanding he had with the customs men whom he paid well.

Rigg bounded off the boat he was on and came aboard the *Sarah*, named after his wife. He shook Brent's hand and Matthew's and the smile on his face indicated everything was all right. As well as arms, Brent was also carrying, as usual, brandy and tea that had come from the big smuggling port of Nantes in France and carried in bigger ships to the Isle of Man and Port Rush. The little wherries which scampered across the North Sea were ideal for the sort of smuggling that Rigg did on such a large scale.

'Sarah bids me bring you home for dinner, Brent. She has a surprise for you.'

'Oh?' Brent was lifting out the baskets of fish from the hold, helped by Matthew and a young lad who worked on the quay. His mind was on fish, but from time to time he thought of the crates of guns on their way across the mountains or paths of Lakeland. He alone had smuggled in enough to equip a small army.

'And Matthew, will you join us?'

'No I cannot, thank you, Mr Rigg,' Matthew said. 'I promised my mother I would be home for dinner. She complains she never sees me.'

177

'We've been busy,' Brent said, 'hardly a night's sleep for ten days.'

'I know. That's why I thought a day or two resting, maybe, at Cockermouth. It can be done?'

Brent glanced at Matthew, saw how tired he looked. He guessed he must look the same. Well, nothing would be gained if their health broke down. Not that he'd ever felt better; just tired.

The devil of it was that his leg had never healed. He walked with a very slight limp and sometimes it impeded his work. It didn't pain him so much; but it angered him. Still, he put it to good use at sea and he never complained. What worried him was what would happen if he had to march. He put it out of his mind; but when he was tired he was conscious that he limped more. Sometimes when he was fit and rested he didn't limp at all.

Now he limped badly down the gangplank, his leg stiff from too much exercise and Matthew and Ambrose noticed and exchanged glances.

'I have my coach waiting,' Rigg said. 'You can rest in that.'

Brent looked at him and burst out laughing.

'I'm no maid you know, Ambrose! You'll be dosing me with laudanum and *sol volatile* for the vapours!'

Ambrose laughed and smacked him on the shoulders leaving one hand companionably around his neck. Sometimes he felt like a father to Brent.

After sluicing himself in the yard and a hearty breakfast of beef-pie washed down by plenty of ale at the tavern on the quayside, Brent and Ambrose walked to where the coach was waiting at the back of the town, the driver of the pair well wrapped up against the cold.

It was a small coach because the road from Whitehaven to Cockermouth though important and busy was narrow in places.

As soon as they settled in Brent fell asleep, his long legs on the opposite seat. After his large breakfast he felt so tired and stupefied that he had not even asked Ambrose what surprise Sarah had in store for him.

Ambrose Rigg's passion, besides the acquisition of wealth – which was an obsession – was extending his home. It had once been a yeoman's low stone house, whitewashed and containing only one floor with a direct entrance to the barns. Indeed at one time, though Ambrose could not remember it, the cattle used to

178

mix freely with the inhabitants of the house, considered just as important.

This land and the house had been in the Rigg family since anyone could remember. After rising from serfdom the 'statesmen' had acquired a special status. The inheritance had passed from father to son though the property still belonged to the lord or squire, monastery or landowner for whom they worked. However, they could not be dispossessed and the yeoman farmer acquired a special role of his own.

But Rigg now owned the house and the land around it outright. It stood on the hill above Cockermouth which gave a fine view not only of the town but of the Lakeland hills to the south and east. For Cockermouth lay flat in the valley of the River Derwent which entered the sea near Whitehaven twelve miles away. The imposing Rigg Manor was halfway up a bracken-covered fell and on either side was a forest of tall fir trees. Ahead was the centre of Lakeland, the mountains and fells surrounding Crummock Water, Buttermere and majestic Ennerdale; and the tips of Hen Combe, Great Borne, Starling Dodd and High Style towered above the soft, undulating folds of the lesser hills.

To the west even Skiddaw could be seen and on a clear day Lake Bassenthwaite glimpsed beneath it on the main approach from Cockermouth to Keswick. Sometimes the hills were obscured in the haze of high summer or the mists of winter and they appeared mysterious and even menacing; but on a clear bright day like this day in September they stood out sharply against the sky and seemed to roll on forever – some high, some low, some hidden or only half revealed – resembling a land of enchantment.

Rigg had bought this imposing site from the descendants of one of the barons to whom it had been given after the dissolution of the monasteries in 1538. There was still a village of Thursby and an Earl of Thursby, but, like the Allonbys, they had not always been wise in their support for the ruling party and had lost a great deal of land as a result. Lord Thursby was never to be seen in Lakeland; but a son and daughter-in-law lived in Castle Thursby and were on nodding acquaintance with the Riggs, largely because of Sarah, needless to say. The Honourable Mrs Rose Thursby would never have had anything to do socially with the former 'statesman' family of Rigg, no matter how well they'd subsequently done in business.

179

Like the Riggs the Thursbys had a young family. It had already crossed the mind of Ambrose that, if he worked harder and the Thursbys stayed as they were, in time his own progeny, half Allonby and therefore socially acceptable, would not be a bad match as far as the Thursby family were concerned.

Ambrose was a contented man as the coach, after climbing the hill, turned through the large gates he had just had installed after being wrought by an ironsmith in Cockermouth. They provided an important link in the wall he had had constructed around his extensive property.

They swung open to a long drive which had formerly been part of a field where his father grazed cows. Now it was being turned into soft lawns and gardens. Shrubberies and flower beds were appearing everywhere, and a fortune was being spent transporting plants and vegetation from the south of England.

The drive ended in a circular sweep in front of the building that had been grafted on to the small humble home where the Riggs had their origins, just a little croft house it had once been. In fact the original building was now part of the extensive stables, and a graceful mansion built by an architect who had studied with Mr James Gibb, architect of St Martin-in-the-Fields and other notable London buildings, had risen beside it.

Like its humble predecessor it was a house built of white stone, but its fluted doric columns supported a Grecian-style arch not unlike that which graced the front of the church of St Martin in London. The porch was wide and was approached by five steps. Double doors led onto a large hallway, showing a tall winding staircase, and a high ceiling from which hung a grand chandelier made of thousands of tiny crystals. It was a rich house, an elegant house, a big house and, if Ambrose had his way, it looked like being one of the grandest houses in this part of Cumberland, rivalling even Castle Thursby itself.

And there, dutifully on the porch to welcome him, were his wife, two small children and his brother-in-law. John Allonby stood behind his sister thus composing what seemed on that beautiful mellow September noon, a very charming family group.

There were even one or two retainers hovering in the background to make sure that the master was immediately served, and barking dogs scampered up to the carriage as it drew into the broad forecourt. A servant ran down the stairs to open the door and Ambrose nudged the sleeping Brent in the ribs.

'Wake up. We're there. 'Tis dinner time.'

Brent, startled, looked out of the window.

'We're there already?'

'You slept the entire length of the journey, my boy.'

Brent looked out of the window, rubbing his eyes.

'My God. 'Tis John. Is *that* the surprise?'

'Aye.'

'I hoped it might be Mary,' Brent said quietly, 'I have not seen her for nigh a year.'

'Ah but that's who it might be *about*,' Ambrose said winking and consulting the timepiece stretched on a gold chain across his large stomach. 'You may have earned your spurs.'

Brent jumped down, and sprinted along the courtyard to where John was coming down the stairs. The cousins clasped arms.

'John, how is it with Mary? No trouble?'

'No, no, none at all. My, Brent, but you do smell.'

John retreated a yard or two and looked at his cousin with dismay.

'Smell? Oh, fish. 'Tis a good healthy smell and in the basket behind the coach we have some fresh herring and mackerel for our breakfast tomorrow.'

Ambrose climbed the stairs slowly because they were affecting his breathing more and more. Prosperity was making him put on too much weight. He greeted his wife with a kiss on the cheek, aware that her belly was nice and rounded. She was presenting him with another child, or so he hoped. She had miscarried earlier in the year and this had worried him, not so much for her health, as lest she should opt out of her side of the bargain to provide him with a fine large family to rival the Thursbys.

But no, he had got her almost immediately with child again despite her protests and the doctor saying that she should rest. Doctors knew naught about it in his opinion; not as much as a healthy virile man like himself, even if he was on the stout side.

'All well my dear?' he enquired letting his hand casually caress the mound of her stomach. She blushed and looked about her to see if anyone had seen his gesture.

'Of course, Ambrose. Desist,' she said agitatedly pushing his hand away from her stomach, and moved away to greet Brent. The smell that had offended his cousin preceded Brent up the stairs and Sarah too backed away, but only with mock dismay on her face. She knew that the Rigg fortune was too well founded in fish to make any real protest about it.

'Why, Brent . . .'

'I know I stink. I declare I had a good wash in the yard of the tavern before we came hither.'

'Not a good enough one apparently. There is a fire in your room and I will have one of the servants take a tub thither and give you a good bath and fresh clothes.'

Brent laughed.

'If you will.'

Then he bent to greet his little cousins, four-year-old Henry, and Elia, who was just one year old and in the arms of her nurse. Brent loved children and they responded to him. He knew he would enjoy being a father when he and Mary had children of their own.

Brent went up the stairs two at a time to his room which was at the back of the house overlooking the fell that rose behind. The lower part was green pastureland, but higher up the forest began which eventually skirted Lake Bassenthwaite.

As Sarah had promised a good fire roared in the grate and soon Thomas the head servant appeared with another, carrying a big iron bath between them. Into this they poured jug after jug of steaming hot water brought up the back stairs by a succession of giggling scullery maids.

Brent sat in his bath and, after Thomas had scrubbed his back, said he would wash himself. As he got out and towelled himself before the fire he was aware of his long muscular body, his sinewy calves which had not lain between a woman's legs for a year. Brent stopped drying himself and thoughtfully looked into the fire.

How had he known that? That he *had* a woman a year ago? Suddenly there was a stirring in his mind, a recollection of trees and moonlight . . . it was like a vision or a dream. Or had it been reality? He remembered what they'd said about the accident. How he had been found. Nothing had disturbed Brent's amnesia since the blow on the head; but now the mists were starting to part. And she . . . He shut his eyes trying to recall who he had been with. He could somehow see her translucent flesh, smell a

182

singular odour, a pungency. She was someone very special, he was sure of that. So why, how had he forgotten her? There was a knock at the door.

'Who is it?'

'Brent it is I. May I come in?'

'I am naked as nature made me; but enter.'

Brent wrapped a towel round his body as his cousin gently turned the door knob and came in. On the big fourposter bed clean clothes were laid with fresh stockings and on the floor newly polished shoes with shining buckles.

'I think we are to have a party,' Brent said smiling. 'If this finery is aught to go by.' He reached for the fine white linen shirt and pulled it over his head. John sat on the chair before the fire and crossed his legs, looking at the fine upright figure of his cousin.

Brent had improved. It was true, hard work and abstinence were good for a man. His body was thicker but with muscle not fat. His face was tanned and lean, and had not that dissolute sensuous look about the mouth that came with too great an acquaintance with the fleshpots. He wore an expression of almost puritanical severity and his eyes were hard and clear. John liked what he saw and was glad that Brent was going to marry his sister.

'Well, Brent, it is almost a year,' he said.

'Aye,' Brent said, getting into his breeches, knowing full well what John meant.

'And you have kept your word.'

'I have that – no women, not one, and hard work.'

'And you still want her?'

Brent stood up straight and gazed at his cousin.

'Want her? *Want* Mary? Do you doubt it?'

'You haven't seen her for a year.'

'Has she changed so much then?'

'No, lovelier than ever, a little fuller maybe. Ready to be married, Brent.'

Brent's heart beat a little quicker. Suddenly those months of chastity seemed an intolerable strain. The thought of Mary, already beautiful, now grown maybe a little plump and more comely; her hips perhaps had filled out a little, and her breasts . . . those small virginal breasts he had gazed upon with the tiny rosebud nipples. He looked at John. It would not do to let her brother know that he had more acquaintance of Mary's body than a chaste kiss. His expression grew sober.

'Well, I am ready if you will it, and she. Let it be done quickly, John. I am still of a mind to serve the Prince, and he is here. He has come.'

'I know,' John said. 'That is in my mind. Stewart is to join him for sure when he comes to England whether it be Newcastle or Carlisle. We have been in touch with your brother Tom. Oh, 'tis all arranged.'

'Then I will go with him.'

'You know, Brent . . . you could make Mary a widow.'

'Aye,' Brent went to the mirror and began the delicate process of tying his cravat. The more he served as a seaman the less delicate his fingers became. 'That is why we wanted to wed a year since. We could have had a child by now.'

'Well we didn't know what was to happen. Besides, I think your mother and I were right. We had to be sure. You have done well Brent. We are proud of you. You have kept your principles, kept the faith . . .'

Brent looked at John, his expression not altogether as warm or friendly as John would have wished.

'I hope for your sake you were right, John. It appeared you thought not of Mary or myself when you sent me out of the house . . .'

'*I* sent you? You left of your own will, aye, and in high dudgeon if I recall.'

'No, *you* sent me as much as if you had pushed me. You taunted me, that I was a womanizer, a coward. Well 'tis done. I have served my apprenticeship John, but I don't know if either Mary or I are in your debt for it. A year has passed when we have not seen each other; have been denied each other's company, wanted each other. Now she could be a widow by Christmas, that is even if we marry at once. I suppose that is what you have come about.'

He shrugged on his coat and looked at the set of his shoulders in the mirror. Then he attended to his hair. He did not wear a wig or powder it. He was glad to hear that Prince Charles did not either. He tied a ribbon at the back and then combed away from his forehead the damp locks that straggled over his brow.

'Mary wants to marry at once,' John said tersely, 'if it be your pleasure.'

'Then let it be her choice. That is decided. My pleasure it certainly is – or will be.'

John hadn't expected this harsh attitude from Brent and he looked into the fire.

'*Must* you join the Prince? Is not your work at sea just as important?'

'I have done my work. The arms are there. Now we must use them. No, I am going to fight. Never let it be said that a Delamain refused to take up arms.'

'You may be fighting against your brother.'

'Aye, likely. I hear he is wed, too.'

'Yes, this summer. In London. We were not asked.'

'Only your mother and sister went to the wedding. I hear George brought his bride to Delamain Castle in August. Henrietta she is called, an heiress I understand. The only child.'

'An heiress? George will like that. Is she pretty?'

'They say very plain.'

'Ah, then George has made another business deal.' Brent dusted his sleeve and settled the lace at his wrists. 'Shall we go and dine, cousin?'

Everyone knew what John had come about and the table downstairs was set for a feast. Ambrose was already at his place carving the beef as Brent and John came through the door; but when he saw them he put down his carvers and took up his goblet already brimming with good red claret.

'Well, Brent. Are you to be a bridegroom?'

Brent smiled. 'Aye, it appears so. At last.'

'Then let it be soon, lad. Let it be soon.'

Suddenly Sarah clasped her head in her hands and burst into tears. Ambrose looked at her with consternation and left his seat to go over to her.

'There my love. Is the emotion too much for you? The thought of having this scoundrel for a brother-in-law?'

'Nay, it is not that,' Sarah sobbed. 'It is only that I fear they may have left it too late.'

Brent stared at her and a feeling of foreboding suddenly overcame him. It was not the war he was afraid of, but, in his mind, he saw moonlight falling in a forest glade, a dark female body twisting beneath his. He closed his eyes to shut the vision out of his mind. Instead he saw the hazy outline of a face, but all that was clear to him was the long dark hair that framed it. He was puzzled and his frown was seen by Ambrose who took his shoulder in that familiar bear-like grasp.

'Now then, lad. 'Tis her woman's time, you know. They get funny when they are wi' child. Of *course* it's not too late . . . Even if there is a war – and I'll wager they'll contain those unruly Highlanders in Scotland – it doesn't mean to say you will be in it. My ships . . .'

Brent, his lips pressed together, stared at Ambrose.

'You know, Ambrose, I must go. You know it and have always known it. I know you care nothing for politics, but I do. I've always said I must support the rightful King and now it is the time. I have my duty to my father and uncle before me.'

Ambrose nodded and went solemnly back to his seat.

'Well so be it. I will keep your place for you, and God knows you might need it. Aye, for you and your wife. For you never know Brent when you might be glad of work and somewhere to go with your bride, to hide maybe. There'll always be a home for you. Eh, Sarah?'

Sarah had dried her eyes and was serving the vegetables. The servants had been sent out of the room as soon as she had burst into tears, except for the nurse who had the baby Elia on her lap. The nurse was a young girl related to Ambrose and regarded as one of the family.

Like her husband Sarah had eschewed politics. They had brought neither unity nor happiness to her family and her aunt's family. Whereas thrift, hard work, independence and non-conformity had made Ambrose very rich.

These things mattered to Sarah as much as they mattered to her husband. His values and hers were the same. The last thing she wanted was a war, with her family divided, fugitives maybe. Both sides couldn't win. The thought of Brent throwing himself away was what had made her burst into tears. Sarah was fond of her little sister, not close but fond, and she had grown to like Brent. Admired him for his hard work and dedication. The folly of the possible war was too awful to contemplate.

Sarah Rigg thought it more advisable at this stage not to answer

186

her husband. Instead she gave Brent a watery smile and made a pretence at gaiety.

'Let's not be solemn,' she said. 'Let's talk about the wedding. When is it to be?'

'The very moment we can arrange it,' Brent said robustly, spearing a piece of prime English beef and raising it to his mouth, 'if not before.'

12

In the large stone-floored kitchen at the back of Furness Grange
Mary Allonby was rolling dough on the baking board. As she bent
energetically over her task her face grew flushed and tendrils of
blonde hair escaped from the tidy coil at the back of her neck. She
kept a firm hold on the rolling pin and she stretched the pastry as
far as it would go, for the crust on the pie should be light and thin.

'Now, miss, the oven is ready for thee,' Betty Hardcastle, who
had been with the family since before Mary was born and had
served in every capacity from scullery maid to nursery maid when
the children were small, was now primarily in charge of the
kitchen. She was one of the few servants left in the house, and
most of these were employed in other capacities on what remained
of the estate.

Her son Nathaniel was bailiff to Mr John and her other son
Francis combined duties as a boatman on the lake with doing tasks
around the house. Her daughters had married and moved away
and her husband Sam had died of consumption many years before.

Betty was past middle age now, but her lean gaunt figure was
almost as precious to the Allonby family as the house itself.

Mary nodded and, cutting the pastry with a knife, put it
carefully over the pie dish, draping it round the pie funnel in the
middle. The ends she tucked under the dish and then she
moistened her fingers and pressed down very firmly. A smaller
piece of pastry she kneaded and began to roll again, this time for
the apple – the first pie was made of succulent pieces of pork and
beef from home-killed cattle, stored in the larder until they were
well hung.

Mary sang as she went about her duties in the kitchen and the
sound gladdened Betty's heart. For too long there had been
sadness and gloom in the Allonby family, which meant that young
Mary had grown up in a harsh and bitter atmosphere unsuited to
the formation of a pretty young maid.

John Allonby had always had the brunt of the hardship, which
had made him naturally quiet and taciturn. His grief he kept to

himself, but it showed only too clearly in his mien and the stoop of his shoulders.

As Stewart, naturally robust and cheerful, had grown to manhood he too took on something of the taciturnity of his brother. But Betty always remembered Stewart as a young boy and how full of mischief he had been – always in trouble, always laughing and tumbling about.

Mary's birth had been the cause of unhappiness to the household. Her mother had taken puerperal sepsis after it and died. Almost at the same time her uncle, Guy Delamain, had died abroad and the sadness that had attended her birth had seemed to leave its mark on Mary who grew into a gentle girl but always with a slightly wistful air – except when in the presence of her cousin, Brent. Betty, if no one else, had noticed how the burgeoning of young love had changed Mary, how a light had come into her eyes and a spring into her step and how she sang as she went about her work.

When Mary was small Betty had been busy with her own family, and it was not until now that she had grown close to the girl, become her confidante and companion.

It was to Betty she had turned when, nearly a year before, her brother and aunt had put paid to her hopes of marrying Brent Delamain. Betty would never erase from her memory how Mary had wept – why, she had thought the tears would never stop. The girl had shut herself in her room and refused to come down for days despite the pleas of her brothers and her aunt. The only person she would admit was Betty, and then it was to hurl herself on that comforting bosom and weep all over again.

In vain had Betty tried to comfort her. That it was for the best, that if he loved her he would wait, he would come back. But Mary seemed convinced that the possibility of attaining happiness had left her; that her chance to have Brent had gone forever.

'Don't they understand, Betty,' she had sobbed, 'I would have had him on *any* terms whether he loved me or no, whether he would be faithful or not.'

And Betty, wise though she was in the way of the world, had been surprised to hear such passion, such uncontrolled yearning from so young, so inexperienced a maid.

In time Mary's tears stopped and she went quietly about her household tasks again. But it seemed to old Betty that she had never forgiven her brother John for what he had done, nor her aunt Susan who used to be like a mother to her – never had nor never would forgive either of them.

All Mary waited for that year was for news of Brent and the short stilted letters she had from him in which he protested his undying love but not much else. She was dutiful and obedient as always, went diligently about her household tasks, cooked and baked and made jam; but her relationship with her brother John subtly changed and became cold and distant, while that towards Stewart grew closer.

Mary put both pies, the apple and the meat, into the oven, the heat from the huge fire in the grate causing her already hot face to flame. The sweat poured down her cheeks as she backed away and closed the big iron door. 'There!' she wiped her hand on her apron and smoothed her hand across her brow. 'That is our dinner! Now Betty, what else is there for me to do?'

She smiled at Betty whose heart filled with happiness at the sight of the smile, the genuine good humour that had pervaded her young mistress since her brother John had told her of his intention to combine business at Cockermouth with a visit to their sister, to try and see Brent. And now John had left, that very morning – and why, he might even bring Brent back with him!

'Why, miss, don't you go with your brother to the wood? Nat is there with him and you could take them some dinner. 'Tis a lovely day and it will take your mind off . . .'

She paused and looked at the young girl because there was, she knew, despite Mary's happiness, a question mark in their minds.

Supposing Brent had changed his mind? Supposing the wind that had framed their love by the side of Lake Derwentwater had grown cold? His letters were like those of a schoolboy, awkward and ill-spelt; they conveyed nothing of the mysterious animal warmth that was Brent – Brent to whom she had been prepared to give herself regardless of convention, whose every glance, whose very touch thrilled her. Who had been wrenched away from her by the strict, overprotective attitude of her brother.

'Betty, do you think he will come back?'

Mary, eyes shining, clasped her hands to her hot face. She knew he would come back. Without any question, any doubt. She only asked again to hear Betty reiterate the words.

'Aye, Miss Mary, I am sure he will, when he knows you are eager for the wedding.'

In the end John, worried by his sister's abstracted manner, her almost permanent air of brooding and silence had relented. He would go and see Brent; a year had almost passed. Anything might happen now that the Prince had come – and if Mary was willing to grasp even at brief happiness, why he would go at once and see what he could arrange.

Wedding . . . marriage to Brent. Was such happiness possible, conceivable? That it would happen maybe in a few days, this very week. All at once her life had been changed beyond recognition. She felt she was on the brink of momentous happenings in her own life and that of their country for, if the Prince did reach London and seize the throne, who knew how it would affect her family for so long persecuted and dispossessed? And Brent, if he fought for the Prince and they won, with what honours might he and others with him not be showered by a grateful sovereign?

It never occurred to Mary Allonby on that bright day in late September 1745 when the world seemed at her feet and her long years of waiting at an end, that the Stuarts might be rebuffed and the Hanoverians remain on the throne. It never occurred to her for a single moment that things could possibly be worse than before.

Mary packed bread and goat's cheese, apples and a flagon of ale into a basket, looked once more at her pies in the oven and ran upstairs to get her outdoor cloak, humming a song as she tripped up the stairs, two at a time.

Stewart and Nat had been hard at work since early morning. They had marked all the trees for cutting during the previous weeks, and now was the time for felling over the long winter months before the sap started to rise with the spring.

Stewart, as he worked alongside Nat Hardcastle, was happy too. He had made his preparations well. All the trees were marked and Nat could work all the winter with the help of his brother Francis the boatman. And by the spring Stewart was sure he would be riding back to Furness with maybe a new horse and a fresh suit of clothes, money in his pocket and the prospect of the Allonby fortunes being restored, after so many years of trial, by King James III. At last, Stewart was convinced, the Allonbys would be on the winning side. Why, the frenzy that had taken hold of

Scotland had spread as far as the Midlands; some even said large numbers were defecting to the Jacobite cause in the south, and that those who had kept their colours hidden for so many years now displayed them openly.

John, more cautious and controlled, less swayed by passion, had pointed out that few really important Englishmen had so far declared for the Prince, in fact none that he knew. All the nobles who owed their wealth and possessions to the Hanoverian Succession stood firm by the King in London and not the one over the water.

But John was like that. He had sunk too far in gloom and a kind of stoical resignation that seemed to suggest he thought his lot had always been an unhappy one and always would be.

It had already been decided that John would not go to the war. He would remain in his important position of linkman between the borders and the north-west, sending note of the Prince's triumphal progress to all concerned, supervising the supply of arms so admirably speeded up since Brent had unexpectedly made an alliance with their brother-in-law. That industry alone had been enough to convince John that Brent had stopped drifting and mended his ways, that he had fitted himself to marry their sister.

And it was the thought of Mary's happiness that made Stewart sing as he and Nat chopped away that morning. To see how lightly Mary trod and how her eyes sparkled and how, overnight, the dark shadows under her eyes had vanished. Stewart had always thought his brother and aunt harsh about Brent. Nursing, as he did, a hopeless passion for Emma he knew for himself the misery of love unfulfilled. When both willing adult parties were forcibly torn asunder in such uncertain times as this, why, it had seemed wicked to him, though he had never told John so. Never dared. John had replaced their father in authority and was a law unto himself.

Nat was chopping at one side of the stout fir that had stood for years, Stewart at the other. When their blades almost converged, at a prearranged signal Stewart, who was broader than Nat, would push the tree while Nat stood aside and they would watch it go crashing to the undergrowth. It was a very difficult moment to judge because, if it was not done correctly, the tree could come bearing down on one or other of them.

Stewart was just about to give the signal to Nat to jump clear when he saw a movement in the undergrowth, and thinking it was his sister who had been so foolish – she who should know to keep well clear of tree felling – he called out with a curse.

'*Mary*, remove yourself quickly from the path of the tree!'

But it was too late, maybe he had misjudged the timing and, with a crash, the tree fell, pinioning the young woman under its top branches. The noise of the tree drowned her cries, and all they saw was the still, apparently lifeless form lying on the ground.

A sob rose in Stewart's throat as, casting aside his axe, he rushed over to where she lay; but even as he approached his step faltered. It was plain to see it was not Mary. It was a slight girl of about the same age, only dark, not so comely as Mary, a ragged gypsy-looking girl. But she breathed! As he knelt down beside her he could see that, although her face was deathly pale, her chest rose rhythmically and that her eyes fluttered and gazed about her as he bent over her. Then he saw that the branch had missed the upper part of her body and pinioned her by one leg only. She had had a narrow escape.

As he gazed at her, having sprinted ahead of the slower-moving Nat, he saw yet another movement in the trees and another figure running, this time calling out:

'Nelly, Nell . . .'

Stewart raised his head to see running into the clearing made by the fallen tree a woman of such remarkable beauty that his mind was momentarily taken off the poor victim who lay on the ground.

He didn't know whether it was the sculptured classical lines of her face he noticed first, or the tall, slender but very womanly body. Her skin was of a soft olive brown, her mouth firm but full, the centre of the lower lip deeply dented, her nose long and straight and her thin black eyebrows imperiously arched. But it was the eyes set deeply into the forehead that had such an arresting quality; they were such a dark brown that the iris was almost invisible. Her lids were half lowered even though her eyes were wide open and framed by luxurious lashes that looked like a fringe. She reminded him of the classical portraits he had seen of an Italian madonna; there was a remote, haunting, vital yet intangible quality about her that made people want to stop in their tracks and stare, as Stewart did then, ignoring the girl pinioned under the tree.

But the face was only a part of this vision. Her long neck swept down to a deep full bosom which was contained in a tight fitting bodice just visible under her cloak, which fell back from her shoulders as she knelt opposite him. A small neat waist broadened into voluptuous hips, and the long shapely legs under the skirt were left to his imagination. He only then observed that she was shoeless, and had the hard calloused feet of one who lived on the road.

Her hair was black as jet and curled down over her bosom as she kneeled beside the girl on the ground, and at the same time looked up at Stewart, her lustrous eyes gleaming dangerously.

'What have you done?'

''Twas an accident. She ran right across our path.'

'You should be more careful.'

'She had no business here.'

Stewart rose to his feet dusting his hands. He was aware that he was talking to a gypsy, or someone part gypsy, because surely no lady walked on her bare feet and had such brightly coloured clothes? Yet, this was no ordinary gypsy girl, of that Stewart was sure. There was something of the aristocrat about her, an indefinable air that his sisters had, his aunt Susan and Emma Delamain had: an absolute certainty of one's heritage regardless of one's circumstances.

She might be poor and barefoot; but she glowed with health and an innate superiority of manner that almost made Stewart feel he was being put in his place.

'*I'm* the owner,' he said, 'of this wood. People trespass here at their peril. Still, I regret . . .'

'I hope you *do* regret,' Analee said with asperity, getting to her feet. 'Lucky for you she lives and apparently is not badly hurt. Now get this tree off her with this fellow here instantly and let me look at her foot.'

Obediently Nat and Stewart picked up the trunk of the stout tree and, with a heaving and groaning, lifted it clear off Nelly's leg. Analee at once took it tenderly in her hands and examined it, stroking it carefully, noting how the skin was broken but how no bones appeared to be.

'Nelly, are you all right?'

She gazed into the pale face of the girl who had become her only friend and was relieved to see a faint smile, a nod of reassurance.

''Twas the shock. I think I am all right.'

Nelly tried to raise herself and Nat immediately gave her

support, gently putting his broad hands under her armpits and helping her to sit upright. Then Nelly winced with pain and Analee realized this was because, in sitting up, she had moved her leg and something hurt.

''Tis the ankle,' Nelly said, bending and clasping it. 'I think I twisted it under the tree.'

Stewart was palpably relieved. What was a twisted ankle when the whole thing could so easily have ended in death? He even smiled at the girl and her bewitching companion, whose expression too had turned from severity to one of gratitude that Nelly was not hurt.

'We are near the house,' Stewart said. 'She can rest there and we can bind up her ankle and tend her scratches.'

He nodded to Nat who lifted the girl in his arms as though she were thistledown. Stewart pointed the way for Analee and they followed Nat towards the house.

It was before they came within sight of the pink walls that they met Mary coming gaily towards them with a basket. It was a strange sight to see appearing from the trees – Nat with a girl in his arms, followed by Stewart and a woman who seemed to Mary, seeing her in the half-light cast by the trees, like some sort of fleet-footed wood nymph. She was so beautiful, with her flowing dark hair, her step so springy, so tall for a woman, that Mary was more puzzled, more disturbed by her than the sight of the casualty in Nat's arms.

Analee knew that she invariably made an impact at first sight on all who met her and she was used to these reactions both on the part of women as well as men. They usually stared, or shifted their stance, or exchanged glances one with another. And then they all settled down, as most people do, and came to accept her except for the men who fell in love with her, the women who took a dislike to her or the Buckland tribe who had never welcomed her.

All she was concerned with now was Nelly's welfare, not this curious trio – a blonde pretty girl and a handsome young man, and a fellow who was obviously the woodman.

Hearing the commotion, the barking of dogs, Betty had come into the yard to stare, and, observing the procession, promptly crossed herself, the instinctive gesture of a good God-fearing Christian when seeing a gypsy. Her first thought was to direct the gypsies to the barn, but she thought better of it when she saw the expression on Master Stewart's face and she hurried ahead into the kitchen.

But to her surprise Stewart directed that Nat should take the girl into the drawing-room overlooking the lake and then he called for Betty to bring water and ointment and strips of clean bandage from the cupboard. In Betty's opinion barefooted gypsies, whether beautiful or no, had no right inside a decent home, let alone the best room. She hoped Miss Mary would impress this clearly on her brother who was obviously distracted by the tall gypsy – very dark she was, so clearly a foreigner – and had temporarily lost his sense of proportion.

But of course Miss Mary wouldn't send the gypsies to their proper place, the barn. She was much too kindhearted and tender. Indeed she even instructed Betty to bring some food to the table because instead of a picnic in the forest they would now eat indoors. She obviously intended to share her bread with a common gypsy!

Mary followed Betty into the kitchen having already detected her mood.

'Now, Betty, we cannot receive guests other than with hospitality, apart from the fact that it was our tree fell on her.'

'No right to be in our wood,' Betty grumbled as she took loaves of bread from the bin and meat from the larder, 'Gypsies!'

'I have naught against gypsies, why have you?'

Mary was smiling as she placed the beef on a platter from which Stewart would serve it.

'They are thieves and rogues. They know not manners or what to do in a house; they are ill at ease in one.'

It was true, both the women had looked around them as though there was something constricting about four walls, something unfamiliar about a floor made of wood.

'We cannot refuse them succour. Besides it is a diversion. It gives me something to think about besides what my brother is saying to Brent.'

When she got back it was obvious that Nelly's foot was swelling and she was feeling a degree of pain now that the reaction had set in. Although she smiled bravely she was pale and Mary could see a glimmer of tears bravely held back.

'You must go to bed,' she said immediately, 'and rest your foot. I shall give you some laudanum to ease the pain'

'Bed?' Nelly said faintly.

'Yes a bed, to lie in and rest. When you are recovered you can be on your way to where you are going. Not before.'

She looked at Analee, who, she saw, was fascinated by the room and the view of the lake from the long low windows overlooking it. She had turned from Nelly and was gazing across at the forest of Lodore, and her face was temporarily transfigured by a look of sheer elation.

'Very beautiful to live here,' she said softly, 'always within sight of the lake and the fells.'

'Yes, we love it,' Mary said gently. 'Would you like to come up with your friend? Nat will carry her and you could help her into bed.'

Nelly stopped struggling and Analee gave in. Besides, she liked the house; it was not the sort of alien place she longed to get away from as she did most times when she was indoors. She felt a welcoming here, almost as if in some way she belonged to it. She was glad they were staying at least for today.

She followed Mary up the stairs into a beautiful room that overlooked the lake. In it was a fourposter bed and furniture that sparkled and shone from age and care. Analee loved the room immediately.

'There,' Mary said, 'we had another invalid here and he recovered, though he was much more badly hurt. He said the view of the lake soothed him. Would you come downstairs and eat with us when you have finished . . . What is your name?'

She looked at Analee awkwardly, the sentence incompleted.

'Analee, I have no other name,' she said simply, 'just Analee the gypsy, and this is Nelly.'

'I'm Mary, and my brother is Stewart. Now we know one another. Pray come and eat. There is a chemise in the drawer for Nelly and the sheets are clean and aired.'

She smiled and shut the door behind her. Analee and Nelly gazed at each other.

'I don't think I ever slept in one of these,' Nelly said looking doubtfully at the bed, 'why is it so high?'

'So the rats don't clamber up,' Analee said laughing. She was suddenly possessed by a feeling of light-heartedness, an irrational sense of happy anticipation as though something nice were going to happen, 'and this chemise is not for over your skirt. You take it off and put this on.'

'*Altogether?*' said Nelly incredulously. 'I don't remember when I last bared my skin.'

'The *gadjé* do it every night – yes, they change their clothes and lie in a bed like this.'

'And these drapes,' Nelly said wonderingly.

'Sheets – one on top and one underneath.'

'Well, I never.'

'It may be the only time you will sleep in a bed,' Analee said, 'best make the most of it. Here, stretch out and I'll help you.'

Quickly Analee divested Nelly of her clothes and assisted her to put her head through the long white chemise; then she drew back the sheets and helped her inside. Once or twice Nelly winced but finally there she was, covered by a sheet, propped up against the white pillow. She looked so ill at ease, so comical that Analee burst out laughing again. She gathered up Nelly's things from the floor and put them across a chair. Then she took her cloak off and looked at herself in the mirror.

Analee hardly ever saw herself, being unused to mirrors in her wandering life. Occasionally she saw her face in the shiny surface of a tin or the clear waters of a lake when she leaned down to drink or wash.

She was surprised now, as she looked in the mirror, to see how unfamiliar her face had become. It looked to her much older, and more knowing in the ways of the world, since she had seen it last. But the sight did not displease her. She saw the way her hair shone and the healthy glow in her face. She bared her teeth and they were even and white, and when she smiled her full red mouth dimpled at either side.

She stroked her bust with her hands and noticed how firm it looked, much smaller now that the milk had gone. For days after leaving the baby she had to pump herself dry twice a day, for the pain was unbearable and her breasts were swollen and hard. But then the milk had dried up and now her breasts were as they had been before Morella was born.

The contemplation of her breasts reminded her of her baby, her loss, and Analee's face became solemn. She lost interest in the sight of herself in the mirror and turned away. She saw that Nelly's eyes were closed. Sleep would do her good.

Quietly Analee tip-toed out of the room.

* * *

There was an atmosphere in the house that Analee couldn't comprehend. She who hated walls and stone and wood felt at peace here. She came down the staircase and into the broad hall. No one was about. She wandered into the long room overlooking the lake and stood gazing at the portraits of the family, hanging on the walls. There was definitely a strong family resemblance that ran through the line. But in the place of honour over the mantelpiece was a portrait of a man with dark beard and moustache, black piercing eyes. It was head and shoulders only, and the head was turned towards the painter so that the full force of his gaze, the sad expression in his eyes, made the viewer almost painfully aware of great, inexpressable suffering.

Analee stared at the portrait for some time, almost spellbound by it. But the sad man bore no resemblance at all to the tall, well-built, blond Allonby ancestors.

'It is Charles the Martyr,' a gentle voice said behind her. 'King Charles who died on the scaffold.'

'Oh.'

Analee knew little about kings and politics, and nothing about Charles the Martyr.

'We are supporters of the Stuart Kings of England here. It is King Charles' great-grandson, Prince Charles, who has landed in Scotland to reclaim the throne.'

'Oh?' Analee looked at her with the interested expression of one always willing to learn. 'I know naught about kings, and take care to keep clear of the law.'

'Well,' Mary said taking a seat by the window, her eyes looking alternately at Analee and the portrait on the wall, 'England was ruled for a long time by the House of Stuart after King James VI of Scotland came to be James I of England . . .'

'He was from Scotland?'

'Yes, but he was related through his mother, Mary Queen of Scots, to Queen Elizabeth I of England who had just died. It was ironical because Queen Elizabeth had Mary beheaded to keep her off the throne. Elizabeth was not married and had no heirs of her own body, or others close enough to succeed her. 'Twas her aunt, Margaret Tudor, sister of Henry VIII of England, who married King James IV of Scotland and their son James V of Scotland was the father of Mary Queen of Scots.'

Analee was listening intently. Mary had a very musical voice and her grave expression and earnestness somehow compelled attention.

'Thus!' Mary laughed, 'if you will pardon the history lesson, it was that the Stuarts came to the English throne in 1603. Ever since the Norman conquest our kings have always been succeeded by heirs of the body and so it continued until in 1688 there occurred a revolution in our country and the rightful King, James II of England, brother of Charles II – the merry monarch they called him – and son of our martyr King, fled abroad. I need not trouble you with the reason for the revolution, Analee, for 'twas complex. King James sympathized with the Catholics, like all the Stuarts, but ever since Henry VIII and the Reformation the Catholics have been persecuted in this country and no monarch was allowed to be a Catholic . . .'

Analee looked at the picture on the wall.

'Oh King Charles I was sympathetic to our faith and they say Charles II converted on his deathbed. But King James was very influenced by his mother Henrietta Maria of France and he openly advocated that the Catholics should have the same rights as everyone else.

'Well he was succeeded by his daughter Mary, a Protestant, and her husband William of Orange and they in turn by his second daughter Anne. Queen Anne was the last of the Stuarts, for Parliament had passed a law decreeing that only Protestants should ascend the English throne so that the Catholic Stuarts should be excluded, and the nearest heir was a fat old German prince called the Elector of Hanover whose mother had been a daughter of Elizabeth of Bohemia, daughter of James I of England and sister of King Charles I. So you can see how far back it went, how tenuous was the connection. The Prince could neither speak nor understand English and came with all his court to occupy the throne of our country . . .'

Mary was near to tears, and Analee moved over to her but feared to show too much familiarity by touching her.

''Twas a scandal. King James II had died, but his son who was born here and was openly a Catholic living in France was the rightful heir to the throne of England, and we who supported him call him King James III.'

'And is he still there?' To Analee it did not appear right at all; gypsy rules of succession were very strict too.

'Yes, an old man now, living sadly in Rome because even the French kings who used to support him would do so no longer. He it was who took part in the glorious rebellion of 1715, in which our family suffered so much, and it is *his* son Prince Charles Edward who has come now to act as regent and fight for his father's throne!'

'Oh may he succeed!' Analee cried clasping her hands. 'I can see it is so right!'

'Yes it is, it *is*! We will drive these odious Germans back to Hanover from whence they came. Oh, Prince Charles is but twenty-four years of age, so bold and handsome, it is said. He came with only seven men and now all Scotland has flocked to him, and so will all England when he crosses the border and marches to London.'

'Will he not be resisted?'

'Oh, there will be some resistance,' Mary said casually, 'but they say that his charm and skill and also the fact he is undoubtedly the rightful heir will carry the day.'

Analee looked at the picture and suddenly there was a whirring sound in her head and she closed her eyes. She could hear the clash of swords, the sound of musket shot, the rasp of cannonballs. There were screams and cries . . . she put her hands to her ears.

'What is it, Analee?' Mary grasped her arm, her face pale with concern, 'are you ill?'

Analee swayed and the sounds abruptly stopped. She was looking steadily at the face of the King, as though nothing had happened. Then she turned to Mary and said gravely: 'There will be much suffering . . .'

'Because of him? The Prince?'

'Yes. For a moment I seemed to hear the rage of battle, cries and screams . . .'

Mary gazed at her guest with wonder – this tall, strange gypsy woman with the bare feet and proud eyes.

'Can you see into the future? Can it really be true?'

Analee shook her head.

'I sometimes can see things, foretell them; but I am not *cohani*, that is a gypsy witch or woman of magic. But things that I often feel strongly about come true . . . in my vision just now I seemed to see much distress for our own people, the gypsies.'

She put her hands to her face and looked at the picture again.

'He was a good man?'

'Oh, he was. Some say a foolish one, a stubborn one; but far far better than any Hanoverian.'

Analee smiled at the young girl, noting the set of the mouth, the hint of passion in her eyes. She was beautiful, and the brother was handsome, too. Analee wondered about the brother and sister living apparently with so few servants in this large house.

'Would you like to walk by the lake?' Mary said. 'I can see it fascinates you.'

'Yes it is very beautiful; and the mountains . . .' Analee looked across the water to Wella Crag. 'You see I normally see everything from outside, not from the point of view of being inside a house. If you are always out of doors things look very different. That window is like . . .' she pointed to the pictures on the wall, 'well, as though that scene is framed like one of those.'

'Yes, I know what you mean. Like a picture.'

Mary led Analee into the hall and out of the wide front door. Almost immediately they could see the lake between the firs. It sparkled as though a handful of jewels, diamonds and sapphires, had been thrown carelessly into it and Analee shaded her eyes against the glare. It was a beautiful day; calm, gentle, serene, no cloud in the sky; not like autumn at all.

'You live here alone with your brother?'

Analee was reluctant to appear curious and glanced at the girl walking beside her.

'No, we have an elder brother John, who is not here today. He will be back soon. Our father died a few years ago. My mother when I was born . . .'

'Oh.' Analee stopped and looked directly into Mary's face. 'My mother, too, died when I was born. You know I felt a strange harmony with you as soon as I saw you. Now maybe this is the reason. We have never known the love of a mother.'

Mary gazed at her strange companion and clasped her hands.

'Oh, do you think so? Is it possible? Tell me about yourself, Analee, why you lead this life. There is something about you that is . . . unexpected. You are not, for instance, like Nelly.'

'I *am* a gypsy,' Analee said simply, 'a wandering gypsy woman. I have nothing special or secret about me. Maybe I have travelled more than someone like Nelly.'

'Are you from overseas?'

Analee paused and looked towards the water; it was a question that people often asked her.

'I? No. I was born here in this country. But as my mother died so young I was brought up by my grandmother and, yes, they came from overseas, from some far distant country – I know not which.'

'From Spain or Italy. That is why you are so dark-skinned.'

'Maybe,' Analee smiled.

'I have spent all my life by the shores of this lake. I never went further than Carlisle and that only once. I cannot comprehend what it is like to wander. Don't you feel afraid?'

'Afraid? No. I feel safer among nature than my own people . . .'

Analee's eyes were tinged with bitterness and her voice faltered. Mary sensed a sadness, but also a withdrawal on the part of Analee, as though she did not want to speak further about herself.

'It's something I can't understand, never having known that life,' Mary said.

'And you are happy as you are?'

'Well, our family has known much hardship. Once we were, well, wealthy and powerful I suppose you'd say, though it was long before my time. Then our father's brother was in the rebellion in 1715 and was executed. Our mother died when I was born, our uncle died, an exile abroad, and my eldest brother finally managed to find some happiness and married a beautiful girl he had known all his life. They had but ten short months of happiness when she died, too, giving birth to a child . . .'

'And the child?'

'Dead.'

'Ah . . .' Analee looked away, not wanting Mary to see the suffering in her own eyes. Then she turned to her again. 'And you . . . what is your future?'

Mary's face assumed so suddenly a look of happiness, almost ecstacy, that Analee was taken by surprise. The deep blue eyes became almost purple and a becoming blush suffused her cheeks. Analee laughed outright at such a sudden transformation.

'I see there is someone special for you . . .'

'I am expecting to be married! Any day he could come galloping over those mountains. My brother has gone to fetch him.'

'Oh, I am so happy for you. Have you known him long?'

'All my life. He is my cousin; but he never showed any love for me until recently. Last year he was very ill and I nursed him back to health. We fell in love.'

'Then why did you not marry last year?'

Mary frowned and studied the ground.

'My family did not fully approve of him. Although he is of noble birth he showed no capacity for settling down, for hard work, and he had no future of his own. Of course I didn't mind that,' Mary said hastily, noting the expression on Analee's face. 'We have never had money, but he also had a reputation as . . . a womanizer.' Mary's voice sank to a whisper. 'My brother thought him too fickle.'

'But all is changed now?' Analee's eyes sparkled at the girl's shyness.

'Oh yes. He has worked hard and been faithful . . . I think, and I expect him any time.'

Analee looked at the happy open face gazing into hers and knew a sudden moment of unease, foreboding . . . there seemed to be a cloud between her and this young girl on the verge of marriage. Was it the intervention of her own unhappiness or was it a foreknowing?

'I must go upstairs,' she said quickly, 'and see to Nelly.'

'What is it, Analee? Have I said something wrong?'

Mary had observed the change in the gypsy's eyes and looked concerned. Analee leaned impulsively over to touch her, then decided not to; Mary might consider her gesture too familiar.

'No, of course not. I was worried that I had neglected Nelly. We cannot stay here long, especially as you are expecting your brother and . . . what is his name, your young man?'

'Mary,' a voice came from the wood and Stewart appeared through the trees, 'can you come for a minute? I want to talk about the thinning of the coppice with you.'

'Ah, I must go,' Mary said. 'We dine at five, and go to bed very early in these parts.'

'I am used to sleeping when it is dark and rising when it is light,' Analee said turning towards the house. 'In fact I cannot keep awake in the dark.'

Stewart who had hoped that the beautiful gypsy would come with them looked disconsolate as she walked towards the house. Mary saw his expression and smiled.

'I think you are smitten,' she said.

'A man would not be in his right mind if he were not,' Stewart replied. 'I don't think I ever saw a woman who struck me more in my life.'

'But she is not for you.'

'Why?'

'She is a gypsy. A nomad; would you wander too?'

'I was teasing,' Stewart said taking her by the arm. 'Maybe she will give me a spell to make Emma mine. If she is a real gypsy she should know about the ways of love.'

'I am sure she does,' Mary said, trembling slightly, for what reason she didn't know. Maybe a chill had sprung up. 'I am sure she knows all about them.'

13

Stewart was at his best at the dinner table that evening, relaxed and full of laughter. In the company of Analee he seemed to bloom, to lose all his reserve. It was the way she looked at him that made him feel so, well . . . manly was the word. Yes manly, and clever as well. She simply had to smile at him and he wanted to open up and puff out his chest like a strutting turkey-cock. He wanted to please her and impress her; above all he wanted to make her go on looking at him like that.

But when she turned to Mary the look was only subtly changed because Mary was a woman and Stewart was a man. Analee wanted to draw Mary out too, and she did this by her smiles of encouragement, the way she nodded her head, seemed completely absorbed by what was being said. Years fell away from the brother and sister as they responded to the impact Analee made on them. She brought out the best in them, caused them to relive childhood memories, remembering when times were not as hard as they were now, so insecure.

It was almost as though . . . she had cast a spell on them, Stewart thought watching his sister's face as she chatted and sparkled, erupting every now and again into long forgotten silvery laughter. Could she cast spells, this beautiful gypsy woman who came from nowhere? Was she, perhaps, a witch?

'Mary has been telling me she is about to marry,' Analee said suddenly interrupting the flow of childhood nostalgia. 'And you, Stewart? Have you no young woman you long to make your bride?'

Stewart looked abashed, less sure of himself. He knew he was blushing, but hoped she did not see it under the brown tan acquired from so many days of chopping trees in the sun.

'Yes, he does have . . .' Mary began impishly, but he looked imploringly at her and she stopped.

'It is true,' he said cautiously. 'I am enamoured of someone; but she will not spare a glance for me. She is younger than I and different, and . . .'

206

'Then that augurs well,' Analee said practically. 'It would not do if she were older or exactly the same in temperament.'

But she could see that Stewart was not joking; he was not amused. He nursed a hopeless passion for someone who did not love him.

'No, she does not like me enough. Maybe you could give me a spell,' Stewart said half in jest, wanting to restore the happy laughing mood of a few moments ago. 'Why not? Can you cast spells?'

'No,' Analee said slowly. 'I do not have the powers. I told you I am not *cohani*; but, well . . . there are one or two ways I do know of trying to capture someone's love.'

Stewart leaned forward impressed, despite himself, by her gravity, the sincerity of her tone.

'Then tell it. I will try it.'

'Well . . . You must pluck three hairs from the neck of the girl you love, better if you do it while she is sleeping. You then put the hairs in the chink of a tree and as it grows her love will grow for you.'

'But,' Stewart protested amused, though he could see that Analee did not speak in jest. 'She is not here. She lives quite far away and I cannot get the hairs from her head.'

'Ah.' Analee stared thoughtfully at the table. 'You really need a *drabarni*, a drug woman who will give you a potion to put into her food. But there again you need to be with her. To win love from afar, that is more difficult. Look, this will be easy for you. You must go to the lake and pick a leaf from a tree hanging over it. Then with your knife you prick your wrist and smear the leaf with the blood while repeating your name. You then turn the leaf over and smear it on the other side, saying over and over again the name of the girl you want to marry. Her name is . . . ?'

'Emma,' Stewart said.

'Then you say "Emma" over and over again. Then you throw the leaf into the lake and watch it flow away.'

She stopped and gazed at Stewart. He was such a handsome, vital young man, looking earnestly at her face. But she did not see happiness for Stuart . . . there was something about this family that bred its own disaster. Looking at brother and sister she could see happiness for neither of them. Neither Stewart nor the girl, not for a long time.

She hoped she was wrong. The mood of gaiety had gone and it was partly her fault. She was not bringing happiness to the house and she wanted to. She felt she already loved this family, the two young vulnerable people who had given her, a rough wandering gypsy woman, so much hospitality. She wanted to help them, to do something for them. But what?

'I must take Nelly some food,' she said getting up from the table. 'She will be better tomorrow. We will go, and presume no more on your kindness.'

'But we like having you here,' Stewart said. 'We get so few visitors. Besides, where will you go?'

'Ah, that I can't say. We are making for over the mountains, towards the sea. Maybe we will cross the water and go to Ireland.'

'You mean you just wander on and on?'

'Yes.' Analee tilted her head at Stewart. 'You cannot understand it can you? You have a house and a bed and fresh clothes to put on. You have food at regular times and warmth in your grate. But I, and Nelly, have known nothing else. The earth is our home; the wild hills and forests. We have always done it and it is how we live. I have . . . for some months dwelt in a gypsy camp and I could not abide it. I hated being tied down. I cannot explain it; it is how I am. How my people are.'

Stewart thought it thrilling to listen to the sombre voice of the gypsy as dark gathered over the lake, and the only light in the room came from the guttering candles on the polished oak table. He thought of her sleeping rough and living like a nomad, no table, no bed. He got up and took her hand and kissed it, noting how fine and smooth it was, the long nails blunted at the ends but not rough or jagged. Although her clothes were poor they were clean and her body was sweet-smelling. She took care of herself.

'I wish you would stay,' he said. 'At least stay and see Mary married. Rest here awhile. Nelly is not nearly fit to go; see if the spell works. I will try it tomorrow. With you.'

Analee laughed into his earnest young eyes. Why not stay a while if he meant it, and it seemed he did? Maybe she could dance at Mary's wedding, reward her like that? She got up and clasped his hand, her eyes shining.

'Well . . . maybe a little longer if you really wish it. Now I must take Nelly her dinner. See how she does. It is late for me to be awake. I am like the birds, as I told you. I will see you tomorrow.'

Betty had already taken up Nelly's food and Nelly was asleep when Analee got to their room. She had come slowly up the stairs, along the corridors. She got in beside Nelly and lay for a long time with her hands clasped beneath her head looking out onto the dark sky studded with stars.

Analee thought that, tomorrow or soon, she and Nelly would bed down as they always did beside a ditch or under cover of a rocky crag. Sometimes they found a cave and stayed a day or two if it were cold or wet. Luxury like this she had never known. But, to her surprise, she did not dislike it as much as she thought she would: the feel of the sheets on her bare skin – for she did not wear a chemise as Nelly did – the boards under her bare feet when she got up. The gleaming table at dinner with silver, and flaming wax candles, plates and the smell of hot food.

It was her first real experience of living in a house and she liked it. It was attractive. It appealed to something in Analee she didn't know she possessed.

Suddenly, her head resting on her hands clasped on the fine white flock-filled pillows, Analee thought of the man who had lain in this room recovering from an illness. He would have looked out on the stars as she did; he and Mary had fallen in love; maybe they had lain together in this very bed.

And suddenly, for no reason at all that she could understand, Analee had a clear picture of the long lost Brent Delamain, and with his image in her mind she fell asleep.

Brent Delamain had ridden hard since leaving Cockermouth at first light, John close behind him. It had been a glorious morning as they left the valley and began the ascent of the foothills just as the sun broke over Grisedale Pike and the fells, covered with heather and brown bracken, had the rich golden gleam of fresh honey. They toiled up towards Whinlatter, and the brown and green fells gave way to the thick forest of tall straight firs through which many a mountain stream cascaded from its source over stones and fallen logs towards Buttermere and Crummock Water.

As it rose the sunlight pierced the trees, dispersing the dense morning mist which spiralled up like smoke through the thick branches. At times Brent's nostrils caught the scent of woodsmoke caused by the charcoal burners who plied a living in the forest.

After a steep descent into Braithwaite they rested, taking bread and ale at the hostelry, and then set off along the narrow bridle paths that meandered through the Newlands Valley by way of Stair and Skelgill and climbed high up to Skelgill Bank and across the top to Catbells. All the way along this last part the lake of Derwentwater gleamed below them, a broad glistening ribbon mirroring the blue sky and clouds, the purple hills that surrounded it and the forest which ran alongside either bank.

From where he waited for John to catch up Brent could see across to Low Moss, Castlerigg Fell and away to Watendlath, and then in the distance the high snowy peaks at the end of Borrowdale.

But below lay the jewel, the prize, its tall chimneys and soft red stone, its gables and mullioned windows reflected in the still lake: Furness Grange and at its core nestled his beloved Mary. He imagined he saw her walking in the grounds and raised his hand to call; but he was too far away. He looked at John who smilingly indicated he should go ahead, and then he dug his heels into his horse and raced down across the fell towards the house.

And indeed it had been Mary walking in the grounds on her way back from taking Stewart and Nat their noonday meal. She clasped her hand over her eyes against the sun as she heard the sound of hooves and there he was towering over her on his horse; and then he had jumped down and she was in his arms.

She could feel his heart beating against her cheek pressed tightly to his chest, and her own arms could scarcely encircle his back he had grown so big. Not fat, she could feel his bones beneath her fingers. He had just developed girth in the months they had been apart. She could feel his mouth in her hair murmuring words of love and then she raised her head, and that face she had seen in so many dreams, that mouth of such gentleness came down on hers, and for Mary Allonby it was the sweetest moment she had ever known in her life. Sweeter than the first kiss, the first embrace. She knew this was so sweet because it was the prelude to giving herself completely to Brent; to becoming one with him, his wife.

His mouth moved from hers to her throat and, lower down, she could feel his hands trying to slip in between the folds of her bodice. Reality came back and with it thoughts of her brother or the gypsy, maybe, looking out of an upstairs window at them.

'Brent! You have grown so broad.'

'Aye, 'tis the good life of the sea.' He held her away from him and took in every inch of her precious body.

'And you have grown too, as your brother said. So comely, yes, and a little rounded. Oh Mary, when can we be wed?'

'You still want to be wed, Brent?'

'Can you doubt it? Urgently. Immediately.'

'It is what I want, too.'

'Despite the war?'

'*Because* of it,' Mary said pressing her head against him again, wanting once more to hear that firm steady heartbeat.

Stewart had heard the hooves and, giving time for his sister and cousin to be reunited, joined them where they had remained by the side of the house. It was a relief to him to see them clinging to each other as though they could never bear to be parted. He, too, had wondered what changes the intervening months might have brought, feared the effects on his sister's happiness. But there, they clung to each other and he knew all was well. He held out his hand.

'Brent.'

'Oh, Stewart! John is coming more slowly over yonder fell.' Brent glanced upwards. 'I think he wanted to be tactful.'

'Aye, he did well. I see you are of the same mind Brent.'

'More than ever. When can we be wed, Stewart?'

'I have told the priest. He is ready to marry you as soon as you wish it.'

'Then fetch him to the chapel as quick as you can and let us get wed.'

Like many of the old Catholic families the Grange had a small chapel where the priest said Mass when he came by. There was a priest at Keswick, Father Bernard, who lived by staying with one Catholic family then another. John knew where he was now and had already sent word to him.

'He will be here by tomorrow.'

'Then tomorrow we will be wed, Mary?'

'Yes. Tomorrow. Oh, Brent I can scarcely believe it.'

'We are just doing, Mary, what should have happened months ago.'

Brent pursed his mouth in the stern expression Mary knew so well.

'Do not be angry, Brent. We have each other now.'

'I am not angry, merely sad we wasted so much time.'

He kissed her lightly and took her hand.

211

'I must wash after my journey. Is my room . . . ?'

'Oh, Brent we have two guests. I'm sure they will bring us luck. They are gypsies and one of them hurt her foot. I'm afraid they are in your old room . . .'

'Never mind,' Brent said, 'soon I will be in *yours*.'

'I put you next to Stewart, that is the room *next* to mine.'

'I'll go and wash and change my clothes and be with you soon, sweetheart.'

Brent waved and went into the house as John clattered up and, eyes shining with happiness, Mary turned to greet him.

The hot noon sun gleamed on the stairs. Huge beams, in which the dust rose, shone through the long mullioned windows that illuminated the staircase, panes of blue and rose and yellow making the sun spots glisten with a thousand colours. Brent loved the old house, the smell of beeswax and candles. He leapt up the stairs four at a time and then went quickly along the gallery that ran the length of the hall.

And there she was, coming towards him as in a dream. The dark hair, the supple body, the face that he knew so well but which had remained shadowy for him, became clear. The most beautiful woman in the world; the goddess always seen in moonlight or in the myriad beams of the dancing, coloured sun. Dancing; she was a dancer and her quick, sure-footed steps, her lithe, graceful body with upraised arms clicking her castanets were as vivid at that moment as when he had last seen her. She saw him; but still she came on and he thought she was a vision, a ghost and would walk straight through him. But she stopped just in front of him and he could smell her tantalizing body smells, a haunting heady perfume that became dear and familiar to him as the mist that had obscured his memory finally dispersed.

'Analee,' he said.

So this was the *gadjo*, this was Mary's betrothed, the man she had fallen in love with as he lay recovering from an illness. Of course he was her cousin, a relation by blood; they even looked so much alike. In a way, she realized, she had always known it. The feel of the house, the familiarity, the peace, the sense of home-coming that was so unusual. She had slept in Brent's bed; had looked on the view that had given him so much pleasure as Mary had brought him back to life – to a life of which Randal had nearly deprived him.

'It *is* you,' she said.

He tried to reach out for her but she stepped back. It was much too dangerous she knew; besides he had easily forgotten her, fallen into the arms of another. Yet the look on his face . . . it was as though something had come to him from a long way away, something strange.

How could he explain how he had forgotten her? Brent gazed at her and saw the bewilderment on her face. In an instant he remembered everything; his first meeting with her, his search for her, hunting her, possessing her. He remembered her dance in the tavern, the way she had danced just for him.

'Analee, how could I have forgotten you?'

'Then you did forget?'

'Everything. Until now, until I saw you.'

'You were very ill,' she said gently. 'After the blow on the head?'

'I remembered nothing.'

'And fell in love with Mary. She is very sweet . . .'

Mary. Brent closed his eyes. Mary . . .

'I . . .'

'She loves you Brent; loves you so much she can't wait to marry you.'

'But I . . .'

'You can't go back on her now. It would kill her. I know her; in a short time I have become her friend.'

He had such a desperate look on his face that she began to suffer too.

'Besides, I am married as well,' she said. 'It cannot be for us again.'

Brent's face seemed to swell with an awful rage and he tried to grab her shoulder, but still she backed away from him.

'*You* married! Then you didn't remember either.'

'Oh, I remembered, but I had no choice. The man who nearly killed you captured me. It is a gypsy tradition that if you capture a bride she must marry you whether she wants to or not.'

'Then you are not really married; not in your heart. It is not too late.'

She began to walk away from him, slowly back down the corridor and he followed her.

'It is too late, much much too late. Make your life again . . .'

'Of course I can't make my life again now I have found you. You *are* my life. Analee let us go now. Let us . . .'

Sadly Analee shook her head.

'No, no . . . abuse the hospitality of the sweet people here? I love them, Brent, and they like and trust me. Mary is a lovely girl, *your* sort of girl . . .'

'She's my cousin . . .'

'*Your* people. We are not meant to live as normal people, Brent. There is something about you and I that is doomed. You would never forgive yourself as a man if you deserted Mary now. We could never be happy in a life built on such sorrow. You would soon tire of the wandering life Brent; life with me . . .'

'I've been a wanderer too on the seas, Analee. Let us go somewhere and talk about this. There *is* some solution.'

He gazed at her and she knew the solution lay with her. She nodded, as if agreeing with him.

'We will meet later, after dinner. We will find a solution.' He grasped her hand, and the thrill of the feel of her flesh was like nothing he had known before or since, not with Mary, not with anyone.

'No,' he said desperately. 'Let us now . . .'

'After dinner,' she said. 'Behave normally now. Do as you would do.'

She gazed up at him, her *gadjo*, Morella's father, and gently let her hand pass across his face as though to etch his features on her palm. Then she turned abruptly into the room she shared with Nelly.

Brent Delamain, his mind in a turmoil, waited for the dinner to begin. How could he guard his expression when Analee came into the room, avoid showing that, for him, she was the only woman in the world – the one it seemed to him he had always sought? In every other woman he had been trying to find Analee, and when he had found her he had lost her, and then found her again . . . and now he was being told it was too late.

He had wanted to follow her into her room, but she shut the door and he stood gazing at it helplessly for some time before finding the one meant for him and throwing himself on the bed. 'Womanizer!' they would all say. 'Brent Delamain never changes. He came to marry Mary and made off with someone else.'

No one would ever trust him again. They would say he was fickle, undependable. Above all, they would say he was not fit to serve the Prince. All these thoughts and more, warred with his own desire. They fought within him, so that when at last he appeared downstairs Mary, running up to greet her beloved and seeing his expression, had asked if he were ill? She had expected him down hours before, anticipating him running into her arms. But he told her he was merely tired and then his eyes had wandered over her head looking for something. He was looking for something now, Mary thought, or someone – his eyes kept staring at the door. He looked ill at ease, unhappy. The relaxed lover she had greeted only hours before behaved now like some sort of fugitive; his face pale, his eyes restless. Was he in trouble?

But Stewart and John appeared not to notice and happily discussed the nuptials that would take place on the morrow as soon as the priest arrived.

'We had best begin,' John said at last. 'I know not where our guest is. What is her name?'

'Analee.'

Analee . . . Brent closed his eyes. Oh that word 'Analee' – it rang in his mind with all the force of an echo that had been lost and forgotten and now resounded louder than ever. 'ANALEE . . .'

'She is very beautiful,' Mary said, glancing shyly at Brent. 'All the men fall madly in love with her.'

'Ah, really?' Brent tried to be jocular. 'Well give us the chance then. Pray, where *is* this Analee?'

'Betty has gone up to fetch her. Maybe she is shy with the company.' Any moment Analee would come through the door, Brent thought. And she would stand and stare and he would . . .

'Miss she has gone!' Betty flurried into the room carrying the large tureen of soup. 'Gypsies! Made off with the family plate for all we know.'

'*Gone?*'

Mary looked up suddenly, but it was not Mary who had spoken. It was Brent. He even seemed half to rise from his seat and then thought better of it.

'How "gone" Betty?' Mary said calmly. 'And Nelly, too?'

'Both miss, and the room as clean as a whistle and the bed turned back.'

'How very unusual,' John said offhandedly reaching for the soup ladle. 'As you say, gypsies I suppose, Betty.'

Stewart too seemed disturbed. He had been so looking forward to wandering in the garden after dinner with Analee, maybe casting the spell together with her by the lake.

'But they were not *like* that!' Mary said, her mind preoccupied by the mystery, but above all by the stricken look on Brent's face, the way he had half risen at Betty's news. 'At least Analee was not. What can have sent them away?'

'Very impolite,' John said. 'Soup, Brent?'

'Please. Maybe they came to some harm?' Brent was trying to control his voice, his emotions, still the pounding of his heart. He wanted to get up and run from the room mount his horse; they could not have gone far . . . He felt panic rising and subsiding in waves, like a terrible fear that is felt and repelled in turns.

'Harm? What sort of harm? No, they have had enough and gone. Never mind.' John passed Brent his soup bowl and turned with a question to Mary.

'Please.' Mary nodded to her brother, 'but I *am* sad about it. I so like Analee. I hoped she would be here for our wedding.'

Wedding. Brent felt a tremor run from head to foot. It was as though he was passing through a nightmare. He was going to marry Mary tomorrow. Analee had betrayed him.

'What is it with thee, Brent? I think you are still fatigued.'

Stewart too had been observing the strange behaviour of his cousin; how restless and anxious he seemed, how he wriggled about in his seat. How pale and haggard he was after appearing so comely and well on his arrival.

'I hope you are not ill,' Stewart added, thinking of the outbreak of the pox that had occurred recently in Keswick.

'No. Naught ails me at all. Maybe weary with the journey.'

'Or nervous with excitement, I'll swear,' John said smiling broadly. 'A bridegroom at last, eh, Brent?'

Brent took a spoon to his soup. The nightmare showed no signs of ending; indeed it was worsening. Every moment Analee was getting further and further away. He put down his spoon and said with pretended calm,

'Maybe we should seek the gypsies lest they have come to some harm in this light. 'Tis dark outside.'

'Aye,' Stewart got up. 'I do not think Analee would behave thus. I agree with Brent. Excuse us, Mary.'

He grabbed a candle from the table and, followed by Brent, hastened through the hall up the stairs. The candle fluttered, lighting up the dark corridor as they passed along, throwing great shadows on the wall. The door of the room was open and, as soon as they entered, it was obvious that it was empty – it had that forlorn, deserted air such as a room does when the inhabitant has packed up and gone away.

Stewart cast the candle into every corner, then went to the window.

'No, they simply got up and left.' He looked dejected. 'I would like to have seen her again. Well . . .'

He turned away and went out of the room.

'Shall we search the fell?'

'Aye, if you like. But they have not come to harm, Brent. They have left of their own free will.'

'We should just see.'

Brent knew he had to keep moving; the one thing he could not do was sit still. Stewart shrugged and followed, noting how Brent preceded him to take the lead. In fact Brent had started to run ahead towards the stable not waiting for Stewart to light his way.

Stewart, although puzzled and upset himself, was intrigued by his cousin's behaviour, having observed his agitated manner at table. Could it be that Brent *knew* Analee . . . or had he met her briefly in the house and become instantly obsessed by her? It was not impossible, having a mind to Analee's looks and Brent's reputation. He followed his cousin more slowly. He came to the stable door and stood behind Brent who feverishly seized the candle and held it above his head.

'My nag has gone. The one I borrowed from Ambrose to ride here today.'

'Then they *are* thieves,' Stewart said, contempt in his voice.

'Nay . . .' Brent swung round, and saw the expression on Stewart's face.

'You know her Brent, don't you? You know Analee. You've met her before?'

Brent said nothing, turned away as though he had hardly heard.

'She could ride well,' he murmured, 'we know not which

direction she may have taken. Aye . . .' he looked despairingly at Stewart. 'She is well away by now.'

'You *did* know her, Brent?'

'Aye.' Brent looked towards the distant hills obscured by the dark.

'There was talk of gypsies when you were injured . . .'

'Yes.'

Brent met his cousin's gaze. What was the use of concealment now?

'She came here to see *you*?'

'No! T'was pure chance. I tell you I had forgotten about her. The memory of her was knocked out of my head by the blow. I swear to you Stewart I never recalled Analee again until today. I fell in love with Mary and wanted to marry her. And then today I saw Analee in the corridor. I thought at first she was a ghost and then, suddenly, I remembered. I remembered everything.'

Stewart was staring grimly at his cousin trying to suppress the contempt he felt about him.

'It *is* true what they say about you, Brent. You are an incorrigible womanizer. It . . .'

'Pray spare me, cousin, your thoughts on this matter,' Brent said wearily. 'It is not as you think.'

He turned to go back to the house when he felt himself seized violently by the shoulder. Stewart spun him around and pressed him against the wall. Brent could feel the prick of steel at his windpipe and, by the faint moonlight, see Stewart's face very close to his. He felt his warm breath and observed the whites of his eyes.

'I'll not have it, Brent – this womanizing. You marry my sister as soon as the priest comes or, by God, you won't live to see Analee or any other woman again. I promise you . . .'

Brent gazed unflinchingly into his cousin's eyes.

'Do not distress yourself, cousin. I will wed Mary tomorrow. I have given my word and I will do it. That was what Analee intended by leaving me. She wants me to do my duty and tells me so in her own way. I will wed Mary because I have given my word; but as for loving her . . . that I can never do!'

Stewart pricked Brent's flesh gently with his knife, so that a rivulet of blood went onto his shirt.

'You . . . will . . . love . . . Mary . . . and . . . make . . . her . . . happy. Do you hear Brent Delamain? You distress my sister, who has suffered so much already, and I will kill you with my own hand. You hear?'

Brent said nothing. He was not afraid of Stewart. Indeed his knife could have provided an end to his ills, for he no longer felt like living. With Analee gone he wished death would come soon.

Mary lay quietly in the bed not knowing whether Brent slept or not. She stared into the dark and tried to understand; to lie with a man and yet not with him. She knew this was not what had been meant by marriage; what had been promised her by Brent in the chapel that morning: 'With my body I thee worship.'

What had happened to Brent? What had come between them? Ever since the gypsy had left, Brent had not been the same as before. Yet he swore he didn't know her. Mary didn't know whether to believe him or not. Only that his attitude had changed after he had entered the house, and soon afterwards Analee and her companion had apparently left. Had she cast a spell on the house? Had she been a witch? To bring more evil and misery to the Allonby family?

They had gone through the ceremony, through the family meal afterwards, with a stiffness and formality that was so different to what Mary had dreamed would be the case. Her ardent wooer had become like a man who walked in a dream.

'Brent. Are you asleep?'

'No.'

'If it is not the gypsy, is it that you did not want to be tied down? Did not want to marry me after all?'

'No.'

He groped for her hand in the dark. He wanted to love her, to keep his promise to her; but all he could think of was the tilt of the proud gypsy head, the gleam in the dark eyes. When he'd looked at his bride it was to see again a cousin, a familial, not a mistress. Someone he wanted to protect and love but could not adore as he adored Analee. He didn't want to sink his flesh into hers and make her his as he did Analee. He had tried but he couldn't do it.

He had lain upon her and kissed her and tried to desire her and to be a husband to her, but it hadn't happened. He had felt her flesh stirring, quivering under his, her legs open with anticipation, her back arched for him . . .

It had been terrible. Terrible for him and terrible for Mary. She had felt humiliated and unwanted, spurned by her husband, her lover, unable to arouse him. He had given up and, instead, had taken her tenderly in his arms trying to soothe her weeping, explain to her that sometimes it didn't happen. It was not always possible for a man to behave in that way; if he was tired, or upset . . .

But still she couldn't understand. She didn't know that his mind was miles away galloping from Furness Grange – whither? To Keswick or Borrowdale, or Carlisle, or South to Windermere? How could he know which way she had gone? And why, why, hadn't she spoken to him, just one last time?

In the dark he was aware that Mary had started to weep again, her face pressed into the pillow. He yearned to take her as she wanted, just to soothe her, to please her; but he could not. He let his hand caress her breasts, feel her slim waist, her rounded thighs, the cavern between her legs . . . all things that in the past would have been enough to drive him mad with desire. He would have mounted the maid and ravished her ten times over. But nothing happened.

It was the first time he had failed a woman, let alone such a nubile desirable one, lying by his side. Mary stopped weeping while Brent's hands ran over her; she turned her mouth to his to kiss, her slender body quivering with desire. She held her breath, hoping that . . .

His hands ceased their exploration and she was aware that he leaned over her in the dark his face gazing down on hers, his expression abject. He was teasing her, tormenting her! She flung herself on her face and, pressing it into the pillow, gave herself once more to a torrent of silent weeping . . . for she did not want her sorrow, her shame, to be known through the house.

'It will be all right tomorrow,' Brent whispered, and he tenderly stroked her wet face.

How could she know that the fault did not lie with her or her beautiful body? That he, Brent Delamain, had been bewitched by a gypsy?

14

Stewart Allonby looked into the face of his cousin Emma and remembered the gypsy's spell. But although Emma's eyes were bright and welcoming there was no expression in them of love such as Stewart had half hoped to see. It was too fanciful. And yet he had done as the gyspy had bidden him and put his blood on one side of a leaf then on another, repeating their names. Then he had cast the leaf on the water and watched it float towards Keswick.

How long ago it seemed, that foolish day in late September when he had gone stealthily to the water's edge to practise the magic love rite prescribed by the gyspy. As he looked at Emma he realized that, despite its foolishness, he had hoped that in the intervening month the magic had had time to work. Then as he looked he smiled at her, aware of his folly. Emma, who always found her Allonby cousin very worthy but dull, was unexpectedly intrigued by the smile and wondered if, after all, he were maybe not as dull as she had supposed. She'd never noticed it before – perhaps because one was conditioned to think of the Allonbys as poor, unsuccessful and not likely to enhance the fortunes or awake the emotions of a pretty young girl.

Unlike many of the young men she had met recently who had pale complexions, well-kept hands and elegant bodies fitted out in the latest fashion, whose hair was concealed in a light periwig or who, if they wore their own, had it beautifully waved about their ears, Stewart Allonby's body was thick-set and sturdy and his face browned by exposure to the elements. He was a smaller, stockier version of her brother Brent. Suddenly Emma thought he was attractive. Really the elegant young men wearied her with their small talk and self-absorption. They danced beautifully and they were not lacking in wit or fine manners, but . . .

'How well you look, Stewart.'

Stewart had seen the change in Emma's expression from a rather bored indifference to a quickening of interest and involuntarily preened himself, realizing that she was looking at him in a more intimate and particular kind of way to the one he was used to.

'And you Emma, a young lady now. Changed since I saw you last, a year ago I think.'

'Yes, it was when we came over to Furness for the betrothal of Brent and Mary. How sorry I was to miss the wedding; but it was so sudden and I was in London staying with Henrietta's parents. How go my brother and his wife?'

'Well . . .' Stewart began guardedly; but Emma was not deceived by the inflection in his voice.

'You seem uncertain.'

'Well, they are in Whitehaven. After the wedding Brent and Mary left for the coast where Brent works for Ambrose Rigg. I reason they are well enough.'

Emma decided that Stewart's lack of enthusiasm was due perhaps to shyness in discussing the relationship of a newly married couple. On the other hand the Allonby brothers had never really approved of Brent. Had they not insisted on a long courtship so that he could prove himself worthy?

Stewart had arrived at Delamain Castle earlier in the day on his way to Carlisle to join the Prince. Because of the nature of his mission Stewart had realized it was unwise to stop over at Delamain, but the presence of Emma was too much of a draw as he made his way towards the city where the Prince was expected any day.

Now he was glad he had come; something in Emma *had* changed towards him. And she was a beauty, grown more imperious perhaps, taller certainly and, yes, voluptuous, why not admit it? Stewart was no connoisseur of women, but to him Emma Delamain outshone any of his acquaintance. But what chance had he got, an impoverished first cousin? A Catholic, a Royalist? Her brother would be looking for a finer match for his only sister than Stewart Allonby. The only chance was a Royalist victory . . . *then* let George see which way the wind blew.

It was nearly dusk and servants were running through the castle lighting candles and fixing lights in brackets on the walls. From the kitchen came the smell of roast meat and Stewart realized that he was hungry, having left Keswick at dawn. He had yet to meet George and his wife. The bailiff had greeted him on his arrival at the castle and given him a room in the wing reserved for guests. His first thought had been to stay with his aunt, but she was not prepared for him and he felt awkward intruding on her hospitality.

Now Emma had entered the drawing room just as he was standing admiring the view from the window of rolling dales and tree-covered hills. Why as far as the eye could see the land belonged to the Delamains and George grew more prosperous and important every day.

'You have not met my sister-in-law have you, Stewart?' Emma said as the drawing-room door opened and a woman of medium height stood looking at Stewart in some surprise.

'Henrietta, may I present our cousin Stewart Allonby? Stewart, Lady Delamain.'

George's wife. Well, she was no beauty as he'd heard; distinctly plain, Stewart thought, as she advanced slowly into the room and gave him her hand. She was plump, not comely but fat. Decidedly fat and because of the fashionable dress she was wearing, which allowed a fair amount of décollatage, her short neck and round stumpy head reminded him of a squat toadstool. In some ways she had a good face, large green eyes and a retroussé nose; but her mouth was small and pursed, as she looked at him now, into a tight little bow as though she did not altogether approve of what she saw. No smile lightened her features as he bowed to kiss her hand; instead he was aware of her bright eyes calculatedly appraising him.

'Stewart Allonby,' she said at last. 'Emma's mother's side of the family. She is dining with us tonight and will be joining us shortly. George did you know to expect your cousin, dearest?'

George Delamain strode into the room and also paused in some astonishment at the sight of his cousin; an unwelcome sight.

'This is unexpected, cousin,' George said, not trying to conceal his displeasure. 'Did you send word of your intention to honour us with your company?'

'No, George. I was riding to Penrith when I realized I should not get there before nightfall, so I took the liberty of begging your hospitality.'

'Penrith?' George said sharply. 'Pray, have you business in Penrith?'

'Yes, cousin. I am buying saplings for reafforestation of our woods.'

'Ah,' George looked instantly suspicious. Everyone knew of the impending invasion of England by the Prince. He himself was taking a leading part in the local militia and permitting them to train in his courtyard. 'Your business has nothing to do with that ruffian Charles Edward Stuart?'

Stewart, who found it almost impossible to dissemble or conceal his true feelings, had expected this question from his cousin and knew that on this occasion it was essential to lie.

'How can that be, George? His Highness as far as I know abides in Scotland.'

'His *Highness* indeed! Scoundrel is what he is, with a price of £30,000 on his head.'

'And I believe he put the same price on the Hanoverian Elector,' Stewart said mildly. 'You know, George, we differ . . .'

'Aye and a mighty difference it is,' George said threateningly. 'You realize you could be hanged for joining the rebels? Like your uncle in the '15. I'll wager you are hell bent on the same path Stewart Allonby.'

'You should not discuss this,' a tired voice said in the background. 'When families foregather it should be in friendship not enmity.'

Stewart turned to greet his aunt who, he thought, had aged in the past year. Her hair was now almost completely white and she walked with difficulty. He knew she was not old and her appearance distressed him.

'Aunt Susan,' he went up to her and kissed first her hand and then her cheek.

'Do you bring news?'

She took a chair and gazed eagerly up at Stewart.

'News?' He was aghast, did she imagine they could openly discuss the Prince in this house? She saw his bewilderment and nodded understandingly.

'Of Brent and Mary.'

'Oh . . . No. I have not seen them since the wedding.'

'But have you heard how they are? Sarah must write, someone must keep in touch. Certainly Brent does not write to me, his own mother.'

'I imagine he has a lot on his mind,' George said darkly. 'I hear he is working hard for his wife's brother-in-law. A fishing hand!

Imagine, Henrietta, did you think to marry into a family where your brother-in-law worked on the deck of a fishing smack!'

Henrietta tittered at her husband.

'Thank heaven you have your own pursuits dearest, or I wager I would not be received at court.'

Sir George and Lady Delamain giggled together, apparently unaware that those in the room were unamused by their derision of another member of the family.

Stewart however was relieved. This scorn of Brent seemed to indicate that George did not really know what Brent was up to. So far the secret had remained safe.

'I daresay Brent would not distress you ma'am if you met him,' Stewart said stiffly. 'You would not find him unworthy as a brother-in-law.'

'Well *that's* as maybe,' George said extending an arm. 'Mother, shall we dine? Stewart would you give your arm to my wife? Emma, would you follow us?'

The little procession walked formally to the dining room where, as always, George Delamin kept a good board and Stewart ate well and appreciatively. His mind, however, was not so much on his food as to be indifferent to the glances over the table of his young cousin. Could it be that the gypsy's spell had worked? No it was absurd; but there she was glancing at him under her lashes and every time he looked directly at her the smile she gave him was, at the very least, provocative.

Stewart began to feel a painful constriction in his chest. Was it possible that the beautiful, worldly Emma Delamain, surrounded as she was by eager young men with fortunes and fine manners, could be tilting her bonnet, so to speak, at him?

Stewart had always been aware of the irony that he and his sister loved their Delamain cousins and that that love was not returned by them, until Brent had had a change of heart and declared for Mary. Stewart's thoughts grew sober. But *had* he made Mary happy? There had been nothing joyous about the couple after their wedding, and John had sworn that he'd heard tears from the room of the newly marrieds, not just once, but night after night until they left.

John had even gone so far as to draw Mary on one side and ask if she were happy, if aught was amiss? But, although seeming to him

225

on the verge of tears, she had vigorously denied that she was anything but blissfully happy. Yet her pale face and lustreless air had not deceived John, or Stewart who more than likely knew the reason for it. He was glad to see them go. Brent was too valuable to the Cause for Stewart to want to have to carry out his threat.

George talked all the time at dinner about his role in the local militia of which he was commander and what they would do to the Jacobites should they so much as see the whites of their eyes. His wife listened to him with approval but the rest of the family were silent. Emma in particular had become contemptuous of George. She thought he took the attitude he did to curry favour with Lord Dacre and his cronies. She had seen too much of their activities in London to feel any admiration for them. To her, half Allonby that she was, there was something stirring about the stories told of Prince Charles. How he had landed with but seven old and ailing men and how, in a matter of weeks, he had captured the hearts of almost every man in Scotland – well maybe not every man, but certainly every woman. Stories had travelled to London about the charm of the Prince, his handsome looks and kingly bearing so different from the bumptious, overweight Hanoverians. All the women were in love with him, so much so that some even lured the allegiances of their husbands and forced them to declare for the Prince. There were even reports of husbands and wives being split and supporting different sides.

Emma Delamain had returned north a dissatisfied girl, aware that there was more to life than pretty manners and dancing feet. The scorn heaped upon the Stuarts by her young friends and admirers had angered her. Had not Robert Allonby perished on the scaffold? Guy Delamain, her own father, had cared enough to live abroad as a wearied impoverished exile and die for the Cause. And there were her Allonby cousins, her own brothers Brent and Tom . . . all hardy, robust supporters of the Stuarts. Beside them her friends looked foppish, their ideas superficial and their hopes frankly mercenary and self-centred.

Henrietta Dacre, her sister-in-law, typified everything that Emma had grown to dislike about London society and the Hanoverian court. She considered her empty-headed, mean-minded and selfish. She and Emma shared not the slightest thing

226

in common and here she was casting derogatory glances at Stewart, eyeing him with contempt.

Stewart had unexpectedly appeared to Emma, meeting him again after a year, in an entirely new light. She could see how angry he was as George and Henrietta between them dominated the talk with their hatred of the Stuarts, their scorn for the Cause; how the muscles of his jaw worked and his eyes smouldered. Suddenly Emma was afraid for Stewart. What was his purpose in Penrith?

She drew him aside afterwards in the drawing-room as Henrietta prepared to play the piano for them and entertain them with some of her excruciating songs, boringly rendered in a monotonous voice. George sat beside his mother eyeing indulgently the talented little wife of whom he was growing so unexpectedly fond. True she was ugly and had apparently little to offer in the way of charm, but in the dark between the sheets she was just another woman's body and a surprisingly accommodating one at that. Although George still kept a mistress in London he had begun to see less of her, and even to prefer the physical comforts provided by his own enterprising wife.

'Do you really go to buy wood?' Emma whispered to Stewart who sat next to her some distance away from her mother.

'Why, do you think I do not?'

Stewart was intrigued by his cousin's question. Could it be . . . He turned and looked at her and his heart missed a beat. Could it be that she *pretended* to be attracted by him, to have changed her mind so as to draw information from him? George and Emma had always been considered by the Allonbys to have much in common, certainly as far as Hanoverian sympathies were concerned.

On the other hand Emma had always been close to her mother. Would she really betray her mother's family? As though wanting to prise the truth from her he leaned his face closer to hers and his eyes met hers, daring her to flinch. Emma regarded him steadily, aware of his warm breath close to her face, the hard rugged masculinity of his sun-bronzed face.

'I am not of the mind of my brother George in case you thought it. *Or* my sister-in-law. A season in London would have changed me if I ever had been. They think of nothing but trivialities. Besides I hear the Prince is *so* handsome.' As she dimpled

227

flirtatiously Stewart realized that he loved Emma Delamain, truly and deeply. It was not something that was just occasioned by her youth or beauty; it would not pass.

'Aye, that's what's won you is it?'

Emma clasped her hands, her shining eyes reflecting the attitude of half if not more of the women in the kingdom.

'Oh, is he not *remarkable*? He is so young, about your age Stewart, and yet he controls an army. He must succeed must he not?'

'Aye, if I have aught to do wi' it.'

'Then you are going to join him?'

'You knew it already?'

'I guessed it. I guessed you would not pass this way merely to purchase wood! I know you, Stewart Allonby. You know our brother Tom is part of the entourage of the Prince?'

'Yes, I have heard from Tom directly.'

'That is why my mother is so worn, so pale. She thinks of Brent and Tom, and you and John. She expects you all to be killed.'

'But why should *we* fail? Why not George?'

Emma looked over to where George sat lounging beside their mother, his legs stretched before him, one arm draped across the back of the sofa.

'There is something about George that is indestructible, don't you think?'

Stewart smiled. Looking at George, Emma's words seemed very apt.

'George maybe, but not what he stands for.'

'Can I come with you?'

'To Carlisle?'

'To wherever you are going to meet the Prince.'

'Of course not dear girl! It is fraught with danger at this instant.'

'But in Perth and Edinburgh he gave balls and soirées.'

'Not in Carlisle or Lancaster. Here it will be business until he reaches London.'

'Oh, is it possible Stewart?'

'Of course, it's possible. It will happen.'

Suddenly Henrietta's singing was interrupted by the arrival of a liveried servant who whispered into her ear. She got up closing the music with a flutter and hurried over to her husband.

'George! It is my cousin who has arrived unexpectedly. George go quickly to welcome him; he awaits in the hall.'

But before George had time to move the door was again thrown open hurriedly by a servant and a tall well-built man resplendent in his military uniform strode into the room, his hands extended.

'Henrietta!'

'Angus.'

The small woman was scooped up by the stranger who embraced her and then turned to survey the room with a quizzing glass.

'George, dearest, may I present my cousin the Marquess of Falconer.' George bowed and shook the proffered hand.

'Delighted, my lord. Lord Dacre was only telling me recently of your exploits in France with his Grace the Duke of Cumberland.'

'And it is on the Duke's business that I am here, Sir George. I am part of an advance party to meet the rebels at the border, if they do not take us by surprise and get there before we are ready. His Grace will stop with Lord Lonsdale at Lowther Castle, but I sought leave to find my quarters with you, dear cousin, if you so permit it.' He bowed towards Henrietta.

'Oh Angus, 'tis an honour. May I present my sister-in-law Emma and my husband's first cousin Stewart Allonby.'

Lord Falconer strode across and kissed Emma's hand, pausing as he raised his head to stare boldly into her eyes. What she saw did not displease her. The Marquess was a man in the Allonby mould, tall and broad but, unlike them, very dark and swarthy with a long rather beaked nose, a firm broad mouth and a deeply cleft chin which jutted at a determined angle – a man used to commanding and being obeyed. He wore no periwig and his thick black hair was tied by a ribbon at the nape of his neck, some straying curls falling over his high forehead to give him an air of brooding authority.

His eyes were of a curious brown-green, like those of his cousin Henrietta, but otherwise he did not resemble her at all, being so startlingly handsome, whereas she was small and very plain. He wore the red uniform of a Colonel with a row of medals, and a long sword at his waist touched the top of his shining black boots.

She liked everything about him except that he was a member of the Duke of Cumberland's army.

'Ma'am,' Lord Falconer rose and turned to Stewart, bowed and took his hand.

'Mr?'

'Allonby,' Stewart said clearly. 'Allonby of Furness.'

'Ah. I think I recall the name,' the Marquess's eyes narrowed. ''Tis well known I believe, in *certain* circles Mr Allonby.'

'Indeed, sir. I believe it is.'

'But in this house you are obviously of the same opinion as your cousin.'

'It is so my lord,' George said angrily, strolling over. 'In this house my cousin is a gentleman, a farmer and noises no political opinions abroad at all.'

'And has Mr Allonby any *purpose* in being here?' his lordship said swinging his quizzing glass and looking appreciatively at Emma again.

'What purpose other than to see my cousin?'

'I hear the Pretender is not far from the border. Know you aught about this?'

'Nothing, my lord.'

'Ah, 'tis well.' The Marquess turned to Henrietta and smiled. 'I know you would not harbour traitors under your roof, my dear. Is there anything for me to eat?'

'Oh, Angus, of course. It will be ordered already.'

'I have ridden hard all day. My men are downstairs being attended to, I believe, in the kitchen. Tomorrow I must ride on, and pray where do you go to Mr Allonby?'

'Penrith,' Stewart said slowly. 'I am buying wood saplings for my forests around Lake Derwentwater.'

'Ah, I shall be in the opposite direction I fear. I have completed my reconnoitre of the border and go back to His Grace who has been recalled from the south to take his position up here. I saw naught to alert me on the Scottish border yet, and Carlisle is very solidly for His Majesty. I have my home on the border,' Lord Falconer explained to Emma who was clearly bedazzled by this splendid creature in his gleaming uniform.

'Your dinner is ready, my lord,' a servant bowed and the Marquess, with a wave, took his cousin's arm and left the room followed by George. For some moments Susan Delamain sat gazing after them until she was joined by Emma and Stewart.

'So that is the Marquess of Falconer. I have heard much about him. He is a very famous, very fierce soldier, known as the Falcon after his family's emblem which is the bird of prey. See, his beaked nose? They say he swoops on his enemies, and once he has his claws on them will not let them go. He is much feared, and hated by some. I think he will have no truck with our Prince and his army . . .'

'Not even the Falcon will rout them,' Stewart said bitterly. 'I too have heard how his lordship is called; but I believe there is more substance in the name than his deeds.'

Susan Delamain shook her head and her hand plucked worriedly at the silk of her dress, 'That is not what I hear. He has spent many years abroad fighting the French. 'Tis where he got his nickname, and earned it too by all accounts.'

Emma shivered.

'He is certainly very awe-inspiring. Why, I think he is vaster than any of the men in our family and they are all good broad, hulking fellows. What a pity he favours the Hanoverians and not our side. I hear he is a disinterested politician; more keen on his soldierly duties, but, yes, a convinced Hanoverian.'

'Enough of the Falcon. I must be gone before dawn,' Stewart said, 'for I am to proceed as soon as I can to Carlisle. It is true Aunt, Emma . . .' Stewart paused, and his voice dropped to a whisper, 'that the Prince marches towards England and I go to join him.'

Carlisle surrendered to Prince Charles Edward on 14 November after some days of siege. The inhabitants of the town had thought themselves surrounded by a large army instead of a few thousand men, and also they were in mortal terror of the Highlanders whose reputation for savagery had preceded them. But once inside, the Highlanders surprised everyone by the mildness of their manners and the Prince, as usual, charmed the masses with his fair-mindedness and sense of justice.

On arrival at Carlisle Stewart Allonby had noticed the siege at the Penrith Gate and watched it in the fog and damp along with the rest. But, on hearing that the Prince was at Brampton seven miles away awaiting an encounter with General Wade's army, he rode there and at once encountered his cousin Tom in the throng surrounding the Prince.

Tom looked gaunt and tired, there were deep shadows under his eyes and his cheeks were cavernous. He immediately asked for news of Brent.

'He is to join us here, as I understand it, as soon as he has made rendezvous with Lord Derwentwater who is bringing arms from France. The enemy is already entrenched in Whitehaven with big cannon pointing over the sea.'

'Aye. I wonder if Brent would be better off where he is – the supplies are vital.'

'I think Brent would not stay. He yearns to fight with the Prince.'

'Then he will meet us when we have taken Carlisle. Let me take you to his Highness.'

Stewart could see the crowd in the distance gathered around the Prince who was preparing to dine but at that point a commotion began in front of the Prince's tent and it was announced that a deputation had arrived from Carlisle to treat with his Highness for surrender. Stewart's interview was postponed and the following day Charles Edward Stuart entered Carlisle and immediately set to making plans with his commanders for the occupation of England.

From the very first Stewart was aware of discord in the Prince's ranks. There were so many Highland companies swearing different allegiances that their rivalry seemed more important than the Cause. Many of the Highlanders had been reluctant to cross the border and had returned to their homes, and those who had forded the River Esk had turned as a man and pointed their swords towards their homeland when they reached the English side. But, more important and damaging, was the fact that the Prince was quarrelling with the commander of half of his Army, Lord George Murray, who was reported to have offered his resignation which the Prince had accepted.

The Duke of Perth was now in sole command of the Army, but the restlessness continued down the ranks to the foot soldiers, many of whom still wanted to go home. Tom told how many commanders were putting pressure on the Prince to reinstate Lord George and eventually this was done, but permanent rancour remained between the Prince and his commander and sustained the unease among the men.

Thus instead of being elated Stewart was depressed and it was not until Brent arrived the following day that he began to take heart again.

For Brent this was the culmination of his life, the purpose for which he felt he had been born. He had ridden hard from Cockermouth where he had left Mary in the care of her sister and now here he was, the bustle and excitement of the Jacobite Army about him at last. As soon as he'd heard that the Prince had crossed the border he reminded Ambrose Rigg of their bargain and had put away his sailor's clothes. The very sight of Brent's rapturous face cheered Stewart and the two cousins embraced.

'Where is Tom?'

'He is with the Duke of Perth. The Prince I learn is not too happy to be attended by a Catholic clergyman; he has to maintain the image of religious indifference because of the possibility he may come to the throne.'

'But the Prince *is* a Catholic!'

'Aye; but 'tis not political to mention religion until King James is established in London. How goes it with Mary, Brent, and Sarah?'

Stewart avoided looking at Brent as he asked him and turned to the window of his lodgings overlooking market street. Their host was a friend of the Allonbys and his house had been the place appointed for Stewart and Brent to meet.

'They do well enough, anxious for the Cause.'

'And Mary is . . . happy?'

'I think so, why should she not be?'

Stewart did not reply for, at that moment the door burst open and Tom wrapped his arms round his younger brother.

'Oh, Brent 'tis good to see you. I thought it would never happen. All the months we plotted and planned. How is the leg?'

'It troubles me hardly at all. I have had many months at sea and this has toughened my sinews.'

'And your wife? A married man, Brent!'

'Aye.'

Tom looked searchingly at Brent, aware of the way he avoided his eyes. He glanced at Stewart, who, too, was looking away. All was not well there. The marriage had surprised Tom who knew the unstable romantic nature of his brother. Well, to all appearances, it had not altered him.

'Come, I will take you to the Prince. He is to have you as part of his very own company.'

* * *

The Prince had just finished a council of war and looked preoccupied as Brent and Stewart were led into his presence.

'Your Royal Highness may I present my brother, Brent Delamain and my cousin, Stewart Allonby – a family well known to your Royal Highness.' The three men bowed and a smile appeared on the Prince's tired face.

'Indeed it is. The name Delamain is well known to me and you, sir, are well called after my own, Stewart.'

'Your Royal Highness.'

Stewart bowed low, too overcome to speak. There was indeed a magic about the Prince; to be in his presence was to be aware of something awesome and mysterious. The Prince, he noted, was tall and slim, his face round and brown from his exposure to all kinds of weather. He had a small but full mouth and lively eyes. Altogether he was very well proportioned and his appeal to the ladies was easy to discern. But he also inspired fierce loyalty in his men, and this was because of his regal manner combined with an easygoing informality that seemed to get the best out of them. The Prince lived as his men, did as they did and he was always cheerful and courteous and imbued with an optimistic and resolute air that it was impossible not to be carried away by.

'You are to serve in my company, as your brother may have told you, both as lieutenants. I am grateful to you, Mr Delamain, for the service you have rendered providing arms for us. Your work is appreciated by me.'

'My honour, your Royal Highness.'

'Thank you gentlemen, and God remain with us.'

The Prince looked preoccupied again and, turning from them, was immediately surrounded by his commanders.

'They are discussing what to do next,' Tom whispered as they left the audience chamber. 'The enemy are approaching on all sides.'

'God grant I get my sword at them,' Stewart growled, his patriotism kindled anew by the encounter with his Prince. 'Let us harry them ahead of us to London.'

But although the Army began its march south almost at once there was no harrying to be done, no encounter with the enemy who were always to one side or the other, or ahead. The Duke of

Cumberland himself blocked their path to London, and the Prince eventually halted at Derby.

There he had to take the hard and, to him, indefensible decision to retreat. There were three Hanoverian armies poised to attack his small numbers. There was no sign of the massive rising he had expected in England nor of the French landing promised by his brother Henry. The Prince had done everything in his power to persuade his commanders to go on, but all had voted against him. They thought to continue would mean annihilation of the Jacobite Army and, with it, the Jacobite Cause. Better to retreat and try again. Yet only Charles, possibly, knew the full importance of what they had decided as on 6 December 1745 the Army started to go back the way it had come so triumphantly and with such hope.

For Brent and Stewart it was a bitter moment when they were told, with their fellow officers, in advance of the men, that they were going backwards rather than forwards. Orders to move had been given at first light and it was not until they were some miles north of Derby that the rest of the army realized what had happened. The officers were hard put to explain to the men, so near to London, the reason for the retreat and the day was spent in recriminations and expressions of discontent.

But the worst thing was the way the whole complexion of the operation changed, even the character of the Prince. From being so cheerful and always in the vanguard he now sulked and kept behind. The mood of the population in the countryside through which they had marched victoriously only a few days before changed quickly to hostility, and the Highlanders who had held themselves hitherto in commendable restraint now set to pillaging, looting and despoiling everything in their path.

To the English officers like Brent and Stewart and others who had joined them – Manchester had provided a complete regiment – it was a horrible sight to see these men, half savages some of them, reverting to their former reputation. And the Prince, although he knew what was afoot, did nothing to try and stop them. Lord George Murray did all he could to keep the Army together but his fellow commander, the Duke of Perth, was now a sick man and the officers discontented and dispirited.

Stewart and Brent who had not once been engaged in battle or even a skirmish, who had not been part of the force that so triumphantly conquered Scotland, felt this disillusion as much if not more than most. Having spent such a large part of their lives preparing for this event it was now unbearable to see it all founder without exchanging a single blow against the enemy. It was galling; it was humiliating.

'They say we will regroup in Scotland,' Brent said one night as they tried to sleep, having been pursued out of Manchester by a hostile crowd. What was more they knew that General Oglethorpe's army, sent ahead by the Duke of Cumberland to harry them, was not far behind.

'Nay, we are done for,' Stewart sighed. He felt ill and coughed frequently. The weather was terrible; it was cold and it never stopped raining. There was not enough to eat and, now that the local people had turned against them, nowhere warm to lay their heads at night.

'Will you leave the Army when we reach Carlisle?'

'No. I'll stay to the bitter end. But we are done for Brent. The Stuarts are finished.'

'Hush,' Brent looked anxiously around though it was dark, 'people will hear you. You will be split in half by a claymore as you sleep.'

'They know. Everyone knows. The Prince knows. It was ill planned this expedition. Five thousand men in all and they say in *each* of the Hanoverian armies awaiting us there were 30,000 men. In each. The country has not risen to the Stuarts.'

'Aye, that is the reason,' Tom said. 'That is the real reason. People are too content as they are. They do not want change; they do not want the Stuarts and the Catholic church back again.'

They had hardly seen Tom. He spent time tending the sick or cheering the faint-hearted. But now as he sat with them, trying like them to keep warm against the bitter night, he nodded.

'That is the truth. The English people will not tolerate Catholicism. It is too foreign to them; it smacks of the French and the arbitrary rule of James I and Charles I. They hate the Pope and that is that. The Stuarts have become alien to them and we did not realize it. We were too distant and our spies did not rightly detect the mood of the people.'

'What will you do Tom?'

'Oh, stay to the bitter end, like you; but we are done for, I agree.'

From Preston on 11 December Charles despatched the Duke of Perth to try and rally forces in Scotland. The Duke was mortally sick and had to travel by coach. Charles announced that he would stay in Preston and await reinforcements from Scotland; but the hooves of General Oglethorpe's soldiers could almost be heard outside the walls, and the dispirited Jacobite army took refuge in Lancaster.

Charles vainly tried to make a stand there to assure people he was merely retiring and not fleeing, but the Duke of Cumberland was said to have arrived in Wigan with 1000 cavalry. Charles set off for Kendal and then more trouble began as the men had difficulty negotiating the heavy ammunition carts on the steep hills in the terrible relentless weather. Charles and Lord George were at loggerheads again. The Prince had gone ahead and peremptorily ordered Lord George not to leave anything behind, not even a cannon-ball. His lordship, who brought up the rear, was said to be angered by this command being aware of the temper of his men and the state of their health. Disease was rampant. In the end he gave his soldiers sixpence a head to carry the cannon-balls over Shap. It was at this point that Brent and Stewart were split up, Stewart going ahead to join the Prince in Penrith and Brent staying behind with Lord George Murray and the rearguard. And it was here that the first chance of action came, unexpectedly, at Clifton near Penrith.

All day Lord George Murray had been aware of enemy activity. They were in the neighbourhood of Lowther Castle and knew that the Duke of Cumberland was expected there. Lord George sent to the Prince at Penrith to ask for assitance, but Charles sent word that he was proceeding to Carlisle and Lord George should follow him there.

Brent could see the distress on Lord George's face at the latest difference between the Prince and his commander. Lord George was a tall robust man, legendary for his bravery; but the weeks of marching, the indecision and unrest had wearied him. He was said to be aloof and haughty, to dislike receiving orders but now his face looked worn and his uniform was bespattered with mud like

237

everyone elses'. The rain came down in a seemingly endless stream and the news of the enemy's whereabouts was conflicting. Some said they were a cannonshot away on Clifton Moor drawn up in two lines, and others said they had dispersed and were heading towards Penrith after the Prince.

As night fell Brent, who had remained close by Lord George, taking his commands and issuing them down the line, was sure that they would not engage the enemy who could now clearly be seen on the moorside. Some dragoons dismounted and came down the hill ready for action, their swords drawn. Lord George conversed closely with Colonel Cluny MacPherson, then a signal was given to the men to align themselves in the shelter of a hedge. Brent lay shivering on the ground, listening to the exchange of gunfire, his clothes sodden, his eyes caked with mud. He gripped his sword in his hand and prayed to God, aware of the blood pounding in his head. The smell of battle was all around and he knew for sure that for the first time he would engage the enemy.

At a signal from Colonel Macpherson the Highlanders from his clan uttered their blood-curdling cry that was said by some to freeze the hearts of an enemy before battle commenced, to frighten them to death in advance. With one accord the force leapt over the hedge and fell on the dragoons who, taken completely by surprise despite their drawn swords, put up little resistance.

Brent could hardly see for the rain and the dusk that had fallen so quickly. The blade of his broadsword flashed about him and as he felt it encounter solid flesh he experienced a feeling not of pity for his victim, but of exultation that at last he was drawing blood for the Cause. Maybe after all the tide would turn; maybe . . .

Suddenly Brent felt a stab of pain in his arm and was aware that he had been hit. He put his hand in the spot and felt it warm with blood; but, though painful, the arm was still usable, and he continued advancing plunging his good broadsword to the right and to the left, echoing the savage cries of the Highlanders.

The rain began to lessen and, in the intermittent moonlight which appeared through the clouds, Brent could see that the enemy, outnumbered and terrified by the ferocity of the Highlanders were in flight.

Around them on the sloping moorside the dead and wounded

lay, men of both sides, but many more dragoons than Jacobites. The stench of sweat and blood engendered even by the brief skirmish was overwhelming and the cries of the injured pitiful to hear. The broadswords did terrible damage, limbs and heads were hacked off and bodies disembowelled.

Yet in all the carnage, his own arm bleeding freely, his stained sword still in his hand Brent felt a joyous, fierce elation. The fact that here were dead men who moments before had lived and breathed disturbed him not at all.

As the retreat sounded he saw the Highlanders creep over the scrub putting the injured enemy unceremoniously to the sword and moving their own wounded to the shelter of the hedge. Brent placed his sword on the ground and, bending down, tore the shirt from the still warm body of a dragoon and began to bind his wound with it. The blood would not staunch and the bandage was soaked. But Brent did not mind. He had been bloodied in battle; he had killed or maybe wounded fellow men. He was no more a talker, a plotter. He was a doer, a man of action. This was a war and he was a soldier, and war was about valour and courage and indifference to death.

Brent knew that life and his attitude to it could never be the same again. More than all the riding, fencing and athletics, all the womanizing, smuggling and heaving huge smelly barrels of fish in rough seas, the skirmish at Clifton had made him a man.

15

Analee opened her eyes and saw it was dawn. Usually birdsong awakened her, but this day it seemed as though the very birds themselves were too chilled to warble. Nelly still lay asleep pressed up against her for warmth, but even in her sleep her slender frame shook with cold. They had found a large overhanging hill beneath whose shelter they had bedded down for the night, making a screen with loose stones and branches to protect them from the wind and rain.

In all her years on the road Analee never remembered such biting cold, such pitiless weather. And the countryside was alive with other dangers; wandering soldiers who had deserted from the Jacobite ranks and who told of disease and defeat. But not only this; they also had to combat the hostility of the population who had so readily turned against them once the Prince's cause was lost.

Some were trying to make their way to Scotland, others to slink back to their Lakeland homes before the terror that was sure to follow the ultimate Jacobite defeat which they knew could not be long delayed. The men were hungry and savage. Rape as well as looting was on their minds as Analee well knew, as she and Nelly hid in a ditch or under the bare hedgerows as the angry, hungry soldiers passed by. Since the Prince had crossed the border and war had been on everyone's mind there was only one thought which drove her on: to reach the Buckland camp which lay directly in the Army's route, to see her baby safe.

For Morella was all Analee felt she had in the world now that she had lost Randal and given up Brent. For she could have had Brent; she knew it. It would have been so easy to have said 'yes', and to have slipped out of the house with him and ridden away. But the sight of the two lovers embracing in the grounds at the grange had decided her. Brent and Mary did love each other and they should have a chance to enjoy that love. It was shocking for Analee, dreaming as much of Brent as she had after leaving the camp, to see that it was *he* who was the betrothed, the object of Mary's love. And then it seemed inevitable – of course he had told her he had cousins in Derwentwater; the sick man nursed to health; the family likeness which she had perceived only too late . . .

. . . Until she saw him wait for her in the corridor and knew from his eyes that his love, his true love was not for Mary. It was still for her. It always would be; the gypsy in Analee knew that. But Mary whom in such a short time she had come to love and admire, who had suffered for so many years . . . to deny Mary that happiness would be evil and Analee had made up her mind and acted accordingly.

Many times she had regretted it as they tramped along the rough uneven paths to Carlisle or left the road altogether and climbed over the mountain ranges, either to shelter from the weather or the bands of marauding soldiers who passed by.

Her baby. Yes she was going back to get her. She should never have left her; that one comfort to her life, that sole memento of her love for the aristocratic *gadjo*. And how beautiful he'd looked that day with the shimmering lake in the background, tall and bronzed, with his fair hair turned golden in the sun and his massive frame . . . and his arms encircling another woman! It had been too much as she'd looked down and seen the tenderness of their embrace, the smile on Brent's face as he'd gazed into Mary's eyes. Analee knew that smile too . . .

No, she must put the memory from her mind. It was not intended; it was not to be. Besides this was a country at war and Brent had meant to go to the war too. What would happen to him and the Allonbys now that their glorious Prince was so near defeat?

Nelly opened her eyes and saw that, as usual, Analee was gazing at some distant spot on the horizon. Analee daydreamed a lot these days; her mind was always far away. There was a sadness in her that distressed Nelly, who loved her and wanted to protect her from the harshness of the world. She had begged her not to leave the *gadjo* when she had found him again, to think of herself, to take the happiness owed to her. But no. All Analee could think of was the joy of the young girl, Mary, when from her room she had seen Brent ride into the grounds; the tearful happiness of her brave young face turned trustingly upwards to his.

'I cannot build my life on destruction,' Analee had said turning

241

from the window; and that had been that. Nothing that Nelly could say, no arguments she could put forward, could convince Analee otherwise.

In a way it made Nelly love and admire Analee more. Such nobility, such sacrifice had convinced Nelly that Analee was more than a mere gypsy; she was someone very special, a queen among women. And she had understood Analee's reason for abandoning her plans to go to the coast and wanting to get back to her baby. Analee should never have given the baby up at all, never been forced to. Nelly could not easily forget the sight of Analee and the expression on her face as the baby suckled so contentedly at her breast.

Now Analee was pinched and cold, her thin bones stuck out from her rags; but her beautiful lustrous eyes remained the same and her body was still round enough to attract the men as they roamed about looking for plunder. There was something about the way Analee held her head as she walked; something disdainful yet provocative, and no man failed to turn his head or quicken his step, however leaden it had been, as he passed by.

Analee smiled at Nelly clinging to her against the cold.

'Come, let us start walking and get the blood going again. Today we should reach the camp.'

'We have been so long on the road and you keep saying that. How do you know this time for sure?'

'Because I know. There are more soldiers heading for the border and Carlisle is very near Scotland; besides, I recognize some of the landmarks.'

They had come a long way; a long roundabout way, since leaving Keswick. They had kept away from the road and skirted Skiddaw and the Lonscale Crags, Saddleback and Bannerdale by bridle paths. They had sight of the River Calder at Tarn Crags and then followed it, saying goodbye to the Lakeland mountains which had provided them with some hard climbs, but also given them shelter in its warm caves protected from the icy blasts of midwinter.

The valley of the Calder was flat, though lush pasture-land had afforded more food than the bleak high peaks over which they had come. But as she walked Analee would often glance back at those magical hills which grew smaller as, just before Carlisle, they reached the busy road which ran down to Penrith.

Analee got up and shook herself like a dog. It was hard to stand, as though her limbs had been petrified by the cold. Indeed she could hardly feel one leg at all and she shook it to make life return to it again. She still wondered that she and Nelly were alive, having slept out every night in this terrible winter except for the mountain caves and the barn they'd once shared with some soldiers. She wondered if they owed their lives to the fact that they had each other through the long cold nights?

Already there were one or two carts on the road, although it was not yet dawn, and groups of people mostly hurrying southwards. Analee and Nelly set off on their way north aware of the rumbling in their bellies and wondering when they would get something to eat. There were no berries at this time of year, and cold and damp had long deprived them of wild animals. Sometimes a family eating by the roadside would give them a crust; but this morning everyone seemed in too much of a hurry, people with carts and sometimes horses, seemingly laden with all their possessions, appeared to have no time to stop and share bread.

Analee was puzzled. As the morning advanced the numbers seemed to increase, only they were all going in one direction and she and Nelly in another. Finally she stopped by a group who had paused to try and straighten a crooked wheel on a cart. The whole family clustered anxiously about the cart on which were piled bedding, eating utensils and even small pieces of furniture.

'Pray,' Analee said to the woman who looked like the mother of the family 'could you tell me why there is all this activity on the road to Penrith?'

The woman looked nervously at her husband mending the wheel bidding him to hasten, before replying to Analee.

'Have you not heard? The Jacobite army is abroad plundering and looting; it has already entered Carlisle and plans to lay waste to the city. We are some of the last allowed out of the gate. They entered after nightfall and terrible tales of pillage are told. The Prince has lost all interest or all control over his men, and a more savage band of murderers you never saw.'

'Then Carlisle is not safe?'

'Nay, the gates are shut and bolted. You will not be allowed in. The Hanoverian army is chasing the rebels and people fear a long

243

battle. We are bound for Keswick in the hope of escaping destruction. You had best turn back.'

The wheel was given a final knock into place and the harassed-looking family set off at a brisk pace along the road. Nelly tugged at her skirt and looked wistfully after the departing family, but Analee shook her head, her heart already cold with fear.

'We cannot turn back. Did you hear them? Pillage and plunder. What will happen to the gypsies who are right in their path? Maybe we are already too late.'

What was left of the Buckland camp still lay smouldering despite the rain. Everything was blackened and no single tent, cart or hut remained standing. The few who had survived the slaughter had fled in all directions and now only the bodies of the dead littered the field: men, women, children, sheep, cattle and even horses.

It was such a terrible sight that Analee had frozen in her tracks on seeing it; even when she felt she could move she did not. Nelly walked around, braver than she, knowing that her family would have moved on long since, though God knew what had happened to them. Slowly Analee walked through the field to join Nelly, not wishing to see what she knew she must see.

First was Rebecca lying on her back, an old woman who had lived over a hundred years, now cruelly despatched with a dirk through her chest and another in her shoulder. Maybe she had started to run, but what chance had she against soldiers in their prime? But she had been lucky, perhaps her great age had saved her for, unlike the other women, she did not lie with her skirts drawn over her stomach, her naked legs stretched wide, the victims of rape before the final hideous slaughter.

The stench was awful and Analee's ears filled with the pounding of hooves, the screams of the women as they clutched their children and ran. This is what she had heard so long ago; it was what she had dreamt. She had known what the war would bring. There, some way from Rebecca, was Lancelot, or so it appeared. His eyes had been gouged out and one could only judge it was him because of his age. Analee shut her eyes but no tears came, just a choking in her throat, a pain in her chest that threatened to cut off her breathing.

And the children . . . the little ones, it was too awful, too pathetic and dreadful a sight. How could men . . . There were babies too, clutched tightly in their mother's arms. But although she dreaded to find what she sought Analee knew, after an hour of searching – the most gruesome task she had ever undertaken in her life – that neither the baby nor Reyora were here. The *cohani* had kept her promise to look after Morella.

Analee's heart filled with gratitude as she looked at the sky. Morella was safe, for that at least thanks to God. It had stopped raining and a weak wintry sun struggled to penetrate the thick clouds. Suddenly Analee heard a groan, an awful sound in that dreadful silent waste. It came from the far corner of the field and she had already been past the bodies which lay in a stricken heap beside the main part of the camp. She hurried over and peered at the faces which stared, some with awful sightlessness, up at the merciless heaven. The groan came again and one of the bodies, slightly under the rest, moved. She bent over and, putting out a hand, clasped the shoulder gently turning the face towards her. The eyes that looked at her were red and glazed with pain, the mouth a rictus of fear.

Randal.

Randal Buckland still lived. Analee's heart cried out with pity at the sight of the man who was still her husband reduced to such pitiful straits.

'Oh Randal, Randal . . . Can you hear me? It is I. Analee.'

Randal seemed neither to hear nor see her; his eyes stared beyond her and then they closed and his head dropped, but he still breathed and started pathetically to try and crawl away from the mass of dead bodies piled near or on top of his.

'Nelly help me!' Analee cried and, as Nelly ran over, she told her to take Randal's legs and detach them from the mangled limbs that surrounded him.

Nelly, her tearstained face shocked from the awful sight, gently took hold of Randal's legs and Analee flinched to see that one was nearly severed at the knee. In fact the blood had almost congealed; even with this massive wound he had lived through the night.

They stumbled over the field and carried Randal to the shadow of the hedge that ran by the side of the road.

'They might come back,' Analee said fearfully. 'God forbid, but let us try and remain out of sight.'

Nelly looked about, pointing to a barn that still, surprisingly, had its roof on although most of the half-burnt timbers swayed in the wind. It was where the gypsies had stored their grain, and this too have been looted by the plunderers.

'Let us take him over there; it provides some shelter.' Once again they made the slow journey across dead bodies and Randal, racked by pain, fell into merciful unconsciousness. His head lolled on his chest as they half-carried, half-dragged him across the field.

But it was better inside the barn. It was dry and sheltered from the strong wind and there was still some grain left to make a soft bed for Randal. Analee sent Nelly to the stream for water while she did what she could to make him comfortable and to see the extent of his wounds. She soon realized she could do nothing.

They were terrible; apart from his almost severed leg he had sword and dirk marks all over his body as though someone had been using it for target practice. His face though was unmarked and even, deathly pale, bloody and dirty as it was, Analee saw the remnants of the dark, handsome gypsy boy with whom she had so many times made passionate love.

She knew he could not survive. Even now his breathing was faint, but he opened his eyes as Nelly brought water and the feel of its cleansing coolness on his body seemed to restore him and recognition dawned.

'Analee.'

'Randal. I have come back.'

'Too late,' Randal gasped sipping the water Nelly offered him to drink. 'Too late.'

'What happened?'

Randal shook his head, tried to speak but could not. His lips hung slack and his eyes began to roll in their sockets.

'The army? The Highlanders?'

Randal nodded.

'They swept through the camp like, like . . .' words failed him and his head sagged on his chest. 'At dusk, as we were eating . . .'

'Randal, what happened to Reyora . . . the *baby*?' Analee's voice faltered as she saw the jealous spark come into Randal's eyes even in this pitiful and desperate condition.

'I don't know . . . never saw . . . Reyora . . .'

He drank again and made another effort, drawing large painful breaths.

246

'Forgive . . . Analee. Always . . . loved you . . .'

Analee's eyes filled with tears as his cracked swollen mouth uttered words that were obviously deeply felt. She bent down to him and, her lips brushing his cheek, she whispered in his ear:

'Forgive me, too . . .'

'If we could start again . . .'

'We will. You will get better.'

But Randal shook his head and his eyes half closed in another spasm of pain.

'Done for, Analee . . . done for.'

Randal suddenly opened his eyes wide and stared at her and, for a moment, it looked to Analee as though he had a sudden resurgence of strength and might, incredibly, recover. But the eyes went on staring and it was then she realized he was dead. Tenderly she laid his head back on the floor and closed his eyelids, gently planting a kiss on each one. She gazed at him for a long time as tears rolled down her cheeks. Randal Buckland, her husband.

''Twas better thus,' Nelly whispered. 'He had the happiness of seeing you again, asking your forgiveness, and you kissed his eyelids in death. It would never really have done . . .'

Analee tried to choke back her sobs, but could not. They racked her body as she lay against Randal, mourning not so much a husband as a lover and the embodiment of a vigorous young gypsy male, cruelly struck down in the prime of life.

'Hist!'

Nelly sat up, her eyes wide with fear. Analee, even as her face lay on Randal's body, could hear the thunder of hooves and then voices, and then a clatter of swords being drawn. She stiffened and closed her eyes. This was the moment.

Let them kill her, too; she would die with her people. But let death be quick, let not . . . she thought of the skirts over the heads of the gypsy women and shuddered.

'What have we here?' a voice said briskly.

'Two gypsy women, sir, with the body of a man.'

'Ah.'

Analee looked up and saw an imperious dark face gazing down at her. Eyes used to such scenes glittered angrily and his full, rather cruel-looking mouth was set in a stern thin line. He was enormously tall and broad and beneath his cloak she saw a red coat and a chest full of medals. She dusted her hands on her skirt and, getting up, dropped a quick curtesy. This splendid man was clearly a general at the very least.

'Do not kill us, sir . . .'

'Kill!' The man thundered in a deep voice to match his forbidding stature. '*I* am not here to kill my good woman! This was done by the barbarian Highlanders, not by soldiers of His Majesty King George such as we are. Luckily you were spared.' He looked around, his face grimacing in disgust at the scene, the stench. 'This man some relation?' He pointed with his stick impatiently at the mangled body of poor Randal.

'My husband, sir, Randal Buckland. This,' she gestured with her arms, 'this was once the camp of the proud Buckland family.' She started to weep afresh. Desolation all around her, and death had never seemed so immediate, so close, so disgusting in its harshness. At her feet, Nelly still crouched in an attitude of supplication.

'Get her to her feet,' the officer touched her lightly with the point of a well-polished boot. 'God knows what we shall do with them.'

'They look starved to death sir.' The soldier who was with him, clearly an inferior, bore an expression more compassionate than that of his superior.

'Are you hungry woman?'

'Aye, sir. Famished.'

'Then get them to our camp and fill them with victuals. After that put them on their way. We want no gypsy camp-followers!'

The officer spun round angrily and walked off to where the body of his men waited at the entrance to the camp. At a brisk command from him they began to disperse across the field, gathering the bodies into piles for burial.

Analee looked at Randal and in his dead face she could see no hope for her, no future. Where was her baby?

'You'll have to leave him,' the young soldier said kindly. 'The Colonel wants us to be clearing here and then on our way after the rebels.'

'What will happen to . . . the bodies?'

'Oh, they will be decently buried. His lordship is a harsh man but just; he will send the chaplain to bury them properly. Now come on quick before he changes his mind about your dinner. The camp is only half a mile away. Can you manage?'

'I expect we can, for some food.'

Analee pulled her cloak about her and dropped once more on her knees to gaze into Randal's face. She hadn't loved him and he had treated her badly; but for a time, a little while, they had shared something that was good and life-giving and her pity was for a young healthy man killed before his time – a tribute to the host of murdered Bucklands. She took his still warm hand in hers and put it to her lips.

'Come.'

Nelly was gently tugging at her shoulders. Analee got up and, leaning heavily on Nelly, they walked after the soldier through the bodies that littered the ground.

At the gate Analee glanced around for the last time at the camp, once her home, and saw that the imposing commanding officer had stopped in his tracks and was gazing after her. When he saw her looking at him he turned sharply away and started to bark fierce, angry commands.

Analee shivered from something other than cold; was it apprehension, fear? There was a keen, penetrating look in the commander's eyes – a tawny green under thick black brows as she could not help observing when he'd looked down at her beside Randal's body. They were eyes that were compassionate yet chilling – compassionate, maybe, because she was a woman and chilling because he was a soldier and this was a war. But the look at the gate had another, more lingering meaning and she caught her breath.

'What is your commander's name?'

The soldier drew himself up and puffed out his chest.

'That, woman, is the Marquess of Falconer, no less. Colonel of our regiment. You were honoured that he so much as noticed you, let alone talked to you.'

'He seems a very stern man. Powerful.'

'Aye, he is. Very. Some say he has a gentle side to him but I have rarely seen it myself. I am his servant, McNeath. He is keen on strict discipline for his men and absolute obedience to his commands. As for the enemy . . . why his name is enough to make them tremble with fear. He is called the Falcon not only after his family name, but because they say he swoops down like a falcon and once he gets his claws in a foe he will not let go.

'They gave him his name in France – "Le Faucon!" they would cry and rush to be out of his way. I tell you I observed it with my own eyes.

'Now hurry so you can be off before his lordship returns. You heard what he said about followers and it would not do for you if he turned his ire towards you. You would see what was meant by the Falcon then.'

His arm bandaged and in a sling, his coat sleeve hanging by his side, Brent rode slowly in the rear of the retreating army. They had reached Penrith after Clifton only to find that the Prince had gone and left orders for them to follow on to Carlisle. The army were weary after days of difficult hill marching, and, despite the skirmish at Clifton, the inevitability of ultimate defeat. They all knew the Hanoverian forces had not properly deployed themselves at Clifton, perhaps not expecting a night-time attack, and thus they were vulnerable to the Highlanders' surprise assault. They knew that with the vast government army massing against them they were hopelessly outnumbered, and now they had lost the support of the people.

Setting off at first light Brent had thought longingly of Delamain Castle only a few miles away, but he knew that to so much as show himself to his brother was tantamount to surrender. He would be handed over to the authorities immediately. Brent didn't want to defect; the die was cast. He only longed for some rest, a real bed and good hot food, some balsam for his aching limbs. His brother officers riding with him did not talk or laugh among themselves as they had on the journey south. Some had only joined it at Manchester. It was a silent, apprehensive group, occasionally shouting a command to the weary foot soldiers to keep in line.

But the soldiers were angry, and restless; their eyes looked haunted and bitter; they roamed around restlessly for the sight of plunder. Thus when they saw the small hunted group of people coming towards them they cheered. Such misery, such dejection would be good sport. It never occurred to them to feel pity for people even worse off than they.

Brent saw the commotion first, heard the screams. A cart fell over on its side and the pathetic bundle of goods inside it tumbled out onto the path. The men started to kick these remnants of whatever worldly goods someone had possessed as though in sport and already one of the Highlanders had thrust a young woman into a ditch and was tearing at her skirts.

It still horrified Brent, this savagery of the Highlanders whom he knew basically to be good men with wives and families of their own. Despite their reputation they had done little to deserve it on the march south; now it was a very different story. This was why he travelled well to the rear of the force. Lord George Murray ahead would know nothing of this.

Brent drew his sword with his good arm and bore down on the marauding men scattering them.

'Pick it up. Pick it up!' he yelled, pointing to the cart. Meanwhile a member of the Manchester Regiment, Matthew Somerset, was hauling the lustful soldier off the shivering body of the nearly naked woman in the ditch. There were one or two women with children but the rest were old, old men and old women. They looked like gypsies. He turned to one younger woman who stared at him, sheltering a bundle in her arms. As he approached her she shrank back and clutched the tiny body more tightly to her.

'Where are all your young men?' Brent asked her.

'Dead sir. Killed by the soldiers.'

Brent closed his eyes in an involuntary spasm of nausea.

'What . . . what soldiers?'

The woman pointed around her.

'Dressed like these; the Scots. They came to our camp the evening before last just after dusk and pillaged, raped and plundered before setting the whole place alight. We only escaped because we were on the edge of the camp. We did not wait.'

Brent leaned over to look at the bundle in her arms. He drew back the ragged blanket which covered it and looked kindly at the woman.

'Don't be frightened. I'll not harm you.'

'The baby is ill sir. I fear she will not last the day. She has the fever and it is no way to travel without warmth, or food in this weather.'

Brent found he was staring at a beautiful fair-skinned baby with golden hair, so unlike the dark gypsy who held it in her arms. The baby's eyes were shut, and her pale face shook with fever.

'You have not stolen this child have you?' Brent said glancing suspiciously at the woman.

'Oh no, sir. Saved her. Her mother is fled and her father dead – killed by your soldiers.'

'She doesn't look like a gyspy baby.'

Reyora looked at the tall fair soldier with the kindly face who was staring down at the baby. The father would have been someone just like this *gadjo*. Reyora wondered where Analee was now; how she had fared.

'The mother was one of our gypsies, sir. The father . . .' Reyora gestured expressively, 'I am not sure.'

Brent felt the stirrings of some peculiar and unexpected emotion inside him as he looked at the baby. A tenderness for the poor little outcast in a harsh world; what chance did she have? Abandoned by father and mother.

'She is a very beautiful baby.'

'Oh she is, my lord. And a lovely nature.'

'Look,' Brent said impulsively. 'My home is not far distant. Have naught to do with my brother Sir George Delamain, but my mother is a compassionate woman. Tell her you met me and I sent my love and asked her to give you shelter until the baby is well.'

'Oh but sir, I am with the remnant of my tribe . . .' Reyora glanced about her and saw how, standing in a pathetic group, their eyes appealed to her.

'My mother could not give hospitality to all even if she wanted to. But for the baby . . . ? Could you not join them when she is better? They cannot go far. The soldiers are all about the place and who knows that the government troops are any better than our own? You are directly in the line of pursuit.'

Reyora's eyes grew speculative.

'Maybe they could camp somewhere in these parts, and I, for the baby's sake, will seek refuge. You are very kind, my lord,' Reyora looked into his eyes, 'kind to a poor gyspy woman and a baby. You will never regret this kindness. I, the gypsy woman, tell you it will only bring you happiness.'

Brent looked at her and the tall lissom body, the lovely face of Analee suddenly danced in imagination before his eyes.

'I owe the gypsies a kindness,' he said suddenly.

'Maybe you loved a gypsy once sir?'

252

Reyora looked at him slyly, but a curious thought had come into her mind. This soldier was being unusually kind . . . she remembered the blond *gadjo* who had loved Analee. Could it be . . . could this possibly be Morella's father? Reyora shut her eyes and tried to conjure up her *cohani* powers of divination, but she was too tired and hungry, weary with shock and numb with exhaustion. This *gadjo* offered rest and it was all she wanted; warmth and rest for the baby. The *cohani* powers told her nothing and she opened her eyes to see the *gadjo* waving to his men.

'I am summoned. I must go. I am sorry for the behaviour of our troops towards your people. Yes, I did once know a gypsy; but I cannot talk of that now, except to say that for her people I will do all I can. Listen, Delamain Castle is just a few leagues south of Penrith, and my mother, Mrs Delamain, lives in the dower house there. Ask your way in the town. You can see it from the hill there in the distance, surrounded by trees. Your people can scatter in the forest and rest for a while if they wish, but take care you or they do not go near the Castle for my brother Sir George Delamain would take a harsh view of gypsies, and I believe he is active with the militia.'

Reyora looked startled as Brent curled his lip and put her hand protectively about the baby's head. 'Oh do not fear; my mother's house is well hidden from the castle and he never goes near her. She is a kind and compassionate woman and will help you if you say I sent you and also my love. Tell her it was her son, Brent, to whom you spoke. Speak only to her or my sister Emma and stay with her until the baby is well. God go with you.'

Weary and sick as he was Brent's voice broke and he looked longingly back the way he had come, towards the hill on which Penrith lay. Would he could go with them and find succour too. His mother would not betray him. But it was not to be. Whatever his destiny was, he had to follow it and, however reluctantly, ride on.

Reyora dropped a deep curtsy.

'And with you, my lord, and bless you for your graciousness. See the baby has opened her eyes and smiles at you.'

And indeed Morella had opened her big blue eyes and gazed, without either of them being in the least aware of it, at her father. But even though he was ignorant of the fact, Brent's heart was filled with emotion as the beautiful baby girl looked at him and a little smile tugged at her lips. She gurgled and held up a hand and he took it and smiled into her eyes and stifled a desire to kiss her soft little cheeks.

'What is her name?'

'Her mother called her Morella, sir. It is the secret name given by a gypsy's mother, but I kept it as a talisman for her daughter.'

'Morella,' Brent said. 'I will remember it. May only good things happen to you, kind woman.'

Brent remounted and gazed at the strange gypsy woman and the lovely baby. Suddenly Reyora darted up to him and, taking his hand, kissed it.

'My lord, sir. You will suffer many things, but you will not die although you will come close to it. In the end you will find happiness, though there are more dark days ahead. Remember it is the gypsy woman, Reyora the *cohani*, who told you these things.'

Brent nodded at her gravely, his eyes unsmiling.

'I will remember it.'

His companion had now separated gypsies and soldiers and sent the latter marching on their way. The sad gypsy remnant stood back from the road as he rode past them; they bowed to him and put up their hands in blessing. Ahead was his struggling, defeated army, but he turned in his saddle before he caught up with them and gazed back to where the gyspy woman Reyora stood a little apart from the others clasping the baby Morella. Brent Delamain stared at them for a long time. Then he put up a hand and waved farewell.

16

Even though such scenes as he had witnessed at the gypsy camp were not unfamiliar to him, Lord Falconer was still sufficiently affected by them to have his temper severely stretched. It was thus in something of a rage that he rode back to his camp and berated his men for their sluggishness and idleness, and bade them clean their muskets and shine their boots for they were hotly to pursue the rebels who were now holed up in Carlisle.

'Rabble!' his lordship muttered angrily as McNeath helped him off with his boots and asked if he were ready for his dinner. 'Aye, though who could eat after that sight, and the stench . . .' The Marquess screwed up his aristocratic nose in a grimace of distaste. 'Tell me did the gypsy women have aught to eat?'

'Yes, sir.'

'And are they on their way?'

'No sir . . .'

'*What*?' His commander rose to his feet gazing threateningly at his servant. 'Don't tell me the men . . .'

'Oh no, sir, I told them expressly not to touch the women, on your orders, sir. They are about to depart, but the older woman, Analee, would like to thank your lordship for your kindness.'

The Marquess waved his hand in a gesture of dismissal and poured himself some whisky.

'Oh no, send them off, send them off. I want no gypsy woman hanging about, nor gratitude.'

But as he looked up Analee stood at the entrance to his tent and he grudgingly told her to enter.

'We shall not "hang about", my lord,' Analee told him with quiet dignity. 'I merely wished to thank your lordship for your humanity towards the gypsies and kindness in feeding us and offering us warmth. We are rested and ready to depart.'

The Marquess of Falconer lowered his glass and looked thoughtfully at the gypsy girl. Now that she was cleaned up and rested he confirmed what he had already suspected on the field –

255

she was uncommonly pretty. She was thin, even scraggy – God knew it had been a hard winter and she must have had little to eat – but as she'd walked off the field he had been struck by the proud tilt of her head, the graceful way she carried herself, the sway of her hips that was distinctly alluring.

'What will you do now woman?' he enquired quietly, turning to refill his glass. 'Where will you go?'

'Why, sir, we are nomads . . .'

'But the place is swarming with soldiers. What chance do you and the girl with you think you will have of escaping rape seven times a day even if you do not lose your lives? Have you not heard about the Highlanders? Have you not *seen* . . .'

Analee shuddered and covered her eyes.

'Ah, pray do not, sir. Pray do not remind me of that terrible scene. We will go westward, away from the army . . .'

She was aware that the Falcon was standing directly in front of her and she looked up to see him towering over her, his thin mouth pursed in a cruel sneer, his eyes gleaming.

'The army are *everywhere*. A force of ours has gone to White-haven to detach the big cannon there to subdue Carlisle; they're to the south, east, north and west. I doubt if you will live the week out. Still, no matter, I have done all I can.' He made a gesture of dismissal.

'Thank you, sir.'

Analee curtsied and turned to Nelly who stood sobbing behind her.

'Come, Nelly . . .'

'Oh, Analee, what is to become of us?'

'Hush girl,' Analee said clasping her arm, 'we have survived before. We shall again. Thank his lordship and come on. He is a very busy man.'

As Nelly started to sob her thanks Lord Falconer lifted his head and gazed at the roof of the tent.

'I am prepared to help you find shelter. My home is not far distant, on the border, and if you go there you can find board and lodging in exchange for some services. You can clean, can you not, and . . .'

'Oh yes, sir,' Nelly said, the flow of tears instantly ceasing. 'And cook and help in the house . . .'

'Nelly!' Analee said quickly. 'Thank you, my lord, but we will be safe. We are used to wandering . . .'

''Tis of no concern to me,' his lordship said, turning to where his dinner was being put on the table. 'You will not survive the week. Go and get killed. Ah, thank you, McNeath, and uncork some claret for me. I have an uncommon thirst after that hideous scene.'

'But, Analee. *I* want . . .'

'You see,' the Falcon observed to Analee with the trace of a smile, 'your companion is not of the same mind as yourself. She would like shelter for some days. Is it not so? What is your name?'

'Nelly, sir. Nelly Driver.'

'Well, Nelly, you go by yourself and present my compliments to my housekeeper. McNeath will set you on your way.'

'I could take her on my horse, my lord,' McNeath said quickly, 'if your lordship will allow it. It will be safer and quicker.'

'Aye,' his lordship started eating his soup. 'Well you may do that, McNeath, and you two women had better say goodbye to each other.'

Quivering, Analee stood looking at the Colonel of the regiment. She was sure she had not misread the insolent light in his eyes as they had run over her body, the appreciative smirk on his face. 'Some services' indeed, 'cooking and cleaning' . . . a likely story! If Analee was not mistaken, or deceived about the nature of men, these services would include some of a more intimate nature. Well . . . Analee looked at the Colonel unconcernedly spooning his soup and then at Nelly trembling with fear. She felt too drained to care over much either about the desires of the one or the fears of the other and, yes, it would be nice to have a roof over their heads, regular food and shelter from the marauding bands of savage Highlanders. At least if she were going to be raped the Falcon would do it in style, whereas the Highlanders . . . she had seen too recently the results of their debauchery.

Nelly by this time was hanging on to Analee's shoulder sobbing, and Analee impulsively clasped her and patted her back.

'There . . .'

'Ah, Analee, *please* come . . .'

'All right, I will if his lordship allows it. I cannot lose my companion can I?' She stood back from Nelly and smiled encouragingly. Lord Falconer, closely observing her behaviour, thought to himself that she was indeed no ordinary gypsy. Here was a woman with style. His heart gave a little satisfied lurch. This was the only good thing that had happened all day. The beautiful gypsy was going to lodge under his roof and she would have every reason to be grateful to him.

'Take both the women on your horse to Falcon's Keep,' the Marquess said with pretended indifference, 'and enough of those female blatherings. And be quick back, McNeath, d'ye hear? Make sure my castle is well protected, but I think the Highlanders will avoid it on their way north. Be off now.'

And the Marquess returned to his soup without another glance at the women who, after curtsying once more, were ushered out of the tent by a respectful and delighted McNeath. If he was not mistaken, the servant thought he had seen a singularly saucy look in the eyes of young Nelly as she had eagerly scoffed up her soup and meat, casting him grateful glances.

At Carlisle where his army regrouped on 19 December, Prince Charles once again set about quarrelling with his commanders. He was gracious enough to congratulate Lord George Murray on his victory at Clifton. This brief period of amity was disrupted however when the Prince announced that he would pull out of Carlisle but leave a garrison there for its defence. His Highness was anxious now to return to Scotland where Lord John Drummond, the brother of the Duke of Perth, awaited him with fresh forces brought from France. From here he would launch another and, he felt, more successful attack on England which would take him to London.

Lord George Murray, still deathly tired after his days in the saddle tried to argue with his leader, but he was not supported by the other officers even though they privately agreed with him that Carlisle was not capable of being defended. Since the retreat from Derby the officers had grown wary of the Prince whose sudden violent and petty moods, whose long periods of silence and dejection, when he refused to talk to anybody, were so much at variance with his erstwhile good humour. No one liked to anger the Prince further at this stage by publicly disagreeing with him.

Accordingly, telling them that as soon as he had reformed his army he would return and relieve them, the Prince left a garrison of about 400 men and marched with the rest to the border which he crossed on 20 December, his twenty-fifth birthday. As he turned from the swirling waters of the Esk and looked back onto English soil little did he know he would never return to it again, at least at the head of an army.

Among those left behind to defend the town was Stewart Allonby. As many of the Highlanders as possible had been taken with the army because of their unpopularity with the townspeople, and most of the men who formed the garrison were English, either local men or men from the Manchester regiment. Many remained at their own wish, being reluctant to cross the border to Scotland.

Stewart was depressed about his chances of survival but determined to do his duty.

'I would dearly love to come with you, Brent, for I think we shall be massacred here.'

'And I would like to stay,' Brent replied, clasping his cousin's hand. 'But it is not to be. Farewell, cousin, we shall soon return to relieve you.'

'Will you?' Stewart said bitterly, sitting on an upturned box in the bare room of his billet. The townspeople had set themselves resolutely against the Jacobites and there were few comforts to be had. The kindly host who had formerly been only too glad to accommodate Stewart now barred him. 'I doubt it. The Prince will not see England again. Can't you see now, Brent, he never had a chance? Why, everything about him is un-English, even his accent, which he cannot help because he was born and brought up abroad.'

'Aye, but they say King George in London speaks with a German accent,' Brent replied dryly.

'It is his manner, his dress. Always the plaid, the kilt . . . you can see how the English people would not take our army seriously, even though some of us are English and wear not the kilt. Very few.'

'We must not give in, Stewart,' Brent replied sternly. 'We have committed our lot to the Prince.'

'Aye, 'tis too late,' Stewart said. 'Too late.'

The bugle sounded in the yard below and Brent saw the ranks of tired dispirited soldiers forming. The Prince and Lord George Murray were at opposite sides, the one looking proud yet and determined, the other bitter, but his haughty head raised higher than ever.

'They never got on, those two,' Brent said, shaking his head. 'You may contribute much of our defeat to that fact. 'Twas disastrous.'

Stewart stood behind his cousin and clapped him on the back.

'You said not to talk of defeat, Brent. Now you do it. Go with them and fight, man, and we shall hold out until you return.'

But the small outnumbered garrison had no hope of holding out, as everyone knew. The big cannon from Whitehaven were rolled up to Carlisle and the Duke of Cumberland himself directed the bombardment of the city. Beside the massed ranks of the enemy without the walls, the garrison knew that not only was the populace not on their side but the government forces outnumbered them by about five to one. When the guns did arrive they knew they had no chance and on 30 December the governor, Mr Hamilton, hung out the white flag.

There was some pretence at bargaining for the lives of the garrison and the Duke of Cumberland concurred, only because he was anxious to go back to the south where he had been urgently sent for to command an anti-invasion force on the coast. But he agreed to the terms to save unnecessary expenditure of lives of his own soldiers and in the sure knowledge that his father the King would mete out justice 'as they have no sort of claim to the King's mercy and I sincerely hope will meet with none.'

The townspeople went wild with joy as the disciplined Hanoverian army reoccupied the town and the ragged remnant of the Jacobite army, some having gone without sleep for nights on end, were herded into the dungeons of Carlisle Castle – Stewart Allonby, bleeding from a wound in the head, among them.

Colonel Lord Falconer was well pleased with the swift capitulation of Carlisle, although to his mind ten days in taking the town had been ten days too long. It was not really until the 18-pounders arrived under his escort from Whitehaven that he knew the end was near.

The Marquess had campaigned hard all year and he was anxious for a rest. He had scarcely left the side of the Duke of Cumberland, a man with whom he had little in common though he admired his qualities as a commander and a soldier. Many times had he personally witnessed the King's younger son's bravery on the field of battle in the Continental wars.

Although the Duke was exactly the same age as his adversary Prince Charles he was very different to look at, being grossly overweight and having the Hanoverian proclivity for self-indulgence. However he was popular with the men who served under him and had given him the name 'Bluff Bill' for his easy-going ways. The Falcon sought an audience with the Duke before he returned to London and asked if he might have leave to visit his estates. The Duke had just enjoyed an excellent meal of fish, five kinds of meat and several bottles of wine provided by the grateful citizenry, and was sitting with his jacket undone over his corpulent stomach picking his teeth when Lord Falconer stood before him with his request. The Duke eyed one of his best commanders indulgently.

'Why, I see no reason not to grant your request, my dear Marquess,' the Duke said in his guttural German-accented voice. Though he had indeed been born in England, German was still widely spoken at the court. 'But hurry south won't you, soon? For I shall need you to keep the French away from our shores. You know how they fear Le Faucon!' The Duke grinned.

'Surely they will not attempt this now, your Royal Highness?'

Cumberland shrugged his podgy shoulders and screwed up his small pig-like eyes.

'The brother of the Young Pretender, Henry, is active in France on behalf of his father. Let us hope now they will not consider such wastage of men worthwhile.'

The Duke belched and summoned a servant.

'A glass of wine for his lordship!'

The servant hurried over and poured some claret into a crystal glass. The Duke raised his glass and bowed to his colonel.

'You will be well rewarded for your help to me in this campaign, Angus. After I have reported to the King my father, I hope he will consent to have you gazetted a lieutenant-general!'

The Falcon bowed very low. He was not a soldier for the honours it brought, but to have his qualities so well regarded was very rewarding. It had never occurred to him for a moment that

261

the Hanoverians might be defeated or the Prince victorious. But now the thought did cross his mind that, had things gone a different way, he would be languishing in the dungeons below this very room where the Duke and himself, glasses raised, were drinking a toast to his Majesty King George II.

The Marquess of Falconer stretched his long legs before a roaring fire and reflected that it was good to be home. It had not taken long to send the Jacobites packing, but the weather had been wretched and his quarters uncomfortable. He was a soldier and used to any amount of hardship, but there was a lot to be said for a warm fire, a comfortable bed, and . . . He thoughtfully got up and pulled the bell rope by the fire.

The gypsy had served him at table, the tall good-looking gypsy, that is: he neither knew nor cared what happened to the smaller, plain one. And what a woman she was, this gypsy as, clad only in her simple skirt and bodice with nothing on her feet, she had plied silently between table and kitchen under the direction of the major-domo.

He had tried to engage her eyes, but to no avail. Her long lids were lowered over her eyes so that he could not see their expression. No matter. To look at her was good enough; he had no need to see her eyes or hear her speak. Her breasts thrust hard against her bodice which was but carelessly laced, and the sight of them swelling above her neat décolletage almost put him off his food. But not quite. Food was just as important as dallying with a woman, or nearly as so. For instance it gave one the strength to employ one's amorous powers to good effect. McNeath entered silently, bowing to his master.

'Your wish, my lord?'

'Fetch me some brandy, McNeath, and you can ask that gypsy girl to come here . . . you know, the tall one. The one who served me at table.'

McNeath raised an eyebrow but said nothing. He understood quite well to which girl his master was referring. Knowing his master's inclinations, he himself had made sure she had waited at dinner. He had seen how his master had observed her when he'd first seen Analee, kneeling beside her dead husband.

'Yes, tell her to fetch me the brandy,' Angus winked and settled in his chair. He leaned his head back and half closed his eyes, remembering her dark, almost savage beauty. He wondered where she came from. And then he heard a movement and, opening his eyes, saw her before him carrying a tray on which there was a decanter and a heavy crystal glass.

'Pour for me will you? What is your name, did you say?'

'Analee, my lord.'

'And have you settled down here Analee?'

Analee didn't reply and his lordship turned to glance at her.

'Well?'

'I do not wish to stay here, sir. I am a gypsy girl, not happy in a house.'

'Well if you want to go into the cold with marauding bands about it is up to you,' Lord Falconer turned and, with pretended indifference, settled in the chair.

'The Highlanders have returned to Scotland, sir.'

'Only for a short time, they hope. Come here girl.'

Analee placed the tray on a nearby table and stood for some time looking at it without moving. She had lain with worse men than Lord Falconer, far worse; but there was something about his easygoing assurance that she objected to.

'You feel you have "bought" me, my lord?' she said pointedly, remaining where she was.

'*Bought* you?' Lord Falconer wondered whether he could believe his aristocratic ears.

'With the warmth and food, the shelter from marauding soldiers.' Analee dwelt heavily on the word 'marauding' for the benefit of his lordship. 'So unlike yourself, my lord. They will pillage and rape regardless, whereas you,' she turned and stared at him derisively, 'wish only to rape in the comfort of your own home.'

His lordship jerked back his head. He was annoyed, indeed dumbfounded. Who did this creature imagine she was?

'I wish no such thing. Leave immediately, if you so desire.'

'Thank you, my lord. I will.'

Analee was about to take the tray and leave the room when his lordship sprang from the chair and within two bounds stood before her.

'Here wait. What did you say your name was?'

'*Analee*, my lord, as I have said.'

'I thought it was maybe *Lady* Analee such is the haughty tone of your speech. How dare you talk to me like that?'

'I apologize, my lord, if I misunderstood your intention.'

The Falcon felt himself flush, while the commotion in his loins engendered by his previously lewd thoughts grew more persistent. The girl, the gypsy brat was looking at him with the most tantalizing, provocative air, her eyes blazing with scorn and her lips half parted. Curse her!

He gave a deep breath but, unable to maintain control, seized hold of her shoulders and crushed his mouth down on hers. At the same time he got a knee between her legs and pushed her against the broad sofa that stood alongside the window. She put out her arms to prevent herself from falling and thus lost all means of protecting herself and all the time, relentlessly, unyieldingly his lordship's mouth bore harshly down on hers thrusting her head backwards.

The Marquess began to straddle her on the sofa, and Analee was aware of the enormous strength and power of the man. But although she was angry she was not frightened. There was something so deft, so expert about his lordship's actions, that she realized she was in the grip of a practised seducer and marvelled at the skill with which he had manoeuvred her into this position. Glancing up at him, Analee was reminded of some great untamed savage with his dark looks and thick black hair falling over his face.

Looking down at her, completely in his power, Angus saw a face not contorted with fear, but one in command of itself, angry, but not as angry as he would have expected almost . . . could one *possibly* say, half amused?

The expression, totally unexpected in one about to be raped, stopped his lordship in his tracks and though he still straddled her he put his hand on his hip, gazing at her with astonishment. Analee smiled.

'Must you *rape*, my lord, when you can take me to my pleasure as well as your own?'

The dignity, the charm with which she spoke, reminded Angus of a London courtesan of his acquaintance who had begun life as the daughter of a French nobleman, but who had taken to whoring when her family were faced with destitution.

She was still a gracious lady, but had completely abandoned

herself to carnal delights and her conversation was as witty as her style elegant. She was, it was said, making a fortune so much were her talents appreciated by those gentlemen who liked their love to be amusing and sophisticated, if ephemeral.

'*Your* pleasure?' His lordship said. 'You mean you will not resist?'

'Does it please you more if I do?'

'Of course not.'

The Marquess of Falconer began to feel rather foolish and backed away from the half recumbent form of Analee putting out a hand to help her to her feet, tantalized by the sight of the mocking curve of her mouth.

Still clasping her hand he pulled her gently over towards him. Her eyes were wide and, as she offered her half parted mouth to him, he could see in them a desire similar to his own. The thought excited him beyond reason and he crushed her body in his arms.

Slowly they sank to the floor and lay there on the thick Persian rug that his late father had bought in the east many years ago.

As he made love to her he could see she enjoyed it too, just as the courtesan in London did, the excellent Marie-Claire. She expressed great satisfaction with love-making and always declared how much it pleasured her, unlike some of his mistresses who never ever admitted to anything other than that they were rendering him a supreme favour.

He saw Analee's dark eyes looking into his.

'Better than rape, my lord?'

'Much,' he gasped. 'How did you learn this art?'

'I am a sorceress.'

'I can believe you.'

The Falcon rose and, going to the table poured more brandy. Then he brought two glasses over to where Analee lay still on the rug, and sat down beside her.

'Drink?'

'Thank you, my lord.' She sat up and took the glass, sipping delicately from it. He saw that her body, though thin, was without blemish and her skin shone with health despite the vicissitudes she must have endured. Her dark hair hung about her face as she drank and the long elegant curve of her breasts reached towards the fire.

265

'You are a mystery,' he said. 'You have just lost a husband and yet . . .'

Analee shook her head.

'It is not as you think. He was my husband but I deserted him many months ago. That is why I was not in the Buckland camp. I had wandered from it and when the war began I decided to return.'

'And Nelly?'

'A companion, a poor woman like myself.'

'Why did you desert your husband?'

'It is too long a story now, my lord,' Analee looked at him and he could see her eyes were sad. 'One I might tell you some day.'

'Some would despise you for what you did just now,' Angus said harshly, 'lying so easily with a man.'

'Do *you* despise me?'

'I . . .' His lordship was again surprised by Analee. 'No . . . but I am a man of the world. I have known many women; but you, Analee, you remind me of a very remarkable woman of my acquaintance in London whom some would call a whore; but . . .' Angus shook his head, 'in some curious way she transcends whoring. I never think of her as a whore though I pay her well for her services.'

'She likes love,' Analee said simply. 'I am like that. I understand it. I need men as much as any man needs a woman. That is why I wanted to turn rape to love, because I knew you needed me and would have me and I . . .' she looked solemnly at him, 'I did not want to have to hate you. I cannot forget the dead gypsy women in the camp with their skirts above their buttocks.'

'No,' Angus drained his glass. 'I can see that. It was vile. Unfortunately I see it often in war. Violence excites men's passions. The same thing can be both horrible and beautiful.'

Analee smiled and moved closer to the black giant.

'Your manservant told us that some said you could be gentle, but he scarcely ever saw it. I think those people who do are mostly women.'

'Aye,' Angus laughed, conscious of her warm body pressed up against his. 'I am a soldier used to war and giving commands. Certainly few of my men consider me gentle. I am glad you do Analee. I am glad I did not take you by force.' He leaned over to her and kissed her shoulder, aware that she turned towards him and nestled her cheek against his. 'Can I take you to my bed and we can do this again in comfort?'

'I think it comfortable here by the fire, but I will do as you say, my lord.'

She smiled at him with mock humility, but Angus Falconer, great lord that he was, was already too besotted by the gypsy to notice.

17

Analee sat in her clean attic room looking out at the snow which fell on the Cheviot Hills surrounding Falcon's Keep. The lair of the Falcon . . . She shivered. Although Lord Falconer's lovemaking was breathtaking, there was something menacing about him as well. She had no objection to the fact that he used her as an object, as a servant she expected nothing more, but his overpowering strength had at times frightened even her, a woman used to the ways of men.

'He is a violent man,' Analee had gasped wincing with pain as Nelly rubbed some ointment on the sore places, 'he admits it. He is a soldier used to war and has never really known a gentle home life. His mother died when he was a boy and he went for the army as an ensign aged only eighteen.'

'I see he tells you everything to gain your pity,' Nelly had said sarcastically.

'But he can be so tender and loving . . .' I think I am more than intrigued by Lord Falconer.'

Her eyes sparkled and Nelly marvelled that one so hostile at first could now appear so enamoured.

Analee seldom had the chance to sit down, and she crouched by her bed looking out of the narrow window. After a night in the Falcon's bed she had crawled upstairs to try and snatch half an hour's sleep before the bustle of the castle began again.

Mrs Ardoine, the housekeeper, had disliked Analee on sight and delighted in giving her the most menial of tasks; grate blacking, floor scrubbing, anything that involved hard dirty work. Even some of the tasks that were normally done by boys Mrs Ardoine gave to Analee, and that morning she had cleaned and laid the fires in the grates of all the main rooms, staggering along by herself with great piles of logs.

Nelly spent almost all of her time at the sink, her arms in water to the elbows. In a great house such as Falcon's Keep there were many mouths to feed, and different hours for the many classes of people who lived there – the family, guests, then the servant hierarchy beginning with the housekeeper, the major domo, the head butler and so on right down to the meanest skivvy like Nelly and herself who were not even allowed to sit at a table but grovelled on the floor for what they could get.

It was a mean existence and Analee looking out longed for the open spaces again where she was her own mistress, alone and free. And now that the master of the house had taken her to his bed? What could she expect once his lordship had tired of her?

Her eyes searched the bare, harsh mountains for a path that would lead her away from the house, out of sight of the narrow road that approached it. Maybe when the thaw came and there was no snow to betray her tracks?

'Analee! Analee!'

Nelly came rushing in nearly tripping herself up in her haste. 'Oh, Analee, you are there! Mrs Ardoine says she will whip the hide off you when she finds you. What ails you, Analee?'

Nelly knelt down looking anxiously into the eyes of her beloved friend. She knew what hour Analee had come to bed; how she had scarcely eased her aching body on to her pallet or closed her eyes when they were harshly awakened. Nelly was fearful for Analee now that the dreaded Falcon, the master of the house, had chosen her as his prey. Why, he was such a terrifying man he would surely treat her even more cruelly and once he had had his way cast her aside, maybe with child, uncaring as to what would become of her. Nelly had been unable to believe that Analee had spent all night with Lord Falconer until, recovering her humour, she had described to Nelly the vastness of the master's bed and how at times she thought she would lose herself in it, but his lordship always seemed to be able to find her again!

But there was no humour in Analee's eyes now, only tiredness and a kind of despair as she returned Nelly's gaze.

'I was so tired after doing the grates, I thought I would faint. I had to come here for some rest.' Nelly tugged anxiously at her arm.

'Oh come down, I beg you, Analee. She knows you are missing and has gone to look for her birch.'

'I will not be birched,' Analee said standing up and straightening her skirts. 'I will birch *her*.'

269

Nelly clutched at Analee's arm dragging her towards the door.

'Oh Analee, pray do not vex Mrs Ardoine. Say you are sorry and . . .'

'Nelly, I am going to *quit* this place!' Analee hissed before they were out of the door. 'I cannot stand it. I am the most menial of servants, hated by Mrs Ardoine. I must go and find my baby! The thought of her whereabouts haunts me. Maybe she and Reyora were captured by the soldiers. I am going to cross the border into Scotland and find where they may be now.'

'They will not have taken a woman and a baby. They . . .' Nelly avoided Analee's eyes.

'They did not kill them,' Analee whispered, 'they were not there . . .'

'No of course not. They fled. They must have gone south, back to Penrith . . .'

'Then I will go to Penrith . . .'

Analee and Nelly were tumbling down the narrow dark staircase that led to the servant's quarters whispering as they went, but when they came to the large stone kitchen which was full of bustle, steam and smoke they fell silent. The awful Mrs Ardoine was standing by the stairs, her arms akimbo, a thick bundle of fine twigs clasped in one hand which she beat against her ample hips. Although she was a large, comely woman who looked as though she might at one time have been a beauty, many years of hard work and disappointment, the loss of all her children in childbirth or infancy, had soured her and she wore a cruel expression on her thin twisted lips.

'Now do we have the servants skulking upstairs away from their duties!' Mrs Ardoine roared so loudly that it penetrated the clamour of the kitchen and a few who scurried about stopped in their tracks to listen and observe. 'Put up your skirts girl and bend over that chair.' Mrs Ardoine pointed authoritatively. 'I will administer to thee such a sound thrashing that your buttocks will be raw like rumpsteak! And I care not who sees thee,' she said gesturing towards the male servants who stood gawping hopefully.

Mrs Ardoine seized Analee by the shoulder, her eyes glistening with malice, and threw her across the room. Analee fell heavily but, before the termagant had time to advance on her to administer further humiliation, she nimbly sprang up and faced her persecutor.

'You lay the canes on me and I will thrash you six times as bad even though you *kill* me for it!'

Mrs Ardoine faltered in her steps, observing the way Analee's lips curled showing her fine white teeth bared in a snarl; so that she had the look of a fierce beast. That blaze in her eyes, the heaving of her breast convinced the housekeeper that the gypsy meant what she said; but it infuriated her the more and she raised her birch to bring it across Analee's face when her arm was arrested in mid air and the birch roughly wrested from her hand.

McNeath stood towering over her, a foul curse on his lips.

'Damn you to hell woman! Would you mark the face of someone who is enjoying his lordship's favours? A small price I'd give for your continued existence here if that were the case.'

McNeath threw the birch on the floor and gestured to Analee who was still staring with some surprise at her saviour, while Nelly gazed with adoring eyes at their liberator for she had no doubts that her turn would have come to bare her buttocks to Mrs Ardoine's birch.

'His *lordship* . . .'

Mrs Ardoine stepped back, her face white with terror.

'Exactly. His *lordship* has pleasured this young woman all night and wishes her to serve his breakfast. *Now* do you understand you old faggot? A mark on her face and I dread to think of his lordship's wrath . . . Analee! Smart now to the pantry where one of the footmen is preparing a tray for his lordship who will take his breakfast in his bedroom. You are to follow the footman and serve him yourself. Do you understand?'

There was no misunderstanding McNeath's leer or the chagrin on the face of Mrs Ardoine. Analee tossed her head and pushed past the housekeeper giving her a little nudge as she did so as if to say 'so there.'

McNeath was looking at Nelly, noting the becoming bloom to her face caused by the heat of the kitchen. She did not have the figure or the presence of her friend, but what she lacked in physical attributes maybe she would make up for in enthusiasm? Besides, her waif-like appearance appealed to him. He winked at her.

'Maybe I should follow my master's path, if you understand me?' Nelly pretended not to and raised an enquiring eyebrow.

271

'Forge a furrow for myself,' McNeath looked at her meaningfully.

Nelly blushed and looked away, her heart beating furiously. Could this handsome, vigorous McNeath possibly desire *her*? He was almost as tall as his master but fair with a red face and sandy hair, fierce blue eyes and ginger whiskers that covered almost all the lower part of his face.

'I will see thee later,' McNeath whispered to her. 'Meanwhile keep out of the way of the dragon and I will see that my master is properly served his breakfast.'

McNeath hurried after Analee and the footman who were already climbing the several staircases to his lordship's rooms. The footman carried a large tray and Analee a smaller one with a pot of coffee and the claret that his lordship sometimes took with his breakfast chops. McNeath ran up behind her and put a hand under her skirts and, from her position on the stair above him, she administered a vigorous sideways kick and hissed, 'If thy master knew thy foul hands had laid hold of me he would cut thy throat!'

McNeath and his master had often shared a woman, but only in the harsh conditions of war when they were few and far between. Sometimes the whole garrison had had to make do with merely one or two poor wenches, but his lordship always had them first, when they were fresh and untainted by the other men. His lordship was very particular about cleanliness and had quaint ideas like that. However, McNeath did not think that this was one of the occasions when his lordship would be passing the wench on. Something both about Analee's manner and the enthusiasm with which the Falcon had called for her so soon after waking made him think his master was unusually struck.

The Falcon was sitting in a chair by the huge fire that roared up the chimney. He wore a scarlet silk morning gown tied round the waist with a black silk sash, the long loose sleeves rolled back at the wrists. His long bare legs were stretched out before him. He looked up as the procession entered and put down a volume he was reading, carefully marking the place before he did. It was nearly noon and the sun streamed into his room lighting up the rich carpet and the folds of the carelessly tossed back sheets. Analee glanced at the bed on which she and her master had tumbled so freely that night and then she looked over at him and caught his eye. His lordship was thinking exactly the same thing.

The footman placed the tray carefully on the table by his lordship's side and bade Analee place the coffee pot and bottle of wine by it. McNeath hovered about, stoked the fire and put on another log.

'Thank you, McNeath,' the Falcon nodded and waved a hand. 'The gentlemen may leave us. This woman here will serve me very well.'

His lordship smiled and the men withdrew as Analee took the covers from the dishes, marvelling at what one man was offered for breakfast. The smells assailed her nostrils and reminded her that she had nothing but some dry bread and water, having declined stale ale.

'Well, wench?'

His lordship leaned back easily in his chair raising his arms above his head and stretching.

'Did you sleep well, my lord?'

'Eventually, yes. Thanks to you.'

'Steak *and* chops, my lord?'

'Both,' said his lordship, 'and pour me some claret. You have given me a fine appetite, Analee. I like you very well.'

Analee filled his lordship's plate and laid it before him, shaking the damask napkin and placing it on his lap. He trapped her hand and held it but Analee swayed. The smell of the food was too enticing, it reminded her of the pain that always gnawed inside her belly.

His lordship threw down his napkin and stood up taking her by the shoulder.

'Why, girl what is it? Are you with child that you are nearly fainting?'

'No, *no*, my lord. You are the first man I have lain with for many a long day. I am tired, my lord, and . . .'

'And Analee?'

The Falcon tipped her chin and looked into her eyes and she saw there, to her surprise, an expression of tenderness, almost concern.

'I am frightened, my lord. I was nearly thrashed.'

'*Thrashed*!' The Falcon roared, 'and by whom? In my house! Here sit down girl and tell me.'

His lordship led her to the sofa and laid her along it so that her body was propped up by cushions. Then he sat beside her.

'I dare not tell you, my lord. I feel I must go from here.'

'Tell me. I command it!'

Analee bit her lips but knew she must obey. Those knowing green eyes, that stern, scowling brow, daunted her. Really he was the most fearsome man she had ever met in her life.

'Mrs Ardoine, your housekeeper, sir. I was away from my duties and it vexed her. I was tired, sir. I have much to do in the house, the grates to clean and all the fires to lay, and the floors to scrub, and with your lordship's need of me last night . . .'

Analee leaned her head back and closed her eyes. This was really like heaven. But it would not last, lying back on silk cushions, the hands of a Marquess – no not just a Marquess, but *the* Falcon, the scourge of the Jacobites – protectively about her, his warm breath on her cheeks. She opened her eyes and saw that his face was very close to hers.

'You poor girl. We do not understand do we? We lords and masters know not what goes on in our own houses. Are servants often whipped, I wonder? I suppose they are. I never thought. And was I cruel to you last night? Did my ardour make me too harsh? Believe me I did not mean it. 'Twas my passion got the better of me. I have thought of you a lot, Analee. I dreamt about you and your face haunted me as soon as I woke so I sent for you. And you scrub and clean the black grates – my poor little Analee.' His lordship held up her hand and looked at it.

'Yes, I see your skin is rough and red, and you have such fine long fingers, Analee; they are those of a lady not a servant. Tell me about yourself. 'Come,' he reached for a hand and drew her down beside him. He put a log on the fire and they watched it catch and flare up. She shivered and he looked protectively at her and reached for his gown which he wrapped about her shoulders.

'My lord is most attentive. But your breakfast will grow cold, sir.'

'Who cares?' Lord Falconer put both arms around her. 'I am warmed by your love, my belly filled by desire for you. I am anxious only to know you better. Can you blame me?'

'Blame you, sir? Could a servant have the temerity to judge her master?'

274

'Ah now you do tease me . . . witch', the Falcon murmured making the loving bond formed by his arms about her even tighter.

Later, the hour for breakfast long past, dinner for Lord Falconer and Analee was served with some surprise but without comment by the footman who, several hours before, had brought up the breakfast which, untouched as it was, he now removed. Now, composed and dressed, Analee sat by the fire and his lordship, also washed, dressed and shaved, strode up and down the room, a glass of sherry in his hand.

Neither McNeath nor the footman betrayed by so much as a flicker of the eye that they thought there was anything untoward in his lordship dining with a servant who, only that morning had been blackening the grate and nearly had her backside scorched by Mrs Ardoine into the bargain. To McNeath it was quite unique to see his lordship so enamoured by a common passing wench as to do her the honour of dining with her in his bedroom! This distinction was usually reserved for fine ladies, sometimes the wives of fellow officers whose husbands were absent on manoeuvres. Not only this, but the Falcon was doing her every honour, bowing to her as he assisted her to her place at table, and insisting that she was served before himself.

And what a feast it was to delight the palate of nobleman and gypsy alike – partridge, roast venison, beef, lean succulent hams, quails' eggs, quinces, tarts and jellies. Dish after dish was laid before them in lavish profusion, and different wines were poured in crystal goblets by an under footman called in to help.

Here was Analee, dining with a lord and waited on deferentially by three servants to each of whom she smiled and nodded graciously as they served her, watched carefully by the Falcon.

At the end of dinner he signified that they should be left alone after McNeath had lit his pipe and placed a decanter of brandy by his side. Outside it was dark; the snow had started to fall again and a thin piercing wind howled round the great house.

Analee belched and gazed at his lordship, noting how seldom his eyes had left her face. The Falcon smiled.

'Analee, ladies do not break wind in public.'

'I am no lady, my lord.'

The Falcon leaned back and twirled his quizzing glass, thoughtfully drawing at the same time on his pipe. He wore a powdered periwig over his dark hair and whereas before he had looked awesome and distinguished now he looked aloof and aristocratic as well. He wore a suit of dark blue silk, and a cravat made of snowy Bruges lace gleamed at his neck. On the little finger of his left hand was a huge ring of solid gold engraved with the family crest – a solitary falcon. But on his middle fingers he wore more elaborate rings of gleaming sapphires and rubies, emeralds and diamonds.

'You were going to tell me about yourself, Analee,' his lordship twiddled the gold signet ring on his finger, 'how you come to have an air of such breeding and refinement yet call yourself a common gypsy. True, you make love like a whore, but it is to my taste.'

'I enjoy it, sir.'

'I can see that you do.'

'As to my origins, I know not, my lord. I am dark skinned like my people. My mother's family came from beyond the seas, I think they call it Transylvania. My father . . .' She lowered her head. 'I know naught about my father.'

'Ah,' his lordship leaned forward. 'I wager he was no gypsy, then. Maybe a little peccadillo on your mother's part, eh?'

'My mother died when I was born, sir. I know no more; naught about my father, little about her. But I am a true gypsy, Lord Falconer. I am not a lady.'

'Maybe I will make you one,' the Falcon said thoughtfully. 'I can see you gracing my salons in London, Analee, clothed in fine silks and satins and bedecked with jewels. How now girl . . . why look away?'

Analee had turned her head sharply to one side, avoiding his gaze. When she looked at him again her eyes glinted.

'Do not mock me, my lord. I am a gypsy. A scullery maid in your home. Have your pleasure with me, do as you will; but do not jest. When your lordship is tired of me you will do what you have done with other women . . . maybe given them a sovereign and told them to be off. Besides, Lord Falconer, I am not made for finery, silks and satins. I am a wandering girl, a vagabond.'

Analee looked up to see a shadow pass over the floor and his lordship, the great bulk of him, stood by her side.

'I do not mock you, Analee. Is it false to say that I am in love? Can it happen in so short a time? Is it possible?'

'With *me*, my lord?'

'With whom else? I have seen no other woman in the last two days and with you I am besotted, Analee. You are no common gypsy, no whore. No ordinary woman at all. With you I have enjoyed love such as I have seldom known before and I believe it was the same with you too, was it not?'

Analee met the Falcon's gaze and nodded. Yes it was the same with her, like no man before, not even Brent, not even her first love. Even now to look upon his lordship filled her with no ordinary emotion – not mere lust, not love, yet . . . Fascination was perhaps the word.

'I will make you my mistress, Analee and take you to London when the war is over. You will be a woman of importance, live in a fine house. I will set you up properly and see you well married in the end. I do not mistreat those I have loved.'

'Oh, my lord . . .'

The Falcon leaned over to her twisting the ring on his little finger. His lips brushed her cheek and she felt herself trembling. He drew her up and stood facing her, towering over her, tall as she was. Then he put a glass into her hand brimming over with wine and took one from the table for himself. He raised his glass.

'To us.'

The Falcon drank and Analee drank but to what she knew not. A house in London, satins and brocades. Was this what she wanted? She looked over to the window but the curtains were drawn. Outside in the thick snow the foxes would be prowling, the squirrels asleep in their burrows. Somewhere there would be gypsies sleeping in caves, in sheltered ditches. Somewhere there would be Reyora and her baby, her Morella. Analee turned and looked at the proud form of the Falcon as he gazed at her, his glass still raised. She shook her head.

'It cannot be, my lord. I cannot see myself in silks and satins, shoes even . . . the mistress of a nobleman.'

'People will honour you, Analee. It will be no shame.'

'It is not the shame. I cannot do it. I belong in the wild.'

Lord Falconer fell to his knees and seized Analee's slender hand.

'Analee, I am making a passionate declaration of love! I *want* you. I will have you! You will be my mistress and I your humble slave. We will have such a time together Analee . . . so much loving . . .'

He drew her hand to his lips and kissed it, then he put his arm round her waist and drew her to him kissing her tenderly on the mouth. She felt something slip into her hand and her fingers closed over the heavy solid gold ring he had worn on his little finger. She opened her palm and gazed at it. There it lay . . . big, much too big for her, gleaming dully, the outline of the Falcon, sturdy and proud, with the obdurate expression on its face that she also observed on her lord's.

She grasped the ring and stared up at him.

'You have only just met me, my lord.'

'I have known you forever, Analee. I knew even when we met on the field 'twas no ordinary encounter. How you struck me, standing ragged and barefoot as you were among all that death and horror, afflicted and grief stricken and yet . . . proud and untouched and invincible. Ah, well I remember that day, Analee. It was destined that we should meet. You are mine and this gift I give you is the symbol of my troth.

'See, the colour of the gold? 'Tis called Falcon Gold and the story of how this came about is a strange one. One of my ancestors, Sir Beyrick Falconer, was a companion of Sir Francis Drake, a sort of brigand who plundered the Spanish Main in the name of Queen Elizabeth. He was captured by the Spaniards and taken to South America where he contrived to escape and have all manner of adventures among the Indians, so much so that they gave him the name of the Falcon because he was so swift and savage.

'So great were his exploits that he was held in veneration by the Indians. Much of what he did is lost in legend, but he became very wealthy by the discovery of a rich vein of gold that was so fine, so pure, so light that they called it Falcon Gold after my ancestor.

'After that he sailed home, the holds of his ship full of booty and plunder and of course of the rich gold he had found. Much of it he gave to the Queen who made him an Earl in her gratitude ('twas Beyrick's son who became a statesman, and the first Marquess of Falconer). But enough of the gold and booty was left to him by the gracious Queen so that he could extend the rough castle on the

Scottish border, from which he and his ancestors had also plundered both Scots and English by turn when it suited them.

'It was called Falconer's Keep because 'twas but a fortified tower such as were built in olden days by the Marcher Barons from whom my family is descended. Beyrick, now an Earl and become respectable due to the trust placed in him by Her Majesty, tore down the fortress and began the gracious mansion we have here today, and he changed its name to Falcon's Keep because 'twas the gold from South America, the Falcon gold, that made his ennoblement, his good fortune possible.

'Much of the gold that was not retained to swell Queen Elizabeth's coffers was made into our family plate from which we dine on great occasions, and some was made into rings and ornaments. This ring that I wear has descended from father to eldest son since the original Falcon, my ancestor Beyrick.

'And in time my son shall wear it too; but now it is for you. The ring of the Falcon is the symbol of his patronage, that he will protect you and look after you. Your life will never be the same again.'

Analee slipped the ring on her middle finger, but it was too large for her even though the Marquess had worn it on his little finger. Falcon gold. The word of the Falcon was law; his command was to obey.

'But it is too big for me, my lord.'

'That I know.' The Falcon held up a chain of fine gold filigree and, taking the ring off Analee's finger, threaded the chain through it. 'This chain too is made of Falcon gold and belonged to my mother, see how it matches the ring? 'Tis almost white, the colour unique. We have it on our crest, on our banners and everyone knows it as Falcon Gold. Now my love let us dally again, and I promise you rest in a fine bed and in a while some sleep to make up for your lack of it last night in the arms of your impatient wooer.

'Never again will you go to the servant's hall, Analee. From this moment you are my established mistress and the gold of the Falconers is your talisman. Wear it between your breasts because I shall think of them often when I am far from you in the war, and know that my talisman is safe and warm and a symbol of our love.'

Analee fingered the ring and then tucked it into the deep cleavage of her bosom so that all that was seen was the chain around her neck.

'And when you want it back, sir? For another?'

'I have never given it before. Methinks I never shall again.'

Analee heard the cry of an owl, or thought she did. Beside her his lordship slept. She gazed at him with regret. She was loath to tear herself away.

Analee stared into the dark and thought of the owl on the cold snowy branches of the tree and of the gypsies huddled on the hillside; the dead bodies of the Buckland gypsies under the ground. She belonged to the earth, to the soil. She wanted to feel the ground under her bare feet, the feel of grass in the spring.

She fingered the heavy gold ring that lay on her breast; it seemed to thud against her chest like a second heart. It was the symbol of his love, his desire, his possession. It was his yoke. She had to wear it always. Falcon gold.

But she did not belong to the Falcon, nor in fine salons, gracing the arm of a nobleman. Analee gently moved and his lordship murmured in his sleep, reaching for her, as though to keep her with him. In the dying embers of the fire she could see his face and the glow of his limbs, the strong chest, the long muscular legs. The periwig was cast aside now and the dark hair lay loosely on the pillow. He *was* like a falcon with his acquiline nose and proud forehead.

How well he suited her, as a lover and as a man. She gently kissed the forehead of the Falcon and he murmured again; but he was deeply asleep. She got carefully out of the huge bed so as not to disturb him and covered his nakedness with the bedclothes.

She dressed quietly and quickly. Then she stood before the fire to warm herself and yet again fingered the gold ring round her neck. Reluctantly she unfastened the chain and put it with the ring on the table where they had supped. He would know what she meant when he awoke. She was his no longer.

Analee swiftly made her way upstairs to the attic she shared with Nelly. She paused at the door and opened it softly. To her consternation she heard loud masculine snores and saw that Nelly had a companion in the narrow bed with her, mostly obscuring her . . . the great bulk of McNeath.

But Nelly, used to the open life, where danger often lurked, was a light sleeper and as soon as Analee crept into the room she peered out from under the form of her comatose lover.

'Analee,' Nelly whispered and Analee ran lightly to her side, 'are you all right?'

'Nelly? Will he wake?'

'No; he is drunk as well as fuddled with love. Hear how he snores. But I cannot move. He has wedged me. What is it, Analee?'

'Nelly, I am going from here.'

'Has his lordship . . .'

'No, it is nothing his lordship has done. It is what he wants to do.'

'Oh!' Nelly said with alarm.

'Nothing unpleasant,' Analee smiled in the dark. 'He is not a monster . . . on the contrary. I feel I perhaps could love him, and he wants me, Nelly. He wants to set me up and give me a fine home. But, Nelly, 'tis not what I want. I must find Morella. I must know if she is all right. Nelly, I must.'

'But *surely* his lordship . . .'

'His lordship is thinking of romance, not babies! He would not help me find her. I must know what has happened to my baby, Nelly. You must see that! If he takes me to London as he says he will I shall never return again. Besides . . .'

McNeath gave a loud snore and embedded himself more deeply on top of poor Nelly who felt as if she were being slowly stifled to death.

'I am not meant to be a lady, Nelly. It is not the life for me and while I am with him I cannot make his lordship see it. I am going now, Nelly. Farewell . . .'

'Oh, Analee. Let me come with you.'

'Not this time, Nelly. It is too cold, too dangerous. Whether or not we shall meet again I know not. But it is something I must do. Tell my lord . . . say it was not that I did not care . . .'

McNeath snorted again and appeared to be waking up. Nelly felt divided between her own lustful longings and her love for Analee. But even if she wanted to move she could not.

'I think he is waking,' she whispered timorously.

Analee smiled in the dark. 'His lordship will protect you. He is a good man; he knows about Mrs Ardoine so do not let her touch you. Farewell, Nell.'

Analee swiftly implanted a kiss on the cheek of her friend, and brushed it gently with her hand.

Then once more she put her few things together in the familiar bundle and, clasping her cloak firmly about her to ward off the cold, made her way to the stairs.

18

Nelly cowered before the Marquess of Falconer, her head hung abjectly on her chest. She had scarcely had time to recover from the delights of her night with McNeath when she was unceremoniously torn from her bed and rushed before his angry lordship. Fully dressed, striding up and down the Falcon fulminated with wrath.

'Just went out into the night in this weather!' his lordship howled looking out of the window where snow had turned to sleet and dashed against the window panes. 'I believe it not! There was a reason. Tell it me!'

Nelly looked even more abject, were that possible, and gazed at her feet. Suddenly a hefty blow sent her spinning to the floor. She looked up and saw his lordship, his fist raised against her, about to strike her again. The sight of his glowering face, the brooding menace in his eyes struck fear into the girl and she knelt before him, her hands raised in prayer.

'I beg your lordship . . .'

The Falcon's fist trembled and then he went to the tassle by the fireplace and pulled it so sharply it nearly came away from its fastening.

'I am not one to hit a woman in anger, God help me. But I know one who will. I will fetch Mrs Ardoine to administer such a beating that you . . .'

The thought of Mrs Ardoine's terrible birch struck fear into the trembling girl and she fell on her face.

'I beseech your lordship. I know nothing.'

The footman summoned to the door was despatched to fetch the housekeeper and her birch while Nelly wept wildly protesting her innocence.

'I only want to know where she is gone girl! I will not harm her.'

The Falcon looked out of the window and thought of his misery on waking, of moving a hand across the bed to embrace his beloved, of finding it empty. And then of the evidence that she had left him . . . the gold ring with the head of the falcon beside the chain on the table where the remnants of their dinner still stood.

Why, why had Analee done this to him? His emotions were torn between anger and misery as the door opened and the housekeeper, clutching the evil looking bundle of thin sticks, came in and curtsied before her master.

'Madam, I want you to administer a punishing to this young woman,' his lordship snarled pointing to the grovelling Nelly. 'Whip her until she begs for mercy.'

'With pleasure, my lord.'

His lordship strolled to the window, his hands behind his back while, with a smile of anticipation on her face, Mrs Ardoine flexed her cane and applied it sharply to Nelly's legs.

'That is a foretaste my girl. Now get across that chair and pull up your skirts.'

'Oh, ma'am, I beg . . .'

Mrs Ardoine seized Nelly by the shoulder and pulled her to her feet, thrusting her across a chair.

Sobbing wildly Nelly covered her face with her hands begging for mercy her whole body taut, waiting for the sharp sting across her buttocks.

'Stop!' His lordship strode up to Nelly. 'I cannot see it done, not to a woman, not even to a snivelling lying wench like this.'

Mrs Ardoine stepped back, her face a picture of frustration. She liked nothing better than administering a good beating, of seeing flesh wobble and bleed under her cane.

'Pray leave us,' his lordship said sharply to his housekeeper. 'Methinks you are too enamoured of the birch, ma'am. One day someone will apply it to you.'

She grovelled at the menace in Lord Falconer's tone and backed out of the room while Nelly looked apprehensively about her. She was wiping her nose on the back of her hand when his lordship came up to her and surprised her by the expression on his face. Gone was the menace, the threat; instead it was replaced by a look of yearning and sorrow that drew pity from Nelly's heart.

'Nelly, will you not tell me where my Analee has gone? Only a few days did I know her, Nelly, and yet she has a place in my heart none has had before. What is it about Analee? Is she a witch?'

Nelly smiled and looked timorously up at his lordship.

'Nay, sir, she is no witch. But she does have a powerful effect on the hearts of men.'

'Ah, I thought so,' his lordship turned away and looked into the fire. 'By her art alone I know I am by no means the first, but I thought I was an important one. How *could* she leave me, having captured my heart?'

Moved by the sight of the arrogant nobleman reduced to such misery, Nelly was more prone to confide in him than if she had been beaten to pulp. The gypsy in Nelly was used to hardship; kindness was something else.

'I will tell you, your worship, for I see you are much moved. It is not that Analee does not love you, my lord. She asked me to say it was not that she did not care.'

'She said that?' The Falcon looked up eagerly grasping at any hope.

'Yes, my lord, when she came to take leave of me. "Tell him it is not that I did not care," she said. My lord, there *is* something else that occupies Analee's heart, a great sorrow.'

'Tell it me. What is it?'

Nelly sighed and wondered if she was doing the right thing. Analee had not told the Marquess, so why should she? Would it destroy his love forever?

'Analee has a child, your lordship. A small baby who was taken from her soon after it was born. She was looking for the baby when she found the Buckland camp so cruelly destroyed. The child was not there.'

'Analee has a baby? But why did she not tell me?'

Nelly hung her head. 'I know not, my lord. It was the child of her husband, Randal Buckland, and Analee never found favour with the Buckland tribe.'

'Ah, I see it now.'

'The baby was brought up by the *cohani*, Reyora, and Analee fled from the camp.'

'So. It is clear to me now. Oh poor girl, if only she had confided in me.'

'Analee was honoured by the attention paid to her by your lordship. She felt that if . . .'

'I knew about the baby I would not love her. Foolish girl! I

285

would have helped her to find it. I think Analee did not apprehend how much she has moved my heart, Nelly.'

'No, your lordship.'

'And I *will* find her. I will go after her, with your aid, and fetch her back here. Then I will help her find her baby. Now, my girl, there is no time to lose. She cannot have gone far in this weather. Where would she go?'

'She thought the gypsies fled south, my lord, away from the fighting.'

'True, they would – those who survived. Towards Penrith?'

'Aye, my lord.'

'Can you ride a horse, Nelly?'

'Not well, my lord . . .'

'Then you can mount behind McNeath. We will go after Analee this instant. Fetch your cloak and be quick!'

His lordship strode to the fireplace and jerked the tassle again, this time so strongly that it did come away in his hands; but the effect produced a bevy of servants swarming about, and quickly he gave orders.

The snow had begun to melt in the early dawn as Analee set out from Falcon's Keep, careful to stay in the shadow of the hedgerows. She knew by the way the light was breaking in the eastern sky which direction she should take and, despite the cold, she felt an exhilaration at being on the road again, even with the sleet beating in her face, the wet earth squelching under her bare feet.

But as she trudged her thoughts became a confusion of emotions. On the one hand she thought of the strapping body and warm lips of the Falcon, on the other the blond hair and blue eyes of her baby Morella. What would she do with Morella when she found her? What life was it for a wandering gypsy and her child?

The rapturous hours she and Lord Falconer had spent together were something Analee had never known before. The ease and comfort of a large feather bed, and the abundance of wine and good things to eat. For one who had always tossed on the ground or, at best, in a loft of hay, such comfort had enhanced the delights of lovemaking and introduced her to a dimension that was new and wholly pleasurable.

But it was an episode in her life. It was over. As the grey, wintry day grew brighter, Analee sighed and, keeping the low mountain range of the Pennine chain to her left, moved steadily south through the valleys and byways of the border country towards Carlisle.

She encountered no wandering bands as she had before, no straggling soldiers. The armies had moved into Scotland where doubtless Lord Falconer would soon join them and forget all about her.

But Lord Falconer had not forgotten. All day he rode hard south with McNeath and another servant William behind him keeping a sharp eye for that figure that had come to mean so much to him. But the weather was against any hopes he had of success. A mist rose from the fells battling with the steady rain and hung about them all day. Soon the mountains became invisible and he was hard put to keep his bearings and those of his companions.

In the early afternoon he stopped and alighted from his panting horse. He bade McNeath and Nelly dismount with William and wipe down the sweating beasts.

'Curse this mist. We have lost her. She is miles behind. We will return the way we came and look more closely, scouring every path.'

'Would it not be better, my lord, to await her in Penrith?' McNeath ventured, stepping forward. 'We know she will be bound thither, and it is a small town. It grows dark, my lord.'

'Aye,' the Falcon looked about him, 'and I am hungry. You are right, McNeath. We shall lodge with my cousin Lady Delamain, and then set forth tomorrow for Penrith. William you will go back to Falcon's Keep and report my whereabouts, for I am daily expecting a summons to rejoin the army.'

'Aye, my lord.'

William's stomach was rumbling, but an empty belly was part of the price one frequently had to pay in the employ of the Falcon, who rarely thought of himself or others when engaged on service, and this was service of a kind.

'Off now, William, and if you should chance upon Analee apprehend her and fetch her straight to me. Understand?'

'Aye, my lord.'

William mounted his tired horse and wearily turned his way back the twenty miles or so they had come, while the Falcon and his diminished party set their face once more southwards.

Sir George Delamain was honoured at the unexpected arrival of the Marquess of Falconer and sent his servants into a spin of preparations for a sumptuous dinner. Maidservants were despatched with warming pans to prepare his lordship's bed and Nelly and McNeath were sent to the servants' hall.

It was a sad and divided home that Angus Falconer found. Emma was grieving for Stewart Allonby, still confined in Carlisle Castle, and her brother George was too ashamed to mention his fate or that of Brent, bragging only about his own deeds.

'I was very active with the militia in routing the brigands, my lord. When your lordship assisted in the final relief of Carlisle I helped to send them packing across the border.'

'And your brother?' his lordship said with a trace of sarcasm. 'He is well?'

'Brent, my lord. I . . .'

'Your cousin likewise is clapped in Carlisle gaol, I hear, waiting to hang.'

Sir George flushed and took a draught of wine while his wife cast him a glance of disdain.

'You know, cousin, that George has naught to do with the rebels. He distinguished himself on the side of His Majesty's militia. We cannot help it if our family is divided.'

Henrietta looked witheringly at Emma who was gazing in front of her.

'My family, too, is divided, cousin,' the Falcon replied gently, looking at Emma. 'I have many members of it on the side of the Stuarts, including two ducal cousins! There are now two Dukes of Athol, a Hanoverian one and a Jacobite one!'

The Falcon laughed and smiled kindly at Emma as if guessing the secret of her heart. Emma had already visited Stewart in Carlisle Castle, seeking to encourage him and give him hope.

Now that he was rested and had eaten well Henrietta ventured to ask her cousin the reason for his journey.

'I would not ask it, cousin, for it is surely on His Majesty's business, were you not accompanied by a serving girl as well as your servant.'

'Ah.'

The Falcon's eyes sparkled and he twisted the stem of his wine glass winking into its ruby depths.

'I am bewitched by a gypsy. A beautiful woman whom I intend to make my mistress. She has already given me her favours, but I wish to establish her in style. I offered her everything: jewels, silks, the gold of the Falconers; but she has run away from me.'

Emma looked up from her sad reverie at the mention of the word 'gypsy'. Drawn to her brother's wife, Mary, by shared sorrow she knew full well the story of Brent's involvement with a gypsy enchantress. Was it possible that the witch was again abroad in Lakeland?

George Delamain sighed and avoided his guest's eyes. These noblemen and their indiscretions! He would never have boasted about pursuing a mistress; he had just very discreetly paid his last one off for fear Henrietta should become suspicious. Henrietta was beginning to show a pleasing fullness in the figure and he was expecting good news about an heir from her soon. Besides there was a sharpness to Henrietta that made him nervous of displeasing her. After all, the Dacre fortune was no small consideration.

'Really, Angus!' Henrietta said, not one to mince her words, 'a man of your eminence sporting with a gypsy!'

'No ordinary gypsy, my dear. I wager she has noble blood in her veins. She is a temptress, an enchantress.'

Emma said nothing. Neither her brother nor sister-in-law knew about Brent and his gypsy lover; but it was an odd coincidence nevertheless.

'And how will you find your gypsy, Angus?'

'By roving the country for her. I think she is coming south to Penrith, and tomorrow I will wait for her there . . .'

Suddenly there was a commotion at the door and McNeath burst in followed by William who had left them only hours before.

'My lord,' McNeath bowed to Lady Delamain and approached his master, 'William scarcely arrived back when a message came post haste from the Duke of Cumberland who would have you rejoin the army in Scotland. The barbarians are fighting back.'

'Curses!' Lord Falconer jumped up; ''twas a summons I expected but not so soon. Where is His Royal Highness?'

289

He began to question the exhausted William while Henrietta gave directions to her own servants.

'I will leave at first light,' Lord Falconer said, 'my duty to my King comes first. McNeath will journey with me, but Nelly and William will continue the search. If you permit us to stay the night, cousin?'

'Of course. I would be offended if you left before you had passed a peaceful night. Your room is prepared.'

'Then I will go straight to my bed.'

The Falcon bowed and glanced at Emma.

'Good night, Miss Delamain. May you be luckier in your next choice of a sweetheart.'

'There will be no next choice,' Emma said thrusting out her chin defiantly. There was something odious about Lord Falconer; arrogant and imperious. She had been about to ask him discreet questions concerning his gypsy but now decided not to. Besides, it was no concern of hers. She was intrigued though to know the identity of this gypsy who had such a powerful attraction over men. She thought of the maidservant who had come with the Marquess and slipped quietly down to the kitchen where Nelly, recovered from her ordeal, was ogling McNeath across the table where they were enjoying a good meal.

'I am looking for an escort to take me to my mother's house. Will you come with me?' she asked Nelly. 'I have heard what a harrowing journey you had this day. Maybe this good soldier will see you safe back here?'

Nelly jumped up and dropped a low curtsy. She had never seen a fine lady in the kitchen premises before, and this girl was both elegant and beautiful, but she wore an expression of sadness as though she had been bereaved.

'I am Emma Delamain,' Emma said, smiling at Nelly. 'In fact,' she whispered, 'there is something I would ask you.'

Intrigued, Nelly pushed her plate away and, nodding to McNeath went to get her cloak and then followed Emma through the long subterranean corridors of the castle into the cold night air.

'Tell me,' Emma whispered, guiding her along the narrow path to the lodge, 'what is the name of the gypsy so sought after by the Marquess of Falconer?'

Nelly stopped in the dark and McNeath, following close behind, nearly cannoned into her.

'Why miss?'

'I assure you 'twill be a secret. Can you tell it me?'

'Could you not ask his lordship, miss?'

'There are reasons I cannot. Is she called Analee?'

There was no moon and Nelly felt confused and uncomfortable in the darkness, uncertain what to say. She saw they were approaching the house and the glow of candles flickered through the thin rain. The door opened and Emma's mother peered anxiously into the darkness.

'Emma, is it you?'

'Yes, Mama. Lord Falconer has arrived at the castle and his servants very kindly brought me home. Please,' Emma whispered urgently, '*tell* me her name.'

Suddenly Nelly heard the sharp cry of a baby and Mrs Delamain disappeared back inside the house. Emma ran forward followed by Nelly and McNeath who thus found themselves all assembled together in the hallway.

'It is all right,' Mrs Delamain smiled. 'She has the colic. We have a baby you see,' she looked at Nelly, 'the most darling little child, do come and see her.'

She put a hand to her lip and crept up the stairs followed by a very puzzled Nelly. To whom did the baby belong? Would Miss Delamain have a *baby*? It was quite a common occurrence for unmarried gypsy girls, but among the gentry . . .

Emma was behind her but McNeath, awkward in this company, stayed on the doorstep. Inside the nursery Nelly could see a nurse fussing over the crib.

'Come see our baby,' Mrs Delamain said, 'she has transformed our bleak lives. A gift from God, the darling . . .'

Nelly leaned forward, a candle held high for her by Emma who was also smiling.

'Is she not perfect?' Emma said, 'she was found quite by chance.'

Nelly leaned over and looked into the face of Morella, little changed since she had last seen her. She was bigger and chubbier, but had the same flaxen hair, the same large blue eyes and cupid's bow mouth as the baby that Analee had given birth to that awful night three months before. Was it only three months? It seemed like a lifetime. Comforted the baby had stopped crying and gazed earnestly up into the eyes of the girl who had helped to deliver her.

Nelly gazed for a long time at Morella, her mind in a whirl. She turned to look at the nurse expecting to see Reyora, but a stranger returned her gaze.

'She is lovely,' Nelly said at last, nervously stepping back, 'is she yours, miss?'

'*Mine*?' Emma laughed. 'I am unwed! No she is not mine, would that she were! She was found by chance, and ailing, among a crowd of gypsies fleeing from the war. My mother gave shelter to the woman who had saved her – her mother and father had been killed by the soldiers. Then this woman wanted to go and rejoin her tribe, but my mother begged to be allowed to keep the baby. Seeing that in these hard times she would be well looked after, the woman reluctantly agreed. Her name is Morella.'

Nelly knew her name; she knew everything about her, her mother and her father. How such an extraordinary circumstance had come about that Morella was in the care of her lawful grandmother she could not guess. She could only attribute it to the will of God.

One thing she knew. She must find Analee and tell her her baby was safe. Only then would Analee have peace.

Nelly looked once more at Morella, noticing the fine lawn of her nightgown, the linen on her crib, the soft shawls and blankets. The room was richly furnished and a fire glowed in the grate. The nurse's only task was to look after her. Morella could not be better cared for. Nelly knew what she must do.

She gave Morella her finger to clutch for a moment, then murmured a silent blessing on her head and stepped back.

'I must get back to the castle, miss. McNeath will be waiting for me.'

Emma followed her down and saw her to the porch. She held the candle high and looked earnestly into Nelly's face.

'I must know,' she said, '*was* she called Analee?'

Nelly stared at Emma, her open country girl's face wide-eyed and innocent.

'Oh no, miss, nothing like that. I've never heard that name to tell you the honest truth.'

Emma searched Nelly's face, but found there only honesty and simplicity. Surely such a girl would not lie? Would have no need to lie?'

'Thank God,' Emma said stepping back into the hall. 'I thought for a moment it might have been a woman also loved by my brother. He cannot forget her either.'

Guessing that her lover might try and find her Analee avoided the roads and kept instead to the hillsides and valleys. She skirted Penrith, it was too full of memories for her; the wood high on the hill was where she had made love to Brent, where Morella was conceived. But once close by Penrith the hills of Lakeland appeared out of the mist in the west and she was drawn towards them as one seeking shelter from an angry and hostile world. Maybe Reyora, fleeing from the armies, would have found refuge in these hills? Almost instinctively Analee set out in the direction of Keswick, scarcely knowing why she did.

As the days passed the weather improved. Although the cold was biting, the rain had ceased and occasionally the sun shone. The nearer she got to the vale of Derwentwater the higher loomed the mountains on either side of the busy road on which plenty of traffic – carts, horses, sometimes a fine carriage and walkers like herself – plied between Penrith and Keswick.

Analee savoured the peace and beauty of the scene around her. Here in the hedgerows, among the pine forests she had found brief happiness. Thinking as she did constantly of the lover she had left and the baby she had lost, the magnificent country-side was a balm to her tired soul. But although she saw many people on their way to market at Penrith, drovers with sheep or cattle, farmers with their produce, the odd pedlar, she saw no gypsies. No one had seen a gypsy tribe, no one a gypsy woman and a fair-haired baby. Of everyone she saw and stopped, she asked the same question.

But the answer was always a smile and a regretful shake of the head.

The purple range of Blencathra and giant Skiddaw on her right, Helvellyn, and the distant mountains surrounding Ullswater to her left, Analee finally saw in the distance the ribbon of blue that was Derwentwater enclosed by its hills. Just as she saw it the sun broke through the clouds lowering over the mountains, and the purple clad hills were bathed in the gentle light of early morning. Suddenly in her mind's eye Analee saw the house on the side of the lake, pink stoned and surrounded by water, almost hidden in the forest of pines.

Would they receive her? Welcome her? Did she dare? At least she would know what had happened to Brent, Morella's father.

Purple Skiddaw now loomed above her and the wide expanse of Derwentwater ahead of her glittered. The mountain tops covered with snow stretched like sentinels of uneven height guarding the entrance to a magic kingdom.

Analee took the path to the right before she reached the town nestling in the valley. At once she began to climb through a forest and when she emerged the hills towered about her, their purples, browns and greens a kaleidoscope of colour while below her stretched a much longer, wider vista of the lake cerulean in the sunlight. Her heart quickened as she rounded a hill and there, perched on a promontory, was Furness Grange, its pink stone and black beams reflected in the still waters of the lake. Analee began to descend until she reached the wood and then she saw the jetty where the boat landed, and the small crofter's cottage that nestled against the mountain side, wood smoke spiralling upwards through the trees.

Analee approached the lakeside and sat on a stone. She pulled up her torn skirts to her knees and rubbed her sore calloused feet. She was very weary. Five days had passed since she had left Falcon's Keep, and now it seemed that even her mind was numbed by the harsh winds that wrapped round her at night instead of the warm blankets she had become used to.

Used? Analee sat up and stared at the distant peaks. Had she become used to the easy life, even the attic at Falcon's Keep? A roof over her head and food, however humble, however roughly thrown at her, to eat?

But the master had offered her much more. He had offered her untold wealth and security, a place of honour and status by his side.

Analee shook her head. It was not for her. She let her feet soak in the clear water even though it was icy cold and stared at the pebbles sparkling beneath. Yes her belly was empty; she was cold and almost permanently damp. Maybe the Allonbys would let her spend a night in their barn? After all, she had not harmed them.

She rose and, picking up her bundle, walked round to the

kitchen entrance from which came the good smell of baking bread. Maybe Betty would be there and . . . Suddenly she stopped. A woman was staring at her from the window; a woman whose face she recognized, but whose expression was hostile, even frightened.

Mary Allonby had on her face a look of such bitterness that Analee stepped back and shielded her eyes from the morning sun to be sure she was not deceived.

'Hey!' a voice called out and Betty Hardcastle stood at the door of the kitchen, her arms on her hips. 'We want no vagabonds . . . why?' She went up, her eyes screwed against the sun which had risen over Walla Crag, and stared at Analee. 'Were you not the gypsy that was here?'

Analee nodded, half smiling, half afraid.

'Then get thee off quick. Thou art not welcome here.'

'But why?'

Analee backed away, frightened and dejected. What had she done?

'Let her stay.' Mary Allonby stood behind Betty, gazing at Analee. Then she brushed past Betty and went over to her, her face a mixture of emotions – pity and anger and curiosity. ''Twas not her fault he preferred her to me.'

'Me?' Analee faltered. Then gradually, intuitively, she understood what Mary was talking about.

'He is not here?'

'You had better come inside,' Mary turned and Analee followed her through the kitchen into the hall, then into the room overlooking the lake she remembered so well. And there was Charles the Martyr on the wall and the heads of all the Allonby ancestors looking, it seemed, down at her.

'I see you are cold and wet,' Mary said. 'Sit by the fire, and Betty will bring you some nourishment. But what are you doing, Analee? What has happened to you?'

'I left a baby when I came here, driven out by the Buckland gypsies. Then when the war started I knew I had done wrong. I wanted to know what had happened to her, where she was. I found the Buckland camp pillaged and half the tribe dead . . .'

'The baby . . .'

Analee shook her head. For once in her life she felt close to tears.

'No. I have sought her. I have not found her. Some escaped. I think they went further south, maybe to Lancaster. I only ask for a night's rest in the warm barn and I shall turn back the way I came . . .'

She stopped and looked at Mary, aware of the things that were unspoken between them.

'I am not welcome here, am I? It is because . . .'

Mary's eyes filled with tears. 'He does not love me, but you. He went mad when you disappeared, tried to follow you.'

'But did you not wed?'

'Oh, we *wed*,' Mary said bitterly. 'My brother held a knife at his throat though I only discovered that afterwards. It was the gentlemanly thing to do, anyway, Brent knew that. But he does not love me, Analee, he cannot. Although three months wed I am still a maid.'

Mary bit her lip and looked anxiously at Analee.

'He has tried but he cannot. He was glad to go to the war, glad to get away from me.'

'And that is where he is?'

'Aye, with the Prince. If not dead. He was wounded at Clifton, but he avoided capture at Carlisle, although my brother Stewart is now imprisoned in the gaol there, awaiting death.'

Analee saw the tears stealing down Mary's face and her heart filled with compassion. She got up and gently put her arm around the weeping girl.

'May I, Mary? Do you forgive me? I liked you so much when I was here before; you were so good to me, so kind. I lay with Brent but once; 'twas a circumstance . . .' She faltered. Mary nodded.

'He told me. He said it was magical, the moonlight, the forest. He said you bewitched him.'

Analee laughed derisively. 'I am no witch.'

The memory of Brent, or Randal, or her first faraway love, seemed so remote now. She thought of her latest love, the Falcon. Her heart lurched at the memory of his vigour, the strange power he exercised over her, the compelling, riveting look in his hooded eyes. Truly she was half afraid of him half – dare she think it – in love? Yes she did have a power over men; but it was not sorcery.

'When you and Brent meet again, Mary, I will be far away. I will go south back to where I came from, maybe find my own tribe.'

'Can you not release Brent from your spell?'

'I have *no* spell, Mary.'

'But Stewart said . . .'

'Oh, that was folly.'

'But she *did* fall in love with him! Emma, our cousin, the one he loved. She said she suddenly seemed to see him with new eyes.'

Analee was aware that she was cold despite the warmth of the fire. She shivered. The power of the *cohani* . . .

'Well,' she shrugged, 'maybe there *is* something we can try . . .' She stopped at the sound of a footstep and stern-faced John Allonby stood at the door.

'John, this is . . .' Mary stepped forward but John brushed her aside.

'I know who it is. Betty told me. Don't you think you have done enough harm, you *gypsy*. . .'

'John, do not speak to her like that! She is not to blame if she is beautiful . . .'

''Tis not beauty, 'tis sorcery. She should be burnt like others of her kind.'

'John, how can you be so cruel? They have not burnt witches for many years in these parts. Analee is my friend.'

'*And* with the rest of her tribe,' John said contemptuously. 'See, more are gathered outside.'

Analee ran to the window, her eyes scarcely able to believe what they saw.

''Tis Nelly. Oh, Mary, 'tis *Nelly*! I thought I would never see her again.'

Nelly sobbed as soon as she saw Analee, and it was a long time before she could explain why she had come. The stout William who had brought her on his horse eagerly quaffed from the tankard of ale he was offered.

'We were on our way back, having waited at Penrith and scoured the countryside, I asking after you constantly, when someone remembered seeing a gypsy of particular beauty,' Nelly looked slyly at Analee, 'on the way towards Keswick. I remembered the house here, and on the chance . . . Analee, you are to come back! His lordship is pining for you. He has had to return to the Army . . .'

Mary and John were looking with astonishment at Nelly and

Analee, embarrassed and realizing they had no idea what Nelly was talking about, put a hand on her arm saying. 'Shh, desist.'

'His lordship?' John said abruptly. 'Lord who?'

'Lord Falconer, sir,' Nelly bobbed, 'he is very smitten with Analee.'

'The Falcon,' John thundered, 'the terror of the Jacobites. *You* and him?'

Analee met his eye boldly, nodding her head.

'His lordship found me when the gypsy camp had been overrun and despoiled by *your* soldiers, sir. The Jacobites for sure it was raping our women before killing them. He had me taken to his home as a servant and . . . he did me the honour of . . .'

Analee, seldom at a loss for words, couldn't for once think quite how to put it. Mary felt her hatred for the gypsy woman evaporating. After all, she had suffered much, too. How tired and worn she looked.

'He fell in love with you obviously,' Mary said with a sad smile, 'as other men have. My brother Stewart half fell in love with you too.'

Mary looked at John and saw how, despite his initial hostility, even his face had grown softer after some time in Analee's company. John, whose heart had turned to stone on the death of his young wife.

'The Marquess of Falconer,' John murmured disbelieving. 'He swoops on his foe like a falcon, is feared and hated . . .'

'He is not as bad as he might appear,' Analee said defensively. '*Once* you get to know him.'

'He saved me from a flogging,' Nelly said supportively, 'mind you he ordered it in the first place, then he changed his mind. Oh, I can see how he could appeal to a woman.'

Nelly was nevertheless thinking of the lusty McNeath whom she personally preferred. She sighed at the very thought of him away at the war.

'Then, Analee, will you go back since you are sent for?' Mary said.

'I? No. I will find my baby and maybe take her to the south away from here, to my tribe. His lordship would have me set up in style as his mistress, but I am not that sort. I am a vagabond, and so I shall remain. As for Nelly, what she will do I know not; but if you will give us a day's rest in your barn we shall be on our way. Eh, Nelly? On the road again?'

Nelly had become extremely attached to McNeath in the short time she had known him and the thought of not seeing him again was almost more than she could bear to contemplate. She stared in alarm at Analee and then said quietly,

'First I have to discuss something with thee. Something very important.'

'Analee, you and Nelly will have your old room overlooking the lake,' Mary said. 'Yes, I insist, and that you dine with us at table. You must tell me what you have seen of the war. I cannot believe the terrible things you speak of of our soldiers. Now you and Nelly go upstairs and I will have Betty fetch hot water for the tub and some fresh clothes for you. No, I am adamant . . .'

Analee was overcome by such kindness on the part of someone she had so unwittingly wronged. Despite her protests, though, she and Nelly were taken firmly in hand and ushered up the broad staircase of Furness Grange.

That night Analee and Nelly snuggled down together in the large bed in the room overlooking the lake. The moonlight rippled along the water, as though moved by a mysterious current, and Analee had spent a long time at the window looking at the broad sweep of Derwentwater, from Keswick nestling under massive Skiddaw in the east right to the jaws of Borrowdale in the west. It was a cold night and snow had started to fall again. Analee thought of the Falcon preparing, perhaps, to do battle against Brent, against the people the Allonbys supported and loved.

Analee sighed and Nelly put her arms around her hugging her, her hand stroking the smooth silky flesh of her back.

'Come, you will not make love to me!' Analee protested laughingly. Nelly blushed in the dark.

'Nay, it is not like that. I do not love you as a man; but I love you, Analee, you know that. I missed you so much. I feared I would never find you.'

'Aye. I thought we had seen the last of each other.'

'Analee, will you not return to his lordship? He . . .'

'No.' Analee lay on her back, her head resting on her hands. 'I am a gypsy. I will find Morella and go south. We . . .'

'Analee . . .'

Timidly, nervously Nelly put her hand on Analee's shoulder. She put a hand up to stroke her cheek, tilting Analee's face towards her.

'What is it, Nell?' Analee was aware of something troubling her friend.

'Analee, I have found the baby . . . Morella.'

'What is it you say?' Analee sat upright in the bed. 'You what? Oh Nell, she is . . .'

'No, no . . . she is alive, she is well. Analee, she was found by Brent on his way to Penrith, he not knowing who she was, sick and ailing with Reyora. Being a kindly man he sent her to his mother at Delamain Castle nearby. The mother took a fancy to the baby, not knowing it was her granddaughter, and has kept her. Is it not a miracle? Reyora had just left when we arrived.'

'And you said . . .'

'I said nothing, Analee. His lordship, who had gone to the castle, had told everyone that he was seeking a beautiful gypsy girl – see how proud he is of you Analee? He does not hide you at all – and Emma Delamain was reminded of the story of Brent and the gypsy. She asked me if she were the same person. Thank God I did not reply until I had seen the baby and when I had, I said "no".'

'She knew my name?'

'Yes. She had it from Mary Allonby.'

Analee leaned back against the pillow her eyes full of tears.

'How is . . . Morella?'

'Oh, Analee, she is so beautiful, a big bonny baby. Her hair is golden and her eyes so round and blue, just like her father's I'll warrant.'

'Yes they were.'

'She chuckles and laughs, she has that dimple on each cheek, do you remember, Analee?'

'I remember. I shall fetch her, Nelly, and . . .'

Nelly pressed Analee's shoulder trying to comfort her. 'Analee, what I have to say is this. Is it right that you should take Morella? She was so ill on the road, nearly died of cold and hunger, and now she is so pampered and cosseted. She has her own room and a soft crib and fine linen; beautiful lawn nightdresses and her very own nursemaid. She smells of sweet oils and unguents and a fire glows in the grate to warm her.'

'You're saying, Nelly . . .' Analee gripped Nelly's hand. 'You're saying I should *leave* Morella?'

'Yes, Analee; she is with her family, her own grandmother. In time, especially if you went back to his lordship, you may have the means to claim Morella. But as a wandering gypsy . . . Is it right, Analee?'

'But I am her mother.'

'What can you give her except hardship and maybe death? She will grow to be a fine lady, and you, too, Analee. As his lordship's favourite . . . in time, who knows? But I think now you must give up thoughts of claiming Morella, leave her where she is. You owe it to her, Analee.'

Analee threw herself on Nelly weeping copiously. Nelly stroked her long hair and her back, hugging her in her arms.

'Analee, you are a young woman. You will have other babies. With his lordship's protection . . .'

'I am *not* going back to his lordship!' Analee thumped the bed. 'I am a gypsy, a vagabond. I want no jewels and silks.'

'But you loved him didn't you?' Nelly murmured softly. 'Was your love not as instant as his own; just as urgent? Even that day on the field when you met?'

'Aye, his lordship has a powerful attraction. He is a fine strong handsome man. Whether 'tis love . . . No, Nelly. My mind is made up. Tomorrow, whatever you decide, I will go from hence and make my way south to where I came from.'

'And Morella? Will you take her, too?'

Analee was silent, the tears still flowing quietly in the dark.

19

To the surprise of everyone – most people having considered them defeated – the Jacobite fortunes improved despite the persistent bickering that still dogged the commanders, and the many desertions as disillusioned Highlanders made their way to their homes. Reinforcements had arrived to swell the Jacobite army to about 8000 men and a new mood of confidence swept through the Prince's followers.

But the Hanoverians had regrouped too, and sent for reinforcements from the South. These began to foregather in large numbers in Scotland under General Handyside and General Hawley.

Lord Falconer, not yet gazetted lieutenant-general, was sent to join General Hawley's command and arrived in Edinburgh just as his troops were leaving to march to Linlithgow.

Hawley was a severe, unpopular man rumoured to be a natural son of George II and thus half-brother to the Duke of Cumberland. However, he and Angus Falconer found much in common. They were both tough disciplinarians and the Marquess did not share the men's opinion that Hawley was a poor military strategist. Hawley was pleased to see Falconer and immediately drew him into his counsel with his second-in-command General Huske.

The objective was to relieve Stirling, which was being besieged by the Jacobites. An advance party, however, under Lord George Murray came upon the government army, and the Prince's soldiers were thus withdrawn from Stirling and drawn up around Bannockburn in anticipation of an attack being made.

But the attack never came. Hawley spent much time in council with his commanders and decided to wait for the Jacobites to expend themselves. He was convinced that the rebel army was a contemptible bunch of rascals, and could never withstand well trained and disciplined soldiers such as his own, the victors of Dettigen and Fontenoy. He did, however, warn his men about the Highlanders' barbarian tactics in order to prepare them and allay their fears.

As the Falcon – eyes hooded ready to pounce on the foe – waited at the head of his men for the Jacobite charge that they knew must come he was possessed by an unaccustomed feeling of unease. He didn't like the fact that the Jacobite army had formed a superior position on the barren moorland ahead of him known as the hill of Falkirk. Moreover, part of the government army had unexpectedly taken off under the impression that the Jacobites were moving south, and now that it had been reported as a false alarm, manoeuvred by Lord John Drummond, Falconer realized how clever the Jacobite reasoning was. Half the government army was still absent, including its commander Hawley who was last seen dining well as a guest of Lady Kilmarnock at Callender House. Falconer had refused the invitation to accompany his commander. He knew Lady Kilmarnock supported her husband who was with the Prince's troops and suspected her motives in offering such lavish entertainment to a government commander.

It was cold and the Falcon shivered in the wind as the storm clouds gathered. Suddenly a bugle sounded and the Jacobite army was observed not a mile and a half away, moving up in the direction of Falkirk Muir.

There was still no sign of Hawley, and Falconer and his fellow commanders began making agitated signals to disperse their troops in order to confront the enemy. Suddenly Hawley, red faced, his jacket still undone, appeared at the gallop and ordered the dragoon regiments to march up the hill before the Highlanders got there; but as the command was given the clouds broke and rain lashed down in the face of the government army, almost obscuring their sight of the enemy.

Lord Falconer's foreboding increased as he ordered his men to draw their swords and advance slowly. Ahead he could see the government forces with their cannon struggling up the hill right in the face of the gale which the Jacobites had to their backs. The cannon stuck in the mud and Angus urged his men forwards to assist the foot soldiers. An order came from Hawley, however, for Lord Falconer's dragoons to break into a trot and as the run towards the enemy began the Marquess forgot his foreboding and plunged into the thick of the fight, swirling his sword about his head regardless of the onslaught of enemy fire.

But the fire took others by surprise and two regiments of

dragoons on their right flank wheeled about and fled the field. The Falcon shouted to his men and, spurring his horse, dived regardless into the line of Highlanders confronting him. Savagely he began trampling them underfoot, his sword flaying to right and left.

The storm gathered momentum and dusk began to fall but, impelled by a new savagery, even for him, Falconer penetrated the heart of the enemy line relishing the crunch of bones as the men fell under his horse's hooves. Even the wild cries of the Highlanders did not disturb him, and he was well into the enemy ranks when suddenly his horse trembled and fell, and a huge Scot, looming out of the gloom, struck Lord Falconer a blow with his broadsword that felled him. As his head crashed to the ground his lordship's last thoughts were that this was the end.

McNeath, perceiving what had happened to his master, rushed to him just as the large Highlander was about to administer a mortal blow, and practically severed the man's head from his shoulders. From under the Falcon's horse another Highlander crawled out and McNeath, in white fury at seeing his lord so badly injured, despatched him to hell as well. By this time more of Falconer's officers had come to McNeath's assistance and, even though they thought their commander was dead, they removed him from the height of battle to the side of a nearby stream. Then they returned to the fray while McNeath tried to unloose his lordship's tight clothes and see whether he breathed or not.

His lordship breathed, but erractically. McNeath saw, to his consternation, that the Jacobite army was triumphant in the field and that many of the dragoons were fleeing in terror at the bloody frenzy of the Highlanders. Even now some of the Jacobite troops were stripping the bodies of the enemy dead for loot. McNeath thought that if he left his master as he was, he was as good as dead, so he heaved him onto his back and lumbered with him into the shelter of the neighbouring forest. There he remained until nightfall when he was able to emerge and seek fresh help.

Both sides claimed victory at Falkirk, but for Hawley it was a bitter blow and he was to wreak vengeance on his own men by the savagery of his actions to those whom he thought had been guilty of cowardice.

The Marquess of Falconer meanwhile knew nothing of this. He remained unconscious and only came to the following day in the bed of a government sympathizer who lived nearby. He had a terrible pain in his head and difficulty in focusing his eyes, and he could hardly move his body. McNeath and his hostess hovered anxiously by and General Hawley, who had personally observed Falconer's bravery, sent word to enquire after him.

'Those beggarly Highlanders pierced the belly of your horse from under you, your lordship, as you passed overhead,' McNeath muttered. 'They did the same to a number of officers, most of whom are dead. Their dirks dug in the animal's belly. Many of them that did it were crushed beneath, but they cared not.'

The Falcon nodded, scarcely able to reply. He looked towards the window and everything blurred. He thought he was done for. He was going to die as he had seen many men do; despatched from the world and forgotten. And who would remember him? His brother James would succeed to his title. His family would mourn for him for a while, but what had he really achieved? What had he to leave behind? No family of his own, no loving wife to mourn his passing, no children.

Suddenly Angus opened his eyes and saw very clearly the face of Analee looking at him, her deep brown eyes tender and passionate. She came nearer to him and her lips parted to kiss him, revealing her splendid even white teeth.

'Analee . . .' he opened his mouth to return the kiss, but she was no longer there.

'Sir?'

'I saw Analee, McNeath, the gypsy woman. Is she here?'

'No, sir.'

'Ah. It was so clear. I am dying then. 'Twas like a vision of an angel. Farewell, Analee, my love.'

Angus' head sank back on the pillow. He had seen her. She had come to visit him; but maybe, after all, to tell him he would recover. Her face had not looked sad. She was a witch, a sorceress. He felt better already. The pain was less severe and when he focused his eyes on the window he could clearly see the skeletal trees outside and the dark, stormy clouds hovering above. He closed his eyes and Analee came to him in a vision again, her body naked and her belly swollen with child. His child. He put his hands on the belly and kissed it and the child inside moved. Analee was going to have his child; he would have a child to leave to the world. He would be remembered.

His lordship opened his eyes and looked at the ceiling his face puckered in a frown. Then he lost consciousness again.

As Analee and Nelly lay in bed at Furness Grange clasped together, half waking half sleeping, talking through the night, the snow had continued to fall and by the following day a white blanket feet thick cloaked the moors and fells of Lakeland.

Mary Delamain had refused to hear of Analee's departure but William, however, insisted on attempting to make the journey, fearing the wrath of the Falcon if he did not return. With trepidation they watched him set out, snow half way up his horse's legs. And still it fell. Considering the circumstances Mary was kindness itself to her guest. The two women resumed the friendship only briefly begun months past. Mary talked about Brent and the Stuart tragedy while Analee, without saying what she knew from Nelly, talked about the baby so cruelly taken from her, as though listening to her own words comforted her.

Nelly set to helping in the house and the kitchen, and the days they spent isolated from the world in that beautiful part of Lakeland were to remain in the minds of all for many a long day. The lake froze over so that even the boat could not reach them, and the hardy Herdwick sheep had to fend for themselves on the bleak snow-covered fells. But the cows could be milked and there were provisions in the larder sufficient to prevent the family and the guests from starving.

One morning Analee woke to see that the thaw had set in and, although still bitterly cold, only traces of the snow remained on the ground. The high peaks around them were still thickly covered and, outlined against the blue sky and tinged by the rosy morning sun, looked like some promised land upon which Analee knew she must turn her back, perhaps forever. She shook Nelly awake.

'Nelly! The snow has almost gone. And I am going too. These good people have been so kind, but it is time I left.'

Nelly shivered in her comfortable bed. The thought of a life on the road again, scratching about for food and sleeping in ditches . . .

'Analee, *must* we go?'

'I am going, Nell. You could make your way back to Falcon's Keep or . . .'

'No. No. I will not be welcome there without you. His lordship will have me well and truly whipped! I will go with you, Analee, be with you where you are. We will find a way together. Besides you will need help with Morella . . .'

Analee stood very still in the act of fastening the laces of her bodice. She looked out of the window for a long time and then at Nelly.

'No. I will not fetch Morella. I have often talked about her with Mary these last few days and, although Mary does not know Morella is my baby, she has told me how well looked after the baby is, how much her aunt dotes on her, like a second daughter. It is all the comfort the poor woman has in the world after the tragedies of these past months. There Morella is loved and protected. What right have I to claim her?'

The tears began again to fall down Analee's cheeks and she quickly finished her toilet and, yet again, started to collect her few things together.

The Allonbys, early risers, were already at breakfast as Nelly and Analee descended the stairs. Mary looked at the bundle and the expression on Analee's face and jumped up.

'Oh, you are not going?'

'Yes, the snow has cleared. You have been so kind to us Mary, dear Mary, more kind than I can ever say or forget. You have helped me more than you know . . .'

Mary looked for a long time into the clear eyes of Analee, trying to fathom there the mystery of a woman who intrigued her more the more she knew about her. Was it not strange that Analee had lost a baby and Aunt Susan had found one? But the baby was fair, not dark, not a gypsy baby, not like Analee at all. Analee had seemed so persistent in talking about little Morella, in wanting to know everything about her. Maybe, Mary decided, to comfort her for the loss of her own.

'Are you sure, Analee? You are welcome here. Betty will miss Nelly in the kitchen, and I talking to you. We are like sisters.'

'I think we shall meet again,' Analee said gravely. 'How or when I know not, but in my bones I feel it.'

They both looked up sharply at the clatter of hooves descending the hill towards the house. There were two men and Nelly ran to the window.

'Oh, Analee, 'tis McNeath. McNeath with William. Oh, he must bring word . . .'

Nelly flew to the door followed by the others. In the courtyard McNeath had descended from his horse which stood snorting and steaming after a rough ride. McNeath's face was red and he was panting hard.

'Ah . . . Analee. William and I have ridden all night. 'Tis his lordship. He is dying and he would see you before he breathes his last. Pray go to him I beg you!'

McNeath who loved his master almost fell on his knees, his face creased in supplication. Analee's hand flew to her heart and for a moment she thought she would swoon. The world seemed to turn upside down, so that the earth was over her head, the sky under her feet. She leaned against the doorway.

'Dying?'

'Aye, badly wounded in battle. We brought him home, but he has not rallied. His days are numbered. He asks for you all the time. William brought word of your whereabouts, but we have not dared tell the master you refused to return. Oh, Analee, you must come home, even to see him breathe his last.'

Analee thought of the mighty, powerful Falcon lying on his deathbed. They had shared so much pleasure, such rapture. But more than that she could not forget him. His presence haunted her mind and his image seemed constantly to hover before her. Now she had no doubt what she must do.

'I will come,' she said quietly and turned to Nelly whose face was alight with joy at seeing her beloved again.

'Nelly? You get up with McNeath. I'll go behind William.' Analee paused and gazed solemnly at McNeath. 'McNeath, this is not a trick to lure me back. You are sure?'

'Oh, Madam, would it were,' the soldier said brokenly. 'Even as we talk my master may be dead.'

The room was very quiet, the curtains half drawn to keep the light out of his eyes. Only his heavy uneven breathing disturbed the silence. His face was ashen and covered with sweat, his great beaked nose and closed eyes already resembled a mask of death.

Analee stood by his side and gazed at him. They had ridden all day and she still wore her cloak, her face grimy with dust. They had not even paused to eat, negotiating the narrow tracks with an ease born of desperation. Lord Falconer was considered to have very little time to live. The servants already crept about as in a house of death.

Analee placed a cool hand on his brow. She closed her eyes and willed him to live; that the life force should pass through her own vibrant body into his. She pressed her hand on his forehead and murmured the only gypsy blessing she knew. If ever she had *cohani* powers she used them now, summoned every force in her being to invoke the spirits of her Romany ancestors.

But the Falcon did not stir. She drew her hand away and saw her palm was covered with the moisture from his brow. Analee knelt by the side of the bed and took between hers the hand that had already been placed crosswise on his breast, in an attitude of resignation to death. She leaned over and kissed his cheek letting her lips brush over his, sending the message of life and vitality.

'Do not die, my lord,' she whispered. 'There are so many good things yet to do.'

Suddenly his eyelids flickered and those standing near gasped. Then they saw his pain-wracked eyes gazing at Analee. He looked at her face for a long time and slowly she saw the colour beginning to creep back to his ashen cheeks. She smiled.

'Am I in heaven?' he whispered.

'Not yet, my lord. I think they would not have you there.'

Analee pressed his hands and put her lips to his cheek.

'Is it real? Is it *you*, Analee?'

'They have brought you home and I have come to you. You are going to get better. I have willed it.'

'You *are* a witch,' the Falcon murmured weakly. But there was a trace of a smile on his lips as he closed his eyes again and fell into a peaceful, more natural sleep.

There were those who had witnessed the miracle they said Analee had performed on the dying nobleman, and went in awe of her from that day. That she had supernatural powers very few doubted. For the Marquess began to recover and from then on Analee never left his side. At night she slept by his bed on the floor. Nelly brought her fresh clothes and she and McNeath supervised the serving of the food, the broths and coddled eggs needed to restore his lordship to health.

He spoke little. In the days that followed Analee's return he could hardly speak at all. But when his eyes were opened they gazed at her, and always when he closed them he smiled as though he were dreaming of her.

The doctors thought it was a miracle, they had given his lordship only hours to live. His wounds were not only severe, but infected with pus. Now even the wounds were beginning to heal. The gypsy woman would go herself into the grounds and, even in the depths of winter, return with herbs and plants which she mixed with her own blood, urine and spittle to lay on his wounds. These she refreshed herself every day. The doctors were horrified by the evidence of this sorcery. She was certainly a witch, otherwise the Marquess of Falconer would be dead.

Analee knew that the powers had flowed from her to her lord. It had felt almost as though her own life was draining away and passing to him. One day they were alone together and, in weariness, she stretched on the bed beside him. She could feel his regular breathing beside her, the pulse growing stronger every day, the healthy complexion returning to his face.

She awoke to feel a hand caressing her and as she turned saw that Lord Falconer's eyes were wide open and gazing at her.

'I think you are recovering fast, my lord.'

The Falcon said nothing but turned her towards him and she laid her head on his breast, listening to the quick healthy pounding of his heart, knowing that his blood still flowed strongly and well.

Analee had restored the Falcon to life.

A week later Lord Falconer was able to sit up in bed, resting against cushions piled high behind him. Analee now slept by his side every night because he would not be parted from her; but she got up before he woke and made sure his food was ready to be served. Then when he had eaten she washed him all over with perfumed soap, drying him and rubbing oils of fresh pine, lavender and herbs into his skin. She then put on him a clean fresh nightshirt and combed his long black hair back from his head, noting the new found vigour in his fine eyes, the healthy flush of his skin. He had lost a lot of weight, but he had always taken such care of his body that his illness appeared to have done him no lasting harm. He was wiry like a young man. His thin face still handsome with the long aquiline nose and the thick brows, the clean shaven cheeks and the ruthless mouth, whose harsh lines were softened by Analee's presence and, more often than not, curled up in amusement at something she had said or done.

For Analee was not only a lover but a companion to him. She entertained him and amused him. Her character delighted him and he made her go over and over again the story of her life, the myths and legends of Romany love. He found her knowledgeable, even profound, and they would discuss life and its deeper meanings, of which both felt they had recently acquired harsh knowledge.

Analee sat by his bedside all day talking or watching him as he slept, for he had still to regain his strength. As he sat there on this day, propped up, the Marquess looked at the woman who daily became more precious to him.

'Analee, do you not get bored here with me all day?'

'Bored, my lord? I?'

'Can you not read?'

'No sir. I was never taught.'

The Marquess laughed and told her to fetch him a travel book from the case by the side of his bed. She snuggled up beside him and he carefully turned over the thick pages, slowly enunciating the words and getting her to repeat them after him.

The printed word was meaningless to Analee but she stared at the pages as he turned them, obediently repeating after him what he said.

'You must be able to read to be a fine lady,' her lover said kissing her ear.

'I? A fine lady?'

'You cannot leave me now, Analee.'

'No, my lord.'

'Say, "my love".'

'My love.' She looked at him.

'Do you mean it?'

'Of course I mean it.'

'I know about your baby, Analee. I have known a long time. When I am well I will help you to find her; but I never want you to leave me. Do you understand?'

'Yes, my lord.'

'My love.'

'My love.'

'Angus. Say "Angus".'

'Angus.'

'There.'

'Angus.' Analee reached out a finger and stroked his chin. 'I know my baby is well and cared for. Do not ask me how but I do. She is happy where she is. Better off. I am content.'

Lord Falconer kissed her hand.

'When I was so ill near death I dreamt I saw you, and your belly was swollen with my child. I wanted you to have my child Analee, I wish it so strongly . . .'

'But sir . . . Angus.'

'I thought a lot about my life and as I have struggled to stay alive I have come to realize how frail we mortals are. I am thirty-six. I have no progeny that I know of though I have loved many women. Nothing to leave, to carry my name. You have become much more than a love to me. I want you to have my children. Do you wish it, too, Analee?' Analee looked at him gravely.

'Now I wish anything that you wish, my lord, Angus. Once it was not so. I thought I was a gypsy, a vagabond; my life was in the wilds. But now in these past weeks seeing you near death, helping you to recover, I have felt otherwise. I know that for as long as you wish it, I belong to you. If you wish it I am content to do as you say, be your mistress, bear your children. I . . .'

There was a knock on the door whereupon Analee jumped up from the bed. Both Mrs Ardoine and Nelly had bundles in their arms and, at the direction of his lordship, who was clearly expecting them, laid on the bed dresses of lavish silks and brocades and undergarments, hoops, petticoats, and bodices, pentelairs and stomachers.

His lordship was looking at the array with satisfaction; Analee with amazement and alarm.

'There, my love. I cannot have you as my mistress without fine clothes. See, Mrs Ardoine and Nelly have been to Carlisle to purchase the best they can. In time the finest dressmakers will be

312

called to serve you. Take no notice of me. Mrs Ardoine and Nelly will assist you to dress.'

'May I not pull the curtain my lord?' Analee said with unaccustomed modesty.

'Well, if you insist!' His lordship smiled and took up the book he had been reading with Analee. Then she drew the heavy curtain across his bed and allowed Nelly to help her out of the simple gypsy bodice and skirt which was all she had ever worn.

Nelly was having a fit of giggles as she held up one undergarment after the other.

'Mrs Ardoine, leave us please,' Analee said noticing the curious, prurient gaze of the older woman as she stood naked. She had never like the housekeeper, but since the attempt to whip her she loathed her. Moreover she knew she was jealous of her position with Lord Falconer.

'But . . .'

'Do as I say.'

Mrs Ardoine cast a glance at her master's bed, futilely hoping for his intervention. Then with a tilt of her chin she left the room, slamming the door behind her. Analee smiled.

'I think I will soon show her who is mistress here.'

Nelly produced a cage-like structure made of whalebone which narrowed at the waist and had laces at the back.

'This is the corset . . .'

'But I *cannot* wear it . . .'

'It will pull your waist in and accentuate the fullness of your breasts,' his lordship said, peeping again. 'My dear Analee, it does me so much good to see you in such finery . . .'

'I cannot wear that!'

But Nelly was already putting her arms through it and pulling hard at the laces.

'Now the hoop,' said his lordship, throwing the curtain right back and settling down to enjoy himself. 'I can see you two women are unfamiliar with such garments.'

'And I see you are only *too* familiar,' Analee retorted glancing at him over her shoulder. 'Ouch, not too tight, Nell.'

The hoop was made of buckram, distended by hoops of whalebone and tied at the waist by running strings, upon which Nelly firmly tugged, following his lordship's instructions.

'Now the petticoat,' ordered his lordship.

Analee gasped as the most beautiful garment of white quilted satin was pulled over her head settling on the hoop, so that it was carried out horizontally from the waist and then hung vertically all round. Nelly was already struggling with an open robe of heavy blue silk damask embroidered with flowers.

'First the stomacher,' instructed the Falcon putting away his book and the pretence of reading. This was made of dark blue ribbon and silver lace with a decolleté neckline edged with lace flounces. Already Analee could see the transformation in the mirror, how slender her waist had grown and how full her bust. Everything fitted so beautifully. She exclaimed as Nelly put over her head the damask robe which opened down the front to reveal the fold of the stiff white petticoat and the beribboned stomacher. It had graceful winged cuffs also edged with lace and stood out at either side.

She turned for approval to the Marquess who nodded and smiled.

'I said you would make a fine lady. Finer than I thought. Always keep your head high.'

'Now the stockings,' Nelly said.

'Stockings!' exclaimed Analee. 'I never wore stockings in my life.'

'Nor a dress like that neither,' Nelly grunted.

'The stockings should have been put on first,' murmured his lordship, 'first to put on and first to take off. No matter.'

'But I cannot wear *stockings*!'

'Why, my love, you will be a lady in damask and silk but with bare feet? Come.'

'You see, Analee, you put your foot in this,' Nelly explained holding out the white silk stocking and looking at it doubtfully. 'I must say I never saw the like of it myself.'

Analee sat on the bed and, watched approvingly by his lordship, stretched first one long leg and then the other encasing them in the unfamiliar hose, which ended just above her knee.

'Garters, I believe,' his lordship said, 'have been forgotten.'

'Oh no, sir. Mrs Ardoine remembered *these*.' Nelly held up a pair of coloured ribbons with rosettes and proceeded to tie them around Analee's legs.

314

'That will be my privilege when I am well,' his lordship observed. 'In fact I feel better already at the sight of the clothes to take off you, my love. 'Tis part of the attraction of dressing up, to get undressed again. Not that you needed adornment . . .'

'The pumps,' Nelly said, holding up a pair of elegant high heeled shoes made of the same material as the dress and embroidered with silver braid like the stomacher. 'We were not sure of the fit . . .'

Analee gazed uncertainly, almost with hostility at the shoes as though they symbolized the final surrender of her freedom. Then she tentatively put first one foot in and then the other, held up her rich skirts and gazed at them.

'You are so much taller!' his lordship laughed. 'I wager you will be higher than me. See yourself in the mirror.'

Analee turned slowly and, hands on her waist, gazed at herself, slowly pirouetting and turning her head as she did. Indeed it was a complete transformation from the short bodice she was used to and simple skirt which hung without artificial aids. She felt cramped and stifled in her whalebone corset, tight stomacher and large hoop. She pulled herself up, her eyes on the Falcon, and walked slowly over to him. His eyes glinted with admiration and he reached for her hand and kissed it.

'My lady . . .' he murmured, 'I have but one thing left to give you. No, two . . .'

His lordship put a hand under his pillow and took from it a small case which he opened to show a huge ring of diamonds and sapphires set in gold. He placed it on Analee's long slender forefinger and she held out her hand unable to believe her eyes.

She remembered all the gewgaws and baubles she had gazed at on the market stalls, all the silks and brocades she had allowed to run through her hands.

'It is . . . mine?'

'Forever. It is a gift; but this . . . this is more precious to me. It is what you left behind and I want you to wear it for me for as long as we love each other. It is more precious to me than all the diamonds, all the sapphires and jewels I could have given you.'

The Falcon took also from his pillow the massive gold ring at the sight of which Analee hung her head. It had engraved on it the head of the falcon, the bird of prey, and the gold was white as though it had been freshly mined.

She had left it on the table the night she fled – a symbolic gesture that she and the Marquess were no longer bound together as he had wished, no longer one. Now all had changed.

He held it up for her to look at, and then he put it to his eye and peered through it.

'I see you, Analee, my mistress. Mine. Remember this ring? Made of the purest Falcon gold brought from South America? A ring is round and has no join; that is why it is symbolic between two people – love cannot be broken. You must never take it off again Analee, or least not leave it as you did before. Well I knew what you meant when I saw that ring gleaming so brightly at me on that dull morning. Now I give it to you again.' Analee bent her head and he slipped the chain around it, himself settling the object between her breasts, against her heart. 'Now it is even more precious because I wore it at Falkirk, and perhaps it saved my life; the talisman of our family. People say I resemble the great Beyrick because I am warlike and ruthless with my enemies. Maybe the French knew about him when they dubbed me "Le Faucon" and my troops took it up; or maybe it suited my style. I know not and now it matters not. The ring is yours. No other gold matches Falcon gold. No other woman, in my eyes, can match you. Like it, you are beyond price. And when our son is born and grows to manhood the ring will be his, and I will have a medallion fashioned for you also of this precious gold. But until he is of age, it is yours.'

Analee felt the heavy ring rest on her bosom. Her eyes had filled with tears which she brushed quickly away not wishing her lord to see how much his words had moved her, how grieved she was to have hurt him by leaving it behind. That she meant as much to him as this was proof that he loved her and would not lightly cast her aside. He was even talking of their children, what could more solidly weld together their flesh?

But his lordship saw her tears and put his arm about her shoulder clasping her to him.

'My Analee. You did not think I loved you so much?'

'A great lord . . .'

'What you have given me is great, too – life. My doctors say but for you I would be dead; they know not how you did it. But I know. It is not sorcery, not magic. It is love. Pure love, as pure as the Falcon gold . . . the white unalloyed gold from South

America. Now my love, I am tired. I must rest in order to regain my vigour and provide you with sons. Go with Nelly and play with your fine new clothes. You will soon get used to them; the constriction will not worry you. You will learn how to carry yourself as the daughters of noblemen do. You must be a credit to me in what you wear and what you do – for what you are yourself honours me already.

'I myself will teach you to read and write for I see you are an adept pupil, and you will be taught to embroider, and the finest of teachers will instruct you in the pianoforte.

'But the gypsy skirt is gone forever, Analee, and that part of you that was at one with the fields and the meadows and sleeping under the hedgerows. Promise me it is gone?'

Analee turned her face away and looked out of the window to where the bough of a tree, heavy with buds, swayed in the gusty wind of an early spring day. How could she promise him anything else? She loved him so completely that any former love, even the very first, seemed like a childish whim. She had brought the Falcon through death and given him life. Her life had gone into him just as one day his seed would root in her, bringing yet more life. Life renewed itself again and again.

'I promise,' she said meeting his gaze and fingering the heavy gold ring at her neck. 'But your lordship will bear with me if at times I kick off my shoes and run about in the grass, for my gypsy ways are hard to lose, and I was born in the wild. I will find it hard to be a lady.'

The Falcon sank back against his pillows and took her hands between his, kissing the tips of the fingers one by one.

'Wild lady,' his lordship murmured. 'I think it will be an irresistible combination. One that I shall find fascinating forever.'

20

By the month of May all the snows had disappeared from the Cheviot Hills and the trees in the great park of Falcon's Keep were dressed with tiny green leaves. Angus Falconer, whose arm had been all but severed from his shoulder, still walked with difficulty but under Analee's care he had grown fit and strong. His recovery had been hastened by the burgeoning of the deep love between them, the understanding of each other's minds and bodies that the long weeks together had only strengthened.

Angus never ceased to be amazed by the accomplishment and intelligence of Analee who, because of his careful tutelage, could nearly read and write. She had even taken over the running of the household after gladly despatching Mrs Ardoine back to her native Edinburgh.

Dressmakers were sent from Carlisle and a whole wardrobe made for Analee consisting of ornate dresses for evening, simpler gowns for morning, cloaks, a riding habit and the ball dresses which Angus insisted she would need when he took her to London.

At times Analee would slip off her shoes and stockings and relish again the feel of the bare earth under her feet; she would wander in the park far from the house and some little yearning would flutter in her heart for the old life. She would finger the silk of her dress and touch the rings on her fingers looking towards the hills, and some part of her would feel like a trapped bird that yearned to take flight.

But then she remembered the heavy gold ring round her neck, and she clasped it and rubbed it between her fingers. The heavy ring of white Falcon gold would remind her of her lover and with it came the realization that her true existence lay in him and the old days were indeed gone forever. She had kept her promise.

The servants at the castle quickly got used to the dominance of one who had once been among their numbers. For Analee did not lord it over them or give herself airs. She was firm and authoritative, but always smiling and gentle. Her commands were softly spoken and accompanied by a smile. It was as though she had been born to it.

One day Analee had slipped away to think, removing first her shoes and stockings and carrying them in her hand; it was a gentle spring day warm enough to be without a cloak. She looked towards the sky and thought of Morella. She wondered if she would ever see her again, and then she remembered what she had just learned and a soft smile illuminated her face. It gave her hope and strength for the future and impulsively she turned towards the house to find Angus and break the news to him.

But his lordship was coming towards her, across the broad lawn between the house and the lake, walking slowly with a stick as he still did, the sleeve of his coat flapping loosely from his left arm which was still inert and strapped to his body. He waved his stick when he saw her and quickened his pace. She waited for him under a tree, her face dappled by the shadows made by the leaves against the sun.

She was so lovely, Angus thought, approaching her slowly so that he could savour the moment of seeing her under the tree, the dark green of her gown merging with the lighter colour of the soft young leaves. He saw the smile on her lips and the light in her eyes and . . .

'Analee! You have still got bare feet!' he roared.

Analee dug her feet into the grass and curled up her toes in a gesture of stubbornness. Then she tossed her shoes on the ground in front of her and laughed as her lover caught her in his arms and gently moulded his lips against hers.

'You are incorrigible . . .'

'What means that, my lord?'

'You will never be a lady. Not a true lady.'

Analee leaned back, flushed from his kiss and smiled enticingly at the Falcon.

'Will you cast me aside then?'

The Falcon groaned and pushed her gently against the tree. Glancing around and perceiving that they were hidden from the house by the overhanging branches of the willow, his lordship cast his stick to the ground and kissing her, drew her gently to the ground.

There, the shadows of the leaves still providing them with cover, the delightful sward of fresh-smelling tender green grass beneath them, they lay for some time. Analee looked at him and eventually their eyes met. She pushed his hand against her stomach.

'This is something I must tell you Angus. Here.' She pointed to her stomach.

He put a hand on hers and understood. 'You are carrying our child?'

Analee nodded.

'My dear,' Angus said proudly, 'The heir to the Marquess of Falconer is the Earl of Blair . . .'

'It may be a girl,' Analee said slyly.

'Oh, Analee, you make me very, very happy. I care not if it is a girl, so long as she resembles you in *every* respect.'

His lordship kissed her passionately and laid her head on the grass, lying beside her. He put his good arm round her waist, leaning over her. His eyes looked over towards the house, the hooded eyes of the Falcon, the sharp imperious beak sniffing the air.

'But first you must be Lady Falconer.'

Analee struggled to sit up.

'I?'

'Why not? 'Tis only a name. You cannot bear my children and *not* be married to me, Analee. 'Twould not be legal. They could not inherit. I swear I meant to ask you before you told me this. I decided I could not take the risk of you running away again. Every time you are out of my sight I grow anxious. Will you have me?'

His lordship bent his head, his eyes an inch from hers. His expression grave.

'If I will have your children I will have you,' Analee said. 'But I will *still* not wear shoes when I do not wish it, even though I be a lady. A proper one.'

Analee became the Marchioness of Falconer at a simple ceremony carried out in the chapel a few weeks after the proposal in the park. Although her condition was not so far advanced as to be noticeable his lordship judged it judicious to have the ceremony quickly and, because he was not fully restored to health, a long and elaborate ceremony was thought unwise. His lordship, looking upright and handsome despite the fact that he still used a stick, was married in the scarlet uniform of a lieutenant-general, with gold epaulettes and several rows of medals. Analee wore a gown of gold brocade richly embroidered with silver thread over a large hoop; her slippers were gold, and jewels and diamonds glittered on her fingers.

Her hair was simply dressed without adornment, her natural ringlets falling over her shoulders and she carried a posy of fresh summer flowers in her hands. But on her bosom between her breasts was the solitary ring on the fine gold chain, the symbol of the love of the lordly Falcon for the gypsy girl.

After the final defeat of the Jacobite army at Culloden in April of that year, 1746, the Duke of Cumberland's affectionate name of 'Bluff Bill' was swiftly changed to 'Butcher Cumberland'. So terrible was the vengeance wreaked on the defeated Highlanders and their allies, that the deeds perpetrated by the government troops on enemy soldiers and civilians alike went down into history, for their perfidy, brutality and inhumanity.

When Lord Falconer subsequently heard the details of the Battle of Culloden, even he was glad he had not been there to share in the doubtful glory of the butchery and savagery that had followed it – Cumberland being determined to put an end to the Rebellion once and for all.

Prince Charles escaped from the field and some of his commanders, incurably optimistic, regrouped to meet in another place and plan to rally. But the Prince was done for. He, with scant thanks for all they had done, bade his supporters disperse while he became a fugitive with a price on his head.

For weeks after Culloden Brent Delamain found it impossible to rid his mind of the sounds of the battle, the screams of the wounded, the savage cries of the Highlanders trying to resist defeat, the relentless sound of gunfire and of steel upon steel. As a special category prisoner Brent had been cast into the dungeons of Edinburgh Castle; special because he had been so close to the Prince, a captain in his Life Guards. Brent had served in all the encounters since Clifton and battle had taken its toll of him; he was a silent man, a man of iron and bitterness. He blamed the undisciplined Highlanders and the personality of the Prince, whose spirits were either up or down but never seemed capable of maintaining that balance, that detachment, that was so essential for a successful military commander. His temperament was too mercurial, too uneven and, in fact, it only flourished at its best when he was hunted as a fugitive although Brent at that time could not know this.

Brent was lucky to be alive. His brother Tom was dead, killed very early in the battle, as the waves of government soldiers bore down upon the tired and grossly outnumbered Jacobite army. Brent had seen the way the wounded were dealt with as he waited to be led away, sabred or shot to death where they lay, just as his men had dealt with the wounded Hanoverians in other engagements.

It was sickening and horrible and now that it was over he was glad to be out of it, although he knew that death inevitably awaited him because of the degree of guilt attributed to him. The majority of prisoners taken at Culloden had been sent to Inverness for shipment to London, and dreadful stories had come back of the conditions in the transport ships in which the men were confined, many of whom died of untreated wounds and disease.

But Brent was incarcerated in Edinburgh Castle along with other gentlemen and members of the nobility including the Earl of Kelly, the Duchess of Perth, Lady Ogilvy and, most important of all, Murray of Broughton who had been so instrumental in bringing the Prince to Scotland. Those who were in prison in Scotland did not expect to remain there long. It was known that the English victors would not attempt to hold trials in Scotland and, uncertain of his fate, Brent nevertheless prepared himself for the end. Whatever happened to him the Cause was lost indeed.

Stewart Allonby, in prison in Carlisle, had waited much longer for his sentence. The lots that had been cast among the ordinary soldiers to stand trial did not apply to officers and Stewart had been sent to London for trial at Southwark. After the vengeance taken on the men of the Manchester Regiment, all of whom had been sentenced to death and barbarously executed on Kennington Common in July, Stewart expected no mercy. But to his surprise his cousin George Delamain, urged on by Emma, spoke for him. It was submitted that he was only a half-hearted supporter of the Young Pretender and that, moreover, he had not drawn sword or fired a gun in battle, which was true, his duties at Carlisle keeping him off the ramparts.

Worn out by months of waiting and repeated bouts of gaol fever Stewart did not deny his lack of fervour, and was rewarded with a sentence to be deported to His Majesty's Colonies and to remain there for the rest of his life. He was then returned to Carlisle to await shipment from Liverpool and, dazed, he still did not know whether it was better to have died or to be forced to live forever so far from the home, the country which he loved.

Two days after his return Stewart was summoned before Carruthers, the Keeper of the Carlisle Gaol, and told he had a visitor. Carruthers was aware of the importance of Sir George Delamain's evidence in securing leniency for Mr Allonby and smiled on him kindly.

'You were lucky, Mr Allonby, in that your cousin spoke for you.' Stewart looked at the floor. He was not proud of George's intervention. He had also been surprised by it.

'I know not whether I prefer death to a life of exile.'

'Oh come, sir. They say his Majesty will extend a general pardon once all is cleared away. You will not be gone long. In the meantime I have a surprise for you. Miss Delamain who accompanied her brother to your trial is here to see you.'

'Emma?'

Stewart's eyes, sunk deep in his head with suffering, momentarily brightened.

'Emma was *there*?'

'You did not observe her in the crowd?'

'I have been in prison six months Mr Keeper. It does not make the senses alert. That and the prison fodder.'

The Keeper turned away and shuffled some papers. He had expected very few to survive their trials, certainly not Stewart Allonby. The prisoners from Carlisle had been very harshly dealt with. The Manchester Regiment who, after all, had played very little part in the war had been savagely butchered. The behaviour of the Scots was considered more forgivable than that of the English who had turned against their King. Carruthers was sorry that he had not treated Mr Allonby better. He was now trying to make amends.

'You may use my room to see Miss Delamain, sir. I will have her brought to you.'

Stewart turned his back and gazed out of the window. He was uncertain whether he wanted to see Emma; how he felt about her. He heard her come softly into the room but still he did not turn.

'Stewart?'

Stewart closed his eyes, his jaw working hard to hold back his emotion. He felt her hand on his arm, her fingers slowly tightening.

'I look awful, deathly pale . . .'

'I know. I saw you in court. But alive! You are *alive* Stewart. You have a chance.'

'Thanks to George.'

He felt Emma remove her hand and her voice was low.

'I knew you would be bitter. But I did not care. I know how you felt about the Prince, how disillusioned you had become with the Cause. You told me in your letters. Not to *die* for him now, Stewart.'

'Oh, Emma . . .'

Stewart turned towards her and she threw herself into his arms. He was so weak that he could hardly support her and for a while they leaned on each other. How beautiful she looked, he thought, stroking her hair seeing the tears cascading down her cheeks. Weeping for *him*? What had he done to deserve it?

'I am not worth the tears, Emma. I am not a hero, not even a brave man, not even dedicated.'

'But you are alive and I love you.'

It was the first time she had told him. She looked up into his eyes, pale gaunt man that he was, tired and disillusioned. He had lost stones in weight and dark shadows framed his eyes. But she loved him, had come to love him through his letters from prison, his need of her.

'How can you love *me*?'

He pressed her close to him again scarcely believing.

'I do. And I will stay with you, Stewart, wherever you go – to the West Indies or America – I will join you as soon as I can. Whatever your circumstances I will be by your side.'

So it was worth it. He had lost a cause, but gained the love of a woman he had always cherished. Was it true, after all, that good did come out of evil?

'Oh, Emma, Emma, I do not deserve you. I do not deserve this.'

He hugged her again then pushed her gently from him and wearily went to sit on a chair. He felt his legs could scarcely support him any longer.

'Unless I recover my strength I shall not survive the voyage. I shall die like those poor men in the transports in Tilbury.'

'Don't worry. I have the measure of Carruthers. He is anxious to please, seeing George is so powerful. You will be well fed.'

'And Brent? What news of Brent?'

Emma's proud noble frame, so upright in front of her lover, seemed to sink.

'For some reason the authorities are treating Brent with severity. There are reports that he was ruthless in battle against the English, his own countrymen. He was seen to strike many down at Falkirk and Culloden. It is this that tells against Brent than anything else. When he was in London George made enquiries in the highest of circles; he even had an interview with the Duke of Newcastle himself. But the English Jacobites are not popular with the Hanoverian Court – hated even worse than the Scots.'

'Then it is hopeless for Brent?'

Emma gazed at her beloved and her eyes again filled with tears. Would they could both be safe – lover and brother. It was too much to expect, too much to hope for. Brent would be hanged and Stewart live out a life of bitterness and misery in the undeveloped American colonies, far from home.

'Our family has suffered too much for the Stuarts,' she said, nodding her head in reply to Stewart's question. 'They have lost everything. They do not even have the advantage of admiration for the Prince although he is hunted all over the Highlands, a price of £30,000 on his head and none betray him.'

'He inspires great loyalty, he has such charm,' Stewart reached up and took Emma's hand, putting it to his lips. 'But he was not a good commander. He would not have made a good king. He was overfond of his own way, his own opinion. Nay, I'm disillusioned, I'll admit. The Stuarts are surely gone forever and Hanover firmly entrenched on the throne of England. Would I were at my home on Lake Derwentwater, going out to hew wood. Would all this had never happened. The Cause lost and I humiliated by my cousin having to plead for me. Now Tom is dead, killed in battle and Brent sure to hang.'

Emma's eyes were wet with tears and she pressed Stewart's hand tightly.

'I didn't know Tom so well, of course; he was older than I and always lived abroad. Mother said he wanted to die if he could not win.'

'How does your mother bear up to all this?'

'She is very brave; also she has had comfort during the past months. The most curious thing, Stewart. Brent sent a gypsy woman with a sick baby to take shelter with us and mother has become very fond of the baby. The gypsy woman, who was not the mother, has gone on her way and mother has taken over the baby.'

'Your mother has taken a gypsy baby?'

'She thinks it is not. She is a dear little thing, very blonde with blue eyes, called Morella. She could almost be a Delamain. Mother mourns, of course, for Tom and Brent and you. But Stewart listen, there is the oddest story I have to tell you that Mary told me. And here I have hope for Brent.'

'And that is?'

'Before they were married a gypsy came to your home, do you remember?'

'I do,' Stewart said bitterly. 'Well I remember her.'

'It seems my brother was once enamoured of her.'

'Mary knows that?'

'Brent told her after the wedding. However the gypsy, Analee, has, by the most curious chain of circumstances, married my sister-in-law Henrietta's cousin, Angus Falconer. They met in the war or something. I know not quite what.'

'Lord Falconer has married *Analee*?'

Stewart could not keep the incredulity out of his voice.

'He was much taken by her and cared not what people thought. Now she is always at his side. It is rumoured her strange gypsy powers even saved his life.'

'So, what is the plan?'

'Mary has gone to Falcon's Keep to plead with Analee, whom she got to know well, to intercede with her husband to save Brent.'

''Tis a slim chance.'

Emma nodded. There was a knock on the door. Emma took

Stewart's hand and looked into his eyes. They had never made love, never even kissed. Now Emma felt she wanted this thin defeated prisoner more than anything in life.

'Stewart,' she said quietly. 'I will follow you. I will find where you are and get a boat as soon as I can.'

'But the conditions . . .'

'No matter what they are I will share them with you. I love you too much to let you go.'

Stewart looked at her and took her tenderly in his arms. The moment he'd always waited for had come too late.

'How can I say no?' he said brokenly. 'Even though I have nothing at all to offer you.'

And for the first time they kissed, before the door swung open and the gaoler came to take Stewart back to his cell.

The Marchioness of Falconer sat at her escritoire in her own salon on the first floor of the mansion which overlooked the elaborate gardens and the lake in the far distance. Beyond that was the uneven range of the Cheviot Hills. She wore a simple pentelair that now suited her more ample figure. It had a round décolletage which emphasized her magnificent bosom and she wore it with a plain petticoat of the same dark green silk which rested on a domed hoop. Like a simple countrywoman a handkerchief was tied round her neck and she wore no rings or jewels except for her necklace which she never removed.

Her feet were bare and tucked under her chair as she tried to grasp the simple arithmetic of her household accounts which she prepared under the tutelage of his lordship.

Analee had taken to her new status with a natural dignity which impressed all who met her – the local worthies and the members of his majesty's army who called to pay their respects to his lordship and wish him health and happiness. At night she entertained regally, dressed in the latest mode, her hair dressed and ablaze with jewels. But by day she wore simple clothes and on retiring she lay, as she always had, naked except for the close companionship of her loving husband.

Analee, looking forward to the future, aware of the child quickening inside her, the heir to the Falconer estates and fortune it if were a boy, thought only sporadically of her former life and the happier she became the less she missed it.

She still loved to wander barefoot around the estate, and she and Nelly would talk of the old times, sometimes with laughter and occasionally with tears when they thought of the fate of the Buckland gypsies, the harshness the war had brought to so many people.

But although Analee often thought of Morella she never spoke of her. She knew she was well looked after and that her future was as good as any she could give her. She felt she owed it to the Falcon to start a new life with him and, apart from telling him that the baby was safe, she had told him no more and he never enquired.

Mrs Ardoine had been replaced by a new and younger housekeeper and with her Analee took care to see that the staff, even the meanest, were well housed with ample food, that no one was ill treated or subject to cruel whippings. Analee infused the large household with her own vibrant personality and it became a happy laughing place full of vigour and good cheer.

Analee found it hard on this particular day in July, with the sky outside a clear blue and the birds singing in the park, to concentrate on her work and was gazing out of the window when a voice cried.

'My lady! My lady!'

Analee, still unused to her new title, looked about her as though to see who could be meant, when Nelly burst in without ceremony, her face alight.

'Oh, ma'am, who do you think is *here*?'

Analee's face was alight with excitement and she jumped up, relieved to leave the accounts, and seized Nelly's hand.

'Who, Nelly? Who?'

No one was more delighted than Nelly at the elevation of her beloved Analee to the peerage or at her own promotion as personal maid to a Marchioness, but she still maintained the informality of their earlier relationship, at least when they were alone together. In public Lord Falconer insisted that his wife be treated with all the deference due to her station and then Nelly never spoke out of turn, or betrayed their intimacy in any way. 'Analee, it is Mary – Mary Delamain and her brother John Allonby.'

'Mary and John here!'

'Oh, Mary is so excited to see you; but she looks sad and drawn . . . I think the business is to do with her husband.'

Analee took Nelly's hand and made quickly for the door running along the corridor and down the stairs, brushing aside the servant who hastily tried to open the door into the main drawing room.

She opened her arms as soon as she saw Mary and the two women embraced, Mary with tears in her eyes.

'Oh, Analee . . . your ladyship . . . I . . .'

Analee put up a hand.

'*Analee*, Mary, no ladyship from you! I am Analee the gypsy and always will be . . .'

Analee stepped back and gestured towards herself, her simple morning dress, her lack of adornment. Mary threw back her head and laughed.

'Analee, what does his lordship say about his wife's bare feet?'

'Oh,' Analee clasped a hand to her mouth. 'That was a mistake. I am allowed to do it, but only if no one is about. Nelly fetch me my stockings and shoes please.'

Nelly bobbed, stifling a giggle.

'And Nelly is with you! Oh, Analee, I am so happy for you. I heard, we heard, about his lordship's serious illness and his recovery . . .'

John Allonby had stood in the background and now came forward bowing stiffly.

'Your ladyship, my felicitations on your husband's recovery and your good fortune. May you be very happy . . .'

'We are, Mr Allonby,' Analee, who had never known this dour man well, took his hand and smiled briefly. 'Now what brings you here? Not bad news?'

John nodded and Mary cast her eyes to the floor.

'We are here to invoke the compassion of Lord Falconer, your husband, hoping that he will help a distant member of his family now in dire straits.'

'His family?' Analee's gaze went from Mary to John.

'Brent, my lady. Brent Delamain, related to his lordship's cousin by marriage, is in mortal danger. He is to be sent to London from Edinburgh to stand trial, and it is certain he will be sentenced to death. The record against him is black. He served in the Prince's elite corps of Life Guards and he killed many of his own

329

countrymen in battle. His cousin Stewart Allonby has been spared the extreme penalty and is sentenced to deportation; but there is little hope for Brent.'

'But how can my husband help? He has no influence at court.' Analee looked distressed.

'*The* Falcon, ma'am? The bravest of soldiers, newly gazetted general? Surely well favoured by the King?'

'Or is it that he would not *want* to help?' Mary moved over to Analee who impulsively grasped her hand.

'Oh, Mary, worry not that Angus knows anything about Brent and myself. That is a secret and forever will be. No, it is simply that his lordship has no time for the rebels, I fear. He says they put the country to a lot of trouble and suffering. He remembers well the gypsy camp . . .'

'But that was not Brent!'

'Of course it was not. He knows in his heart that there were many fine and upright men on the Jacobite side, though you would not think it to hear him talk. But my lord is,' Analee inclined her head as though searching for the right word, 'he is not an *easy* man. He is personally a kind man and a wonderful husband; but . . . stubborn.'

'Not the Falcon for nothing,' John Allonby murmured.

'He has strong views on loyalty.'

'It is a matter of ideals, Analee.'

'I know, Mary; but Angus, for right or wrong, believes the Jacobites to be traitors to the rightful King of England. I know he will do nothing.' She shrugged. 'However, we can try. I will ask him. Unfortunately he has still not recovered from his serious wound which nearly killed him, and lies abed until nearly dinnertime. But you will stay with us and see him then.'

Mary shook her head.

'We must go at once. There is no time to lose. If only to say goodbye . . .'

Mary leaned her head on Analee's breast and gave herself up to a torrent of weeping. 'Oh, Analee, and to know that he does not even love me. That he thinks only . . .'

'Shhh.' Analee patted her shoulder looking at John who nodded and moved towards the door just as Nelly entered with Analee's shoes and hose.

'My lady . . .'

'Take Mr Allonby into the garden, Nelly. He wishes to take some air.'

Left alone Analee took Mary to the sofa and sat beside her.

'There, my dear, cry to your heart's content. How unhappy I am that Brent has behaved to you as he has; it spoils my own happiness. But if he could see, if he could know how happy his lordship has made me!' She put a hand on her stomach, 'and we are to have a child, Mary, to solder our love. I am nearly five months gone.'

Analee saw the expression on Mary's face and smiled.

'Are you shocked little one? We have been married only two months I know. But his lordship and I were always meant for each other; there was never any question . . .'

Mary looked at the gypsy, now no longer a gypsy girl despite what she said. Analee had in some subtle way changed; she had the air and regality of a lady. With her customary sorcery Analee had already achieved the part. Why there she was, a real marchioness with one of the great lords of the land for a husband. Yet it seemed perfectly natural for her. It was not only the way Analee looked – it was her bearing and the way she held herself; a dignity as though she had been somehow born to it.

'If Brent lives, Analee, can you use your powers to free him from your spell? *Can* you?'

'Mary I have told you I have no extraordinary powers. I am no *cohani*, no witch. But, yes, if Brent lives I will do what I can. Why . . . here is my lord.'

The door opened and the Falcon came slowly in, his eyes searching.

'Ah, Analee, they told me you were here. My dear . . .' his gaze fell upon Mary and he stopped.

'My lord, Angus, this is Mary Delamain who was so kind to me when I was snowbound.'

The Marquess walked over to Mary and bowed over her hand.

'You are very welcome, ma'am, and thank you for your hospitality to my wife. How long will you stop here?'

Analee got up and took her lord's arm.

'Angus, Mary is the wife of *Brent* Delamain your distant cousin by marriage.'

'Ah,' his lordship cried, understanding dawning. 'That will be why she is here. I understand he is on the list for trial in London and almost certain to be condemned. His is one of the names of those thought most culpable.'

'You knew it, my lord?'

'Aye. I heard it yesterday from Colonel Worth who stopped here on his way back to London. He knew we were very distantly related.'

'Oh Angus, cannot you do something for your cousin!'

His lordship thumped the floor with his stick.

'No I cannot and pray do not ask me. You know how I feel about the rebels. There is nothing I can do anyway. His Majesty is determined to punish them and stamp them out by his example. I know it.'

The Falcon shook his head and moved to the window. Analee could see from his stormy gaze that he was angry; that brooding Falcon stare that had struck terror into the hearts of so many, friend and foe. But now it was never directed at her; the only expression she ever saw on the face of her husband was one of love and tenderness. She went over to him and leaned her head against his arm stroking his sleeve. The Marquess fidgeted with his stick and tried to move away.

'Analee, pray do not. It is no use . . .'

'My lord, Angus, did you never have anything you felt very passionately about?'

'Only you,' he whispered so that Mary could not hear.

'Very well. You defied society to marry me. But only supposing it had been against the law? Would you have done it then?'

'You know it. I would have defied everyone and everything to have you as my wife.'

'Then think how Brent Delamain and those like him felt. They are zealots. They are not criminals.'

Reluctantly Lord Falconer, who was still tantalized by the proximity of his wife even though he knew her so well, freed his arm.

'My dear Analee . . . even if I wanted to I can do nothing. I am powerless. There!'

'Can we not contrive to *rescue* Brent before he is sent,' Analee said quietly. 'There must be a way. Even Lord Nithsdale escaped from the Tower of London itself after the '15 Rebellion. It is a famous tale. Can it not be done from Edinburgh Castle?'

'No it cannot!' his lordship thundered. 'You want me to lose my title? Forfeit my commission in His Majesty's regiment? We are undone, Analee, if we so much as lift a finger to help these traitors! I will not risk my life, my inheritance, the inheritance of our child, for something in which I do not believe. *You* I do believe in, but the Stuarts no!'

There was a silence only broken occasionally by the sound of Mary weeping. Analee gazed stormily at her husband.

'When you are married, my lord, do you not take on obligations owed by your spouse?'

'You have obligations to Brent Delamain?' his lordship said incredulously.

In Analee's mind there flashed the thought of a moonlit scene; a handsome blond god – a beautiful baby girl. She found she was trembling, but she tried to hide her emotion. Much as she knew Angus loved her he was not ready now to hear about Morella, if he ever would be which she somehow doubted. He was too jealous, too single-minded to countenance hearing about her relationship with Brent, to know about their child. It would not make him want to help Brent; he would probably volunteer to hang him with his own hands. Her lord was much too savage for magnanimity at this stage in their relationship, which was still so dependent on physical passion. No, she would not tell her husband the truth. Even Mary did not know the whole truth.

'I have obligations to the family of Allonby. They were very kind to me and Nelly and offered us shelter when we needed it on two occasions. I would like to do a favour for Mary, more particularly than Brent. As you love me, sir, so does she love her husband and would have him by her side.'

'But they would be exiles, outlaws . . .'

'No matter,' Analee said firmly, 'they would be alive and together. For *me*, my lord, won't you help?'

For answer his lordship shook his head angrily and stumped out of the room.

Mary turned her ashen, tear-stained face to Analee who, she was surprised to see, was smiling.

'I think he will do something,' Lady Falconer said. 'I know my lord.'

'If my name is ever brought into this plan,' his lordship said over dinner when the room was cleared of servants, 'I and future generations of my family will curse the name of Delamain . . . and Allonby,' he added scowling fiercely. 'I am doing this solely for my wife, whom I adore. It is much against my better judgement. It is a token of my love for her; she has asked it and I will do it. I know she will not be ungrateful and will show me so in many ways; thus, my motives are not altogether without self-interest . . .' Lord Falconer paused and looked meaningfully at his wife who bent her head and suppressed a smile, her eyes shining. 'We shall vigorously deny any connection with the plan to free Brent Delamain and say our name was used basely because of my relationship to the family. 'Tis all I have to say. D'ye hear?'

John Allonby was gazing with open admiration at the man he had hated; the Falcon. Not only had a committed Hanoverian and a member of the government army to boot consented to help free his cousin, but the plan was so simple it was perfect.

'You are a born strategist, my lord,' John said respectfully.

'Aye,' his lordship replied modestly. 'I have that reputation, which is why I am today a General in His Majesty's regiment. You see then why my name must never become associated with this, even though you are put to the rack . . .'

'Never sir. I swear,' John got up and bowed to his host.

'And you *may* be racked, Mr Allonby, or worse. You will be the one left behind in your cousin's place. Maybe they will take your head instead of his.'

'They are welcome to it, sir, if they so decide,' John said slowly. 'Do not think it has not occurred to me . . .'

'Oh no, John . . .' Mary, who had been so happy as the plan was revealed, looked aghast.

'Yes, Mary, I have done no wrong that they know: I have not fought with the Prince; but . . . I shall have contrived to help a traitor escape. However, my love, do not grieve if it is so. I shall die cheerful. I am a single man and you and Brent have all life and all the happiness in the world before you. I am half dead since Charlotte died, anyway. Furness Grange may be sequestrated and sold . . . but you will be free, starting a new life, maybe overseas in the Indies or Africa.'

''Tis nobly spoke,' Lord Falconer said. 'Now to the details of the plan. For if you are to be in time you cannot delay a moment. They are despatching the criminals like hens in a farmyard I hear.'

21

The governor of Edinburgh Castle, Colonel Guest, was a stern man. He ruled his castle and its garrison with a fist of iron and gave little quarter. He shared with the Tolbooth and Canongate prisons responsibility for the large number of captured Jacobites who had supported the Prince, in battle or otherwise. He had many noblewomen in his castle, too, who had rallied to the Prince – either by raising bodies of fighting men themselves or by selling their jewels or by defying reluctant husbands.

Most of his prisoners were of the rank and file and in batches they left the castle to be taken for trial at Carlisle, Chester, York or Lancaster. Once in England lots were cast among the men for those who were to be tried, one in twenty. The rest were deported or, ultimately, pardoned and freed according to the degree of guilt. Colonel Guest cared little as to what happened to any of them.

He had one or two special prisoners, like Murray of Broughton and Brent Delamain, whose offences were deemed enough to hang them. These were kept apart from the rest while a strong escort was awaited to take them to London.

An orderly stood at the door and the Governor, who had been studying papers, looked up.

'A Mrs Delamain to see her husband, sir. She has come from Keswick and knows he is soon to be taken to England.'

'Is there permission?'

'From General Hawley himself, sir,' the orderly handed the governor a note which he barely glanced at. He had no time for these sentimental gestures on the part of the authorities. In his opinion rogues like Delamain should be denied all privileges.

'It may be the last time she sees him, sir. She is said to be unwell and her brother has accompanied her.'

'Is *he* to be admitted, too?'

''Tis on the order, sir.'

'Oh get it over. See 'tis kept short. Traitors have no rights in my opinion; they all deserve the gallows. Have the prisoner Delamain brought up.'

Mary stood trembling in the small room near the entrance to the prison. Even though John was with her she was terrified. Lord Falconer's plan had seemed so simple in the shelter of Falcon's Keep; but here it seemed impossible. As they waited John tightly held her hand and she pressed it, unable to speak.

She hardly recognized her husband when he was brought in. He was so thin and gaunt and he dragged his leg with pain. He blinked his eyes against the light and scarcely seemed able to recognize her.

'Brent, it is Mary.'

'Aye, so I heard. Why did you come, Mary, to distress yourself thus? I have not been a good husband to you. Start life again . . .'

John moved quickly over to Brent and seized his arm.

'Do not waste time talking. Remove your clothes.' Brent stared at him and held up his arms.

'How can I remove my clothes in chains?'

Curse, they had forgotten that!

'Then your breeches merely. My jacket will conceal the chains.'

'You are . . .' Brent gazed at him in amazement.

'Rescuing you. I am taking your place. We are the same colour, the same build . . .'

John had not reckoned with Brent's emaciated appearance; but it was too late now. The best laid plans always misfired so he had heard. He was prepared to brazen it out now, whatever happened.

'Haste man. We have no time to tarry.'

'But they will try you in my place.'

'We think not; but it is a chance I must take.'

John had removed most of his clothes and kept glancing anxiously at the door. As if accepting the inevitability of what was happening, Brent stumped out of his breeches with Mary's help and donned John's clothes.

'We will never get away with it.'

'We might. 'Tis dark in here. Here now, my hat, pull it well over your face which has a ghastly prison pallor. There. Good-bye sweet sister. Brent come!'

'John I cannot . . .'

John gazed at his cousin, at his sister.

'It is all I have done for the Cause, Brent. Is it too much to ask I be allowed my contribution? Even if I die I die happy; but I think I will not. Even the Hanoverians do not kill innocent men . . . at least officially. Now call the guard. It is important he does not come in first. Say Mary is too upset and I will tarry here until they come for me. Mary must create a commotion with her weeping. 'Tis part of the plan. Quick.'

Mary began to wail loudly and Brent limped over to the door. John observed the limp and bit his lip. How they had ever hoped to get away with this . . .

The door opened and the guard peered into the gloom.

'What is it?'

'My sister is greatly distressed and her husband would have us go.'

'Ah . . .' the guard shrugged and opened wide the door, glancing at the prisoner slumped dejectedly by the window. He had seen it happen so often lately as all the men were being sent to England; it was a sorry business. He locked the door and shepherded the weeping woman to the gate having little regard for the man who walked slowly behind her. He knew only one woman had come in and only one woman had gone out. No one had warned them to take much notice of the men. He saw the weeping woman through the gate and returned to the darkness of the prison. He would just finish his game of dice before taking the prisoner back to the dungeons. There was no hurry.

Analee sat in the carriage holding tightly to Nelly's hand. She stared anxiously at the castle gate and shared with those inside it the strong conviction that the plan would not succeed. Now that it had happened it seemed idiotic to suspect it would. Forging General Hawley's signature had been foolhardy, though Angus had a letter from him and they tried to copy his hand. They were being a long time and she stared anxiously at Nelly.

'It has gone wrong!'

'Hush,' Nelly comforted, 'you are too impatient. They have only been gone for a few moments. There is the governor to see and all sorts of things.'

Lord Falconer had not wished his wife to accompany Mary and John; after all, what had she to do with it? And if she was discovered? He had been foolish enough as it was. But the Falcon, if he did not know it before, was becoming aware of the stubbornness of the woman he had married. She would not take 'no' for an answer. If she wanted a thing she would get it. The only place he found her at all submissive was in bed, and even there she also seemed subtly to exercise her own particular kind of dominance. She was remarkable. He had let her go after warning her not to expect a visit from him when she was lodged in the castle as a prisoner of His Majesty along with Lady Strathallan and Lady Ogilvy.

But Analee had felt she owed it to Mary to see that she got Brent back; and she wanted to talk to Brent. They had stayed the night on the way with Jacobite friends of the Allonbys who had so far been spared persecution by the government, and they would stop there on the way back. After that Analee would return to her husband and see Brent no more.

The gate of the castle swung back and she clasped Nelly's hand and closed her eyes.

'Oh, Nelly . . .'

'Aye 'tis them. 'Tis Mary and . . . why, Analee, it *is* Brent. There is no doubt for he drags a leg and Mr John walked in quite firm and straight.'

Nelly tumbled out of the carriage at the same time as McNeath jumped from the box. They had thought to effect the escape in a light coach driven by McNeath so as to involve no further members of the household. Nelly ran up to Mary and put her arm about her, but, as planned, McNeath stayed by the coach. To anyone looking on, any guard or soldier, they must appear to be merely a sorrowing family, not the escort for the escape of an important Jacobite passenger.

Yes it was Brent, but how changed. So changed, so unlike John except in height that Analee wondered how they had achieved it. She leaned forward and held the door open, clasping Mary as she stumbled in. Then Brent followed and almost before they had sat down and closed the door McNeath had whipped his horses into a fast trot down the hill from Edinburgh Castle into the teeming streets of the town clustered in its shadow.

Everyone was breathing hard and now Nelly was also crying. Analee had tears in her eyes as she looked at the face of the exhausted man, his head back on his seat, his eyes closed. Analee studied his face to see whether she felt any emotion . . . tired or starved or ill or whatever, he was still Brent, her one time lover, Morella's father. Yes, there were traces of the handsome man he had been, eyes made even finer now by suffering, the curve of the mouth, the fine arch of the brow . . .

Brent opened his eyes and looked straight into those of Analee: then he quickly shut them again. He reopened them cautiously as one does when expecting a shock. She smiled at him reassuringly.

'Yes, Brent. It is I, Analee. I have contrived to help your escape.'

'Analee . . .' Brent leaned his head back and closed his eyes again. Analee. Was it possible? But she did not look like Analee in those fine clothes, that gorgeous cloak, the elegant hat with a plume.

Analee with a *hat*? Brent opened his eyes and looked again. It was not Analee, could not be. Why this person undoubtedly had her eyes and resembled Analee; but . . . she wore shoes, and carried a bag and her hands were gloved. No it could not be Analee, the wild gypsy he had loved.

'It *is* I, Brent,' Analee said gently knowing full well what was going on in his mind, 'but I am married now to a man of substance, a lord . . .'

'The Marquess of Falconer,' Nelly said firmly, '*General* The Marquess of Falconer.'

Brent opened his eyes and his lips trembled in a faint laugh.

'The Falcon? This is a joke someone is playing on me. He is a Hanoverian soldier, a man known for his mercilessness in battle. I thought he was killed at Falkirk and we all said "good riddance". Why should he be married to Analee? No I am dead and this is a dream.'

'It is no dream, Brent, and we shall explain all by and by. For the moment rest and be thankful that you are alive.'

Rory Macintoch had fought with Brent in all the Scottish battles. He had escaped from Culloden and was overjoyed to see him again. They were to spend the night together in the priest's hole in the house because they were loyal Catholics as well as Jacobites. Servants kept a twenty-four hour guard in the grounds of the house; but even during the day Rory kept out of sight.

Luckily in this remote part of Scotland few people outside the house would even be aware of the visit of Mrs Delamain and her brother, nor would it be noted as exceptional. Fiona Macintoch and Mary Allonby were old friends.

Fiona was a girl very like Mary in upbringing. She had known deprivation all her life, though it was especially bad for her family since the Act of Union. Up to that time Scotland had had its own Parliament; after that the country was ruled from London. At least Queen Anne, in whose reign the union took place, had been a Stuart; but after her death and the German Elector of Hanover usurped the English throne – according to her family's view of things – there was no going back. The English were hated and opposed at every turn. If the Allonbys thought they had martyrs to the Cause the Macintochs had more. In the present rising alone Fiona had lost another brother, killed, and a father who was in hiding with Cluny Macpherson in his cave in the highlands.

But to see Brent alive, even if he looked far from well . . . And to hear the part played by Lady Falconer, of all people. But Fiona was sworn to secrecy; that was a trust she would never betray. Like many Scots people near the border she had heard of Lord Falconer's sudden marriage to a fascinating gypsy – the Falcon was a law to himself, so everyone expected him to do something different. But a gypsy! How would *she* be received at the court of George II?

Fiona had taken to the new bride immediately, sensing her warmth and concern for the Allonby family. She had also trusted her. There was a strength about Analee that had convinced Fiona that if anyone could pull off the audacious coup she could. Mary jokingly said she was a witch but would not admit it.

Seeing Brent now among them and hearing how it was carried out, of the forged letter and the risky plan that had succeeded, Fiona was convinced Analee *was* a witch. How otherwise could she possibly have succeeded?

What was more the Marchioness, despite her beautiful clothes, was not the one to stand on ceremony. She knew that the Macintochs were poor and what servants there were patrolled the grounds of the house. Her ladyship set to in the kitchen and insisted on helping Fiona prepare the dinner while Mary, still shocked, rested in her room and Brent was put to sleep in the priest's hole after his sore leg had been bathed and his chains cut off, with some difficulty, by McNeath.

'My lady, I insist you should not come into the kitchen.'

'Nonsense,' Analee said. 'You know I am a simple gypsy woman?'

Fiona, a bonny girl of nineteen with auburn hair smiled.

'I have *heard* it said, your ladyship. I do not know I believe it.'

"Tis true,' said Analee, 'now tell me what I have to do and I will do it. Do you have meat to carve? Bread to cut?' She stared at Fiona noting her amazed expression.

'I see you do not think I am a gypsy. Is not my face dark and my eyes black? If I could show you my feet through these fine stockings you would see that I spent most of my life barefoot. It is the one thing my lord complains of, the scratch of my feet in bed. He says it is as though I wore boots!'

Fiona threw up her hands and laughed.

'Oh, Lady Falconer . . . you are very droll. Still Mary did say that you were a gypsy; she saw you as one. She says you have magical powers.'

'I have not; but we gypsies have a certain . . . way with us, you know. Maybe it is that. Now let us eat, girl, for I must be away at first light to my husband. You will see that Brent and Mary go on from here?'

'That is the plan. They will travel on horseback to Cockermouth where Mr Rigg has agreed to give Brent shelter until a boat may be found to take him to Ireland. Mary will stay for a while with Mr Rigg and her sister . . .'

'Mary must go with her husband,' Analee said firmly. 'I will speak to him about it.'

At dinner Brent could not take his eyes off Analee; everyone noticed it, especially his wife. Yes it was his Analee, the same. But married to another . . . Her gypsy husband had died and she had married the scourge of the Jacobites . . . the Falcon himself! It was incredible! But he still loved her; he always would. He looked into her eyes unaware of Mary next to him, unaware of anyone except Analee . . . But Analee seemed unconcerned and ate heartily as though she had spent a tiring day which in fact she felt she had. She spared Brent no special glances and entertained the company

342

with stories of her wandering life as a gypsy and how his lordship had found her at last and taken her into his home.

'And do you miss the life, Lady Falconer?' Fiona, very much taken by her guest, had listened, her chin propped on her hands, her eyes shining. To her it sounded like a fairy story.

'I can't say I miss it now,' Analee replied truthfully. 'It was a hard life; but sometimes, yes. I look about me and see the trees burgeoning and the hard winter earth breaking open with life. Then I recall that special kinship with nature that I had when I was not the wife of the Marquess and a very different sort of world is now before me.'

'But how did you come to be up here?' Mary said, also caught by Analee's spell, 'so far from home? What made you come to the north?'

Analee drew from her bosom where it rested between her breasts the talisman of her husband's love, the ring of Falcon gold, twisting it thoughtfully in her fingers as she often did. Yes, today she was dressed like a marchioness with a corset and hoop, underclothes of lace and fine cambric and a one piece gown made of crimson brocade. She glanced at the rings on her fingers, the diamond and sapphire Angus had first given her and a rich ruby on her little finger. Although she had not married him for them she loved fine things. She'd fingered silks and baubles on the market stalls of the town through which she had passed whenever she had the chance. She remembered the vision she'd had that one day she would be a grand lady.

She knew they were looking at her and admiring her, the set of her hair, the elegance of her dress, the glitter of her jewels. The ring of Falcon gold was like a lucky charm to her and she rubbed it between finger and thumb. What should she say? The truth? At last?

She looked at the young faces gazing at her – Rory Macintoch and Brent Delamain who had fought in battle, Mary and Fiona who had known suffering and deprivation and the agony of waiting for their men to return. Maybe she did owe them something, the knowledge that out of much misery happiness could come, that victory could take the place of disaster.

She leaned her chin on to the palm of her long brown bejewelled hand which glistened in the light of the guttering candles so that the audience knew not which dazzled them more, the diamonds and rubies on her fingers or the blazing dark eyes set in the imperious, beautiful face.

'I will tell you,' Analee said at last sighing deeply, 'though it is a secret few know. Not even my husband knows, though of course I will tell him in time. I tell it you now because you all have suffered much in recent times – you have gambled and appear to have lost. You, dear Mary and Brent, will be exiles in a foreign land, maybe forever. You Rory and Fiona – who knows where you will be in a twelvemonth? I tell you this little tale because it may give you hope and show that out of bad times good times can come, as I pray they will for you.

'It so happened that I was orphaned at birth and brought up by my grandmother. We were wandering gypsies, part of a nomadic southern tribe, not stationary as were the Buckland gypsies, into whom I eventually married. We rested sometimes for days, sometimes months and, from being a maid, I knew that I interested men a good deal and they me.

'My grandmother wanted to preserve my purity and marry me to a good gypsy boy because she could see, even at fourteen, how developed I was, how interested in love.

'But I was wilful and didn't heed my grandmother. I flirted with the boys and teased them and earned a name for myself for fickleness and inconstancy. I loved to dance and enjoy myself as young girls do; but I liked all the boys who admired me, and my grandmother despaired.

'My grandfather was already dead and then one day when I was seventeen my grandmother took a chill and died, and I found I was on my own. I had no near relations and no one really cared for me or was concerned about me, and I passed many months in despair until one day I met a gypsy boy who was far more serious minded than any I had known before. He was a fine horseman and taught me to ride expertly, and he had many skills which he wanted to develop only he lacked the education and means to do it. Oh he was such a fine, handsome, proud young man only a little older than I, and with such promise. He taught me really how to love and he cared for me and I was his woman. That was how it remained until one day we met up with another crowd of travelling gypsies and among them was a brilliant dancer with whom I discovered an immediate affinity. He was taller and more beautiful than my man and such a wonderful dancer that whenever I was with him I felt lost to the world.

'We continued with this group on the road and I soon realized I was in love with two men, or fancied I was. I was happy with both. My lover, by whom I was now expecting a child, became savagely jealous and this only spurred the dancer to flirt with me anew although he merely did it to anger my love.

'I know not what got into me at the time. I was young, and although I loved my man best and wanted his child, some devil in me made me pay more attention to the dancer and I flaunted myself in front of him, pretending to prefer him to the other.

'One day my lover, insane with jealousy though I was too blind to see it, asked me outright if *he* was indeed the father of my child. I smiled and played and teased and then shook my head and, before I knew what had happened, my love had drawn a knife and plunged it into the heart of the dancer who, even then, was looking incredulous at what I had said. For we had never even lain together, and deep in my heart I had kept constancy for my man.

'I shall never forget the look in his eyes as that beautiful youth lay dying, the bewilderment and the silent way he rebuked me, for he was incapable of speech. And then, turning to my love and seeing the jealousy and hatred die and turn to remorse, I threw myself into his arms and said I had merely teased him.

''Twas too late. The authorities took him and hanged him and no one pleaded his cause. I waited by the gaol, but I was not even allowed to see him again, beg his mercy. We gypsies have always been treated as a low form of human life.

'Meanwhile the winter came on and I was alone and friendless, big with child and prey to a remorse that all but killed me. Would that it had, I thought at the time. My baby was born before term and died immediately for lack of care, and I had no one but a strange woman to comfort me and take away my dead child . . .'

Analee paused, her eyes glistening with the sharpness of the memory. She saw that Fiona was silently weeping; that Mary had her eyes on the table, and Rory gazed at the floor, the muscles in his jaw working. Only Brent, who still loved her, met her eyes, gazing at her with the stormy jealousy she had once seen on the face of her lover, the one who had hanged. She had, he now knew, borne another's child – what if he knew she had borne his, too? She gazed at him tenderly and smiled.

'So I wandered on, forever trying to rid myself of the dreadful memory of what my wanton flirtatiousness had done. Two men cut off in their prime on account of me. I often dreamed that my lover came back and asked the truth, but however much I told him that the child was his he did not believe me and he would vanish, crying reproaches in the wind.

'Because it is my nature to love and to want to be admired I consoled myself with other men, in time. Randal Buckland who forced me to marry him I did not love at first, but I grew attached to him and grieved on his death.

'And now at last I have found my *true* love; my husband, Lord Falconer. I did not marry him for his title or wealth, but because we too had grown to know and love each other through suffering shared after he was nearly mortally wounded at Falkirk. I knew his reputation but he is not a bad man. He is a soldier and an aristocrat. A strong man. The man for me.'

Analee looked at Brent, saw the pain and suffering in his eyes, and then at the gentle unloved Mary, so long denied the bodily joys for which she yearned, which she had a right to expect from her husband.

Analee felt with all her heart that she wanted to make things go well for them before she returned to her own life of happiness with the husband who so anxiously awaited her at Falcon's Keep.

After dinner Analee indicated that she would like to speak to Brent alone. The table was cleared and they were left in the dining-room, one on either side of the fire. Already rested and in fresh clothes Brent looked better. He would soon be the tall, upright, well-built man she remembered.

'Analee . . .' he said to her as the door closed and came quickly to her side, but she put out a hand to stay him and he was surprised by the distant expression on her face.

'Come no nearer Brent Delamain.'

'But Analee . . . you did this for me. Took this risk.'

'I did it for your *wife*, for Mary and the Allonby family whom I love.'

Brent dropped his arms, extended to take Analee, and turned away.

'She is not my wife. I cannot love her. I have tried but I think only of you. You bewitch me Analee. Even though you have told this tale tonight of your love for another man – I speak not only of Lord Falconer but of your first love – even though you emphasize that you have lain with so many of whom I am merely one, I still love you and want you, and I always shall. You pretend you are a strumpet but you are not. You are *my* Analee! Thinking of you prevents me from even performing the act of love with anyone else.'

Analee sat down and placed her hands in her lap. She pursed her beautiful full mouth into an expression of severity and looked at Brent.

'Why sir, I am surprised to hear that a vigorous man like yourself is unable to give pleasure to a woman even if his thoughts lie with another. But, Brent, you must get over this fixation you imagine you have for me. I confess that for me you were *not* someone casual; you were someone very special, Brent, and always will be.'

She remembered their blonde daughter and her eyes momentarily clouded with thoughts of a happiness that was now lost but which might have been. Yes she did love Brent; he was part of her. Morella was part of them both; but it was a love that lay in the past, encapsulated in time. She wanted to take the stricken youth in her arms and tell him how much she had loved him, what she had done for him, suffered for him. Instead she gazed at him, her imperious head, beautifully coiffeured, tilted to one side, her eyes masked to hide her true feelings.

'Brent,' she said slowly, softly, 'I am married to the Marquess of Falconer, a man of fascination who dominates me body and soul. What happened between you and me is in the past and will never occur again. Let us remember it as a beautiful moment, captured forever in the moonlight. My husband is a masterful, jealous man and expects much from me. Compared to my love for him my feelings for you were like that of a young infatuated girl. Angus and I have a very deep bond. See . . .' She took the chain around her neck and showed him the ring of palest gold with the head of the falcon engraved on it. 'Angus gave me this as a symbol of our

347

enduring love – a ring of purest gold, Falcon gold it is called. Our love is binding like this gold, eternal like the ring.' Analee dropped the ring back into her bodice and folded her hands on her lap. 'You and I are not for each other, Brent, whatever you say. If I ever thought it, I think it not now.'

'You may think what you like,' Brent said. 'If the Falcon has captured you now, so be it; but it will not last and when it ends I will be waiting for you as I was meant to do, as I should have done before. My life of suffering these past months has made me realize what a fool I was to give you up, to put someone's happiness before mine. Not only was I not happy; but I made Mary desperately unhappy.'

'I know,' Analee said quietly, 'but listen, you are a fugitive and are bound for Ireland and, Brent, I want to ask you this and tell it you at the same time. Be a husband to Mary. Forget me, for you can never have me again. Like Mary nursed you, I nursed him to health and that way my love for him was cemented. I love Angus much more than I ever loved you. I can't tell you why but 'tis so, and now . . .' Analee crossed her hands meekly over her stomach and gazed at Brent, 'I am carrying his child and his blood runs with mine. It is final . . . It is settled. It is done. We are to raise a family and I am to become a fine lady with a house in London.' She smiled mischievously.

'My husband is teaching me nice manners, how to conduct myself like a lady and how to read and write. You might not believe it, but I have taken to the life far better than I expected. Although I am always Analee the gypsy, nothing can change that, I am also the Marchioness of Falconer – and nothing can change that either, or will.' Her ladyship patted her stomach and gazed complacently at Brent.

Brent's face, still contorted, was more livid than ever.

'I don't care whose child you are carrying or how many more you have!' he shouted. 'You are *my* Analee . . . *my* gypsy and you always will be.'

Analee lowered her eyes and felt a sickening moment of defeat. She got up and walked slowly to the door turning at the threshold, her hand on the doorknob. 'I will see you no more, Brent, and I can say no more; but if you love me then do as I ask. God bless you.'

She saw that tears had come into his eyes, as there were in hers, as she quietly shut the door behind her. Then she went to find Brent's wife. There was only one thing left to try and do.

Mary had heard everything. Even down the corridors Brent's shouts had penetrated. She wept as Analee came to her room, sat on her bed, took her hand.

'It is no good, Analee. He has eyes only for you.'

'Now listen,' Analee said practically. 'I have done all *I* can; there is still something *you* can do.'

'I? What can I do?'

'Well the only thing left is a gypsy spell . . . oh I know I have denied magical powers; but some things are passed down in gypsy lore and I have known them since I was a little girl, they came from my grandmother, who was foreign. Whether they work or not depends often on the intention of the one who wants to win the man's love. You *must* believe it. Well, Stewart was successful was he not?'

'Yes, but you said . . .'

'Maybe I was wrong? Maybe it *was* the spell? We can only try. Now listen, this is what I want you to do. It is simple and you must repeat it after me. Will you do it?'

'I will do anything to win Brent's love.'

Analee squeezed Mary's hand and leaned forward.

'Now when you have your woman's time I want you to take some of the blood and add it to the powdered pips of apples and pears, quinces and berries, and fruits you have in your sister's garden or wherever you are. These you must previously have burnt and ground to a powder. This you add to the little phial of blood you have procured and then you get some pieces of Brent's hair or, if you can, parings from his nails and add these to the mixture which you must then put in his food. Oh do not wince . . . It sounds unpleasant but 'tis tasteless if the food is well flavoured. You can add this mixture to his food up to three times, after that . . .'

Analee got up.

'I have told Brent I am with child by my lord and want nothing more to do with him. We are building our own life together, we and our children, which Angus urgently desires. He is of the government, bound for important duties in the army, at Court perhaps. Our lives must sunder, Mary. But I will always have a place for you in my heart. I hope you escape to happiness, and wish you and your family well. Now I am going . . .'

'But it is dark . . .'

'No matter. McNeath will drive carefully and we shall lodge at the first hostelry we come to. When Brent finds I am gone you will see he will soon realize how lucky he is to find such a wife as yourself. And you *will* be happy Mary. I know it. You have remembered the spell? Say it again.'

Mary nodded and repeated it until Analee was happy. Her eyes were on Analee the enchantress, the witch.

Moments later she heard the rattle of the coach, the barking of dogs.

The Marchioness of Falconer was returning to her lord, to the great mansion of Falcon's Keep in the heart of the Cheviot Hills. The Cheviots marked the end of the Pennine Range so that Analee had in some senses finished her journey. The past was behind her. Like the Allonbys, the Delamains, the defeated Jacobites and their fugitive Prince, she, Analee the gypsy, was beginning life again.

BOOK II
Falcon Gold
1748–1750

1

Analee put down the tapestry on which she was working and gazed once more out of the window. It was the tenth time she had done so in less than an hour. The day called to her to be out of doors; to feel the grass, still covered with dew, beneath her feet; to dabble her fingers in the cool waters of the lake.

It was no use. She was not a fine lady. Oh, she might look like one – she had the airs of one and now the manners of one. But inside in her heart, where it mattered, she was still Analee the gypsy. For the first twenty years of her life she had scarcely ever slept in a bed or known a roof over her head, until the aftermath of the shattering events of the '45 Rebellion had transformed her life and made her the wife of a great lord, Angus, Marquess of Falconer.

The Rebellion. How long ago it seemed! Analee idly eased off her shoes and pressed her nose to the window pane. The lake sparkled and shimmered in the early morning sun which peeped over Lodore but was still low in the sky, so that half of Derwentwater was still in the shadows.

The Grange always caught the first rays of sunshine. They streamed through Analee's bedroom window to arouse one who was used to rising with the dawn. Then, as the sun moved throughout the day, it illumined first one part of the big house and then another so that in Analee's mind, when she was away from it, she always saw a home drenched with sunshine, as though, symbolically, it was full of happiness.

And for her Furness Grange was happy. She had been happy there ever since she first came as a wandering gypsy and Nelly had caught her foot in the undergrowth and sprained her ankle. That had been their introduction to the Allonby family, and now the Allonbys' house was hers. Analee sighed and started to walk to the door just as it opened and Nelly came in, the baby in her arms.

'Oh Nelly, I *cannot* embroider! The day is too lovely for tapestry work. My lord will be disappointed in me yet again. Come Nelly. Let us walk as we used to, pretending we are gypsies once more.'

Nelly glanced at her mistress's feet and laughed. 'I think his lord-ship likes you too much, Analee, to mind about the embroidery.'

'Aye, or the reading. I simply cannot follow the print, Nell. I know it well enough but it makes me so tired. Come, Betty can attend to Clare and we shall take some bread and meat and eat by the lake. We can wander up over Manesty and Maiden Moor. Come, 'tis a lovely day.'

'Oh very well – I see you have a mind to it. Look, Clare has yet another tooth.' Nelly gently eased open the slumbering baby's lips and proudly displayed the tiny new pearl.

'Nelly, I declare you love that baby more than I do.'

'No, that is not possible,' Nelly said softly, looking adoringly at her mistress. 'For I know you love her better than any.'

And indeed Analee was a good mother. She nursed and cared for her baby by herself whenever she could; whenever she was not in London with her husband or journeying about the country with him. Rather than get a wet nurse Analee had fed the baby herself, preferring to remain with her at the risk of incurring his lordship's displeasure. And the results were there to see. Clare had thrived; she was bonny and sturdy, almost too heavy at fourteen months for Nelly to carry. She could walk by holding onto the furniture; she was a smiling contented child with a mop of black curly hair, black eyes and a determined chin. These characteristics she inherited from both her parents, but her fair skin she got from her father, for her mother's skin was dark olive like that of her forbears, wandering gypsies who had sought refuge in England from persecution abroad.

Yes, she was the Falcon's child. And how he adored her, his first born! The first thing he did when he returned home after an absence was to fling off his cloak and top coat and romp on the floor with his daughter. Seeing them together sometimes brought tears to Analee's eyes and, watching them, she would think that the family would really be complete when she fulfilled her duty and bore her husband the son he wanted, the heir to his great estates.

There was time, plenty of time, but what they had not had since Clare's birth was much opportunity to be together. As a General in His Majesty's Guards, Colonel of his own regiment, the

'Falconers', the Marquess had been continually abroad fighting the French in the closing days of the war to establish Maria Theresa as Austrian Empress in succession to her father.

Now the war was nearly over and negotiations for peace were in progress. The Falcon wanted her in France by his side and Analee knew that the happy carefree days she had spent in her beloved home by the lake were drawing to a close.

And indeed that April day was the last that Analee was to spend for some time at the home which, to please her, the Falcon had acquired from the commission dealing with forfeited Jacobite estates following the failure of the Rebellion. The Allonbys had twice given Analee succour before tragedy overtook them; like so many others who had supported Prince Charles Edward Stuart in his abortive attempt to regain the throne of England for his father, they had been severely punished. John Allonby, the head of the family, had been imprisoned for a time for his part in rescuing his brother-in-law Brent Delamain. He now lived in France. His brother Stewart had been deported to Maryland to serve as an indentured servant for seven years. Their sister Mary Allonby was in France too with her husband Brent, and the Crown had declared the historic Furness Grange forfeit by the Allonby family and had put it up for sale.

At Analee's request her husband had gladly bought the house, seeing that it was so dear to her. He gave it to her as her own home to be used whenever she wanted rest and peace by the tranquil lakeside, away from the cares of running a huge castle like Falcon's Keep on the Scottish border or their great London house in Piccadilly. Secretly, in Analee's mind she was but custodian of the Grange in the event that the Allonbys should be pardoned and should return, but her husband did not know this. He had hated the Jacobites and helped to defeat them, and the only fault he could find with his adored wife was that she had any truck with the Allonbys at all. He was glad to see them all safely out of the country and hoped they would never return.

Like girls, their hands sometimes entwined as they helped each other over uneven ground, Analee and her friend and servant Nelly Driver climbed ever upwards until they stood on the brow of Maiden Moor. Beneath them lay Borrowdale, that beautiful valley through which the river Derwent tumbled from its source high up by Allen Crags down to the huge lake to which it gave its name, Derwentwater.

From where they stood laughing and out of breath, their faces alight with cheerfulness and good health, Analee and Nelly could see across to Glaramara and, in the far distance, the glittering snow-capped tips of Scafell on one side and the Langdale Pikes on the other. It seemed like the very top of the world.

Analee recalled the time she had spent travelling in the district with the gypsies of the Buckland tribe. Her intimacy with the dales and mountains had relieved those days of tedium and lifted them into the realm of enchantment, so that Analee remembered them with a sharp nostalgia that almost amounted to regret.

They sat at the top of Maiden Moor and Nelly unpacked the fare she had brought, bound gypsy-fashion in a scarf. She and Analee shared the food as they had in those far off days when they roamed about together.

'Only this time we have plenty,' Analee said as she sank her teeth into the white flesh of the newly baked bread, still warm from the oven.

Nelly nodded, knowing what she meant, their minds always attuned. 'Aye, then it was berries and a stale crust if we were lucky. Oh Analee, we are more fortunate now I think! It is true his lordship still does not permit me and McNeath to wed, and this grieves me; but I am happy with you, serving you and seeing you contented and well.'

Analee grasped Nelly's hand and squeezed it. 'Nelly, he will! I promise it. Now that the war is nearly over he will let you marry. It was only that he wanted you to take care of me while he was away, Nell, and he thought that maybe – ' Analee looked at her friend slyly, 'if you had other preoccupations, like a little McNeath . . .'

'I would not take such care of you? Oh, Analee!'

Nelly's plain face, made comical by its grimace, filled Analee with affection for this companion who had shared so many of her trials.

'Oh *I* know it! But his lordship did not – you know how fearful he is for my welfare. But now that Clare is over a year old and the war is at an end – why I know he will keep his word and you and McNeath will be wed as soon as I can arrange it. Think, Nell, this time next week we shall be on our way to Paris! Maybe we shall see John and Brent and Mary.'

'You think his lordship will allow it?'

'That I meet them? If I can find them, why not?'

'I think he does not want you to have aught to do with them. That is my opinion. You would do well not to cross him in this matter, Analee. I know my master.'

Analee selected a young shoot of new grass and put it between her even white teeth. She sat back on her hands and studied her bare toes.

'Nelly, I do not mean to let my lord control me body and soul. You know that and he knows it too. I will have who I want for friends and he will not stop me.'

Nelly said nothing. Formal with Analee in public, familiar with her when they were alone, she felt she knew her better than anyone in the world and she loved Analee better than her life, better than McNeath – loved her like a sister, a mother, a daughter.

She had known that the marriage would be a stormy one. Both Analee and the Falcon, fourteen years older than his wife, had characters as unyielding as the rocky mountainside around them; each was stubborn and wilful as the other. Moreover Analee had not been brought up as a well-born lady, such as his lordship was expected to marry. She had not behind her a history of dutiful obedience to her parents, a grounding in manners, deportment and letters from a governess, the tradition of a life of ease with servants to cater for every need.

It was a marriage of equals, of stormy self-centred beings whose interests were separate, but whose one enduring bond was passion. Love had moulded the Falcon and Analee together as sure as fire bonds steel with steel. It seemed in those first days that they could never have enough of each other. Even now, after two years of marriage, Analee pined constantly for her lord and, despite the difficulty for her, wrote to him daily.

She could have gone to the Continent with him; but her duty as a mother called her too and so she had stayed with Clare, true to her gypsy upbringing – children on the whole being more important to gypsy mothers than to noblewomen with every comfort and servants to command.

The Falcon and Analee had quarrelled about this; he wanted her constantly at his side, but Analee had been resolute and Clare had flourished. Now she was old enough to be left while Analee fulfilled her wifely duties.

Nelly knew how badly the Falcon, always surrounded by the danger of death or disease, wanted a son. If he died his estates would go to a brother, and Analee would be much worse off. Looking at her girlish form silhouetted against the bright blue sky, her skirts swirling about her, her long dark hair caught in the breeze, Nelly knew that Analee would soon be with child again. These carefree days were numbered.

And as though sharing Nelly's thoughts, a solemn look supplanted the laughter on Analee's face.

'These are still days full of trouble, Nelly. His lordship has much to do to help secure the peace with France. Oh doubt not that I will do his bidding, will not anger him. So much I have learned: that to please him is my duty next to that of being a mother. Maybe I will become a mother once more as he wishes. Then I will be able to spend more time at Furness.'

The smile came back to Analee's face and she looked below her to where the buds were appearing on the trees and fresh young leaves on the bushes. Little fronds stretched up obscuring in places the crystal clear waters of the Derwent as it bubbled and tumbled over the stones and shingle of the river bed. The rocks and boulders that stood like sentinels on either side of the narrow track were known as the Jaws of Borrowdale, and from where they sat they saw it gradually broaden into a wide valley dotted with farms and small crofts. It curved towards the steep pass at Honister over which the packhorses plied carrying ore – plumbago, lead and tin – and merchandise of all kinds to and from the port at Whitehaven. It took a laden packhorse the best part of a day to go from Borrowdale to Buttermere, steeply up one side, perilously down another, the panniers swaying on either side of the laden horse. The men in charge trudged wearily alongside, doubtless too preoccupied with keeping their nags on the narrow path to glance back and survey, in all their majesty, the mountains and peaks of Lakeland stretching way to the south and westwards towards the sea.

The sea. Analee recalled how, as gypsies, she and Nelly had sought the sea and how it was that on their way they happened to stop at Furness. Thus had their destinies been shaped, a little accident that had transformed their lives. But for that they might have come to the sea and crossed to Ireland where they would still be wandering, seeking but never finding, Analee always thinking of her lost daughter Morella left behind with the Buckland tribe.

''Tis in odd ways that our lives are transformed,' Analee said as she got up and shook her skirts of crumbs and grass. She inhaled the pure air and looked about her.

In her mind's eye she seemed at the same time to see both the past and the future. The past was clear, but the future obscured by a haze – things dimly perceived and not understood. There was happiness there, but sadness too; there was the challenge of the unknown.

Analee's nostrils flared as she savoured with animal relish the thought of what lay before her. Many nights of love with the Falcon, more children, journeys across Europe and England, new people to meet, the excitement of the Court in London, perhaps that of Louis in France . . . She threw out her arms and stretched them high, exhilarated by her destiny, welcoming it.

Then the Marchioness of Falconer gathered up her skirts and, tossing her head in the air, began a very unladylike scamper across the moor back the way they had come. Laughing and breathless, her cheeks red from the wind, Nelly flew after her mistress, admiring the swiftness of her foot, her litheness as she skipped across the turf, her long black hair flying in the wind. She looked, thought Nelly, like a child of nature, innocent and free, yet at the same time like a spirit from some other world – indeed an Enchantress, as so many who knew of her powers called her.

His lordship's body, though so familiar to Analee, was yet more precious for the time that had separated them. The Falcon was over six feet tall and his huge muscular frame was scarred by many battles. He had almost been killed at Falkirk during the '45 Rebellion and the place where his arm had nearly been severed from his body was still an ugly angry livid scar. Analee ran her hand lightly over his body and felt him tremble even though he slept deeply.

She was aware of her own body by the side of his – tall and supple, curved thighs and rounded buttocks, long legs entwined in his.

She had arrived in Paris the previous day and gone straight to the house taken by her lord in the Rue du Faubourg near the Luxembourg Gardens.

She looked about her at the large room, the wide bed, the elegant drapes hanging across the windows, the tall furniture. Then she looked down at herself – a woman loved and capable of giving love, not just a chattel for pleasure, but an artist in creating harmony through the body, the stimulation of the senses, the mutual gratification of desire. In this she and her husband were one; it was their great bond, their most intimate source of satisfaction in each other.

Angus and Analee lay in bed until the sun was high, slumbering, caressing, gossiping, their bodies never far from each other, their faces close together. Analee observed that her husband's eyes were red and tired-looking and that at his temples were touches of white she had not seen before. She took his lined face between her hands and embraced it, letting her tongue caress it gently as though rejuvenating him with the elixir of her own young vibrant life.

'My lord, you look so weary.'

'Aye, 'tis not only the night we have spent, my love. I rode hard from Flanders to be with you on your arrival.' Angus stretched and smiled at Analee. 'And I am tired of war.'

'But the war is over, my lord.'

'Yes, Maria Theresa is firmly established on her father's throne, the Austrians and Hanoverians are victorious and England is on the right side yet again. Now the Duke of Newcastle has asked me to help supervise the peace, and the devil of a time we have with Louis XV! Since the death of Cardinal Fleury, he has governed by himself – or rather has failed to govern properly. He has a council of ministers to advise him but in reality he is under the thumb of his mistress, Madame de Pompadour. Indeed, she enjoys such power that ministers pay more court to her than the King and tell her all the state secrets.'

Analee sat up in bed clasping the sheets around her, her face alight with excitement.

'Have you met the Pompadour? They say she is the most beautiful woman in France. I stayed briefly in London on our way here and was with the Prince and Princess of Wales at Leicester House. The Princess confesses to a longing to meet her.'

'Does she indeed?' Angus glanced at his wife. 'I like you not keeping company with the Waleses at Leicester House; they are in disfavour with His Majesty and I am his loyal servant.'

'Ah, but they are so much more amusing than King George, confess that my lord!'

'And also a hornet's nest of Jacobites surrounds them. That is why you were there, I doubt not.'

'Not so Angus. The dancing is much better than at St James's and the company more pleasing. What is the Pompadour like? Tell me.'

The Falcon fastened his eyes on the ceiling, his head propped on his arms.

'Let me see. She is about twenty-six, a little older than you, my love, and is tall with a mass of chestnut hair which she wears elaborately coiffured. She is slim and has a beautiful figure; her face is round and her features regular. But what there is about her that is so attractive is a puzzle. Even the Duc de Luynes, no flatterer and an intimate friend of the Queen, says she is *fort jolie* . . . strikingly pretty.

'Myself, I think the secret is in her eyes because it is hard to say exactly what their colour is, whether they are grey or green or blue. They seem to be of no particular colour, yet of all colours, like a kaleidoscope. And her expression changes with lightning rapidity to show pleasure, astonishment, grief or amusement. Her features are so vital and mobile, so alive . . . I think it is this that is the Marquise's special quality. When she laughs her teeth are perfection, and she moves with such a grace and style you would think she had been born to be the King's mistress instead of being of the *bourgeoisie* – in fact her family is slightly scandalous and her mother, a beauty like her daughter, a notorious whore.'

'I think you are half in love with her yourself,' Analee said, her eyes smouldering, letting the sheets fall so as to reveal her bosom.

The Marquess observed her gesture and, knowing its reason, laughed. He fingered the heavy gold ring that lay between her breasts, supported by a thin chain. It was almost white, so pure was the gold mined two centuries ago in Ecuador and brought home by Sir Beyrick Falconer to lay at the feet of Elizabeth I. The great queen, in appreciation of this gesture, had called it 'Falcon Gold', and enough of the precious metal had remained with him to enrich the house of Falconer.

Angus had given Analee this ring as a token of their love: '*A ring is round and has no join; that is why it is symbolic between two*

361

people – love cannot be broken.' She was to wear it always as a symbol that she and the Falcon were one.

He studied the outline of the falcon bird engraved on the ring and looked into her eyes.

'I promised you a medallion when we had a son, made of Falcon Gold as this is. But first you have to do something to achieve that, my love.'

Analee stroked his cheek and reached up to kiss him. 'I long for the medallion made of priceless Falcon Gold that you promised me, my lord, and know well what I should do. But, alas, I cannot achieve it by myself . . .' She leaned back, a wicked gleam in her eyes, and Angus put an arm around her waist.

'So much for the Pompadour,' she said at last with satisfaction.

'The King is a fortunate man if she does half as much for him,' said Angus, cupping her narrow waist between his broad hands. 'I hear, in fact, that the act of love does not please her as much as it might and, as you know, the King – like all his Bourbon ancestors – is greatly enamoured of this art that you practice so well, my love. Still, her effect on the King is very pronounced, and all try to please her, except – ' his lordship smiled with satisfaction, 'that ass, the so-called Young Pretender, he who would have wreaked so much harm on our land. He has offended her by affecting to despise her bourgeois origins. They say she is behind the King's efforts to have Charles expelled from Paris. Ahh . . .' Angus said no more as his love brought his face down to hers. Nelly knocked timidly on the door at noon and when there was no reply entered with their breakfast of hot chocolate and freshly baked rolls.

His lordship opened his eyes at Nelly's approach and gently shook Analee, trying to cover their nakedness. Nelly busied herself putting down the tray, and by the time she had gone to the window and asked permission to draw the curtains, her master and mistress were neatly and decorously tucked under the sheets, only their heads visible, their eyes sparkling mischievously.

'I trust you slept well, my lord and lady,' Nelly said primly, bringing the tray to the bedside. 'McNeath said I should call you, as his lordship has an engagement with a French gentleman whose name I cannot pronounce.'

'Zonks! The Marquis d'Argenson!' His lordship raised himself on one elbow. 'He is a powerful man I would not annoy; no lover of the King or the Pompadour either. My love, will you rest and amuse yourself while I am gone? No doubt you are fatigued from your . . . journey.' He gazed at her slyly over the rim of his cup as he sipped his hot chocolate. 'Me, I feel remarkably invigorated.'

Analee winked at Nelly as she took her chocolate, allowing Nelly to prop up the pillows behind her. Analee ached with pleasure and repletion, longing for the hot bath Nelly would give her after the Falcon had gone out. She gazed out of the window at the houses across the street. From below came the sound of voices, footsteps and the clatter of horses' hooves on the cobbles, the rattle of carriage wheels.

'Nelly, pray pass me my robe,' said the Marquess, 'and send McNeath to help me dress. He can wash me and shave me in my dressing room so that her ladyship is not disturbed.'

Nelly passed Angus his robe and averted her eyes as he lumbered out of bed. Beside him Analee looked neat and even fragile, though she was tall for a woman. Nelly was quick to cover her with the bedclothes and then she went swiftly to the stairs to summon McNeath who waited in the hall below.

For the next hour while his lordship prepared himself Analee slumbered, aware only of his lips pressed lightly to her cheeks, a hand caressing her brow, words of endearment murmured in her ear before he was gone.

'His lordship says tonight you will go to the French court,' Nelly said excitedly, soaping Analee's long limbs in the bath that had been placed in the bedroom before the large fire. 'You are to spend the whole afternoon preparing yourself . . .'

'Indeed!' Analee laughed and bade Nelly pick up the towel. 'Now we must discuss my wardrobe, and Nelly you must wash and dress my hair. I think I will powder it tonight, it is sure to be the fashion at the French court. Oh we have such a lot to do! Fancy Nell, to see the French King and Queen . . . oh and the Marquise de Pompadour. Imagine seeing *her*! Nell, I declare I am well and truly excited. I have come from the Court in London to the Court of the great King of France. Is it not strange, Nell? To think, if you had not sprained your ankle we should both be gypsies wandering over the roads, set upon by any man who would take us . . . and here I am the wife of a Marquess, fit to be presented to the Kings of England and France!'

As Analee stood there, glowing with excitement and beauty, Nelly thought – as she had so often thought before – that it was no strange accident that had brought her here: it was Analee's destiny, woven before time in the stars perhaps, to enchant, to be enchanted.

2

Nothing Analee had heard could have prepared her for her first visit to the Château of Versailles on that warm summer evening in the year 1748. The road from Paris ran straight as an arrow through the great forest where the Kings of France hunted, and because it was used such a lot with people coming and going to and from the seat of power, the surface was smooth. Drawn by four horses, the carriage ran swiftly until it burst out of the forest and the vast château that seemed like a small town in itself was suddenly revealed. Louis XIV had turned his father's hunting lodge into one of the most magnificent palaces in the world.

Besides this, Analee thought as the carriage turned through massive gates into a huge courtyard, St James's Palace and even Hampton Court were like dolls' houses. Coaches of all sizes were crammed in the courtyard and people scurried about – menials about their duties, or dignitaries and government officials come to attend the court. Sedan chairs bearing some fashionably gowned lady or portly gentleman bustled in and out among the traffic, dogs barked, horses shied, and smoke rose from the great kitchens. Flaming torches burned in the sconces set in the sandstone walls and the many windows were golden with the soft molten glow of candlelight. Servants rushed forward to open the door of the carriage and the postilion jumped down to assist the Marchioness of Falconer who, indeed, looked regal herself in a dress of dark green satin embroidered in coloured silks and metal thread to give a woodland motif. The open bodice of her dress was filled by a stomacher with a ladder of *échelles*, ribbon bows, which decreased in size down to the waist. Robings embroidered in the same manner as the skirt ran from the neck to the hem of the gown. Her close fitted sleeves, ending just above the elbows, were edged with deep ruffles of Brussels lace which Angus had brought her from Flanders and which had been sewn on that very day by Nelly.

Her hair was powdered and dressed with artificial flowers and tiny pearls and she wore a corsage of fresh flowers at her bodice.

Her very low *décolletage* exposed the deep cleavage, wherein lay the ring of Falcon Gold which her husband had given her before their marriage to cement their love. The fine gold chain supporting it was her sole adornment apart from the jewels which glittered on her fingers.

Such an important man as the Marquess of Falconer and his wife were preceded by two liveried servants through massive doors and up a broad staircase to the first floor, where Mansart's magnificent Gallery of Mirrors ran almost the entire length of the front of the château. By day it was a vast concourse of people going about their business, servants fetching and carrying, courtiers bent on some errand or other, sedan chairs carrying members of the royal family, and occasionally the odd cow or ass driven through to provide fresh milk for the royal nursery.

By night it was transformed into a gigantic reception room, lit by thousands of candles flickering in the silver candelabra and chandeliers whose reflections danced in the mirrors that gave the hall its name. The mass of shimmering winking pin-points of light were multiplied many times over so that there seemed a multiplicity of gilded walls and ceilings, inlaid panels, silver consoles and ornate orange trees in silver tubs.

But if anything outshone the splendour of the setting it was the throng that milled about, ladies in dresses of gorgeously embroidered silks, satins and brocades, with stomachers sometimes patterned and sewn with pearls, or filled with brightly coloured *échelles* in the style favoured by the Pompadour. Hairstyles were rich and elaborate and diamonds, rubies, sapphires and emeralds seemed in as plentiful abundance in this city of the wealthy as stones on the sea shore. Snowy bosoms, enhanced by priceless necklaces, were high and prominent and waists were nipped in by corsets tightly laced under the elaborate stomachers.

The men were almost as splendidly apparelled as the ladies with full bottomed wigs, close-fitting waisted coats collarless and with buttons from neck to hem curving away to reveal dazzling waistcoats of gold or silver brocade, damask, silk or satin heavily embroidered or patterned with gold and silver lace. Cravats were full and edged with lace, and breeches which matched the coat were sometimes bound at the knee by buckles like those on their shoes.

Such were the proportions of the room that it seemed it could contain two or three times the number that gathered there, and the laughter and chatter was like a hum of bees carried away out of the open windows into the ornate gardens beyond.

Amidst all this splendour, even in this vain self-centred crowd of nobles gathered around the King in *ce pays-ci* – 'this country', as it was called, a special realm with its own laws and customs – there were those who did not fail to notice Lord and Lady Falconer as they made their way along the gallery towards the private apartment. Angus, wearing a full powdered periwig, looked every inch the Falcon whom so many had cause to dread, in his scarlet military coat with very full skirt and deep cuffs, gold lace intricately woven at his pockets and button holes. It fell away to reveal a plain buff waistcoat and breeches and there were no regimental colours or facings to distinguish him as a General in the Horse Guards. His high black boots had been polished by McNeath until they gleamed like pitch.

Angus acknowledged one or two people whom he knew, but Analee, nervous in this large unfamiliar crowd, kept her head high and her gaze strictly on the backs of the two men in front of her. Nothing she had seen in either of the courts in London came anywhere near this in splendour or magnificence.

The courtiers, always anxious to congregate near royalty, hung about the doors which were flung open by one of the servants preceding Analee and Angus.

'The King's antechamber, my lord.'

The chamber was crowded and noisy, but at the entrance of Angus and his wife the chattering subsided and a lane was made for them to the doors opposite which swung open, pulled by invisible hands. Through them Analee could see a small group of people surrounding a tall man who leaned nonchalantly against the chimney piece. A young man approached and bowed and Angus acknowledged him, returning the bow.

'Monsieur le Prince, may I present my wife, the Marchioness of Falconer. Madame, the Prince de Croÿ.'

Analee made a deep curtsy and gave her hand to the gorgeously dressed young man, who bowed low over it, kissing it.

'I am here to present my wife to His Majesty.'

'Indeed my lord. His Majesty is expecting you, and also Her Majesty who is in her apartments.'

Analee looked up and her heart lurched in a strange way when she saw the tall man by the chimney looking at her. It was King Louis XV, she was certain, for not only did his demeanour betray the majesty of his office, but he was wonderfully handsome as she had heard he was, not as tall as her husband but still very tall with a powerful physique. His large eyes, infused with melancholy but expressive and controlled, gazed at her for a moment before they were transformed by a smile that broke on his large generous mouth and he came over to her as she curtsied low to the floor.

'Sire,' said the Prince, 'the Marchioness of Falconer.' The King smiled and murmured a few scarcely audible words, and then the Prince helped Analee to her feet while her husband made a deep bow.

'Lord Falconer,' Louis said, jutting out his strong chin and speaking French in a pleasantly low husky voice. 'You did not tell me you had such a beautiful wife. Where have you been hiding her?'

'Sire, my wife has been in England with our young daughter.'

'And *you* of course have been busy fighting my army.'

The King looked momentarily severe but his face relaxed as Angus returned his gaze unflinchingly. 'I like you, Falconer. I wish I had you in my army among my generals, then we should not have been brought to such a sorry pass. The common people already express dissatisfaction with the terms of the Treaty – "*bête comme la paix*" they say, stupid like the peace. We have lost not only Madras but all the territory occupied by my brilliant general Maréchal de Saxe in the low countries.'

'Alas Sire, I am not responsible for the terms of the Treaty,' Angus began diplomatically. 'I am only a rough soldier, but devoted to Your Majesty.'

He bowed again and the King was about to speak when there was a commotion at the door. A woman was entering the room, preceded by a number of others who glided before her with the special sliding footsteps which were a characteristic of the court at Versailles. At first Analee thought it must be the Queen because of the deference shown to the woman smiling so regally at those who bowed as she passed. When she reached the King she dropped a deep curtsy, and Analee saw the reserve she had noticed in his eyes replaced by a warm tenderness. He put out a hand to take that of the curtsying woman, raising her to her feet.

'Monsieur le Marquis, have you met la Marquise de Pompadour?'

'I have had that good fortune, Your Majesty.' Angus bowed low over the very white elegant hand outstretched to him. 'I was talking in glowing terms about the beautiful Marquise to my wife.'

Madame de Pompadour gave Angus her brilliant smile and Analee could see how she had mistaken her for the Queen, though she had heard the Queen was no beauty. She had a poise and dignity that not even the Princess of Wales could claim, the highest degree of female royalty that Analee had met, since the English Queen Caroline was dead. The Marquise too glided and this movement enhanced the perfection of her slim figure, her tiny waist, her dress of blue and silver brocade embroidered with grey and silver roses and stretched over a large pannier. Her stomacher was also of silver brocade embroidered with small pearls. Around her neck she wore a blue ribbon and in her powdered hair silver and blue artificial flowers and jewels.

The Marquise was tall for a woman but shorter than Analee, yet her majestic air made her seem her equal. Her gaze lingered for a while on the features of the handsome Falcon and then she turned to Analee who was uncertain whether she should curtsy or not. She compromised by giving a short bob and bowing her head and this seemed to please the King's mistress who also inclined her head, her eyes fixed shrewdly on Analee.

Indeed they were remarkable eyes, the colour uncertain as the Falcon had said. They were not very big – not like the King's large brown limpid ones – but sparkled with gaiety and wit and, yes, friendliness.

'Have you been long in France, Madame?' the Marquise said, speaking in low musical tones, the conversation being translated by the bi-lingual Falcon.

'I arrived but yesterday Madame.'

'And it is your first time in Paris?'

'Indeed.'

'Then I hope you will enjoy your stay.'

The Prince de Croÿ who had been looking over his shoulder in an agitated manner now coughed and bowed low to the King and Marquise.

'Her Majesty is expecting the Marquis and Marquise de Falconer. If you permit . . .'

'Of course,' the King smiled. 'We hope to make your acquaintance again Madame, Monsieur.'

Analee curtsied deeply once more and when she had risen the King had turned and was talking to someone else; but the Marquise de Pompadour continued to look at her, and from her to her husband, smiling.

'The King sometimes gives little supper parties. The Prince de Croÿ, I am sure, will get in touch with you.'

'Deeply honoured Madame.' The Falcon bowed and touched Analee's arm.

'A word before you go, Monsieur le Marquis.' The Pompadour lowered her voice, leaning towards Angus. 'I believe you are as anxious for one of the clauses of the Treaty to be implemented as His Majesty.' The Falcone looked serious and bent his ear. 'We are most anxious for Prince Charles Edward to be got out of France,' she continued.

Angus noted the 'we'. He had heard the Pompadour was becoming increasingly interested in politics. This seemed proof, if proof were needed.

'Indeed Madame? Then we have a common interest. I shall do everything I can to assist you, if not apprehend the scoundrel myself and take him for trial in England.'

The Pompadour threw back her head and gave a peal of silvery laughter. 'Ah, I think that is going too far, my lord. It will not commend itself to the Queen who is fond of the rogue. Remember – the supper party!' She gave him a smile that Analee could have sworn was mildly flirtatious but which quickly turned to friendliness when her eyes caught Analee's. 'And you Madame. *Au revoir* for now.'

'Hurry,' the Prince de Croÿ hissed. 'Her Majesty has especially interrupted her dice game to receive you.'

Now that the King's back was turned, Analee and Angus were able to walk out of the room in the wake of the Prince de Croÿ who had been joined by an emissary from the Queen, and two ladies.

The little procession moved once more through the King's

antechamber to the Queen's room, where an even larger crowd was gathered, eager to see the English General with such a fearsome reputation and – the rumour had quickly spread – his ravishing wife. The Queen of France, Maria Leczinska, was seven years older than the King and looked far more. Indeed Analee was shocked by the appearance of the woman who had borne Louis ten children and been his wife for over twenty years. She seemed to crouch petulantly on her chair and her plain face was stiff and unsmiling as Angus bowed and Analee made her deep curtsy. Behind her stood a fat young man with small black eyes that gazed about him suspiciously, so different from the warm friendly brown eyes of his father. Indeed the Dauphin did not resemble the King at all and was known to have an evil temper. Like his mother, whose favourite pastime was embroidering altar cloths, he was excessively pious and was said to throw himself flat on his face at the Elevation of the Host during Mass. Beside him, next to the Queen, sat his second wife whom he had recently married, Marie Josèphe of Saxony. She looked very young – she was just fifteen – and kept her eyes on the floor so that Analee could see little of her face except to note her straw-coloured hair and flat broad nose.

The Dauphin was supposed still to be in mourning and still in love with his first wife Maria Teresa of Spain who had died after the birth of a daughter, and Analee thought that explained the sour look on the face of the unattractive young man and the sad way his wife hung her head.

None of the Royal Family spoke and, at a word from the Prince, Analee curtsied deeply again and she and Angus backed out of the room.

'What a contrast,' Angus murmured as the door shut behind them. He shook himself and Analee saw beads of perspiration over his upper lip. 'I know now why Louis has mistresses. Of course they do not like me because they know I am against Charles Edward, who is related to the Queen. That is why nothing was said.' He took care that his remarks should not be heard by the Prince de Croÿ and the Princesse de Conti who had accompanied them. Etiquette was very important at Versailles, and this included loyalty, in public at any rate, to both King and Queen – what was said behind their backs was another matter.

'His Majesty is anxious that you should be well looked after,' the Prince said, 'and that I should give you refreshment.'

The Princesse de Conti smiled at Analee but was unable to converse with her because she knew no English and Analee no French.

They were back in the Gallery of Mirrors, still thronged with people hoping to catch a glimpse of the King or members of the Royal Family as they made their way to the card tables or to dine.

Suddenly the Princesse de Conti stopped and beckoned to an attractive woman who was deep in conversation with a tall dark man. The Princesse moved towards them, talking and nodding in the direction of Analee and Angus. Analee guessed they were the object of the conversation, and the Princesse brought the two over to her, stretching out a hand and saying in French, 'Madame, I have brought to you the Princesse de Talmond who not only speaks your language well, but is here with her friend Lord St March, who is from your country.'

Angus translated quickly for Analee and she smiled at the Princesse and extended her hand to her companion who bowed low over it kissing it.

'The Marquis and Marquise de Falconer,' the Princesse de Conti said. 'And now I must return to Her Majesty who is anxious to play.'

'And I to the King.' The Prince de Croÿ made a low bow. 'I am sure I can leave you with Madame de Talmond and Lord St March.'

'Of course I have heard of the Princesse de Talmond,' Angus said kissing her hand, 'but Lord St March?' The Marquess quizzed the stranger with his glass noting how his eyes were fastened on Analee as though he recognized her. 'Do you know his lordship, my love? It seems he might have made your acquaintance.'

'Not that I know. My lord?'

'I think we *have* met ma'am, but I do not recall when, I confess.'

His lordship appeared shaken by the encounter with Analee and in the glitter of lights his face had grown visibly pale. Analee felt uncomfortable, knowing they had not met and disconcerted by the look in his eyes. She turned instead to the Princesse de Talmond who was watching the proceedings with amusement. The Princesse was not young, yet she had a vitality and warmth that took years away, and she was elegantly dressed and beautifully made up to take advantage of her clear eyes and fine skin. She wore a pink dress embroidered with gold and pink rosebuds and trimmed with gold lace at her wrists and throat. Her *décolletage* was very low, revealing a full white bosom on which sparkled a magnificent diamond necklace.

'Shall we go and sup? The Prince de Croÿ gave you into my charge. Lord Falconer, I hear you are here to discuss the Peace?'

'Yes, ma'am . . .'

The rest was lost as Angus and the Princesse preceded them through the throng to a room off the Gallery where tables were laden with succulent food and wines. There were all kinds of fish elaborately dressed, and chicken, quail, ham, sides of beef, and whole sucking pigs glazed and with their heads intact. Servants stood behind the tables, serving the food, and others moved among the guests filling glasses with champagne or red wine from Burgundy. The sounds of a small orchestra came from another room, and through one of the doorways Analee could see people seated round the card tables. She was still aware of the gaze of Lord St March; it was disconcertingly familiar and she was at a loss to explain it.

'Perhaps we met at Court in London my lord?' Analee's eyes studied him over the rim of her glass. Lord St March was older than Angus, tall and extremely bronzed as though he spent a good deal of time in sunnier climates than England. The cut of his brown velvet suit was severe and he wore no adornment in the way of jewels, flounces or laces. His hair was powdered and swept back off his high forehead. His eyes were darkly brilliant, his nose large and aquiline above a sculpted mouth and a firm chin. He was an attractive man.

'I think not ma'am. I have spent the last few years on my estates in Spain, the death of my wife having driven me abroad for consolation. I am on my way back to London to pay my respects to His Majesty and called to see Madame de Talmond whose husband is an old friend of mine.'

'Monsieur de Talmond is not here?'

'He is seen infrequently at Versailles but prefers his estates in Lunéville where the father of the Queen, King Stanislaus of Poland, has his court. Madame de Talmond was born Marie

Jablonowska and is a cousin of the Queen, and indeed only comes to court to see the Queen and the Dauphin of whom she is very fond.'

'And the King?' Analee lowered her eyes and deftly speared a piece of carp in aspic on her plate.

Lord St March bent his head so that his lips almost brushed Analee's ears. 'Madame, it can be no secret to you that there are two factions at court – the King's and the Queen's – and each have their adherents. Besides, Madame de Talmond is the rumoured mistress of Prince Charles Edward who also takes the side of the Queen. She, of course, is related to his own mother, who was a Polish Princess. The Queen is full of tenderness for the Prince and makes him tell his story of the '45 Rebellion over and over again, listening with tears in her eyes. I should say "made" for he is seldom at court now though some say he visits the Queen in secret. The King is anxious to be rid of him, and also of the Princesse who is plotting and scheming for all she is worth. He has threatened to exile her to Lunéville.'

'Take care not to let my husband hear you,' Analee put down her plate and wiped her mouth with a napkin. 'He is after His Royal Highness too. It is part of the Peace Treaty to have him expelled.'

Lord St March was looking at the smart figure of Angus deep in conversation with the Princesse de Talmond who appeared to find him very interesting, throwing back her elegant head and laughing a good deal.

'His lordship is in the army?'

'Does he not wear the scarlet coat of His Majesty's Guards?'

'Indeed ma'am. I am unfamiliar with military uniform. I believe King George has changed it a great deal. His lordship, although looking most distinguished, could almost be a private gentleman.'

'My husband has been in Flanders with Lord Ligonier. He is now detailed to Paris to help implement the Peace. Tell me, Lord St March – ' Analee made sure Angus was still engrossed in his conversation and put her lips to the Earl's ear, 'I have many friends who were on the losing side in the Rebellion. I would dearly love to know what has become of them. Though devoted to my husband and loyal to the King, I cannot help admiring the Prince and those who served him.'

Lord St March looked into Analee's eyes and smiled. 'I am sure I can arrange it, but not now. I will have words with the Princesse after we have gone. I have to escort her back to Paris . . .'

'But it *must* be secret.'

'Oh it will be. Have no fear.'

'We are in the Rue du Faubourg. Number 93.'

'I will remember it. Well my lord, what think you of Versailles?' St March was now addressing Angus, who had moved closer to Analee.

''Tis very grand sir. I am grateful, though, we have not such splendour in England or else there would be a revolution . . .'

'But we already had that did we not, sir, in 1688?'

'I am thinking of a revolution by the people against the misery and squalor of their lives while the nobles live protected by the King in opulence. I have noticed great suffering in the country through which our army passed.'

'I think many of the nobles find it a prison too,' the Princesse said keeping her voice low. 'The King keeps them here so that he can see what they are up to. It is the bourgeois who govern. How, otherwise, would the Poisson have achieved such eminence?'

'The Princesse is talking of Madame de Pompadour,' Lord St March murmured to Analee, 'whose father, Monsieur Poisson, was but a steward to the Pâris brothers, court bankers who practically governed France. Even though she is said to be remarkably well educated, the Marquise had to be taught the special ways of court etiquette before she was allowed into Versailles.'

'At which she now excels,' the Princesse said bitterly. 'She is so artful that she even manages to please the Queen who goes and sees her theatricals, occasionally allows her to travel with her in her carriage and invites her to dinner.'

'They say the Queen is happy to be relieved of His Majesty's attentions,' said Lord St March, 'having borne him ten children in just over ten years and complaining that she was forever in bed, pregnant or being brought to bed. She has not sought to keep her looks or attraction for him, not that they ever amounted to much. No, the Marquise is very considerate to the Queen, who much prefers her to the Mailly family who provided mistresses for the King over a number of years.'

'I see you are very well versed in the French court Monsieur,' the Princesse smiled knowingly at Lord St March.

'Madame, in Spain where the court is related to that of France we miss nothing I assure you, though it is a good deal duller.'

'Do you care to play cards?' St March turned to Angus who yawned and shook his head. 'I see the games have begun in earnest.'

'Not this evening. It is nearly midnight and I have much to do tomorrow. Besides my wife is also tired after her journey. If you will excuse us, Madame? Lord St March?'

Angus bowed and took Analee's arm, somewhat peremptorily she thought. She was not in the least tired and would have liked to watch the Queen at play; there had been a commotion in the card room as the Queen and her suite took their seats at the Cavagnole table. She thought Angus looked angry and in the carriage on their way back to Paris he told her why.

'That cursed man was ogling you unashamedly Analee, I'll not have it before my eyes!'

'But Angus he is so old – older even than you!'

'Not too old to make love. He never took his eyes off you.'

'And I thought you rather taken by the Princesse de Talmond . . .' Analee said archly. 'You were huddled closely together much of the time.'

'That is a different matter. I had a purpose. The Princesse is the rumoured mistress of the Young Pretender. If I can make myself pleasant to her she might lead me to him . . .'

'And how do you propose to make yourself *pleasant*, my lord, may I ask?'

Angus groped for her hand in the dark and squeezed it. 'By diplomacy, of course. How else? You think I have eyes for another woman while I have you at my side? I meant business with the Princesse, naught else.'

376

3

Analee was to make several more visits to Versailles in the weeks following her presentation to the King and Queen. The King seldom came to Paris – except sometimes incognito at night for pleasure – and conducted all his business with his ministers at his château in the forest. Analee had the opportunity to sample court life at close quarters, to observe the customs that were unique to that curious, enclosed world where she was able to confirm that the nobles were trapped in a vast beautiful cage – a veritable prison. Even to get the meanest apartment in the château was a great honour, while banishment to their country estates for misdemeanours was a punishment not only worse than death but often one that produced death itself, a sort of physical wasting away in exile. Away from the sun, the centre of the universe, a banished courtier did not wish to live.

There were rules and regulations about behaviour, speech and manners that were quite incomprehensible to the outsider. Madame de Pompadour had only learned them after months of gruelling instruction by the Abbé de Bernis and the Marquis de Gontaut before being established by the King as his *maîtresse en titre*. There were customs that governed the Royal Family and the various degrees of nobility, who should curtsy or bow to whom and how low; who should sit where, how and above all on what.

Happily such behaviour did not concern Analee who was received politely at the Court and looked after while her husband and his colleagues were in conference with the King and his ministers. She was shown the various parts of the huge building: the two vast wings, one for the Princes of the Blood and their establishments and the other for the nobles; mazes of corridors and rooms where people lived, sometimes forgotten, if they were old or feeble, for years.

But above all Analee delighted to walk in the gardens which the great André Le Nôtre had constructed for Louis XIV. The formal fountains, lakes and flowerbeds were a picture now in the fullness of summer, interspersed with trees and blossoms – tuberoses, stocks, wallflowers, jasmin. The straight walks leading from the château were full of people promenading in the sun, some of whom Analee, accompanied by the wife or wives of nobles in discussion with the Falcon, was gradually getting to know.

Analee thought she would be stifled by life at Versailles. Her mind often flew back to Falcon's Keep or Furness, especially the latter – the freedom of the hills and fields, the tranquillity of the lake in its natural setting so unlike the confined, though beautiful, scenery that man had constructed around the greatest château in the world.

It was during one of these promenades, in the company of the Comtesse d'Estrades, a cousin of Madame de Pompadour, that Analee again saw Lord St March walking, his hands behind his back, in earnest conversation with two men Analee did not know. Lord St March saw Analee at about the same time as she became aware of him and, excusing himself to his companions, he came quickly over to her and kissed her hand.

'Madame la Marquise! How beautiful you look today. I was hoping to call on you when I returned to Paris.' He bowed to the Comtesse and her friends.

'You know Lord St March?' the Comtesse said in surprise, turning to Analee.

'We met here the night I was presented to their Majesties. His lordship was in the company of Madame de Talmond . . .'

'Ah.' The Comtesse's prim little mouth shut in a disapproving rosebud. Of the bourgeoisie herself, she owed her position at court entirely to the rise of her cousin. She was not very beautiful, but she was lively and amusing and, besides enjoying the trust of the favourite, the King also liked her. She was the mistress of the Comte d'Argenson and was on the way to being the most powerful woman in France after the Marquise de Pompadour.

The Comtesse, through the complex web of court gossip, knew quite well that de Talmond was the mistress of Prince Charles Edward and that St March was sympathetic to the Jacobites. Analee could see from her face and the confusion on that of the Earl's that she had made a *faux pas*. She tried to remedy this by making some general remarks about the weather and the beauty of the scenery, but soon after the Comtesse excused herself and made

378

her way back to the château, leaving Analee and Lord St March alone together.

'I'm afraid I blundered,' Analee said apologetically. 'I could see by the frozen expression on the Comtesse's face that I had said something wrong. She does not like the Princesse de Talmond?'

'She does not *approve* of her, Madame. I've told you there are two distinct factions in the Court – the King and the Marquise on one side, the Queen on the other. Little d'Estrades is an intimate of the Pompadour to whom she owes everything. She knows the Pompadour was insulted by the Prince when she had just come to court and she has not forgiven him.'

'How did he insult her?'

'Oh after the '45 he was fêted by everyone in Paris. The Pompadour, quite recently the King's mistress, wrote him some little *billets doux* to which the Prince did not even reply. He made it quite clear that he would have nothing to do with someone so bourgeois, whatever her position in the King's favour. He said rude things about her which the Queen and her entourage made quite sure were repeated. The Pompadour has a long memory; she is too aware of her humble origins and she has never forgiven him.

'Louis is good natured, easy-going, easily led. He is fond of Charles to whom, after all, he is related. But the Young Pretender has been reckless and wayward since his return from England. He drinks too much and throws his money around.

'And Charles has done his best recently to irritate the King. He had medals struck with his head on to celebrate recent victories of the British fleet over the French. Worse than that, he insisted that the King's goldsmith should make a dinner service for him before the King who also ordered one. Thinking it was for Charles to take with him to Switzerland, Louis agreed that the goldsmith should serve the Prince before him, but Charles had no intention of going and used the plate to give a magnificent entertainment for the Princess de Talmond and others of the nobility.'

'But how can the King tolerate such behaviour?' Analee was aghast. Much as she admired Charles, Louis XV was one of the most powerful monarchs in the world.

'He is such a nice man. A kind man. He is sorry for his cousin. He knows he should quite properly be in line for the English throne and would prefer him to the Hanoverians; but what can he do? The Hanoverians have now been on the throne since 1714 and the English people are happy, prosperous and secure. They do not want civil war again. All that is behind them.

'Louis and his ministers are realists. And now they have come badly out of the war of the Austrian Succession in which England was on the opposite side. England demands that Charles be expelled from France, from the whole of civilized Europe. They want the only possible place he can go to be Rome where his father and brother are, and thus demonstrate to the world that the Stuarts are in the pocket of the Pope.'

By this time Analee and the Earl were approaching the court-yard from the garden side. The Earl stopped and looked at Analee.

'I see I have troubled you Madame. You think of your friends?'

'And of the poor Prince. I hear he is so captivating.'

'Ah yes, the ladies still adore him. The Princesse de Talmond and the Duchesse d'Aiguillon are said to have fought over him. But you will have a chance to meet him. That is what I was about to come and tell you if I had not met you here. Madame de Talmond has invited him to a dinner she is giving. She has asked me to bring you.'

The Earl gazed into Analee's eyes. He had a smile on his lips; but a nostalgic, almost unhappy expression on his face belied the smile. She was aware of an intimacy between them, despite the bustle of people and animals around them, the constant comings and goings of carriages, horses and the excited barks of hunting dogs. Suddenly there was a stir and a troop of horsemen cantered through the gates followed by one or two light phaetons. Analee immediately recognized the central horseman as the King and, together with the other women present, swept a low curtsy as Louis dismounted and walked towards the first phaeton which contained Madame de Pompadour with some ladies. He leaned over the rim of the carriage and, smiling at the exquisite Marquise, helped her to alight, giving her his arm to escort her into the château. Analee noticed how they gazed at each other as though they were alone, not surrounded by a great throng of people.

'How tender he is with her,' she sighed.

'She has just recovered from yet another miscarriage. She yearns to have a child by the King but has been dogged by ill health. She lives on a diet of milk and vanilla.'

'Oh dear – and I thought she looked so well and happy,' said Analee, looking at the Earl.

'She is happy, no doubt. She never rests enough after these miscarriages, but is up within a day or two forcing herself to look beautiful and happy for the King. She lives for him entirely. Of course she gets a lot in return. He buys her houses and spends a fortune on her. And then she has power, which some say she values more than possessions.'

The arrival of the King and his mistress from hunting had interrupted the *tête à tête* between Analee and St March and she turned as if to go into the château.

'You have not told me how to answer the Princesse de Talmond's invitation, Madame.'

Analee bestowed on his lordship a meaningful look and tilted her chin.

'It is without my husband?'

The Earl shrugged, still smiling. 'If you wish it Madame . . . but what would His Royal Highness say?'

'But what must I say to my husband?'

'That you must decide for yourself, Lady Falconer. I would have thought that a woman as beautiful as yourself . . .' He faltered.

'Would have ample experience of making excuses to her husband? You are wrong sir. Oh I know affairs are common among the nobility, but I am faithful to my lord.'

'The Marquess is indeed fortunate,' Lord St March murmured, 'in a wife of such virtue. But I am not asking your ladyship to forfeit that virtue. You expressed a wish to meet your friends, to see the Prince. I thought merely that I was doing you a service.'

Analee looked thoughtfully at the man standing beside her. She was drawn to him, yet she did not know why. It was not a carnal attraction. She was at a loss to explain it. It was as though he was someone she had known all her life, like a beloved relation.

'Madame . . .' The Earl seemed about to say something to her and then changed his mind. Was it something to do with the rapport that both knew existed between them?

'I will come, my lord. My husband is occupied with affairs of state all day long. Next week he rejoins the army for a few days in Flanders so I have no need to lie. I merely wanted you to know that I was not an adventuress.'

He bowed. 'That was the last thought in my mind, Madame. Until next Tuesday when I shall call to escort you to the Princesse – *au revoir*.'

The Prince de Talmond kept himself pretty continuously out of Paris. For many years since their marriage eighteen years before he and his wife had judiciously gone their separate ways. Whether he knew of her liaison with Prince Charles no one knew; but he was not present the night a week later when Analee arrived with the Earl of St March to dine with the Princesse.

Madame de Talmond embraced Analee warmly as soon as she was announced.

'Madame! How fortunate that you are able to come. I am sorry that the Marquis is away. Such an *attractive* man.'

Analee smiled and murmured a platitude. Her eyes roved the room looking for familiar faces. But there was no sign of the Delamains or the Allonbys, only a cluster of exiled Jacobites and French sympathizers – and that strange man the Earl of St March, whose eyes followed her everywhere.

Analee had just arrived when there was a stir of excitement and necks craned forward to see the guest of honour – Prince Charles himself. The Princesse had gone to greet him as soon as his carriage was announced and he entered with her on his arm, standing just inside the door as the guests rose to greet him with deep bows and curtsies.

The Prince at twenty-eight was still handsome enough to deserve the epithet 'Bonnie' which he had been given in the '45. Analee thought him heavier than she had expected; but his presence was a striking one and his air majestic. He wore a suit of dark blue satin with the Garter badge on his left breast and the ribbon of the Garter across his richly embroidered silver waistcoat. His hair was lightly powdered and he wore matching knee and shoe buckles of sapphires and diamonds.

The Prince bowed to the assembly who started to applaud him as he walked through the drawing room with the Princesse, greeting friends and being introduced to new ones, until they stood

382

before the Earl of St March and Analee who dropped a deep curtsy.

'The Earl of St March, I think Your Royal Highness has met?'

'Indeed yes, ma'am. St March.' The Prince nodded and fixed his piercing eyes on Analee. Here was someone born to command, to reign, Analee felt and she could scarcely meet his gaze. No one had ever impressed her with such regalness of manner, not the Kings of France or England or the Dauphin of France. His eyes were so experienced, so world weary, so . . . bitter?

'May I present, sire, the Marchioness of Falconer who is in Paris with her husband.'

The Prince nodded his head but did not smile. '*Falconer* Madame? Any relation to the Falcon, the scourge of the Jacobites?'

He spoke in a low voice but Analee felt herself involuntarily start to tremble.

'Lady Falconer is not of the same mind as her husband, Your Royal Highness. That is why she is here.'

'How do we know Lady Falconer is not sent to spy on us? Are we not surrounded by perfidy? Really, Madame de Talmond . . .'

The Prince frowned and seemed as though he was about to turn his back but Analee looked up at him, her body still inclined in a curtsy.

'Your Royal Highness, I am no spy. I am an admirer of yours and a friend of your cause. I had many friends in the Rebellion. The Allonby family, sir. Brent Delamain . . .'

'Ah . . .' The Prince stopped and looked at her with interest. 'Then we shall be able to have you vouched for ma'am. Brent Delamain is in my retinue this evening. See, here he is . . .'

Startled, Analee looked up. Brent Delamain, her one-time lover, the father of her daughter Morella, stood staring fixedly at her, as though rooted to the spot where he had entered.

Yes, she was dancing in the tavern, how could he ever forget her? He saw her twirling skirt, her twinkling bare feet on the sawdust-strewn floor, the movement of her lively supple body, the gyration of her hips, the swell of her half exposed bosom, her hands above her head clicking her castanets. Their eyes had met and she'd danced for him; she'd flaunted her beautiful body just for him, and later they'd made love in the moonlight. He'd only seen her twice after that – once at the house on Lake Derwent-water, and once when she helped to rescue him from Edinburgh Castle where he'd been awaiting trial and almost sure death after the failure of the Rebellion. Yet he loved her for life.

Now here she was again – no longer the bare footed dancer, but a titled lady, a Marchioness clad in satin, her fingers sparkling with jewels. But her face was still the same, sculpted like a Bernini madonna with high cheek-bones and a proud tilted chin, and those eyes – almost fathomless, deep set and half concealed by eyelids that opened wide when she was angry or amused, the eyes flashing with indignation or laughter.

She was his Analee. He moved towards her, oblivious of the Prince or the other guests around him. He would take her in his arms. This time he would never let her go.

'Brent . . .' She extended her hand for him to kiss, but in the gesture he saw a warning. It was as though she were pushing him back, telling him to come no nearer. It was emphasizing the distance between themselves, both now married to other people, no longer lovers in a forest glade. Brent looked at her eyes and saw they were more than usually inscrutable, half hidden by lids, thin and almost transparent like the finest porcelain. The eyes were smiling and friendly, but distant. He bent and kissed her hand.

'Lady Falconer . . .' How he choked on the words! *Lady Falconer*. She should have been his; she *was* his. He looked at her with smouldering eyes.

Her *gadjo*. Analee had not forgotten him either; not forgotten the night she had met him, how he'd thought she was a horse thief stealing his brother's horses. The lock of his fair hair fell over his brow . . . Then in the tavern a few days later, she'd seen him standing at the back of the smoke-filled, noisy, crowded room, his lean aristocratic features unmistakable. He had eyes only for her.

The Prince was unaware of the undercurrents between his henchman and the Marchioness of Falconer. In a room full of devoted followers he was busy talking while Brent approached Analee and bowed over her hand. But the Princesse de Talmond noticed. Passionate and jealous of the Prince, she was aware of the fascination of the Marchioness; everyone in Versailles was talking about her. She was rumoured to have been found by the Falcon as a bare-footed gypsy, yet now she looked every inch a noblewoman. Everyone vied to entertain her and try and discover more; but the women, jealous of their husbands or lovers, were wary of her and watched every move fearfully. Some said she was called the Enchantress and had a strange power over men and women alike.

The Princesse saw how Brent walked towards Lady Falconer, like a man in a trance, and she watched the Marchioness put out a hand almost as a rebuttal, as though to warn him to keep his distance. But his kiss lingered on her hand and then he kept her hand in his as he gazed at her, searching her eyes.

'Ah Delamain,' the Prince said, glancing at them. 'I see you *do* know Lady Falconer.'

'Indeed sir,' Brent bowed, 'I had the honour to meet her several years ago.'

'But you know the Marquess of Falconer?'

'I do not know him, sir, but I know of him. No I knew her ladyship before she . . .' Brent nearly choked on the words, 'became his wife.'

'Maybe she inclines to his way of thinking?'

'About us? No sir! Lady Falconer is no Hanoverian, of that I can assure you. Indeed it is to her that I owe my life – '

'That is quite untrue sir.' Analee interrupted suddenly, casting a warning glance at Brent. For Brent to say she had a hand in his rescue would be to betray not only her but the Falcon.

Brent realized he had erred and corrected himself. 'That is to say, her ladyship was of great assistance to me at a dangerous period in my life.'

The Prince smiled and looked lazily at Analee as if appraising her.

'Then the Marchioness is no spy?'

'I would give my life on it sir.'

'Pray do not. I need you, and she has already saved your life once, you say. Lady Falconer, forgive my suspicion. But with a husband such as yours and leading the life I do . . . *You* are welcome here: but your husband . . . he is doing all he can to have me harried from here.'

Analee bowed her head; once again she found she was inwardly trembling. 'He sees it only as his duty sir. Believe, me, if there were aught I could do . . .'

'Maybe we will find something for you, Lady Falconer, by and by to show your loyalty. Now, Marie, are we eating tonight?'

The Princesse dropped a low curtsy. 'Yes, Your Royal Highness, dinner is ready and after that there are cards and dancing. Lord St March, will you escort Lady Falconer? and Mr Delamain could you give your arm to Madame de Vassé?'

'I see you are well acquainted with Mr Delamain,' Lord St March murmured, tucking his napkin in his waistcoat once they were seated at the table.

'I am a friend of his wife,' Analee said quietly, aware of Brent gazing at her across the table.

'Indeed? That does surprise me. All the world knows they are ill suited; yet he greeted you so warmly.'

'I think he recalls happier times. And *you* sir? I know so little of you. Are you a Jacobite?'

'Ah ma'am. Am I? Am I not?' His voice was very low. 'My father was a convinced Jacobite, yes, and fought in the Rebellion in 1715. He was exiled and died abroad just as I was growing to manhood. I saw at that time the folly of the Jacobite cause. Even then I knew they would not succeed. The Old Pretender was no splendid figure like his son, you know. He was uncertain and timid, and lacking in character. He was excessively pious. I saw little to choose between him and King George I whom my grandfather supported. With my father's death I was heir to the estates of the Earldom of St March. Much as I loved my father, I thought he was hot-headed and didn't wish to follow him into exile. So I became . . . uncommitted, supporting neither one side nor the other. In the end I got the best of both worlds – my grandfather's estates and the property my father had bought after his flight to Spain, and there I have spent most of my life. My late wife was delicate and the climate suited her; but I have frequently travelled to England, spending some time in the courts of Europe and thus familiarizing myself with what was afoot. I confess I have a love of intrigue.'

'It is a wonder the Prince does not suspect you of being a spy.' Analee looked cautiously around, but no one was paying any attention to their conversation.

'Ah poor man! He trusts no one and sees spies everywhere. He uses people ruthlessly and yet because of his charm they work for him. So many of his supporters are penniless and rely on him or his father for succour; but of course Charles has nothing to give. Yet he lives well and one wonders where his money comes from, since it is said he will not take a penny from King Louis. I know not what will become of the Prince. He is frittering his life away, drinking too much, intriguing too much and angering the King of France, who wants only to be rid of him.'

'And women?'

'The Prince has never been a womanizer. He is too aware of his dignity and consorts only with well-born women like the Princesse and Madame de Vassé. The Princesse is very jealous of him and they have frequent fights. They say he tires of her rages. See, now he is looking at you! Indeed, Madame, I think you have intrigued everyone here tonight; I see many eyes stray in your direction.'

'I think they expect my husband to come through the door on a charger,' Analee said laughing. 'I am too dangerous as the wife of the Falcon.'

When the lavish dinner finally ended the Princesse led the way into the drawing room where the carpets had been pulled back for dancing. A trio that had played throughout the meal took their place in a corner and began tuning their instruments for a gavotte. The first to claim Analee for the dance was Brent and he led her to join the couples who were forming.

'I shall dance with you all evening.'

'People will talk.'

'I care not. Only to hold your hand, Analee, is enough. How long have you been in Paris?'

'Several weeks. Lord Falconer has taken a house in the Rue du Faubourg.'

'Mention not his name to me.'

'Brent, he is my husband.'

'I still feel the same as ever I did.'

Analee was silent and went gracefully through the motions of the gavotte. She loved dancing, even these measured formal dances that were hardly, to her, like dancing at all. The sway of her body, the tilt of her head caused everyone to comment on her grace or to stop their chattering just to watch her.

'What of Mary?' Analee said when the steps of the dance brought them together again.

'She is living with her brother in a house in Passy.'

'You do not live together?'

'I am constantly with His Highness. I am shortly to go abroad again.'

'I would like to see Mary and John.'

'Then I will arrange it. Analee, when can we be alone together again?'

Analee avoided his eyes, shaking her head. 'What you mean is not possible, you know that Brent. I told you before to forget me, and you must.'

She curtsied to her partner as the dance came to an end and Brent escorted her back to her place.

'I can't forget you, whatever you say. You have bewitched me Analee, changed my life. I need – '

'Ah, Delamain, do you think you could release Lady Falconer to dance a measure with me?'

'I am sure her ladyship would be honoured sir.'

Brent bowed to the Prince who took the surprised Analee's hand, raising her to her feet.

'I think we have a minuet, Madame. You dance remarkably well. I could not help observing you during the gavotte.'

'Thank you sir.'

Analee was aware of the Prince's eyes on her whenever the steps of the dance brought them together. He was still fascinating, she thought, whatever St March said. Strong and powerful and masterly, a leader. No wonder so many had adored him, followed him still. She knew all eyes were on her and the Prince as they danced, and then he claimed her again for the next dance until the Princesse de Talmond waspishly intervened.

'Comte Dampierre has come especially to see you sir. I think he has something of importance to say. He waits in the salon.'

'Oh very well,' the Prince shrugged reluctantly. 'Lady Falconer, I hope you will partner me again.'

'My pleasure sir.' Her cheeks flushed, Analee curtsied low and did not rise until he had left the room, having noted the expression on the face of the Princesse de Talmond.

'I think the Princesse does not like me,' she whispered to Lord St March who came immediately to her side.

'She is very jealous; but what she says is of no importance. She depends on him emotionally and he can do what he likes. The Prince finds it hard to engage his affections with women. He lets them worship him and, when he wants to, uses them to satisfy his lust. Above all he uses them for the Cause and to give him money.'

'Does the Princesse give him money?'

'Who else? And other women. But I can see he was taken with you.'

'I have no money.'

'But perhaps you have something else.' Before Analee could ask him what he meant, she saw Brent bearing down on them.

'Oh here comes another swain! If the Prince is smitten, here is a man drowning in love if I'm not mistaken. And you are so unkind to him, Lady Falconer . . .'

Lord St March's tone was full of mock reproach and, glancing at him, Analee thought suddenly that here was a man who did not appear to want her body, whose interest in her was detached. Could it be that here was someone who wished genuinely to offer her friendship – was it possible between a man and a woman?

He saw her glance and smiled, and not for the first time she wondered what really lay behind those dark eyes.

4

Brent called upon Analee a few days later and was shown by a very excited Nelly into the drawing room where Analee had yet again resumed the same piece of neglected tapestry.

In moments of quiet like this she would let her mind wander back over the years and tried to ask herself honestly what sort of life she preferred – that of a gypsy or a lady of title and money? Looking around at the elegant furniture of the rented house, the rich carpets and lavish furnishings, the brocades and satins covering the chairs and sofas, the heavy damask curtains held in place by ropes of gold thread, Analee recalled her life in the open country. The only time she saw into a house then was when hunger forced her to beg bread from a farm or a crofter almost as poor as she was.

Yet she was the same person – nothing inside her had changed. Maybe she preferred this life, she thought, letting the tapestry rest on her lap. She had only changed her circumstances. She was still happy and able to give happiness, to give and receive love. She had the affection of a devoted husband, an adorable child – two adorable children. Analee's eyes clouded; the first daughter she had not seen since a week after her birth. She was now three, a pretty blonde child she had heard. Analee sighed and resumed her embroidery. She had done the right thing by Morella, and one day . . .

'Oh ma'am he is here!' Nelly burst in with her usual lack of ceremony, her hand stifling a giggle.

'Who Nelly?'

'Mr Brent, ma'am.'

'Oh . . .' Analee sank back in the chair and cast her eyes to the ceiling. Just when she had been thinking of Morella, Brent's daughter. 'Oh bring him in, Nell, though what I can say – '

'Analee . . .' Brent came straight over to her and clasped both her hands. 'Oh my darling Analee . . . !'

'Brent!' Analee wrenched her hands away and looked at him severly. 'I tell you, I will forbid Nelly to admit you.' She gazed at him, her expression wavering between disapproval and amusement. How could she not be partly in love with Brent?

Nelly hovered in the background, hopeful that something would happen to divert the day.

'Nelly, would you fetch some madeira? Or – Brent what would you prefer?'

'No, madeira will do well.' Brent smiled at Nelly. 'I see your good servant is with you yet Analee.'

'My good *friend*. Nothing has happened to make my old gypsy friend into a servant. Nelly is my right hand. True, circumstances have elevated me, but at heart . . . I was thinking just before you came, Brent, nothing has changed. Here, sit beside me.' Analee sat on the sofa, covered in gold brocade with wooden surrounds of inlaid marquetry, and patted the place beside her. Brent eagerly sat down and faced her. 'I am the same woman I always was. Only things about me have changed.'

'Oh Analee, you are the same for me.'

'But here things have changed, Brent. You and I are married to different people. I love the Falcon deeply, with all my heart. You . . . I have tender feelings for you, Brent, how could I not? But 'twas all a long time ago.'

'But yesterday for me. Why did I ever allow – '

'What happened, happened Brent.'

'Yes, you are the wife of a rich Marquess, and I am an impoverished exile. *That* happened.' Brent smiled bitterly and clenched his fists. 'You would not want to be married to one such as me.'

'If it had been meant,' Analee said quietly, 'I would have shared your exile, willingly and happily. I care nothing for riches or titles. But it was not meant, and I love Angus – not for his wealth but because he is my lover and my husband, the father of my daughter Clare and soon, I hope, of another child.'

'You are with child again?' Brent cried, looking outraged.

'Alas, not yet. It is his lordship's earnest desire to have a son; but so far . . .' Analee looked away. In her experience she conceived very quickly. What could be preventing the magic happening this time? She knew it was not that either she or Angus lacked ardour; indeed their love-making was more passionate than ever.

'Analee, may I not be your lover? Share you with the Falcon if it is your desire, much as I hate it. But to have you in my arms, to see you again . . .'

Analee's hand flew to her mouth stifling a cry. 'Brent what *can* you be suggesting?'

'Oh Analee do not play the innocent with me. Everyone has lovers and mistresses, even the fondest couples . . .'

'Then they cannot be so fond if they need another. Those are marriages based on money and position, not on love. I could not conceive of having another man besides my lord. I do not need another. I am shocked at you Brent.'

Brent leaned forward and grasped her hand. 'Can you mean it Analee? That I am nothing to you? That you do not feel still for me the attraction that once drew us together?'

Analee tried to free her hand but could not. His warmth seemed to transmit itself to her, infusing her blood, rushing through her veins like quicksilver. Yes, there was a powerful attraction. His face came nearer and his lips brushed hers. Analee shuddered and was aware of the pounding of her heart. She saw the longing in his deep blue eyes, the tenderness and care. He had always loved her. He freed her hand and drew her into his arms . . . and the door flew open and once again Nelly rushed in, without the madeira.

'Oh ma'am, ma'am! His lordship is here. His carriage is in the courtyard.'

Analee flew up from the sofa and smoothed her bodice. Her hands moved to tidy her hair, cover her flaming cheeks. Brent still sat transfixed. He had just been within a second of capturing her, but now . . . Caught by a husband! The most ridiculous of situations, lampooned by every comedy writer.

'Brent, you must go.'

Analee made for the door to try and forestall her husband's entry, but at that moment his voice was heard booming outside and there was a flurry of activity in the hall. The door to the drawing room flew open and there he stood, still wearing his travelling cloak and sword, an expression of anticipation on his face. Analee flew into his open arms and hugged him, burying her face in his cloak to hide her confusion.

'Oh Angus, I have missed you so much. I . . .' She looked up to see that a frown of great severity had replaced the smile on her

392

husband's face. He was staring at Brent, who slowly got up, not bothering to conceal the dismay and frustration on his face.

'And this gentleman is, Madame?' The Falcon's words were icy.

'My lord, this is Brent Delamain, Mary's husband. You remember, I – '

'I remember nothing. That is a subject we agreed never to discuss. And where is his wife, pray?'

'My wife is in Passy, sir, in a house there.'

'We were discussing visiting her,' Analee said quickly. 'Brent has only just heard that we are in Paris. I think he wanted to thank your lordship for the plan that saved his life.'

Brent bit his lip and avoided Angus's eyes. It was true Lord Falconer had formulated the plan whereby Brent had escaped from Edinburgh. But Brent thought the success was due not to him but to Analee who had carried it out, boldly sweeping up to the castle in her carriage and carrying him away. Brent could not bear to look at the man who had not only married the woman he loved but who had been responsible for the deaths of so many Jacobite soldiers. He felt then that he hated the Falcon more than any man on earth, and his lip curled in a bitter snarl which he took no trouble to conceal.

'I care not to see Mr Delamain in my house or near me ever again,' said the Falcon. 'He is a renegade and a traitor. I hear he consorts with the Prince and plans yet again to invade our shores and disturb innocent peace-loving Englishmen and women in their beds. Mr Delamain may consider himself fortunate I do not apprehend him and convey him back to England to be tried and undoubtedly hanged.'

'Oh Angus!' Analee said in distress, 'I hate to hear you talk like this. The Delamain family is related to you by marriage. Brent is married to a dear friend of mine. I . . .'

'Hold your tongue my good wife! In this house I am the master. I deplore the fact that I am associated with Mr Delamain in any capacity, no matter how remote; though my cousin Henrietta and her husband Sir George are loyal to His Majesty King George, no doubt of that! You are to be ashamed of yourself sir, for . . .'

Brent raised his head and his eyes challenged the Falcon. Looking at them, Analee could not help feeling that the men she loved were a pair, well matched, tall, strong and vigorous, the one fair, the other dark like her. She had had children by both these men and each daughter resembled her father: Morella blonde, pink skinned and blue eyed; Clare a dark ethereal beauty with white skin and curly black hair. She, Analee, was the vessel – proud to be loved by two men worthy of her. That they hated each other violently was obvious. The room vibrated with hate and distrust. The Falcon was suspicious, there was no doubt about that. Analee and Brent had been about to kiss, the tension like an unsprung coil between them. To recover and compose themselves in a few seconds was an impossibility and the Falcon was a jealous man. What else did he know or guess, apart from the fact that Brent was in his eyes a traitor? Did he also know that Brent had been his wife's lover, and would be again if he could?

'I am ashamed of nothing sir!' Brent said proudly. 'I am ashamed neither of my family nor my allegiance to the rightful King of England. Only a hundred years ago His Majesty King Charles II was restored to the throne after he had been in exile for ten years and all had given up hope. The Stuarts came back to England then, and by God sir, they will again!'

'A hundred years ago, Mr Delamain, is a hundred years ago. 'Tis a long time.' His lordship nonchalantly unfastened his cloak and threw it over a chair. He wore his military red coat, but this time with badges of rank as he had come from his regiment. His blue cuffs and blue collar patches were conspicuous amid the gold lace with which his coat was adorned. His buff waistcoat was edged with gold and a gold knot glowed on his right shoulder.

The glamour of his uniform gave the Falcon an advantage over Brent, but only in matters of dress for Brent was his equal in physique.

'In that time, since the restoration of King Charles, we have had King James II who was despatched after a reign of only three years because of his popery, a characteristic of all the Stuarts who would have England the fief of the Pope in Rome. For over thirty years we have had peace, and our country has grown great under the rule of Kings who are also properly descended from the Stuart line. The only time our country has suffered is when you and your friends have sought to overthrow the established government, and small support you have had. Scarcely a person of note moved. We do not want you sir, and you cannot put back the clock.

'Besides, I hear our would-be king wastes his time in drinking and dissipation. He makes himself a laughing stock in the French court and I, for my part, would be ashamed to call him an Englishman.'

Brent jumped at the Falcon, catching him off his guard. His fist shot out and caught Angus on the chin and, in trying to deflect the blow, his lordship's boots slipped on the polished floor and he crashed heavily to the ground, clutching at a chair to try and break his fall. Nelly screamed and ran out of the door shouting for McNeath and Analee rushed to kneel by her husband's side. His eyes were closed and a little rivulet of blood came from the side of his head.

Brent gazed down at him, the fury on his face giving place to concern.

'Is he . . .'

Analee cradled her husband's head and kissed his cheek, taking no notice of Brent.

'Angus, oh my lord . . .'

His eyelids fluttered and opened, gazing at her, and then past her to Brent who stood hovering threateningly. McNeath came in followed by Nelly and seized Brent by the shoulders, pinning his arms to his sides.

'Oh leave Mr Delamain,' the Falcon said wearily. 'I think he will not be so brave another time when he is not at such an advantage.' He sat up, holding his head in his hands, then heaved himself to his feet, staggering slightly. Analee led him to a chair and made him sit down while Nelly and McNeath fussed about him. Analee slowly turned to Brent, her face white with anger.

'How *dare* you strike my husband in his own home? You must be gone lest I myself do you damage and scratch your eyes out with my bare nails.' Analee held up her hands – ten fingers spread in front of Brent's face, ten wickedly long nails. Brent, his face pale and distressed, looked first at Analee then at the Falcon sitting slumped in the chair nursing his jaw.

'I should apologize but I cannot. He insulted a man who has suffered much, and in abusing that person he abused me.'

'Oh fine words sir! See you do not live to eat them. Now do as my wife says or when I recover my strength I shall throttle you with my bare hands and throw your body into the Seine.'

McNeath hurried Brent to the door and drew Nelly out with him. He knew his master had been humiliated and would want time to recover. He had seldom seen the Falcon so disadvantaged or shaken.

Analee put her arm round Angus and her cheek against his. But no answering hand came up to caress her, his cheek did not press against hers. He remained impassive, slumped in his chair. When he did raise his head he straightened his shoulders and squared his jaw, but said nothing. Analee went over to the window and looked into the bright sunlit street. She could not bear to see her husband brought so low, even though the blow was swift and unexpected and could not possibly have been foreseen or deflected. But she knew something else was troubling him. She sensed it in his withdrawal from her.

'I think something brought Mr Delamain here other than mere concern for the Prince,' Angus said quietly. 'I detected a light in his eyes as I came into the room. It was for you, Analee, that light. I swear he is in love with you.'

'Oh Angus, how could he be? We scarce know each other.'

'But you have met before?'

'Aye, when I helped with his rescue.'

'And only then?'

Analee lowered her eyes. 'Only then, Angus, and briefly.'

It was partly true; they had only ever met briefly. They had never spent the same night under one roof, in one bed. How could she explain what was between Brent and herself? She could not tell her husband that Brent had fathered her first-born daughter, or that he still nursed a reckless obsession for her.

'Then that brief time was enough for you to enslave him. Oh I know how easily you do it; it happened to me. But I'll not have a rival wooing you in my own house Analee. If I see Brent Delamain once again I'll do as I said. I shall kill him with my own hands.'

Analee turned as the Falcon heaved himself out of his chair and lumbered from the room. He was still hurt and probably in pain. She waited for a few minutes then ran quickly into the hall and upstairs. From inside his room she heard voices and knew that McNeath was with him. She knocked timidly and after a long pause McNeath opened the door. He shook his head sadly when he saw her.

'His lordship does not wish to be disturbed, ma'am. He said I was to tell you.'

McNeath hung his head in embarrassment, but his huge frame effectively barred the way. Analee did not know what to do. It was the first time she had been barred from Angus's room. She would spare McNeath and save her pride, and not insist.

'Take care of him McNeath. He will feel better when he has slept.'

McNeath nodded gratefully and closed the door. Sorrowfully, thoughtfully, Analee made her way downstairs again into the wide hall and back into the salon. Nelly was straightening the furniture and the rugs, patting the cushions and picking up one or two broken objects.

'There Analee,' she said with a bright, forced smile. 'No one would ever know.'

'Except those who were here, Nell, especially me. My lord bars me from his room. He has never done that before. He has always needed me, whatever his mood, his feelings. Oh Nell . . .'

Analee sank into a chair and for once in her life she wept. Her heart was heavy with sadness – and with a presentiment that worse might come. 'I feel such a dread, Nell, such concern in my soul.'

'Oh Analee . . .' Nelly knelt by her and took her hand. 'It is because his lordship loves you so blindly. He is proud, and upset that you should see him so disadvantaged. He will get over it in an hour or two.'

Analee shook her head. 'No Nell, it is worse than that. His lordship observed the light in Brent's eyes, maybe the confusion on both our countenances. He knows that Brent is in love with me. It was so obvious Nell.'

'It *is* obvious Analee,' Nelly agreed stroking her hand. 'Even as he came towards you I saw it. You must be rid of Brent Delamain, my lady. You must never see him again.'

'I'd hoped that by this time he would be happy with Mary, maybe have children and have begun a new life. But he is indifferent to reason. He is quite blind.'

'It is a great passion Analee!' Nelly's eyes were shining. 'Indeed I think it is quite beautiful.'

'*Beautiful!* When it threatens my marriage? Nell, you must be touched in the head,' Analee cried scornfully.

'Nay,' Nelly said slowly. 'Not touched, dearest Analee, but if you would have the truth, I have always found his lordship a fearsome man. Brent, as well as being big and strong, is so gentle.'

'His lordship has always been kind to me.'

'Not always, my lady, if you remember the marks on your body when he first bedded you.'

'Oh Nell that was for a very short time!'

'Aye but I saw them. I knew then he was a man capable of great cruelty and, indeed, McNeath tells me he is merciless on the battlefield, cutting about him like a butcher, despatching his foes and showing no mercy to the weak either on his side or that of the enemy.'

Analee took Nelly's hand and pressed it. 'I know he is a soldier and a hard man. I have always known it. Yet he gave me his love and his name and treated me with consideration and tenderness. Maybe I do fear him too, because of the dread I have inside me at this moment. Oh Nelly, I hope this will not turn him against me, because the wrath of the Falcon would be unendurable.'

An unaccustomed gloom fell over the house in the Rue du Faubourg and continued all day as the Falcon lay upstairs nursing his bruises and his wounded pride. Analee tried again to see him but was turned away by McNeath.

By night-fall Analee's sense of dread and foreboding had increased but she made no more effort to see her husband. She had her dignity too. She had Nelly make up a bed for her in a spare room. She dined by herself and went early to bed, lying fretful and awake almost until dawn.

And then she only slept fitfully because she could hear the Falcon calling to her in her dreams, needing her. He was hurt and in danger. She woke up, but the house and the street outside were silent, apart from birds singing. The dread she had felt the day before returned again and she got quickly out of bed and tiptoed along the corridor to the room which she was in the habit of sharing with her husband. She opened the door and peeped in. No McNeath came to bar her. The Falcon lay in the great bed, barely illuminated by the soft grey light of morning.

Analee silently approached the bed and gazed at him, her heart swelling with pity and love. How she longed to lie beside him and comfort him! But dare she? He stirred in his sleep and grunted, and she wondered if he was dreaming about her. She slipped out of her nightgown and lay alongside him, her breathing rapid and irregular because she was afraid.

Suddenly she felt him stiffen and she knew he was awake. His hand, feeling the place beside him, encountered her bare flesh. Analee trembled with desire as much as with fear.

'My lord? Angus?' she whispered.

Angus gave a fearful cry and rose from the bed, leaning over her, his face contorted with rage. He straddled her roughly and, seizing her throat with his hands, thudded her head again and again on the pillow until she felt she would lose consciousness. He sat on her stomach, his huge knees on her chest, and she knew she could not breathe like this for much longer. Angus was going to kill her, as he said he would kill Brent.

'What is this strumpet, in my bed? This whore? I have got it out of McNeath that you *did* know Brent Delamain. When you were a gypsy you met him on the road. Aye, and laid with him for all I know . . .'

'No my lord. No!'

'Aye, coupled with him in the ditch where you belonged and where I should have left you.'

'But McNeath knows nothing about my past.'

'He knows enough.' The Falcon's fingers tightened their grip and Analee felt her eyes bulging from their sockets. 'I threatened to have his testicles off if he did not tell me all he knew. Then he would never enjoy the delights of Nelly again, or lie between her ample thighs. Aye, talking of thighs, what is one whore apart from another?'

The Falcon stretched out on her body, taking his hands from her throat and seizing each of her legs, roughly dragging them apart. She was so unprepared for him that as he forced himself into her she cried with pain, and then he grasped her neck again and pressed his thumbs against her windpipe.

Suddenly he wrenched at the chain around her neck with such force that it caused a gash which made her bleed. The clasp broke and it fell onto the pillow. He snatched up the ring from where it had rolled, the ring of Falcon Gold, and holding it up in the light of the dawn gazed at it, turning it for a moment in his hands.

'See this my whore? The likes of you are not fit to wear it. You do not deserve to bear the honourable name of Falconer or wear my ring.' He flung it roughly on the floor and continued his violation of her with more force than before. 'This is what the soldiers do before they kill – they rape first and then they stick in the sword, sometimes in the same place, so that they can sunder the body in two. Or they may leave the wench to be raped by more, maybe ten or twenty or half the regiment. But the end is always the same . . . Death.'

Analee though this *was* the end. Nothing in her life had prepared her for such torment. She who had always relished the act of love was being violated by her own husband – ravished and strangled at the same time. She felt her senses reeling as he suddenly released her neck and lay inert on her unresponsive body, his heart thudding against her chest. When he recovered he got unsteadily to his feet and leaned over her quivering body. The tears rolled down her cheeks and, as the daylight advanced into the room, she saw his eyes were still red with anger and lust and that he had not finished with her.

'Well my whore, not dead yet?'

He seized her by her long black hair and pulled her roughly to the floor, then sat astride her once more and started to strike her about the head and chest. Analee had stifled her cries up till now, but when he started to pull her hair and hit her head on the floor she gave a frenzied scream, which only made his lordship hit her the harder. He clenched his fist and punched her nose, her mouth, first one cheek, then the next, then her chest, her ribs . . .

'No, no Angus, oh please . . .'

Yes, she was going. The pain was less; her vision was blurred; there was a commotion in her chest, something wet trickled out of her mouth. She was dying. Analee closed her eyes and all sensation ended.

Gradually there was Nelly. The room was dappled with sunlight; beneath her was a soft mattress; she could hear the birdsong. Were they at Furness? If she looked out of the window she would see the beautiful lake and the hills on the other side. No, all she saw were the tiny window panes and . . . but it was painful to raise her head. She sank back on the pillow and slowly the pain reclaimed her body infusing every limb.

Nelly leaned over to stroke her mistress's brow, her face alight with happiness. Analee lived! They had been terrible days since McNeath had wrenched his master off the unconscious Analee. Servants had carried her to bed, bathed her wounds and covered them with balm; but Analee's face was grey, her lips blue, and from her mouth came an ominous trickle of blood.

Nelly had sent for a doctor, who examined Analee and shook his head mournfully. There was little he could do, he had said. He was not hopeful. Analee's ribs were cracked, her lungs damaged, and one cheekbone broken. Fortunately the internal bleeding had stopped, but Analee remained unconscious. For days she lay inert, the weeping Nelly always beside her.

The doctor came twice a day, and sometimes brought a colleague to give a second opinion. Slowly, the news got abroad, though no one was sure of the truth. Had the Falcon really attacked his wife? And if so, why?

Once she had regained consciousness, Analee knew she would recover. She lay quietly in her bed and fastened her thoughts on happy memories of England, of those days when the fields and lakes were drenched with sun as she and Nelly wandered idly along, stopping to pick wild berries in the hedgerows or stalk a fat pigeon for their dinner. Then there were the days when she had first known Randal and his brothers and sister. Those were simple, happy days close to nature; she should never have left them. She was unsuited to this life and it had nearly killed her. When she was well she would leave Angus and renounce her rights as his wife. She would return to the road again. It was solely her longing to resume her gypsy life that was making her well.

Each day Analee grew a little stronger under Nelly's tender care, and one day she was fit enough to be propped up against pillows. It was a beautiful day, and Nelly opened the window wide to allow the sun to stream in. From the street below Analee heard chattering and laughing and the merry cries of children, the barking of dogs and the neighing of horses as they clopped along the cobbles.

'It is good to be alive after all Nell,' she whispered, and for the first time for days Nelly saw that wide beloved smile and knew that her mistress wanted to live. 'Shall we go back to the fields when I am well? Take to the road again?'

Nelly smiled and nodded but put her finger to her lips. 'I have a surprise for you. There is a visitor who has come repeatedly to see you.'

'Oh not Brent . . .' Analee began weakly but Nelly shook her head.

'His wife. Mary is downstairs.'

'Mary is here? Oh Nelly bring her up. How do I look?'

'Better, much better. Your bruises are nearly healed and you have that light in your eyes again Analee.'

'And his lordship, where is he?'

It was the first time Analee had mentioned the Falcon, and when she did it was in a distant voice as though she were making an enquiry about a stranger.

'His lordship never leaves his room ma'am. He is prostrate with grief and remorse and asks constantly for you. But the doctors refuse to allow him near, for fear you will sicken again.'

'Ah.' Analee leaned back. She had hardly thought about him at all, because every time she did she saw his body, in the act of raping her, beating the breath out of her lungs. It was ugly, not beautiful, not an object of veneration as before. It bore no relation to the man she had known and loved. Could it have been the same man? But yes. As Nelly had said, the Falcon was a violent man. She no longer knew whether she loved him or not. She tried not to think about him.

'Show Mary in. I long to see her again.'

Analee hardly recognized the woman who came timidly through the door. Once buxom and comely, Mary had grown as thin as a wraith and her face was drawn and prematurely lined. She wore a drab gown of some brown stuff and an unbecoming bonnet concealed her once thick golden hair. Analee recalled the days she and Mary had spent at Furness, in that bright summer of '45 before tragedy had struck and blighted the lives of so many, including hers. But the smile was the same, and the warmth, as Mary came over to Analee and gently kissed her.

Nelly brought a chair to the side of the bed and Mary reached over and took Analee's hand, gently pressing it.

'So you heard?'

Mary nodded. 'And I know why. Brent told me. I had to see you Analee, if only to say . . .'

'There is nothing to say. 'Twas not Brent's fault. What he did was no excuse for my lord to half kill me.'

'They say he nearly succeeded.'

'Does everyone know?'

'Most people have heard, one way and another. 'Tis a small English community here. They say the Falcon was deranged from a wound in the head he got in the war, but I know the truth. Brent cannot control himself for grief. He still loves you, Analee, and he always will.'

Analee gazed at the woman she loved so much, felt such pity for. Mary deserved happiness if anyone did. How she had loved Brent, her cousin, how thrilled to be his wife.

'I am sorry Mary. I did all I could.'

'I know, and I performed the spells you taught me; but nothing Analee, nothing . . .' Mary bowed her head and a tear slid down one cheek. She quickly brushed it away, trying to hide it with a smile. 'But God has helped me Analee. I think He has shown that He wants me for Himself. It was hard, but I have accepted it as His will.'

'You mean . . .'

'I am seeking annulment of our marriage to enter a convent. The nuns have been so good to me and have shown me where true love lies. How ephemeral and treacherous is the love of man. In God I have found peace and freedom from torment.'

'And you love Brent no more?'

Mary sighed. 'How can I say I don't love him? But I love him as a sister loves a brother, as Heloise learned to love Abelard. He has left me a maid, did you know that Analee? I am a virgin still and thus will seek to be the bride of Christ.'

'Does Brent know this?'

'I told him the other day when he came to tell me about you. He was so distraught, that he had brought these injuries on you. Yet he dared not come to the house. I told him then. That I would free him to . . .'

'But I am married to Lord Falconer,' Analee said gently. 'I do not wish to wed Brent.'

'After this?'

'You know he was deranged. He enquires constantly after me. I shall go back for a time to England; but my place is always by his side. You must tell that to Brent, Mary.'

'Brent is going to England too. Oh he is in cahoots again with Rigg, smuggling arms and preparing for the next rising. I care not what he does, Analee. I think God has always meant me to be a nun and as soon as the formalities have been arranged I will take the veil. In Him I will find peace.'

'I hope I may come and see you Mary?'

'Always, my dear friend, and where I am you will always find God, and God alone is happiness.'

Analee thought for a long time after Mary had gone. Yes, she had spoken truly. Her place was by Angus's side. It would do him too much damage to leave him; it would confirm what everyone was saying, but did not know for sure. It would ruin his career maybe, sully his reputation. Her duty now was to be seen with her husband. But whether she still loved him or not it was too early for her to know.

5

The house in the Rue du Faubourg had a small paved garden with ornate shrubberies, a little fish pond and a sundial in the middle. In time Analee was well enough to sit out in the sun though the days were drawing into autumn. She would sit, well wrapped up, watching the birds as they hopped along looking for food or gazing at the fish swiftly darting in and out of the weeds in the pond.

One day she heard a step behind her and a shadow momentarily obscured the sun. She felt herself tremble and her heart began to beat rapidly. She knew it was him, but she didn't turn or look up until he stood in front of her, his gaze abject, his expression tender. Their eyes met.

'Analee?'

'My lord.' She couldn't bear to meet his gaze and lowered her eyes.

'May I sit with you?'

'It is your house, sir.'

'I do not mean that. I will be gone from it at once if you so desire.'

The Falcon sat down beside her.

'I thought I might go back to England, sir. With your permission.'

'Oh Analee . . . do not speak to me so. Do not be so harsh with me. If you knew how much I have suffered.'

'But not marked, I think, my lord.'

The Falcon seized her hand and fell sobbing on his knees beside her.

'Oh my darling; do not be so cruel with me. You know I love you to distraction. It was my love for you that made me so jealous, insane with grief. I knew not what I did. For days, weeks, I neither knew nor cared whether I lived or died. And they would not let me be by your side.'

Analee looked at the sobbing man; but she still felt nothing, neither pity, nor rage, nor love. He was just a man on his knees, sobbing, and looking rather awkward and ridiculous on account of his large build.

'Pray get up, my lord; the tiles are dusty.'

But her words made him sob the more and he grasped her hands, covering them with kisses.

'I love you, I love you Analee. If you had died I would have killed myself. My love, say that if you cannot forgive me now, you will try. That I may be by your side, and help you to forget.'

Yes, he was her husband; a general in the army. What was happening to the Peace without him? She had a duty, for the time being. She felt cold inside, and detached, and there was certainly no love for the man covering her hands with passionate kisses, watering them with his tears. But maybe it would grow again? Something might grow in the place of the great love she had once had for him; a different love, tenderness, perhaps affection, she didn't know. Now there was nothing – none of these things.

'I forgive you, Angus, because you were provoked and scarcely knew what you did. Whether I can love you again in the same way I don't know, yet. But I will be a dutiful wife and stay by your side . . .'

'But you *must* love me, Analee. I shall die without your love. I can't live without our passion.'

He drew her to him and tenderly kissed her neck, her cheeks, and then gently his mouth brushed her lips. She felt no spark, no flame of desire, and she could almost feel the pain again of his rapacious attack. She closed her eyes and willed herself to love him, to desire him, to forget the past or remember only the good things.

They dined together that day for the first time, sitting opposite each other, waited on by Nelly and another servant. McNeath had been banished to the servants' quarters. Analee found it hard to forgive McNeath for what he had told the Falcon. Indeed it was McNeath who had provoked the attack as much as anyone else. But Nelly swore McNeath had been in no doubt that his lordship would keep his word and sever his vital organs; the words had been forced out of him – that Analee had met Brent Delamain before the day on which she rescued him. More McNeath did not know, Nelly wisely having kept her own counsel on the subject.

In the afternoon the Falcon took Analee for a drive in the

carriage, along by the Seine and through the Bois de Boulogne. They occasionally saw people they knew and bowed and smiled. Analee was doing her duty: she and Lord Falconer were together again – everyone could see it. The news would soon spread.

That night he came to her bed, timidly, like a shy first-time lover. She quivered as he lay beside her and fear again took possession of her at the memory of that other time.

'My love, you are trembling.'

He thought it was desire, and tentatively caressed her belly. But she lay there very stiff, her body shaken by this slight tremor.

'You are afraid Analee?'

In the dark she nodded. Any minute now he would turn on her and thrash her, lose control of himself again . . .

'Oh my love, do not be afraid. I love you so much. Oh Analee, let us be as we were. Let us make a child that will cement our love, cause it to grow again and burgeon. My love for you has never failed; but I must woo you again and I shall.'

He slipped his hand between her thighs, and with his other hand raised her gown so that the firm mound of her breasts were exposed to his embrace. Then he made love to her, trying by the tenderness of his caresses, the gentleness of his actions, to atone for what he had done.

But Analee felt nothing. The wonderful fusion of their flesh, the merging of their essences, evoked in her nothing but memories of what was past, resignation to what was happening at the present.

He lay beside her afterwards, his hand still stroking her body. 'It will happen,' he said, 'you will love me again; you will want me and desire me. And I will be patient and tender with you, my Analee, because no woman can love as you do. I will merit your love and win it from you, my darling wife.'

But as he slept, Analee wondered if what he said would happen; if she could ever feel for him in that way again.

In October of that year, the Treaty of Aix la Chapelle was ratified and the official end of the War of the Austrian Succession made England and France at peace once again. The English flocked to Paris, and Prince Charles continued to defy the French King, refusing to leave France.

The King gave a ball at Versailles to celebrate the Peace and it was notable how many English joined with the French in thronging about the Royal Family.

Angus and Analee had been seen together constantly and for the ball she looked particularly resplendent in a robe of gold brocade that showed off to perfection her olive skin and the raven black hair which glittered with diamonds. There were jewels at her wrists and on her fingers, and around her neck a gorgeous necklace of diamonds and emeralds which was Angus's most recent present. He now continually showered her with presents, trying to buy back a love he had lost and which before he could have had for nothing.

But the token of their love that she had once worn round her neck, the ring of Falcon Gold, now lay in a drawer in her bureau. She had silently vowed to herself when her husband had wrested it off her neck that she would never wear it again. He knew why she did not wear it; but he never mentioned it. When he saw it round her neck again he would have won her love.

But to the outward world Angus and Analee appeared reconciled. They were always together – smiling, dancing, chatting with friends old and new. All traces of Analee's injuries had gone and she appeared vibrant and happy. Only Nelly knew of the horror that still scarred her soul, the nightmares she had when she relived the assault by her husband. That night they danced at the ball at Versailles and many were the comments made about them – their happiness, their love for each other was apparent to all.

For the Falcon *was* in love, and showed it, and Analee was a very good actress, discovering skills in the art of deception she hadn't known she had. Only she knew that inside, beneath the satins and the jewels, her heart once so full of love, had turned to stone.

'Lady Falconer, may I have the pleasure of a dance if you should have one free.'

Analee, in conversation with the Duc d'Ayen, a boon companion of the King and an admirer of pretty women, turned to see Lord St March smiling at her.

'My lord! I heard you were in England.'

'Indeed my lady, and now on my way back to Spain.' He turned to greet Angus who hardly ever left his wife's side. 'Have I your permission, sir, to dance with the dazzling Marchioness?'

Angus grunted and resumed his conversation with Madame de

Brancas, an intimate of the Pompadour who was dancing with the King at the far end of the room, looking alluring in grey and pale blue. Yet as Analee moved off Angus kept his eye on her, jealously following every movement she made around the room.

'I was sorry to hear of your indisposition, Lady Falconer. I am so happy you are recovered. His lordship too. I hear he sustained a nasty wound in the war. And your accident was caused by a fall I believe.'

'From the top of the stairs to the bottom,' Analee said, meeting his gaze. 'I lost my shoe at the top. Happily we were both well looked after.'

The Earl had a quizzical look in his eye, and Analee thought that by now the whole world knew the truth.

'Now tell me, my lord, we are out of touch. What is happening with the Jacobites?'

'Ah then you *do* think I am a spy, Lady Falconer?'

'Or maybe you think *I* am one!'

'Well, the Prince will still not leave France. The Princesse, who is being threatened with exile by the King, urges him to defiance; the Duchesse d'Aiguillon urges acceptance. He is promised a pension and a house by the King – *two* houses if you please! – to be specially built at Neufchatel, and a position worthy of his illustrious station. The Prince, however, is obstinate.

'But I have something even more interesting to tell you. The Prince has asked me about you. He would like to meet you again. He was very struck by you at Madame de Talmond's dinner.'

'By *me*?'

'Yes – he particularly asked after you. I always pay my respects of course when I pass through Paris. My father was a great friend of his father's. Besides, I like to know what is going on. He would like me to arrange a dinner for you. Would you accept?'

'I know not what to say.' Unusually for her, Analee looked confused.

'You may not see him again. I do not think he will last here long. 'Tis a great honour.'

'A very great honour.'

'He is living at the moment in the house of the Prince de Rohan at St Ouen, but I have friends who would gladly arrange to entertain His Highness.'

'*And* my husband?' Analee said archly.

'I am sure you will think of something to tell your husband ma'am.'

'I will say I am dining with the Allonbys. He likes them not.'

The Earl's face lit up. 'Capital. I see I may accept on your behalf?'

Analee inclined her head, her eyes sparkling with mischief.

Analee felt happier than she had felt for weeks at the thought of her assignation with the Prince. She knew it would be a harmless amusement but even the thought of it did her good, causing a transformation that made the Falcon think she was beginning to love him again.

Analee continued to be unresponsive to his embraces, indifferent to his ardour. It was beginning to wear him down and make him resentful. Their private life was so different from the one they acted out in public. She lay with him, but reluctantly, and let him make love without responding. Increasingly they slept in separate rooms. The Falcon felt his eyes wandering more and more among the pretty women they met at the many balls and parties they attended in Paris and Versailles that autumn.

In the end Analee did not have to lie to her husband. His duties called him out of Paris again and Lord St March arrived to escort her to her dinner with the Prince. Analee had spent hours at her toilette, her gown of red damask newly made by the best dressmaker in Paris.

'You look a picture,' Lord St March murmured. 'His Highness will be enchanted.'

'And will the Princesse de Talmond also be there?'

The Earl looked at her with amazement. 'You think he would ask her there with you? Do you not know your dinner is to be *à deux*, madame?'

'We are to be *alone*?'

'I thought you had understood it, Marchioness.' The Earl gave a discreet cough.

She had not understood so much – such a bold move by the Prince surpassed her expectations. But now that it was upon her Analee smiled in the dark. She was to be alone with the most attractive man in Europe.

'Nothing need happen that you do not wish. His Highness is . . .'

'Oh you need not tell me these things, my lord. I am not a simpleton – I know the Prince is not a philanderer. I think he has a political motive for this dinner.'

'We shall see by and by, Madame.'

The carriage rode down the broad sweep of the Rue Saint Victor and then turned off into the Rue du Murier where it stopped outside a small house set back from the road.

'His Highness will see that you get home. *Bonne chance*, Madame.'

The door opened and Analee was handed down by a footman who let her into the house, closing and locking the outer door behind him. Analee's heart beat lightly in her breast and she handed her cloak to another footman who bowed and showed her into the salon. The Prince was alone, sombrely dressed in black velvet without decorations, standing by the mantelpiece with a glass in his hand. He hurried over to her, a smile on his lips.

'My Lady Falconer, how kind of you to come.' He bent and kissed her hand and she dropped a deep curtsy. The fire roared in the chimney and the lights of the many candles were reflected in the polished mahogany and satinwood of the furniture. To one side, a table was laid with two covers.

'Pray sit down, Lady Falconer. A glass of champagne?'

'Thank you, Your Royal Highness.'

The Prince went over to a great oaken brass-bound wine-cooler and poured a glass of champagne for Analee, refilling his own glass. He brought hers to her and raised his glass in a toast.

'God save the King.'

'The King, Your Royal Highness.'

The Prince sat beside her and she saw for the first time the lines under his eyes, the deep crevices by the side of his mouth. He looked older and more tired than when she had last seen him.

'I mean the King in Rome, Madame. James III of England, my father.'

'I know that, Sire. God save His Majesty.'

'Then you *are* one of us, Madame?'

Analee looked towards the fire. Was she getting revenge on the Falcon? Was this how she paid him back?

411

'I am very sympathetic to your cause, as you know sir.'

'I hear, Madame, that your husband has treated you very cruelly.'

'Oh no, sir. That was a rumour brought about by the fact that we were ill at the same time. His lordship sustained a wound in the war and I fell down the stairs in our home at the same time.'

'You are a very loyal woman,' said the Prince, smiling faintly. 'Your husband is a lucky man. I would value such loyalty beyond price. Shall we dine, Madame?'

The Prince rang a bell and took Analee to the table exquisitely set with fine linen, crystal and silver. He helped her into her chair and sat opposite her. The door opened and two servants entered, one carrying a tureen of soup. This was followed by fish, saddle of lamb and sweets.

'I think you wondered why I wanted to see you Madame.'

Analee gazed directly into the Prince's eyes.

'Oh – do not doubt that it was to savour your beauty again Madame; but I also wanted your help.'

'How can I help you sir?'

'I want the Falcon to try and dissuade the authorities from expelling me.'

'Oh sir – how can my husband do that? It is written in the Peace. Besides he . . . he hates Your Royal Highness and all you stand for. I must be honest.'

'I appreciate that Madame. But I hear you have great power with him. I need friends, Lady Falconer, powerful friends. For a man like the Falcon to say I was harmless, no danger . . .'

The Prince was pleading with her. He needed her. Analee the gypsy was the confidante of the son of a King, perhaps a future King himself. How vulnerable he looked – how handsome, how imperious! Yet at the same time, how lost. She was half in love with him already. If only she could help him. With her wiles, to extract a promise from the Falcon . . .

'I will do what I can sir. How I will do it I know not; but I will try.'

Her reward was an enchanting smile. Then he started to tell her of his adventures since he left Scotland, of his journeys to Spain, the defection of his brother Henry, his refusal to see his father. He talked in a soft mellifluous voice, slightly accented – a mixture of

412

French and Scots. But it was his eyes that Analee found so exceptional – alert, intelligent, hungry for success, for recognition, for love.

After dinner he led her to the sofa; the fire was stoked and brandy brought and they were left alone.

'You are a wonderful listener, Lady Falconer. I feel that I have known you all my life.'

He put out a hand and touched the lock of hair which fell over her bosom, the rest being coiled high on her head. He had drunk a quantity of claret at dinner and, though certainly not intoxicated, undoubtedly had his reserve relaxed and his senses roused by the wine.

'I hear you are called the Enchantress, and you are indeed enchanting. It is true you were a gypsy?'

'I *am* a gypsy sir. I was born in the wild and lived there until his lordship found me and took me to his home.'

'I wish you would bring me luck, Analee. May I call you Analee?'

'Of course, sir. I wish I could bring you luck. I wish it with all my heart.'

The Prince leaned over and kissed her. It was not the expert kiss of a practised philanderer, but an artless clumsy kiss of a young boy. Yet it filled Analee with a fierce desire and she leaned towards him, tenderly clasping his face between her long hands and gently inserting her tongue just inside his mouth, flicking it along his lips.

'You will bring me love tonight Analee? And maybe luck for the future?'

'I hope so sir. I will summon all my gypsy spells to bring you what you desire most.'

'The throne of England.'

The Prince led Analee through the quiet house, up a narrow staircase and along a corridor. There was no sign of the servants. At the end a door stood open and Analee could see a roaring fire and candles, also a bed with the sheets turned back. The Prince shut the door and locked it, casting the key on a table.

'I am surrounded by enemies. I must always be careful.'

'Is there no one to protect you here sir?'

'Against you?' The Prince laughed and sat on the bed pulling off his boots. She could see he felt at ease with her. 'Oh there are men to protect me. My servant waits opposite the house to take you home. He will keep watch. The house servants have gone to bed and no one knows we are here except Lord St March and the friends who lent me this house.'

'They know you are meeting me?'

'Only Lord St March knows that. I trust him.'

'He is a Jacobite?'

'Oh yes – and his father before him. David St March is a clever fellow: he is in with both sides, but his heart is with us. When I am king I will grant him rewards, though not as great as to those who have offered their lives. When there is trouble he is never to be found. But he gives us money and without that we would have no chance at all.'

The Prince sat in his shirt and breeches gazing at Analee, who with her usual lack of modesty had removed her dress and hoop and stood in her petticoat, her stomacher still laced about her. She had taken off her jewels and loosened her hair, so that it fell across her bosom and down her back.

Charles Edward stood up and went over to her, clumsily putting his arms about her from behind and kissing her cheek.

'Could you unlace my stomacher, sir?'

The Prince laughed and deftly undid the laces which released the garment, leaving Analee half naked, revealing her full proud breasts. She turned to the Prince and began unfastening his shirt; then she thrust her breasts against his bare chest and kissed him expertly, removing his shirt as she did so and feeling for the fastening of his breeches.

The Prince's eyes burned with passion and he started to fumble with the cord at her waist which released her petticoat. Then he held her away from him and gazed at her full, naked beauty.

'You are the loveliest woman I ever saw. Oh Analee . . .'

Analee went over to the bed and removed the warming pan which had been thoughtfully put there. She lay in the centre of the bed, without covering herself, hands behind her head. She knew that like this she looked at her most enticing.

The sight made the Prince move eagerly, struggling to remove his breeches as he did. She could see he was an inexpert lover, which somehow did not surprise her, but she thought that a man as

414

handsome and as youthful as he should have lain with many, many women of all kinds not just a handful of aristocratic ladies. This much she could do for the Prince if she could not restore his throne: teach him the art of love.

He would have leaped upon her like a young animal, but she moved deftly to one side and turned swiftly towards him, encircling his body with her arms and gently entwining her legs with his. Then she began to kiss his neck and his chest; but his passion, the sight of his red face, his moaning and panting made her realize there had been no need to rouse him after all.

The Prince's performance confirmed what doubts Analee already had as to his skills as a lover. She herself had not even begun to feel aroused, but she did not mind. He clung to her almost piteously like a young boy and she remembered all she had heard about his unhappy childhood in Rome, the separation of his parents, the early death of his mother, and his apparently loveless existence until the Princesse de Talmond had entered his life.

And what of the Princesse now? She certainly had much to put up with if the Prince always made love like this. No wonder they quarrelled a great deal. She must be very dissatisfied, unfulfilled. His hand lay on her breast and he slept, snoring slightly. His hair was tousled and his face looked very young. She gazed at him and stroked his cheek, feeling a tenderness which was that of a mother rather than a lover. She was his refuge from the harsh world that fate had created for him. In her arms she held not a future King of England but a helpless boy who some said had no future at all.

After a while he opened his eyes and gazed at her.

'You *are* an Enchantress,' he said. 'Everything they say about you is true. Would you, could you be my mistress and live with me always? You would make me happy, Analee.'

'But I hear you are much sought after, sir, by the ladies.'

'Ah!' The Prince sighed. 'They want me not for myself but for who I am. Oh Madame de Talmond is different perhaps. She has a good heart. But she can be a wild cat, and she is much older than I am and very jealous. Then there is Madame de Vassé and the Duchesse d'Aiguillon. They smother me, Analee. I am tired of them all. Come with me and I will gladly go into exile as Louis wishes.'

'I think, sir, that the magic of the moment and this room makes

415

you talk thus. I know you do not want to leave this city; and even if you did, for me to come with you is out of the question. Now that we have cemented our bond by this act of love, and you have so honoured me, I will always be Your Royal Highness's slave and seek constantly to further your cause.'

'Ah Enchantress, love me again.'

Analee summoned all the expertise she knew to make love to the young Prince. To make it an experience he would remember. For the first time since the Falcon's attack on her, she herself knew again the delights of carnal desire and, despite the fact that the Prince was fifty times less experienced than the Falcon, she enjoyed his fumbling embraces and inexpert kisses the more. He was not rough and he did not hurt her, though he did not seem to know how to please a woman.

Analee left the Prince's bed towards dawn. She did not want to wake him to say goodbye. Constantly on the move as he was, he obviously needed the rest. She glanced at him slumbering and blew him a kiss, then dressing quickly and silently, she went down to the street where a servant appeared from the shadows to greet her. He led her to a small waiting chaise and drove her swiftly home just as the morning light was breaking over the rooftops of Paris.

Nelly was awake and went silently with her up to her room where a solitary candle burned and embers glowed in the grate.

'I fell asleep, Analee, forgive me.'

'Oh Nelly – I have made love to a Prince!' Analee clasped Nelly, feeling her face wet with tears. 'Nell, why do you cry? I am happy!'

'Oh Analee, to think only a few short years ago you were a gypsy vagabond, and now . . . One day he may be King!'

'Even if he is not, I care not. Oh Nell, he is no great lover; but I see why the women adore him. There is something very helpless about him. He is very lovable. I don't think he meant to make love to me, you know. I think he just wanted to get me to use my influence with his lordship.'

'What influence, Analee?'

Analee allowed Nelly to help her undress and brush her hair. Then she lay on the bed, her hands behind her head.

'He wants me to try and persuade his lordship to take his side, to enable him to stay here. But I know his quest is hopeless. His fate is already sealed and nothing Lord Falconer can do will alter that. Even if he wanted to he could not, and he does not want to.'

The following morning Analee awoke late. Her first memory was of the Prince, and the fact that in her body she contained the seed of kings. A startling thought took hold of her. This was her fertile time and how proud she would be to bear a child of the Prince's. Yes, to bear the Prince's child: what an honour! She curled her legs against her stomach and ran her hands over her body. She knew she would not lie with him again; she felt it in her bones as she had felt many things, and been right.

But the Prince did not think so. When Nelly entered Analee's room at noon she brought a posy of flowers and, in a large white envelope, a note on which the Prince had written in his large untutored hand.

'Enchantress, thank you. When will I see you again?'

Angus had been again with the army which was disbanding and returning to England. The Falconer regiment was staying in Flanders for the time being and it was two weeks after Analee's encounter with the Prince that Angus returned home.

The gap now between him and Analee had seemed wider than ever. He resented the fact that she could not forgive him, or rather could not forget, for she said she had forgiven. As for Analee, her time had been spent day-dreaming about the Prince. She had willed his seed inside her to take root and become part of her, constantly letting her hands rest on her belly as though invoking a spell. She had hoped to hear from him again, despite what she'd felt in her bones; but Lord St March who had called a few days later told her he had had to leave Paris. Lord St March was discreet enough not to enquire what had happened on the night of her dinner with him. All Analee volunteered was that the Prince had asked for the Falcon's help and that she didn't believe it possible. Lord St March agreed.

'I must return to Spain,' he said. 'I have two younger children there – a daughter who is a little wild and fully ready for marriage and a son who wants to enter the army. Madame, I must take leave of you and I hope only to see you again before long. I shall be bringing my daughter to be presented at court in England after I have settled the career of my son.'

'I hope we shall see you in Piccadilly, my lord. Take care to call.'

'Madame, I shall.'

He took her hand, bowing low over it. As they looked into each other's eyes, Analee felt she knew this strange man very well. Then he was gone.

Finally Angus returned from Brussels where he had left his regiment camped outside the town. They greeted each other awkwardly, as if they did not know the lie of the land, and at dinner they sat at opposite ends of the long dining table, scarcely speaking. Angus was preoccupied by his thoughts, Analee by hers. The monthly time she had been expecting had not come. If it did not within a day or two, it could only mean her wish had been granted and she was pregnant by the Prince. The Falcon drank a lot of wine and sat afterwards in the salon drinking brandy.

'Well, Analee what did you do with yourself while I was gone?'

'I waited for your return sir, like an obedient wife.' Analee kept her secret joy out of her eyes and looked gravely at her husband.

'Did you go out at all?'

'I visited Mary Delamain at her convent in the Rue des Fosses. She is to become a nun.'

The Falcon's face grew puce and he stood up glowering over his wife. 'And her husband?'

She met his eyes fearlessly. 'Their marriage is to be annulled. I believe he is abroad. Angus, you know I will have naught to do with Brent Delamain ever again. I am committed as your wife.'

'But do you love me? Do you love me Analee?' he thundered, bending down until his contorted face was close to hers. Analee shut her eyes in an involuntary shudder. She knew that every time he did this she would be reminded of that terrible night.

Then she thought of the Prince and the secret she hoped she carried inside her. To have lain in his arms! She owed him something for the honour he had done her – the gift he maybe had given her. She would at least ask the Falcon to help him. And the Falcon would only help him if Analee pleased him.

So, out of duty and despite the contorted face smelling of drink, Analee tried to recall the days of their love and she took his face between her hands and kissed his lips gently.

'Of course I love you Angus.'

'Oh Analee . . .' The Falcon groaned and fell to the floor, his head on her lap. 'How I have yearned to hear you say that again! Come my delight and let me make love to you; let us recapture the joy we once shared.'

Analee closed her eyes as he began to undo her bodice and unloose her robe. She would give herself up to love with another man – for the Prince.

She would not think of the Prince tonight, but of her husband. Her robe fell off and the Falcon took her hand, pulling her to the floor. Gazing at her he said: Now that you are back with me, now that you have forgiven me, I intend to remain with you as much as I can. Analee, I long so much to have a son. Give me a son!'

After they had gone to bed they slept and made love intermittently throughout the night, as they used to in the beginning when their ardour was at its peak; those days, far off they seemed now, when the Falcon had been recovering from his injuries sustained at Falkirk.

She summoned all her powers to relax and enslave the Falcon all over again, both to disguise the fact that she no longer loved him and to put him in a mellow mood for her request on behalf of the Prince.

When he woke the next morning he found that she had already risen and washed, brushed her hair until it gleamed, and donned a fresh nightgown of pale blue silk with embroidered cuffs. The room had been tidied and a fire roared in the grate before which was a table laid for two. When she saw he was awake, she came over to his side and planted a kiss on his mouth.

'Seeing that we have gone back to the past, my lord, I wonder if you recalled the times we dallied all day long in your bedroom eating and sleeping . . .'

'And making love,' the Falcon growled, reaching for her. Analee skipped agilely aside and, with a coquettish smile, drew back the bedclothes and held out for him his morning robe.

'We have fresh coffee and newly baked bread, jams and ham.'

The Falcon scratched his chest, gave a mighty yawn and folded Analee into his arms.

'My dearest wife – my wife *and* mistress! I confess I have a prodigious appetite.'

He went over to the table and they sat facing each other, Analee pouring the coffee and wondering how she could bring up the question that was the object of her night's work.

'When shall you have finished in France, Angus?'

'Oh in six months or so. Like you it not here my love?'

'I miss my home and my baby Clare.'

'Then we shall have her sent to us.'

'Angus, could we not go home for Christmas? Back to Furness?'

The Falcon raised an eyebrow and spread butter thickly on his roll. 'Furness? Not Falcon's Keep?'

'Furness is so intimate and friendly. Falcon's Keep is so grand and cold . . .'

The Falcon smiled and reached for her hand. 'I love you so much today, my darling, that you may ask what you like. We *shall* spend Christmas at Furness Grange.'

'Oh thank you Angus.' Analee rushed round the table and embraced him, then she whispered in his ear. 'Angus, you have everything on earth you wish, is it not so?'

The Falcon raised his head and a wary look came into his eye. 'Yes, my love, but why do you ask me this?'

'Is there aught you can do for . . . Prince Charles Edward?'

The Falcon shut his eyes as though in pain. He opened them again and shook his head.

'Do my ears deceive me? Have I heard aright? Prince Charles Edward! What on earth is he to you – or me for that matter? You have been seeing Delamain again . . .'

He was about to rise from his chair, his face turning scarlet with anger, but Analee, who still had her arms about his shoulders, held him down. As she had seen him rise she remembered his anger, his strength; and the affection she had begun to feel for him again the night before, withered in her heart.

'Hush, sir. I have not been seeing Mr Delamain, but I have been seeing other English people, Lord St March and such, and all feel sorry for the way the Prince is being harried. His Majesty King George is so secure on the throne, they say, that the Jacobites have no chance of a return. The activities of the Prince and his friends are but a passing irritation. They say it is undignified the way he is pursued from pillar to post. I am just telling you what people say. They know how powerful you are. A word from you and he will be allowed to stay in France. He swears to behave himself.'

The Falcon rose, pushing back his chair with an angry gesture and at the same time almost knocking over his wife. By now his face was quite purple and his eyes bulging.

'He *swears*! Do you know that man is quite incapable of keeping his word? He is an idiot, a liar and a rascal. He is a plotter and an inveterate maker of mischief. His spies rove all over England and the Continent creating havoc and discord wherever they can. They are like parasites on the earth. My dear Analee we are being merciful in insisting he is despatched from the secular states of Europe. If he stays here he will surely be killed by an assassin, so many are they who hate him.

'Now please, my good wife, provoke me no more with your foolish and thoughtless remarks.'

The Falcon thumped his chair on the floor and resumed his seat on it once more. Analee had gazed at him during his outburst with steely indifference; the fury was in her heart. Observing his contorted face, his bursting veins and bulging eyes, she wondered how she had ever loved him, could ever expect to find him merciful and compassionate. He was used to issuing commands and being obeyed; his authority must never be thwarted.

She had failed the Prince, as she had known she would.

'Besides,' the Falcon growled, his mouth full of ham. ''Tis much too late. The Duc de Gèvres is charged this very day to hand him a letter from the King ordering him out of France, and if he will not go he is to be arrested.' He turned to Analee, still standing by his side and attempted to take one of her stiff cold hands. 'Those Jacobites are everywhere, my love; they are an infernal menace to our King. And the Prince's *amie*, the notorious Princesse de Talmond, had the audacity to present Lady Ogilvy – she that escaped from Edinburgh Castle like your friend – to the French King only a week or two ago! Her impudent ladyship was large with child, and his lordship is forming his own regiment to use against *our* troops!' The Falcon spluttered with rage. 'Really my love! How you can countenance acquaintance with these people I know not.'

'Lady Ogilvy is only nineteen years of age. I cannot help but admire her spirit,' Analee said boldly, stepping back in case he felt like striking her again. But her husband banged the table, causing the cups and plates to rattle and a dish of quince jam to fall on the floor.

421

'*There!* You will go on arguing with me and defying me. I forbid you, Analee, to have any further truck with Jacobites, however faintly tainted. Forbid, do you hear? I want no more visits to that blackguard's wife in a convent, and to make sure you do as I say we *shall* go home, as soon as we can, my love, and *you* for good. I shall not bring you back with me when I return.'

The Falcon got up and began to pace back and forth. 'You sadden me, Analee. After the night we have spent I thought you wished to please me; but your sentiments are an affront to me, an outrage to my position in the army. And Lord St March, what do we know of him? He is another! He wheedles between the Courts of St James's and Versailles with an ear there and an ear here. He is a spy in both camps.

'Nay, I forbid you to have truck with any of them again. Back to the country for you. The sooner you start breeding sons for me the better; that will take care of your time. Keep you out of mischief. Now, summon McNeath to help me dress. You have put me in a right irritable mood.'

The Falcon stamped into his dressing room and banged the door. Analee went to the window and gazed out at the pale wintry sun which was glittering dully over the rooftops.

She would not miss Paris or the glitter of Versailles. For it was here that she had lost her love, the great love she had for her husband. No, not lost it; he had wrenched it violently from her. What would sustain her now that she no longer loved him, now that she saw him for the tyrant everyone had said he was?

She put a hand on her belly, glad of the secret within her, willing it to take root and grow like a fine tree – a fine young sapling of the house of Stuart. For if she did carry a child in her womb, Analee knew for certain it was not that of her husband. Maybe one day, in the curious way that marks the affairs of men, recompense would unwittingly be made by the Falcon to the man he now harried and pursued. For a son of a Stuart Prince would inherit the great Falconer estates and justice would be done. With all her heart Analee willed that it might be so.

6

Ambrose Rigg leaned back in his chair and consulted the large timepiece that hung from a gold chain stretched across his corpulent stomach. Of recent years the stomach had increased in girth, his face had grown more purple and his large nose more bulbous. To the admirer of human beauty Ambrose was not a pretty sight; but Brent Delamain had cause to be grateful to him. Rigg was a good man at heart, a firm and loyal friend, and an ample provider for Brent's cousin Sarah who was married to him.

'Well, Brent lad, 'tis good to see thee and talk to thee again, and now 'tis dinner time!' Ambrose got up and clapped him on the shoulder. 'You did right to come to me. I will employ you again; you were a good worker and an honest sailor. But I wish you would give up these foolish thoughts of another Jacobite rising. We in England are happy with our King. We are glad that the war is ended although I must say, as one who engages in the smuggling trade, that we had a very profitable time of it smuggling brandy and silks from France, and wheat and woollens back into the continent of Europe. Aye, we always do well out of wars; but then this country is on the road to prosperity. There are great opportunities overseas; no doubt of that.'

'Does Sarah hear aught of Stewart?'

'Only that he is fortunate in being quite comfortably placed. Seems well and not unhappy, but you will hear this for yourself boy. Come, she awaits us at dinner.'

Brent hung back, reluctant to confront his cousin. 'But how will she receive me?'

'*Receive* you? I know not what you mean.'

'There is the matter of Mary . . .'

'Aye, well . . .' Ambrose gave Brent the hearty clap again which he often used when he was at a loss for words.

''Tis very sad of course, you and Mary . . . but she writes that she is happy in her convent. Sarah says she was always very religious. Do not blame yourself, my boy.'

'I do blame myself,' Brent said sombrely. 'Although my brother was a monk I think a woman's place is not in a convent. I did not do the right thing by Mary . . .'

'You must put it out of your mind. Marry again, raise a family! A fine fellow like you should not be without a woman. You have not seen the latest additions to *my* family Brent – a boy born two years ago and a baby scarce three months old.'

'You are the family man, Ambrose!'

'I am that,' Rigg smiled, 'and building a fine house and fortune to leave them. Property, Brent, that is the thing. Property – ships and houses and money.'

Sarah was waiting for them in the dining room, casting a final glance over the fine fare on the sideboard – the dishes of steaming vegetables, the carving board laden with joints of beef and lamb. The table was gleaming with fine plate and silver, the best wax candles glowed in the candelabra. Ambrose had brought Brent from Whitehaven under cover of night so as to avoid being seen because he was still a fugitive.

Sarah looked up as Brent came in and her smile, although pleasant and dutiful, lacked warmth. He went over to her and kissed her hand, noting that she had grown plumper and more matronly, her bosom fuller and her hips broader than when he had last seen her. Her mouth was thin and her eyes had the cautious look of the thrifty housewife whose business was entirely to do with the care of her husband and the wellbeing of her family.

Sarah, again unlike Mary, had not married for love. The Allonby family, through always being on the wrong side, had over the centuries declined from nobility and riches to poverty. Now their family home, Furness Grange, had been sold to Lord Falconer, the hated Hanoverian general. But some said that his wife, the extraordinary gypsy he had married, had bought it to save it from falling into worse hands; that she loved the place and, if ever the day should come, intended that it would be restored to the Allonbys. Mary had written warmly from Paris of her visit to the Marchioness and spoke of her kindness and graciousness during her visit to her in return before she left for England.

But these things did not concern Sarah, comfortably secure in the mansion that Ambrose had built and to which he was constantly adding so that it was on the way to becoming one of the great houses in the county. She had a large staff, four children in the nursery and enough to do about the house and estate to make her forget, for a greater part of the day anyway, that all these good things came from commerce and the labour of the gross, uneducated man she was married to.

Sarah could never forget she was an Allonby; that the family went back to the Marcher Lords left by the Conqueror to control the wild north country, that Furness had once been only part of their large estates, and that in feudal times they had been one of the greatest families in Cumbria. It was the tenacious way that the Allonbys, like many old families, had clung to their Catholic faith and later to the Stuart line that had caused their downfall and brought about the state to which they were now reduced.

But Sarah had put all that out of her mind. She had known precisely what she was doing when she gave herself to Rigg. She was marrying not so much the person but the estate of one of the new rich; people who by dint of hard work had dragged themselves up, as Ambrose had, almost from a state of servitude. It was the next generation, her children, who would form the new gentry based on wealth and property and not on ancestry.

Mary was not mentioned until the end of the meal. Ambrose, who liked to talk in the comfort of his own home and in the presence of people close to him, had conducted almost a monologue about trade, shipping, the government and the state of Europe. Preoccupied with his own thoughts, his own guilt, Brent only commented when Europe was mentioned and then to attack France and defend the Young Pretender who had finally been expelled, as Louis had promised, and was in hiding.

'Have you seen Mary recently, Brent?' Sarah asked in a tone as casual as she could make it.

'Aye, I went to take my leave. She does not wish to see me again until she is . . . professed.' Brent bowed his head and bit his lip, stammering over the word 'professed'.

'She is set upon it then?'

'Yes. I can do naught to make her change her mind.'

'Except be a husband to her,' Sarah said bitterly.

'Now, now!' Ambrose roared. 'We said we would not talk about the whys and wherefores that Brent and Mary do not get on. They are not a match 'tis all.' Ambrose wiped his mouth on a fine linen napkin, picked his teeth with a blunt finger nail and took a final quaff of wine before pushing back his chair. Then he belched and, stretching his arms in a yawn, scratched under his armpit – all to the evident disgust of his wife who averted her gaze. 'I'll be for my bed. We'll talk again in the morning Brent. I think your best base will be the Isle of Man. You can lodge with John Collister. Best not to have your face seen in Whitehaven or about these parts for a while. In time you'll apply for an indemnity – the King is granting them all the time now that the Rebellion is firmly quashed. But tomorrow you can stop here. We have a guest coming I think you will want to see.'

'Oh?' Brent looked at Ambrose, who winked at his wife and then made for the door, bidding them goodnight as he went.

'Emma, your sister, is coming from Delamain Castle,' Sarah explained.

'Does she know I am here?' Brent said excitedly. He had not seen his sister since his betrothal to Mary in October 1744.

'No, she wants to talk to Ambrose.'

'To Ambrose?'

Sarah sat back in her chair, clasping her hands before her. 'Emma wants to try and join Stewart in Maryland. She cannot get him out of her mind, and now he has not written for some time and she is desperate.'

'Well, let her go. What is to stop her?'

Sarah eyed him frostily. 'You think a maid on her own should cross the Atlantic Ocean looking for a man? To my mind, it is not seemly. Anyway, George will not hear of it, or your mother. I have given them my word I will not let Ambrose give in, and for her to see you will soften the blow. George quite rightly wants to send her to London to do a season and meet young men. She is twenty-two, Brent; she will soon be on the shelf.'

Brent said nothing. He knew that Sarah had been twenty-six when she married Ambrose, and glad to accept him. Sarah would have taken almost anyone rather than remain an old maid – and his money was about the only acceptable part of Ambrose; he had been forty-one at their marriage, a paunchy rheumy-eyed bachelor, set in his ways and not too particular about his personal habits. The very last spouse, one would have said, for the fastidious Sarah Allonby who, though not beautiful like her younger sister, was both personable and presentable, and in happier times would have been considered a suitable bride for some sprig of the aristocracy or landed gentry. As it was, she had grown up poor and almost solely in the company of the family at Furness Grange.

Emma could hardly believe it was Brent who came running out to open her carriage door – tall, bronzed and very fit looking, yet he seemed much older than the excited young man, newly in love with Mary, who had greeted her and her mother in Keswick four years before.

But Emma looked older too. Time was robbing her of her girlish beauty, Brent thought, kissing her cheek and handing her down from the carriage. Time – or the sufferings of unrequited love, whose pangs Brent knew only too well, but which often affected a woman more than a man because a man was kept busy and occupied while women had little to do but remember happier times and pine for their return.

Emma was almost pitifully thin and her face looked pinched and lined. Her eyes, great brown eyes, were almost sunk in their sockets and glowed with a strange light, and her thick dark hair, now lustreless, was coiled in an unbecoming bun. She clung to Brent as though aware of what he was thinking and when she looked at him her eyes were wet with tears.

'Oh Brent, you are in danger in this country! Why must you take risks? Have we not lost enough, we women?'

'Hush, Emma. I am well protected here. The servants are too loyal to Ambrose to betray me, and too scared of losing their jobs because work is hard to find. As soon as you are gone Ambrose will have me shipped to Laxey in the Isle of Man and I'll man his wherries from there.'

'Brent you *must* help me! I know that they have all plotted to stop Ambrose . . .'

Sarah walked slowly down the steps and over to Mary as though to forestall Brent from answering, although she could not have heard what was said. She gave Emma a frosty peck on the cheek and took her hand.

'Did you have a good journey?'

'Yes, thank you, though parts are blocked with snow.' Emma shivered.

'Come quickly inside girl, and warm yourself.'

Thoughtfully, Brent followed them and the servants who had collected her box into the house. His sister had changed; she was no longer a beauty. Time and grief had done that to her. He clenched his fist and banged it against his thigh. Time and grief had done its work too well among the followers of the Young Pretender – how many lives had been wrecked, hearts broken, fortunes dispersed among those who had followed the Stuart cause?

Brent knew he was risking his life in England, but he had come partly to get away – away from the Prince, and away from Analee, the wrecker of hearts, the breaker of homes. Analee! Brent's heart always contracted when he thought of her. How glad he was he'd knocked her husband down, yet at the same time full of remorse because of the consequences to Analee. He never ceased wanting her and, although so much was stacked against him, something told him that one day she would be his. He remembered the gypsy he had met on the road during the '45, the woman with the sick baby whom he had taken pity on and directed to his home.

'*You will suffer many things*,' she had told him, looking into his eyes. '*But in the end you will find happiness, though there are dark days ahead.*' And they had been dark; he had faced death but escaped it, escaped from its very jaws, as she had promised. In the end, though, in the end he would find happiness – and the only happiness for him in this life was reunion with Analee.

On the other side of the ocean, three thousand miles away, it was midwinter too in the valleys that ran off the Chesapeake to form the county named after Queen Mary, daughter of James II. For Stewart Allonby it was his third winter and on the bitter February night of 1749 as he sat in front of a great fire, his feet on the table in front of it, his pipe in his mouth, he reflected that life had on the whole been good to him.

Not only had he survived the Rebellion, a time in gaol, a trial; but also the stormy journey across the Atlantic and the separation from his family, especially Emma. Emma: Stuart gazed into the fire and stirred the logs with a foot. He often thought of her, briefly, guiltily. He hadn't written to Emma for nearly a year, and yet her letters continued to arrive regularly week after week. He had them all in a pile in a box under his bed, many of them briefly perused, whereas before he would savour every word and read them many times over.

Yes, in many ways Stewart had been lucky. He had been indentured to a plantation owner, Hector Cameron, as a forester and he could not have been more fortunate in his placement, for Hector was by inclination a through and through Jacobite. From the very beginning he had treated Stewart more like a guest than a servant, so that Stewart now had a warm comfortable cabin to himself near the family mansion and some Sundays he took dinner with them. Increasingly he was invited to evening parties, and Hector made no secret of his preference for him and his ambitions regarding him.

Hector's family had been among the first settlers in Maryland, carving a way through the lush forests and pasturelands to make homesteads on the banks of the Chesapeake. A thriving industry was built up based on the tobacco plant imported from the West Indies. Now Hector was one of the first men in the region, a rich thriving merchant whose wealth was based on the acquisition of land, and the planting of that magical, money-making crop – tobacco.

Unlike slaves, who were bought for life, indentured workers were free men who sold their labour to an employer for a fixed term and received a small wage. At the end of this time they were free to go elsewhere. They also had better food and conditions than the slaves with whom they did not mix, except sometimes sexually although it was forbidden. Indentured service was a way favoured by the British government for dealing with its transported prisoners; it meant they were confined for a specified time to a certain place and their whereabouts were known – it was a cheap form of imprisonment. The better a man's clan, the better his terms of service and the conditions of his employment.

Only one thing marred the life of Hector Cameron; he had three nubile daughters but no son to succeed him, to carry on the enterprise started by his forefathers and triumphantly continued by himself. As he was a comparatively young man still, this was of no consequence – not that he would have any more children, his wife being like him in her forties. But he had to make provision for his daughters, see that they were well married to men who would take care not only of them but of the wealth and possessions their father would leave them in the course of time.

For a year Stewart had worked diligently and well, but in a menial capacity, sharing a bunk in the communal house for the indentured labourers and eating good but rough food at the long table with them. Among them were prisoners from England, like himself; a few ne'er-do-wells who had come to America hoping to find that gold grew on trees; and some second generation Americans whose families had tried to make it like the Camerons but failed. But increasingly Stewart was picked out by Hector for more important jobs. From being one of the many foresters he was put in charge of several hundred acres, and then he was taught the tobacco business and worked as a foreman among the slaves in the field. Now he was an under-manager with his own cabin and servant.

Gradually he had been invited to the house more often, provided with better clothes. But always he was aware of his place as a hired servant, knowing that the likes of the Camerons with their lowly Highland origins, who had worked hard to get where they were, would easily take offence if a servant were to push himself forward.

Stewart couldn't remember exactly when it was that he realized he was being slowly groomed for preferment by Hector, and also that Elizabeth his second daughter was casting eyes full of meaning in his direction. Up to then – it must have been a year ago at Christmas time – he had thought only of Emma, longed for the day they would be reunited either in his country or elsewhere, despairing of it ever happening.

The idea of himself as a citizen of Maryland, maybe a farmer like Hector owning slaves and vast acres of country, had only come gradually to Stewart. Why *should* he go back to the life he had left? Why had he automatically taken it for granted that he would? There was nothing for him in England; he was forbidden anyway to go back, ever, by the terms of his deportation. What was there for him on the Continent except as a soldier of fortune, clustering with the others round the pathetic Pretender in Rome, dependent on him for a few shekels to keep him from starving?

The Stuart cause was lost and Stewart – who had been named after the Royal Family – found that now he hardly cared. It was time to make a new life and start again, and what better than in this new and exciting country? It was rich beyond man's dreams, beautiful and fertile; a way of life was being built up by the people who, for whatever reason, but many of them political, had flocked here from the old country.

A whole new society was growing up, beautiful mansions being built. The women's gowns were made of the finest stuffs imported from England and France, and the fashions were the latest as seen in Europe eagerly copied by diligent dressmakers. There was good food to eat, wine to drink and money to spend. The local legislatures were developing into a self-governing form of democracy that had never been tried before and which took very little notice of directions from the government in London. Many of the new Americans were only second generation English; a lot of them had now been born in this country and thought of it and not England or Scotland as home.

And about the same time that Stewart felt himself beginning to look forward to an exciting future, casting off the past and its hopeless futile memories, there was Elizabeth, twenty-one years of age – not beautiful but comely and ogling him at every opportunity. Elizabeth Cameron, with her two sisters, an heiress. Perdita, the eldest, was married to the son of an already wealthy merchant, and the youngest, Anna, was only fifteen. But Elizabeth, red haired and ambitious . . .

Soon after this awareness of her interest had occurred he had stopped writing to Emma.

There was a knock on the door and Stewart took his feet from the table.

'Come in.'

Elizabeth! Just as he had been thinking of her. She peeped round the door at him, eyes twinkling, a shawl round her shoulders against the cold night. She was not supposed to visit him here, but she did, creeping through the yard after nightfall while her old servant Cicely kept watch in the big house.

Stewart drew her in and shut the door. Hungrily she turned to him and their mouths met in a long embrace. Behind her the flames leapt in the grate; he had not yet lit the lamp. He felt her hard young breasts against him, her body yearning to merge with his. Stewart freed his mouth and groaned, pushing her away, but gently.

He went over to the table and, taking a spill from the fire, lit the oil lamp. She stood in the shadows of the room, panting a little, a smile on her lips. Then she walked slowly over to him and stood against him again, slipping a hand under his shirt. The feel of her cold hand against his skin made Stewart groan again and, taut with desire, he drew her into his arms covering her face with kisses, crushing her body to his.

'It must be soon,' she said, 'soon . . .'

'If it were *now*,' he whispered, 'who would know?'

Elizabeth laughed and teasingly freed herself. 'Well *I* would know, and maybe the whole world would know if I were to be got with child. No, Stewart, it is no way to begin our lives. My father would not have me the laughing stock of the district. His daughter must be a virgin when she is married . . .'

'Married . . . !' It was the first time the word had been mentioned.

'And why not?' Elizabeth flounced up her skirts and sat on a chair. 'The Allonbys are much better born than the Camerons, or at least our branch of the Camerons. You must know father likes you. I thought it was obvious.'

'But for a son-in-law?'

'Are men around here so plentiful? Most that I know are too old or too young or too far away. Father knows it too. Besides, he admires you Stewart. He says you did not brood on your defeat or humiliation, nor did you despise the work you were given as a common forester. You did not try and take advantage of your birth or worm your way into his favour. He is a self-made man and he liked all that. Besides, he knows we are fond of each other . . .'

'Has he asked you?'

'He has observed it, he says, in my eyes and by your demeanour. I think you would not find him reluctant if you asked for my hand.'

'But Elizabeth, I am but an under-manager. I have no fortune, I live in a hut . . . I must *seem* to be marrying you for advantage.'

'But anyone who knows you will not think that.'

'No, I cannot do it.'

She reached for his hand and pulled him down beside her. 'You *must* do it. For me. I want you, Stewart, for my husband. There – *I* am proposing. If you want me, there is nothing in the world to stop you . . .'

Suddenly Stewart thought of Emma's dark eyes, the promise they had made in Carlisle gaol. She would come to the ends of the earth to be with him, she'd said, and always in her letters she asked – when could she come? Nothing would deter her. Only he, he knew, had deterred her. For a year he hadn't replied, or answered her a word.

He had made her fall in love with him. Years ago Analee had given him a spell and he had cast a leaf covered with his blood on the lake. The spell had worked, had captured the eager beautiful young girl, and she had remained true to him, through all his misfortunes. It was she who had made her brother George plead for him at his trial in London; she who had the sentence changed from death to transportation . . . Emma.

Elizabeth's eyes were tawny, flecked with white like an owl. Her cheeks were pink and she had a fiery temper to match her hair. She was imperious and would brook no opposition; she meant to have him. She was the plainest of the sisters, but the one with the most character. Her loud voice could be heard throughout the house, commanding and exhorting; she was her father's favourite, his right hand, more powerful than her gently reared mother, an Edinburgh woman who pined for her native land and did not enjoy good health. Maud Cameron hated this wild pioneering country to which Hector had brought her as a bride, the lack of culture, where the main event was the weekly arrival of the boat from England. She had borne her three children in fear and pain back in the hard days, before they had this fine house or as many servants, and was grateful she could have no more, even the son Hector longed for so much.

Maud always felt that she had failed in her duty by not providing an heir, and from then on the painful and debilitating symptoms she had always suffered from grew increasingly severe until she spent a good part of her time, especially in the winter, in bed.

But Hector had thrived and prospered without much help from Maud. He hadn't needed a woman's help. This was a man's world, this business of farming and growing tobacco and importing slaves.

But now they had one of the finest houses east of the Chesapeake and acres of cultivated plantation as far as the eye could see. The children were almost grown up – Perdita well married, Anna a beauty; there would be no trouble there.

It was only . . . Elizabeth. She should have been a boy, her mother always said, half fondly, half in spite. She was forthright and aggressive and capable. With her fiery red hair and decisive manner she should have been the son Hector had always wanted. Elizabeth was always going to be the awkward one, the difficult one to marry – few men would be able to cope with that temper or would want to, despite the fortune Hector would leave her. But Stewart Allonby was one of them; he was strong enough to handle Elizabeth, and above all he needed the fortune.

Elizabeth knew he was ideal and she was determined to have him. Beside the fact was handsome – of average height but thick-set, with a strong hard body that did not go amiss with his sensitive aristocratic face – she could see how he would develop. He was not overbrainy, but straight and honourable. His forbears had contributed to his make-up: loyalty and courage counted for much in this pioneer country. She also knew that his taciturnity concealed a passionate nature and this she played on by letting him kiss and fondle her, occasionally touch her breast or feel her bare thigh . . . but no more. She was seducing him by stages, handling out rope and drawing him in by inches.

'Do you want me, Stewart?' Elizabeth was saying, her voice hoarse with urgency. Emma faded; only the present opened into the future stretching out before him.

'Oh Elizabeth, of course I want you!'

She leapt away from him laughing, and did a whirl about the floor. 'Then father wants to talk to you!'

'About *this*?'

'No, about your position. He knows how you feel, that you are a man of pride. He knows you want to be well-established before you marry me. Go and see him. Quickly!'

'Now?'

'Now. This instant!' Elizabeth laughed and scarcely gave him the chance to put on his coat before she dragged him to the door and out into the cold.

* * *

Hector Cameron had ordered a fine dinner to be served that night, also a good suit of clothes to be put out for his prospective son-in-law if all should go well. Yes, he was a fine choice – Elizabeth was lucky and so was he, Hector. He had observed young Allonby closely for three years and he had not done a thing wrong, made a false move. It had even been Elizabeth who made the advances – although Hector knew, as Elizabeth did not, that Stewart received almost weekly letters from a lady in England. Hector wanted to sort this, as well as other matters, out on this night and he had a roaring fire in the grate and a decanter of whisky on the table close by.

Stewart entered, apologizing for his appearance. 'I have not shaved or changed sir, but Elizabeth said 'twas urgent.'

Hector looked with approval at the young man standing diffidently by the door – shyly, but not timidly. There was a difference between diffidence and timidity. Why, all Stewart had, or was about to have, he owed to Hector, and this showed in the respectfulness of his demeanour towards the older man.

'Come my boy, sit down. I have a good fire for you and some whisky after a day's work. What think you of the new contingent of slaves?'

'They are good specimens but weak sir. The winter gales caused terrible sufferings at sea I hear, and many of them died while others jumped overboard to escape their torments.'

'Aye . . .' Hector grimaced. 'I like it not this business, I'll be honest with you. Seizing people, no matter if they're black, and bringing them here by force don't seem right. But what can we do? Without slave labour this new country would never achieve greatness and prosperity. The most I can do is look after them properly when they are here and feed them well. It is also the best way, incidentally,' Hector chuckled, lighting a cigar, 'to get the most out of them. They are so grateful.'

'Oh you are a good master, sir, no doubt about that. But I hope this land will not long depend on slave labour. There is a move already afoot in England to get it stopped . . .'

'Oh well, that is England! We all know how out of touch they are with the realities of colonial life. But look, Stewart, I have not brought you hither to discuss with you the rights or wrongs of slave labour . . .' He sat down opposite him and gazed at the tip of his well lit cigar. 'I have things of much greater importance to discuss with you than a few miserable blacks. You know, I think, what it is about?'

'It is about your daughter, sir. Elizabeth.'

'She wants to marry you.'

'I know that sir.'

'And you?'

Stewart looked up and met the gaze of the man he had come to like and respect. Hector had all the good Scottish qualities that Stewart most admired – forthrightness, thrift and honesty. He was a good man: a good businessman and a good master. To lie to Hector would be to betray his trust.

'I like her very well sir, but . . .'

Hector raised his chin, the question in his eye: '*But?*'

'I have nothing to give her, sir. How could the daughter of Hector Cameron marry an indentured worker? You have bought my labour and I have another four years to go. It was the condition of my transportation.'

Hector got up and refilled their glasses. Then he started to pace up and down in front of the fire. 'Stewart, we all know the terms and the reason for your transportation. It is not as though you were a common convict, a felon as are so many who find their way to these shores. Nay, you were a soldier, a zealot who happened to find yourself on the wrong side. If the Young Pretender had gone on from Derby to London, as many say he should, we would have had King James III on the throne today and you would be a landed gentleman with your family's estates restored, maybe new honours, too. Is it not so?'

'Yes sir, it is so.'

'As far as I am concerned, you are a worthy choice for my daughter. Why or how you are here has nothing to do with it. I am willing, Stewart, to make you my estate manager. Oh – I thought of this before I knew Elizabeth had you so firmly fixed in her mind. Derwent, although not old, has had a hard time here. He is not a well man. I could send him to another of my smaller plantations in Virginia and he would consider it a promotion. I will free you from your indenture and you will move into the house here with us and live as the family. You will be a free man with a salary. You will have earned your right to marry my daughter. If you agree, in six months we shall announce the engagement not to an indentured labourer but to my manager, my right-hand man, a member of an old and honourable English family.'

Stewart bowed his head, then took a draught of the whisky in his glass. 'I do not know what to say, sir.'

Hector put his coat tail to one side and sat down again, leaning forward in the chair, his finger jabbing the air in front of Stewart. 'There is one thing, young man. Do you love her?'

So the question he had dreaded had come. No, he didn't love her. He liked and admired her; he wanted her comely proportioned body and she was willing enough to give it. But Elizabeth wasn't lovable, not in the way that . . . that Emma had been. Elizabeth was too domineering, too masculine. How to be honest with Hector without sounding mercenary?

'I . . . respect and admire Elizabeth, sir. I think . . . love will come, because up to this day I did not know how much she cared for me. I did not dare let my feelings . . . run away with me. I did not dare . . . hope.' Stewart took another draught of whisky and felt it warm his body. He noted the look on Hector's face and thought he had spoken well.

'Ah, I like that my boy! You are honest. And I'll be honest with you. Elizabeth is not a very *womanly* girl, in the old fashioned sense. My wife has always said she should have been a boy. She has always liked horses and riding and things to do with out of doors. But she is a good girl, a clever one. I think that in time, as her qualities become more apparent to you, you will come to love her, as she undoubtedly loves you.

'Now Stewart, there is one more thing. As you know, I see the post when it comes off the packet . . . Every week, for years, letters arrive for you from England. A woman, eh?'

'My cousin, Emma Delamain, sir. I was at the war with her brother Brent who married my sister Mary.'

'Ah – ' Hector looked relieved, 'a sort of family thing?'

'Not quite sir. Emma and I grew up together. But we did become briefly attached when I was in gaol. It was one of those things . . .'

'Caused by the war. These things happen, I know. Perhaps an infatuation on her part?'

'I have not written to her for a year sir, since I first became

437

aware of Elizabeth's . . . charms, and also her apparent interest in me which I found I reciprocated.'

'Capital!' Hector stood up and squeezed his prospective son-in-law's arm. 'No need to mention this to Elizabeth, but I should write to the young lady telling her of your intentions. Get it clear. Just in case she labours under any misapprehension.'

'I will do that sir.' Stewart sighed with relief. The die was cast; his fate sealed. And it was a good fate; the right fate. What point in him and Emma trailing round Europe lost and unhappy like Mary and Brent? Apparently it was all over with them anyway, and no wonder. Such a life was enough to destroy anyone. It would have destroyed them.

No, it was better like this. He now had prospects and a future. He would have a wife whom he did not as yet love but who would be a helpmeet in this hard and foreign country. She would always be capable and efficient; a good manager of a home, a healthy breeder of children. She was the sort of woman he needed.

Romance had died for Stewart with the defeat of the Young Pretender and the cause that he had spent his life longing to serve. It had died when he crossed the Atlantic in close confine with nearly a hundred other transportees; their journey only differed from that of the slaves in that they were white and eventually would be free – something the slaves could never hope for. It had died when he realized how hopeless things were for him and Emma, how futile to expect they could ever be happy. What chance had he to make her happy, working off his indenture, then having to start at the bottom of the ladder?

Now he was half way up. It was better this way. He would write and tell her. As Hector Cameron's son-in-law he was tantamount to being his heir. Perdita's husband was the eldest son of wealthy neighbours – he would have his father's estates to see to. He would work hard and prosper, raise a new family of Allonbys . . . a race who would succeed as the old one had not. He, Stewart Allonby, scion of a noble line, was starting again . . . in this free and glorious land of America.

7

As the carriage trotted along the path between Penrith and Keswick, Analee recalled the same journey she had made on foot years before after she had run away from Falcon's Keep to look for her baby. She had arrived hungry at the Grange and been taken in by Mary, only to be found there by Nelly who told her where Morella was and that she was safe. There had followed a week of peace and happiness in that place, quite unexpected because they had been forced to stay there on account of the snow.

It was at the end of that week that a messenger had ridden post haste to tell Analee the Falcon was dying. She had fled to his side, cured him by her mysterious gypsy powers and a few months later married him.

Lady Falconer thought back on those days, twisting the rings on her fingers as she gazed out of the carriage window. Opposite her Nelly slumbered with Clare lying against her on the seat. They had made an early start so as to be there before nightfall. To her right the peaks surrounding Ullswater appeared out of the mist, reminding her of her journey up Patterdale with the Buckland family when she had had to decide either to go back with them or to go on by herself. That had been a decision that changed her life.

Had it been the right decision after all? She and Angus had journeyed from Paris first to London and then to Falcon's Keep for Christmas. But it had not been a happy time; she and her husband were increasingly estranged. He was almost abnormally suspicious of her, jealously watching her at any ball or dinner, questioning her closely afterwards about who she had talked to and what had been said. She did not know whether he suspected her of plotting with Jacobites, or planning to capture the attention of some man. Perhaps both.

For her part she still nursed the resentment born on the night he had attacked her. Try as she might to put it out of her mind, she could not. Every sudden move on his part she saw as a prelude to an attack, especially if he had been drinking. She felt she did not know where she was with him. Their love-making had lost its frenzied passion and had become automatic, sustained largely with indifference by Analee.

However the Falcon thought he had achieved one thing: his wife was with child. Satisfied with his prowess he had left to return to France after giving her permission to go to Furness Grange, where she would be out of circulation for balls and the possible attentions of other men. Analee would be safe at Derwentwater, so reckoned the Falcon.

Now they were under the shadow of Blencathra and great purple Skiddaw was ahead of them. At last, in the distance, Analee could discern the narrow ribbon of Derwentwater; it grew broader the nearer they got to it until she could almost see its entire sweep ending in her beloved Borrowdale. In her mind's eye she could see the Grange nestling in the hollow by the side of the lake, the smoke rising from the chimneys that would have been lit in anticipation. Nelly opened her eyes and sat up.

'Where are we Analee?'

'At Keswick, nearly. Oh Nell, I feel as excited as a young girl.'

Nelly smiled at Analee and sat back. Perhaps she too was recalling those old gypsy days, and wondering if she were better off. At times she didn't know. Now both the Falcon and Analee were opposed to her marriage to McNeath; the Falcon because he wished McNeath to be his body servant, and Analee because she had taken against McNeath after he had told the Falcon about her and Brent. Nelly understood; in her heart she thought he'd been weak too, despite the threat of losing his most precious possession. Ever loyal to Analee, Nelly had become less enamoured of her swain.

Nelly shook the sleeping Clare, sighing deeply. She would be a spinster, that was for sure, serving her beloved Analee all her days. Oh well, there were worse fates. She had Analee's little girl to care for, and soon the new baby already nearly four months in Analee's womb. And what a special infant that would be! Indeed, the fact that she was carrying the Prince's child seemed to have done something to Analee, given her a serenity that enabled her to withstand the Falcon's jealous taunts, the sneers and criticism of her that had so transformed their marriage.

When the Falcon had been particularly slighting or abusive

440

Nelly would observe Analee resting tranquilly, her eyes on some far distant place that only she could see, her hands joined protectively across her belly. And then she might catch Nelly's eye and give her a smile based on mutual understanding and complicity, as though to say 'Let him talk as he likes. We have a secret, have we not Nell?'

Clare was a lively, excited child and she bobbed up and down looking out of the window as they rolled into Keswick and drove up to the landing stage at the side of the lake. There they were greeted by Nat and Francis Hardcastle who had served the Allonby family since they were youths and whose mother, Betty, was now housekeeper at Furness Grange. Little had changed in the Grange since Lord Falconer had bought it for Analee. She liked it as it was and, except for a coat of paint and some refurnishing, the addition of more staff, the place remained the same.

Nat Hardcastle had been working in the woods with Stewart Allonby the day Analee and Nelly had first arrived in the autumn of 1745. As he went to get her boxes Nat could not help recalling the day, and thought that though the gypsy had changed and become such a lady there was still the same earthy quality about her now as there was then, the same good humoured charm and friendliness that she bestowed on all, high and low. To Nat this was the mark of quality; it was what distinguished the nobility from the new rich like Mr Rigg who was either too familiar with his servants or too severe.

'The boat is ready, my lady. Your servants arrived with your luggage yesterday and the house is warm and the beds aired, not that my mother doesn't keep the place in good condition all the year round.'

'I know she does Nat; but it is nearly a year since we were here.'

'Is it as long as that, my lady?'

'Yes, ten months ago. We were here in April. How is your mother Nat?'

She allowed him to hand her into the boat and make her comfortable while Francis stowed the bags in the stern and helped Nelly to settle. Nelly felt the firm clasp of Francis's strong hand and gave him a quick glance. Yes, he was looking at her alright, out of the corner of his eye.

She was facing him as he took up the oars and pulled away from the shore with firm strong strokes. It was a fully laden boat, containing baggage and five people, yet Francis handled it as though it were a mere skiff. His muscles bulged under his thick jersey and his thighs rippled beneath his breeches as he pulled strenuously backwards and forwards. He wasn't a bad looking man, Nelly thought idly, clasping Clare against the cold – strong too. He wasn't as tall as McNeath, but he was very well built . . . Nelly gave a satisfied little half-smile and gazed across the lake to where in the distance she fancied she could see the Grange.

It was a cold day in late February and the sky was of that washed wintry blue that seems to presage the spring. The mist rose at the end of the lake so that the hills surrounding Borrowdale appeared to rise out of nowhere. The high peaks were tinged with the late afternoon sun, but the lower fells were deep in shadow. Nelly thought how clearly the contrasts were defined in this cold beautiful landscape. Everything was etched so distinctly on one's eye the birds flying low over the lake, the fish seen skimming beneath the surface as though aware of their predators, the islands that lay between here and Furness; above all, the reflection of the hills and fells, the trees and sharp rocky crags in the crystal clear water.

Pulled by Francis's strong muscles the boat flew swiftly over the water as the house on the lakeside loomed gradually nearer. Then they were there, and on the jetty more servants waited to catch the painter and tie it securely and help the mistress of the house alight.

Analee, weary from travelling in the cramped confines of the coach and boat, shook herself as she sniffed the sharp pungent air. 'Oh it feels so good! The air here is different from anywhere in the world. It is compounded of heather and woodsmoke and the cold clear water that falls from the hills. I know nothing like it. My spirits soar just to know I am here.'

'And right glad we are to welcome you, ma'am.' Betty Hardcastle, pink cheeked and jovial, dropped a curtsy. 'It has been a long winter without you.'

'Oh Betty, did you miss us?'

'Aye, we did; we know how well you like it here. See, ma'am, all is prepared for you.' Betty turned round to scold the servants scurrying here and there with boxes and luggage. 'Be quick now with her ladyship's things, don't dally. And how is my little Lady Clare?' Betty bent down and took her by the hand, planting a warm kiss on her pale cheeks. 'Cold my little one? Give old Betty a kiss then.'

'Get her inside, Betty and Nell, because it is cold. I just want to go on looking at the sight around me before it is dark.' Analee took a deep breath and was wandering off away from the jetty when Betty gave her an agitated look and made another respectful curtsy.

'If you please, ma'am, a gentleman is awaiting you.'

'A gentleman? Who?' Analee could see the nervousness on Betty's face, the way her eyes darted from one side to another.

''Tis Mr Brent, ma'am, Miss Mary's husband.' Betty pursed her lips in an expression of severe disapproval and shrugged her shoulders.

'Brent Delamain *here*? Tell him to be gone at once!'

Analee put out an imperious hand in a gesture of dismissal and looked as though she was about to resume her walk.

'Oh, begging your ladyship's pardon, but I cannot do that. I have not the right, ma'am, not the power.'

Analee looked at Nelly, who raised her eyes heavenwards in a gesture of despair.

'Then, Nelly, you must do it. He has no right here. If it came to the ears of his lordship . . . I would be sent straight back to Falcon's Keep.'

'I think he does not mean to linger, ma'am,' said Betty. 'He has had his horse saddled and ready since dinner time when he arrived. He says he has something urgent to say. He says he will not detain you.'

'He had better not.'

Analee threw back her shoulders and walked purposefully in through the front door, across the large hall where a fire was leaping up the chimney and into the drawing room that ran the length of the house facing the lake.

Brent was standing with his back to the fire, his hands clasped behind him. In the dusk the bright gold of his hair silhouetted against the fire seemed like a halo around his head. He wore travelling dress and high boots grimy with dust. When he saw her

443

enter he did not move, but she perceived how he raised his head and seemed to stiffen.

'Analee,' he whispered.

'Nelly, fetch candles,' Analee called out to Nelly who had hastened in behind her, and Nelly promptly doubled back to do her bidding.

Whenever he saw her he felt the same pounding of the heart, the constriction in the throat. Now she was outlined against the candelabra in the hall, the glow of the great log fire behind her. The hood of her black velvet cloak had fallen back from her head and to him she seemed like some shadowy emanation of the past, her proud head raised interrogatively, her eyes like deep molten pools gleaming in the flickering orange light of the fire.

'Brent,' she said scarcely above a whisper. 'What madness is it that brings you here? His lordship . . .'

'Oh I am well aware of his jealousy, and I would not imperil you for an instance my love. I know that the servants here are loyal to you; but even then I will not tarry for a moment longer than I need.'

Brent came swiftly over to her and seized her hands, kissing them and then holding them to his breast.

'Oh my Analee, always mine and one day completely mine, I know. I am here just to ask you a favour on behalf of my sister Emma. You are the only one I can turn to. But quick, before Nelly comes with the candles, let me feel your lips beneath mine.'

She raised her head and saw once again those eyes, the curve of the mouth, the cleft in his strong chin. Whenever she saw him it was but briefly, yet each time it was as though they had never been parted, that their life was one long journey together instead of a series of disconnected episodes. Yes, she did want Brent Delamain, and she opened her lips as his mouth approached hers. Tenderly at first, then, as he felt her own desire, he kissed her with increasing passion. He closed his eyes to try and imprison in his memory forever the rapture he felt. But when he opened them again he saw Nelly advancing into the room with the candles, and he gently withdrew his mouth from hers, with a final tender kiss.

Analee's eyes were closed as Brent drew back. He still possessed a strange power over her, so that she felt an urgent and immediate desire to yield to him as she had in the forest.

444

'The candles, ma'am.'

Nelly glanced curiously at her mistress and Mr Delamain entwined in front of the fire. She would gladly leave them alone together and lock the doors if they wished, so that her mistress, after suffering so much at the hands of the Falcon, could find some happiness with Brent.

'Thank you, Nelly. Leave us now; but keep the door open. I do not want tales to go back to his lordship. You may stay by the door, Nelly, and be sure no one else approaches.'

'Yes ma'am.' Nelly obediently positioned herself by the door, her ears hopefully alert. What a pair they made! He led her over to the fire and seated her in the tall chair in front of it. With her cloak open over her red velvet dress, what a picture her ladyship looked – enough to excite the heart of any man!

And Mr Delamain . . . he seemed to get more handsome as time passed, his face leaner and more attractive, yet his body still sturdy and muscular. Looking at them, Nelly thought it was the contrast between the blond and the dark that made them such an impressive couple. Would that they could always be together! His head was bent towards Analee and he was speaking very swiftly.

'Analee, I have promised help to Emma who wishes to join Stewart in America. I am the only one who can help her and you are the only one who can assist us.'

'How?'

'By inviting her to stay with you. They know what she has in mind and my elder brother George keeps her like a prisoner in his castle. She came to see Ambrose last month and he would have helped her but his wife forbade it. Ambrose is fearful of offending George with whom he does much business. Anyway, he thinks it foolish, nay even wrong, for my sister to run after a man who no longer writes to her.'

'Stewart no longer writes to Emma?' Analee looked up, startled.

'No, not for a year. Up to then he wrote regularly about his life in Maryland where he was a forester to a Scottish plantation owner.'

'Maybe he has come to harm?'

'That is what Emma fears. Ambrose opines that he has found another sweetheart.'

445

Analee stared into the flames, aware of Brent's proximity. She thought that she always felt so close to Brent because of Morella – the daughter he did not know he had. One day she would tell him; but not yet.

'And what do you think?'

'I know not; but whatever anyone thinks, Emma has a strong mind and is determined to go and find Stewart.'

'Can you not write to him and ask?'

'There is no time. I have found a boat which will take her to Nantes and then to America at the beginning of April.'

'Why should you help Emma if everyone is against it? Is it wise Brent?'

'It is because everyone *is* against it that I will do it, to spite my brother above all. And it is Emma's happiness I wish. Knowing as I do what it is to love and have my love rejected . . .'

'I do not reject your love, Brent. But it is impossible, things being what they are. Another time, another place . . . all might have been different.'

'But he is a monster. I heard he almost disfigured you . . .'

'He is very jealous. He was mad with jealousy over you. He sensed something between us and it turned his mind after the blow you fetched him. His servant McNeath fuelled the flames which ate into his brain by telling him we had met before, when I was a gypsy. He guessed the rest though I did not tell him he was right. Since then he has grown increasingly suspicious and watches me all the time. It is the reason he does not take me back to France and forbids me to go to our house in London. He sees lovers or Jacobite traitors everywhere.' Analee gave him a mischievous smile. 'I think he would have a seizure if he knew that by letting me come here he was putting us directly in each other's paths!' She put up a hand to take his, and he kissed it and held it to his heart.

'One day we will be together Analee. I know not how, but 'twill happen. A gypsy told me so.'

'A gypsy! Another one!' Analee laughed.

'I met her on the road as we retreated towards Scotland. She carried a sickly baby in her arms and I told her to go to my mother who was nearby. My mother has kept the child – you may have heard – and the gypsy moved on. But she looked at me and told me I would suffer much but one day I would find happiness.'

'And her name?' Analee asked, to confirm what she already knew.

'Ah I have forgot . . . let me see.' Brent clasped his hand to his eyes in an effort to remember. 'She said . . . yes, I have it. "Remember it is the gypsy woman Reyora, the *cohani*, who told you these things."'

Reyora. What a part fate played in her life! Reyora – who had attended her when Morella was born, who had saved the child from death when the Scots decimated the camp of the Buckland gypsies. She had known that Brent and Reyora had met on the road . . . Now Reyora had promised him happiness.

'Do you know her?' Brent said eagerly.

'I . . . can't remember. 'Tis of no importance. Now Brent, if you are determined and Emma is determined, then I will help you. Tell me what I must do.'

'Simply ask her to stay with you. Your husband is Henrietta's cousin. 'Twill seem quite natural. Then I will fetch her from here and take her to Laxey in the Isle of Man from where I operate to Nantes in France and Port Rush in Ireland.'

'What do you do, Brent?'

'I smuggle for Ambrose – wine and brandy from France, tea from India, tobacco from America. It all goes through Nantes and Port Rush and Whitehaven and then by packhorses over the fells of Cumberland and Westmorland and into England. But I also smuggle arms to be lodged in Scotland and various parts of the north of England in the event of another rising.'

'A *Jacobite* rising?'

'Of course. What else?' He smiled at her gently, but Analee could detect a weary note in his voice; gone was the enthusiasm of the past.

'You think it is possible?'

'Anything is possible – though I do not think it likely. The Prince is in hiding, hunted by spies and would-be assassins sent by King George. The King of France will have naught to do with him because he wants peace with England. However, we go on hoping. 'Tis all we can do . . .'

The Prince. Analee remembered that magic night when the last hope of the Stuarts had held her in his arms . . . a frightened young boy seeking only love and protection. One not well versed in the art of making love. She had never seen him again. She put a hand to her belly. How incredible that she was carrying his child . . . how proud she felt! Yes, she and his Cause were one, and she and Brent were one.

'I will help you all I can, in any way, at any time. But now, Brent, you must go. I will write to your mother . . .'

'Could you not go over? Offer to fetch Emma back with you? I know it would help. Otherwise they might think of an excuse to prevent her.'

'You want me to go to Delamain Castle?' Analee was aware of her heart racing. She had left Morella when she was a week old. Morella, her daughter . . . Brent's daughter.

'Yes I urge it. It is the only way. Then I will come and fetch Emma in the last week of March. Will you do it for me, Analee?'

Analee looked up at him, feeling her love for him deepening with every moment they shared.

'For you, anything Brent.'

He looked at her and he looked at Nelly, sitting quietly by the wide open door. He bent and swiftly brushed Analee's lips.

'Farewell, my heart. I will see you again soon, and one day it will be forever. Remember the gypsy.'

Analee smiled and pressed his hand, kissing it lightly. 'I will remember.'

She sat still as he swiftly left the room preceded by Nelly. She was aware of voices, doors opening and closing and then the thud of a horse's hooves receding from the house, taking him away from her. Despite the heat she felt a sudden chill and pulled her cloak about her shoulders, and then she sat for a long time staring into the fire, her eyes wet with unshed tears.

The snows had left Lakeland and a few birds were making tentative sorties to the bare hayfields looking for straw for their nests when Analee drove up, unannounced, to Delamain Castle to keep her promise to Brent.

She had let a week pass to rest and gather her thoughts after his departure. There was plenty of time, and in that week the tranquillity of life at Furness had infused itself into her soul, and given her fresh heart and hope, and resolution. Yes, she was committed to Brent and the Cause, and the Prince. The powerful, brutal Falcon, who she knew organized spies to seek out the Prince and kill him, was her husband in name only. Whatever destiny she and Brent had she would wait for, patiently, knowing that it was far off but that, if Reyora had said it would happen, it would.

Lady Delamain was resting when Analee was announced. She was expecting a child and had not been well, following the pattern of her first confinement – sickness and headaches, nausea and dizziness all the time.

The first child, Mildred, had nearly died at birth and Lady Delamain had been warned not to have another. But as long as she could breed Henrietta Delamain would. Without an heir to his estates her husband would lose interest in her. She knew quite well he had married her for her money and her breeding potential and, having fulfilled one part of the bargain with her dowry, she was determined on honouring the other.

If she did not produce an heir, in the event of George's death the estates would go to his hated brother Brent, a Jacobite fugitive and renegade.

Lady Falconer. The name was enough to make Henrietta rise from her bed immediately. She had never met this intriguing gypsy Angus had married. True, a common gypsy was the last person someone of her quality would in ordinary circumstances expect to be acquainted with. But the circumstances were not ordinary and this was no common gypsy. Besides, Angus had made her his wife, an honour sufficient to ennoble the meanest. As one of the most eminent men in the country, he was practically above the law.

Henrietta had the maid dress her hair and help her into an afternoon robe in a becoming shade of pink that she hoped would reflect a little colour onto her sallow cheeks. Then she dabbed on plenty of rouge and descended quickly to the drawing room.

Lady Falconer, resplendent in a black velvet travelling cloak open to reveal a royal blue costume, was standing at the window gazing out over the forest of Delamain that stretched away from the formal gardens as far as the eye could see. She turned as Henrietta came towards her, her hand outstretched.

'Lady Delamain, pray do forgive this unexpected call. I . . .'

'There is no need to explain my dear Marchioness. I am most honoured by your visit. Besides I have longed to meet you. Angus has always promised to show you to us but never has.'

The women embraced and Henrietta took Analee's cloak and showed her to the comfortable sofa that faced the window, sitting down beside her.

'Alas, his lordship has been at the war since his recovery from his wound. I scarcely saw him myself until he took me to France with him.'

'And now he leaves you again, Lady Falconer?'

Analee ignored the malicious tone of Henrietta's question and inclined her head in the direction of her hostess's protruding stomach.

'Like yourself I am *enceinte*, Lady Delamain. I expect a child in the summer. I asked his lordship's permission to stay in the countryside I love so much and he was good enough to agree.'

Henrietta digested this interesting scrap of information, and patted her own distended stomach.

'Alas, I suffer from sickness all the time I am carrying my baby. It was the same with the first. I have not been well, dear Lady Falconer, I regret to say.'

Analee could see she was ill and her sympathetic nature gave her a bond with Henrietta she would not otherwise have felt. Nothing could have been more different than the personalities of the two women: Henrietta small, plain, calculating, aware of her money and her position; so different from Analee whose looks and disposition were enhanced by her generous nature and compassionate impulses.

She had heard nothing but ill of Sir George Delamain, Brent's brother – how he was grasping, ambitious and mean natured and had turned his brothers out of the family home on the death of their grandfather.

Suddenly Analee leaned forward, her eye caught by movement on the lawn and the sound of childish laughter. Her heart missed a beat as she saw a small girl, well wrapped up against the cold March air, running up and down with a puppy, both chased by a woman who looked like a maidservant. Morella – it could only be Morella, that fair haired beauty, issue of herself and Brent one moonlit night, oh such a long time ago, before the Rebellion.

How vividly she remembered Morella's birth in the gypsy tent, attended only by Nelly and the occasional ministrations of Reyora the *cohani* – how the child had seemed to wedge in the birth passage until Reyora and Rebecca the *phuri-dai*, headwoman of the tribe, had made a magic incantation to relieve her.

'What a beautiful child!' Analee said when she had gained control of her emotions. 'But she is too old to be yours, I think, Lady Delamain?'

'Mildred is but a year old Lady Falconer. This is the ward of my mother-in-law, a foundling left with her during the Rebellion. Her name is Morella.'

'I did hear about her,' Analee said slowly. 'She belongs to a gypsy woman who met Brent Delamain on the road.'

'My husband's brother can never do anything right. He directed this woman and child to my mother-in-law as the child was ill. It was obviously just the gypsy woman's wiles to be rid of her responsibility and run away. She said she was not the mother of the child but no one believes her. She had obviously lain with some non-gypsy, a soldier maybe, and got herself into this disgraceful condition, and when she saw she was well off abandoned her baby.'

Analee bit back the words which rose in her mouth like bile. Instead she forced a smile. 'She is a very lovely little girl.'

'Oh she is enchanting, there is no doubt. My mother-in-law is devoted to her; but Sir George is insistent we do not let her into this house if we can help it for fear her influence, her bad blood, should corrupt our own children. Oh here is my husband.'

Analee, frozen into fury by Henrietta's words, tried hard to compose her features in front of Sir George who crossed the room to greet his visitor.

'Lady Falconer, may I present my husband, Sir George Delamain. My love, this is Angus's wife come to pay us a visit.'

Sir George bowed low over Analee's hand.

'Indeed, ma'am, I heard you had arrived and came as quick as I could. We have heard of the beauty of the Marquess's bride,' he gazed at her as he raised his head, 'and now that is confirmed for us to see.'

'You are very kind, Sir George. But I am not here without a purpose. I have come to ask you a favour.'

Yes, she had a job to do, a promise to keep. Analee tried hard to conquer her dislike of Brent's brother and sister-in-law.

'Say it, Marchioness, and it shall be done.'

451

Sir George sat down with a flourish and took his tortoiseshell snuff box from his vest pocket. He was as tall as Brent and well proportioned, but as dark as his brother was fair, with deep set brown eyes and thick brows that met over his long supercilious nose. He had a very thin mouth, quite unlike Brent's full generous one, and the lower part of his face was dark as though he could not get a sufficiently close shave. He wore a plain brown suit over a yellow waistcoat, yellow stockings and shoes with large square buckles. He had on a full bottomed wig, and a cambric handkerchief edged with lace and stained brown with snuff trailed out of his large coat pocket.

He did not look the aristocrat as Brent and the Allonby family did; more a man of business, a successful merchant whose life was dominated by greed and ambition. Had she not good reason to dislike him already, he was not a man who would in any way have attracted Analee.

However these emotions she kept to herself, aware that he was ogling her in front of his wife. A silly simpering smile on his thin mouth made him look shifty and dishonest.

'I would borrow your sister for a few days. I need company and I have heard she is such an attractive girl.'

'You have met Emma?'

'I have never had that pleasure; but his lordship speaks so well of her and 'twas he made the suggestion.'

Although this was not true, Analee knew it was a lie that would have a good effect on her host and hostess. They were quite obviously so in awe of the power and importance of Lord Falconer that for him even to wish something was to have it obsequiously put into immediate effect.

'Ah the Marquess *has* met my sister. I recall it now, do you not my dear Henrietta? He came here during the Rebellion and stopped the night. How kind of his lordship to think of her! Indeed Lady Falconer, I'll not hide it from you, we should be glad to have Emma from hence where she is moping about all day.'

'George wishes to send her to London,' said Henrietta, 'but we do not have a chaperone for her, my interesting condition keeping me at home. It is the very thing Lady Falconer! How perspicacious of his lordship and kind of *you*.'

Sir George got up and swept her a deep fulsome bow. Then he

went to the fireplace and pulled a bell to summon a servant, who appeared almost immediately as though lying in wait behind the door.

'Fetch Miss Delamain from the dower house. I have a visitor for her.'

Sir George paced delightedly up and down rubbing his hands. 'Capital. She will be in safe hands and it will give her some occupation.'

'Pray, in what way is she not safe Sir George?' Analee raised her naturally arched eyebrows.

'She is in love, ma'am, I regret to say, with her worthless cousin Stewart Allonby.' Sir George turned away, his face registering apparent despair. 'That rogue whom I saved from the gallows at her behest, using the influence I had with men of importance in London. Indeed, I confess I also had the family name to think of, as my own brother was incarcerated in Edinburgh Castle, and my first cousin in Carlisle. You may imagine the shame on our family ma'am, I being among the most loyal of King George's subjects. As I knew Stewart had taken little part in the fighting and was apathetic to the Pretender's cause, I bestirred myself to please my sister. And I was successful. His sentence was commuted to deportation and there he languishes, Marchioness, on a plantation in Maryland out of harm's way – unlike my brother Brent who is up to all sorts of mischief again, so I have heard.'

Sir George gave a realistic growl that reminded Analee of a ferocious mastiff which had had its teeth drawn and so could not get at its prey.

'My sister pines for Stewart, instead of being grateful that her cousin is spared; instead of putting him out of her mind and looking around for a suitable young man, of whom there are plenty eager for her, as I needn't tell you Lady Falconer. She is *my* sister, and we Delamains go back to before the Conqueror; besides which I have considerable estates, a substantial town house and am by way of making a fresh fortune in business – '

'Yes George,' Henrietta interrupted testily. 'I am sure Lady Falconer is not concerned with your fortune – it is evident enough – but more with the *reason* that your stupid sister pursues this young man who is so unworthy of her in every way.'

There was a common, boastful streak to her husband that

Henrietta despised. Sometimes she wondered where it came from, because the Delamains were in fact impeccably descended.

'I think I can understand a young woman's heart,' Analee said softly. 'She loved him, and now that he is an exile why should she love him less?'

The logic of this did not appeal to the Delamains who, each having married the other for their own practical ends, gazed at her uncomprehendingly as though they had absolutely no understanding of how the heart could overcome the head.

At that moment there was a rustle by the door and, pale-faced and anxious, Emma Delamain stood there gazing half fearfully at her brother, half curiously at Analee.

'Ah my dear Emma . . .' George went over to her and seized her arm effusively. 'Look who has come to visit us. None other than the Marchioness of Falconer, the wife of Henrietta's famous cousin, Lord Falconer, whom you met here some years past.'

Emma – who hated the name of Falconer, knowing what harm he had caused to the Jacobites – shuddered involuntarily. Yet, although she did not know for sure, she suspected Analee had helped to free Brent. It was a matter he said he was sworn not to discuss. So the powerful Marchioness *might* be a friend, though married to a foe. She went timidly over to Analee and dropped her a brief curtsy.

Analee saw a tall unhappy looking girl, who had once been beautiful. She had fine features, deep set eyes, brown like her brother George's. But whereas they tended to make him look devious, in her they were feminine and attractive. But there were dark hollows around them as though she did not sleep well and what had been a buxom figure, judging by the way her dress hung upon her, was now thin and scraggy.

Analee saw the suspicion in those brown eyes as they looked at her and her heart went out to her in pity and also in rage – rage at the circumstances that had taken the looks of a young nubile girl who once had everything to live for, and rage at the Delamains who understood her so imperfectly. Besides, this was Brent's sister. How often her thoughts turned to him in tenderness and love, and this emotion shone from her eyes as she gazed at Emma trying to convey to her that she was here indeed as a friend.

Analee got up and went over to Emma, not to embrace her

because that would have embarassed and maybe angered her. But she took her hand and pressed it and the full force of her tender, understanding gaze was enough to transform Emma's prejudice and suspicion into curiosity and even hope.

'Lady Falconer would have you visit with her. *There*.' Sir George puffed out his chest importantly. The suspicion returned to Emma's eyes and she backed away from Analee.

'But I know not her ladyship . . .'

Sir George intervened between Emma and the door and grasped her wrist.

'Come, come child. Her ladyship is related to my wife by marriage. It is the Falcon himself, none other, that has spoken of you. He would have you keep her ladyship company in that beautiful castle on the Scots border.'

'Oh no,' Analee said quickly. 'I am at Furness – on Lake Derwentwater . . .'

'Furness! Your ladyship is at Furness?' Emma clasped her hands in front of her, her eyes shining.

Analee nodded, speaking quickly. 'My husband bought the Grange for me because I love it so well. Your cousins were so good to me there. I hold it in trust against their eventual return.'

'You mean you would give it back to them?' Emma said incredulously, and Sir George and his wife looked aghast at such un-Delamain-like altruism.

'Of course. I thought if we had the house it would be in good hands. Rather that than have it go to complete strangers. So if John or,' Analee looked keenly at Emma, 'Stewart or their sister Mary were ever to be in a position to claim it again 'twould be restored to them. I want you to think of it as a home for you too, Emma . . .'

'Stewart grew up there,' Emma said brokenly.

Sir George looked annoyed and cleared his throat. 'I must confess I thought your ladyship was at his lordship's border home, Falcon's Keep. I did not realize that Furness, which has so many memories for Emma –'

'Oh but George,' Emma cried, her face completely transformed in joy, 'I would love to go there! It would revive my spirits. How kind of her ladyship, *and* his lordship to think of me. May I accompany you back Lady Falconer?'

'Of course child, if your brother and mother allow. I hoped they would.' Analee thought George was about to demur, but Henrietta got heavily to her feet and put a restraining hand on his arm.

'Of course they will. How fortunate, George, that Lady Falconer will escort Emma there. Is it not so?'

'I suppose so,' George said ungraciously.

'Then quick, Emma, go and ask your mother's permission and pack as soon as you can. That way we shall be there by nightfall.'

'But Lady Falconer, do stay a night with us. You will have a long journey. How is it that you were here so early?'

'I stayed at an inn in Penrith. If we leave within the hour we shall be home today. Thank you Sir George; but I should like to return to Furness. May I go with Emma, do you think, and meet her mother?'

Brent's mother – Morella's grandmother. Analee felt her voice choke with emotion and hoped her host and hostess would attribute it to some indisposition of the throat. Analee knew that part of her motive in coming here was to see Morella, despite Nelly's advice. Nelly had been against it. But Analee, daily observing Clare, yearned to see her first-born. Just to see her, she promised Nelly, nothing more.

With a lot of fussing and bowing, George escorted his sister and Analee over to the dower house where Mrs Delamain lived with her daughter and, although she did not know it, her granddaughter.

8

From the open doorway of the house they heard laughter. The happy scene Analee had seen being enacted on the lawn was carrying on inside the house. A little colour had come back to Emma's face and she smiled at Analee who was trying to conceal her own nervousness. Why had she done this? Why had she not left well alone? After all . . .

'Come here, come here child!' A door burst open and the little blonde girl came tumbling into the hall pursued by her nurse.

'Miss Morella! I have told her . . .'

'Oh leave her, Grace . . .'

Emma's mother, Susan, leaned heavily on a stick. Although only in her early fifties she looked as though she carried ten or fifteen years more. She was tall and gaunt and her sunken cheeks, white hair and bloodless lips made her seem quite an old lady. Susan, born an Allonby, had seen more tragedy than most people either expected or deserved seemed to have nothing left to live for until darling Morella had come so unexpectedly into her life. Morella, her treasure . . .

Susan was staring at the woman George had brought – a lady rather, undoubtedly a fine one. She was the tallest woman Susan had ever seen and her figure, though voluptuous, was slender in the right places – the neck, and the waist which curved under her well fitting royal blue jacket bodice. She had a very full bosom which rose from the round *décolletage* and her hair, which gleamed like black lacquer, was pinned up in a high knot while a thick stray lock curling up at the end fell onto her bosom.

But it was the expression on the woman's face that Susan found riveting. She appeared quite unconcerned with those about her, indeed seemed not to know they were there, while she gazed at the small child who was trying to escape her nurse's clutches in the hall, screaming with delighted laughter at the same time.

Little Morella, cornered in a right angle of the wall, started squealing and giggling as the nurse caught her and raised her high

457

above her head, squeezing her fondly at the same time. From high up over the nurse's head, Morella gazed down upon the scene of visiting grown ups, and she too seemed as taken by the visitor as the lady was with her. She stuck a finger in her mouth and her expression became very solemn. Her large blue eyes grew wide, and it was as though she had set to studying her as she would an object of intense fascination.

Analee held out her arms and went over to the nurse, still heedless of the company.

'May I take her?'

Analee reached up for Morella and clasped her in her arms drawing her against her bosom and pressing her cheek against the curly blonde head. Analee shut her eyes, knowing they were moist with tears and prayed that she would not shed them. Oh the darling, the treasure . . . her own baby, smelling of soft scented soap and lotions. She wore a dress of pretty patterned blue muslin with long sleeves, and the leading strings sewn to the back armholes trailed over her mother's dress.

Morella lay quite happily in her mother's arms, resting her head on her breast in an attitude of quiet contentment. The scene seemed to be encapsulated in time so that it was remembered long afterwards by those who observed it and later came to know the truth.

'She is such a darling,' Analee murmured unsteadily, taking hold of herself, willing the tears to evaporate. 'I could not resist hugging her. My daughter Clare is a little younger. They would make lovely playmates.'

Carefully she put Morella down on the floor and then knelt and put her arms round her.

'Do you say anything darling? Can you tell me your name?'

'Morella,' her daughter obliged in a clear silvery tone.

'My name is Analee.'

'An'lee,' Morella repeated, still fascinated by the stranger, magnetized by the colour of her dress, the lustre of her eyes, the warmth of her expression.

Analee hugged her again and got to her feet.

'She is adorable.'

'Mother, may I present Lady Falconer – the Marchioness of Falconer, mother.' Then, quick to realize her mother's initial reaction would be the same as her own, Emma hurried on. 'Lady Falconer is a great friend of Mary's, mother. She has bought Furness Grange and says she means to hold it in trust for the Allonbys . . .'

'Should they ever return, Mrs Delamain.' Analee went over to Susan and took her hand. 'And I know it was your home too. I received at Furness the most wonderful hospitality which I shall have cause to remember all my life. It came at a desperate and important part of my life and I shall never forget it.

'I also fell in love with the place and its beauty. I would like Emma to be with me there and I have come to ask if I may borrow her from you?'

Susan Delamain was aware of the warmth emanating from the person who was addressing her, but also of another curious quality – power. Somehow Analee had a control over their lives, their destinies, in a way she could not then understand. It was as though she was standing in the presence of someone familiar, someone she had known for a long time – not a total stranger at all.

She felt as if she trusted Analee so implicitly that she would put her life in her hands; hers and that of her daughter. It was an odd sensation, and as she looked deep into those fathomless dark eyes she felt as though she was being drawn into a vortex that was both all enveloping and wholly beneficial. She smiled at Analee. 'If Emma wishes it, of course. I know she has been unhappy of late. Do you wish it, Emma?'

Her mother turned to her, aware already of the change that had taken place in her daughter. The awful lifelessness that had possessed her since her return from Cockermouth had given place to something more like her usual self – hope and vitality. If anyone could restore her daughter it was this remarkable woman.

Analee stayed half an hour with Susan Delamain while Emma quickly packed. They talked and played with Morella and, drawn together by love for the child, they established a rapport that Susan never remembered forming so quickly with a woman before. Susan told her about Emma and Stewart, of her own fears that he had formed a new attachment. For her part Analee didn't dare betray Brent's trust, hoping that in time the mother would forgive her for letting her daughter go. Something in the way she spoke, however, made Analee think that Susan knew the purpose

459

of her visit – that it was to take her daughter from her, maybe for a long time.

But above all Susan observed how Analee played with the little girl, with such gentleness and love, such tenderness, that she might have been her own daughter. And how the child responded to Analee, so much so that when she stood holding her grand-mother's hand waving from the door she kneaded her little fists in her eyes and began to cry.

'Pretty lady,' she wailed, 'nice lady!'

The nice lady looked out of the window of her carriage which had been brought to the door of the dower house and waved and smiled. When the horses set off she kept her head turned towards the doorway and her eyes on the small child who stood there, until the carriage disappeared round the drive and was out of sight.

Susan Delamain clasped Morella's hand tightly in her own and walked slowly indoors. She had always thought that Reyora was the baby's mother, though she said she was not. Susan imagined she had lain with a non-gypsy and was ashamed of the fact.

Now she wondered again. Reyora had said Morella was the daughter of a gypsy woman, but nothing more.

And Susan, who was wise in the ways of the world, wondered to herself if Analee could possibly be the baby's mother, but was unable to admit it for reasons Susan could guess.

The tenderness with which she had embraced her, played with her, kept her eyes on the child until the carriage was out of sight . . . and the baby had loved her too.

Susan took the child on her knee in front of the fire and played with her blonde curly locks, hugging her close. 'Maybe you saw your mother today my darling. Maybe you did. I wonder, shall we ever know? Imagine, if the great Lady Falconer were Morella's mother.'

Emma leaned back in the carriage and watched the turrets of Delamain Castle recede out of sight. Beside them was the river that ran all the way to Penrith and they largely followed it until they took the turning off to Keswick just out of the town.

Analee too was gazing at the river and thinking of her last visit to Delamain Castle – as a horse thief. Brent had surprised the intruders in the grounds and had almost captured her. Then she had returned to Appleby and thence to Penrith with the Buckland family, following the course of this same river.

It was strange how a part of the country, the north of England, that she had never seen in her life before 1745 was becoming as dear to her as any native land. It was much dearer than the south where she had been born and through which she had wandered for the first twenty years of her life.

So, wrapped in their thoughts, the two women passed the first few miles of their journey in silence. The road, because it was much used, was a good one. It formed one of the main highways from the north to the south and the horses, fed and rested, maintained a good pace, the steady rhythm of their hooves providing a restful accompaniment to the preoccupations of the two women in the coach.

Analee glanced at the girl opposite her, only two years her junior. Yet what a wealth of experience divided them: Emma, carefully nurtured in a castle, expecting to marry a man of her status, a wealthy northern landowner like her brother perhaps. Then the circumstances that brought about the '45 Rebellion, her love for her brave cousin Stewart, and her subsequent unhappiness.

She looked a girl accustomed to sadness, but to whom hope had come within the last few hours. Emma saw Analee's gaze and smiled.

'You have come to take me away, haven't you?'

'You knew?'

'Well . . . Brent managed to get a message to me that he would contrive to have me taken from the Castle without George suspecting. Now I know it must be you. At first I was afraid of you because of the reputation of your husband; but I am sure you must be a friend.'

'I *am* a friend,' Analee said. 'I am doing as Brent asked me. He has found a boat to take you to America.'

Emma clasped her hands and her eyes shone. 'America and Stewart!'

'My dear, I have to ask you this – are you sure you should go?'

'Sure? Quite sure. Stewart and I are pledged to each other forever, Lady Falconer. He gave me his word and I mine to him. He had loved me for a long time, you know, and blindly I did not see his qualities. But the Rebellion changed all that. How proud I was of him: he gave up everything for the Cause just like my father and my Uncle Robert. I began to despise the foppish young men who surrounded me, whose concern was only with idleness and dissipation.'

Analee remembered the spell she had given Stewart; he had been in despair over Emma's indifference to him. It was she who was responsible for Emma falling in love, and now she must take the responsibility for helping to reunite them again. But was it the right thing? Analee was weighed down by her doubts.

'Would it not be better, my dear Emma, for someone to try and discover why Stewart stopped writing to you? Maybe . . .'

'He has found someone else?' Emma burst out indignantly. 'You do not know Stewart, Lady Falconer. He is a steadfast man if ever there was one. He would never betray his word to me. No, something prevents him writing – he has come to some harm or he is unhappy. A deep depression has taken hold of his spirits, maybe, and he can see no future for us. I *must* go to him and, with me by his side, everything will be different!'

Analee was impressed by Emma's spirit; but her doubts remained. She knew what separation could do to the human heart. It could distort men's ideas, make them fickle. She sighed; she could recall only one man who had remained constant through the utmost provocation, and that was the brother of the girl sitting opposite her: Brent Delamain. Would that he had proved less steadfast and she, Analee, would not have Mary's unhappiness on her conscience.

Spring usually came late to Lakeland, but that year soft breezes stirred at the end of March, wafting warm air from the south and from across the sea. The trees were still stark and bare, but little tendrils of green appeared on the bushes, and the daffodils and crocuses peeped through by the side of the lake and under the trees in the surrounding woods.

Analee and Emma spent a lot of time out of doors, walking along the shore with baby Clare toddling along with them as energetically as her little legs could carry her, carefully followed by Nelly. Usually when Nelly was around, Francis Hardcastle seemed to appear out of nowhere and walk beside her under the pretence of clearing their way through the leaves and thick undergrowth that sometimes impeded their progress. Analee observed how Francis gazed at Nelly, the way he seized every opportunity to put an arm around her, to help her over a fallen log or across a busy stream.

Analee was glad. Francis was a fine young man, and undoubtedly helped Nelly to put McNeath out of her mind.

But Emma was impatient for news of Brent. She spent hours gazing up at Catbells waiting for the first welcome sign of him riding down towards the Grange, or sitting in the dark listening for the sound of the horse's hooves.

The two women got on well enough, but Analee found Emma reserved, as though a prisoner of her thoughts. She also wondered if Emma slightly mistrusted her, because of her association with the Falcon, if she felt she had to be continually upon her guard. Emma certainly didn't confide in her, but seemed content to pass her days of waiting by reading, walking or looking dreamily out of the window.

Analee, however, respected her wish for solitude and did all she could to restore Emma's health and looks by ensuring that she ate and slept well, had plenty of rest and did not worry. But now that she had partly embarked on her journey Emma seemed more relaxed. The waiting time was over and her cheeks filled out, the dark surrounds disappeared from her eyes, and the lustre was restored to her thick dark hair. She would be a beauty again for Stewart, providing the rigours of the voyage did not undo all the good the tranquillity of Furness had done.

One day Emma was wandering in the woods in the company of Nelly and Clare. Analee had correspondence to see to and had told the others to take their exercise without her. Suddenly Emma looked up to the skyline and there, on the top of Catbells, sat a tall man on his horse about to begin the descent to the house.

'Oh Nelly, he is here! Brent is here!' Emma drew up her skirts and began a race along the shores of the lake, having to slow down from time to time because Clare was heavy in the arms of the panting Nelly.

Analee was at her desk, writing a perfunctory and dutiful account of her life to the Falcon in her slow careful hand, when she became aware of excitement in the yard followed by the sound of a horse's hooves. Her heart began beating quickly in her breast and she sat very still, willing herself to control it.

Then suddenly he was there. The sound of quick footsteps and his arms were around her, his face nuzzling into her neck. Oh the very feel of him, the familiar masculine smell, the panting breath on her cheeks after a hard ride!

'My love,' he murmured. 'Just a few fleeting moments alone with you. Why is it always thus?'

Analee turned to him, entwining her arms about his neck, pressing his face down on hers, their lips melting together, their bodies close as though they were one.

And it was thus that Emma found them, having run hard and left Nelly and Clare far behind. She stopped suddenly at the sight of the pair embracing, her face aflame with embarrassment and . . . was it anger? She coughed loudly.

Brent wrenched himself away and then, their arms still entwined, he and Analee gazed at Emma, their faces serene from the peace and satisfaction the knowledge of their love gave them.

'I'm sorry Emma,' Analee said at last parting from Brent, 'that you should find us thus. It must shock you.'

'I have loved her for years,' Brent said.

'I know you *once* loved her,' Emma said. 'But now she is wed, and a mother and expecting another child – '

'You are expecting another child?' Brent turned to Analee, his face pale with sudden anger.

'Yes. I am still my husband's wife, Brent. I have my duties to perform. You didn't think I could keep him out of my bed?'

'I hate the thought of him, that is all,' Brent exclaimed bitterly. 'And another child . . . !' He threw himself into a chair.

'Mary told me that you had once loved Analee,' Emma said as she walked slowly into the room, 'and that your love for her was such a passion it destroyed your marriage. She has written to me of her love for you, and now she has given up hope and gone to live in a convent as a nun! The Marchioness of Falconer is still a danger, I see. Having destroyed one marriage she now deceives her husband. I am surprised at you Lady Falconer.'

Analee felt herself blush under that stern gaze. She had thought she had eventually made a friend of Emma during the days they had been together. They had exchanged confidences like girls and

Analee told Emma to call her by her Christian name – but now that hard won rapport seemed to be lost. In her way Emma was quite a Puritan, thought Analee. Yet she and Brent were very similar; both obsessed by an old love.

'I am sorry to have upset you, Emma,' she said. 'I have discouraged Brent for all I am worth, as he will tell you. I loved Mary and never wanted her unhappiness. I also loved my husband and was content, but of late my husband has used me ill, become jealous and possessive. I find my love for him . . . growing cold.'

'And Brent is always here to warm you again!'

'Hush, Emma!' Brent cried. 'You must not talk like that. I have made a positive assault on my beloved Analee's virtue, but she has not yielded to me since she became Lord Falconer's bride! Would that she had, and I would be the happiest of men. She is true and faithful to her husband and, as you see, bears his child. But one day I hope and pray Analee will be mine . . .'

'I assure you we do not meet here like clandestine lovers,' Analee added. 'My lord would not let me accompany him to France and Brent had your interests at heart, not his, when he asked me to help you get away from home.'

'Then I am grateful,' Emma said shortly. 'If that is the truth. I will go and get my things together.'

Emma abruptly left the room and Analee turned in dismay to Brent. 'Now what have we done?'

'Aye, she is vexed. I suppose in a fashion she is jealous though she would not admit it. She is denied her lover, and you have two! She knows not what the future will bring for her, and here you are with one husband and another waiting to take his place.'

'Yes, maybe she is put out.' Analee walked to the window and stared for a long time across the lake. 'Emma is a funny girl, Brent. I would you could dissuade her from going to America. She has very high ideals; she expects a lot from people. What if Stewart has weakened and found another love? I worry what would happen to her then.'

'You don't know my sister. She is strong, a survivor.'

'I hope you are right. I am sorry I have failed Emma. Our relationship was not easy; I felt Emma was suspicious of me, but that at last she was growing more relaxed and we had begun to be friends. I never realized she knew you and I were once lovers. She

465

never mentioned it; she must have been watching me and wondering about me. I feel I have disappointed her.'

'The Rebellion brought her and Mary together,' said Brent. 'They found they shared common ideals. I imagine I have disappointed her too. Yet nevertheless she will use us both to get her ends – she wants Stewart and get to him she will. Oh my love, let us not talk of Emma in the few moments we have together. I thank God I am going away so that I shall not see you grow big with the Falcon's child. Curse that man! Would it were *my* child you carried . . .' He pulled her to him and held her close.

Analee thought of Morella playing happily on the lawn at Delamain Castle. Should she tell him? No, not now. Like his sister Emma, she did not know how he would react to such news. One day, maybe she would tell him, when she judged the time to be ripe.

'Where will you go Brent?'

'I am operating out of Laxey in the Isle of Man, as I told you. From thence to Port Rush, Whitehaven and the Scottish coast. It is dangerous for me to be seen too much ashore. And I must go back to France and report to the Prince.'

'Where is he?'

'He is at Avignon where he has a house, but for how long I know not. Avignon has been debarred to him too. The man is hunted like a fox. It cannot be right.'

'It is wrong,' Analee said quietly, 'very wrong, to hunt a man like an animal. Give my respects to His Royal Highness if you see him, Brent. I met him in Paris, as you know.'

'Aye, I remember him looking at you. I think you took his fancy, Analee, as you do so many men.'

If only Brent knew he had done more than look at her. Analee warmed to the memory. But that was a secret for her and the Prince. It was certainly not for Brent.

On a horse borrowed from the Furness stables, Emma followed Brent up the narrow bridle path that wound over the top of Catbells, across the broad sweep of Newlands Valley and down the steep tortuous track into Buttermere. Emma had few things with her because, in her mind, she was leaving everything behind – family, home, friends, possessions – and starting a new life. She

466

was crossing the vast Atlantic in order to make a break with her past that was symbolic as well as actual: the beginning of a new life with Stewart. What would happen after that was God's will.

From the top of Long How, Buttermere was merely a streak of silver in the distance. It was surrounded on all sides by high peaks which still bore the traces of winter's snow – High Crag, Great Borne, Grasmoor and Robinson. Once by the edge of the lake they stopped to give their horses water and rest while they themselves partook of the nourishing fare provided by Betty Hardcastle.

Emma looked around her as one who was seeing a well loved scene for the last time. She sniffed the air and gazed up at fells covered with brown fern or tough green grass on which the sturdy Herdwick sheep wandered in search of food. Here and there a stream trickled down from its source high up to feed Buttermere or its neighbour, gentle Crummock Water, and scatterings of loose stones and boulders which had fallen from the craggy rocks above looked like dark scars on the faces of the mountains.

The shores of both lakes were lined with coniferous woodland and it was finally through the upright fir trees that they skirted Buttermere to make their way along a narrow path that climbed high up over Scarth Gap. From there they had a breathtaking view of Ennerdale Water before the track dipped down into the forest that ran alongside the River Liza as far as the lake itself.

It was beginning to grow dark, and as they rode round Ennerdale and came to flat ground at Cleaton Moor Emma looked back at that beautiful peaceful scene – the beauty of Ennerdale and its surrounds, the high snow-capped peaks, the great forest of firs.

'Goodbye dear Lakeland,' Emma murmured, her eyes filling with tears, for she had no idea if she were seeing it for the last time. Then she spurred her horse after Brent along a flat dirt road that quickly led to the coast.

They arrived well after dark, making for a cottage that Brent knew on the edge of the little port of St Bees. Emma was tired, but her journey was far from over. The cottage was owned by a boatman who worked for Ambrose Rigg and who kept an eye on the goods smuggled across Lakeland from nearby Fleswick Bay, where Brent was due to rendezvous with a wherry later that night.

467

'I thought you'd be spending the night in the open,' the boatman said letting them into the warm room. A fire burned in the grate, on which steamed a pot from which came an appetizing aroma.

'Nay, I know my way like the sure-footed Herdwicks,' Brent laughed, chafing his hands in front of the fire. 'I have done it often. My sister stuck close behind me and did not falter. Besides, we soon had the moon to guide us.'

'You rode well to come this far in a day.' The boatman's wife was putting plates on the table. 'Best eat now because you have a two-mile walk to the bay and time is short.' She looked at Emma, pale with weariness, and smiled. 'Here you are love, a good mutton stew to warm you. Nothing like it.'

'Aye, and some ale to wash it down.' Jed the boatman brought an earthenware jug and two mugs from the dresser.

Emma and Brent tucked eagerly into the fare before them, but barely had time to finish their ale before Jed was putting on his cap and bidding them hurry.

'Thank you,' Emma said to Jed's wife who was looking at her with motherly sympathy – not knowing the reason for her secret departure and not liking to hazard a guess. She nodded and waved, then closed the door on the cold blustery March night with the wind coming in from the sea, thankful that she was not obliged to sail that night.

They had to leave the horses behind because there was no path from the cottage on the outskirts of the village to the smugglers' cove which Brent had got to know well over the years. The ground around them rose and fell, the going heavy over the freshly turned earth, and Brent put an arm through Emma's to give her support.

'We're nearly there.'

'Thank God, I am dead of weariness.'

Brent squeezed her arm, wishing he could see her face in the dark. They had hardly spoken during the journey and he wondered if in her mind Emma still reproached him for the scene she had witnessed.

'Think not hard of Analee, Emma,' he said nervously. 'She is a good friend.'

'Aye, a very good friend to *you* I think.'

''Tis not like that! Oh I know you would have a woman virtuous; but Analee . . . well, she is not like other women. I can't explain.'

'I hope, by the way, you never mentioned this love to our mother?'

'Never!' Emma said firmly. ''tis not a thing she would comprehend. She is . . . She is a witch,' Emma continued. 'She bewitches men, aye and women alike because Mary was much taken by her.'

'But not you?'

'I liked her well enough; though something about her disturbs me. She seems to see everything, the past and the future. 'Tis as though she knew all there was to know about one. It made me want to keep my distance and not reveal too much about myself, no more than I could help.'

Brent smiled into the darkness. 'I love Analee and one day I will have her,' he said. 'A gypsy promised me as much, and so far her word has come true. Ah here we are – and look yonder, the ship awaits us!'

They stood at the top of the cliff overlooking Fleswick Bay. Silhouetted in the dim light of the moon which occasionally peeped from behind the scudding clouds was a small ship, bobbing about in the choppy water. Emma shivered. This was only the beginning . . . she had never been to sea before.

They trod wearily along a narrow path that zig-zagged down to the shingle beach whose remoteness and inaccessibility made it such an ideal rendezvous for smuggling, lying as it did tucked away around St Bees Head and just before Whitehaven. A longboat lay waiting and, after they had clambered in, Jed launched it expertly into the water and jumped in, pushing off from the beach with one oar while he paddled furiously with the other, making deep firm strokes in the choppy water.

The moon came out as they rowed towards the ship tossing at anchor in the bay and Emma gazed silently at the receding shoreline, not knowing when – if ever – she would set foot on it again.

9

Ambrose Rigg's corpulent frame quivered with anger as he tossed the letter over to Brent.

'There! That could cost me thousands of pounds' worth of legitimate business. The fellow blames me!'

'But he *knows* it was not you.' White faced, Brent picked up the letter and read it slowly. It was to Ambrose from his brother George Delamain and it accused him of conspiring with Brent to spirit his sister out of the country. If Ambrose did not dismiss Brent forthwith, he threatened to make it known to all his business contacts that Ambrose did not keep his word, and to the authorities that he smuggled not only illicit goods but arms for another Jacobite rising.

All of which perturbed Ambrose a good deal. In his trade a man's word was his bond, as good as a signed piece of paper. A deal was completed on a handshake; the paper was mere formality. If Sir George Delamain accused that respected merchant of defaulting on his word he would be believed and Ambrose's business would suffer accordingly. Those who had known him a long time would go on trading with him, but many wouldn't. There would be others who would not risk offending the baronet in an age when bribery and influence counted for so much. Sir George was growing increasingly powerful, not only in the north but in London where patronage and privilege held sway.

As for the authorities, they already knew about Rigg's smuggling activities as the handouts they received to keep quiet about them formed a sizeable part of the income of the Whitehaven customs men. Everyone smuggled and many, the highest in the land among them, bought from smugglers. In the days when he was chief minister Sir Robert Walpole himself had his personal supplies of smuggled wine from France and linen from Holland brought to Westminster in an admiralty barge.

But what was not tolerated, what was by its very nature a treasonable activity, was the smuggling of arms. The government was constantly on the lookout for another Jacobite rising and this sort of activity was highly punishable.

'Nay, your brother knows *you* were involved. He knows I would not stir myself to offend him; but he knows I still employ you.'

'How does he know?' Brent threw the letter onto a table and took a chair, staring broodily into the fire. They were in Rigg's office overlooking the harbour at Whitehaven. Brent seldom went further than this when he came ashore, and then usually under cover of dark like tonight.

'Word gets around. Too many people know. But my wife Sarah and your brother were determined Emma should not go to America. They joined forces over this one – and now you have worsted them and Emma is on her way. You have let me down Brent.'

'I couldn't help it. She was determined and would have found another and maybe more dangerous way. She was in a curious mood, Ambrose, possessed of a sort of ruthless determination that is not uncommon in our family, both men and women. She regarded going to see Stewart as a sacred mission.'

'Aye, well . . .' Rigg poured himself a balloon glass of the fine French brandy that he brought in by the cask. He was a practical man and when he was defeated by something, his next thought was how to make the best of it.

'You'll have to go, lad.' He slapped his thigh and put the glass to his lips, tossing back its fiery contents.

'Go . . . ?' Brent stared up at him, his face mottling with anger.

'I can't employ you any more, not for a while. You must see that. I can't have you working for me on this run now. Look . . .' Ambrose went over to his desk and began to write. 'I'll drop a note to Pierre Furet of Nantes recommending you for a job of some sort.'

Brent got up and poured himself a drink without being asked. 'Oh I know Furet and many others. But I do not want to work in France, Ambrose. I have built up a safe line here, both for you and . . . our cause.'

'I know, and you have done well. I have no complaints, had you left your sister where she was. She'd have got over it; women always do. You should have left well alone, Brent lad. But you didn't – you wanted to provoke your brother as much as help your sister, I'll wager.' Ambrose shook his head. 'I don't have any option. See, I have an ultimatum here from Sir George written by his own hand. He wants his own back.' He thrust the letter once again under Brent's nose.

Brent knew he was defeated. Gone now was any chance of a fleeting trip across the hills by moonlight to visit Analee. He had to make the best of it with good grace.

'Well Ambrose, you've been a good friend. I didn't mean to abuse our relationship.'

'But you did use my ships and you did use my agent John Collister.'

Brent nodded dejectedly. 'Yes, I did. Pray God that things turn out well for Emma, seeing that helping her has been the undoing of me.'

Ambrose came up to him and put an arm around his shoulder. 'Brent lad, I have grown right fond of you, I think you know it. I respect you – aye, and I respect your ideals though I do not share them. I think your cause is quite lost and in my opinion rightly so. There is naught to be gained for any of us in restoring the Stuarts. My advice to you, lad, is abandon that cause. If you cut yourself off from the Jacobites, in time you can apply to the King for an indemnity. He is giving them all the time, aye even to those who opposed him as vigorously as you. *Then* I will employ you again. We are related by marriage, and I always hoped you would follow me in the business; look after it for me until my sons are old enough

'Oh Brent lad, settle down. I know things with you and Mary didn't work. Maybe it was the Rebellion unsettled us all, I don't know. But she is in a convent and you are free. Marry, raise a family, grow roots. There are rich pickings to be had in these days of prosperity. Take advantage of them, like your brother who well enough knows 'pon which side of the bread his butter lies. I'll write to him . . . nay I'll go and see him, so that nothing is committed to paper. I must do all I can to re-establish myself with Sir George again.'

Henrietta Delamain would have put down her foot quite firmly about receiving Ambrose Rigg in her drawing room were it not that he was accompanied by his wife, who after all was her husband's first cousin. Sarah Rigg, for her part, rarely accompanied her husband on his business trips; but this time he had prevailed upon her for the sake of reinstating his business and himself in Sir George's favour. He even decided to make it a family occasion, and brought his two eldest children Henry and Elia with him.

Henrietta was near the time of her delivery and found it comfortable neither to sit, stand nor lie down. Consequently she alternated between sitting and standing and Sarah, watching her evident discomfort, was sorry for her. Henrietta was a small woman and she looked like a ball rolling about as she paced across the drawing room while the men talked business in Sir George's study. On the lawn Elia and Henry ran about watched over by their nurse and Mildred's nurse who had brought the baby out for some air.

'You have chosen a fine day for your visit Sarah.' Henrietta paced restlessly to the window again, a supportive hand on the small of her back.

'Yes, the countryside looked so lovely as we drove over – the daffodils, the fresh new buds, many lambs cavorting about in the fields. On such days 'tis good indeed to be alive!'

Henrietta looked at Sarah, a woman she scarcely knew. She had the Allonby air of aristocratic detachment, of one who was used to her place in the world, commanding and being obeyed. No matter how far down in the world the Allonbys had come, they had never lost that. George's mother had it, and so had Stewart and John. Sarah sat upright in her chair, her hands in her lap, her lips pressed together, prim and daunting.

'We hardly know each other, Sarah,' Henrietta said suddenly. ''Tis a pity is it not? We are related by marriage and your children, what pets they are. Oh how I pray that my next baby is a son! Sir George so pines for a son.' She pressed her hands against her belly longingly, as though by sheer will power she would draw forth an heir from her womb.

'Let us hope so, in that case. If not now, another time maybe.'

'Oh do not say that!' Henrietta raised a hand to her brow. 'If you knew how I *dread* childbirth! If this child is a son 'twill be my last. I suffered so much in giving birth to Mildred, I have had such a hard time carrying this one . . . constant sickness and pain; I do not think I could go through with it again. I don't think I can.'

Henrietta suddenly sat down and to Sarah's consternation burst into tears. Such a display of weakness was not the kind of thing Sarah was accustomed to. She gazed at Henrietta with embarrassment and then she went over to her and lightly placed a hand on her shoulder. A sudden surge of pity for the poor woman took hold of her and she clasped her in her arms.

'There, there, Henrietta. I am sure all will be well this time. You will have a son, and then – '

'Oh but what if I do not? Sir George did not marry me for love, Sarah. He married me for my money, and to have sons. He would think nothing of putting me to one side if I failed to provide an heir . . .'

'Then he would not have your money,' Sarah observed drily. In her case she had married Ambrose for his money, and he her to give respectability to his name.

'Oh, the money is no longer important.. It is taken care of – wisely invested and multiplied ten times over. My father has the greatest admiration for Sir George's business acumen. He has not wasted my money, but used it shrewdly. Now he does not need it. No, he would divorce me and marry again . . .'

'But divorce requires an Act of Parliament!' Sarah expostulated. 'Even Sir George would not go that far, with the opprobrium it would bring him. I think you exaggerate Henrietta.'

'Oh no I do not! He *hates* Brent so much, and if George were to die before his time all this would belong to Brent or his heirs. Everything that Sir George has fought so hard to achieve . . .' Henrietta wrung her hands, and a fresh outbreak of sobbing began.

'But Sir George looks very healthy to me,' Sarah said sensibly. 'And anyway, Brent is attainted for his part in the Rebellion; he could not inherit. So put these things out of your mind, I beg of you. You will make yourself ill otherwise. Ah look . . .'

Henrietta followed the direction of Sarah's gaze and dried her eyes. On the lawn Henry and Elia had been joined by a third child.

'It is Morella,' Henrietta sniffed. 'The child adopted by your aunt.'

'But she is a beauty! I thought she belonged to a gypsy.' Sarah went up to the window and gazed thoughtfully at the trio who were now running up and down shrieking with joy.

'Well . . . the father was no gypsy, that much is obvious.

Sometimes I think that all your aunt has suffered has made her take leave of her senses . . . to adopt a changeling! I would be careful about letting your children play with her, Sarah.'

Sarah opened her eyes wide and stared at Henrietta. 'Does she have some disease?'

'Oh no, no, nothing like that. And you can see she is well looked after. No, but you know . . . bad blood. Sir George had forbidden that she should ever play with our children.'

'Poor little thing . . .' Sarah gazed at the child, much taken by her fair ringlets bobbing about in the sunshine. 'She has a look of our family, do you not think? Fair hair and blue eyes. She is quite lovely. Ah, there is my aunt watching her. How she has aged poor woman. I must go and talk to her.'

'Do you mind if I do not accompany you Sarah? Even walking a few steps is hard for me. When you come back the men will doubtless have finished and we can take tea together.'

'Of course, you must rest and not disturb yourself. And have no fear, I will not bring Morella back with me in case she should somehow distress the child in your womb.'

Sarah gave a frosty smile and swept from the room while Henrietta surrendered herself to a fresh onslaught of tears. Some days she could do nothing right, and she had wanted to be friendly with Sarah Rigg.

Susan Delamain had only known of her niece's arrival when she saw the children on the lawn. She hardly recognized them, or Sarah whose slim outline had become more rotund and matronly since they had last met. Susan couldn't even remember when that had been, because although Ambrose Rigg came quite often to the Castle on business, he was never received by Henrietta to whom breeding counted such a lot. The two women embraced warmly and then Susan held her niece at arm's length.

'When was it we last met? Surely not when Brent and Mary were engaged?'

'No, aunt. George brought you over for dinner two years ago, after the extensions to our house were finished . . .'

'That's right. It was after the Rebellion when I was so worried about Brent and Stewart – and you were with child if I remember.'

'Ah yes, that was Norman and since then I have had Caspar who is but three months old. Mr Rigg is determined on a dynasty, aunt.' She ran a hand lightly across her stomach and laughed. 'Thank God they and I are in good health. Whereas poor Henrietta . . .'

'Ah yes, Henrietta does not breed well. But then she does not confide in me and treat me like a friend, and as I don't see her much there is not a lot I can do to comfort her. You haven't seen my little Morella have you?'

'I have heard about her, but I was saying when I saw her from the window, how enchanting she is.'

Susan's expression grew tender. 'She is like a gift from God, the darling. She looks so much like Brent when he was tiny, with her soft blonde locks and big blue eyes.'

'And yet you have no idea who the father was?'

Susan shook her head and laughed. 'Most certainly not Brent! Nor the mother either, except – ' No, she must not tell her niece; she had not spoken of her suspicion to anyone. It was too fanciful, and too dangerous even to hint abroad that Morella's mother might be Lady Falconer. Susan had decided to keep that to herself, no matter how tempted she was to do otherwise. 'No, only I did not think the mother was the gypsy who left Morella with me. But who can say . . .'

'Aunt, have you heard from Emma?'

Susan nodded. 'Yes, she wrote me from France. She was about to board ship for Baltimore. Oh pray God . . .'

'You know that Brent was involved?'

'Of course I know, and Lady Falconer . . .'

'Lady *Falconer*!' Sarah's mouth fell open.

'She took Emma from here pretending that she wanted company. I can't say I am angry – I only wish they had confided in me. Emma longed to be with Stewart. She was never the same person after he was sentenced and deported.'

'But how can you know for sure? Did Emma say so?'

'No, she did not mention Lady Falconer in her letter. But that was how 'twas done. Brent took Emma from Furness and on to Whitehaven, and then to France.'

'But why should Lady Falconer do such a thing?'

'That is what George wants to know. He is in a fair rip I can tell you, and can't decide whether to write to his lordship or not about his wife's meddling.'

'You think Brent *knows* Lady Falconer?'

'Oh yes. I think she helped Brent to escape from Edinburgh – Emma was sure she did. Why, I know not.'

Susan's eyes turned again to Morella. So like Brent as a child . . . There had been talk of Brent and a gypsy woman who caused his injury. No, it was too fanciful. Besides if Brent had had a child by a gypsy surely he would know it. All she knew was that she could not love Morella more even if she knew for certain she were her own grandchild. There was a feeling of kinship between them. Susan put an arm on Sarah's. Her niece was a funny woman; no one quite knew where her sympathies lay.

'Sarah you must take care to say not a word . . .'

'Oh aunt, fear not. I keep enough secrets as it is, Rigg is engaged in so many dubious activities. I am solely concerned with domestic matters I assure you, and am not likely to gossip. Why, who have we here?'

A stranger had strode onto the lawn towards them. He was a tall slim young man, dressed modishly in a green riding coat, double-breasted with brown buttons and buttonholes. His sleeves were deep and decorated with matching buttons, and he wore breeches of the same material as his coat, and black leather half jackboots ending just below the knee, with turned down tops of soft tan deerskin. His wig, with its long queue tied with black ribbon bows above and below was of the style known as 'Ramilles' and went with his generally smart and military appearance.

His face was lean and handsome with curved lips and high cheekbones, slender black brows over piercing blue eyes. He gazed for a while at the children, a smile on his lips, and then he walked casually over to the ladies and bowed deeply, a saucy eye staring quite boldly at Sarah.

'My dear, may I present a house guest of George? Mr Hugo Fitzgerald. Mr Fitzgerald, my niece Mrs Ambrose Rigg.'

'Charmed, Mrs Rigg. Indeed I just had the pleasure of meeting your husband, ma'am. He told me I would find you out here, and your children. Charming.' Mr Fitzgerald, looking like one well pleased with himself and the world, stood with hands clasped behind his back watching the children running on the lawn. 'I have many sisters all of whom breed prodigiously, Mrs Rigg, and I have left scores of beautiful nieces and nephews at home in Ireland.'

477

'So I detect from your accent Mr Fitzgerald, though 'tis very slight.'

'I have spent a long time overseas, ma'am, with the Irish Guards – in the service of His Majesty King George, I hasten to say, ma'am, and not the rebel Jacobite Irish Brigade. I have now sold my commission and, being penniless though well born, desire an entry into commerce, which is becoming quite respectable these days. Sir George was kind enough to undertake to procure a position for me. I believe he might have spoken about it to Mr Rigg . . .'

'You would bury yourself in these parts Mr Fitzgerald?' Sarah could not keep the amazement out of her voice.

'And what is wrong with these parts Mrs Rigg? I find them quite charming. The beauty, such as I have seen, of this countryside almost surpasses that of my native land. No ma'am, I am of a mind to secure a good position and settle down, maybe marry . . . Are there marriageable ladies in these parts d'you know?'

Susan threw back her head and laughed. 'Mr Fitzgerald, there are marriageable ladies in *all* parts of the country. I don't think you will have difficulty on that score. Indeed, if you think of taking a position with Mr Rigg, I believe Keswick and Cockermouth – not to say Whitehaven and many surrounding villages – will furnish a number of eligible and presentable young females. But first, you must make your fortune.'

'Ah that I intend to do, Mrs Delamain, without delay. I did hope Sir George, who I hear has a very eligible sister, might take me into his employ; but he regrets to have no place for me at this instance.'

'And my daughter, Emma, is abroad too Mr Fitzgerald.'

'So Sir George tells me, ma'am, and not too happy about it neither is my impression. Well, well – so be it. My loss, another man's gain I understand is the case. Here are Sir George and Mr Rigg, their discussions satisfactorily completed I take it.'

Both men, hands clasped behind their backs, smiles of satisfaction on their faces, strolled over towards them pausing on the way to admire the children playing on the lawn.

'Ah my dear, you have met Mr Fitzgerald I see, a young man warmly recommended by Sir George to help run my enterprises. He has a good military career behind him and seeks a position in commerce.' Ambrose was eyeing Fitzgerald up and down as one might a good horse.

'So Mr Fitzgerald was saying,' Sarah said. 'He also has a mind to find a bride.'

'Capital. We have a number of worthy families in this area, have we not Sir George? Moreover we could do with upstanding young men like Mr Fitzgerald settling here too. Why should they all go to London?'

'Why indeed?' Sir George took a pinch of snuff and fastidiously dusted his fingers. 'This is the age of expansion through trade and our Colonial possessions, and the north of England has a rich and prosperous future. We need new families, new blood, new dynasties like that of Mr Rigg here.'

Sir George beamed benevolently on Ambrose Rigg who had demonstrated a pleasing degree of respect and subservience by getting rid of Brent and coming over personally to apologize. He had also brought a cask of brandy for Sir George and some bolts of fine silk for Lady Delamain and these presents were none the less acceptable for being, Sir George imagined, free of duty. Ambrose also had some business to put in the way of Sir George – almost pure profit with very little outgoings. And now here he was offering to take on young Hugo Fitzgerald, whom Sir George had come across in London staying with Sir Tollemy Redpath, another friend of his and a well respected business colleague, to whom Sir George was anxious to render a favour.

Sir George was not sorry that Emma was no longer available. He would certainly not have been eager for a match between her and young Fitzgerald who was absolutely without fortune, though his family was an old and well respected one in Ireland. Not that George cared very much what happened to Emma, now that she had put herself beyond the pale of family care and concern. Let her find Stewart, marry him and go to hell for all George cared.

'Well, let us go indoors and take tea with my dear wife.' Sir George turned to lead the way back into the Castle. 'Mother, will you join us?'

'No thank you George. Sarah, would your children care to have tea with little Morella?'

'Why mother – ' George began warningly, but Sarah burst out.

'That would be lovely aunt. See how well they get on! I believe

Henry has an eye for beauty already . . . taking after his father no doubt.'

Henry Rigg at seven was big for his age, being both broad and long. He was very much the Rigg rather than the gentle Allonby-like Elia who at five was fair and petite, a fragile rather pensive child resembling, Sarah thought, Mary when small. But if Henry had the Rigg girth and robustness he did not share the boisterous Rigg temperament or the coarseness of his father. He was good tempered but serious minded, already interested in nature and how things worked. He had his own tutor and did well at his studies. And all the time Sarah instilled into him the virtues of good manners above all. Physical characteristics apart, which she could do nothing about, she wanted him to be every inch an Allonby.

'I'll come and get them when we are ready to go, aunt, and say goodbye.' Sarah smiled and waved as the nurses shepherded the brood off the lawn towards the dower house. Ambrose hung back to escort his wife, his thumbs in the armholes of his waistcoat.

'Shall you mind, my dear, if young Hugo lodges a while with us? I want to break him in gently.'

'Mind? Why should I mind? The house is big enough. Fitzgerald is to replace Brent?'

'That is the idea.'

'Then let us hope he has none of his *other* inclinations.'

'Oh have no fear there. Fitzgerald is Hanoverian through and through. That's why I've taken him. To please Sir George.'

Hugo Fitzgerald was an immediate success, charming everyone with whom he came into contact. He rode back to Cockermouth with the Riggs and the following day started work at the docks in Whitehaven: greeting the boats, inspecting the cargo, paying the men. Then he spent endless hours supervising the clerks who did the accounts, checking them himself, logging orders and making sure they were filled. After a few weeks Ambrose Rigg began to wonder how he had ever done without Hugo Fitzgerald to keep his business in order.

Hugo amply carried on from where Brent had left off. Hugo didn't do anything better than Brent; but he did things as well. The trouble was that for a long time Brent had only been doing half the work for which he was originally employed, and since the Rebellion he had been continually at sea in order to be out of the way of the authorities. Ambrose had been too long without a right-hand man; Hugo was just what he needed.

Everyone liked Hugo – he was happy, hardworking, polite, free but not too familiar with underlings and respectful but not too obsequious with his superiors. He dressed like a dandy but worked like a navvy. He took lodgings in Whitehaven so as to be at the docks every morning by first light, when the boats which had waited for the tide came in with their catch. By the time Ambrose had ridden from Cockermouth to Whitehaven, most of the day's work was done and Ambrose could saunter around like the man of property he was, inspecting his ships, his catches and his warehouses stocked from floor to ceiling with merchandise both lawful and unlawful – the latter carefully out of sight to the unobservant eye.

In mid-afternoon Ambrose would usually drive back again to the bosom of his family which was an expression of all those things he had worked for so many years to obtain – a fine large house with stables and outbuildings and enough servants to assure a man every comfort he could wish for. Then there was his wife: a fine well proportioned woman, a good breeder and a diligent mother who came from an ancient line so that her blood, mingling with his to produce a new breed of Riggs, was noble. Yes, his children would not only have all that money could buy; they would have breeding and education as well, good speech and fine manners. Above all, they would by virtue of their Allonby ancestry be of the gentry – fit for the highest offices in the land.

For them there would be no need to toady, as Ambrose had had to all his life, to those who were less able than he was, but whose blood had accorded them a station in life to which he, the son of a mere 'statesman' – a yeoman farmer – could never aspire. The George Delamains of this world would only be accorded the respect that was their birthright, nothing more – and the Riggs of the future would be able to hold their heads as high as the next generations of Delamains.

Hugo came back with Ambrose at the weekends and there he charmed Sarah and the Rigg children every bit as much as he charmed those among whom he worked. Sarah preferred Hugo to Brent. Not only was there no family tie to trouble her, but no hint of Jacobitism either – not a suspicion of it. The Fitzgeralds, Hugo assured her, were through and through supporters of the Hanoverians; had he not served for many years in His Majesty's Brigade of the Irish Guards?

'Did you know Lord Falconer?' Sarah enquired suddenly, in the middle of a large Sunday dinner when meats of various kinds, pies, potatoes brought from Ireland, pastries and sweetmeats were accompanied by a rich variety of rare and costly wines imported especially for his own use by Rigg from France.

'Falconer?' Hugo wiped his mouth and took a sip of wine. 'Aye, the Marquess of Falconer. Who does *not* know the Falcon? The terror of the Jacobites, aye and of the Frenchies as well. Mind you I never got to greet his lordship personally as his regiment was part of the King's Household Cavalry, and I was never directly in an engagement with his lordship. But his reputation, 'tis legendary . . . a respected but much feared man.'

Hugo drained his glass and tucked into the loin of pork freshly killed on the Rigg estates and hung until it was just ready for eating.

'We are acquainted with the wife of his lordship,' Rigg began importantly. 'Lady Falconer is – '

'Lady *Falconer*?' Hugo put down his knife and fork and leaned the palms of his hands on the table. 'Lady Falconer! The Enchantress! I caught a glimpse of her once at Court . . . My goodness, what a beauty! And you *know* her ladyship?'

'She is called the Enchantress?' Sarah wondered idly, a smile playing on her lips. 'She certainly enchanted my cousin . . .'

'And many others who come in contact with her,' Rigg muttered, spearing his teeth with the new gold toothpick his wife had insisted on providing for him, being sick of the sight of his thick blunt finger digging into his cavities on all occasions.

'Would I had the sight of her ladyship myself. Aye, we are acquainted through Brent Delamain who married Sarah's sister Mary Allonby, and made her right unhappy into the bargain. All, they say, because of Lady Falconer – Analee she was called, a common gypsy girl.'

'Analee the gypsy . . .' Hugo sat back, the fine loin of pork forgotten. 'Aye, that's the story I heard in France but I could not believe my ears. That his lordship found this woman on a field where her gypsy camp had been ravaged by the retreating Jacobite troops. That he took her to his home as his whore and later married her, making her one of the greatest in the land.'

'But first of all she cured him from a near fatal wound after Falkirk. His life was despaired of, and 'twas considered a miracle that he lived. I have never met her myself, but her influence on my family has not been inconsiderable.'

Sarah thoughtfully bit into a piece of crisp duckling. She knew she was putting on weight but her fondness for food was growing prodigious, not that it worried Ambrose. As long as his wife was happy and cared for her family he was not over concerned with her appearance. He mainly took his pleasures in the whorehouses of Whitehaven where a plentiful supply of nubile young women fresh from the farms, like young plump hens, were constantly available. Ambrose was content on the whole to leave her be, to use her to satisfy his demands only occasionally. This arrangement appeared to work well and she even seemed to have grown fonder of him in recent years.

'How I would like to meet the Enchantress again,' Hugo breathed. 'I confess that I recall every detail of her appearance, and I only saw her at a distance among a group gathered round the King at Hampton Court.'

'Why Lady Falconer resides not twenty leagues from here,' Ambrose chortled winking at his wife. 'She is at Furness Grange which is on the shores of Lake Derwentwater. She was sent thither by her husband to await the birth of a child.'

'Lady Falconer at Lake Derwentwater!'

'Furness was bought for her by her husband,' Sarah said. 'It was forfeit after the Rebellion. My husband was not interested in acquiring it and did not bid. I believe Lady Falconer loves the place and spends a great deal of time there. I even hear it rumoured that she and the Marquess are not as fully in accord as they used to be. But I must confess this is all tittle-tattle.' Sarah got up from the table and rang a bell for the servants. 'I care little about Lady Falconer and have enough to do in my own home. Pray put her out of your mind Mr Fitzgerald. I wager you have enough to do without having Analee the gypsy interfering in your life. Whether she means it or not I cannot say; but I believe her to be a dangerous woman and best avoided.'

But try as he would – and this was not very hard – Hugo could not get the tale of the fascinating Marchioness of Falconer out of his mind. Her image came up to haunt him as he went about his work or rode between Whitehaven and Cockermouth. To think that just across the mountains, only a few leagues distant, there she was! Often on his way home he would imagine turning his horse towards Whinlatter and the Newlands Valley; but instead he made it trot obediently along the road to Rigg Manor where a warm welcome, a soft bed and a full board awaited him after a hard week's work.

But one day, Hugo thought as the nights lengthened, the trees put on their leafy dress and summer came to Lakeland, one day he just might . . .

10

That summer brought forth the full magnificence of Lakeland. The sun and warmth nurtured the wild plant life; trees were heavy with new growth and flowers bloomed in glorious profusion, attended by an abundance of honeybees and butterflies. The sparkling lake was a kaleidoscope of colour – like so many jewels, thought Analee, cast into the water, iridescent, reflecting the cerulean sky, the soft pink and white swirls of cloud, the variegated greens and browns of the woods and fells, the blossoms of the rhododendrons and gorse that bordered the lake.

When Analee had been expecting Clare, the Falcon had been constantly by her side, loving and protective; but now – save for Nelly and the servants – she was alone. She did not feel lonely, however, surrounded as she was by the beauty of the countryside she loved so much and by the affection of her servants. Indeed, as she walked slowly through the grounds of Furness Grange, lingering by the lakeside, she was overcome by the tranquillity of the scene and she felt a deep exhilaration that the child she carried would be a direct descendant of the Stuart Kings of England.

As her time drew near, her happiness was not diminished by the absence of the Falcon or even word from him; she would sit by the banks of the lake, gazing over to the purple-clad fells opposite, the soft ridge of fir trees beneath them. She felt the same affinity with nature that she had known so vividly in her gypsy life, a deep primitive instinct of oneness with all living things.

It was in the image of the primeval goddess that Hugo Fitzgerald saw Analee again as he approached her without bothering to stop at the house. He had seen her as he rode along the top of Skelgill and Catbells, and even from afar he had recognized the woman who had remained in his mind as such an outstanding adornment to the court of George II the day he had been there.

Nelly had propped Analee up in a low chair, her back against fat comfortable cushions, her feet on a low stool. Her morning gown was arranged about her in graceful folds and she had loosened her

485

hair so that it fell across her bosom in thick dark curls. A book lay open on her lap, but she had scarcely looked at it. Instead she alternately dozed and gazed at the scenery surrounding her, savouring the mood of high summer through its smells, sensing it through half-closed eyes, feeling its warmth penetrate her skin.

The crunch of footsteps on the gravel made her open her eyes and sit up.

'Nelly is it time for my chocolate?'

She half turned and there confronting her was a tall young man, fashionably dressed in a dark fustian frock coat with brass buttons and a turned down collar made of velvet. His heavy jackboots, with wide bucket tops, reached above the knees and at the heels were broad spur leathers. He wore a periwig made of natural dark hair lightly powdered, the short queue being tied at the nape of his neck by a black bow, and under his arm he carried a large cocked hat with button and loop in the fashionable style known as the Kevenhuller Cock.

Hugo Fitzgerald was gazing at Analee in a way that made her think they must have met. He seemed to know her, but he bowed and said nothing, his eyes never leaving her face.

'Do we know each other sir?' Analee raised herself, leaning on an arm.

'Indeed, ma'am, I have seen you but I do not think you observed me. It was at His Majesty's Court at Hampton Palace before Christmas last. I think you had just returned from Paris with your distinguished husband, ma'am.'

'Yes, we were there once only before travelling north.'

'It was therefore with great pleasure, Lady Falconer, that I heard from Mrs Rigg that you were staying here and I have come over to bring you her respects . . .' Hugo faltered and Analee, seeing his confusion, smiled in order to help him out.

'How very kind of Mrs Rigg sir. We are not acquainted but have friends in common.'

'Aye, that is what she said ma'am,' Hugo continued quickly. 'And I was passing on my way to Keswick . . .'

'Pray how are you acquainted with Mrs Rigg, Mr – ?'

Hugo bowed low, sweeping his hat to the ground. 'May I introduce myself: Hugo Fitzgerald, Lady Falconer, lately a lieutenant in the Irish Guards. But when the war ended, my regiment, that of Lord McQueen, was disbanded and I decided to seek my fortune in commerce, ma'am, having breeding but no fortune. I was acquainted with Sir George Delamain who was kind enough to recommend me to Mr Rigg whom I now serve as a factor, ma'am.'

'You know that Lady Delamain is related to my husband?'

Hugo looked taken aback and glanced round for somewhere to put his hat. 'Now that I did not know Lady Falconer. How fortunate it was that I called, for I am bound for Delamain Castle on business for Mr Rigg after I leave Keswick.'

'Then you may convey my respects to Sir George and Lady Delamain, though I do not think I enjoy their good graces at this moment.'

'Oh Lady Falconer, that I cannot imagine . . .' Hugo began.

'No, it is true. Emma was staying with me when she was mysteriously spirited away to join her lover in America. I confess I know nothing of it except that Emma left me a note . . .'

Hugo held up a protesting hand. 'Lady Falconer – as if one could attach any blame to you on that score! Sir George has blamed his brother Brent Delamain for their sister's misadventure, and now he has completely washed his hands of the unfortunate young woman. I'm sure not a whisper of suspicion is directed at you.'

Analee closed her book and folded her hands in her lap. Mr Fitzgerald was very amiable, she decided, a welcome diversion on a hot summer's day. Besides, his admiring gaze was not displeasing to a woman heavy with child and neglected by her husband.

'How happy I am to hear that!' she said, smiling up at him. 'Pray give Sir George and Lady Delamain my warmest regards. I hear that her ladyship is delivered of a daughter.'

Hugo's features arranged themselves into a grimace. 'Aye ma'am. A sad affair. Her ladyship had the most difficult labour which all but caused her to quit this world, and the child likewise. The baby is still sickly and her ladyship unlikely to conceive again. All of which is a sorry business for Sir George whose heir – apart from his rebel brother who cannot inherit – is a distant cousin. Sir George has worked hard to build up his estates, and to what end? I hear he would not see her ladyship for several days, such was his chagrin.'

'Men – !' Analee shaded her eyes against the sun. 'There is not much to choose between them in my opinion. 'Tis not, after all, as though Lady Delamain had done a deliberate mischief to her husband; she must be as much out of countenance as he is. Poor lady – she has my deepest sympathy. Ah, here is Nelly with my morning chocolate. Would you take a drink with me Mr Fitzgerald? A glass of madeira wine perhaps?'

Hugo looked eagerly around and drew up a chair which he placed beside Analee. 'May I ma'am? I would enjoy a glass of wine before I proceed on my journey.'

'You have ridden this morning from Cockermouth?'

'Aye ma'am, I came over Whinlatter and across Newlands, thinking to break my journey by paying my respects to the woman – dare I say it, ma'am? – I have heard they call the Enchantress.'

'Ah, has it travelled so far afield Mr Fitzgerald?' Analee's face broke into a smile. ''Tis quite false. I am no sorceress, no enchantress . . . alas, I wish I were.'

She fell silent, thinking of the Falcon and how her love for him had been torn asunder. Had she really been an enchantress she would have kept his love; he would not, could not have abused her so.

Nelly placed a tray on the table beside Analee and looked with interest at the handsome young stranger.

'I do not recall admitting this gentleman, ma'am.'

'Nelly, this is Mr Hugo Fitzgerald, an acquaintance of Sir George and Lady Delamain and in the employ of Mr Rigg. Would you fetch him a glass of chilled madeira and some biscuits.'

Hugo inclined his head and Nelly dropped a smiling bob before hurrying off.

'I think you must have taken the position occupied by Mr Delamain, have you not Mr Fitzgerald?'

'I think I have ma'am, though I understand Mr Delamain has not been working for Mr Rigg since the Rebellion. As I hear it he has been skulking in the Isle of Man up to no good. But I ask no questions on matters that do not concern me, Lady Falconer.'

'How wise, Mr Fitzgerald.'

Analee felt a cramp in her stomach and turned in her chair. Then she tried to get up, putting her feet to the ground, her hands round her belly. Her face was twisted with discomfort.

'You must excuse me Mr Fitzgerald; it is nearly my time. I think I will go in out of the sun.'

'Oh pray let me help you Lady Falconer.' Hugo jumped up and Analee held out a hand. He gently helped raise her from the chair and, at the mere touch of her hand, a current seemed to pass through him. For a moment they stood gazing at each other; even large and cumbersome as she was, Hugo could feel her magic permeating him, thrilling him to his very heart. Her face was full and radiant with the glow of impending motherhood, but it also possessed something else: a knowingness, a hidden core of wisdom that penetrated his being. It infused him with a sense of slave-like devotion that was something completely new to one whose considerable success with women lay in making *them* slaves to his charms.

Suddenly Analee felt the familiar fire pierce her belly and knew that her labour had begun. She gave a cry and would have fallen had she not been sustained by Hugo's strong arm. The pain came again and she gasped. 'Take me into the house Mr Fitzgerald. My time . . .'

Hugo put an arm gently about her and, supporting her, led her slowly into the house where Nelly, having espied them from an upstairs window, flew to greet them.

'Oh Analee . . . !'

'It is time Nelly, you must send a servant for the midwife.'

'But Ned and Francis are not here ma'am, and of the other servants who can ride swiftly?'

'Oh let *me* go!' Hugo volunteered eagerly. 'I will go quickly and fetch her back with me.'

'Nay 'tis not – '

'Yes, yes let him go Nelly!' Analee said. 'I think we have urgent need of her and I am sure Mr Fitzgerald is the ablest horseman here.'

'I will fetch her on my horse. Pray tell me where she lives.'

Nelly swiftly gave him instructions while the other servants, alerted by the commotion in the hallway, ran about making preparations for their mistress's lying-in. Warming pans were rushed up to Analee's bedroom and clean sheets pulled from the linen cupboard. Little Clare was taken to the nursery by her nurse, and the crib and layette which had been prepared for the new baby were placed ready in Analee's room.

Hugo leaped on his horse and galloped off towards Braithwaite where the midwife lived, and Nelly and Betty Hardcastle helped Analee slowly upstairs. At times she grasped the bannister for support and hung onto it while the spasm of pain passed.

The pains were coming in quick succession and Analee only wanted to reach her room and lie down. Thankfully she sank onto the bed, while Nelly helped to remove her clothes and put on the loose robe that had been prepared for her confinement.

The sun was high in the heavens, the lake sparkling beneath her window; but her own room lay in the shade except for a sunbeam glancing in from a side window. This was Analee's fourth lying-in and as she lay there panting, memories of the others passed through her mind. The first baby had been born in a barn and lived only long enough to utter a brief cry; the second, Morella, was born with much fear and pain in a gypsy tent; Clare was born at Falcon's Keep, with a midwife, two doctors, and her husband in protective attendance. That had been an easy joyful labour.

And here she was at Furness . . . giving birth to a royal child. For it was a royal child! Oh the awe of knowing that she was about to bring forth the son of Prince Charles Edward Stuart! A sudden calm seemed to possess her and her heart slowly filled with peace and joy. Then the slow rhythm started of pain and relief, pain and relief, as the process of birth once again began for Analee.

Hugo felt exhilarated as he rode swiftly over the hills towards the village of Braithwaite lying at the end of the Newlands Valley. His first chance to do a service for Lady Falconer – and what an important one! He felt like some knight errant and his duty to his employer was swiftly forgotten.

As luck would have it the midwife had just returned from an all-night call in Keswick and, when she heard the august name of her new patient, lost no time in putting her instruments together again and gathering up her bags. Her pony and cart were still saddled, but it would take time to ride over the narrow path to Catspaw and she agreed to sit behind Hugo Fitzgerald on the broad back of his mare. The midwife was a middle-aged agile woman, country-born and bred, and this presented no difficulty to her. In fact she was flattered at riding behind this elegant nobleman with his fashionable clothes. She eagerly grasped his trim waist as he rode his horse swiftly back by Portinscale, and through the narrow forest track that bordered the lake almost as far as Furness.

At the house all was commotion, servants running hither and thither and sharp commands coming from both upstairs and down. A servant rushed out to take Hugo's horse and another took the midwife's bags and ushered her quickly up the stairs to Analee's room. Hugo would have followed her up, but he was stopped at the foot of the stairs by Betty Hardcastle who took him into the dining room and gave him a glass of port.

'Excuse the haste, sir, but we are of a to-do.'

'That's all right. How is her ladyship?'

'Oh she does well enough; she is a fine strong woman. Nelly her faithful servant is with her.'

'And his lordship – is he expected, or was the birth early?'

Betty averted her eyes. 'I know nothing about his lordship's movements sir. 'Tis but my duty to serve her ladyship when she is here and not enquire into the doings of my betters.'

Hugo moved to the window. He felt nervous and yet excited, anxious and yet full of anticipation. It was almost as though he was the father of the baby himself, so anxious was he for Analee, so proud of the outcome.

'She *is* an enchantress,' he muttered to himself, his nose pressed to the window-pane. 'I have known her but a few short hours yet I care for her as much as my own life.'

Analee held tightly to Nelly's hand, her lips clenched between her teeth. She would not scream and make her household already more anxious than they were. She was not merely Analee the gypsy, she was the Marchioness of Falconer; although as a gypsy she could scream and swear as much as she liked, as the wife of one of England's premier noblemen more dignity was expected of her. So she gripped Nelly's hand and clenched her teeth until the veins stood out on her temple and the muscles bulged at her neck.

The midwife, once in the presence of her illustrious patient, felt an unaccustomed sense of awe and began to wish that the doctor had been sent for too, but one look at Analee was enough to show her that the labour was very far advanced and that all would be over before the doctor was found. She was a woman well experienced in the profession, however, and quietly, so as to infuse the patient with her own calm, she rolled back her sleeves, put on her apron and scrubbed her hands thoroughly in a basin of water.

Then, with the help of Nelly, she gently drew back the bed-clothes and lifting Analee's chemise placed a hand on the swollen moving belly. She bent down, placing a practised ear close to Analee's navel and listening carefully. She nodded at Nelly. 'All is well; the baby is far down the birth passage.'

The pains were now coming so quickly that Analee was continually in agony without respite and she thrashed about the bed, biting at the cloth Nelly had given her and pressing her hand hard.

She shut her eyes and thought of the baby's father, the Prince; of the beauty of the lakeland scenery surrounding the house; of her previous *accouchements*; of the Prince again and his clumsy boyish way of making love. Yet, like any grown man, he could produce a child. Finally she thought of the Falcon, but this image of masculine domination, of love withdrawn, she banished as quickly as she could from her mind. She continued thus for the next few hours, while the midwife and Nelly hovered beside her.

Suddenly Analee felt as though she wanted to push and bear down and she looked at the midwife who had gently inserted a hand in the birth passage.

'Do not push yet, my lady, hold on for as long as you can.'

Analee bit hard on the cloth once more, the pain excruciating. She felt an enormous desire to push, then suddenly there was no more pain and the midwife kneading her belly cried, 'Push push, my lady.'

Nelly grasped her hand and Analee pushed, and gasped for breath and cried. Then she pushed again and the midwife crouching at the end of the bed seized the baby's head with her hands and drew it carefully into the world.

For a moment all was still. The sweat poured down Analee's brow; she could feel her heart hammering in her chest; her body was wet and from between her legs she felt a small body, and then the gush of blood. She could hear the birds singing almost with piercing sharpness as they flew low over the lake, and somewhere a horse neighed. Then came the sound she had waited for, the sweetest of all sounds in the world: the cry of a new born baby

492

announcing to the world that it was safely delivered, a member of the human race. The lusty cry penetrated the room, drowning all other sounds, and then the midwife placed the baby on her belly. Suddenly suffused with joy, Analee raised herself on her arms and looked down at the tiny creature, the new life which had been a part of her.

Both Nelly and the midwife laughed through their tears of happiness.

'It is a boy, my lady, a fine lovely healthy boy! Oh Analee!'

Nelly wiped her mistress's sticky brow and smoothed back her wet hair; then she hugged her and kissed her while the midwife took the baby and cleaned it, wiping away the blood and protective yellow covering in which it had been born. Analee reached out her arms and the midwife gave the naked baby to her. Analee clasped it, hugged it and kissed it, noting how fine and sturdy he was, the thatch of dark hair, the imperious tilt of the chin. Why it was as though he knew his father was a prince, his ancestors kings of England.

The baby nuzzled against his mother and Analee rubbed one of her big ripe nipples against his lips. The baby eagerly grasped it and sucked, instantly assuming an expression of ecstatic concentration, while Nelly and the midwife continued to exclaim with delight and admiration.

'I never saw a child want to suck so soon,' said the midwife. 'This one is confident of his place in the world. There is no milk there ma'am, you know that.'

'I know, Mrs Pybus; but the baby takes comfort, if not nourishment from the thin liquid in my breasts. Oh is he not *angelic*?'

'He is a large angel,' Nelly said, 'a big healthy boy.'

'His lordship will be pleased,' Mrs Pybus said deferentially, 'I believe it is the heir.'

'Yes, it is the heir,' Analee said softly, 'the heir to great estates, a great name.'

Oh the exquisite feeling of the baby at her breast! Analee leaned back and shut her eyes. It was an emotion like no other; so erotic that it made her think of making love – love-making and giving birth were part of the same process, both marvellous and life-giving.

The baby stopped sucking, his head falling back against

Analee's arm, and the midwife took the sleeping baby gently away. Then she went to the door to summon the maid who had waited outside. Suddenly the sounds from the rest of the house broke into the quiet peacefulness of the birth room, pails of hot water were brought in, basins, cloths freshly warmed, towels and soft snowy sheets.

Nelly sponged Analee with the warm water as she had after the birth of Morella and Clare, gently over the entire body, across the breasts, under the arms. Analee still lay with her legs apart, feeling that any moment the afterbirth would be expelled and the process of birth complete. Yes, she felt the pain again and once more pushed while the midwife, who had delivered the baby into the care of a maid specially engaged for the purpose, reached into the birth passage and skilfully pulled away the spongy, gory mess and put it in a bucket.

Analee smiled. 'Gypsies consider the afterbirth precious, Mrs Pybus; they dry it in the sun and use it for potions and unguents.'

Mrs Pybus made a grimace of distaste and covered the bucket with a cloth.

'If you will excuse me saying so my lady, them are filthy habits and have no place among civilized folk such as us.'

'At least my origins haven't reached the ears of this good woman,' Analee whispered smilingly into Nelly's ear.

The midwife came with clean sheets, and rolling Analee to one side they deftly removed the spoiled birth sheet, replacing it with soft white linen embroidered with lace and the arms of the House of Falconer. Nelly puffed up the pillows behind Analee and helped her to raise herself so that she lay comfortably against them. Then she put a fresh sheet on top and a light blanket woven from the fleece of Lakeland sheep.

After a while the baby – carefully washed and swaddled and still fast asleep – was brought to his mother who took him in her arms, hugging him gently and putting her cheek against his soft dark head. She felt peaceful and a little tearful with joy and relief that all had gone so well. The sun was now low in the sky and through the window she could see the swallows and gulls fly low over the lake. The swallows would soon be departing for a warmer clime and already the nights were growing shorter. The Grange now lay in shadow and the purple tops of Lodore, Castlerigg Fell and High Seat glowed in the setting sun.

Analee dozed, and around her the house seemed to settle into its slow customary routine, but with a joyful sense that all had gone well with the mistress, safely delivered of an heir to the great Lord Falconer.

Hugo Fitzgerald had declined to leave until he knew the Marchioness was safely delivered. He had heard the cry of the new born baby, the bustle in the house, the voices of the staff raised in joy. A boy: Lord Falconer had an heir. If only it were *his* child! Hugo's heart beat more quickly at the thought of possessing such an adorable mistress, so fecund, vital and alive. If only it were possible; he would go to the ends of the earth to achieve such a dream . . .

The door opened and Betty Hardcastle came in, her good country face wreathed in smiles, followed by two servants carrying trays. Over her arm Mrs Hardcastle carried a cloth which she swiftly put on the table, while one of the servants proceeded to lay it quickly with cutlery and glass from the first tray.

'Her ladyship has insisted that you dine and stay here for the night sir. But for you the midwife would not have arrived so quickly and the birth might not have been as smooth.'

'Her ladyship has been informed that I am still here?'

'Her ladyship *asked*, sir. As soon as she was recovered she asked immediately for you.'

Hugo clasped his hands together in an attitude of ecstasy. 'She asked after *me*? She is an angel even to think of such a thing at such a time.'

Mrs Hardcastle cast him a shrewd look and set the dishes from the second tray on the table.

'Pray be seated sir,' she said. 'Her ladyship is always most thoughtful, which is why she is so loved by those whose privilege it is to wait on her. She thinks of the smallest thing to do with the household or the care of her staff. If they are ill she must know of it, and she herself will travel to far off cottages to take food and succour to the poor and needy. Indeed she is an angel sir, and deserves better of those . . .' Mrs Hardcastle quickly remembered herself and spoke sharply to the footmen to bring in the hot meat and wine. 'Your pardon, sir, I was forgetting myself.'

Hugo came slowly to Mrs Hardcastle's side, and bent his head so that his large blue eyes gazed into hers.

'It *is* his lordship?' he whispered in a tone of soft confidentiality.

Mrs Hardcastle seemed confused. He looked so kind, so sympathetic . . .

'I should not speak so sir, in front of strangers.' She looked quickly to the door to be sure they were still alone. 'But his lordship has neglected my lady *most* shamefully. All this year he has not been near her; nor would he permit her to be with him. She is most diligent in writing to him, that I know from my son Francis who takes the mail to catch the post at Keswick; but none comes back from the Marquess – oh no! I have heard, sir, though I pray her ladyship has not, that he dallies with women in London and cares not who knows it. Fortunately her ladyship is protected from gossip here by her loving servants and by Nelly who would not have her mistress disturbed by rumour; nor her tranquillity threatened as she has waited the birth of his lordship's son.'

'He is a swine!' Hugo snarled. 'Such a wonderful woman. Her beauty alone . . .'

Betty shrugged and pointed to the table as the footman came in with a steaming dish of roast meat and a bottle of the best wine from Burgundy.

'Pray sit down, Mr Fitzgerald sir. I hope the beef is to your liking. It is from our own farms, best Cumberland beef. And the wine from his lordship's personal cellar. I saw to that myself.'

Hugo sat down, seizing his napkin and bestowing on Mrs Hardcastle a smile of such sweetness that her heart turned over with pleasure. Although he was very different in looks from Mr Brent Delamain, being dark while the former was blond, he had the same roguish self-confidence, the same blend of modesty and self-assurance, the same degree of perfect good manners that gave Mr Brent such charm. It was the inexplicableness of his subsequent behaviour towards his wife that made him such a mystery and such a sorrow. Betty had never been able to understand it. Hugo tasted the meat and drank some of the wine, put one hand to his heart and the fingers of the other to his lips blowing her a kiss.

'Divine, Mrs Hardcastle. Perfection. The wine is insurpassable, and the Cumberland beef . . . exquisite!' He bent his head and ate for a few moments having been unaware of the degree of his hunger. Then he looked up at Mrs Hardcastle who, on the pretence of making sure all was well at the table, seemed inclined to linger.

'Believe me, I grieve to hear about his lordship, and ever may I be her ladyship's most humble servant to do for her all I can. Do you think she would receive me?'

Mrs Hardcastle looked rather startled and her fingers clutched at her ample bosom.

'*Tonight* sir? Oh I hardly think . . .'

Hugo leaned over and put a hand trustingly on her arm. 'Pray ask her for me; I must be off at dawn or else there will be a hue and cry after me. Ask her for me, you good soul. Perhaps she would personally wish to thank me for fetching the midwife – she may be vexed if I go without seeing her.'

His blue eyes looked pleadingly into Mrs Hardcastle's and she smiled and nodded her head.

'I'll see what Nelly says. You bide here.'

She went to the door and looked back at him tucking into the good food she had provided. He was a charmer, no doubt about it, ready to twist any woman round his little finger.

From the threshold it seemed to Hugo Fitzgerald as though everything was bathed in a white radiance which emanated from the bed where Analee lay. The bedclothes and sheets were white, the chemise Analee wore was white, the baby tucked up in the crib beside her bed was in white swaddling clothes, and the candles by the side of the bed were of pure white wax.

Yes, she was an enchantress: her smile beckoned to him, as he advanced into the room, and she held out a hand in greeting, her eyes shining with joy and fulfilment. Her well brushed hair hung over her shoulders curling in chunky black locks on her full bosom which was only partly concealed by the neckline of her chemise.

He kissed the extended fingers, his lips touching her hand while his eyes scanned her face. Her skin was smooth and brown, the colour like that of a ripe olive from the groves of southern Spain; but it was her huge dark eyes, brown yet almost black, fringed with long black lashes, that seduced him.

He felt there and then that he wanted to throw himself upon her, sink his head onto that enfolding, copious bosom, feel her arms around him, her long fingers caressing the nape of his neck. Her hand gripped his and a thrill passed through him that was only compounded by the essences and fragrances that emanated from her.

'Enchantress,' he murmured, 'my felicitations on the birth of your son.'

'And thanks to you Mr Fitzgerald for making it such an easy one. The midwife would never have been here so quickly if you had not fetched her. She told me she left her pony and cart at home and rode behind you on the horse.'

'Lady Falconer, it is my greatest pleasure to have assisted in any way I could, however humble; may I take a look at his lordship?'

Analee, startled, looked about her as though expecting to see her husband.

'His lord . . . ?'

'Your son, ma'am, he is Lord . . . ?'

'Oh my *son* . . .'

Yes, there was a distinct relief in the way she sank back, Hugo noticed. She was afraid of the Marquess.

'My son. I believe it is Lord Blair, the Master of Blair. Fancy the little darling being a noble lord!'

They both looked at the crib in which the Master of Blair slumbered, unaware of the great honours to which he had been born, unaware of the greater ones to which he might aspire.

'Has he a name, ma'am, other than Blair? A Christian name, that is to say.'

'No, we have not given thought to it. My husband . . . has been abroad.'

Hugo stood over the crib aware of his size and power compared to that of the weakness of the child who slept so peacefully. He drew himself up even more and filled his chest with air. He could father a child; he, Hugo Fitzgerald, could lie upon a woman and make her conceive. In his many amours he had never thought of it this way before – this gift, this power of fatherhood. When he turned, Analee was gazing at him thoughtfully, almost as though she had divined what he was thinking. He smiled and exhaled the air from his chest, shaking his head and gesticulating with his hands.

'He is so small, the Master of Blair. He made me feel so big.'

Yes he was well-built, Analee thought, eyeing his frame as he looked at the baby. Whereas the Falcon was cast in a massive mould and Brent was tall and thick-set, this man was very well proportioned, inclining neither to being too fat nor too lean. And whereas the Falcon was particularly dark and swarthy, and Brent predominantly fair, this man was brown complexioned, with large blue eyes and doubtless thick brown hair under his wig. He had a charming soft brogue to his lilting voice, and yet he was very masculine.

Analee was aware of herself having just given birth, of the issue of her femininity, of her powers of procreation, of her weakness as a woman – of the result of the nine long months of gestation lying asleep in the crib. And as he had stretched himself she had also become very aware of this strange new male come so suddenly into her life, of his power and vigour and . . . kindness. His eyes were soft and smiling as he glanced from her to the baby and she could imagine him dandling a child on his knees, and being careful and concerned. He would never have abandoned his wife for almost the entire time that she was carrying a child. She could never see Hugo Fitzgerald doing a thing like that. And even if the child wasn't his, for sure the Falcon didn't know that. Thank heaven anyway that the child seemed to resemble her.

There was sensuality in the room as well as motherhood and domesticity. She wished this strapping young man would sit on the bed and take her hand, maybe put his arms around her. She sighed . . . but it was not to be. It could never be. It was a fancy in her mind, disoriented after giving birth.

The longing and the yearning, unspoken between them, continued for some moments. Each wanted the other, yet knew that for now – forever, perhaps – it was not possible even to touch. Hugo looked down at the beautiful woman, so strong and yet so fragile, lying in her bed; he wished he could take her in his arms and comfort her, giving her his own strength. He knew she must be lonely and unhappy despite the joy in her child.

'I would do anything I could for you, ma'am. You have only to ask.'

Analee looked up at him, her brown hands lying on the white counterpane, her dark eyes sparkling.

'It is good to have a friend like you, Mr Fitzgerald. I know not why, but I feel a bond between us, though it is only this day that we have met.'

'But I felt it too! When I saw you at Court I saw no other woman. When Mrs Rigg spoke of you I instantly remembered your every feature, your beauty, your grace – I felt I *had* to see you. Lady Falconer, in ages past noblewomen had squires. May I not be your squire?'

Analee laughed in pure enjoyment at this Irish romanticism. 'It is beautifully put, sir, and apt too. For, if I remember, the squire only paid courtly love to his lady. Believe me the Marquess of Falconer is a very jealous man, and would have no other sort of attentions paid me.'

'I understand Lord Falconer is scarcely ever here ma'am . . .' Hugo began.

Analee tilted her chin defensively. 'Lord Falconer is a very busy man. Even now that the war is settled there are still, as you know, hostages in Paris that each side agreed to provide. His lordship is constantly abroad on business. It was his care for me that I should be well protected and tranquil at my beloved home on Lake Derwentwater.'

Hugo bowed his head, so as to hide the disbelief in his eyes.

'And now, ma'am . . . may I ask if you will rejoin his lordship again?'

'If he sends for me, of course. Or he may summon me to Falcon's Keep. I do not know his wishes until I hear from him.'

Hugo said nothing; such wifely docility was admirable, if distinctly false. His lordship was a rogue and a philanderer, that much was clear, and his Marchioness too intelligent not to know it. But whatever she said, enough had passed this night between them to make him feel that a bond already existed, a bond sacred and true. He would be her swain and, if ever he could bring it about, he would do all he could to make her his mistress.

11

The Falcon gazed for a long time at the child lying so peacefully in the crib, whose eyes returned the speculative gaze of the tall dark man. The child didn't seem at all daunted by this apparition and finally gave a huge yawn and, putting a finger in his mouth, closed his eyes.

The Falcon stepped back appreciatively. 'Aye, he is a true Falconer. He cares not for authority. See, he is indifferent to me, his father.'

'He is but a month old, Angus,' Analee said mildly, thankful that the child had her colouring and resembled her rather than his natural father. With his innate jealousy and suspicion she had feared for a moment that Angus would somehow have sensed that the child was not his, the way he had instinctively sensed that day that she and Brent were about to kiss.

The Falcon had just arrived, unexpectedly, on his large bay horse accompanied only by McNeath. His presence had immediately filled the house, disturbing its order and tranquillity, as a gale disrupts a calm and peaceful day.

Analee had not seen him since the previous January and it was now September. He had not written to her or sent word at the news of the birth of her son. Now he had arrived and she felt a chill in her heart as overpowering as the cold that comes in with the gale. What would he want of her? Would he just depart, or take her with him, or order her back to Falcon's Keep? Suddenly Analee was aware that her tranquil days were over, and the future was bleak and uncertain again.

The nursery faced the Borrowdale end of the lake and for a moment Lord Falconer stood gazing towards the high peaks that were barely visible in the distance, Great Gable, Glaramara and, towering above the rest, giant Scafell. The Falcon shook his head and turned to his wife.

'I cannot abide this solitude. I know not how you endure it Analee. Well, my dear, you look well.' He went over to her and

501

kissed her on the cheek, chastely like a brother. Analee could not help recalling the days when their proximity, their nearness to each other, created a kind of fusion so that they had to kiss and to embrace, to possess each other instantly. Momentarily she leaned against him, longing for those days to return, almost willing them back, but the Falcon turned away from her and, looking once again at his heir, walked over to the door.

'Come my dear, we must discuss names and such,' he said, as he held the door open for her.

After Clare was born he had seldom left her side and as soon as he decently could he reintroduced her to the delights of love again. But he had also become a companion and a friend, and the memory of those days hung like a burden on Analee's heart as she walked down the staircase, aware of his heavy steps behind her.

Maybe it showed on her face as they re-entered the drawing room because, as she turned, he caught hold of her and looked for a moment as though he would embrace her, as though he too had felt the same need as she.

'I thought of Duncan,' he announced. 'Duncan Alexander Blair. They are family names, and my next son will be Beyrick after the first Earl of Falconer, Beyrick ennobled by Queen Elizabeth.'

'As you please Angus,' she said obediently, rejoicing in her heart that the mighty Falcon was cukold, that his heir was not of his own blood. If their days together were to continue in this fashion, it was a knowledge that would cheer her every time she thought of her husband or looked at Duncan. Would Prince Charles Edward have approved of Duncan? Assuredly; it was a good Scottish name. Analee smiled contentedly at the knowledge.

'You are very docile, my dear Analee,' the Falcon remarked approvingly. 'Not the termagant I recall. Maybe these days in the country have tamed you?'

'I recall, my lord, that 'twas not I who needed taming,' Analee said, her old spirit showing in her eyes. ''Twas you who raped, maimed and near strangled me.'

Angus came over her, his arm raised so that she thought once again he was about to strike her.

'Now I'll have no more of that!' he shouted. 'That was an aberration, a momentary derangement and, although I humbly tried to atone for it, you took less notice of me than a cat one of

502

the fleas on its body. I, Angus Falconer, chose to give my name to a common gypsy, to make her the mother of my children, to have her accorded all the honours and dignities of my station – and what did the gypsy do? Repulsed me, her own husband; left me in no doubt that my embraces were loathsome . . . Now Analee, I am going to give you one more chance. You must love me and show that you love me, and respond warmly to me as you did in those far off days. Otherwise I will put you away and take another wife. The King will willingly grant my petition for divorce as it is well known that he cares not for the nobility marrying into the commonality, especially such riff-raff as you hail from.'

'His Majesty was very kind to me,' Analee said, rage again consuming her heart. 'He was even gracious enough to say how fortunate your lordship was to secure my hand as a bride.'

'Oh fie!' Angus said wrathfully. ''Tis well known that the King can be taken in by any pretty woman. And you *are* uncommonly pretty, my love.'

The Falcon's tone changed and he went up to her and closing his eyes caressed her gently as if recalling all the delights they had once shared. Analee felt her knees weaken at his touch; her heart-beat quickened with desire and she wished he would take her in the abandoned way he had in the old days, whenever and wherever the fancy pleased him. She could see the veins standing out on his temple and knew that he did feel desire for her, as she did for him. It was months since she had lain with her husband. Her only infidelity in their married life had been with the Prince, and that would never have happened but for her husband's brutality towards her.

How she had once craved his body, did so still. He was her husband, had been her greatest love – maybe they should try and forget the past, as he wanted to; despite the callousness of his expressions, the threat to 'put her away', the disdain in his voice when he talked about her origins.

Analee's heart was dancing. The old magic was returning; she and the Falcon wanted to know each other again, to merge his desire and her desperate need after all these months of enforced abstinence.

Angus looked at her flushed face, her eyes darkened by desire, and wondered how he could ever love anyone else, ever want anyone other than this enchantress, this woman who was his wife? What folly had possessed him to treat her as he did, what wanton profligacy made him abandon her in this dark northern clime? Never, with all the women he had lain with since he last saw Analee – and he had not been parsimonious with his favours – had he experienced desire so sharp it was almost agonizing. And he had to do nothing to find such fulfilment – she was his.

Unable to believe his good fortune he gazed down at her and gently kissed her lips, then her eyes, her chin and her forehead. He put out a hand and stroked her, beginning at the neck, over the bosom, across the flat stomach while Analee gazed at him with that expression he now recalled so well, but had not seen for such a long time. But she was not smiling and he saw that her bright dark eyes glistened with tears.

'Oh my dearest Analee,' he murmured, 'forgive me . . .'

She touched his body marked with the many scars he had sustained in a life of fighting, and these gave him an added virility, a lustre – to have such a brave soldier for a lover, a husband . . .

Yes, he was her husband; whatever he said, however brutal he was, they were wedded, she bore his name and she had his child – Clare was the bond that had cemented their love. The dark bubble-haired Clare, vivacious and impetuous, so like her father.

She *would* bear sons for the Falcon – she would do what she could to erase the memory of his brutality, the hurt of his words, and remember that he was not only a great lord and warrior, but her lawful husband. If only he would keep on loving her like this, reminding her constantly by his nearness, by his physical presence, that he loved and needed her . . .

He was looking at her, as though reading her thoughts. 'You must come with me to London, Analee, be by my side. I need you. I love you Analee, and only you; I never want to be parted from you again. I thought to punish you, but I have punished myself by depriving myself of your company, your body, your love. I need and desire you Analee. What passed between us was a cruel misunderstanding. Tell me, Brent Delamain – '

Analee put one of her fingers to his lips. 'Do not mention his name; do not torment yourself with something that never happened.'

'It did not?'

'Of course not.'

The Falcon looked at her as if satisfied and groped for her hand.

'Then his name shall not arise again. I am a jealous man, Analee. What I did was because I was tormented with jealousy. Oh I know I treated you cruelly, my love; my fantasies made me into an ogre – and I have neglected you for many months. Can you forgive me?'

Could she? Would he forgive *her* if he knew Duncan was not his son? No, he would never forgive her; he would perhaps kill her and consider himself justified. Was what she had done to him worse than what he had done to her? He had raped and beaten her, nearly killed her . . . but she had borne an heir to the Falconer estates who was not a Falconer.

Yes, Analee reflected: what she had done was far worse, in the eyes of the Falcon, in the eyes of mankind. Many men beat their wives and treated them ill, but the wives who were unfaithful were often put away. Why, everyone knew that even the mother of the present King had been locked up by George I for infidelity. She was imprisoned for over thirty years until her death and never saw her children again – and she was a great princess, not a common gypsy.

But in her own eyes, Analee did not feel she had done wrong. She had borne a son to a Prince, a man deprived of his heritage and great estates; now *his* son would one day have great estates in the England and Scotland over which his father so much wanted to rule. There was a justice in this. Let it be. She would have other sons for Angus.

In the balmy September days that followed Analee and the Falcon basked in the happiness of the renewal of their love. It was as if they relived the first days of their relationship, after the Falcon had returned to his home and taken Analee the serving girl to his bed. In no time lust had been transformed to mutual love, and so it was in the days following their reconciliation at Furness Grance.

'Furness has worked its magic on us,' Analee said one day. By lifting her head she could see from the bedroom window the shadow of Castlerigg Fell opposite them. The purple heather on the fells was in full bloom and the russet leaves on the trees were thick and heavy with the moisture of autumn. Analee rested her head on one arm as she gazed out of the window of the room across the still waters of the lake.

'See my lord, that crag opposite is known as Falcon Crag. It was a portent.'

'How so my love?' her husband said.

Analee smiled, that lingering amorous smile of a woman who knows her own powers, is confident of her own success.

'A portent of our love, Angus. It was doubtless called Falcon Crag long before we came here. 'Twas meant that our love should be renewed here.'

'It was never lost, my love, it will always be like this,' the Falcon said. 'We shall never be parted again, my Analee.' He turned to the table beside the bed and, from a soft leather pouch that lay there, he drew forth a medallion, wafer thin and exquisitely wrought with the delicate imprint of the falcon bird engraved in the middle. He held it up on its fine chain and it spun round, its white gold almost dazzling in the light.

Analee felt the tears come into her eyes as she looked at it and, as he bent and put it around her neck, she closed them tight, hoping he would not see. She knew the meaning of the medallion, made of Falcon Gold; but now to him it was one thing and to her another. To her it meant that, in her way, she was always loyal and faithful to the Falcon. For him it was the celebration of the son he had always wanted. But he saw the tears steal from under her lids and, misunderstanding the meaning, kissed her.

'I promised you this when we had a son, my darling. It is both a reward and a renewal of our love.'

Still she did not speak, but fingered the smooth roundness of the medallion which lay on her breast. The ring no longer symbolized their eternal love, nor did the faultless oval of the medal. It was no longer a symbol of enduring unity, but of mistrust and deceit. Still, she would wear it for him. She smiled through her tears and he thought they were tears of joy. He raised himself on one elbow and gazed at her. 'I am glad it has given you so much pleasure, Analee, but I must leave soon, my dearest. I have to go to London, then to France, and I want to take you with me. Will you mind leaving this place of heavenly peace?'

'I shall mind Angus, but to be with you, to have your love and tenderness I would give up anything. We always have this place here, as a refuge from the discord of the world. I have been here nearly a year and it has been a good time for me – a time of reflection, of giving birth, of making love with you my dearest husband.' She reached up and stroked his cheek with her long slim hands feeling his lips, his nose, the hollows of his deep-set eyes, the bristles on his face and chin. Even after being satiated by love-making she still felt hungry for him. Having so unexpectedly had their love restored after supposing it lost forever, Analee had begun to wonder if indeed she had powers that other people had not; if the magic of her gypsy forbears had in fact transmitted itself to her. Was she a spell-maker, an enchantress, after all?

She had once again enslaved the Falcon, and been enslaved by him. After what he had done to her the previous year in Paris that in itself was magic enough.

Suddenly that pleasant period of somnolence that follows love-making was shattered by thuds, cries and loud female screams which appeared to come from the courtyard behind the house. The Falcon had leaped out of bed in one bound and hastily donned some clothes while Analee swiftly followed him, pausing only to slip into a light morning gown. As they rushed to the top of the stairs they saw Betty Hardcastle panting up, her hands to her flushed face. She paused as she saw them, the Falcon in the act of hastily buttoning his breeches.

'Oh my lord, my lady . . . there is a terrible to-do in the yard. Pray come quickly sir . . .'

'But what is it? Where is McNeath?' Angus asked testily. 'This is outrageous.'

'Indeed sir, it is McNeath that has caused the commotion.'

'*McNeath* caused this commotion? Nonsense woman!'

'No sir. He is fighting with my Francis in the yard. He will kill him sir.'

The Falcon brushed past Betty on the stairs and Analee, followed him, pulling Betty with her.

'It is about Nelly?' she whispered.

'Aye ma'am.'

'I thought as much.' Analee spoke rapidly as they walked along. 'She has been playing them off one against the other all this month.'

'Aye ma'am. McNeath caught her naked in the barn with my Francis. She does not have a *stitch* of clothing on, ma'am!'

507

'Oh my goodness!' Analee's hands flew to her face as she reached the kitchen door and saw the scene in the yard. McNeath and Francis Hardcastle, both stripped to the waist, were lunging at each other like prize pugilists. Their bodies were covered with sweat, and Francis had a wound on his head from which blood was pouring. Nelly was hovering on the other side of the yard, near the out-house barn where the horses were stabled, the loft being used for storing hay. It was a favourite place of dalliance not only for Nelly, but for all the amorously inclined servants of the house, being comfortable, warm and protected from the gaze of the curious. It was true that Nelly had not a stitch on, except for a piece of sacking which she held over the top portion of her anatomy; the lower part was exposed to the view of the entire household who were now gawping at the spectacle with evident enjoyment.

The Falcon gave an angry roar and ran across the yard, grabbing McNeath with one huge hand and practically flinging him against the wall of the house. The spectators gave a unanimous gasp of admiration at this demonstration of prowess, McNeath being nearly the equal of the Falcon in build and strength.

Francis who had been taking the worst of the battering stood bent and gasping, his face obscured behind a mask of gore, his eyes blinking away the blood. Analee ran over to Nelly and began to drag her inside; but Nelly could not stop crying and screaming, clutching at the meagre sack which half covered her bosom.

'This is outrageous Nell,' Analee hissed. 'His lordship will have you dismissed and the men whipped. What a scene, and you with no clothes on! Have you *no* shame?'

'Oh Analee!' Nelly gave vent to a fresh outburst of tears on hearing the words of her beloved mistress and turned to her for comfort. Analee pressed the weeping girl to her, so that the shame of her nakedness could be concealed – not but that those around had seen all there possibly was to see.

'Oh ma'am, Analee. Francis and I were just dallying a bit and McNeath comes up and flings him down the steps of the loft ma'am. I thought the horses would trample him to death. I flung myself after McNeath begging for mercy, but he throws me to one side, rather as his lordship has just thrown him, and kicks Francis into the yard where he starts to pummel him as though he would kill him. Oh ma'am, what am I to do?'

'You will have to choose, Nell, you will have to choose.'

Analee patted her shoulder; but she could not help smiling across at her husband who had just pulled McNeath to his feet and was giving him a talking to, while the hapless Francis, half-blinded with blood, was led into the house by his mother, now sobbing hysterically.

'Now get back to your work and forget this disgraceful business,' Angus cried, gesticulating angrily. 'Go now. Go.'

The servants, having thoroughly enjoyed the break in their morning routine, shuffled back to their tasks, one or two of the men taking a last look at Nelly whose former gauntness of frame had filled out in the last few years due to the good living she had enjoyed. Her figure was now round, wholesome and eminently desirable, as the fight between her two lovers had proved.

Later that day, cleaned up and decently dressed, Nelly stood before Lord and Lady Falconer, her head bent, her hands clasped before her in an expression of abject misery. Tears stole down her cheeks and she let them fall regardless onto her clean pinafore. The Falcon's expression was stern, but Analee's was gentle and encouraging.

'You must choose, Nell, if either will have you, which I wonder. His lordship blames himself that he did not let you wed McNeath before; but as you know I did not exactly favour him myself.' She gave a meaningful glance at the Falcon who averted his eyes. 'However, all that is over and forgotten. McNeath is a fine man. He has loved you, and bedded you, for years. Francis Hardcastle too is worthy – a good robust son of the soil who will make you a fine husband and father to your children. But Nell, his lordship and I are soon to go from hence. First back to Falcon's Keep and then London, to our house in Piccadilly. If you do not choose McNeath I shall have to leave you here, much as I love you; for if you choose Francis he and McNeath could not abide for long in the same household. Now will you say, or do you want time to consider?'

Nelly wailed afresh, kneading her fists into her tear-stained eyes.

'Oh ma'am, my lord, I have no hesitation at all – if . . . if he will have me,' she blubbered, wiping her eyes on her apron. 'Oh he was so fine, so strong! Did you not observe his muscles rippling, ma'am, in his fine body, the wrath on his face – ' Nelly's face was shining through her tears.

'Who Nell, who . . . ?' For all her concern Analee could hardly stifle her laughter while even the Falcon's severe countenance was beginning to crease into a smile.

'Why ma'am, sir . . .' Nelly dried her eyes, the pinafore by this time helplessly crumpled, and broke into a radiant smile. '*McNeath*, ma'am! Oh you should have seen his ire as he threw Francis down the stairs! And as he stripped I thought he was going to ravish me ma'am; but no, he tossed down his coat and jumped after Francis, kicked him into the yard and began such a pummelling of that poor fellow that I wonder he has the ability to walk or the breath to do it.'

'Maybe he has neither Nell, for his mother has kept him in her room bathing his face and bruises with boracic.'

'And he did it for *me*, ma'am! Inflamed he was by desire for me, red hot jealousy! Oh ma'am, if he would have me I would never stray again.'

'Well let us ask him,' Angus said, striding to the door and flinging it open. Outside stood McNeath, proud and upright like a turkey cock, his civilian dress of shirt and breeches, white cravat, red stockings and black buckled shoes clean and neat. He had not a mark on him and his face was scrubbed and shining, his red whiskers freshly combed and springing from his face. He smiled when he saw his master's face, and his eyes immediately flew to Nelly. The Falcon stood to one side, gesturing towards her with his hand.

'She is all yours McNeath . . . if you will have her.'

'*I* have her sir? Why . . .' McNeath walked rapidly to Nelly's side and awkwardly grasped her hand.

'She is a strumpet,' his lordship thundered, 'no doubt of that. All the time you have been faithful to her, McNeath – ' here he winked broadly at his servant, who had been rumoured to enjoy a different woman every night during their absence from Furness, '*she* has been cavorting with this country bumpkin, who – '

'Oh now sir,' Nelly protested, looking fearfully up at her loved one. 'He is a good man, a kind man. I'll not have that said about Francis. But he is not like McNeath here, your lordship, not a patch.' Nelly gazed up adoringly at him. 'And if I did happen to stray once or maybe even twice, the temptation proving too much for me, I swear I will never do it again.'

'I'll say you won't my girl,' McNeath said threateningly. 'I shall keep such a strict eye on you that if I catch you so much as ogling another man I'll have the skin off you.'

'Ohhh!' Nelly clasped her hands and squealed with delight.

'Aye, well that appears to be satisfactorily settled,' Angus said, rubbing his hands together. 'Then let us get ready for our departure as soon as possible from this place.' He turned to Analee, smiling. 'I confess that now I have come to love Furness and I shall miss it. It has restored our love and joy in each other, thank God for that. Furness to me is a happy place, a talisman, and I shall return here as often as I can. It has cast its spell over me.' The Falcon put his arm lightly around Analee's shoulder and kissed her cheek. 'But I have duties in London at Court and abroad and you, our good and faithful servants, will accompany us.' He looked at Nelly and held up a warning hand. 'But the moment we are in London, the very instant, I shall have you two wed by the vicar in St James's Church across the road from us. Then you will belong to McNeath right proper, Nelly, and he can do what he likes with you.'

Nelly gazed at her victorious lover with rapture in her eyes, seeing which Analee could only think ruefully that she and Nelly were alike in one thing: they liked strength in a man, and power; passion, certainly, and maybe, though they would not care to admit it, violence. Angus and McNeath were both fighting men, warriors who bore the scars of battle on their bodies, its passion in their hearts. They would drink from the fountain of life to the full, for tomorrow they might be dead. They could be cruel, false even, but they had the means within them to drive their women to a frenzy, to enslave them entirely and completely, ruthlessly and forever.

In each case, master and servant, mistress and maid were alike. Perhaps, Analee thought, this was the way fortune meant it to be. Deep in her heart, she prayed that now their happiness would last forever.

12

Lady Delamain could scarcely contain her excitement as the Falcon's impressive cavalcade swept through the gates of the castle and up the long drive. His own heavy travelling coach was preceded by a light barouche containing his two children and their nurses, and followed by another coach which held the baggage, and McNeath on horseback. Lady Delamain had spent many anxious days making preparations for her distinguished cousin's visit and had been at the window hours before they were expected.

At the sight of the procession she gathered up her skirts and rushed out of the drawing room, cannoning into her husband who was issuing from his study at the same time.

'Oh George . . . !'

'I have seen them, Henrietta. Pray try and control yourself.'

But Henrietta Delamain, who had little enough diversion in her dull life, was quite unable to subdue her excitement. Her face aflame, she flew down the great stone stairs and along the hall, out onto the porch which stood above the broad marble steps leading down to the drive. The Falcon's coach was just completing a neat arc as it came to a stop at precisely the right point, and two liveried footmen hurried over to open the doors emblazoned with the arms of Falconer.

The Falcon alighted and turned to assist his wife, who was dressed in a heavy travelling cloak to keep out the cold, her face almost concealed by a monk-like cowl. The Falcon tenderly and firmly clasped her hand until she was safe on the ground and then kept hold of it as he escorted her up the steps and presented her once again to Henrietta who took Analee in her arms, kissing her warmly.

'Lady Falconer, how glad I am to see you again! And safely delivered of an heir since I last saw you. How fortunate you are to have so pleased your husband in a way that, alas . . .' Henrietta faltered, her eyes bright with sudden tears as her husband came behind her and put a warning hand on her arm.

'Hush, my dear. Her ladyship is not the least interested in our domestic affairs.'

'Oh but I am, Sir George,' Analee said quietly. 'I hear you have a lovely baby girl and you are to be congratulated too. Even if this world unfairly gives precedence to male children it is still a delight to welcome a new born baby, of whichever sex, into the world.'

She looked meaningfully at Sir George Delamain to whom her remarks were pointedly addressed and her husband, still lightly holding her hand, threw back his head and laughed.

'Now, now Analee. Of course any child is to be welcomed; but it is the law of the land that only a male can inherit certain titles. Let us hope that my cousin and her worthy husband will, in due course, be blessed by God with an heir.'

Lord Falconer bent and kissed his cousin on the cheek, noting her pallor and the fact that she had become more plain than ever, as well as more buxom. Sir George, on the other hand, seemed leaner and older and the expression on his face one of almost permanent severity, the line of his mouth grim and unrelaxed.

The nurses now approached with Lady Clare and the young Master of Blair and both were fussed over by Henrietta, especially the infant heir wrapped in his shawls.

'He is the very image of you Angus!' Henrietta had turned down the warm blanket to peep at the tiny face gazing wonderingly up at her.

'Aye, they all say it,' the Falcon agreed with a satisfied smile. 'The spitting image; but then we Falconers are a fine breeding strain and imprint our likeness on all our progeny.'

'That is not to say that he does not resemble her ladyship, somewhat,' Henrietta said quickly, looking at Analee who had a curious expression on her face as though she had been amused by some secret thought.

'Aye, my wife and I have a certain resemblance ourselves; we are both dark and quick tempered. Now, Henrietta, we have been abroad since dawn, will you not give us food and drink?'

Henrietta's hands flew to her scarlet cheeks and she sped up the stairs as quickly as her plump little legs could carry her, calling for the servants to carry his lordship's bags, conduct him and her ladyship to the best guest chamber prepared for them and make sure that the sumptuous repast was ready in the drawing room.

The Falconers, having visited Falcon's Keep, were on their way to London, breaking their journey overnight at Delamain Castle. Sir George was anxious to ingratiate himself with the powers in the land and his wife's cousin was among the highest. Henrietta also had something very special to ask of her cousin's wife and looked all day for an opportunity to be alone with her.

It was late October and the days were drawing in, the air cold. Analee yearned for a sight of Morella and, just before dusk while Angus was ensconced in a business discussion with Sir George, she slipped out of the castle and hurried across the broad lawn to the dower house that stood on the edge of Delamain forest. At first she knocked in vain; but for the fact that she had seen a light in a lower window, she would have thought the house was deserted. Then the door was opened slowly by an aged footman who peered cautiously into the dark.

'It is I, Lady Falconer,' Analee said quickly to reassure him. 'Is Mrs Delamain at home?'

The footman stood to one side and beckoned Analee in, closing the door after her.

'Madam is not well, my lady. She is resting in her room.'

'Oh, I am sorry to hear that. And Morella, the little girl . . . ?'

'She is with her nurse my lady. May I take you to her?'

'Oh please.' Analee shut her eyes with the intensity of the emotion – to see Morella again, to hold her in her arms! Clutching her cloak to her, because it was cold in the house, she followed the man as he ambled arthritically along the hall and knocked at the door at the end, opening it for Analee and bowing low as she passed.

Few candles burned in the room, but a warm fire roared up the grate providing a welcome blaze in the gloom. Morella was sitting on her nurse's lap, her head against her breast as she crooned her a lullaby, her great blue eyes gazing into the fire. Analee stopped abruptly, alerted by the melodious voice, the gentle words of the song. They were in the *Romani* language.

She hurried forward and bent towards the nurse and the child who appeared unaware of her entry. Morella was the first to see her and struggled out of her nurse's arms, but Analee's eyes were on the woman who seemed riveted by the glow of the flames, and still did not stir.

'Reyora!' Analee stretched out her hands and the woman half rose, looking around her as though startled. She stared at the tall woman in front of her, diamonds glistening at her throat, the rich stuff of her dress discernible beneath her velvet travelling cloak. She stared at her, unrecognizing, uncomprehending.

Analee shook her head free from her hood, her bejewelled hands clumsily untying the laces which fastened her cloak.

'Reyora, it is I . . . Analee.'

'*Analee!*' Reyora sat down quickly again and put a hand to her heart, staring up at the woman before her. 'Analee?'

'Yes, Analee the gypsy, Morella's mother,' Analee whispered, trying not to let the child hear.

'I cannot believe it is Analee,' Reyora said. 'I cannot believe it, and yet the voice is Analee's, the looks are Analee's . . . but the *clothes*!'

'Ah the clothes are not Analee's, but I am she. Oh Reyora what fortunate chance brought me here today, how often have I thought of you, longed to see you, to thank you for saving Morella . . . !'

'I thought you were dead. I knew not how you could have survived with all those marauding soldiers on the road, the famine, the dreadful winter. It was hard enough for us travelling in a troupe, which is why I left Morella here. But you are not only alive, you . . . why you are a fine lady! Analee, did you *steal* those jewels?'

Analee smiled, but first she bent down and tenderly picked up the little girl who was tugging earnestly at her robe. She kissed her soft cheek and nuzzled her, her hands running through the fine golden hair while her eyes filled with tears.

'How are you my darling? Do you remember me?'

''Course I 'member,' said Morella clearly. 'Fine lady. Nice lady.'

'Oh you darling – you see, I came especially to see you! I have not forgotten you either.'

Analee sat on a chair opposite Reyora, letting her cloak slip from her shoulders, Morella still on her knee. Reyora could not take her eyes off the magnificence of Analee's clothes, the glittering jewels at her throat and on her fingers, the fashionable hairstyle, the smoothness of her skin.

'Reyora, I have become a noblewoman.'

'You a . . . ?'

'I am married to the Marquess of Falconer, these three years.'

'The Marquess . . . ? *You* are the Lady Falconer that the household has been in such a tizzy about for days?'

Analee nodded, her eyes shining at the expression on Reyora's face – Reyora, the *cohani* who had delivered Morella, who had undertaken to save her from the wrath of the Buckland tribe. Reyora, looking much older and thinner now, but still as serene and dignified as when she was a power in the Buckland tribe.

'Yes. I met Angus when I came upon the remnants of the Buckland camp, after it had been ravaged by the Scots. Oh Reyora, and I found Randal and held him in my arms while he died.' Analee put her hand in front of her eyes and bowed her head involuntarily, choking at the memory. 'Oh what a terrible time that was, one I can scarcely bear to recall. But the Marquess of Falconer came at the head of the government troops and found me there. He took me to his house and . . .'

'And you are Lady Falconer.' Reyora sank weakly back in her chair. 'I cannot credit it. Analee the gypsy, once the wife of a wandering gypsy boy, now the wife of a *lord*.'

'And I have children by the Falcon. A girl and . . . and a boy,' Analee said, hesitating only slightly. She was so aware of Reyora's magical powers that somehow she felt sure she would divine the truth about her new-born son. 'The boy born just three months ago. They are here with me, Reyora – how I wish you could see them! Come with me to the house . . .'

Reyora shook her head and glanced at Morella. 'No. I am relieving the nurse who has the same feverish chill as Mrs Delamain. I cannot go just now. How long will you stay?'

'We are going tomorrow, back to London. We are on our way south. But Reyora, tell me what has happened to you, and how is it that you came here.'

Reyora shrugged and pulled her thick shawl around her shoulders as though reminded of the cold. 'Well, I quickly divined that Mrs Delamain, that good lady, was related to the child, having in mind what you told me about the blond *gadjo*.' Reyora glanced quickly up at Analee. 'I was poor and hungry, and the cold was bitter. The child was not well, and I knew I would be leaving her behind where she would be looked after far better than I ever could, chance and God having brought us here.'

'Oh yes – you did the right thing Reyora, you did.'

'I then went south with what was left of the Buckland tribe; but many fell sick and died in that cruel winter. Time passed, however, and I became the *phuri-dai* in place of Rebecca who was killed in the camp.'

Analee shuddered and closed her eyes, remembering the awful sight of carnage. 'I know, I saw her. Oh what a terrible thing it was.'

Reyora shrugged once again, not with indifference but as though shaking off the pain.

'We could not go back to the site of our former camp with its terrible memories. It is accursed ground forever more. We have made a new camp not far from here and from time to time I come to see Morella and assure myself that all is well. And so I have found you. It is good Analee.'

'Oh Reyora, it is *very* good! I will tell you where I live so that you can always come and see me too.'

But Reyora smiled and shook her head.

'I will not visit you Analee, fine lady in your great house no doubt. But if you ever need me I will come. We are lodged not far from Appleby in the place they call Hanging Shaw, though there has been no hanging there that I know of for many a year. If you are ill or in need, send for me Analee and I will always come, but you and I are now in different worlds and it is best that we should stay that way.'

'But Reyora, can I not do something for you? I have money . . .'

Reyora shook her head. 'You know us gypsies, Analee. We have sufficient for our needs; we have warm tents, and fires that glow at night, enough tinder to light them. We trap birds and rabbits and catch fish from the streams. We lack nothing Analee, certainly nothing that money can buy.'

'I would love to come among you again,' Analee sighed, wriggling her feet in her soft shoes. 'Sometimes I yearn for the open, for the life that I knew . . .'

Suddenly there was a noise and Nelly popped her head round the door.

'Oh there you are, my lady; Lady Delamain is asking for you. Rather than have her come to find you I guessed where you were and came myself. Why . . .' Nelly advanced into the room, looking uncertainly at the woman sitting by the fire.

'Is it . . . ?'

517

'Aye, it is I, Reyora, and I scarce recognized you Nelly. Have you become a fine lady too?'

Nelly blushed and laughed, smoothing her neat seersucker dress with her hands.

'No Reyora, but I am the maid to a fine lady. Analee . . .'

'She has been telling me of the change in her fortunes. I have often wondered what became of both of you. I am glad all is well.'

'Nelly is to be married as soon as we reach London,' Analee said. 'She has for long loved a handsome soldier who is my husband's manservant.'

'That I am glad to hear. Then the story has a happy ending.' Reyora got up and stood gazing at Analee and her little daughter, who sucking her thumb, stared tranquilly up at her mother. 'What about this little one?'

'She is happy here. If my husband knew . . .' Reyora nodded sagely. 'Besides she is well looked after, Reyora. If it were otherwise I would not hesitate to tell him; but he is a wrathful man, a jealous man . . .'

'I understand and I think you are right. She gives the old lady much happiness. But Analee I fear she is not long for this world.'

Analee clasped Morella to her anxiously. 'Is her illness serious then?'

'No. 'Tis a chill and a fever. She will recover from this. But the old woman is frail Analee. She has had a hard life, many griefs and bereavements. I don't say this year or next year, but one day . . . what will you do then? Sir George Delamain has no love for his mother's ward.'

'Then when that day comes I shall do what I have to Reyora. Have no fear; I shall face my responsibilities.'

'I am sure you will Analee. How fortunate we met again and I could reassure myself as to your fate.'

'Reyora,' Nelly stepped timidly forward, 'did you ever hear aught about my family? My father, Brewster Driver . . .'

Reyora shook her head firmly. 'No, I never did and I never wanted to. You were well rid of that man Nelly, and are better off where you are. Put them out of your mind.'

'But my mother, my brothers and sisters . . . ?'

'All tarred with the same brush. A bad lot. I never saw such discord in the camp as when they were there. You are lucky to have escaped a fate with them Nelly Driver. Now you are a maid to a fine lady and to be married to a good honest man. Think yourself lucky and forget about the Driver family.'

She held out her arms, but Morella clung to her mother. Reyora gently prised her hands away from Analee's arms.

'There my pretty, my baby, come to your old Reyora. See this fine lady has to go. She will come again, many times.'

'Oh yes.' Analee could not bear to let the little body out of her arms and hugged her close, aware of the tears welling in her eyes, the emotion in her bosom. Much as she loved Clare and Duncan, this child, her first live-born child, was very special. She felt such a maternal longing for her that she was almost tempted to run to the Falcon and tell him everything, to take her with her. But no . . . She kissed the child tenderly and handed her to Reyora.

'Go with kind Reyora, Morella. I will come back, never fear.'

Nelly helped her on with her cloak and she turned to face Reyora, but the tears streaming from her eyes obscured her vision.

'Dear, kind Reyora . . .'

'Say nothing. Go in peace.'

And Reyora turned towards the fire, gazing into it as she had before, just as though Analee had never come.

Lady Delamain sat in her boudoir twisting her hands anxiously. Analee noted the moisture on her lip, the obvious agitation in her heaving bosom.

'I hope your ladyship does not mind my confiding in you; but I have heard that you . . . have powers.'

'Of course I do not mind my dear Henrietta – and you must call me Analee as we are cousins; but my powers are only a legend. I was not able to help Mary Delamain to conceive, and I don't see how I can help you.'

Analee had listened to the story with considerable sympathy. Of how Henrietta had had two difficult confinements, how she nearly died during the last one, how the child had been extricated from her womb only with the help of murderous surgical instruments which had caused the poor baby's face to be permanently scarred, and how the doctors had said that, in the state her inside was, she would never conceive again. Sir George was desperate for an heir. He would not believe she could not conceive and ruthlessly put her

519

to the test every night which was wearing down her health. She was willing and anxious to be impregnated by her spouse, but if it was all to no avail . . . Henrietta had gazed piteously up at Analee.

'But despite these manifestations of his ardour my husband despises me. He does not do it for love; he does it for revenge. It is like . . .' Henrietta averted her eyes, lowered her voice, 'rape, if you will forgive me Analee. It is disgusting, and he used to be considerate and tender. Now all my regard for him is crumbling under these onslaughts.'

'I do not wonder, my dear Henrietta,' Analee said gently. 'I wish I could at least help to restore your husband's love if not your procreative powers. It is very hard for you . . .'

'I am anxious to please him . . . to regain his love,' Henrietta started to sob into a fine cambric handkerchief, 'but how can I if he is more like a beast than a man? How can I help myself? Oh what am I to do?'

Thinking of the grim-faced Sir George, the firm set line of his mouth, Analee did not know what Henrietta could do. He was a man she had always instinctively disliked, exhibiting a mixture of bullying and obsequiousness that Analee found peculiarly repulsive. To live with such a man must be a torment. Suddenly Analee thought of Reyora who undoubtedly had magical powers, and who was but a short distance away from where they were now. She got up and walked slowly to the window, staring out in the dark to the house by the edge of the forest.

'Henrietta there *is* someone who may be able to help you. She is called Reyora and is in your mother-in-law's house at this moment.'

'Reyora, but was she not . . .' Henrietta began, her voice rising with indignation.

'Yes, you may not like her and you may not want to see her. She brought Morella to your mother-in-law, and she has come back to visit her. I knew Reyora in my past and she has great magical powers. She lives not far from here now and can perhaps help you . . .'

'But a common gypsy . . . !' Henrietta grimaced with disgust.

'*I* am a common gypsy,' Analee said quietly, closing the curtains and walking back to stand by the fire. 'Even though I am now a marchioness, at heart my gypsy origins are still there. You could allow me to help you but not her?'

520

'Well . . .' Henrietta considered doubtfully and shrugged. 'If you say . . .'

'But you must never tell your husband or ask her any questions, is that clear? And you must do as she says whether you find it distasteful or not. Gypsies sometimes use substances repulsive to ordinary people in their potions. You must do exactly what she says, and Henrietta – ' Analee walked over to her and took one of her languid white hands, 'you must be *sure* her connection with me remains secret. Do you promise?'

Henrietta looked up at the fiery dark eyes and began to tremble. Oh, the thought of ever disobeying that command . . .

'I promise.'

'Then I will send word to her by Nelly that you wish to see her, and then you will tell her how and when.'

Analee and Angus were late to dinner that night as the Falcon led his wife into the drawing room where the invited guests were assembled. Hugo Fitzgerald caught his breath at the sight of her. She was even more beautiful than when last he had seen her on the day she had given birth, alight with the bloom of new motherhood.

The keen eyes of the Falcon had noticed Hugo's gaze as soon as he came into the room, and glanced at his wife. Analee, however, had not seen him and greeted Sir George who began to introduce his carefully assembled guests to her while the Falcon stood on one side gazing at her moodily. The fact that men universally admired his wife both annoyed and satisfied him. They wanted her, but he was the one who had her. What he did not know for sure was, how much did Analee want them? Did she ever think of others apart from him? He thought forward to their visit to London and immediately regretted his decision to take her with him. He should have left her by the tranquil shores of Lake Derwentwater – a flower to be visited and pollinated at intervals during the year, a special treat for a man weary of the cares and pleasures of the world.

For the Falcon did have other pleasures; his appetite for women was insatiable. Even so lovely and versatile a woman as Analee could not satisfy his needs. What mattered to him was variety, and Analee – lovely and skilled in the art of love as she was – could not supply that. She could only ever be herself. What now if his wife

521

found out about his amours in London, in particular the young debutante freshly arrived from the country who had caught his fancy so much during the season? He had not yet won her, since she was too well brought up, too well chaperoned; but the idea of conquest was ever in his mind and, by the wanton look in her eyes, the whispered messages on the dance floor or across the table, he knew she was not averse to the idea. The challenge was irresistible.

And now he was taking Analee with him! His new infatuation for her had blinded him to the obvious dangers. Supposing she should find out . . . The Falcon shrugged and applied himself to studying the guests just as Hugo approached and clasped Analee's proffered hand warmly, kissing it, gazing up into her eyes. Lord Falconer flushed. The cheeky puppy! He could not mistake that glance, and Analee's smile of recognition meant that they were acquainted.

'Mr Fitzgerald, my lady. I believe you are acquainted.'

'Indeed we are, Sir George. 'Twas Mr Fitzgerald who kindly rode to fetch the midwife when I was delivered of my son. My lord, may I introduce Mr Fitzgerald whose promptness eased my labour.'

'Indeed,' Angus growled and kept his hands behind his back not even attempting to bow, his eyes coldly appraising.

Hugo straightened up and looked into the eyes of the man he considered his rival, for he was deeply in love with Analee having been quite unable to rid his mind of the memory of her during the past weeks. Hugo and the Falcon stared at each other, neither liking what they saw, both squaring their shoulders as though for a fight.

Hugo saw the famous Falcon – a tall man with a lean dark face and smouldering jealous eyes. The Falcon observed a much younger man almost as tall as he was with a tan complexion, large blue eyes and his own hair not even powdered, secured at the nape of his neck by a brown velvet ribbon, the locks falling carelessly over his brow. His beard was scarce on his chin, Angus thought contemptuously; he was but a boy, much younger than his wife!

'How came you to be visiting my wife sir, may I ask?'

'Certainly my lord,' Hugo smiled and, despite the Falcon's rudeness to him, bowed. 'I was sent thither to bring greetings to her ladyship from Mrs Rigg, who is acquainted with your wife. I work for Mr Rigg sir, and was on my way to bring a message to Sir George here. I was pleased to be of service to her ladyship and subsequently privileged to observe your fine heir, on whose birth may I offer your lordship my congratulations.'

'If I detect any impertinence in your tone of voice sir . . .' Angus began when Analee hastily intervened.

'My lord I detect nothing but politeness in Mr Fitzgerald's tone of voice, and respect for your lordship, if I mistake it not – am I not right Mr Fitzgerald? I thought so. Goodbye then for the moment Mr Fitzgerald.' Analee firmly took the Falcon's arm, aware of his body quivering, and strolled with him towards a quiet corner of the room.

'Angus what is the matter with you?' she whispered.

'I saw the way he looked at you. Young puppy . . .'

'But there . . .'

'And he *knows* you then. I guessed it as soon as he entered the room, his eyes raking your body . . .'

'Oh Angus! You are absurdly jealous. If you feel like this about every man who observes me – '

'I do.'

'Then I should best go to a nunnery.'

'Ah you know it, you are aware of it, your power . . .'

'Of course I am aware of it Angus.' Analee turned to him in surprise. 'How could I not be? But I do not respond to it, as I am sure you do not to every woman who ogles you – ' Angus started guiltily, but Analee proceeded smoothly. 'I love only you my lord, and desire none other. I could not even recall Mr Fitzgerald to mind as he was introduced. There now.' She patted his arm as the steward came in and announced dinner. Analee was escorted in by Sir George, and Henrietta by Lord Falconer.

Hugo Fitzgerald was very far down the line, and almost out of sight at the long dining table. But from where he was he caught glimpses of the Enchantress as she smiled and sparkled at the top end of the table, never giving him so much as a glance.

But Hugo didn't mind. He was content to gaze, to feast his eyes on her and bide his time. Because in his bones he felt that it was just a matter of time.

* * *

'So we meet again, I didn't think it would be so soon.'

'Lady Delamain said I had to come while you were here,' Reyora replied clasping Analee's hand, marvelling to herself at the profusion of jewels that graced it, the quality of the heavily embroidered silk robe and beribboned stomacher that she wore. She thought back to the time when Randal Buckland had brought Analee to the gypsy camp trussed in the back of a cart; but Analee always had dignity even then. It had not surprised Reyora to learn about the change in her fortunes; she had never been as other gypsies.

'We must be quick,' Analee whispered. 'The men are at table talking and will shortly expect to join us in the drawing room.'

Analee had been summoned after dinner to Henrietta's boudoir and, on approaching it accompanied by Nelly, found Reyora waiting outside. Now she knocked on the door and a timorous voice bade them enter.

Inside Henrietta was standing in the centre of the room, wringing her hands in the nervous gesture that Analee had seen so often in the brief time she had been at the castle. Henrietta wore a gown of magenta silk damask, a colour that ill became her as it clashed with her red hair. An elaborate stomacher, fussily trimmed with *échelles*, and a quilted petticoat over a dome-shaped hoop made her look much plumper than she actually was. Her hair was arranged in the style known as *tête de mouton* with a clump of false curls at the back of the head which now, in Henrietta's agitated state, were awry and fell forward over her face. To try and restore her fading youth Henrietta made heavy use of rouge and white face powder, her eyebrows blackened by the use of a lead comb, and she wore a large silken patch on her right cheekbone.

The effect was of someone vastly overdressed. Henrietta only succeeded in looking grotesque, and the quantity of make-up carelessly applied on her face had started to run in the heat from the many candles in the dining room.

She looked a pathetic figure and Analee, knowing the cause, found that her heart went out to her in pity.

'Henrietta, this is my friend Reyora. You have heard of her but not met, I think. She is a very clever woman with many medical and magical skills, as I know well for I have benefited from them.'

Henrietta, who previously had scorned the gypsy woman to

whom her mother-in-law had given shelter, looked embarrassed and did not smile.

'We have very little time, I understand madam,' Reyora said moving over to Henrietta. 'You must trust me and let me examine you, and I will do it as swiftly as I can while Analee is here as you wish.'

'*Examine*?' Henrietta said falteringly.

'I must look at you, madam; for if you cannot conceive it is no use if I do not know the condition of your womb and that I can only know by feeling with my own hands . . .'

'Oh I *cannot*!' Henrietta backed away looking appalled, 'I cannot allow . . .'

'I *cannot* prescribe something when I do not know the condition, madam,' Reyora said persistently, looking to Analee for help.

'Reyora is very skilled Henrietta,' Analee said gently. 'She has delivered many babies in her time, and treated many cases of infertility. You need have no shame in front of her.'

'There, if you will lie down, madam, it will not take a moment.' Reyora moved over to the bed and, turning back the cover, smoothed the sheets.

When the examination was over she got up, signalled to Nelly to rearrange Henrietta's clothes and went over to the washbasin where she sluiced her hands. Henrietta was trembling as Nelly smoothed her clothes, rearranging her hoop and her heavy quilted petticoat.

'There,' Analee said, helping her to sit up on the bed, 'I said it would not be too bad.'

'It was awful,' Henrietta said petulantly, but gazed hopefully as Reyora came once again over to the bed. She stood looking gravely at her patient and shrugged her shoulders.

'All is not well inside my lady, as you have been told. Your passages are twisted and blocked; had you had skilled help in your last delivery it might have been avoided.'

'But I had the best doctors in this part of the country.'

Reyora raised her eyes momentarily to heaven. 'The best doctors, madam, are butchers when it comes to these intimate things concerning a woman. They know nothing about them. I have borne four children myself and, as Analee said, helped many many others into the world – and some out of it before they were born. I know the inside of a woman like I know the palm of my own hand.'

'So . . . there is no hope?'

Reyora shook her head. 'There is always *hope* madam, but very little chance. I will prepare a potion for you to drink and a poultice which you must leave for as long as you can without letting your husband come near you. You can pretend you have your woman's time and are unclean. We can try this remedy three times. After that . . .'

'Yes?' Already Henrietta was gazing trustingly at this masterful gypsy woman who seemed so certain what she was doing, who knew so much about the mysteries of a woman's body.

'After that, if it is unsuccessful I will try and make your husband love you again, madam, be gentle with you. That is the best we can hope to achieve if all else fails.'

'Reyora is very honest,' Analee said softly, bending to dry Henrietta's eyes with her own sweet-scented handkerchief. 'It is best not to give false hope.'

'Oh yes, you are right,' Henrietta exclaimed gratefully.

'And do you trust her?'

'I do, yes I do! I will do just what she says, however unpleasant. I will do it.'

'Better than the embraces of a man who does not love you,' Reyora muttered.

'Much better,' Henrietta agreed. 'If only my husband could love me again and be content with our daughters I would be happy. But oh I think he will not . . . he will look for another woman.'

'Even *then* I can help you madam,' Reyora said meaningfully. 'Trust Reyora.'

'I will – and I do. I feel better already. Thank you Analee. Thank you Reyora, Nelly. I think you are leaving me with a true friend Analee, one I can trust.'

'Better than the doctors, they are rogues,' Reyora said. 'I am leaving tomorrow, but if madam will send a trusted maidservant with instructions as to when I can come again, it will be done.'

'Oh thank you!' Henrietta, completely transformed and recovered from her ordeal, clasped her hands and pressed them. 'I *know* I can trust you and all will be well.'

'I will see Reyora out,' Analee said consulting a fob watch at her waist, 'and Nelly will help you arrange your hair and your make-up, so that we can rejoin your guests.'

Outside the door Analee seized Reyora's arm and tugged her along the corridor.

'You must see my babies before you go. It is a chance I did not think we should have.'

Reyora smiled. 'Now I will have seen all your children. Her ladyship will never have more children, Analee; she is completely twisted inside. She is infertile.'

'I guessed it,' Analee said sombrely.

'It is a wonder her last child ever survived. But I did not want to make her lose hope immediately. It is good for her to accept the situation gradually, and I will prepare her for it.'

Analee nodded her head. 'That's what I thought you were doing. Even if you can make her husband tender with her again it will be something.'

'Indeed it will,' Reyora snorted. 'He is a beast. I know how he treats his mother.'

Analee opened the door to the room where Clare and the baby were slumbering, watched over by a nurse. Clare lay on a small bed, her eyelashes curled on her rosy cheeks, her little mouth slightly parted, the strands of dark curly hair falling over her brow.

'Such a beauty!' exclaimed Reyora. 'So different from . . .'

'Shhh!' Analee pointed to the nurse who dozed in a chair by the fire, 'See,' she whispered, 'here is the heir to my husband's estates.'

Proudly Analee drew back the coverlet from the baby Duncan, also asleep in his crib. His eyes were tightly shut and his pink lips pursed in an expression of arrogant determination. He even appeared to puff importantly as he breathed in and out. His brown curls were covered by his tight fitting bonnet and he looked like a bald little gnome. Reyora gazed at him for a long time, nodding her head. She shut her eyes tightly and then, opening them wide, gazed at Analee with a curious expression.

'You *know*?' Analee whispered wonderingly.

'I think I know. He is the son of someone more important than your husband.'

Analee nodded, her eyes shining.

'Maybe a king?'

'One day, maybe a king.'

'He will be very powerful.' Reyora reached down and took his tiny hand. 'He will be a strong and powerful man, that is all I can tell you. And you, Analee,' she looked up and passed a hand over Analee's face, 'you, my dear friend. Your troubles are not over.'

'No?' Analee looked startled then sad. 'There is worse to come?'

'I know you have trouble with your husband. He does not treat you well? He is a violent man?'

'Only at times. One time especially. Other moments are ecstatic. We have just spent some wonderful weeks together, and I feel I love him very much – I hoped that the bad times were gone.'

'Yes I know, you have just had a period of great happiness. I think there are stirrings again in your womb. Treasure that time, Analee, for there is fresh hardship to come.' She clasped Analee's hand tightly. 'But you will survive it. Just be warned by Reyora the *cohani*, who loves you: prepare for it, and you will survive, you will overcome. In the years ahead you will have more children and also much happiness to counteract the many sorrows that will be in store for you. And I, Reyora, will always be there to help you when you need me. And I think you will need me, one day.'

Reyora clasped her again briefly to her bosom and swiftly went to the door, closing it quietly after her. Analee, her face dark with apprehension and dismay, gazed for a long time into the face of her sleeping son.

13

Analee had found that her fortunes began to change as soon as she and her husband arrived in London. Reyora's words came true far too quickly. There was an almost immediate dropping off in the Falcon's ardour and he was away from the house in Piccadilly for long periods at a time; where, she did not know. He never told her and she did not ask; she didn't want to become the nagging, shrewish wife.

Analee thought it was the effect of living in the city. It did not suit her; the artificiality of life at both courts was stifling. At the court of the King in St James it was routine, dull and governed by George II's passion for time-keeping and doing exactly the same thing at the same time every day. At the rival court of his son Frederick Prince of Wales at Leicester House everything was intrigue, gossip and speculation. Analee was actually more drawn to the court of the Prince which favoured the Jacobites – in fact he was rumoured to be plotting with Bonnie Prince Charlie to give him the throne in place of his father. Frederick and George hated each other as much as George had hated his father – it was almost a tradition among the Hanoverians that father and eldest son were at enmity with each other.

The Falcon, however, abhorred Leicester House and favoured St James's Palace. But because the King was old and in ill health and his demise expected at any time, it was wise to keep a foot in both camps, as it were – to pay court to both ruler and heir. So at least one night a week the Falcon was to be found either at Leicester House or Richmond where the Prince had his country house. The rest of the time the Falcon danced attendance on King George and his German mistress Lady Yarmouth, formerly Madame Walmoden, who had been sent for after the death of the King's greatly loved but much abused wife Queen Caroline in 1737. Lord Falconer and Lady Yarmouth got on very well together; people even hinted that she shared her favours between him and the King – but those who knew Lady Falconer said that no

529

man in his senses would want to go to bed with the aging Lady Yarmouth when he could enjoy the same delights with his wife.

Analee was unhappy and suspicious. She was jealous of her husband but tried not to show it. She saw how he flirted and ogled the women and she thought this idle life became him as little as it became her. Here he became a different person, a courtier, a practised flirt – it was only on Lake Derwentwater or at their home on the Scottish borders that he became hers, her husband and her lover.

The weeks seemed to drag by for Analee, restless and unhappy in her vast London prison, the great Falconer mansion on Piccadilly. She liked neither reading nor playing cards nor sewing, nor gossiping for hours on end with other idle women, the main preoccupations at the court. In Lakeland or Falcon's Keep she always found plenty to do inside the house and then there were long walks and rides outside it. Here, except for an occasional canter in Marylebone Fields or sometimes at Richmond, there was nothing to do. Many times she looked back to her days as a wandering gypsy and thought of them with excitement and nostalgia.

And then one day a familiar face appeared at Leicester House and once again her life was changed.

Lord St March had been observing Analee for some time before she became aware of him. She was chatting to the Princess of Wales who admired Lady Falconer, and would have liked to take her into her suite but for the well known opposition of her husband. Princess Augusta knew that Lady Falconer was suspected of having Jacobite sympathies and she never lost an opportunity of passing on information to her or finding out how much she knew. But she never got far. Lady Falconer was as close as an oyster. Her Royal Highness observed Lord St March staring at the Marchioness and waved her hand, beckoning him over.

'I see you have yet another admirer, Lady Falconer.'

'I ma'am?' Analee started and turned round just as Lord St March, in obedience to the Princess's command, approached. He was dressed completely in grey except for his stockings and cravat, the Brussels lace at his wrists and the periwig on his head all in white. 'Why – 'tis Lord St March. I have not seen him since Paris a year ago.'

Lord St March bowed deeply to the Princess of Wales and kissed her hand, then that of Lady Falconer.

'You do me an honour, ma'am.'

'I too have not seen you for a long time my lord. Have you been plotting?' the Princess enquired merrily in her heavy German accent. Usually she spoke French, but as Lady Falconer did not speak the language she did the best she could in her halting English.

'*Plotting*, Your Royal Highness? Why should I plot? I am completely loyal to His Majesty, and to His Royal Highness, of course.'

'But they say my husband plots against the King,' the Princess said slyly.

Lord St March pretended to be shocked and held up his hands. 'That I cannot believe ma'am, knowing as I do the devotion of His Royal Highness to his father the King. May I say how well you look ma'am, and your family well too I hope?'

'Indeed all my family are very well thank God. May I leave you to entertain Lady Falconer, my lord? I see Lord Egmont is trying to engage my attention.'

The Princess beckoned to her husband's favourite to join her, and Lord St March and Analee, after making their obeisances, withdrew from the Royal presence. Analee suddenly felt awkward in the company of St March, recalling the previous occasion on which they had met. He was one of the very few who knew of her assignation with Prince Charles. But she longed to talk to him of the Prince, how he did and where he was.

'You look particularly enchanting Lady Falconer, if I may say so,' Lord St March began. 'Have you been long in London?'

'Since November my lord.' Analee passed a hand across her forehead. 'I am afraid the city does not agree with me. I yearn to go back to the country.'

'And the Marquess? I hope he is well.' Lord St March looked around. 'Is he here tonight?'

'He was here but I believe he has gone.'

The Earl looked surprised. 'You believe, you do not know?'

'My husband does as he pleases Lord St March. He is a law unto himself. He only makes token appearances at Leicester House, preferring the Court at St James and apparently the company there.'

The Earl said nothing but could not help noticing the inflexion in his companion's voice. How beautiful she was, how like . . .

'I have my eldest daughter Constance with me ma'am. May I present her to you?'

'Oh please do!' Analee clapped her hands. 'Is she here?'

'She is surrounded at the moment, or was when I last saw her, by a bevy of young men. She resembles her mother, my late wife, who was very attractive to the opposite sex.'

Lord St March coughed and gave an apologetic laugh.

'How is the Prince?' Analee said in a voice scarcely above a whisper.

Lord St March looked cautiously around before replying. 'He is well ma'am, but in hiding as usual. More careful than ever though since the English forged a letter saying that he had died of pneumonia. By this they hoped the Jacobites would deny it and give away his hiding place. But those who are loyal to the Prince are very careful. He has been much at Lunéville and has I believe become interested in medicine. Of course he was overjoyed when Lady Yarmouth was pelted with eggs on the occasion of the recent visit of the Comedie Française to London.'

'You sound as though you have seen him recently.'

Lord St March glanced round again. 'I have ma'am. In Paris. He gave me a letter for you – he said I had to deliver it to you personally.'

'A letter for me? You have it here?'

'Oh no ma'am, not on my person. I wondered if I might bring it you at Falconer House, maybe tomorrow? May I have the pleasure?'

'Of course.'

'You must be very careful my lady that his lordship does not get wind of this. I know he neither likes nor trusts me.'

'He is suspicious of everyone,' Analee said sadly, 'and jealous. He thinks that every man would seduce me. He cannot conceive of a mere friendship between the sexes.'

Lord St March looked at Analee and thought her husband was not without justification. He remembered her visit to the Prince and how the Prince still talked of her, despite his known infatuation for Madame de Talmond which still continued, albeit stormily. He had trusted St March with a letter for her.

'Give it to the Enchantress,' he had said, 'personally into her own hands.'

Suddenly there was a commotion at the end of the room, roars of masculine laughter and a high tinkling feminine laugh, and a beautiful girl burst out of the throng of men, her hands covering her red cheeks. Even the Princess of Wales looked up from her earnest conversation with Lord Egmont, together with another of the Prince's cronies, George Bubb-Dodington, and a sudden silence fell on the room.

'That is my daughter, I regret to say,' his lordship said in a tone of embarrassment. 'She is always drawing attention to herself.'

Analee stared at the very pretty girl who was coming towards her, but also at one of the men in the group she had just left. The tall spare figure of Sir George Delamain stood slightly apart from the others and she saw how his eyes followed her progress through the room.

'May I present my daughter Constance,' Lord St March said. 'My dear, the Marchioness of Falconer.'

Lady Constance gazed haughtily at the fabled beauty who looked at her with such a kindly and charming smile. She was younger than she'd thought and far more beautiful than she could ever have imagined. Her father had raved about her, and no wonder. Apparently she had even attracted the attention of the Young Pretender who was no womanizer and had not even so much as glanced at her, Constance, when she was presented to him. She was so aware of her beauty that she regarded all woman as rivals, but there was something so simple and friendly about Analee that at last she smiled and curtsied.

'Lady Falconer, my father has spoken much about you.'

'And he has told me a lot about you, Lady Constance. I see why.'

Analee smiled past her at the men and Constance turned and giggled.

'They are all young and stupid, except I think for that one.' She pointed at Sir George who, not having seen Analee, had turned his back and was talking to a smaller group.

'Sir George Delamain? You know him?'

'I met him yesterday at the Court of His Majesty. He said he came here specially to seek me out.'

'Indeed,' said Lord St March, his face dark. 'I will seek the scoundrel out . . .'

'But why papa, he is harmless. I quite like him.'

'He is a married man,' St March said, 'and has no right to be making eyes at a young innocent girl like you.'

'Oh father, he is not making eyes, do not be so naive. He talks to me like an intelligent woman and I like him for it. I care not whether he is married or no. He was simply being pleasant.'

'I believe Sir George is most uxorious,' Analee said pleasantly. 'I am acquainted with his family and know his wife Henrietta. I hear they are a happy couple.'

'There!' Constance laughed at her father. 'And he is years too old for me, almost as old as you.'

'That is very old indeed,' her father said. 'Why Lady Falconer, I believe you were wrong; see, your husband is here after all.'

Analee looked up as the Falcon approached, his eyes searching everywhere as though he were sniffing out his prey. He looked so well and handsome in his court dress that her heart yearned for him again, to have him as her own and share him with no other.

'My lord may I present Lady Constance Craven? The daughter of Lord St March.'

The Falcon bowed and took Constance's hand and Analee observed how his eyes raked her elegant form, lingering on her full bosom, her long slender neck.

'My lady, what a pleasure,' the Falcon murmured. 'I confess I was beginning to find this company tedious, but now . . .'

'You are very kind my lord,' Constance faltered, looking up at the awe-inspiring man whose name was a legend throughout Europe. 'I have heard . . .'

'*Upon* my word, Lord and Lady Falconer!' Sir George, having espied the disturbance caused by the entrance of the Falcon, hurried over rubbing his hands. 'What a great pleasure to see you here my lord, my lady. I did not expect to find you at the Court of the Prince of Wales.'

The Falcon straightened and eyed him through his quizzing glass.

'Indeed sir, and why not pray? His Royal Highness is the next King of England after all, and it behoves us all to pay our respects to him.'

'Indeed, indeed Lord Falconer, my sentiments exactly.' Sir George cleared his throat and looked nervously about him. 'Still one must be careful. They say His Majesty receives notice of everyone who attends the Court of his son and if those attendances prove too numerous they count against one when seeking advancement.'

'And do you seek advancement Sir George?' the Falcon said imperiously. 'I thought you were a farmer and businessman.'

'Oh but I am most interested in politics Lord Falconer. I hope to be returned to Parliament shortly having a borough in my pocket where the member is retiring.'

'As a Whig or a Tory, Sir George?' the Falcon enquired loftily as though putting him through a process of interrogation.

'Oh, as a Whig Lord Falconer, of course as a Whig,' Sir George said deprecatingly, rubbing his hands in the obsequious fashion Analee found so odious. She thought of poor Henrietta and wondered how she was.

'Then I shall support you,' the Falcon smiled. 'Too many damned Tories have too many Jacobite sympathies, eh St March?'

The Earl took a pinch of snuff from an elegant snuff box made of ivory inlaid with mother-of-pearl, and brushed his fingers before replying in a leisurely gesture that Analee admired. It contrasted with the deference of Sir George and seemed to mark the Earl as a power in his own right. The Falcon was never happy unless he was establishing his supremacy, forcing all metaphorically to kneel before him.

'I have no means of knowing my lord,' St March said offhandedly, 'as I am neither and do not even dwell in this country. Now Lady Falconer if you will excuse me I shall take my daughter home.'

'I hope you will bring her soon to Falconer House,' Analee said smiling, 'and, depend upon it, before the week is out I will be sending you an invitation to dine with us. Sir George how long do you stay in the City?'

'Oh I know not Lady Falconer. I am hoping for an interview with the Duke of Newcastle and until that is arranged . . .'

'I can arrange it for you any day, my good man, you have merely to say,' the Falcon said. 'I was only today dining with His Grace. I have his ear at all times.'

'Oh my lord, what can I say,' Sir George began when he saw someone across the room and waved, 'young Hugo. Excuse me my lord, but an acquaintance . . . oh I think you know him. You met when last at the castle on your way to London.'

The Falcon was staring frostily at Hugo Fitzgerald who, having espied Lady Falconer was making straight for them, pushing through the courtiers who thronged the room.

'Ah Hugo . . . when did you arrive? Hugo was out to supper,' Sir George confided to Lord Falconer, 'and I told him to find his own way here.'

'You are in London together?' the Marquess enquired.

'Indeed my lord, we came in my coach. We are both on business. As you know Mr Rigg . . .'

'*He* is not here I trust,' the Falcon said scathingly. 'Otherwise it would appear the world and his wife were welcome at Leicester House.'

'You have objection to me my lord?' Hugo said, bristling.

'None at all sir. In fact I cannot recall having met you before.'

Hugo flushed, but turned to Analee and bowed deeply. 'Lady Falconer. What good fortune to find you here . . .'

Analee smiled, admiring his spirit, his tone of voice deliberately defying the Falcon – such a contrast to the fawning Sir George. How well he looked tonight she thought, young and vigorous. He had a look in his eyes especially for her, she knew it . . . and yes, deep inside she felt something that she could not quite describe for him. It was not love, it was not admiration . . . tenderness perhaps. In her heart she thought of her new-born son and the eager young man with the same emotion.

'My lord, young Fitzgerald here was at Delamain Castle when you and her ladyship did us the honour . . .' Sir George began painstakingly.

'Ah yes, I *do* recall . . .' The Falcon raised his eyebrows as though the memory were fresh to him. 'I think I do recall . . . a soldier I believe you were Mr Fitzgerald.'

'Yes my lord.' Hugo, his youthful face still flushed, reluctantly turned his eyes from Analee to her husband.

'What regiment pray sir?'

'The Irish Guards my lord. Lord McQueen's regiment.'

'Ah then you saw service overseas? At Fontenoy perhaps?'

Hugo flushed even more deeply and stepped up to the Marquess as though he would knock him down.

'You mistake me sir. I was in the Irish *Guards*, not the Jacobite Irish *Brigade* which caused such havoc against the English at Fontenoy. You try to insult me I think sir.'

'Oh forgive me,' the Falcon said mockingly, 'a lapse of memory. I can't recall if Lord McQueen's regiment was ever overseas.'

'It is well known my lord that Lord McQueen's regiment was part of the Pragmatic Army and served with His Majesty at Dettingen. However when I joined it the war was nearly over and I saw no service.'

'You look scarcely old enough,' the Falcon observed with a sneer and Hugo again appeared on the verge of raising his fist when Analee put a restraining hand on the Falcon's arm.

'My lord I think it is time we went, do you not?'

But the Falcon, who had been enjoying his attempts to humiliate Fitzgerald, was now ogling Lady Constance who, reluctant to leave, had been listening to the proceedings with mouth agape.

'You must not heed me, my dear young lady. I am an old and experienced soldier and like it not when young fledglings try and behave as though they rule the army.'

'It did not occur to me that Mr Fitzgerald made any such pretensions,' Lady Constance said boldly. 'I thought your lordship was trying to needle him unnecessarily.'

The Falcon bent his head, a smile playing about his lips. His long legs were apart and a hand rested nonchalantly on his hip.

'*Did* you Lady Constance? I see that you, on the other hand, have a wisdom in advance of your years. I congratulate you Lord St March. We do indeed look forward to the pleasure of dining with you and your charming and clever daughter. And Sir George, my wife will be in touch with you doubtless. In the meantime I will have a word with His Grace of Newcastle, aye and his colleague Bedford too if you so desire, that is if I can get hold of him. He is an idle rogue who spends most of his time at Woburn and not at his department of State in Westminster. You see I am well versed in these things. I have my finger, as it were, on the pulse of *every* aspect of the government, especially when it comes to administration of the army, or the activities of the Jacobite rebels.' The Falcon's gaze strayed from Lady Constance to Hugo Fitzgerald who still glared at him wrathfully though he appeared to have simmered down. At a new jibe from the Falcon his rage mounted again when Analee firmly took hold of her husband's arm and, bowing, led him over to the Prince and Princess of Wales to take their leave.

The Prince of Wales, known as Fretz, was nervous, insecure and by nature a schemer. He particularly detested his younger brother William Duke of Cumberland who was dearly loved by the King and was Captain General of the army. Frederick had always begged his father to be allowed to go soldiering, but it had never been allowed. He was even quite old before he was brought over to England from Hanover, or permitted to marry or have his own household.

Now he delighted in plotting against his father with his cronies who included all the disaffected members of the administration, displaced politicians or aspiring ones such as William Pitt, and those who feared that the King would soon die and the lightweight irresolute Fretz would reign in his place.

Among the men Fretz was forced to have at his Court, but whom he detested, was the Marquess of Falconer. He suspected the Marquess of being behind the latest refusal of his father to let him go soldiering, and he knew that the Falcon and the hated Duke of Cumberland were as thick as thieves. He also knew how Lord Falconer loathed the Jacobites and how he had reported to His Majesty the fact that two of the tutors to Frederick's eldest son, George, were suspected of being Jacobite sympathizers.

The Prince of Wales never spoke to the Falcon unless he could help it, but tonight he took a malicious pleasure in making remarks that were bound to irritate the powerful nobleman. He unashamedly ogled Analee and engaged her for five minutes in low, ribald conversation apart from his wife, while Analee smiled, blushed and generally began to look uncomfortable. The Prince was thought to be an ineffectual lover – his own mother had doubted his virility to such an extent that at one time she doubted if he could have fathered his first child – but he still indulged in the affairs obligatory for a man in his position.

Analee considered the Prince among the least attractive of men. His complexion was yellowish, and he had a large curved semitic nose as a result of which it was maliciously rumoured that his real

538

father had been one of two favoured Turkish servants, Mustapha and Mohammed, employed by the King. Yet although she was embarrassed by his suggestive remarks made in a loud German-accented whisper, she knew that the Prince was too in awe of the Falcon to go any further. However, she was still relieved when the Princess intervened and asked Analee how long she was to be in London.

'I do not know Your Royal Highness. It depends upon his lordship.'

'And that ma'am I do not know either,' the Falcon said puffing out his chest importantly. 'I believe His Majesty may require my attendance upon him on his next journey to Hanover. He has been so good as to intimate as much. As for my wife, she is carrying a child ma'am and will doubtless go north to give birth as she did on the last occasion.'

The Falcon gazed at Analee in a proprietorial manner. The last thing he wanted was that the Princess should suggest appointing her a lady-in-waiting. Now that the Queen was dead it was one of the highest honours open to women in either court – the Princess taking precedence over the King's daughters.

'You are to be congratulated Lady Falconer.'

'Thank you, Your Royal Highness.' Analee curtsied and swept a glance at the Prince who appeared nonplussed at the news. He had wasted five minutes flirting with a pregnant woman.

'Shall you *mind* the country Lady Falconer?'

'I love it ma'am. I prefer it to the city.'

'Indeed?'

'I was a gypsy ma'am before his lordship did me the honour to take me as his wife. I prefer the out-of-doors. It is in my blood.'

The Princess's plain pock-marked face assumed a look of embarrassment at such frankness and she averted her eyes.

'I had heard as much,' the Prince said. 'I did not believe it could be true.'

'It is quite true sir,' the Falcon said testily. 'And my wife brags about it too much. I think it is of more importance to her than being Marchioness of Falconer. Now if Your Royal Highnesses will permit . . .'

The Prince bowed and smiled at Analee. 'I think you are very fortunate in your wife Lord Falconer. See you take care of her.'

'I think Your Royal Highness may depend on *that*.'

The Falcon bowed low and Analee curtsied. And then they slowly made their way through the salon to the waiting coach outside.

The Falcon sat brooding silently as the coach travelled the short way between Leicester House and Piccadilly. The flares in the sconces on the buildings lit up the rain-drenched cobbles and the few soaked dismal beggars who stood in the gutters, or huddled against the buildings for warmth. Analee had begun to fear his moods again and she leaned back and watched the rain patter against the window of the carriage. She was feeling tired, and somewhat dejected. It was February and a gloomy time to be in London. She felt restless and ill at ease. She was frequently sick and found this the most difficult pregnancy she had yet had. The others had been completely trouble-free. The child of their love in the autumn would be remembered as a creature of the storms and stresses that followed.

In London and Paris Analee saw a completely different man from the one she had loved and married in the north of England. He appeared superficial and vainglorious, intent on impressing people with the influence and sway he claimed to enjoy in high places. He moved with a swagger among the highest in the land and was indeed on intimate terms with all the great from the King downwards. The only person she had ever seen him positively toadying to was Lady Yarmouth, the King's powerful German-born mistress. She knew about the rumours that they slept together if only for the fact that he seemed to get more favours from the King than other men, and her ladyship was known to admire his virile charms.

But it was the attitude of the Falcon to younger women that pained Analee more. She herself was but twenty-five in this year of grace 1750 and, in the eyes of many, still young and beautiful. But the Falcon, forty this year, seemed to prefer them even younger, more nubile like the seventeen-year-old Lady Constance Craven whom he had immediately ravished with his eyes. Now as he sat grim-faced in the flickering light which came from the flarebearer who ran alongside the coach to light the way, she knew what was the matter with him: he was wracked with jealousy.

'That Hugo Fitzgerald,' the Falcon muttered, 'would I could have him horsewhipped out of the town.'

540

'Why sir? What has he done to you?'

'It is what he has done to *you*, my good woman,' the Falcon roared, reaching out and seizing the neck of her cloak. 'He has been intimate with you, that I swear. From the look on his face . . .'

Analee struggled, feeling his knuckles against her windpipe. In a panic she quickly unlaced the cloak and it fell off her thus allowing a welcome passage of air into her lungs again.

'My lord! You are not off on this track *again*? Intimate with Mr Fitzgerald – how and when?'

'That is what I'd like to know.' The Falcon folded his arms against his chest and spread his legs. 'You had obviously met before. He knew you. He was there when Duncan was born. Well?'

'Do you suppose I lay with him *then* my lord?' Analee said scathingly and then, involuntarily, shut her eyes as her husband's hand stung across her cheek.

'Do not mock me woman! Then or whenever. It is all the same.'

'I doubt if I could have obliged him then my lord,' Analee said shakily after a pause, one hand rubbing the sting on her cheek. 'It is not a gypsy custom to lie with a man for some weeks after childbirth, as you well know. We consider a woman unclean so long as she bleeds from the womb. I had only just recovered when your lordship joined me at Furness, as should have been obvious to your lordship.'

'Hmm!' the Falcon snorted but said nothing.

'Your lordship is blinded with a jealousy that has familiar and painful overtones for me, reminding me of the occasion in Paris when you nearly killed me. Will you do the same now every time a man looks at me?'

'But he wants you. It is the way he looks at you, and he will have you. I see it in his eyes, if only to spite me. He hates me and I think I know why.'

'Why, my lord?'

'He is a Jacobite spy! I am convinced of it. The Irish Guards indeed! And what is he doing at the coast working for Rigg when, as a gentleman, he should be lolling about the Court in idleness in London?'

'Because he has no money.'

'Fie. Let him marry it then. He is presentable enough. I warrant he is a spy and I will catch him. He ingratiates himself with my wife maybe in order to spy on me.

'It is well known that you favour the Jacobites. Is that it Analee?' He put out a hand again to grasp her bodice but Analee moved quickly along the seat so as to avoid him. She felt chilled without her cloak and longed to be at home.

'I think you are obsessed with Mr Fitzgerald Angus. I neither know him well nor care for him and am, as like as not, not going to see him again. He interests me not at all. I think you merely do this to hide your own attraction towards younger women, whose age would make me appear a grandmother. I should take on at the way you ogled Lady Constance. She has just had her seventeenth birthday I believe.'

'Aye, a good looking wench,' the Falcon mumbled appreciatively. 'This is no concern of yours Analee. A wife is meant to be faithful even if a husband is not – and I do not say I am not, mind you. The late Queen was a model in this respect about the amours of His Majesty, even allowing his mistresses to become her ladies-in-waiting. With a man, it is quite a different thing.'

'Oh is it?' Analee said bitterly. 'I think not. I am not Queen Caroline to be made such a fool of, no nor Princess Augusta – for it is said she turns a blind eye on the Prince's affairs. You must choose me or another and if I ever got to hear . . .'

'Yes, my little minx?' The Falcon suddenly relaxed and smiled in the dark, aware of his passion for his wife reasserting itself.

'If I ever got to hear . . . remember I am a gypsy,' Analee said darkly. 'Beware of my spell.'

14

Lady Constance Craven laid down her book in surprise.

'Lord Falconer? To see me?'

'Yes my lady. He asked specifically for you, although I told him the Earl was out of town.' The maid, impressed by the stature of the caller, kept glancing nervously over her shoulder.

'Then you must show him in, Bell. Do not keep the Marquess of Falconer waiting.'

Bell hurried out, her face aflame. She hoped Lord St March would not dismiss her for admitting a man in to see his young unchaperoned daughter. She knew that Lady Constance was brought up on the Continent and unlike the English in these matters, but still it did not do . . . for a young unmarried woman to receive a man, alone.

Constance was hurriedly smoothing her hair and arranging her dress when the Falcon strode in, carelessly casting his hat on a chair. He stood and looked about the room as though he had lived there all his life. Yes it was one of his attractions, Constance thought, looking at him. He had great presence, great self-assurance and command. Constance curtsied and the Marquess bent and kissed her hand.

'Lady Constance.'

'Will you be seated Lord Falconer. Is . . . her ladyship not with you?'

Constance pretended to peer expectantly over his shoulder as though any moment Bell would reappear with Lady Falconer. The Falcon still held onto her hand and smiled.

'You little hussy! You know perfectly well my wife is not here. 'Twas *you* I came to see – alone.'

Still keeping her hand in his he led her to a sofa and sat down facing her.

'Constance . . . I cannot stop thinking about you.'

Constance blushed and her free hand flew to her face.

'Lord Falconer! What is this?'

'Oh I know you are a young unmarried girl, only just turned seventeen and have never heard the like and so forth. Though with your beauty I doubt it. 'Tis enough to make a monk forsake his cloth. I know all that. But tell me . . . tell me you like me too.'

'Of course I like you Lord Falconer; but I hardly know you. We have met . . .'

'But three times,' the Falcon said raising his eyes ecstatically to the ceiling. 'The first time at Leicester House when I observed you first and saw how you tried to put me in my place when I needled young Fitzgerald. Beauty allied with such spirit was irresistible to a man like me, jaded with the world. Then I saw you two nights later at St James's Palace when you were playing cards with the Princess Amelia and trying as politely as you could to make Her Royal Highness, who is rather deaf, hear your calls. I watched for a long time from across the room and I know you were aware of me, but trying not to show it.'

'I was aware of your wife looking at me too.'

'Oh she is jealous of you all right. Analee is skilled in these matters, and she observed at once how smitten I was with you.'

'I hope she will not bewitch me. I hear she is called the Enchantress. My father is very taken by her.'

'Many men are taken by my wife and many would take her,' the Falcon's face darkened, 'but I keep her in pod as much as I am able and, in the little time when she is not breeding, I frequent her often to keep other bees away from my flower.'

'Her ladyship is therefore *enceinte* now I presume?' Constance said lowering her lashes. The Falcon's heart nearly burst with desire. Oh she was a minx. He came even nearer to her and put his other hand over her free one so that he now enclosed both.

'The third time I saw you was two nights ago at Lady Yarmouth's and then you very clearly gave me a sign that you found me not unattractive . . .'

Constance pretended surprise and opened her very wide blue eyes.

'I? My lord!'

'Nonsense. You kept looking up at me from the card table and flashing those eyes . . . oh I could smother them with kisses this very instance. Then when you were dancing did I not observe the glances from behind your hand . . . and *not* in the direction of your partner.'

544

'But my lord, you are old enough to be my father!'

Now she laughed outright, teasingly, and the Falcon unable to restrain his passion seized her in his arms and stifled her pert remarks with his kisses. The lips were so mobile and tender under his, so beautifully formed, so . . . experienced?

He held her away and looked at her in some surprise. 'I do not think I am the first man to kiss you, Constance?'

She flicked her pink tongue over her moist lips and gave him a saucy smile. 'Spain is such a hot country, my lord. Women are said to mature early there.'

'You . . .' He crushed her to him again, one hand trying to ease itself inside her bodice. Her flesh was hot to the touch and so yielding . . . But she grasped his hand with surprising strength and stayed its eager exploration.

'My lord . . . only kisses. I am not ready to be ravished.'

'Yet,' the Falcon said, tenderly brushing her hair back off her forehead. 'But soon . . . I desire you so much, it overpowers me.'

Constance sat up straight and moved away from him, smoothing her stomacher. She gazed at him severely. 'Lord Falconer, you are one of the premier noblemen of England *and* married *and* a father. You are old enough to be my father as I have said. I cannot possibly entertain the thought of, of . . .'

'A liaison with me?' The Falcon casually placed an arm along the back of the couch so that the tips of his fingers rested against her bare shoulder.

'Of *course* I cannot entertain the idea of a liaison with you! It is scandalous. It is even . . .'

'Yes?' he enquired, leaning forward so that the hand moved down across the swell of her full white breast.

'Dangerous,' she whispered.

'Oh it is very dangerous; but I like danger. Do you not? Or is it my wife's gypsy powers that frighten you?'

'It *is* that, and also the fear that you may leave me with a child my lord, and that I will be disgraced and sent home to Spain. I love my father very much and do not wish to vex him.'

The Falcon stroked her cheek with a strong brown finger and then traced the curve of her delicious mouth. 'Oh I see. It is only that. You do not fear being seduced, or losing your precious virginity which most girls hope to cling on to until they are married. You are apparently not afraid of a man's ardour. Since you do not mention it, I gather it is lost already? Most girls, at any rate those of my acquaintance, mention it first.'

Lady Constance pursed her lips and gave what Lord Falconer considered a saucy but enigmatic smile. 'Is it?' insisted his lordship, his passion at the thought rising.

Still she said nothing and he was aware of the hammering of his heart, the powerful stirring in his loins.

'I shall have to find out for myself, I can see that,' he said quietly. Expertly, delicately, he began kissing her neck and the top of her bosom, gently so as not to disgust or frighten her. He could feel her melting, knew that she wanted him. But rape or ravishment was not in his mind. He was too experienced, too sure in his dealings with women, too knowledgeable about the delicate nature of their physical and emotional mechanism, to attempt anything so clumsy.

Although he did not acknowledge the debt, he had much to thank Analee for in his perfection of the art of love. At first he had been inclined to be rough with her, but she had taught him how gentleness and tenderness were preferable to violence, and many men of war such as the Falcon were violent, choosing to take by force rather than by stealth. She had shown him that a woman was bound to a man by understanding, by gentle caresses, soft murmurings and lingering kisses in intimate parts of the body, rather than by any show of masculine strength.

Now his mouth lingered on the full snowy part of the bosom for so long that when he came to ease her breasts out of her bodice Constance was eager to help him by loosening her stomacher herself. She then detached it altogether in an abandoned manner, so that the upper part of her was completely bare and she lay back against the sofa moaning and sighing, indicating by her panting and the trembling of her body that she was ready for more.

But the Falcon, practised in the art of seduction, knew when to stop. Anticipation was often better than achievement, at least for so young a girl, and if he took her now she might regret her impulse in an explosion of self-disgust. Whereas if he left her at this point, quivering and eager for him, she would want to see him again so as to enable him to achieve that culmination which he so eagerly desired.

Her breasts were ripe and full for a young girl, indicating the level of her maturity, and he kissed each one tenderly before reaching for the stomacher from the floor where it had been cast aside and gently beginning to fasten it on her again.

'But what are you doing?' Constance cried in dismay. 'I thought . . .'

'My dear young lady, my beautiful darling Constance, I let my emotions get the better of me. I apologize. I . . .'

'No, no, but I want it – don't you see? Can't you feel it?' She seized his head in her hands and stroked his cheeks with her fingers, her eyes appealing.

'My dear, I know,' he said very gently. 'It is what I want too, above anything in the world, to possess you, and yet . . .'

'Yet what? I am ready, I am willing.'

The Falcon finished fastening her stomacher and reluctantly prised her hands away from his face. 'My love, you are young, a mere girl. As you said I am much older than you. I am married, I . . .'

'Oh, do not taunt me with my foolish remarks now,' she cried in distress. 'That was said to tease. Besides,' she looked at him slyly, 'that was before I knew of the delights of your caress, your embraces. I want to lose my virginity to a man such as you, a great soldier, the Marquess of Falconer. I desire it above all things.'

'Ah . . .' The Falcon sat next to her, putting a predatory arm around her waist, a smile playing on his lips. 'Then you are a virgin? You do not taunt me now, I see.'

'Don't mock me,' Constance pouted. 'I was playing with you. Of course I am a virgin! You do not know how closely protected we are in Spain. Each girl has her own duenna who is with her always. My duenna would be here had she not fallen ill, and my father thought I would be safe in England away from the hot-blooded Spanish nobles. Little did he know about Lord Falconer!'

'Or his own daughter,' the Falcon said silkily. 'Little did he know what a minx he had, ripe and ready for seduction by any practised rogue.'

'Not by anyone, I assure you,' Constance said hotly, 'but yes, you do exercise a strange fascination over me. You are so famous and so powerful, and when I saw the beauty of your wife I did not think you would so much as glance in my direction. You are like some fabled prince out of a story book. But not only did you glance at me, you sought me out, following me around in an obvious manner. It was like a dream coming true for a young untutored girl, and of course I have had my fantasies of love like any other. I matured early, I knew I was well developed. I wanted love, hungered for it. And what better than to find it in the arms of someone such as you.'

'Then you *are* asking me to seduce you, my pretty love?' the Falcon said, leaning forward and caressing her cheek.

'Yes,' she whispered, 'soon. Please, soon.'

The Falcon let his cheek linger against hers then sat back. He thought this was proceeding most satisfactorily. 'When is your father returning?'

'I don't know. He has gone north where he has an estate. Tomorrow or the next day.'

'Ah.' The Falcon looked vexed. 'I cannot return today. I have to see Lord Hardwicke the Lord Chancellor, and maybe also the King. Tonight we are dining with The Duke of Cumberland. But tomorrow . . .'

'What is wrong with now?' Constance said urgently, her eyes pleading. 'I am ready. I might think differently tomorrow.'

'You will not, my dear. Besides, you said you did not want to be got with child. I agree – nothing would spoil your introduction to the arts of love more. I can get something that will protect you and this I have not got with me.'

For a moment Constance looked frightened. 'What is it? Is it something unpleasant?'

'Not at all. And it will give you protection. As far as I know I have never fathered a child other than by my lawful wife and it is all due to this simple little expedient. Tomorrow afternoon, my love, be ready for me. Can we go to your bedroom?'

'Oh.' Constance looked thoughtful. 'I don't see why not. I will try and contrive it and give Bell the afternoon off. I shall say I am going out. Could we meet in the park?'

'No my dear. Everyone in London knows me. Try to open the door yourself. I will not knock but will be outside just after three. Be there.'

The Falcon got up and looked down at her, aware of a wave of passion such as he had not felt since he had first known Analee and, although their colour was very different, Constance had something of Analee in her, a wanton abandon, a readiness for and enjoyment of love that he had not found in many women.

'Tomorrow,' he whispered, kissing her on the forehead, closing his eyes in anticipation.

Tomorrow she would be his.

Analee gazed at Hugo Fitzgerald and shook her head. He disturbed her more than she cared to admit. It was not only the hot-headed persistence of his youth, but an animal quality that attracted her. He was not unlike many of the wild healthy gypsy boys with whom she used occasionally to sport before her life took such a drastic change. The shake of the head was meant to indicate disapproval; but she knew it was also a gesture of despair. She did not quite know what to do about him.

'My husband is already jealous of you. Why, if he knew you were here . . .'

'I waited all morning until I saw his carriage go out.'

'But what can you hope for?'

'I want to be your swain, to be given the privilege of loving and protecting you.'

'But I do not need your love and protection,' Analee protested, beginning to smile. Something about him made her feel better. She had been violently sick and ill that morning and her guts still ached. Now she felt well again, more alive. It was refreshing to be so wanted and admired after her husband's increasing indifference to her. The Falcon did not love her as he used to, no longer venerated her. She had become just another woman despite all her efforts to keep and please him, to excite him and make him desire her. Maybe it was her pregnancy, but she felt she had lost him.

'Yes you do,' Hugo was saying as he paced backwards and forwards, his hands behind his back. 'Your husband is a beast. He riles me whenever he can, he ignores you, leaving you to go through childbirth by yourself – and then how long was it before he came to see you?'

Analee gestured deprecatingly. It was six weeks, she knew. He had not come near her until she was able to make love again – was this the reason? At the time she hadn't thought about it, it seemed so impossible and then he had made up for his neglect – oh how he had made up for it.

'Mr Fitzgerald, much as I like you, I can see no reason for you to call or to continue calling. I am married and I am yet again carrying a child by my husband . . .'

Hugo looked aghast and stopped his pacing. He stared accusingly at her stomach.

'You . . . ?'

'Yes. In my belly, where your eyes are fastened. I am four months gone and shall again give birth in the summer.'

'But how *can* you?'

'How can I what Mr Fitzgerald? Make love to my husband?'

'Permit him . . .' Hugo's face was creased with disgust.

'He is my husband sir. He has a right, whether I wish it or not. But I do wish it! I love him. That you cannot seem to realize.'

'How can you love him?' Hugo had raised his voice so much, his emotions getting beyond his control, that Analee feared the servants would hear him.

'Just because you do not like him and he does not like you, that is no reason *I* cannot love him or welcome his embraces. Besides in this land a wife is subject to her husband, she has few rights apart from what he permits.'

'Then it is monstrous! The law should be changed.'

'Not when a man is good and, by many standards, his lordship is very good to me. He gave me his name when I was simply content to be his mistress. I am the mother of his children, of the future Marquess of Falconer. It is a great honour that I, a mere gypsy, came to such a high estate. If I have regretted it at times and missed the freedom of my former life, I am constantly reminded of my good fortune when I see my children and the happiness I am able to give my lord . . .'

'I want to hear no more,' Hugo said wrathfully. 'It is true I detest the man, and he me.'

'He knows you are interested in me,' Analee said softly. 'That is why. Indeed, anyone who did not know it would be a fool; you make it so obvious.'

'I can't be the first man other than your husband to admire you.'

'No, but one of the most persistent.'

'Oh Analee. Lady Falconer . . .' Hugo threw himself on his

knees and seized her hand, 'if you knew how much I wanted to love you and protect you. I know I am not rich or noble like his lordship; but I would never leave you to bear your children alone. I would be with you every minute of the day.'

'I confess, that *might* be tedious,' Analee said laughingly, but touched despite herself. 'When I married a soldier I did not expect to have him constantly by my side. In many ways the Marquess and I suit each other. Thank you.' She squeezed the hand that still held hers and tried to raise him to his feet. 'Believe me I am flattered by your attention and grateful for it. But pray leave me now, and do not come back . . . for I fear that if his lordship found you here he would not hesitate to kill you. For my sake stay away.'

'Then you do like me, a little?' Hugo's eyes pleaded. 'You do not wish me harm?'

'Of course I do not wish you harm, and yes I do like you. But I am also older than you, don't forget that, and twenty times more experienced in the ways of the world – at least I think I am – and I assure you that, despite certain vexations, his lordship and I suit and shall undoubtedly stay together until we die.'

Her body was so beautiful on the bed that it took the Falcon's breath away, although in his time he had looked on many beautiful naked women. He had resumed his caresses the moment she closed the bedroom door upon them. While she still stood by the door he had taken her masterfully but tenderly in his arms, kissing her neck and easing her breasts from her bodice, then unfastening her robe, untying her hoop and helping her to step out of her petticoats until she was naked.

Her body was very white and the little triangle of hair at her groin was a dusky blond, slightly darker than the thick golden hair of her head which she had unloosened and which lay about her on the pillow. She lay now with one leg half up and her arms wide in an attitude of abandon. As he had thought, she had little shame, no false modesty. She had permitted him to undress her without a murmur, without one forbidding gesture. He undressed, then he went over to the bed and sat beside her, gazing at her. He found it difficult to swallow; she was so beautiful, her eyes like liquid sapphires, her high cheekbones giving her an air of almost oriental mystery, her full lips provocative. When she smiled and her mouth parted he saw her small white teeth like evenly matched pearls. He began to caress her, moulding her slim waist. It was such an exciting prospect that it made him feel dizzy. He had never known such rapture as this, not even with Analee. He lay alongside her and began to embrace her even more. At his touch she started to tremble and clutched at him violently.

'Do not be afraid my darling . . .'

'I am not afraid,' she whispered. 'But it is a milestone in my life, is it not? Something that can never happen again. I want it to be perfect.'

'It will be,' the Falcon promised her.

Later, when she opened her eyes he saw that they twinkled with satisfaction and merriment. Thank heaven. It often took time for some women, even the most enthusiastic, to recover from the embarrassment of their first experience.

'Did you enjoy it my darling?'

'I had never expected anything like it,' she said hoarsely. 'I can't describe it still. I can't believe it. Such total abandon! I never knew it to be like this.'

The Falcon lay alongside her and drew up the sheet. It was cold in the room but their bodies glowed with the heat they had engendered. He wrapped his arms about her.

'You are a woman now, a perfect woman, made for love. We shall have such a glorious affair.'

'But how can we contrive it?'

'We shall manage, though alas I am to go abroad with His Majesty in May. But I will send Analee north and then we can meet more freely. I am so obsessed with you my darling, we must meet every day. Do you wish it too?'

She turned her limpid eyes to him and her hand caressed his chest. 'You know it, my lord.'

'I must go my heart,' said the Falcon, raising himself reluctantly.

He dressed swiftly, and then sat on the bed and tenderly kissed her cheeks. She sighed and smiled.

'Thank you,' he whispered. 'I love you.'

She looked at him lovingly, her eyes filling with sadness.

'Can you love two women my lord?'

'I love only *you*,' the Falcon said, 'and will give you frequent proof of my love. Until tomorrow my darling. I will send a note and before that flowers and maybe a jewel; but you must be discreet and not tell your father from whom they come.'

Then he kissed her again and quietly left the room.

15

The Marquess of Falconer studied the letter he had found by chance in his wife's boudoir. It had been tucked in one of the compartments of the elegant escritoire at which she wrote letters and kept the household accounts.

Normally the Marquess would never go into Analee's boudoir; but on this occasion he had been looking for the phials of aphrodisiac that he knew she kept for the infrequent times when her husband was tired or his carnal appetites jaded. Then she would restore him to potency with the aid of her gypsy medicines added to her own considerable skills and charms. There were certain drugs that heightened desire and excitement and these he wished to use on his new young mistress to arouse her to a frenzy of ardour that he would have the delight of assuaging.

For Constance was a continual revelation to him. She had quickly made up for her inexperience by proving a ready pupil, a subtle and ingenious improviser in the arts of love. The only frustration they had now was the infrequency with which they could meet in secret; but already Constance's effect on Lord Falconer was becoming the talk of court circles. Wherever the Marquess was, Lady Constance Craven was never far away, and there were many who had observed how she had seemed to bloom and mature in the space of only a few short weeks. The only people who didn't appear to notice these things were her father and Lady Falconer.

What excuse to find for sending Analee away failed even the resourceful Marquess, and also in his heart he was reluctant to let her out of his sight. For faithless he might be and sick and pregnant she might be; but Hugo Fitzgerald was in the north and the Falcon loathe to put him and Analee in proximity.

But this would settle it; he would send her to Falcon's Keep and have her carefully watched and guarded like a prisoner.

'Adorable . . . avec toute la tendresse possible.'

There was no signature and no address, just the date in French,

Janvier 1750. The writing was large and childish as though it had been written by a schoolboy. The Falcon swept out of the room, bellowing for Analee at the top of his voice. Nelly, who had been bathing Duncan, heard it in the nursery and her heart filled with apprehension. She could not recall the master using this tone of voice since those early days when Analee, not yet his wife, occasionally disobeyed him. But never since they had been married. Never.

Analee heard it too, lying on the sofa, looking out of the window and trying to get a little cheer from the pale March sun that lit up the small paved garden outside. She had been terribly sick that morning and had had violent pain. She began to think she might lose this baby and she hoped if so it would be soon. The suffering was wearing her down. It was the reason she hardly ever accompanied the Falcon to court but remained at home resting.

She didn't even attempt to get off the couch but remained where she was, her breath coming quickly, a tight band of fear gripping her heart. The Falcon hardly ever shouted or stormed unless he were very angry indeed.

He burst into the room, waving the piece of paper before him, then he thrust it under her eyes, his face transformed by a brutish snarl.

'*Adorable . . . Avec toute la tendresse possible!*' he shouted. 'Who is this from?'

Analee recognized the paper immediately and she thanked God that she was pale already or the blood draining away would have betrayed her completely.

'How came you upon it my lord?' she asked coldly, trying not to lose her composure.

'Never mind how I came upon it. How did you get it? That's the question.'

'I was given it.'

'Reasonable, reasonable,' the Falcon said mockingly backing away from her. 'That I can understand. But by *whom*? By whom were you given it?'

'That I cannot say.' Analee tried to stay the beating of her heart by taking a deep breath and placing her hands on her stomach. Even the slight press of her hands gave her pain and caused her to shift uncomfortably on the sofa.

'Don't try and wriggle out of it,' he shouted. 'I can see you squirming with guilt.'

'I am shifting with pain in my belly, my lord. I think I will lose this child.'

'Child of sin!' he snarled again. 'A bastard! No child of mine.'

'That is not true sir. It is your child for I have lain with none other. There is naught on my conscience. You know I have men who admire me – you have noticed it often. If they write me notes I cannot help it.' She gave a helpless gesture but the Falcon would not be placated.

'But who is this?'

'I have forgot,' Analee said. 'I swear I have forgot. Some common youth judging from the handwriting.' She shrugged her shoulders inconsequentially.

Lord Falconer appeared nonplussed by her calm, by her pallor, her air of injured innocence, and the obvious pain she was in. He turned to the window and fidgeted with an ornament on the low gilt table which stood under it.

'I am sending you away, Analee. I know not who your lover is; but I will not be cuckold in my own home. When you are well I will wring the truth out of you, but as I see you in distress . . . Doubtless it is the punishment of God upon you for deceiving me.'

'I have not deceived you, sir,' she cried. 'This is your child, as I swear on the heads of my other children. May God strike me if I lie. Where would you have me go Angus?'

'To Falcon's Keep. I will have you guarded there like a prisoner. McNeath may be Nelly's husband but he is loyal to me. McNeath and Nelly shall be your gaolers.'

'May I not go to Furness?'

'No!' But the Falcon looked thoughtfully out of the window and then strode over to Analee, playing with a fine jade paper knife. 'On the other hand maybe, yes, I fear not young Fitzgerald while you are *enceinte*. In fact I fear him less since I have come upon the most surprising information about him . . .'

'And that is . . . ?' for some reason Analee felt fearful and there was a painful lurching in her womb.

'Fitzgerald is a violent anti-Jacobite, a Hanoverian supporter. This is why he was so needled by me saying he was a Jacobite. His family suffered grievously at the hands of the Jacobite supporters in Ireland, having their house burnt down by miscreants and their effects seized. He hates them venomously and he was released from the army after offering his services to track them down.'

'He is a *spy*?'

'Aye, and a government spy. He knew what that arch villain Delamain was up to in Whitehaven and he has taken his place to follow in his tracks. Already a few Jacobites have been apprehended, thanks to him. Now they are waiting for Delamain to make a false move and try to return home.'

Analee was overcome by a wave of nausea and lowered her head. 'I do not believe it,' she whispered.

'You liked him, didn't you my dear? Maybe you are not so enthusiastic now to hear that he lies in wait for your beloved Brent Delamain.'

'That is why he is so friendly with George Delamain,' Analee said faintly, 'who hates Brent with heart and soul.'

'Aye. I learnt of it from the Duke of Newcastle who himself is involved in the affair and regards Fitzgerald as one of his most trusted agents. I must confess it made me feel better about the fellow, even though he ogles you.'

'Why are you telling me this?' Analee asked quietly.

'Because, my love, I know your secret sympathies are with the Jacobites. I know you will hate one sent to spy on them. On the other hand I also know that you, as my wife and the Marchioness of Falconer, will not betray my confidence and try and alert Delamain. Thus I have you doubly at my mercy. By all means go to your beloved Grange and stay there until I send for you. I will be going with the King to Hanover in May and know not when I shall return. But it will be time enough for you to think on the wrong you have done me, the slur you cast on my family name.' The Falcon contemptuously cast the Prince's letter on the floor and left the room.

Later that day Analee went slowly up to her boudoir and for a time stood there looking around her. It was a small cosy room, but she never felt as happy there as she did at Furness with the broad expansive sweep of the Lake constantly before her. Why had the Falcon come into this room at all? What had he been after? Simply to spy on her? To inspect the household accounts? She did not think so.

She looked carefully in the pigeon holes and drawers of her escritoire, but nothing was amiss except that the papers were in disorder. She had nothing else to hide. Then she looked round the room and the fact that the door of one of her cabinets was ajar caught her eyes. It was one she very seldom went to these days as it contained aphrodisiacs and potions for amorous stimulation, and in recent weeks Angus had seldom approached her so there had been no need of them.

A sudden conviction took hold of her as she walked slowly over to the ebony cabinet and opened the door. The Falcon had been very sprightly indeed recently, unusually happy and carefree even though he neglected her. He was out a lot and always came back in a good humour. Now . . . yes, some of her phials were missing and also, she perceived, several of the tiny sponges that came from the West Indies, and which she always kept in case she wanted to prevent conception or one of the servant girls did. But maybe the culprit this time was Nelly, who did not want to become pregnant by her husband while Analee was carrying a child. She pulled the bellrope and waited until Nelly arrived, her face anxious.

'Yes ma'am?' she bobbed.

Analee pointed to the cupboard. 'Nelly, have you taken anything from my cabinet? Either sponges to prevent conception or potions to stimulate McNeath?'

'Oh no Analee. I have my own store which you gave me. Besides, my husband needs little stimulation.' Nelly giggled.

'And you have not replenished it?'

'No ma'am. I swear.'

'Then I believe you. Nelly, we are going north again. I am banished; but to me it is a blessed relief. We are going to Furness.'

Nelly at first clapped her hands, her eyes shining, but then a thought struck her and she looked downcast.

'Oh ma'am, Analee, what about McNeath?'

'His lordship is sending him with us to be my gaoler. He is to make sure I do not flee and join the Jacobite insurgents.'

'Oh ma'am, McNeath is loyal to *you*.'

'But surely first to my husband?'

'Nay ma'am. He says it is owing to you that we were allowed to get married, his lordship would never have permitted it. Also, he perceives how his lordship neglects you and . . .' Nelly blushed and hung her head.

'And, Nell?' Analee prompted gently, but Nelly shook her head.

'I cannot say it Analee.'

'Goes with other women? McNeath will know because he accompanies him everywhere. Ah well. Pray do not tell me more; I thought as much when I saw the cupboard open. His lordship was snooping round and found the letter the Prince sent me. I think he is using it as an excuse to get rid of me. He knows I have many admirers and is not really jealous because I have no opportunity to satisfy them, being incommoded and constantly ill. Oh Nelly, hasten and pack. I can't tell you how I long to be gone.'

The heavy travelling coach made good progress through the Midlands and towards the north, but Analee was wracked by pain and sickness all the time. McNeath wanted to stop but she was so fearful that she begged him to go on so that she could be ill in the comfort of her own home. A servant had been sent on ahead by horseback to alert the staff at Furness to prepare for the arrival of their mistress; but the further north they got Analee knew they would not last the distance. At one of the inns in which they spent the night, a doctor was sent for and he advised Lady Falconer not to travel further; but she was up by first light and insisted that they press on.

At last the familiar outline of the Pennine Chain appeared to their right and a feeling of such joy and relief stole over Analee that she sank back in the coach.

'We will make it to Delamain Castle at least, Nelly. Send McNeath at once for Reyora and tell him to bring her there. She will help me.'

McNeath on receiving his instructions saluted and rode off and Analee sat back and waited for the turreted battlements of the castle to appear. How beautiful it was to be back among the lush green fields and forests of the north! The excess of rain in these parts made everything so rich and fertile, and the tilled soil through which young crops were beginning to appear that much darker and more fecund than in the south.

Analee recalled her journey north all those years ago when as a young, ragged barefoot gypsy, she strode through the fields, leaping over the hedgerows, eating berries and drinking from the waters of the clear streams. Now she was a Marchioness travelling in a fine carriage with a maid and an outrider; a mother of three children and the wife of one of England's premier noblemen. Sadly she thought of the Falcon. He had not even bade her goodbye.

'Look Nell . . . there it is, Delamain Castle. Oh thank God!' Analee leaned forward and immediately felt a stab of pain in her belly so that she found it difficult to sit up straight again. 'Oh Nell, we shall just make it in time.' And she leaned against her companion, thankful for her strong arm of support, watching as they got nearer to the huge castle which seemed such a refuge in her time of need.

The unexpected arrival of the Marchioness of Falconer threw the whole place into an upheaval. When her distressed condition was perceived a bed was prepared, two warming pans set up and a large fire lit in one of the best chambers. In the absence of Sir George, Henrietta admirably took charge and it was not until her guest was tucked comfortably in bed that they had time to exchange more than a few words.

'Oh thank you Henrietta. I think I am about to miscarry.'

'I shall send for the doctor immediately Analee.'

Analee laid a hand on Henrietta's arm. 'I have sent for Reyora. McNeath went on ahead to fetch her. Is that all right?'

'Of course,' Henrietta said softly. 'I can't tell you how much I owe to that good woman. She has been healer and friend in the months since you introduced her. She has given me renewed confidence and hope. It is true I will never conceive again, but Sir George underwent a gradual transformation towards me and became tender and loving, and ceased reproaching me for my barrenness. His attitude completely changed after Reyora gave me some potion to mix with his food. That in itself is a proof of her powers.'

'I am so glad,' Analee said, but she could not help thinking of the young girl that Sir George had been ogling in London – Lady Constance Craven, daughter of Earl St March. Maybe because of her he found himself able to leave his wife alone. She was certainly a lovely girl, full-blooded and mature in her charms. Analee recalled the way Sir George loitered on the outskirts of the group, his covetous eyes fastened on Constance. But every man's eyes had focused on her, even those of the Falcon and he was old enough to be her father! Analee had felt a momentary jealousy that, in her presence, men had eyes for another woman. But then Constance had her youth and nubility on her side – the promise of delights as yet untapped. Suddenly Analee had a very clear vision of the classical profile of the beautiful Lady Constance and for a moment the meaning of it worried her – and then she was wracked by a fresh spasm of pain and the image faded. Observing her, Henrietta held tightly onto her hand and wiped her brow with a damp perfumed cloth, delighted to have the chance of returning a service Analee had once performed for her.

By the time Reyora got to the castle Analee's belly seemed like a seething ball of pain and Reyora, quickly appraising the situation, set to mixing her herbs with coloured liquids in phials that she drew from her old hemp bag.

'Reyora . . .' Analee said weakly. 'Help me.' She drew up her legs with pain and twisted in the bed. Reyora put a cool hand on her hot brow and, swiftly drawing back the bedclothes and lifting Analee's chemise, put both her hands on her belly and closed her eyes.

'Oh . . . Reyora thank you.' The relief was immediate. The pain lessened and Analee felt calm. She gazed into the deep eyes of her friend who was looking at her thoughtfully.

'Shall I lose it?'

Reyora nodded. 'I'm afraid so. But there will be others. I will not let you be deformed inside like Lady Henrietta.'

Henrietta, standing with Nelly in the shadows of the room, came forward. 'Trust Reyora, Analee.'

'Of course I trust her.' Analee managed a weak laugh despite the pain. ''Twas what I told you all those months ago. Oh!'

'Take Lady Delamain away from here, Nelly,' Reyora ordered tersely, placing her hand on Analee's belly, her eyes tightly shut, as though she were saying an incantation.

'It is coming away. It will not be long. So this is what his lordship has done to you. Made you miscarry at five months!'

'He thinks it is not his child and my sufferings a punishment from God.'

'And is it?'

'It is his child, yes.'

'Ah.'

Nelly reentered and quietly took her mistress's hand. Analee gazed up at her gratefully, thinking how Nelly was always there at those important moments of her life. She had seen birth and now she would see death. For the next few hours she clung to Nelly while Reyora massaged her belly gazing at her, willing her to have courage.

Looking at her patient Reyora could not help thinking back to the time she had tried to abort Morella, but without success. How glad she was she failed. This time she could do nothing.

Suddenly there was a rush of blood and Analee felt her belly drain in a blessed feeling of relief as the foetus came away. Reyora quickly gathered it up from the bed and, after looking at it, put it in a cloth and wrapped it up. For a moment there was silence in the room – Analee experiencing the first freedom from pain for days and Nelly gazing sadly at the tiny form wrapped in a bloodstained cloth. She was amazed that such a small thing could cause so much pain, such upheaval.

'Good, it has all come away, no harm has been done.' Analee lay back against the pillows and closed her eyes, puffy and underlined with deep purple shadows.

Reyora mixed another potion which she put to Analee's lips and watched as the blood gradually returned to her face and she grew more rested.

'There, you will sleep my beauty . . . a good long peaceful sleep.'

'Thank you Reyora,' Analee murmured. 'My good and faithful friend. Without you I would have been lost.' She opened her heavy eyes and gazed at the *cohani*. 'Could you tell the sex? Was it . . . ?'

'It was a boy,' Reyora said briefly. 'You will have others. Go to sleep.'

And gradually Analee sank into the shadows, sadly aware that the legitimate first-born son of the Falcon was dead.

Analee spent some days at Delamain Castle before journeying on to Keswick and ultimately her beloved Furness Grange. The kind

Henrietta Delamain could not do enough for her and the women became friendly and spent a lot of time together. When she was better they walked in the garden, Analee on the lookout for little Morella playing with her nurse. But the memory of the child she had lost was too heartbreaking and she felt she could not meet Morella just yet; if she sought her out she would break down.

Analee took a long time to recover from her miscarriage. Even when she was back at Furness, surrounded by the love of her servants and the beauty of the countryside, a bleak feeling of loss and despair would often overtake her and nothing could rouse her from it for hours, sometimes days. She would just sit and gaze at the lake, her face unsmiling.

'Her ladyship's morbid spirits worry me,' Nelly said one day to her husband who was polishing his musket in an outside shed. 'Think you we should send for his lordship? I have heard of women who do away with themselves in cases following the loss of a child.'

McNeath grimaced and spat on the butt of his gun. 'Methinks his lordship would be indifferent to what you say about his wife. He has eyes for another, as I told ye. I never saw a man so taken in love, not even when he first met her ladyship, do you recall, and they used to spend days closeted together in the bedroom.'

'Aye,' Nelly smiled ruefully, feeling her own belly. She had a notion that the sponge had let her down. Nelly wanted a baby and, now that Analee was no longer carrying one, maybe it was a good time. 'But you tell me this girl is very young?'

'She could be his daughter; but she is a fine wench. I reckon he got her ladyship out of the way in order to bed her more easily. For her father looks after her carefully all the time.'

Nelly put her hands to her face and shut her eyes. 'Oh I cannot bear the thought of my lady being so deceived. And all the suffering she has had to endure on his account. It is too cruel.'

'Nell, say naught is my advice,' McNeath said casting an eye on his comely wife. 'Naught to him and naught to her. He will not come to her and he cannot help her in the state he is in, wild with love.'

563

16

Analee came but slowly out of the depression of spirits that had afflicted her for so long. Nelly had finally despatched McNeath to Reyora for a potion and Reyora had sent it, promising to come herself if Analee was not better. But from then on Analee did get better because she first became aware of the glories of the spring around her, the verdant greenery, the sparkling waters of the lake and the little tendrils of cloud in the clear blue sky. Yes nature had made her better, she thought one day, smiling for the first time for many weeks – nature and Reyora's cure which came from the elements. For the first time too that morning she had looked at her babies with pleasure and even noticed that Duncan had grown and was more agile. The thought had sent her back to the Prince's letter which she kept constantly near her. '*Adorable . . . Avec toute la tendresse possible.*' With all the tenderness in his heart he found her adorable. Her loneliness and isolation from the Falcon made her reflect more on that brief encounter with the Royal exile so that, in her mind, she venerated him even more and developed a fierce devotion for his cause.

Gradually through the sunny days of April and May she got better and her depression gradually lifted. The Falcon had sent brief word that he was going to Hanover with the King and the fact that he did not intend to see her before his departure filled Analee with grief, but also with a steely determination to put him from her mind in any other sense than that of a dutiful wife.

And now that she was better she longed to be more active. She was busy about the house and spent long hours in the garden with the gardeners learning from them but also teaching them, for few people knew as much about wild flowers, herbs, berries and strange grasses as Analee. She would walk into the wood with Nat Hardcastle and discuss the clearing and planting of trees. She took an interest in the farm and the animals, in the housekeeping accounts and the ordering of food and, in order to let the pregnant Nelly rest as much as possible, she put in a fair amount of time in the nursery playing with her children who had come to mean so much more because of her separation from her husband.

The invitation from the Riggs arrived quite unexpectedly. It was brought over by a messenger who waited for a reply. Analee did not hesitate. It fitted in with her newfound energy, her renewed zest for living, and although she had never met Ambrose Rigg or his wife she accepted with alacrity and agreed to stay the night with them.

Suddenly then she thought of Hugo Fitzgerald – would-be swain, and apparently a Hanoverian spy. He had not been near her even to try to ease her distress – so much for the swain who had wanted to love and protect her. But then, possibly, he did not know. She realized that the reason she had so swiftly accepted the Riggs' invitation was curiosity about Hugo Fitzgerald, and a knowledge that he would probably be there made her take special care over her appearance for her visit. She sent to Keswick for materials for new dresses and she took as much nourishment as she could, for her illness had made her so thin that her ribs and clavicle showed through her skin diminishing the effect of her still voluptuous bosom.

Analee had never been to Cockermouth and, because the air was balmy, chose to go in the open landau so that she could admire the long blue expanse of Bassenthwaite Lake over which towered great Skiddaw. One could peer through the thick firs of Thornthwaite forest observing the shafts of brilliant sunlight that illuminated glades across which birds flew and rabbits scampered, while beyond rose hazy spirals of woodsmoke from the fire of some itinerant wanderer or charcoal burner. Analee sniffed the air. The pungency of smoke and pine made her feel it was good to be well, and alive.

She went with only her coachman and a manservant riding postillion. Nelly was left in charge of the children and McNeath had long since disregarded his master's orders to keep a watch on his mistress – for what could happen, he wondered, and who could she possibly see? Besides, as Nelly frequently pointed out, it was not his place to act as guardian to his mistress.

Sarah Rigg still nursed the conviction that, unwittingly or not, Lady Falconer had done ill to her family, especially to her sister

Mary. But Mary had found contentment in her convent and all that had happened was now in the past. So when Hugo Fitzgerald begged her to invite the Marchioness, she did so more out of curiosity than a desire to please him or her husband, who was so gratified at the thought of having such an eminent person in his house for a night.

She waited anxiously with her husband and children on the porch for Lady Falconer to arrive, hoping that everything in the kitchen was happening as it should and her ladyship's bed had been properly warmed and her sheets aired.

Sarah was completely unprepared for the sight of the beautiful woman who gazed at them from the open landau. She wore a cloak of fine red camlet and a striking feather-fringed tricorne hat made of black beaver.

Rigg puffed down the steps importantly to help her alight and when she did Sarah drew in her breath at the elegance of the Marchioness, so tall and lissom with her jet black hair flowing from beneath her hat. Yet the smile was of great friendliness and charm and Sarah's apprehensions diminished as she hurried out to greet her followed by her brood in ascending order of age, the youngest, Caspar, still clutching his nurse's hand.

Analee extended her arms to the children especially baby Caspar who had a sturdy little body and red cheeks. As though sensing that someone special and unusual was here the children rushed up to her, leaving their nurse and grasping at her skirts, while baby Caspar reached up his tiny hands to be lifted. Analee bent and took him in her arms, and the younger two clamoured to be picked up as well while the eldest, Henry, stood gravely by entranced by the magnificence of the visitor. Suddenly there was a commotion of childish voices and laughter, and parental rebukes all coming together in a vast chorus.

'Really children!' Sarah at last sternly restored order by giving Caspar to the arms of his nurse, gently propelling Henry away and telling him to take his sister Elia indoors, and firmly seizing Norman by the hand.

'I am so sorry, your ladyship,' Sarah began but Analee interrupted her with a laugh.

'Mrs Rigg, pray do not rebuke them. I am devoted to children.'

'And they to you, ma'am.' Ambrose Rigg made an exaggeratedly low bow which, in view of the corpulence of his person, was no easy task. His face was florid and his bulbous pock-marked nose quite purple with excitement. He wore a satin suit in yellow, a colour unbecoming to a man of his appearance, and from the pocket of his long embroidered waistcoat hung a large handkerchief covered in snuff stains. Analee at first thought this must be some elderly relation, so difficult was it to imagine him as the husband of the tall statuesque Sarah Rigg who, besides being so much younger than he, was decidedly of better breeding. But he had introduced himself as Ambrose Rigg and, yes he undoubtedly was the master of the household. 'We are greatly honoured by your ladyship's visit,' Ambrose continued. 'And everything is ready for you ma'am.' He bowed the way ahead walking in a curious side-step so that he faced Analee while continuing to move forward, rather like a waddling duck.

'It is a great pleasure for me Mr Rigg I assure you,' Analee said following carefully so as not to cannon into him. 'And what a beautiful house you have, and such a lovely situation overlooking Cockermouth. I barely caught a glimpse of it on my way here; but the scenery is very fine.'

'Oh it is Lady Falconer, it is. Some call Cockermouth flat, but the town lies in a valley and there are hills on all sides. A fine straight road leads to the ports where I have my business.'

'I have never been to the sea in these parts Mr Rigg. I was once on my way there, but destiny prevented me ever reaching it.'

Ambrose rubbed his hands together in a gesture of enthusiasm. 'Then you must come to Whitehaven ma'am! And I will show you round and entertain you there as no royalty was ever entertained. Ah see who is here, come post haste from that very place to welcome you.'

Analee glanced back as Hugo Fitzgerald leapt up the steps to the porch three at a time and came bursting into the hall his face alight with expectation.

'Lady Falconer!' He came over and unceremoniously grasped her hand, imprinting a deep kiss on it. Then he raised his eyes and gazed into hers – to see nothing there but an icy remote expression. He felt taken aback by the utter immobility of her features and backed away bowing as he did.

'How do you do Mr Fitzgerald,' Analee said politely, barely smiling, and turned once more to Rigg as though anxious not to miss a word he said.

The procession moved into the drawing room where a large fire roared in the grate, though it was a warm day, and tables were set with cakes and sweetmeats, jugs of cordial, delicate porcelain cups and pots of tea. Analee glanced appreciatively round her at the spaciousness of the room, the opulence of the furnishings, the elegance of the furniture.

Sarah poured the tea and herself brought Analee's cup.

'This is to refresh you Lady Falconer, after your journey.'

'Oh it was not at all wearying,' Analee said, taking the cup with a smile, 'but tea is welcome after all. What a beautiful house you have here Mrs Rigg, and furnished with such taste.'

'Aye, *my* brass and my wife's taste,' Ambrose said overhearing, and preening himself by thrusting out his great corporation encased in yellow satin. 'This used to be a tiny crofter's house Lady Falconer; but my father bettered himself and started a small business in Whitehaven. Then, when I was but a boy of nine I started work for him and now I control vast interests, have a fleet of twelve ships, several warehouses and ever year I add to this fine house to make it bigger and better for my heirs. For I am determined my sons shall have everything I did not and come into my business and provide for me in my old age. We have three sons Lady Falconer, and maybe . . .' Ambrose winked and placed a podgy, well manicured hand on his wife's belly, 'maybe another, for my wife is in pod.' He chuckled gleefully while Sarah, her face burning, quickly brushed his hand away and smoothed her petticoat. Her waist was still neat and trim so she was not far gone, Analee thought.

'You are to be congratulated sir, on your progeny and also your good fortune in capturing such an accomplished wife,' Analee said, noting the expression of irritation on Sarah's aristocratic face. There was dissatisfaction there too, and disgust at the spectacle of her overweight husband with his red face, thick lips, huge nose and long bob wig which was askew so that it tipped more to one side than another. Analee was immediately intrigued by Sarah. She knew the Allonby history and the poverty that had come from their loyalty to the Stuarts; but why Sarah had married this undoubtedly genial but personally rather gross and offensive elderly man seemed difficult to understand.

However, as Sarah later explained to her in an unaccustomed burst of confidence, the Allonby women were unlucky with their men. 'My Aunt Susan's husband died in exile, and then Mary made that unhappy marriage with Brent. I knew Mr Rigg could give me things I could never otherwise have had, and he is good to me. I want for nothing. And our children will inherit a fortune, and a place in the land we never had, despite our birth.'

'You are very fortunate,' Analee said tactfully, watching the evening clouds gather in the sky. It really was perfection on this hillside with its view across the town of the uneven ridge of mountains that hemmed in Loweswater, Crummock Water and Ennerdale, scarcely discernible now through the mist and the growing dusk. The late spring evening promised a foretaste of summer and, as Analee stood by the open window, a breeze came out of the forest wafting with it the scented woodland smells of Lakeland. She breathed deeply.

'It is so beautiful here, and quite a contrast to the Grange. Oh . . .' She turned to look at her hostess. 'You do not mind me mentioning it Sarah – for I may call you Sarah may I not?'

'Of course.'

'I feel I know your family so well, and love them. Mary was so good to me when I came to Furness, a vagabond on my way to the sea.'

'Mary has a very sweet nature,' Sarah said quietly, aware of a sudden constraint in the conversation. 'Oh do not look like that Lady Falconer. I know what happened was not your fault. My cousin Brent was always impetuous and foolhardy, he caused such trouble as a boy. It was natural he would grow up in the same mould. He was always chasing rainbows, though I must admit I was and am fond of him. He lodged with us for a year and there was not a single criticism I could make of him. And then he married Mary, and there was the war. It unbalanced him again and you are,' Sarah turned to Analee and looked at her sadly, 'aware of what happened next. He felt he could not love her as he should or be a husband to her.'

Analee looked at Sarah, wondering how much she knew about her role in the affair. If she knew the proud, stoical Allonby clan, not much. She could not see Mary divulging to her sister the reason for her husband's lovelessness, and Brent would have remained as silent on the subject as a tomb. There was a reserve to Sarah that made Analee that much more surprised when she started to confide in her so soon after showing her to the long bedroom on the first floor overlooking Cockermouth and the distant hills. Sarah had immediately started making excuses for being married to Mr Rigg, as though to say it was not the sort of thing that an Allonby would do in normal circumstances, marry so much beneath them.

'I believe Mary is happy now in the convent,' Analee said gently. 'It appears that she thinks she always had a vocation to serve God. Maybe this is why her marriage was not successful.'

'It is said, Lady Falconer,' Sarah said avoiding Analee's eyes, 'though how much of it is true I know not, that my cousin fell head over heels in love with you. So much was told me by Emma, though what part speculation took in it I know not.'

'I think speculation did play a big part in it Sarah,' Analee said, her eyes veiled enigmatically, 'and please call me Analee. I am a gypsy as you know and detest formality. And *what* news of Emma?'

Sarah sighed and sat down in a comfortable low chair clasping her hands together.

'Emma came home last week.'

'Emma is *home*?' Analee said in a voice of amazement.

'No. Emma is here,' Sarah replied softly. 'She dare not go home and face her brother and mother straight away. In fact she has become a recluse and wants to see no one. I have persuaded her to take dinner with us tonight in your honour.'

'But Stewart . . . ?' Analee already knew what Sarah was going to say.

''Twas as we expected Lady . . . Analee. Stewart's heart was engaged to another. The daughter of the wealthy plantation owner for whom he worked. Emma saw him but once; no twice. First unexpectedly at a ball in Baltimore where she was staying, and then he came to see her in a very gentlemanly manner and explained he wanted to start life again.'

'He could have told her before,' Analee said quietly. 'I wish I had not helped her to go. I had grave doubts at the time.'

'Well, you did what you thought best, though we were against it, Mr Rigg and I. Brent however was quite determined and so was Emma, so you are really an agent and played an insignificant part. Do not blame yourself; no one else does, only the depth of Emma's foolish love and Brent's headstrong nature.'

'I was involved nevertheless and I am sorry it turned out badly. But she went a year ago. Surely . . . ?'

'She did not like to return home so soon and she had no money. She went to Virginia where she had friends and became a governess. In the meantime she wrote to Mr Rigg who sent her the money for her passage.'

'He is indeed a very kind man.'

'He has a good nature,' Sarah said wryly, 'and means no harm. He was fond of the girl and hoped she would find happiness as we all did. But she has gone very into herself and . . . her looks have changed. She is no longer a beauty.'

'Beauty is not important,' Analee said. 'If Emma is bitter that is more important. Bitterness mars the soul. Do you think she would speak to me?'

Sarah did not want to offend her distinguished guest; but she knew that all had not gone smoothly when Emma had stayed at Furness. Something had happened whose nature she had not divulged to her cousin; but that had made her bitter too. She had only been persuaded to attend the dinner this evening to please Mr Rigg, who was like a second father to her now.

'I do not know, Analee. Let us see how it goes this evening.'

The dinner party was to precede a gathering to which all the local worthies had been invited. Analee hadn't realized the occasion was to be such a splendid one and marvelled at the range of Sarah's talents in being able to provide a sumptuous feast followed by a reception for fifty or more people. The long mahogany table in the Riggs' dining room was lit by gleaming candelabra and the pewter and silver, the crystal and delicate bone china were reflected in the highly polished sheen of the wood. Besides Ambrose and Sarah Rigg, Analee, Emma and Hugo Fitzgerald, the dinner guests included the Honourable Harkus and Rose Thursby from Castle Thursby in the neighbourhood, and Arthur Croft, a local merchant recently widowed, to make up the number.

The sideboard groaned under the weight of roast beef, neck of mutton boiled and garnished, stuffed woodcock, plum puddings, currant puddings, cheeses, sweetmeats and a variety of the best French wines.

Analee provided most of the conversation with accounts of Court life in London, the tittle-tattle of the battles between St James's Palace and Leicester House, the influence of Lady Yarmouth which was now so great that even ministers went to her before seeing the King to beg her intercession.

'But I am sure you are weary of this,' Analee said, sipping her wine and gazing at the company over the brim of her glass. 'I much prefer the country myself.'

Hugo Fitzgerald had never taken his eyes off her, and indeed the rest of the company were enthralled. When she told a story she had the gift of transporting her listeners there immediately as though, in imagination, she could make them travel vast distances and visit strange and exotic places. Hugo recalled her at the Court, scintillating, gaining everyone's attention, and on the other hand lying in her bed at Furness nursing her new-born child. Hugo had expected to find her heavy with child now for when he had last seen her she had told him she was carrying another child by that accursed man, the Falcon. Yet her ladyship, although dressed with elegance and wearing a gown of blue ribbed silk over many petticoats and a large hoop, was so slim, her waist almost within the grasp of a man's joined hands, that it was obvious she was not breeding.

The ecstasy to have heard she was at Furness, the effort to get Sarah to invite her, and oh the bliss that now she was here! Hugo had worked hard in Whitehaven all week and had hurried back today to find that his love had already arrived. Since then he had walked on air.

Harkus and Rose Thursby, although unable to resist an invitation to meet the fabled Lady Falconer, nevertheless felt they were dining beneath them. Everyone knew she had been a common gypsy, and as for Ambrose Rigg . . . he was so vulgar and of such an unsavoury appearance that it was all Mrs Thursby could do to stay in the same room as him. It was true Sarah Rigg was an Allonby, but since the Rebellion the Allonby stock had fallen lower than ever; with the exile of John and Stewart and the sequestration of their ancient house by the authorities, it could almost be considered extinct. Blood counted however with the Thursbys, an old county family who had judiciously combined loyalty with expediency over the years.

Harkus and Rose Thursby had five children of roughly the same age as the Riggs, and Harkus ran a profitable farm and kept the castle in good order and repair while his widowed father flitted between a small house in London and a palazzo in Venice. But the pace of modern times worried Harkus Thursby, schooled in the steady painstaking tradition of his forbears. There was all this business of trade overseas and new industrial processes; there was the rise of the new rich: men like Ambrose Rigg, who surely did not deserve by any standards, other than financial, to be where he was, or to have a house that almost rivalled Castle Thursby in size and extent, and indeed exceeded it in opulence.

What was worse – the Thursby money was staying pretty much as it always had been and was not expanding to meet the rising inflation caused by costly foreign wars and the extravagance of the Hanoverian Court. If he was to maintain the standards created by his family Harkus needed more money, and Ambrose Rigg had assured him that if some of the Thursby money was to find its way into his business it would be increased fourfold – far better than holding government bonds or investing in disasters such as the South Sea Company which had led many to ruin some thirty years before.

Harkus Thursby knew he was lowering standards by any association with such a person as Rigg, and now Sarah Rigg was inviting his wife to tea and the children to play with hers. Rose Thursby was even more conscious of social class than her husband, having come from the landed gentry, established in the north of England for as long as the Thursbys. No Wentworth would ever have anything to do with trade or commerce no matter what the inducements. They were landowners and farmers, good country stock, the backbone of England.

Rose Thursby, a beauty at nineteen when she had made such an excellent marriage to the Honourable Harkus, heir to the fifth Baron Thursby, was at twenty-nine an attractive and accomplished woman if set in her ways and with a very strong idea as to the place of everyone in the scheme of things. For Ambrose Rigg to have jumped from being a mere 'statesman' to the landowner on the scale he now was was quite monstrous. Sarah Rigg was another matter, a lady by birth and breeding. This fact made it easier to consort with the Riggs which was so necessary because of the financial difficulties that Harkus had confided in her. But Rose inherently despised someone who married so obviously for gain as Sarah Allonby had; it was the sort of thing you never got over or came to terms with, someone marrying for gain in such a blatant fashion. You were always reminded of it every time you looked at her and that repulsive beast of a husband beside her, always breaking wind or belching or sticking a fat ugly finger up his broad nose.

As for Lady Falconer . . . it was almost beyond belief how one of the premier nobles of England could marry someone who had gone barefoot and slept in ditches. She didn't even try and hide it. She was certainly beautiful and of an undeniably aristocratic bearing; but you would think one would have kept that sort of background to oneself and not loudly vaunted it abroad as Lady Falconer did. Here she was saying she preferred the country and Harkus, obviously impressed by her, was agreeing with her not realizing that she obviously meant that she wanted to be running around the fields with no shoes on and doubtless not much on her upper half either.

'We are not people for the Court ourselves Lady Falconer,' Harkus said politely. 'We stick to the north of England where we are known and where we came from. One of my ancestors did have some truck with the Court of Queen Elizabeth, but he was exiled to the West Indies for his pains and never heard of again. A salutary lesson!'

Emma had turned to look at him at the mention of the West Indies and Analee, who had been observing her as unobtrusively as she could, was aware of the longing in her eyes, the sick pallor of her face. Her figure was gaunt so that she appeared to have no bosom at all and her sunken cheeks and hollow eyes made her seem prematurely aged. Her dress was drab and her hair, simply and naturally dressed, lacked lustre. Analee recalled the proud young woman of just a year ago, and many had said even then that Emma was not the girl she had been before the Rebellion.

But then there had been a life and vigour to Emma sustained by her love for Stewart, her desire to cross the ocean and be with him again. Now she was lifeless, and the formerly brilliant dark eyes were dull and disinterested. She had taken no part in the conversation at all and had avoided looking at Analee.

But Analee was determined to speak to her and did so during the reception, when the double doors between dining room and drawing room were flung open to create a small ballroom sufficient for twelve couples to dance at a time. A five-piece orchestra had discreetly appeared from nowhere, the long dining table had been removed and in an adjoining salon a delicious supper was laid out temptingly amid a welter of white china plates and tall crystal glasses. There were different kinds of cold fish done in a variety of ways – in aspic, with sauces or served plain dressed with prawns or baby crabs – and meats, fowl and game again sumptuously disguised in pastry or herbs or potted in dishes and lavishly garnished. There were jugs of mead and ale, and bottles of wine – the white in silver coolers topped with ice, the red served in decanters made of crystal with moulded silver bases.

The other guests – of all kinds, local gentry as well as trade and minor aristocracy – were introduced to the Marchioness of Falconer, the legendary Falcon's wife, and then went off to partake of the delicious fare or dance a few measures on the floor.

Hugo trailed after Analee, vainly hoping for a word until at length he was sure she was at pains to avoid him. Emma was about to disappear to the privacy of her bedroom when Analee spied her and caught her gently by the arm.

'Do not go yet Emma! We have not spoken.'

'I have little to say to you Lady Falconer,' Emma said dejectedly not meeting her gaze. Analee had noted this downcast expression at the dinner table, how Emma had studiously avoided looking at people directly in the eyes.

'I am sorry you returned in such a wretched and unhappy state Emma. That is all I wanted to say. I am sorry for my part in it.'

Something about the tone of Analee's voice made Emma look up and a little colour returned to her cheeks.

'Yes it was a failure. I am sorry too. It has ruined my life.'

The crowd of people, their gaiety, the tinkling sound of the orchestra in the corner suddenly reminded Emma of the ball in Baltimore where she had met Stewart, and her eyes filled first with an expression of panic and then unexpectedly with tears. Vainly she tried to brush them aside, whereupon Analee took her hand and led her through the door into the corridor, its gloom a contrast to the brilliance on the other side of the door. Emma broke down sobbing and Analee reached for her head and held it against her breast stroking her hair and murmuring words of comfort.

'There, my dear, there, there. No life is ever ruined. We are all given the capacity to pick up the pieces again.'

'No, no . . . I . . . l-l-loved him and he . . . he . . .'

'I heard. He was engaged to another.'

''Twas . . . 'twas not only that. He wanted to start a new life; to forget the past.'

'It is understandable,' Analee said gently. 'In view of what he suffered.'

'But I would have come to him.'

To this Analee had nothing to say, knowing as she did that the intricacies of the human heart had little to do with logic or reason. Of course Stewart could have sent for Emma, and she would have gone gladly, whatever the circumstances. Only he did not. Her eyes rested sympathetically on Emma's face. 'Come and stay with me at Furness, Emma. It is beautiful there now. Come back with me.'

But Emma continued to cry, shaking her head, her fingers nervously plucking at the embroidered robings of Analee's bodice.

'No, I am waiting for a note from Mama. As soon as George goes to London Mama will send for me.'

'But she can send to Furness for you. Come, I would like the company.'

'No I cannot. Not now.' Emma raised a tearstained face to Analee. 'But thank you. I am sorry to cause such a scene. You are very kind Lady Falconer.'

'It was Analee – may it not be so again? And pray don't thank me. Why?'

'For being kind to me, for what you have done tonight. But you will never really understand, Lady Falconer – you have all the beauty and wealth in the world and all the men admire you. And I have nothing.' And bitterly, tearfully, Emma rushed upstairs.

* * *

Hugo Fitzgerald managed to get a dance with Analee; but during the elaborate measures of the gavotte, even as danced in Cockermouth, it was difficult to get a word in edgeways. They were forever turning or bowing or sidestepping and Hugo was puce with frustration. Once off the dance floor some fat old worthy would be waiting to claim her, and after that another – and so it was, just as he had predicted. She was taken into supper by Ambrose and out of it by Harkus Thursby who smiled more than anyone could remember – he being naturally a sombre man – at the beautiful Marchioness on his arm. And the night wore on. It was almost dawn when Analee thankfully said goodnight to Sarah at the door of her bedchamber and any chance Hugo had to talk to her was gone.

But at breakfast late the next morning, at which the Marchioness appeared as fresh and well groomed as though she had had ten hours' rest, there was a surprise for her.

'Mr Fitzgerald insists on escorting your carriage back, Lady Falconer,' Sarah said. 'We however would like you to stay. Is it not possible? Just one more day. I promise you a quiet evening, a good dinner and a game of cards.'

'Dear Sarah, nothing would give me greater pleasure; but I cannot. I am expected back today and I miss my babies. But I want you to come over very soon and spend the night with me. Is it a promise?'

Sarah's eyes sparkled. The evening had been a great success; the best party the town had known for years. No one had snubbed her husband and the Thursbys' frostiness had noticeably thawed. Mrs Thursby had even suggested for the first time that Sarah should bring *her* children to tea, and now the Marchioness of Falconer was asking her to stay! Money, Sarah thought grimly, seemed to have more pull these days than breeding.

'I would love to Lady . . . Analee.'

'Then we shall fix a day soon, when the weather promises to stay bright and you can see my lovely lake with its colours changing in the sun, and the magic of the early morning haze when you could imagine fairies and hobgoblins were abroad. But as for Mr Fitzgerald, I am quite safe without his kind attention. Thank him for me though.'

'He insists, I'm afraid,' Sarah said. 'He is out this very moment preparing his horse.'

17

Hugo Fitzgerald followed Analee into the house without waiting to be asked. He leapt off his horse as they arrived at Furness and handed her out of the carriage in advance of the servant who rushed forward to perform the same task. Analee hadn't exchanged a word with him either before or during the journey. She wasn't exactly rude, but she behaved as though he were not there.

Now after greeting her staff, arranged before the house to welcome her, she gave her cloak to a servant and hastened into the drawing room, Hugo eagerly at her heels. Once inside she swept round and faced him.

'Now Mr Fitzgerald, what exactly is this charade?'

'Charade, ma'am?' Hugo quietly closed the double doors and stood against them looking at her. 'What charade?'

'The charade of pretending to be enamoured of me.'

'But I *am*, Lady Falconer!' Hugo approached her with the gentle stealth of a cat. 'I scarcely think of anyone or anything else. It has been like that since last summer. I am in a torment.'

'It *is* a charade, sir,' Analee said briskly, 'and I believe you have ulterior motives.'

'Oh?' Hugo looked at her with genuine surprise. 'What other than to capture the heart of the Enchantress?'

'I think that is a blind sir, and that you have been put up by my husband to spy on me.'

Beneath the scorn of Analee's gaze Hugo appeared to falter, but a dark angry flush suffused his face.

'A spy sent by your husband? Madam, I beg you . . .'

'My husband has informed me that you are a committed Hanoverian agent. That you are spying on Rigg and trying to trap any Jacobite you chance upon. In particular you are waiting to betray Brent Delamain should he return to these parts. Knowing my husband – he is a thorough man – I believe this to be true. What is more, by allowing me to come here, near you, despite his jealousy of me, I think it proves you are not what you pretend. How much does he pay you, *Mister* Fitzgerald?'

Analee turned her back on him scornfully and went to the fireplace. On account of the mildness of the weather, there was no fire in the grate, just a large urn of budding twigs and spring flowers. Over the mantelpiece hung the portrait of the martyred Charles I which Mary had explained to Analee all those years ago when Analee had come to the house as a gypsy. Analee gazed at it, her heart beating quickly and her eyes full of tears. She heard a step behind her and knew he was very close, but still she did not turn.

'Lady Falconer, Analee . . .' Hugo said quietly and hesitantly. 'I am not a spy, perish the thought! I am a devoted servant of the Stuarts, and follow in the fine tradition of my family who fought for James II in Ireland and were ruined at the Battle of the Boyne. We nurse a hatred for the Hanoverians and the curses they have brought on our country. And as for spying on you my lady . . . I would cut my throat before you rather than have you entertain the thought for a second longer.' Hugo made an expressive gesture with his finger across his windpipe and Analee, for the first time, began to doubt the conviction she had gradually formed that he was in Angus's pay.

'But my husband . . .'

'Your husband is right in one thing, my lady. I *pose* as a government spy; but in fact I scatter pebbles along their way instead of boulders.'

'But he said you have betrayed men . . .'

'True my lady; but only knowing they were of such little importance that they would soon be released. From time to time I also discover a quantity of arms or close a route inland from one of the coves. That way the authorities think that I am doing my business and leave me alone. In fact I am preparing for a fresh landing by His Highness, maybe in this very part, so that he will land in England. He does not make for the south where he is expected and has more opposition and Scotland is ruled out altogether.'

'*Here*?'

'Aye, at Whitehaven even. I assure you it is imminent. Now do you believe me Lady Falconer?'

Analee looked uncertainly at him and then away. 'I know not what to say,' she said at last. 'A counter-spy is a most difficult person to believe. Know you Brent Delamain?'

'*Of* him my lady; we have never met. I had to be careful before I wormed my way into the confidence of the government and then that pompous and ridiculous man Sir George Delamain. I made use of him too.'

'A landing in Whitehaven . . .' Analee said wonderingly. 'He might come here . . .'

''Twould be ideal my lady!' Hugo said eagerly, while Analee thought of the sleeping baby Duncan upstairs. 'Oh I knew you were for us! There was the rumour and now I know. Your husband is a man I detest – not only because he is married to you but for his politics too. I could not be sure you would help us until now.'

Hugo moved forward as though to clasp her in his arms, but Analee sidestepped him and went to the bell-pull to summon a servant.

'You must go now, Mr Fitzgerald. You have given me much to think on. I hope you are telling me the truth, because . . .'

Hugo stepped up to her and, taking her hands, pressed them to his lips. Analee, conscious of that strange power drawing her to him, allowed her body to relax and respond to his respectful kiss. As if aware of her change of attitude he kept her hands clasped tightly but, raising his face, kissed her lips very gently and with a tenderness that only hinted at the passion that was to come. Analee closed her eyes, susceptible to his maleness, the rugged powerful smell of him after cantering his horse all those miles from Cockermouth. His bulk almost encompassed her and she felt his harsh cheek against hers. It was months since she had lain with a man, an abstinence enforced on her by her husband. His mouth left hers and he kissed her chin, her neck, the top of her lovely bosom while his powerful arms encircled her, almost squeezing the life out of her.

Analee remembered she had pulled the bell-rope to summon a servant and struggled away from him, laughing teasingly.

'Desist I pray you! A servant will be here any minute and he may be in the pay of my husband who has promised to have me guarded.'

'He is a blackguard,' Hugo said breaking away reluctantly. 'Oh

Analee, my darling, I have you. Next time you will be mind. I know it in my bones, I have always known it. 'Twas merely a matter of time.'

'You have, it is true, been most persistent,' Analee murmured. 'But do not presume too much.'

'Oh I do not, my lady. I, the most fortunate of men were I to attain my goal, certainly do not presume on the magnanimity of the fabled enchantress. But now that I have shown I am not a cursed government spy, I hope, I trust that you will favour me . . . I know your husband neglects you, and that he is soon to go away with the King. In the meantime he amuses himself . . .'

Analee held up a hand. 'Pray, no more rumours, sir. I do not wish to know.'

There was a respectful knock on the door and a servant entered just as Hugo and Analee had pulled apart and were standing some distance away from each other.

'Good day Tom,' Analee smiled at the footman. 'Pray bring a glass of wine to refresh Mr Fitzgerald who is about to leave us.'

'Oh my Analee,' Hugo murmured, 'not for long. Not for long.'

Lady Constance Craven lay in the great bed at Falconer House and gazed at the form of her sleeping lover. It was a warm May day and there had been no need for bedclothes.

For the most part they were content to make love wherever and whenever they could. Usually she came to Falconer House, admitted by a back door, because her father had begun to be suspicious asking about the flowers that came for her every day, the beautiful jewels she received. But Constance was enigmatic – 'an unknown admirer' was all she would admit to.

Now this perfect time was coming to an end. The Falcon was to go to Hanover the following week. This might be the last time they met.

Lady Constance gazed at her own body, no longer virginal but much used, fulfilled by love. How could she support life without the Falcon? How could she continue in her despised role of the aristocratic maiden on the look-out for a husband? For she knew she wanted no husband other than he; but it was impossible. He had told her many times that it was impossible, though their love would endure forever even if she married another, as in time she must.

'I will cuckold him from the start!' the Falcon had mocked. 'So make sure he is an ass. You need only look for his money, not his manly qualities. I will provide you with all you need of the latter my love.'

It hurt Constance to think that he could talk of her marrying another man; but she grew to realize how well versed he was in the ways of the world, how cynical, mostly how right. Yes, she would marry some nincompoop chosen by her father and continue to love the Falcon . . . . all her life.

Lord Falconer stirred sleepily and reached out an arm for his love. Oh the feel of that soft yielding girlish flesh! Constance had the most beautiful skin the Falcon had ever encountered. It had been pampered from babyhood with creams and unguents and the warm waters of the Spanish coast where Constance used to bathe unobserved by any except her duenna. How different she was from Analee whose skin, though vibrant and beautiful, had the oily translucence of an olive, a resilient quality that she had got from her many years spent in the open air.

The Falcon fingered the soft flesh of the girl next to him and his desire increased, made more poignant by the thought that he was soon to leave her. God knew when he would see her again, or if she would still want him. Her father was here to marry her off, and maybe she *would* fall in love . . . . It was a risk he had to take; though for the moment he was quite sure of his power over her. Constance, he knew, would prove inconstant. All she really wanted was a vigorous lover like him to ease the yearning of her flesh.

'Oh my heart,' he murmured, 'whatever shall I do without you? Oh Constance . . .'

'*Constance!*'

Her name seemed to echo; her eyes were closed and it came from the far end of the room. But it was not the gentle soft murmur of the Falcon. It was strident and angry and then, when she opened her eyes and peered over the shoulder of her lover, she saw the sight she had always dreaded. Her father stood at the door, an expression of loathing and contempt on his face.

'I might have known this was going on,' he said at last. 'People tried to warn me, dropped hints but I could not believe it of my own daughter, gently reared and chaperoned by a duenna. I could

582

believe it of Lord Falconer because of his reputation; but I did not think that even *he* would stoop so low as to seduce a girl of noble birth scarcely out of the school room, and turn her into a whore.'

Constance said nothing, but her large frightened eyes gazed at her father. The distress on the face of a beloved and indulgent parent moved her far more than his obvious disgust and the meaning of what he was saying.

The Falcon finally seemed to realize that they were not alone – at first he had scarcely been able to believe his ears and lay there inert and stupified – then he raised his head and looked straight into the eyes of Lord St March.

'Oh my God,' he said and sank his head into the pillows.

'Aye Lord Falconer – defiler of my daughter! How dare you sir!'

'Pray get out and let me dress St March,' the Falcon said weakly. 'Save your daughter further embarrassment, I beg you. We'll discuss this afterwards.'

'Yes father, please.'

The Earl appeared undecided as to what to do but then he nodded his head. 'Five minutes. I'll wait outside the door.'

As soon as the door was closed the Falcon vaulted out of bed. Constance was aware that she was trembling. Seeming to have little concern for her predicament, he rapidly put on his breeches, his shirt and waistcoat and began to tie his stock.

'Curses,' he said. 'To spoil such a wonderful interlude.'

'*Interlude* my lord? I thought it was the love of a lifetime.'

The Falcon bent quickly to the bed and sat down, pulling on his socks. 'Of course it is my love . . . but you are a very young girl. Who knows what changes I will find in you on my return?'

'You will find no changes in *me*, sir,' Constance said, staring at him as though some sort of recognition of his nature was beginning to dawn. 'But I fear I may find you changed. I have heard a man grows indifferent once he has seduced a maid.'

The Falcon put his feet into his shoes and then leaned over her, stroking her hair. 'Do not mistake me, my darling Constance. I will never forget you nor this idyll of our love. Nor would I ever be indifferent to you. But circumstances . . .'

Lord Falconer drew back the sheet to gaze once more at her beautiful body, at the erotic image he would bear forever in his mind. And that's all he would bear, he thought ruefully, now that her accursed father had found out. He would personally slit the throat of the servant who had let him in. Yet it had never occurred to him to have his own house guarded.

Constance, observing his lecherous expression, snatched the sheet and pulled it back up to her chin.

'Pray my lord, leave me while I dress,' she snapped. 'And do not think you can continue with these liberties as if I was just a plaything to while away a few weeks before you went to Hanover . . .'

'Constance, I *never* . . . my love, believe me . . .'

'The five minutes are up sir!' Lord St March bawled from the other side of the door and the Falcon, looking confused and uncertain for one of the few times in his life, stood up and reached for his coat, shrugging it on and smoothing the stiff white ruffles of lace that fell from his full shirt sleeves banded at the wrist. He took his wig off its stand, adjusted it in the mirror and then without another word opened the door and confronted the injured parent.

'Now sir, shall we proceed to my study?'

'I am obliged to you sir,' Lord St March said stiffly and followed the Falcon down the wide double staircase, across the large hall and into the small room that overlooked the patio and was lined with books and pipe racks and jars of various kinds. Two comfortable leather armchairs faced each other on either side of the fireplace, and the sun streamed in through the window on to the persian rug which lay on the polished oak floor.

'Pray sit sir.' The Falcon pointed to a chair but Lord St March put his hands behind his back and stuck his chin in the air.

'I will stand sir. I am going to call you out, Lord Falconer. You may name your seconds.'

The Falcon bowed his head and, moving to one of the pipe racks, thoughtfully selected a long meerschaum pipe which he slowly proceeded to fill with tobacco from one of the earthenware jars. 'I pray you will not be overhasty, my lord. Your daughter came to me right willingly.'

'But you will not deny you seduced her sir, a virgin scarce seventeen years of age. You found her a virgin, I believe?'

The Falcon tried to hide the flush which suffused his face, occupying himself in striking a tinder with which to light his pipe. 'Aye,' he said at last. 'In the physical sense your daughter was intact, but . . . . She almost besought me to seduce her.'

'You could have resisted Lord Falconer. You should have resisted.' Lord St March's voice took on a brittle, bitter tone and his eyes never left his adversary's face.

'Well sir, take a young woman who makes eyes at you all the time and follows you about . . . what would *you* do?'

'Though I have not led a blameless life I do not recall myself ever seducing a seventeen-year-old virgin, Marquess. Think of the consequences for her . . .'

'Oh I assure you sir, they are minimal . . . unless you call me out and then everyone is bound to hear of this affair. Your daughter is not with child, that I know of, and I feel I have only increased the pleasure she will have when she is married, the further delights she will be able to offer her fortunate future husband.'

'Only if he is a roué like you sir!' Lord St March snarled. 'If he is a well born young man, such as I expect to find for her, the fact that she is not a virgin will disgust him and he will ask for an annulment of the marriage . . .'

'Oh I think not sir. Young blades today . . .' The Falcon casually waved his pipe in the air, blowing smoke towards the window, quite unprepared for the swift harsh slap across his face administered by the Earl, whose patience had been more than severely tried. The Falcon stepped back and his pipe fell to the ground just as the door opened and Constance, neatly gowned and her hair brushed, stood timidly in the doorway.

'Oh father!' She ran to the Falcon and put her hand on his cheek. He brushed her away and adjusted his wig which the blow had knocked to the side of his head.

'It is no matter Constance. Your father is right to be angry. I got no more than I deserved . . .'

'You will get more sir!' the Earl said threateningly, rubbing his hand, so hard had been the force with which he struck his daughter's seducer.

'Your father means to fight a duel with me.'

'Oh no!' Constance ran from her lover to her father and cast herself upon him, sobbing. 'Oh father, you must not do such a thing!'

'But I must, my dear,' her father said gently, pushing her away from him. 'He has dishonoured you. I will fight him in France so

585

that His Majesty will not hear of it and thus save him some opprobrium, if he remains alive, for I shall mean to kill.'

'Oh father I beg, I beg . . .' Constance threw herself on the floor at her father's feet in a torrent of weeping, but he looked at her as though he scarcely noticed her.

'France I'm afraid it cannot be,' the Falcon said removing some ash nonchalantly from his sleeve. 'I have to leave with His Majesty at the weekend . . . if I am alive. I have friends with a quiet estate in Sussex – but I shall not mean to kill *you*, sir. I tell you that now so that if you kill me it will be premeditated murder.'

The Earl stared at the Falcon, ignoring the hysterical sobs of his daughter. 'In that case you do not have long to live, Marquess. Pray send your seconds to my house sir, and name the place. I choose pistols.'

Lord Falconer nodded and bowed his head. 'If you will have it so. Believe me, I love Constance . . .'

'You are over twenty years older than her,' St March said angrily, 'and in no position to marry, having a lovely wife of your own and two children I believe. You had no right to let yourself love her, or to sully my family's name with your lust. What chance did a silly wench have to resist a man of your eminence and fame? In my heart I grieve, but I cannot blame her. Would I had been more vigilant. Get up girl and come with me.'

Tremblingly Constance rose to her feet, her eyes red, her cheeks streaked with tears. She didn't even look at the man who had initiated her in the arts of love, in whose arms she had lain only an hour before. She knew without any doubt – both from the expression on her father's face and the sheepish, guilty look on the Falcon's – that it was over. Over for good.

18

The Earl of St March stood uncomfortably in front of Lady Falconer and looked at the floor. Her distress, though dignified, was hard to bear, as well as the fact that he had been the instrument of it.

'I assure you ma'am, all his lordship has is a flesh wound in the arm. I did not shoot to kill, and his shot went into the air as he told me it would. He is a brave man, I'll say that.'

'Oh my husband lacks not courage, sir,' Analee said, determined not to let flow the tears which welled behind her eyes at the news of her husband's perfidy. 'What he lacks is wisdom in certain other matters.'

'He is an unscrupulous rogue, Lady Falconer, and a vile seducer. He is unworthy as a husband for a woman such as you.'

'Oh I think not sir,' Analee said, a wry smile on her lips. 'As you know in my time I have been unfaithful to my husband. You arranged it did you not?'

The Earl coughed and once more studied the floor. 'I believe that was a very different matter, my lady. A summons to a mature woman from royalty is not quite the same thing as the seduction of a young and innocent virgin by a seducer more than twenty years her senior. I could not disobey the Prince's request . . . nor you either I believe, ma'am.'

'I think of His Highness with affection,' Analee said impulsively, 'and the deepest respect.'

'Ma'am, before I caught your husband in the arms of my daughter – *in flagrante delicto* I believe they call it – I was of a mind to come to you anyway with a fresh message from the Prince. He is to be here in the autumn!'

'Here? Then it is true?'

The Earl, an expression of surprise on his face, took a step back. 'You have heard?'

'Yes. The news was brought to me but recently by someone who is arranging the matter.'

'Then ma'am I am dumb,' the Earl said wiping his brow with a spotless handkerchief. 'I thought I was the only one entrusted with this information, other than those with whom he is to stay.'

'But it was thought he might stay with me. It was suggested . . .'

'*You* my lady? At Falconer House?'

'Nay, here in Lakeland.'

'But the Prince will not be *here*, ma'am. He is only to be in London for a matter of days. He wishes to join the Church of England and abjure the religion which keeps him and his father off the throne.'

'The Prince is not coming to Lakeland?'

'Not that I know ma'am. As one of his most trusted emissaries I would surely have been the first to be told of it.'

'Nor a landing at Whitehaven?'

'Never my lady, I swear. It is to be a private visit to London in the autumn, probably staying at the house of Lady Primrose in the Strand. Where came you upon this other information Lady Falconer?'

The Earl, puzzled but relieved that the matter of her husband's perfidy was over, began to relax and moved towards the chair indicated by Analee, waiting for her to sit down before he did so.

'There is a man, sir, who works for Mr Rigg in Whitehaven. He succeeded Brent Delamain and he recently told me that he was a Jacobite agent preparing a landing for the Prince.'

The Earl shook his head. 'It cannot be. There is no such plan, my lady.'

'His name, sir, is Hugo Fitzgerald. I believe you met at Cart?'

'Fitzgerald!' The Earl shot up out of his chair. 'He is a well known Hanoverian supporter, nursing a fervent hatred for the Prince. He has betrayed many of our men . . .'

'That is what my husband told me,' Analee said quietly. 'It is the truth then?'

'Undoubtedly. They say Fitzgerald has the ear of the Duke of Newcastle personally and has access to him at all times.'

'Could he be . . . a Jacobite too?'

'You mean a counter-spy?' The Earl shrugged. 'They say there are many who work for both camps, but if Fitzgerald were of our persuasion I would know it. I know all our kin and where they are in England.'

'He said his family were defeated with King James at the Battle of the Boyne . . .'

'What nonsense. They helped to drive him out and eventually to bring the Elector of Hanover over here. Fitzgeralds are very prominent in the Irish Guards, loyal to the King.'

''Tis a common name doubtless . . .'

'I know *this* Fitzgerald, do not fear my lady. He was snooping around that night at Leicester House just to see what the Prince of Wales was up to. Everyone knew his business and shut up like oysters.'

'Is it true that the Prince plots against his father?'

'Well . . . I have to be discreet my lady, but they do not get on. 'Tis said the Prince has a plan to take England for himself and give Hanover to his brother William and get him out of the way. This was what was wished by his grandfather George I – and indeed he wrote it in his will. But his son, our present King, snatched the will and bribed others that were named and no more was heard of the matter.'

'Then where does Prince Charles Edward come into this?'

'Oh ma'am, these counsels are too profound and too secret for me to divulge. Although I know your ladyship's affection for our Cause, your husband is a Hanoverian general. I also know that, despite his perfidy, you retain some affection for him. Do you not Lady Falconer?'

Analee gazed at him, her eyes filling with tears. She nodded her head. 'I think I shall always love the Marquess no matter what. I know, you see, the power of his attraction, the rapture of his love. He has many faults but these are quickly forgotten, especially after the anguish of so many months of loneliness. It would kill me to lose him; but I would never betray others for his sake. But maybe it is best to tell me nothing although I would never repeat it. What I do not know I cannot tell.'

'I think I can trust you, ma'am, despite the love you continue to bear for your husband; but I cannot divulge certain matters of state. But the Prince asked me to tell you that he would be in London in September and that he desires to see you again. As for my daughter . . .'

The Earl got up and walked over to the window. Although it was June the weather was cloudy and misty and a breeze ruffled the calm waters of the lake so that little white crested waves rode in towards the shore. 'As for my daughter, Lady Falconer, she is packed back to Spain. She is no longer a virgin and doubtless much depraved in her ways; but she is young and can start life again. Under the careful eye of her duenna in Spain she can reflect on her misbehaviour before I let her return to this country. Indeed I might marry her off to the son of a Spanish grandee who has asked for her for many a year, since she was scarcely a baby. It would be a good match with a strict Catholic family, which would do her no harm, and keep her wild impulsiveness in check.'

'In that case you should take care to have her maidenhead restored,' Analee said slyly. 'For I believe the Spanish are very particular in this matter.'

The Earl raised an eyebrow. 'It can be done Lady Falconer?'

'I believe it can be contrived,' she said casually. 'And a bladder of pig's blood inserted in the love passage so that the "newly deflowered" bride can bleed to the satisfaction of all concerned, and honour is saved.'

Lord St March was looking at her with admiration. 'You are a constant surprise to me Lady Falconer, you are so knowledgeable in so *many* things.'

'Do not forget that I am a gypsy, my lord, and these personal things to do with the human body are part of every gypsy woman's upbringing. It is also because I am a gypsy that I wish to win back the love of the Falcon.'

'You have a spell for that too, ma'am?'

'Oh yes, and I will weave it with all my power while he is abroad so that he will come back to me. I believe the Falcon does love me, Lord St March, above any other; but he is a passionate man, vain and flattered by his power over women. He cannot resist putting his virility to the test and about this I fear I can do little. But in his heart I know his lordship enjoys a deep affection for me and it is better that I am constantly by his side and not away from him although, I grant you, it did little to prevent him ogling your daughter; but she was a girl of unusual attraction. No, now that this business has been resolved and he is in Hanover with the King, though nursing a wounded arm, and your daughter is safely back in Spain, I will send for my friend Reyora who is the *cohani* of her tribe. She will help me weave a powerful spell which I shall send through the air all the way to Hanover.'

Analee joined her hands together and smiled bewitchingly at her guest, her head on one side, her hands clasped loosely in her lap.

'They call you the Enchantress, Lady Falconer, which indeed you are. A woman more beautiful than is just, and with a wisdom beyond your years. My lady . . .'

The Earl got up and, pressing his hands together under his chin, began to pace up and down the room as one deep in thought. 'My lady I know not how to put this; it is a difficult thing for me to say; but since I first saw you I was struck not only, as other men are, by your beauty, by the dignity and poise of your demeanour but also by something . . . quite other.'

'And that is, Lord St March?' Analee prompted, puzzled by the obvious difficulty which beset his lordship, by the stress he was under, and the way that he clenched his hands so that his knuckles showed whitely beneath the frilly cuffs of his shirt. Surely Lord St March was not about to make a declaration – after what had just passed? He saw her worried glance and his face softened.

'Do not look alarmed Lady Falconer. I am not about to proposition you – nothing is further from my mind. You see, when I was a very young man living on my grandfather's estates in Devon I became enamoured of a beautiful girl. She was so lovely, so divinely gifted that I not only wanted to possess her but I also wanted to marry her so that she could be mine for always.' The Earl wiped his brow with his handkerchief and continued his uneasy pacing. 'It happened, Lady Falconer, that this beautiful girl was a common gypsy belonging to a tribe camping on my grandfather's ground. They were wandering gypsies, but they passed some months there in the winter and I was fascinated by them and their way of life and spent some time with them. This beautiful girl was attracted to me as I was to her. I promised her marriage, which I fully intended when I was of age – I was then nineteen. But alas, I could not wait to possess her. We became lovers, and my love was got with child by me as we were both young and ignorant. I went to my grandfather to ask permission to marry, but he packed me off to Spain without ever allowing me to see my love again – for when I went to find her the gypsy camp was gone. And I never knew what became of her . . . or her child.'

Lord St March looked at Analee who found that her mouth had gone dry, her flesh cold, and that her breath came unevenly because of the hammering of her heart in her chest.

'You see my lady . . . you so much resemble that love of my life – and she remained the love of my life even though I later married, and honoured and respected my dear wife who bore me five children. When I saw you I saw her, not only in looks but in every movement; and in your spirit, your resilience, you resemble her. She too was meant to marry an Earl as you have married a Marquess.'

'And her name?' Analee heard herself whispering, although she knew already.

'Morella. That is all I know. Beautiful, heavenly Morella . . .'

For a time there was a silence as the room seemed to reverberate with the word, *Morella . . . Morella . . . Morella*. Analee heard it in the waves lapping against the jetty, the wind blowing in the trees and through the long corridors of the house. *Morella . . . Morella . . .* the echo whispered and then she found herself gazing at him and saying softly, 'Morella . . . Morella was my mother's name. That much I know. Nothing more but that, as you told me, she loved a man to whom she was not married – I was never told who and died after my birth. She was only sixteen. I was brought up by my grandparents . . . and our tribe came from Devon.'

'Then I am your father,' Lord St March said simply, sitting down abruptly, but the hand he raised to brush away a tear was shaking and the words came with difficulty.

Analee looked at her father and thought she had always known that somehow he and she were united. His appreciation of her had never had the meaning of other men, and she had felt a deep rapport with him from the start. The thought that she not only had a father, but that he was alive and in this room with her, was somehow overwhelming and left her with nothing to say. Lord St March finally got up and pulled the bell rope and almost immediately a manservant entered the room.

'Pray bring some cordial for my lady and a brandy for me.'

'Nay, a brandy for both of us,' Analee said, her voice shaking. 'Thank you Tom.'

'Analee . . .' Lord St March went over to her and held out both his hands. She looked up at him, her eyes brimming with tears, and clasping them brought them to her lips.

'Oh father . . . !' she said. 'Now I can call you father.'

'It *must* be true,' he said, his voice still registering the astonishment he felt.

'It *is* true. There was so much secrecy about my birth.' Analee pressed his hands to her cheek, unwilling to let them go. 'Both pieces of the story fit. I know one half, you the other. And her name was Morella . . . and I resemble her.'

'You not only resemble her, my dearest daughter, you *are* her,' St March said, his voice shaking. 'When I saw the great Lady Falconer it was as though I had seen my darling Morella reincarnated. Even your voice is like hers. I thought it might be a case of possession, that somehow her spirit inhabited you; but the Church tells us that is evil, and you were so gentle and sweet. Yet how to approach you I knew not. Maybe by coming here I hoped to be able to discover the truth.'

Tom re-entered, bringing a tray on which stood glasses and a decanter of brandy. This he put on a table and, pouring two glasses, handed one to Analee and another to her father. Then he withdrew closing the doors quietly after him, while Analee and her father raised their glasses silently, toasting each other.

'To the memory of your mother . . . who has surely brought us together to be reunited.'

'To my mother,' Analee said, 'and to yet another Morella. For I must tell you, father, that you have a granddaughter who is named for my mother. She is the result of a love affair I had with a nobleman before I married Lord Falconer . . .'

'But where is she?' St March jumped up, his eyes sparkling.

'She is not here father, but is well looked after. That is all I can tell you at the moment.'

'The Falcon does not know?'

'Not yet. He is a jealous man . . . and the nobleman I spoke of, well, he is known to the Falcon too. But dear father – ' Analee took his hand and led him to the sofa, 'we have so many things to talk about that this will be just a part of the story. For me to know that I have a family, a father and brothers and sisters – it is the most glorious thing in my life.'

'Constance is your sister too,' the Earl said quietly.

'Ah yes. What a good thing that affair was stopped in time. My lord would be horrified if he knew he was sleeping with his sister-in-law. As no one was aware of the relationship – surely it was not a crime?'

'Shall you tell him?'

'About you? Of course I will shout it from the housetops if you will permit it.'

'Oh dearest Analee,' the Earl said putting a fatherly arm around her slim waist. 'I will trumpet it abroad to all the world. I am so proud of you, my dear, and so glad that, after all your suffering, now I can be by your side to help you.'

Lord St March stayed with Analee for five days and during this time they hardly ceased talking. They wandered about the woods bordering the lake, or sometimes rode over Manesty to Maiden Moor following the narrow bridle paths of Derwent Fells. At night they returned and sat by a large fire – the Earl in a chair, Analee on the floor leaning against him. Analee learned all about her brothers and sisters – Brinsley Viscount Hepworth, aged twenty and at Oxford; the Honourable Rollo and Edward Craven, both still at Eton; then Lady Constance, about whom she knew all too much; and finally the Lady Antonia Craven who was still in Spain. She learned about her grandfather and grandmother and about the estates the family owned in Spain and the north and south of England. She learned more about her mother, and could not hear enough of the beautiful gypsy who had borne a daughter all those years ago to the heir to the Earl of St March and had died soon after. Every time they referred to this melancholy event they shed tears; but somehow they felt her presence was with them, so sure were they that she had brought them together.

On the last day, her father made Analee promise she would visit him on his Yorkshire estates and then they would journey to London together and, after the Falcon had been told, announce the news. Analee still could not bring herself to tell her father the truth about her son Duncan. She thought that was something too secret, too sacred . . . even for him. Analee promised to come to Yorkshire as soon as she had done just one thing, and this she discussed with her father before he left, to get his approval. Like her, he agreed that the thing must be done. His only worry was that she herself should come to harm, the precious daughter whom he had just found.

'Do not worry, dear father,' she said pressing his hand and kissing him. 'Can you doubt that, after all that has happened, the protection of my mother's spirit will fail me now?'

The candles shone on the newly polished silver and the red wine in the tall crystal goblets glittered, Analee thought with foreboding, like freshly drawn blood. Hugo Fitzgerald, however, had no such dismal thoughts. She had sent for him . . . the Enchantress, and this night he would surely make her his. They were alone together dining at Furness and, the dull weather having given place to warm sunshine, this June evening was a perfect one. A full moon shone on Lake Derwentwater with such radiance that the whole of the surrounding countryside was bathed in a bright golden light making it seem like day.

They had walked for a while in the garden before dinner and, although her manner was mysterious, she had allowed him to hold her hand. Now as she gazed at him across the table, the same enigmatic smile hovered on her lips – although he thought her eyes seemed dark and unfriendly. A little tremor of apprehension shot through him and he remembered the Furies and what they did to those who betrayed them.

But he had not betrayed Analee. His love for her was pure and above all the sordid political intrigues in which he was engaged. It was the one good thing in an otherwise distressing and crumbling world, in which he played a part of which he was not proud. He put out a hand and took her fingers, pressing them to his lips.

'Enchantress,' he murmured. 'Tell me why you sent for me.'

'Because you were right. I have heard that the Prince is coming.'

Hugo looked up, his thoughts far away in the realms of love, the delights of lying in Analee's arms, his head on her soft bosom.

'The *Prince*, my lady . . . ?' he said with bewilderment.

'Prince Charles Edward.'

'Ah yes.' Hugo looked confused. 'Oh, you have heard he *is* coming?'

'But you told me as much.'

'I was not sure then ma'am. And pray how have you heard this good news before me?'

'Because, Mr Fitzgerald, I think you are not as *au fait* with the Jacobite plans as you told me. For one thing, the Prince has not and never had any intention of coming to Lakeland. Yet you are very familiar with the Hanoverian plans. Very few people knew that my husband was going to Hanover with the King, yet you knew it. You must have the ears of very highly placed persons to get such information so easily.'

'But I have Lady Falconer,' Hugo said uneasily. 'I told you I . . .'

'Served both camps.'

'Yes, but my true loyalties are . . . oh why do we talk about this? It is of no consequence, my love, my Analee.' Hugo hurriedly threw down his napkin and went quickly to Analee's side, bending his head to kiss her. 'This is a night for love. We can talk politics tomorrow . . . but first let me assuage the deep longing that burns in my loins, my beautiful Analee.' He turned her head towards him, his lips about to crush down on hers, when a sharp blow from behind caused him to stagger, knocking over Analee's glass of wine.

Brent Delamain, enraged already by the discovery that Hugo Fitzgerald was a traitor, nearly took leave of his senses when he saw the monster bend to kiss his beloved. Analee, who had observed Brent's quiet planned entry, quickly got up to take herself out of harm's way. She had done all she could. The rest was up to Brent.

Through Emma, the only one with knowledge of his where-abouts, Analee had sent a letter to Brent outlining what she knew of Hugo and his plans to betray him. He had insinuated himself so well that Ambrose Rigg trusted and respected him. Brent, who still operated out of Laxey staying with the Collisters, knew there was a spy somewhere at work – guns destined for Scotland disappeared at the quayside, and detachments of government troops had an odd way of stopping the packhorses laden with arms in the middle of nowhere.

When he got Analee's letter he knew at once the cause – Hugo, in an ideal position to influence events under the guise of being a Jacobite sympathizer.

Staggering against the table, Hugo managed with difficulty to right himself and turned to face his attacker. There he saw a man equal to him in stature if a little taller, with his own blond hair unpowdered and wearing a double breasted hunting jacket and breeches of good quality brown broadcloth. The long aquiline nose was slightly flared as if with anger, his lips bloodless and pressed tightly together and his clear blue eyes blazed with scorn.

'And pray who might *you* be?' Hugo stammered in bewilderment.

'I think you seek me, Mr Fitzgerald. Delamain is my name. Brent Delamain. I am told you wish to betray me to the authorities so that I will doubtless hang from Carlisle Castle like many illustrious men before me.'

'*I* sir?' Hugo said in simulated amazement. 'I am a loyal Jacobite at heart . . .'

Brent had drawn his sword and pointed the tip lightly at Hugo's chest.

'At heart sir – there where I touch you lightly with my sword – you are a foetid spy. The very worst kind, because you pretend to work for both sides while your own interests are paramount in your mind. Many of our men have disappeared because of you; some of our ships have foundered, doubtless by wreckers instructed by you. I think even your paltry life is not sufficient to pay for the harm you have done. Now put up your sword sir so that I may kill you in a fair fight.'

'Oh Brent!' Analee rushed forward. 'I pray you will not fight here. I thought your plan was to capture this wretch and take him away.'

'I had to come by myself, Analee. I could not bring more men. It was the safest way to cross the hills at night even though the moon is full. I want to kill this rogue and throw him in the lake. *En garde* sir!'

But Hugo, too shaken to move, was staring at Analee, the one who this very night he had anticipated holding in his arms.

'*You* betrayed me Lady Falconer?'

'With pleasure sir, since you have betrayed so many of those whom I admire. You wormed your way into my confidence by false professions of ardour, doubtless to find out even more about Jacobite plans than you knew already. Doubtless too when we were lovers you expected me to tell you everything I knew . . . oh do not deny it sir. You expected me to betray my true friend, Brent Delamain, into your hands.'

'No such thing Lady Falconer. I swear! I am growing tired of these political intrigues. I am satisfied working for Rigg and the work I do there. True I think the Jacobite cause is lost forever; but the Hanoverians are not much better. The King is a ridiculous figure, and the high taxes we have to pay to keep a standing army defending Hanover iniquitous!'

Brent prodded Hugo again gently with his sword.

'I am going to kill you, Mr Fitzgerald, if you do not defend yourself. You have told too many lies for anyone to believe a thing you say. I will throw your body in the lake, and none will ever be the wiser. As you are a double spy each side will blame the other for your disappearance.'

Brent threw his coat onto a chair and, loosening his cravat, put up his sword in the offensive position.

Hugo, looking helplessly at Analee, disengaged his sword from its scabbard, put off his coat as well and then, in a swift movement which took Brent by surprise, thrust at him, the sharpened steel almost piercing his chest. For so big a man Brent was very nimble and he quickly stepped back, his face mottling with rage at one who so disregarded the etiquette of swordsmanship.

A glint came into Brent's eye, every bit as dangerous as the steel he carried in his hand and, with a rapid forward thrust, he parried Hugo's attack, counter-attacked on his own and lunged forward, the tip of steel deeply embedded in Hugo's arm.

Hugo dropped his sword, swayed and clutched his arm from which a torrent of blood poured, soaking his shirt and dripping onto the carpet. Analee ran up to him and quickly ripped open the shirt sleeve, binding the wound with a linen napkin. Hugo had gone as white as the napkin which was soon soaked, indicating the severity of the wound. Analee, reminded of the blow the Falcon had sustained at Falkirk, which had almost deprived him of a limb, said urgently:

'We must get him upstairs, Brent. And quickly or he will bleed to death.'

'I yearn to finish him off,' Brent said menacingly, reluctant to put his sword back in his scabbard. But by now Hugo had lost consciousness and even Brent could not despatch a wounded man, as he had often seen done in the bloody battles in which he had fought. He turned away in disgust and poured himself some wine.

'What is to be done with him now?'

'I will dress his wound with some herbal medicines I have. Tomorrow I will send him by coach back to the Riggs. He can make up what story he likes as to how he came by his wound. I do not think they will hear the truth from him.'

'But the rogue will continue to thwart our plans . . .'

'I think not Brent,' Analee said applying a tourniquet to Hugo's arm. 'He has been found out, wounded and yet remains alive. If he is sincere about settling down to become a merchant, indeed this is his chance. I will get Tom to take this creature upstairs, and Nelly will help me dress his wound. He will recover.'

'Analee . . .'

Brent came swiftly over to her and, taking her face between his hands, kissed her lightly on the lips. She shut her eyes and felt the familiar surge of passion for Brent course yet again through her veins. Yes, tonight she would lie in the arms of a man – not Hugo Fitzgerald, not her husband, but Brent Delamain who had loved only her ever since that night, years ago, when they had become lovers in a forest glade by moonlight.

This night there was moonlight too. It came flooding in through the window where Brent and Analee lay, tightly clasped in each other's arms. She thought the moonlight had woken her up, for her lover breathed evenly, or maybe it was the cry of a nightbird; and she watched the moonbeams stream across the floor illuminating the wide beautiful room with its mullioned windows overlooking the lake. A peacefulness suffused Analee's soul such as she had not experienced for many months. There had been her unhappiness in London followed by her miscarraige; her depression afterwards and the long road back to recovery and, what was more important, acceptance.

For Analee now realized she had to accept the nature of the man she was married to. It seemed to her that she had been struggling against this fact from the beginning. He was used to commanding, being obeyed, having his least whim gratified. Everyone, even his wife, was there for his convenience, his pleasure, to serve him in some way or the other. Very few were his equals and, except for the King and certain high ministers or generals, there were a mere handful above him.

The Falcon was a law to himself. What right had Analee, a mere gypsy, to expect anything else?

Brent tossed in his sleep and Analee curled around him, putting her arm about his waist.

And yet, she thought, she was no longer Analee the gypsy. She was the daughter of the Earl of St March, acknowledged and recognized by him as such. He would petition the King to have her legitimated, he had said, and the King was sure to agree. So in her own right she was Lady Analee Craven.

Roused by her proximity Brent turned to her, his hands gripping her slim waist. He could see her face outlined in the moonlight, sharpened by the whiteness of the pillow on which it rested. Dark skin, shining dark eyes, jet black hair. He couldn't believe he was seeing her again like this. How often had he done so in his dreams, only to wake and find himself alone? He etched her features with the tip of his forefinger feeling her eyes, her nose, her lips, like a blind man whose chief sense was through touch.

'What are you thinking, darling?'

'That I am a lady,' Analee said.

Brent half rose on one elbow and looked at her in amazement. 'A *what*?'

'I am a real lady, you know. Not merely Lady Falconer by right of marriage; but Lady Analee Craven by birth.'

'I prefer you as Analee the gypsy,' Brent said smiling and kissing her lips, her hair, her cheeks. 'A wanton wild gypsy as you were when I first found you and you cast your bond of enchantment around me – forever. 'Twas thus we first loved each other,' he whispered. 'In the moonlight in the forest. I have never forgotten it. I cannot believe it has come true again; that for five years I have fruitlessly yearned for you, my Analee.'

Analee gazed at him, her *gadjo* – her blond handsome god. Only she shared her love for him with Angus, whereas he loved her exclusively.

They didn't speak for a while or move, but lay as they were. Then rising, Analee walked to the bowl on the washstand. Crouching, she washed herself carefully before joining him in the bed.

'What are you doing my love?'

'It is to protect me from having a child. Since my husband has not lain with me for months he would know it was not his.'

'But my darling,' Brent said sitting up. 'We are together for always. What does *he* matter?'

For a while she didn't reply and he repeated the question, getting angrier. 'I say what does he matter?'

'I am married to him Brent.'

'Yes but now . . .'

'I am not going to leave him Brent, my beloved.'

'But you must! Analee how can you . . . ?'

She caught his hand and made him lie down again. 'I am married to the Falcon for life, Brent. I made the promise at our wedding and I shall keep it.'

'But he is a monster! He is cruel and never faithful to you.'

'He is not a monster. He is a violent and passionate man. He needs me, and he loves me. I know it.'

'But *I* love you and *I* need you! I always have. My love for you keeps me chaste, pure. I do not go after every woman, young or old, in town like I hear he does.'

'Oh, so you know that too.'

'Everyone knows that the Falcon has an eye for the ladies. I heard it in Paris and I have heard the same thing happens in London. He is unworthy of you Analee.'

Analee appeared to consider and finally shook her head. 'No. He is a law unto himself. I will never leave him, Brent. But I love you. That is the only consolation I can give you.'

'And you love him too?'

'Yes, I do.'

Brent threw back the sheets and got angrily out of bed as though to put as much distance as possible between his love and himself. Then he came back and stood over her, his face distorted with wrath.

'You cannot love two people! You cannot! I tried and I failed. I loved Mary until I saw you again, and then I loved her not at all. I couldn't bear to touch her. You can't love two people, you can't!'

'In different ways, you can,' Analee insisted gently. She held out a hand and took his, drawing him gently to the bed. 'Here, sit by me, and listen. You say I put a spell on you, but I did not. It is the way you are Brent. I wanted you to love Mary – I did everything I could; I cannot help what you are. But I am married to Angus Falconer and, although in many things he is not admirable, he is a man much stronger than I am, a man I can fear and admire.'

'And me. You despise me, is that what you are saying?'

'I love you Brent. Deeply and passionately, with the whole of my heart. I do not fear you; I admire you and like you. You are brave and courageous. I do not *like* the Falcon very much. 'Tis an entirely different emotion I have for him. He masters me.'

''Tis an illness you have, if you ask me,' Brent said bitterly. 'He treats you like an animal and you lick his hand.'

'No he does not treat me like an animal. In his way he looks up to me. But I am a woman and, to a man like my husband, women are always inferior. They do not make war or play politics and to him these are important things. But he loves me, and he needs me. Soon he will come back again.'

'Then all this was just . . . playing with me.'

'No, it was the expression of my love.'

'It is also to help you get even with the Falcon.'

'A little,' Analee admitted with a faint smile. 'If he has his diversions I am not above them either.'

'I am a *plaything*,' Brent said wrathfully and hurriedly began to dress. 'I will go from here with that fool and dump him in the lake. I will never see you again Analee. You treat me like a child . . .'

Suddenly he stopped, aware of her arms about him, her cheek pressed to his. His body trembled as from behind she moulded herself to him and he turned and crushed her in his arms.

He loved her, and yet she could share him with another. And he knew he would share her, that he would continue like this for as long as she wanted. Visiting her when she called, meeting when they were able. But he remembered the gypsy woman on the road to Penrith all those years ago, and he knew that one day – he didn't care when but it would come – he would have Analee for himself.

When the sun came up they embraced once more, sated with love, happiness tinged with sorrow, and longing only relieved by tears. They had no idea when they would meet again. For Brent had told her how tired he was of the wandering life, how little hope he had for the Cause.

602

'Because of the nature of the Prince,' he explained.

'How is that?' Analee said softly.

'He has changed. He is almost unrecognizable from the man who led us only five years ago. His worst qualities have got the better of him. He believes no one, trusts no one and drinks to excess. He is proud and overbearing so that even some who love him have deserted him. He offends anyone who tries to help him and his quarrels with ladies in public are notorious. He grieves his father by never seeing him, and ignores his letters and those of his trusted secretary, James Edgar, who is a kindly man wishing only good to the Prince. The Earl Marischal who has lived in permanent exile from this country because of his and his family's support of the Stuarts, will have nothing to do with him now. It is the Prince who has lost us the Cause and many, I among them, are beginning to lose hope. That is why the activities of such as Fitzgerald, though detestable, are no longer really dangerous.'

'Would you have killed him?'

'Nay. I meant to teach him a lesson and turn him loose. I'll take him back to the Riggs and Emma can nurse him. I believe she's taken a fancy to him, and he has brought her out of her lethargy and depression.'

'I'm glad,' Analee said. 'I think in many ways they would suit. But what will you do Brent?'

'I may go to America to see Stewart, see how he does, if you will not have me Analee and I believe you mean what you say. Anyway what life would it be for you with a penniless exile?'

He had looked at her wryly and she leaned forward and kissed him squeezing his hand.

'It is not that! I am used to a life as a wanderer.'

'I know. I know it is not that. But it is true nevertheless. So, in time, I may petition the King to be allowed to return home. I will go into commerce, maybe into ships. I am a fair sailor and I'll try and build up a fortune, get the better of my brother George. In the meantime, my beloved Analee, I will never forget you. I will never marry unless it be to you, and if that is not possible I will die without wife and children of my own.'

Analee thought of Morella, Brent's daughter; but she said nothing. Now was not the time or the place for revelations of this kind. Now she knew what he would do, but if she learned about

Morella she had no way of predicting his actions. One day she would tell him. One day.

Brent left at noon. Fitzgerald was well enough to sit on his own horse, sullenly and without looking at Analee or speaking a word to anyone. She felt that his humiliation had punished him more than any wound could do, and she was glad. He rode in front of Brent's horse, his reins in one hand, the other arm slung in a bandage. He would survive.

Brent and Analee said little before he left. Their hearts were too heavy with words unsaid, tears unshed. He had taken a long passionate leave of her in the bedroom, so that he did not kiss her before leaving but mounted his horse and then stood looking at her, his hand raised.

'Farewell,' she whispered and blew a kiss into the air. Then she watched him ride slowly along the narrow path that took him up Catbells, until he was over the top and vanished out of sight.

19

The Falcon's boredom at Herrenhausen, the King's estate in his beloved Hanover, was growing intolerable. George II was obsessed with routine and liked to do the same thing at the same time every day, so that Court life was governed by the clock – whether it was eating, going to church, riding, playing cards or attending the theatre. For a man of Lord Falconer's temperament such order was extremely irksome.

It was true he had been on two diplomatic trips which had broken the monotony, one to Frederick the Great at Potsdam and one to the Empress Maria Theresa in Vienna. The King of Prussia, a nephew of George II, took to the Falcon enormously. He invited him to stay at his favourite palace of *Sans Souci* – to which he admitted only his intimates; even his wife had never been there – and drilled for him day after day his regiment of enormous Prussian guards famous through Europe.

As a military man the Falcon admired Frederick the Great, the skill with which he had captured Silesia in the War of the Austrian Succession, his recklessness and ruthlessness in battle. But he was immune to the attempts of the King to lure him to his Court, even the promise of a senior command in his army. The Falcon had too much to lose to do that – he could have a senior command in the British Army any time he felt like it. Besides who knew how long Frederick's star would shine?

Though inclined to despise women, even powerful ones, the Falcon was impressed despite himself by Maria Theresa. She was an attractive woman with a regal presence and manner and her grasp of the European political scene was as great as her hated rival Frederick's. Moreover she had fought like a tigress to retain the empire left to her by her father and, despite the opposition of such powerful European powers, she had succeeded. She did not try to lure the Falcon to her side, but treated him most graciously, even having a ball and play performed in his honour. He returned to Hanover from both visits confident that whichever side Britain would be on in the next war – there was sure to be one, and it could not be both for they were implacable enemies – he would be received well in either Court.

But his visits were brief, and in between times the Falcon was not only bored; he was frequently ill and in pain from the wound in his arm sustained in the duel with St March before his departure for Hanover. As it was the same arm that he injured at Falkirk he had been able to tell the King that it was the old wound troubling him again. But his physician he could not deceive and, though sworn to secrecy, the doctor feared that some deep rotting infection might set in which would necessitate amputation.

Now the Falcon was suffering again. The fever had returned and he lay on his bed at night wracked with pain and also with fear – because what use was a one-armed general in battle? At night the Falcon's fears seemed overwhelming and, with this terrible dread went visions of his wife drowning in the Lake of Derwentwater, lost to him forever. He would wake up crying and McNeath, rushing in, would find him leaning out of his bed, his arms outstretched attempting to save Analee from the water.

By September the Falcon had grown weaker and his condition was giving cause for concern. The physician considered that the amputation of the arm was but a matter of days away, and he tried to prepare the Falcon for what would be a very hazardous operation.

'It cannot be put off my lord, or else you will lose not only your limb but also your life . . .'

'My wife . . .' the Falcon murmured. 'Analee . . .'

'It is too late my lord to send for your wife. Too late . . .'

Analee awoke and felt a burning pain in her arm, a sensation of fear. Her forehead was bathed in sweat and she knew that she had a fever. She lay in her bed waiting for the panic to subside and then the pain left her and her forehead grew cool in the night air which came in through the open window.

What had caused the panic? Was it the prospect of leaving her beloved Furness to journey to London? Was it fear of the Prince and what she would find? Analee got up and went to the window, leaning out to gaze at the stillness of the lake bathed in moonlight.

It had been a lovely summer and she had been happy. She had spent a few weeks with her father near York and then returned to Lakeland where, wrapped in solitude, she had been able to reflect on the past and plan for the future, while helping to care for Nelly who was approaching the time of her confinement. McNeath had gone over to Hanover to be with the Falcon who found it impossible to do without his devoted body servant.

Yet all summer she had been plagued by a nagging worry about her husband. He was not well, he wrote, he had a fever which came and went. His arm troubled him. But then he was better again and a guest of the King of Prussia in Potsdam. There was even talk of him going to Russia to the Court of the Empress Elizabeth on a mission for the King.

But although the Falcon wrote to her, he never asked her to join him; he never told her he missed her. She had not broken the news to him about her father, preferring to tell him rather than put it in writing.

But why this apprehension, this fear? She went to bed and slept badly, but it happened the next night and the night after. Always the pain in the arm, the fever, the unreasonable panic.

On the fourth day, pale and haggard through lack of sleep, Analee sent a servant riding hard to Appleby at first light with orders to bring back Reyora with him and not to delay.

Reyora, fearing Analee was ill, came at once riding behind good sturdy Tom and they arrived in the evening of the same day. But when she saw Analee, she appeared in good health though pale and looking tired.

'Every night I wake with a burning pain in my arm, a fever and a terrible sense of fear . . . my heart palpitates wildly and my hair is damp on my brow. Then I walk about the room and the pain and fear pass. But I cannot sleep. I am haunted by the notion that this concerns the Falcon, that he is mortally ill. Oh Reyora what can I do?'

'Calm yourself,' Reyora said squatting on the floor of the drawing room and placing her fingers on either side of her forehead in an attitude of profound concentration. She closed her eyes and her breathing was very slow and deep until she appeared to be almost in a trance. Finally she opened her eyes and, looking at Analee got up, shaking her head.

'I can see nothing. If I can touch something that belongs to him, preferably something alive . . .'

'Something alive. *Clare!*' Analee cried. 'Clare belongs to him.'

'Clare.' Reyora nodded her head with satisfaction. 'The very thing.'

They crept into the nursery where the four-year-old Clare lay asleep in her cot. Her nurse slept with her and a candle still guttered by the side of the bed for she was afraid of the dark. But this night she slept deeply and contentedly, her long dark lashes curling up on her cheeks, her black hair spread on the pillow.

'She grows more and more like you,' Reyora said.

'She is like him too . . . also with his fiery temper.'

'Good . . . the more like him the better.'

Reyora put the palms of her hands on the temple of the sleeping child and went again into the trance-like state – only this time for much longer. At times she swayed a little and nearly fell and Analee, alarmed, caught her and held her tight. Finally Reyora opened her eyes and stared into space as though she were still seeing the visions in her trance.

'It is to do with your husband,' she said. 'Come, I will sleep in your chamber tonight and see if you have your dream again. Or rather I will not sleep. I will watch you.'

Analee went early to bed and Reyora sat on a chair watching her. She saw her undress and slip into a chemise and she marvelled at the finery that Analee now wore compared to her days as a gypsy. And her figure, it was still that of a young girl despite three children and a painful miscarriage. Any man would be proud to love Analee; but there *was* something wrong. Reyora could tell that by communicating with the spirits through the child. It was not infidelity; it was far worse. She knew about the infidelity and about Analee's father. Analee had stopped on the way to York and told Reyora everything, and Reyora rejoiced and grieved at the same time – grieved at the Falcon's perfidy and rejoiced that Analee had discovered her origins at last. Not that it surprised Reyora; she had always known that Analee was no ordinary gypsy. Known it from the beginning when Analee had been married so reluctantly to Randal Buckland.

Now she watched the sleeping woman, saw the even rise and fall of her breast, the fluttering of her eyelids in her dreams. Suddenly

Analee started to shake as though she had a fever and a sweat broke out on her brow. She clutched her arm and began to moan and her eyes opened and shut quickly, showing only the whites as though she were having a fit. Her teeth chattered and she thrashed about on the bed all the time clinging to the arm as though she were in the severest pain.

Reyora stepped forward and shook Analee rousing her from her nightmare. Analee sat up, her face constricted with fear, baring her teeth like a frightened animal, the sweat pouring down her face. Her arm hung loosely by her side and Reyora seized it and shook it while Analee looked dumbly at her.

'I can feel nothing. No sensation at all. First there was this terrible pain. Now . . .'

'The Falcon is mortally ill,' Reyora said.

'I must go at once . . .'

'You will not be in time. We shall send a spell through the air. It is the only way. It is not easy to achieve, but we must will it to succeed. Only that can save him from having his arm cut off, perhaps losing his life. Get up now Analee, we have no time to lose.'

Analee got up and dressed quickly, all symptoms of her fever gone. Reyora took out her bag in which she carried her medicines and began mixing various powders in a bowl.

'Come, I want you to make water for me,' she said and without hesitation Analee, well versed in gypsy magic, lifted up her skirts and squatted over the chamber pot, handing it to Reyora when she had finished.

Reyora poured a little of the steaming liquid into her mortar and beat again with the pestle, murmuring soft incantations.

'Can you catch a bird at night?'

'I never have.'

'A pigeon would do, or a rabbit. Come quickly.'

Taking her bowl with her Reyora followed Analee down the stairs of the darkened house and out into the garden. It was nearly dawn and, with the first glimmerings of light over the mountains, life was stirring among the plants and flowers. The bright eyes of a rabbit shone through the gloom and Reyora, taking Analee by the hand, bade her be very quiet. Then she gave her the bowl and, lifting her skirts, crept across the lawn her eyes gazing intensely into those of the rabbit, willing it not to move.

In the grey light of dawn the frightened rabbit could be observed halted in its tracks, one paw raised, its body poised for flight – but no movement could it make. Its eyes were fixed on Reyora and it only trembled slightly as she quietly bent down and grasped it by the neck, expertly breaking its spinal cord as she picked it up. The rabbit jerked and lay still and Reyora hurried back to Analee.

'Fetch a knife from the kitchen, a very sharp one, and then we shall catch a bird. Hurry.'

There was still no one about as Analee went swiftly to the kitchen and found a sharp pointed knife in the drawer of the large table where Betty Hardcastle made all her pies and cakes. Reyora was moving stealthily among the trees on the edge of the lawn and suddenly there was a squawk, a fluttering of feathers, and she emerged with a small live bird in her cupped palms.

'I have a female thrush. It is ideal,' she said. 'Now quickly pierce the neck of the rabbit and let the blood run into the bowl. Then gather me some leaves of myrtle, rosemary and thyme and scatter them in the mixture, being careful not to break them.'

Analee did as she was bid carefully and efficiently while Reyora spoke quietly to the bird, caressing it so that it ceased its agitation and lay quietly in her hands. When the mixture was ready the first beams of the sun were reaching over the mountains, bathing the house in the rosy kiss of dawn and making the tiny mullioned windows wink and sparkle like a thousand diamonds. The fresh herbs floated on top of the pungent, blood-coloured mixture which was thin and opaque like soup. Reyora took a bunch of grasses and, dipping them into the bowl, sprinkled the bird all over, then very carefully saturated its back, but not its wings, with her potion. Finally she dipped its beak in, and it came out of the bowl dripping as though blood were issuing from its mouth.

Reyora then whispered something to the bird, passed her hand across it three times and lifted it high in the air, pointing it in a southerly direction. Then she released it and, shaking the drops of moisture from its feathers, the bird flew swiftly across the lake in the direction Reyora had pointed and they watched it until it vanished in the trees on the other side.

'We can only hope,' Reyora said, looking gravely at Analee. 'It's the only chance he has.'

* * *

In his dream the Falcon saw Analee come to the window and tap on it, urging him to let her in. He struggled to rise from the bed but because of the pain he could not. Her knock became more urgent and he could see her white anxious face peering through the glass, her long brown fingers stretched against the pane. The Falcon fought and struggled, summoning all his massive strength, now so sadly depleted. The sweat poured off his face and he clenched his teeth with pain, but he did it. He got out of bed and staggered to the window, fumbling at the clasp, murmuring 'Analee . . . Analee . . .' before he collapsed on the floor, his hand clutching at the windowsill. But before unconsciousness claimed him he felt the sweet cool air coming through the open window and Analee knelt by his side, one hand on his injured burning arm.

Hearing the commotion McNeath, who slept near his master, rushed in and found the Falcon lying on the floor by the open window. He thought he was dead and called urgently for help while he tried to lift the huge bulk himself. The Falcon was cold; he was surely dead. McNeath felt a lump come into his throat and then two more servants ran in and, taking their master's feet and shoulders, lifted him tenderly onto the bed.

'Look,' McNeath said going back to the window. Where the Falcon had lain was the dead body of a thrush. McNeath picked it up and threw it out of the window with an exclamation of disgust. The bird smelt putrid and was covered with blood. 'His lordship was doubtless freeing the bird,' McNeath said, and shut the window firmly.

But the Falcon was not dead. The doctor who had come running in his nightshirt ascertained that immediately. A look of astonishment stole over his face as he felt the pulse of his patient and looked under his lids, put a hand on his brow. The doctor then examined the wound on the arm which, though still angry, was less severe than the day before and the swelling had definitely subsided.

'His lordship is on the mend,' the doctor said. 'His crisis is passed. I simply do not understand it.'

'Could it be anything to do with the bird, doctor?' McNeath said, looking towards the window.

'*Bird*, man?'

'His lordship went to free a bird. Maybe the air and lying on a cold floor helped.'

'Oh nonsense. It is my good medicine and care that has cured the Falcon. 'Twas a matter of time. Thanks be to God,' the doctor muttered as an afterthought, having been convinced of the inevitability of amputating his arm this day and burying him the next. 'We must tell the King at once.'

The Falcon improved rapidly. He was bled again, but it only seemed to make him weaker so it was stopped. Every night he slept calmly in his bed and as soon as he closed his eyes, his wife came to him and told him she had made him better. She reminded him about Falkirk and how she had saved his life. He said that he loved only her and always had. That a bond united them that none could sunder. He had already forgotten Lady Constance or any other of his amours of the years and repented his folly. He wanted only her. He yearned to possess her again, but when he held out his arms to take her she vanished. All day he thought of Analee and longed only to sleep so that he could dream about her again.

At the end of the week he was up and about and he asked the King for permission to return to England. The King, who was old and ailing these days, only really felt well in his beloved Hanover. He was surprised everyone did not feel the same and looked at the Falcon.

'But, Marquess, I am not due to return until next month.'

'With your permission, Your Majesty, I yearn to see my wife again.'

'Indeed?'

The King smiled and glanced at Lady Yarmouth, who turned to her lady-in-waiting so that smirks and smiles were exchanged all round the Court. Everyone knew about the Falcon and Lady Constance. The only surprise was that he hadn't touched a woman, to anyone's knowledge, since he had been in Hanover.

'When I nearly died I was reminded of how neglectful I have been of her and, since it is so near our return, if Your Majesty . . .'

The King, a small dapper man but now with a pronounced paunch, smiled indulgently at his beloved Falcon, one of the few men he felt he could really trust.

'Dear General, much as I shall miss you, I understand your reasons. Such a beautiful woman must not be alone too long. Are you sufficiently recovered to make the journey?'

'Indeed sire. The thought of her makes me stronger every moment.'

'Then lose not a day,' said the King and gave him his hand to kiss.

Lady Primrose tapped on the door and then opened it for Analee before stepping back and closing it behind her. She listened for a moment at the door, but the voices were too faint for her to hear. Reluctantly she tiptoed downstairs to where Miss Walkinshaw had been waiting to see the Prince all day.

'I'm afraid His Royal Highness will be a long time,' she said. 'I have taken Lady Falconer to him, and he particularly wished to see her.'

Clementina's plain, impassive face didn't alter.

'I will wait,' she said in her soft Scots burr. 'I am sure he will remember me. I nursed him when he developed a severe cold after Falkirk. I was staying with my uncle Sir Hugh Paterson at Bannockburn House. He is bound to recall it.'

Lady Primrose shrugged. Miss Walkinshaw could wait as long as she liked, but, herself, she doubted whether the Prince would remember one so self-effacing and unattractive.

Charles Edward Stuart held Analee's hands between his for a long time, gazing into her eyes. Then he took her to a sofa by the fireside and placed her beside him.

'Enchantress,' he murmured. 'I have never forgotten you.'

'You are very kind, sire.'

'I sent you a letter.'

'I received it. Lord St March is my father.'

'So I hear, so I hear. I am delighted. Any fool could see, however, that you were of noble birth and the Earl I treasure as one of my most trusted friends.'

The Prince had changed, there was no doubt of that. Although not yet thirty he had the air of a man much older and he looked older too. He had grown heavier, particularly about the face, and his eyes had the rheumy look of the habitual drinker. But he was still a fine figure of a man, royal, still handsome, of superb deportment. Duncan's father. Analee could see the likeness much more clearly now.

'Analee,' the Prince said, getting up and standing over her. 'I would like you to serve me, as your father does, only in a more particular way.'

Analee felt a thrill of apprehension and looked at her royal host. 'In what manner sir?'

'I want you to tell me all the Falcon's counsels with the King and generals.'

'But he is in Hanover sir.' Analee smiled with relief. Despite his continued association with the Princesse de Talmond she thought the Prince was going to ask her formally to be his mistress.

'He will soon return. The King returns next month, which is why I am here now. I have come to make my plans, Lady Falconer. There is much unrest in the country. I have already talked to the Earl of Westmoreland and the Duke of Beaufort. They are convinced the time is near. The King is old and unpopular, hated by his son who has even been in touch with me. I believe he would be willing to give me England if he had Hanover! These Germans are only really happy in their own country. All I need is a spy very close to the King.'

'But I am not close to the King sir. And my husband keeps his own counsel.'

The Prince took her hand again and kissed it lightly, holding it for a moment against his breast.

'But you are a magician. Can you not worm it out of him? Look at his papers? I have heard you are very skilful.'

'Did my father suggest this sir?' Analee said quietly.

'Oh no! I would not ask him. I wanted to ask you.'

She looked at his eyes, his mouth, his firm rather fleshy chin. They said he had developed a fondness for whisky during his days in Scotland, and that his subsequent troubles had made him only more dependent on the stuff. He wore a sober suit of dark blue broadcloth with a white embroidered waistcoat and a crisp white starched cravat at his neck. His bob-wig was powdered and the short queue down the back was tied with blue velvet ribbon. She noticed that his hand shook a little and there was a glass of whisky on the table by his side.

She still venerated him because he was a Stuart, a member of an ancient royal family. But now she realized she could never see him on the throne of this or any other country. In her heart she knew it could never be. Analee got up and dropped a low curtsy.

'Your Royal Highness, as a brave and loyal man yourself you would not have me betray my husband? If you knew I was base enough for such a deed how could you ever trust me?'

'But it is for a very great cause Lady Falconer. It is above the loyalty of husband and wife.'

Analee shook her head. '*Nothing* is above the loyalty between husband and wife. I would dishonour myself sir, if I did as you asked.'

'But in the campaign, ma'am,' the Prince said testily, 'during the Rebellion, *many* husbands and wives were of opposing loyalties.'

'But I believe that was honest and open sir. What you are asking of me is underhand. I cannot do it.'

'Very well Lady Falconer. Good day,' the Prince said brusquely and went to the door. 'You disappoint me. But I cannot help admiring you. You would have made a good friend. I wish I had more like you.'

Although he was angry, the expression on his face was sad as he gazed at Analee and suddenly her eyes filled with tears. She sank to her knees and, taking his hand, kissed it.

'May God bless you and look after you, dear Prince,' she said. 'I will never forget you or what you have done for me.'

'*I* have done something for *you* Lady Falconer?' The Prince had a smile on his lips.

'You have given me a most priceless possession sir, one I shall treasure all my life.'

'And may I know what it is?'

'Yourself, Your Royal Highness,' Analee whispered.

The Prince threw back his head and laughed, his good nature restored. 'Thank you Enchantress. I wish all my mistresses could be as grateful. 'Twas a pleasure for *me*, too, I assure you.'

He held out a hand to raise her and then kissed her on the cheek. She slipped out of the door without another word, her heart too full.

By the time she rejoined Lady Primrose and Colonel Brett, who had accompanied the Prince to London, Analee had recovered her self-possession. The Colonel looked at her shrewdly but asked no questions. No, he had doubted very much whether Lady Falconer would turn into a spy. He had told the Prince as much. Clementina Walkinshaw, however, was another matter. Though not so highly placed, she had a sister who was in the service of the Princess of Wales. In her own way she might make a much more valuable ally. Besides, she was besotted with the Prince and had besieged him with letters, whereas everyone knew that Lady Falconer loved her husband no matter how badly he treated her.

As Lady Falconer put on her cloak Colonel Brett smiled encouragingly at Miss Walkinshaw and took her arm.

'I believe His Royal Highness will see you now, my dear. Pray follow me.'

Shyly Clementina followed him from the room, bowing to Lady Falconer as she passed.

His coach waited in the courtyard. There was no mistaking it, dirty and dusty from the long drive from Hanover. With a cry Analee ran into the house, up the stairs and into the drawing room on the first floor. He stood by the fireplace clad in his red general's coat, buff breeches and high shining black boots. One arm was in a sling.

He had been there for hours, gazing at the door just waiting for her to come in. To see her again, to hear her step on the stairs, her excited cry in the hall . . . What had he done to deserve such a wife? And now here she was looking at him, radiant like a bride, his love, his very own love.

'Analee . . .' he said and took a step forward as she flew to him taking care not to touch his bad arm. He put the good one tenderly about her and for a long time they stood clasped together, listening to the sound of each other's hearts.

'I came home specially to see you,' he said.

'I know.'

'How do you know?'

'I sent a bird to bring you.'

'I am obsessed by you Analee, my dear wife. And once more you came to me in a dream and saved my life. I am never going to leave you again, or look at another woman. And we are going straight to Furness to renew our love. Will that please you?'

He held her away and looked at her dark vibrant eyes, her curved mouth slightly parted with expectation, the arch of her brows, the high smooth forehead, that translucent brown skin that made her look so youthful and alive. How could he ever have looked at another woman? There was no one like Analee in the whole world.

And there, on her breast, lay the medallion that she always wore, no matter what other diamonds and jewels sparkled beside it.

'Falcon Gold,' he murmured, touching it. 'It is a talisman; no misfortune can befall us so long as you wear it – no *real* misfortune,' he said rather sheepishly, noting the gleam in her eyes. 'I do not talk of little, trifling matters, like – '

Analee put a finger to his lips to silence him. 'Do not say it, Angus. Let us look to the future, not the past. Of course Furness will please me, my lord. And you too, I think?'

And she returned his gaze, her glance amorous, her eyes alive with mischief, with anticipation of all the loving they would enjoy in the peace of Lakeland, the only place they were really happy together.

Only good times, she was sure, lay ahead.

BOOK III
Lady of the Lakes
1755–1761

Author's Note

As far as I can ascertain them, all the historical references in this book are true. For many years after the failure of the Rebellion in 1745 Prince Charles Edward Stuart wandered as an exile until 1766 when he went to Rome on the death of his father, the Old Pretender.

His obscure life during his years of exile has been pieced together by many authors and I have consulted all the sources available. He did form a liaison with Clementina Walkinshaw who had met him during the Rebellion, and she did join him in France and bore him a daughter, Charlotte. She left him in 1760 and never saw him again though Charlotte joined her father in Rome in his old age and was created Duchess of Albany by him. Her story alone is a fascinating one.

Clementina Walkinshaw's sister Catherine did serve the Princess of Wales and at one time the court of the Prince and Princess of Wales was known to be a hot-bed of Jacobite intrigue. So it is surely not idle to speculate that Catherine's own feelings about the Prince, whom her family had served for so long, may have been equivocal. It is however pretty certain that, with the rest of the family, she disapproved of her sister's relationship with the Prince. There were those however who still maintained that she was a Jacobite spy, though the evidence seems to suggest very strongly that she was not.

In writing the present volume, the third in the series, I am especially indebted to the following:

Berry, C. Leo. The Young Pretender's Mistress. Charles Skilton, Edinburgh and London, 1977

Corbett, Julian S. England in the Seven Years's War. Longmans, Green & Co., London, 1907

Savory, Sir Reginald. His Britannic Majesty's Army in Germany During the Seven Years' War. Oxford, 1966

Sherrard, O. A. Lord Chatham: Pitt and the Seven Years' War. The Bodley Head, 1955

Williams, Basil. The Whig Supremacy 1714–1760. Oxford, 1962
Williams, Basil. The Life of William Pitt, Earl of Chatham.
  Longmans, Green & Co., 1913

N.T.

1

Watching the children play by the side of the lake on the small safe beach that Nat Hardcastle and his men had constructed especially for them, Analee smiled. The contentment in her heart was, she knew, secure and lasting. Her husband had loved only her for over five years now; he was never far from her and when he went to London or abroad on the King's business he wrote to her every day. The proof of their love was two more babies, little Charlotte, now four, and three-year-old Beyrick who romped on the pebbly shore with young Robert, Nelly's child, a year older than Charlotte. Clare and Duncan, more grown-up, were sailing home-made boats from a tiny wooden jetty and around them nurses and servants fussed while Analee gazed contentedly at her brood, feeling that she had at last achieved some satisfaction in a life full of turbulence and heartache.

To compare Beyrick and Duncan was to realize how truly her husband's child Beyrick was – even at three he was a small edition of that huge man with his great hooked nose and massive frame. Such was his size that his birth had been difficult even for a woman as strong as Analee. He seemed to enter the world fighting so that even at the commencement of his life he resembled his father, the great warrior known to friends and enemies as the Falcon, the bird of prey.

'See how different they are,' Analee murmured to Nelly who sat beside her in the shade because she was expecting her second child. Analee liked the sun and sat with her head back to receive the full benefit of its rays on her healthy olive skin. She closed her eyes and her body was suffused with warmth as from a lover's embrace; she thought with longing of the tender ministrations of her husband – away in Hanover to be with his ailing monarch George II, who in his dotage spent more time in his beloved native land

'Beyrick is the very image of his lordship,' Nelly concurred, twisting awkwardly in her chair as though unable to find a comfortable position. Analee opened her eyes and glanced at her

623

with sympathy, knowing well that cumbersome feeling as the baby, nearing its time, shifted about in the restricting confines of the belly. 'There is no doubt that *he* is his son.' Nelly glanced slyly at Analee who, with a smile on her face, shut her eyes again and once more succumbed to the rays of the sun.

'You are the only one to know the truth, Nell.'

'It is sealed in my heart forever,your ladyship.'

Suddenly there were sounds of scuffling on the tiny beach, childish voices raised in anger and Duncan, Lord Blair, heir to the great Falconer estates, administered a blow to his sister Lady Clare and sent her reeling into the water. Her ladyship fell on her bottom, her legs rising high in the air, her curly locks resting on the lake's still surface. For a moment Lord Blair glared at her and then, glancing at his mother made off for the shelter of the wood as fast as his long legs could carry him. The three younger children stopped their games, gazing at their elders with concern.

Analee jumped up and made swiftly for the water's edge, but Nat Hardcastle was there before her and scooped Lady Clare, crying more from humiliation than actual bodily harm, into his arms. Eight-year-old Clare kicked her legs furiously, showing the many flounces of her petticoats, now soaking wet, and demanded to be put down, vowing all the things she would do to her brother when she caught him.

Analee took her in her arms, gratefully accepting her from Nat and set her down gently on the ground, kneeling so that she was scarcely taller than the child and gazing into the dark eyes resembling her own. 'Clare,' she said chidingly, taking her daughter's hands in hers, 'I foresaw this. You must not goad Duncan. He is by inclination good, but you tease him so that all he can do is to hit out, because otherwise he is the mildest and most polite of boys.'

Indeed Duncan's manners were impeccable, his disposition regal, invariably gentle and courteous. Everyone remarked on the dissimilarity between him and his father, at a loss to account for the difference that was one of temperament and mien rather than looks.

'He has no need to cast *me* into the water, Mama,' Clare said, looking threateningly in the direction of the wood where Duncan was being pursued by two of the menservants. 'For he is stronger than I am.'

'But his nature is milder. If you call him a coward he will react like a strong man, like Papa. You would never call your Papa a coward, would you?'

Clare's expression softened; a look of hero-worship came into her eyes. 'Oh, Papa is no coward, Mama. I wagered Duncan that he could not swim the lake, that he dared not. Papa would have dived immediately into the water. . .'

'But Papa is a grown man!' Despite herself Analee laughed and took the child in her arms, kissing her. 'Of course Duncan cannot swim the lake and doubtless even your Papa, the mighty Falcon, would not care to venture into its icy water. For despite the temperate nature of the day, the streams that feed the lake are cold, my darling, even in the most benign weather. They come from high up in the mountains, from the hidden recesses of the rocks, and maintain their crystal quality even when they are absorbed by the vastness of the lake.'

Clare, wide-eyed, stared at her mother as though she was expounding mysteries that, although beyond her childish comprehension, she knew to be exciting. Already Clare was tall, with a sturdy, pliant body. Unlike her mother her skin was fair but her eyes were dark and surrounded by exquisite long lashes which she fluttered unashamedly when wishing to make a conquest of the opposite sex. She flirted outrageously with her father who sat her on his knees and laughingly called her a minx, saying that she was just like her mother.

Analee watched anxiously as she heard the servants crashing about in the wood and then sighed with relief when she heard Duncan squeal and knew that he was safely captured. She smiled at Nelly. 'They have got him. I must punish him for hitting his sister; but not too hard. It was not altogether his fault.'

'It was not his fault at all!' Nelly snorted.'She is a virago, that one. She is too like her father and . . .'

'Her mother?' Analee raised an eyebrow, the gentle rocking continuing, a smile on her lips. 'Aye, she is our child, the fruit of our loins. Do you recall those days, Nell, when I was a servant at Falcon's Keep? Do you remember Mrs Ardoine and her birch? It was all so long ago.' Analee sank lower in her chair and stretched her feet out before her, wriggling her toes and gazing at them. Analee had never got out of her gypsy's habit of easing off her shoes whenever she got the chance; she scarcely ever wore them in the house and was not averse to walking barefoot through the woods, the soles of her feet hardened from years of trudging over the land.

'I remember.' Nelly said quietly. 'I am not likely to forget and am thankful those days are past.'

'I too am thankful they are gone,' Analee said, raising her hand to shade her eyes from the bright glare of the sun which was almost directly overhead, reflecting up from Derwentwater with the fierce unrelenting brightness of a shining mirror. 'But sometimes I wonder . . . you remember the freedom, Nell, of our way of life? Waking in the morning with the sun as it rose from behind the mountains, the fresh dew on our faces . . .'

'Aye, and an ache in our backs,' Nelly said practically.'Our bellies empty and not likely to be filled. No thank ye, Analee, I much prefer being the maid of a fine lady, my husband the man-servant of a great lord!'

'A *maid*, Nell?' Analee looked incredulously at her beloved companion. 'Nay, a friend. The only true friend I have or am ever likely to have. No servants you and McNeath, but friends, true friends, of my lord and myself.'

Nelly looked at her mistress, her eyes brimming with tears of emotion. 'You are no gypsy, as you know, Analee, but a great lady, the daughter of a lord. Now that we know the truth of your birth, a truth which I always guessed, you honour me more than ever in saying that. When I think of my own humble birth, the shame of my brutal father and compare . . .'

Analee stretched out a hand and grasped Nelly's. 'Do not speak so, my dear friend. Put all those sad memories behind you, as Reyora once bade you. Do not think back on the past.'

But Analee knew that Nelly had once been got with child by her father and such bestiality was hard to forget and forgive, even though among the gypsy people it was not uncommon. Brewster Driver had been a rough, harsh man and his family went in constant fear of him.

'Perhaps he has been hanged long ago as a horse thief,' Analee went on thoughtfully, remembering those far-off days when she had briefly stolen horses for him. 'It would be no more than he deserved.'

'My father a horse thief and yours a lord,' Nelly sighed,

nursing her swollen belly. 'There is such a gulf between us, Analee.'

'That is stupid talk, and let us have no more of it. Ah, here is young Lord Blair, safely captured I see.'

The Master of Blair, squealing pitifully, his legs hanging against his capturer, Nat Hardcastle, was brought over to his mother and deposited gently on the ground by the side of little Clare who, her tears dry, was gazing at him with the contempt of the first-born. When she saw Duncan set down beside her she kneaded her fists in her eyes and looked as though she was about to start bawling all over again. Analee held up a warning finger.

'Now hush, Clare. If there are any more tears you will be sent inside. Do not taunt Duncan and he will not harm you or if he does I shall soon put a stop to it, and if your father hears of it . . .'

Duncan's face clouded with fear. He seemed to go in mortal dread of his father, who indeed with him was a stern parent, whereas to the rest he was tender and indulgent. He told Analee it was because Duncan was his heir and he must grow up accustomed to fear and respect his father; but Analee often wondered if there was another reason – if, in some intuitive way, Angus knew Duncan was not his child but the offspring of a man he despised and hated, Prince Charles Edward Stuart, the Young Pretender, now an exile wandering on the Continent. This hostility between supposed father and son saddened Analee, who thought of the relationship between the King of England and his eldest son, traditionally one of mutual dislike. But how sad old King George had been when his heir Frederick, poor Fred, had suddenly died four years before. Angus said that he had been a broken man ever since.

'There is no need to fear your father, Duncan,' Analee said gently.' Do not look so anxious. As long as you do as you are bid he will always be just; but he would not like to hear of you knocking your sister into the water.'

'Oh pray do not tell him, Mama,' Duncan pleaded.

'I will say nothing,' Analee patted his shoulder, 'as long as there is no repetition.'

'There will not be, Mama.'

Duncan glared at Clare and toddled away as swiftly as his six-year-old legs would carry him.

Despite the quarrels of her children the scene was one of such domestic bliss that Analee's good humour remained undisturbed. It was good to be a mother, a beloved wife eagerly looking forward to the home-coming of her husband. Yes, despite what she said, it was even good to be a marchioness, the natural daughter of an earl, a woman of society with a high place in the hierachy of the country. Had she not met the Kings of England and France, been on good tems with the Pompadour, and also with the Princess of Wales who had even invited her to be a member of her suite? But, more than this had she not lain with the man who fascinated so many women, the last of the Stuarts, regarded by many as the heir to England's rightful king? Had not his seed grown within her and produced a fine sturdy child? Her eyes followed young Duncan to the shoreline and, briefly, her eyes misted with tears at the thought of the hapless fate of his father, a penniless exile and now, according to reports, a feckless rake and drunkard.

In many ways little Duncan seemed to emulate his real father. He was a beautiful-looking child with enormous charm. Yet he was moody and capricious, alternately sulking and giving vent to moods of wild elation. He was unfailingly courteous and polite and yet he could be very wild and savage as when he had thrown Clare in the water, not caring whether she sank or swam – or was it that he knew that in his small protected world there would always be servants to guard his behaviour, to prevent him or those he upset coming to any real harm?

Analee was almost asleep in the sun when she was aroused by one of the servants, who, dressed in the full Falconer livery, correctly attired even despite the informality and the heat of the day in scarlet coat and breeches and snow-white cravat, was entering the quiet glade by the lakeside, a few hundred yards from the house. Analee sat up as the servant bowed low, his eyes lingering for a moment on the bare brown feet of his mistress.

'Madame, Miss Delamain begs that you will receive her.'

'Miss Delamain? Emma is here?' Analee looked at Nelly and quickly rose from her chair. 'Did you hear that, Nell? I have not seen Emma since I went over to Cockermouth, oh let me see, it was shortly before his lordship's terrible illness . . .'

'It was five years ago, your ladyship. I remember it as though 'twas yesterday. It was the year 1750 and I was expecting

Robert.' Nelly glanced at her son, who had resumed his romping with little Charlotte and Beyrick.

'Aye, and our paths have never crossed since. I had the feeling Emma was avoiding me. She never accompanied the Riggs when they came over here and was never there when I visited them. I must go and see her at once. Nelly, I leave the children in your care and do not hesitate to administer rebuffs and rebukes when you think it necessary. I will try to persuade Emma to join us for luncheon by the lake.'

'It is almost ready, my lady,' Tom the manservant bowed. 'I know cook is well advanced in her preparations for it.'

'Let us make haste then.'

Analee smiled at Tom and, gathering up her skirts, bade him precede her along the path through the wood that led to the house.

Inside, Emma was standing by the long, low window that overlooked the lake. She was still thin though not as haggard as Analee remembered her; certainly not the beauty that she had once been before she journeyed to America in her fruitless quest to recapture her love, Stewart Allonby. Momentarily Analee felt a pang on account of Emma's resemblance to her brother, Brent. It was something in her expression rather than facial similarity or colouring; also her gestures and the way she turned aside from the window and regarded Analee as she came into the room.

'Emma!'

'Your ladyship.'

Emma dropped a slight curtsey.

'Oh, Emma,' Analee grasped her hands. 'Do not "your lady-ship" me. I am Analee, your old friend. Am I not?'

Emma's hands were limp in hers. The expression in her eyes when she met Analee's gaze was hostile and suspicious. She ignored the question. Analee let her hands fall, gesturing towards a chair.

'Pray sit down, Emma. I am delighted to see you.'

'Your ladyship is very kind. I came on a whim as I was journeying between Cockermouth and Delamain castle where I am once more living with my mother.'

'You are living there permanently again? I did not know.' Analee gazed for a moment over the lake, seeing in her mind's eye a small laughing creature darting across the lawn. Morella. It was impossible ever to put Morella completely out of her mind; not a day passed but she spent some part of it thinking about her. It was as though she had lost her first-born, even though she lived only a few miles away.

'Mama is very frail now. She needs me.'

'I am sure she does.'

'It really was because of Mama that I came.'

'Oh?' Analee's eyebrows were raised interrogatively.

'Mama is pining for news of Brent. The worry about him makes her ill. She thought . . . you . . .'

Emma gazed searchingly into Analee's eyes.

'I have heard no word of Brent since he departed from here some years back. He is no longer part of my life, Emma. All that is finished.'

'We thought you might know something.'

'Nothing.' Analee shook her head firmly, feeling a little band of steel encircle her heart. She had, she *must*, put Brent Delamain, Morella's father, firmly out of her mind. He had only ever brought trouble, alienated her from the Falcon. It was on his account that the Falcon had once nearly killed her; it was really because of Brent that that great fissure had occurred in their lives. Yet he had said he would love her forever. In her heart she knew it was true. She sighed. 'I am sorry, Emma; sorry to know that in her old age your mother still grieves for her son.'

'Of *course* she grieves for her son,' Emma snapped. ''Twould be unnatural not to. I am sorry I disturbed your ladyship.' She pursed her lips and Analee could see her jaw working as she gritted her teeth. Emma would be about twenty-seven. Already she had the markings of an embittered old maid.

'Will you not take off your cloak, Emma, and stay with us awhile?'

Far from removing her cloak, Analee perceived that Emma was actually fastening it and drawing her gloves over her ringless fingers.

'I thank your ladyship, but I wish to proceed with my journey. I must apologize for disturbing you.'

Emma turned towards the door but Analee ran in front of her and barred her way.

'I cannot let you go like this! You know that I regard your family as my own; that I venerate your mother and love your cousins the Allonbys, aye, and your brother Brent. Too much has passed between us over the years, Emma, for you to regard me with such scorn.'

'I do not *scorn* you, Lady Falconer.' Emma's lips began to tremble and Analee realized that she had been keeping herself strongly under control. 'I *fear* you! I fear the impact of the woman known as the Enchantress on all whom I love.'

'But that is absurd . . .'

'It is not absurd! Did I not know of the passion my brother Brent had for you, so much so that it destroyed the very foundations of his marriage? And did I not know of the impression you made on Hugo Fitzgerald so that he put his own life in danger. . .'

'Hugo Fitzgerald!' Analee looked sharply at Emma. 'You spoke of my impact on all whom you love. Is Hugo Fitzgerald among them then?'

Emma's pale face was suffused with colour, her eyes bright. She lowered her head.

'I did not mean to say his name.'

'Ah, but you did. You also said I endangered his life. I did *not*, Emma. He was that perfidious type of person who is known as a double spy. He pretended to be loyal to Hanover and at the same time to favour the Stuart cause. To this day I swear I know not where his true allegiances lie.'

'Brent nearly killed him. For *you*. Because of that he would not look at me again when he returned wounded from here. He moved to Whitehaven and never again set foot in the Riggs' home at Cockermouth, at any rate as long as I was there. Yes, I found him personable and attractive. I also thought he looked with favour on me; but no, it was the Enchantress . . .'

'Oh, Emma, this is nonsense.' Analee stamped her foot with anger and went to the window, her arms akimbo. The sun was now directly above the house. She hoped the children were being given their lunch as it was long past noon. 'I am a married woman, the mother of several children. I am happy and contented and in love, aye,' Analee turned to Emma, her fine eyes blazing,'in love with my *husband*. There is no other. Now he is in Hanover but he returns soon and I will go to London with him for the rest of the year. He allows me a few weeks in Lakeland at the best time of the year, the late spring and early summer. There is no room in my heart for any but Lord Falconer.'

'You told me that before, but it was not true. Every man who sees you is enraptured by you.'

'Oh that is absurd! I assure you I am chaste as a nun while my lord is away. I look at no other men and if they look at me I cannot help it, I am sure. I have not seen Hugo Fitzgerald or Brent Delamain for years and know not what has become of either of them.'

'You once gave Stewart a spell,' Emma whispered urgently, the colour of her cheeks growing higher. 'Will you not do the same for me?'

Analee vividly recalled the day that she had given Stewart Allonby a spell here at this very house, and he had cast it on the lake to flow in the direction of Emma's home.

'I will do anything for you, Emma, but I have not cast a spell for years. I have forgotten my gypsy ways. Besides, my spells do not always work; they did not work for Mary, for Brent did not fall in love with her again and she remained estranged as his wife. Hugo Fitzgerald and I parted on such bad terms I doubt if he even thinks of me.'

'Then why does he not look at *me*? What have I done to him?'

'Because your brother wounded him maybe?' Analee said gently. 'His pride was hurt?'

'Or because I am too plain,' Emma said bitterly. 'I am not sufficiently attractive for him.'

'That you can do something about,' Analee said. 'You do not need a spell to enhance your looks; but I have a suggestion to make. If you will stay with me for a day or two I shall send for Reyora, my old friend the *cohani*. She is full of magical spells that will surely be sufficient to ensnare Hugo Fitzergerald, if you are sure you want him.' Analee lowered her voice and gazed at the floor.

'Why should I not be sure? He is a very personable man.'

'Oh there is no question as to his looks. It is his disposition and nature that worry me.'

'All that has changed. He is a solid businessman working for Ambrose Rigg. He has no truck at all with politics now. I know that, Analee. Times are very different, the Hanoverians securely on the throne. No one any longer believes the Stuarts have a hope.

Hugo has become the very model of respectability; a pillar of society.' She clasped her hands together, her eyes alight.

'I do not think you need any spells,' Analee said gently. 'If he could see you as I see you now, flushed with love and alive with hope, he would desire no other. The ability to entrance him is there, in you *yourself*, Emma.'

'But he will not even see me, Analee. If he hears I am with the Riggs he will not come near. I beg you to help me. I beg you.'

Emma watched as the blood from the rabbit dripped slowly into the pot containing her own menstrual blood. Fascination at the process warred with horror and repugnance. She had gathered herbs under Analee's direction from the surrounding hills and ditches and ground them into fine powder with a pestle and mortar, mixing them with her spittle and urine. When Reyora had come and discovered that her woman's flow was due, she said that this was the most suitable, most propitious time for a spell of such power that it would enslave any man – for the rabbit's blood represented his, and her own menstrual blood was a sacred fluid, a symbol of potent fecundity.

The blackbird wriggled in the secure clasp of Analee's hands as Reyora spread the mud-coloured liquid over its back, murmuring soft words of incantation.

'How will it work?' Emma said breathlessly.

'The bird will alight on his head or shoulder and he will be immediately transformed and will think only of you. This is a most powerful spell; I myself have to spend some time preparing for it in order to be strong enough to send the power. Analee and I once sent a bird as far as Germany where it cured the Falcon stricken with a mortal illness. But this is a softer spell, a love spell, and the bird does not need to die as the other did.'

'Why did it need to die?'

'To give life, of course. This on the contrary must not die. It is a female ready for mating. By the time she finds your beloved she will have mated and by settling on him will impart some of her own fecundity, filling him with lustful thoughts.'

Emma blushed as Reyora looked gravely at her.

'We are dealing with elemental things, my dear – you must not be afraid of love.'

'But why will his thoughts turn to me and not another?'

'That is part of my spell. It is because your essences are mingled in my magic potion. As the need in his loins grows urgent, a picture of you will appear in his mind, as an object of desire. He will find he cannot rid himself of it and will seek you out. When his eyes alight on you he will realize that it is *you* he wants and he will fall deeply and irrevocably in love with you. You must be sure that you want him, for the spell is binding.'

'Do you really want him, Emma?'

The bird wriggled again in Analee's hands and for a moment looked as though it would fly off, but her hold on it tightened.

'Yes I do.'

'Plighting your troth over this bird is more important than the wedding vow. Now you must place your hand on the bird's head and repeat some words after me. Are you ready?'

Reyora took Emma's right hand and dipped it in the murky liquid. A powerful stench assailed Emma's nostrils and she felt a spasm of nausea.

'Now you must stroke the head of the bird and say these words after me. Are you ready?'

'Yes.' Emma felt herself begin to tremble as Reyora took her stained fingers and placed them on the head of the bird.

'I, Emma Delamain.'

'I, Emma Delamain.'

'Do swear.'

'Do swear.'

'That I wish to be bound to Hugo Fitzgerald.'

'That I wish to be bound . . .' Emma voice trailed away and she swallowed hard. She glanced at Analee, who gave her a reassuring smile. Emma's voice strengthened. '. . . to Hugo Fitzgerald.'

'That I wish to lie with him and give myself to him.'

'That I wish to lie with him . . . and give myself to him.'

'In the marriage bond forever.'

'In the marriage bond forever.'

'I swear by the gypsy lore.'

'I swear by the gypsy lore.'

'There, it is done.'

Analee suddenly released the bird and it flew upwards, scattering drops of the liquid onto Emma's head. It appeared to hover momentarily over her as though seeking direction and then it turned its beak westwards towards the coast, flying low over the lake towards the Borrowdale valley before it disappeared from sight.

Emma, gazing at her hands stained with the muddy, nauseous liquid, was overcome by a feeling of total revulsion; her forehead, too, was stained with the drops left by the bird and she felt unclean, putrid like the liquid.

But Reyora gazed at her with satisfaction, cleansing her own hands with grass she had pulled from the side of the neatly cut lawn.'The spell has gone well,' she said. 'The drops of liquid shed by the bird are an excellent sign. Now tip the remaining liquid in this bowl in the lake, in the direction the bird has flown, and then go up to rest resisting the impulse I know you have to cleanse yourself. As you sleep you will dream of your beloved. Before morning breaks the bird will have mated and before evening will rest upon him.'

'I know not what to say,' Emma said falteringly, looking from one to the other. Then she knelt and emptied the bowl into the lake.

'Say nothing,' Analee reassured her. 'But go upstairs as you are bid and lie down. Nelly will rouse you later and help you to wash and change your things; but now obey Reyora and all will be well.'

The two gypsies stood watching Emma go slowly towards the house, keeping her dirty hands well away from her dress like someone fearful of being caught in a foul deed.

'Well, you cannot blame her,' Reyora said, taking up the bowl that Emma had left by the side of the lake and cleansing it with grass. 'I hope she is not mistaken in this man. It is a very strong spell I have woven.'

'I know it, dear Reyora. You have lost none of your *cohani* powers.'

'Indeed they are more potent than ever. I recently killed a man from two hundred miles away. He had defiled one of our young girls, scarcely thirteen years of age; taken her in a ditch and left her almost dead. We knew not who he was nor where he had gone. Some weeks later he was found in a field in Kent, pierced through the heart by a stake. Everyone said it was a witch. Indeed it was. It was I.'

'But how did you come to know this?'

'He carried in his pocket a bracelet he had stolen from the young girl; his first motive was theft before his gross passions overtook him. He was a member of another tribe, the Louth gypsies from Cornwall. They had passed this way. One of the women of our tribe was married to a Louth gypsy. She knew the story and returned the bracelet knowing it was he. The tribe have done all they could to make recompense for the deed of one of their number. I relieved the poor child of the result of this carnal encounter.'

'She was with child?'

'Unfortunately. But I took it very near the time so she felt very little pain. I healed her mind, too, and she has forgotten everything.'

'Dear Reyora, clever Reyora,' Analee said fondly, remembering Reyora's successes with her in the past. 'How glad I am to have you for a friend.'

Reyora put an arm about her as they strolled towards the house. 'Now, Analee, tell me how it is with you? I told you, did I not, that things would be better. And have they been?'

'Oh yes!' Analee stopped and looked at her friend, her eyes shining. 'I have two more beautiful children and the undying love of my lord. I . . .' her smile faded and she came nearer to Reyora. 'Why do you look like that old friend? Is aught amiss?'

'I told you, Analee, that for you life would be sorrow mingled with joy, joy with sorrow. You have just had great happiness as I said you would. Now you must be prepared for a little change. But do not despair. Things will right themselves again, after a time.'

'It is to do with the Falcon?' Analee whispered anxiously, and took hold of Reyora's arm as the sage nodded her head.

'Oh, Reyora, do not let him be faithless to me yet again. I cannot bear it. Oh surely it is not another illness? Do not say . . .'

'I say nothing, my dear,' Reyora said calmly, fastening the large carpet bag she carried after depositing in it her phials of potions and spells. 'I cannot deflect the course of events. I can only prepare you for them and assure you that evil will not triumph forever. It cannot. Now show me your children once again, dearest friend, and I will give them my blessing before I go. I love them all as though they were my own and anything I can do to protect them from life's ravages, I shall. You can depend on Reyora.'

2

Hugo Fitzgerald stood on the jetty at Whitehaven watching the hatches being battened down on the fishing wherries that would go out with the evening tide. The cargo of French brandy which the boat had carried was safely out of sight in the warehouse, hidden under bales of legally imported cotton and tobacco. Hiding the contraband was merely a formality because all the customs men in Whitehaven were in the pay of Ambrose Rigg, whose smuggling activities formed the basis of his considerable fortune.

He himself was growing richer every day, Hugo thought with satisfaction, because his share in it was increasing, too. It was a fine prosperous business in which nine-tenths went to Mr Rigg and a tenth to the revenue. There had to be some token payments to the Exchequer because the scale of Rigg's activities was so vast. He was one of the most important men, if not *the* most important man, in Whitehaven.

Rigg had always been lucky in the men he employed. Brent Delamain had served him faithfully until circumstances had obliged him to leave, and Hugo had taken his place. Hugo was even better than Brent because Brent was essentially a man of action, whereas Hugo had a keen business brain. Hugo liked figures and his acumen had enhanced the business which Rigg had built up so assiduously over the years, and which he was now content to leave to run itself because his own interests were in his large and growing family and his fine estate on the outskirts of Cockermouth.

Hugo looked at his watch and then up at the pink sky. It was a fine evening. He was due to dine with the Riggs and give his report to Ambrose, who came into Whitehaven far less often than he used to. Hugo hailed the master of the wherry and head, turned towards the quay when an object seemed to drop out of the sky and land on his shoulder. Startled, Hugo swiftly moved his hand: there was a flutter of wings and a bird flew off, ascending swiftly towards the sky. Hugo brushed his shoulders with his hand and swore, examining his fingers.

'Curses! Damned bird!' he exclaimed and getting out his handkerchief, wiped the bird's dropping off his shoulder, irritated that a good coat should be soiled. Once in the warehouse he climbed the stairs to his room and removed his coat, rubbing the shoulder with clean water until the stain had gone.

That it was a curious incident never occurred to him. He combed his hair and whiskers, changed his cravat and, putting his hat on his head, went round to the back of the warehouse where his horse was saddled and ready for him

A great white napkin was spread over the vast circumference of Ambose Rigg's belly. Above it, his face was red and his greying hair frizzy but sparse. His nose was full of large pores, resembling a pincushion, and threaded with tiny red and purple veins. The hands which frequently raised his glass to his lips were soft and podgy, and a large diamond glittered on his middle finger. Ambrose liked the sound of his own voice. He wanted everyone to know about his success however often they had already heard the tales of his inauspicious start, his childhood of respectable poverty. Although he was only in his early fifties, his experiences seemed to have stretched a lifetime. He remembered Queen Anne and the accession of George I, the 1715 Rebellion and the discontent at home.

'They were very uneasy days,' Ambrose said, trapping a large belch in his napkin and looking guiltily at his wife. 'Pardon, my dear, but that was an uncommonly good dinner. Mutton and caper sauce is, in my opinion, an unbeatable combination.'

Sarah Rigg smiled her frosty smile. Her husband's manners were certainly better than when she had married him, but they would never be those of a gentleman. She fanned herself with her own napkin and pushed back her chair. 'It is very hot,' she said. 'Too hot for mutton. I think.'

'It is never too hot for mutton. What, Hugo?'

Hugo had been looking at Mrs Rigg, noting the sour expression on her face, the downward turn of her mouth. There was little doubt she was carrying a child again. He marvelled that such a corpulent man and such a disagreeable woman could ever contrive to couple at all. The thought of it quite stretched the imagination.

'No, sir. I enjoy mutton at any time, but if Mrs Rigg . . .'

638

'Aye, she is with child again. I saw your glance. She breeds every two years. Is it not so, my dear?'

'Alas, yes,' Sarah said, tetchily fanning her hot face. 'So it seems.'

'It is the will of God, my dear,' Ambrose said complacently. 'The will of God and my own not inexpert endeavours . . .'

'Please, Ambrose!' Sarah said sharply, looking at Hugo. 'I do not care for this kind of conversation.'

'I'm sorry, my dear.' Ambrose winked at Hugo and then looked at the door as a servant entered bearing another dish. 'Good, plum pudding I hope. Boiled mutton and plum pudding . . .' He slavered with greed, rubbing his podgy hands.

Hugo felt a spasm of nausea and closed his eyes at the sight.

'Are you quite well, Mr Fitzgerald?' Sarah was kooking at him curiously. 'Does the food not agree with you?'

'On the contrary, Mrs Rigg. It is so good I . . . I am bereft of words.'

'Then you will have some plum pudding?'

'If I may.' He leaned over and took the plate from Sarah's hand, observing a look of grim satisfaction in her eyes. She was a woman he did not understand. He knew she did not like him but he did not know why. He was polite, hard-working and dependable. Yet she never tried to increase their intimacy or call him by his Christian name. He felt she merely tolerated him. She was, of course, Brent Delamain's first cousin. Maybe that had something to do with it, yet she was said to disapprove of him too. Even when he thought of Brent he felt his stomach curdle. If ever there was a person he detested . . .

Ambrose had two helpings of pudding before he spoke again. Sarah, Hugo noticed, enjoyed her food, too. He thought of her breeding again and the idea seemed quite incredible. How did such a formidable, severe woman even bring herself to the requisite degree of tenderness, and submission? He felt a stirring in his loins and was shocked. Surely thoughts of Sarah could not . . . ? He did not desire her in the very least.

'It is time you were breeding, too,' Ambrose said, as if reading his mind. 'You must be thirty.'

'Thirty-two, sir.'

'Aye, I thought so. Well, I did not marry until I was turned forty.

But if I knew then what I know now I would have started sooner. One cannot enjoy one's children if one is older, as younger folk do. They romp on the floor with them and all kinds of things. And now a new baby. I will be in my seventies when he is grown up.'

Hugo saw Sarah look at Rigg. He could tell the words on her tongue although they were left unsaid. She wondered why he didn't stop and leave her alone. Hugo wondered the same thing. He knew Ambrose always patronized the best brothel in Whitehaven when he was in town. Maybe there was some satisfaction in bedding the severe Mrs Rigg, getting her with child; or maybe he deemed a very large family an essential tribute to the memory of one who had started with nothing?

'I have a mind to marry, sir,' Hugo surprised himself by saying. 'But who?'

'Who?' Ambrose roared. 'There are any number of pleasant damsels in Whitehaven and Cockermouth.'

'But I do not know any, sir.'

'Then that is your fault. You work too hard.'

'Does female company not attract you, Mr Fitzgerald?'

Sarah Rigg's tone was rather taunting. Hugo thought.

'Indeed it does, ma'am. Maybe it is true that I do work too hard.'

'I would have thought you would be most sought after.'

Sarah Rigg gazed at him and Hugo felt himself blushing. It was as though she had divined the lascivious course his thoughts had taken. He actually saw her smile, a rare expression. In fact the smile transformed and softened her features and made her seem younger than he thought she was although he had heard that she was a good bit younger than Rigg. Maybe not much older than himself.

'I am not in the circle of balls and parties, ma'am. I do not have the time.'

It was true he had no time. He worked as hard at Ambrose's business as though it had been his own. And indeed it was his hope that Ambrose would make him a partner. He worked hard with this object in view. 'Rigg and Fitzgerald', why not?

Hugo Fitzgerald slept badly. He tossed and turned in his bed and seemed to wake every few minutes. Yet he only heard the cry of a night bird, the whinny of a horse in the stables. Towards morning there were the sounds of the servants stirring early in the house, of water being drawn in the yard and the cattle being fed. He got up and looked out on the pleasant rural scene that lay before him, the mountainous range that led to Ennerdale and Wastwater or over in the west, towards Derwentwater. The early morning mist obscured the most distant hills and the pungent smell of wood smoke assailed his nostrils. He saw a young girl busy in the yard below, hauling a bucket of water from the well. She was tall and well-built and as she turned, bent over by the weight of the pail, she seemed to look up at him and his heart turned over.

Emma. It was Emma Delamain. He leaned over the window sill but the young girl passed nonchalantly beneath. Of course it was not Emma at all. Emma. He went over to his bed and lay down, his hands cradling his head.

He had not thought of Emma Delamain for years. Why should he think of her now? He had scarcely known her: a subdued, ill-looking girl who had been jilted in America and had crept home to lick her wounds. He now recalled her height – she was tall for a woman – and the beautiful rich quality of her chestnut hair. Her face was pale and too thin, but her eyes were deep in their sockets and her lids rather opaque. Her nose was long and straight, her mouth firm. It was said she had once been a beauty. He wanted to kiss the mouth, to encircle that slim waist with his arms. He suddenly felt an overwhelming desire for her and he leapt out of bed and stripped off his nightshirt, dowsing his throbbing body with cold water.

At breakfast he was like a man in a trance.

'Did you not sleep, Hugo?

Ambrose was tucking into a dish of ham, lamb chops and coddled eggs. He lifted a tankard of ale to his mouth and took a large draught. His attitude was that of a man in the last stages of starvation.

'Not very well, sir.'

'Ah! You need a woman.'

'I think I do, sir.'

Ambrose looked at him with surprise as though not expecting his remark to be taken seriously. 'I meant it in jest. Doubtless the mattress was too soft or the pillow too hard.'

'No, I think I do need a woman, sir. A wife.'

'Ah,it was my remark about breeding that troubled you.' Ambrose wiped his mouth on the sleeve of his coat, and smirked. 'Yet your wages should buy you enough in the way of carnal satisfaction, eh? They have some very good wenches at Mrs Earnshaw's.'

'I was not thinking of prostitutes, sir, but of a wife. As you said, I should be wed. I am of age.'

'Ah, you are certainly that!' Ambrose chuckled and, pushing back his chair with difficulty, waddled to the sideboard where he helped himself to devilled kidneys, fried potatoes and a piece of liver. 'Is that it, eh? Come, my boy, you can tell me.' Ambrose sat heavily in his chair, then leaned conspiratorially over to Hugo, putting a hand on his arm. 'My good lady suffers from sickness in the morning and will not join us.'

Hugo leaned back, pushing his plate away from him.

'You have lost your appetite, too! Who is it? Who is the fortunate wench?'

Hugo put his hands in his pockets and gazed at the ceiling. 'What think you of Emma Delamain,sir?'

Henrietta Delamain clasped Analee's hand and held it briefly to her bosom. 'Dear, dear Analee, how lovely to see you again! But such a brief visit? Can you not stay longer?'

'Not now, Henrietta,' Analee said, following her hostess into the long drawing room of Delamain Castle. 'I have only come to enquire after your health and then I must go to Falcon's Keep to await my husband.'

'So your holiday in Lakeland is over?' Henrietta pointed to a chair and also sat, facing her guest.

'For the time being. We had some beautiful weeks there. But I miss my husband.'

'Of course.' Henrietta searched the face of her guest, about whom there were always so many rumours – that she had been a gypsy, that she was the daughter of a nobleman, that she possessed magical powers. None or all of them could be true for all Henrietta knew. Cooped up in this grim castle in the middle of the country, seldom visiting London, she often felt cut off from life. 'And how are your children, Analee?'

'Oh they are very well. The younger ones are adorable; Clare full of character and spirit; and Duncan . . . well, very much his own person.' Analee glanced out of the window as though willing herself to see that curly blond head bobbing about on the lawn.

'Oh you are so fortunate in your children.' Henrietta passed a hand across her brow. 'To have sons, what would I not have given . . .' Henrietta wrung her hands and looked at the ceiling.'But still, thanks to you and good Reyora, the matter seems no longer to trouble my husband. He has become reconciled to my barrenness and accordingly more tender towards me. The question of an heir to this great place continues to trouble him. Brent, of course, could not inherit because he is an outlaw. Unfortunately the title would pass to a distant cousin, but our eldest daughter, Mildred, could possibly inherit some land and part of the estate. George has lawyers seeing to the matter,'

'But surely he is in good health and not like to die?'

'Oh yes, he is in excellent health; but you know there are always unforeseen circumstances and my husband is a very cautious man. He so longed for an heir.'

'Maybe you will have one in the course of time.'

'I doubt it, dear Analee. I doubt it very much.'

'And what news of Mrs Delamain and Emma?'

'They are well. Emma lives again with us, you know, or rather with her mother. She seldom visits us at the castle, being content to brood on her thoughts. Alas, I fear she will never marry, but be an old maid, an embittered spinster dwelling on past memories. I never saw a girl so changed. She was such a beauty. Charles Edward Stuart has a lot to answer for; the ruin of some of our family and many a broken heart, to say nothing of broken lives. Happily George took care to make prominent display of his loyalty during the Rebellion. He commanded the local militia and has at least saved the honour of this branch of the Delamain family.'

Henrietta looked searchingly at Analee who, it had been rumoured, had also shared a double loyalty during the Rebellion – to her husband, a Hanoverian commander, and to the renegades. But Analee was still looking out of the window, filled with an understandable sense of agitation. For she had not come to see Lady Delamain or even Emma, but her own daughter Morella who lived with her grandmother in the dower house of the castle.

'Sir George's loyalty indeed does him credit,' Analee murmured. 'Could we walk in the garden do you think, Henrietta? It is such a lovely day.'

'But you need not journey on today, surely? At least stay the night. It is past noon.'

Analee had risen early, the journey across the lake and from Keswick to Delamain Castle had taken most of the morning. It was true she was tired. The Falcon was not due until the following day. Moreover if she wanted to see Morella . . .

'I will stay,' she said. 'But I must leave first thing tomorrow. Pray be good enough to send one of your servants to bring my bag from the carriage.'

'Of course.' Joyfully Henrietta got up and went to pull the bell rope. 'Nelly is not with you?'

'Nelly is about to have a child. Oh how I dislike being parted from her at this time. I am hoping my lord, who comes with her husband, will allow us to return to Furness for the birth. But she is well looked after. The midwife who assisted me is waiting to attend her.'

'And Reyora?'

'Reyora is only called if there are difficulties. We do not expect them with strong Nelly.'

'That woman is a treasure. I am sure it is she who has brought about this change of heart in my husband.'

'It is possible,' Analee said, fastening her cloak loosely about her. 'It is quite possible.'

'She comes over to see Morella and always pays me a visit. She is strangely drawn to that child.'

Analee felt her heart skip a beat.

'Morella must be what, ten or so now?' Analee was sure her voice would give her away, but Henrietta prattled on without appearing to notice anything.

'She was born in the year of the Rebellion, 1745. Yes, she is ten. She is a tall, strong child, a curious girl. I never understand her myself.'

'Oh, why?'

'She is so grown-up. One would think her a lot older, and she is so wise! I find myself listening to her with great respect.'

'Oh, you do see her then?' Analee murmured. 'I recall you once said that you did not have her in the castle for fear she would contaminate your own children on account of the mystery of her birth, the obscurity of her origins.'

A blush of embarrassment spread over Henrietta's homely features and she avoided Analee's eyes. 'Did I really say that? What an odious person I was. You see it is since, through you, I came to know Reyora that I think I have discovered the true meaning of goodness, and anything connected with Reyora could not be bad.'

'I am glad to hear you say it.' Analee said, following her hostess along the stone corridors of the castle, down the broad staircase and out of the great double doors.

It was a beautiful day, warm but balmy, and the trees stirred in the wind. Only in the north country did one find such a profusion of greenery, Analee thought, due to the heavy rain, the dark richness of the soil. She thought of the hot streets of London, of the bustle and confusion of the court and her heart ached to remain here; but it was not to be.

'Would you like to see Emma?' Henrietta said when they had taken a measure by the side of the rose garden, admiring the profusion of blooms, inhaling their heavenly scent. 'She returned much refreshed after seeing you. I believe she stopped a few days longer than she intended?'

'Yes, she did. We got on well, I am glad to say.'

'Poor girl. She will never wed. She will remain a spinster to look after her mother. Another heart broken by Charles Edward Stuart!'

'Has her mother forgiven me for helping her to go to America? I often think how different Emma's life might have been if I had not assisted in that folly.'

'Oh you meant well. I know Brent was behind it, and Emma is stubborn like all the Delamains. Well, she learned her lesson. No man is to be trusted. Ah look, the door opens and there is Emma.'

Analee turned as Emma started to run along the path from the dower house to the parterre between the rose gardens, her arms outstretched.

'Analee! They did not tell us you were here.'

Analee went towards Emma and caught her hands, kissing her. 'I was not sure I would be able to call. I am on my way to Falcon's Keep. But I couldn't resist it.'

'*And* she is to stay the night. I insist that you and your mother dine at the castle. Sir George will be delighted. He is due back from Whitehaven this afternoon.'

'Whitehaven?' Emma's voice faltered and she looked at Analee.

'Aye. He does a lot of business with Rigg, you know. Uncouth though Rigg may be, he is related to Sir George through Sarah. I would be the first to disclaim the connection but it appears he is on the way to being a very substantial landowner. Money, of course is no respecter of persons; providing one has the knowledge, anyone can make it.'

'I found Mr Rigg very agreeable,' Analee said, looking sharply at Henrietta. 'He is a kindly man, his hospitality quite lavish. Like me he was not brought up to be used to the finer things of life and consequently appreciates them the more.'

Henrietta's chin trembled at the implied rebuff and Analee thought she was about to burst into tears.

'My brother thinks very highly of Mr Rigg,' Emma said quickly, 'and of his business acumen in particular. He . . .'

But Analee was looking at the house where a tall, fair child stood in the doorway gazing at her. Without speaking or looking back, Analee walked slowly towards her and stopped in front of the child whose gaze remained unwavering. Then she dropped a curtsey.

'Do you remember me, Morella?' Analee bent down and lightly clasped her hands. 'You have not seen me for some time. What a big girl you have grown into.'

'Lady Falconer,' Morella said in a high, clear voice. 'Aunt Susan saw you from the window.'

She turned and behind her was Brent's mother, Susan Delamain, supporting herself on two sticks, a rictus of pain vying with the smile on her face. As Analee gazed over Morella's head at her, she knew that Susan knew everything. She dropped her head in acknowledgement.

'Mrs Delamain.'

'Lady Falconer, what a very pleasant surprise. I wanted to thank you . . .'

'Thank me! I thought you would censure me.'

'Oh no.' Susan hobbled slowly over to her and Analee could see the painful, swollen joints of the hands that clung to the sticks.

'What had to be had to be. Emma would have contrived somehow to get her own way; but since her last visit to you she is a different person. You have given her life and hope – how, I know not.'

Still holding Morella's hand, Analee turned to watch Emma walk slowly up the path chatting to Henrietta.

'She is beautiful again.'

'Yes, her looks have returned. It is as though the past nine years of bitterness had never been. I think she is reconciled to her lot. They call you the Enchantress, I believe. You have enchanted Emma.'

'Oh not I,' Analee said gently. 'I think she felt rested and, yes, peaceful by the side of our beautiful lake. Derwentwater never fails to weave its spell on those who seek its balm. Many a time I have journeyed there depressed and ill at ease and within a few days . . . How Morella has grown!'

Analee looked at the child, who was still staring at her, a grave, thoughtful look on her face. How like Brent she was. There was not a trace of her mother about her. She had Brent's blue eyes, Brent's blond hair, the firm Delamain mouth, slightly stubborn like Emma.

How foolish it was that no one knew the truth, Analee thought bitterly. How absurd to pretend . . . but no, what purpose would it serve? If the truth got out it would undo her marriage to the Falcon and cause only unhappiness and resentment among those she loved. Yes, she was sure Mrs Delamain knew; the look in her eyes still told her so. She knew, or she had guessed.

'I remember you very well, Lady Falconer,' Morella said clearly. 'I remember the last time you were here, and I remember you driving away with Emma, and Aunt Susan crying afterwards.'

'Oh, did you cry?' Analee looked compassionately at the frail woman in front of her. In years she was not old but she looked it; the skin over her face was like parchment and her large luminous eyes bright, as though with incipient fever.

'I knew Emma was going away and I did not know when I should see her again. But I trusted you, Lady Falconer. I have always trusted you,'

'Come and see my dolls,' Morella said, pulling Analee by the hand. 'And the doll's house Uncle George had built for me.'

Laughing, Analee allowed herself to be dragged along the corridor and pulled upstairs. When they got to Morella's room she

realized they were alone and no one had followed them. It was the
first time she had ever been alone with her daughter, her first-born,
in many ways her dearest child because the most deprived. Her
room was large and airy and overlooked the river that ran
alongside the castle, stretching all the way to Penrith. Analee
recalled passing by the side of that river when she set off with the
Driver family on the journey that was to change her life. She had
passed by this castle . . . it seemed like another age.

'What are you looking at, Lady Falconer?'

'The view, my darling. It is so pretty, is it not?'

'Why do you call me your "darling"?'

Analee felt a lump come into her throat and she leaned against
the window sill, willing the tears to go from her eyes.

'I think you are a very sweet little girl. You *are* a darling. Now,
show me your dolls.'

Beautifully dressed and kept, they sat on Morella's bed,
propped against the wall. There were fair dolls and dark dolls, rag
dolls and wooden dolls. And there was a sumptuously dressed
doll with long dark hair, the expression on its face familiar . . .
Morella picked it up and held it out.

'This is you, Lady Falconer. See how like you it is.' Analee
grasped the doll and stared at it. She felt a prickle run down her
spine and her heart began to pound with apprehension.

'This is an incredible likeness. See, this dress is even like one I
have. How came you by this?'

'Reyora gave it me. She is the gypsy who found me when I was
abandoned by my mother. She brought me here and left me with
Aunt Susan. I am an orphan, Lady Falconer, and but for Reyora I
would have died. She gave me the doll because I admired you
when you were here last. I said what a lovely lady you were . . .'
Morella sighed and pushed her flaxen hair away from her face. 'I
said I wished I had someone like you for a mother.'

'Oh, Morella!' Analee fell to her knees and clasped her daughter in her arms, pressing her close, feeling the vibrant warmth of
her young body. Her eyes were wet with tears which ran down her
cheeks and onto the blue basquin bodice of her elegant gown.

'Why are crying, Lady Falconer?' Morella pulled herself away
and stood gazing at Analee.

'Because you have a mother, I'm sure you have, and one who

loves you. One day perhaps you will find her and then be happy ever after, as in the story books.' Analee brushed the tears from eyes and stood up.

'I don't know how you can say that. I have no mother. She abandoned me. Why should she look for me now? I hate my mother for abandoning me, for leaving me to die before Reyora found me. I hate her, I hate her!'

'Oh you must not say that,' Analee seized her again and held her by the shoulders. 'What did Reyora tell you of your mother?'

'That she could not look after me. That she had to go away. She *said* she loved me very much. I do not believe it.'

'Oh she did love you! I am sure of that,'Analee said, her voice breaking. 'I feel it in my bones.'

'Are you really an enchantress?' Morella said shyly. 'Can you see into the future and the past?'

'No, I am not an enchantress but I have certain powers. I know you have a mother and that she loves you, and that one day you will know who she is and you will be happily reunited.' Analee knelt and kissed her face, hugging her close. 'I promise you that.'

'In the meantime will you pretend to be my mother?'

Analee laughed and got to her feet. 'You have very kind people here who look after you. Your Aunt Susan, Emma, Sir George and Lady Delamain. They love you and will look after you . . . until your own mother comes. Now we must go down.' She put the doll back on the bed and smoothed its clothes. 'There, Lady Falconer,' she admonished the doll in a grave voice. 'Be sure you look after Morella and see that she behaves.'

Downstairs there was the sound of a commotion, doors banging and dogs barking. They hurried to the window to see what was happening and there below, on the lawn in front of the house, they saw a man approach and Emma shyly waiting to greet him, while a groom held the man's horse and dogs yapped at his heels. In the background Sir George Delamain sat on his large roan watching, a smile on his face. Then he turned away and rode up to the castle.

The man quickened his step and, when he was near to Emma, held out his hands. His face was alight with happiness and something else: love. Hugo Fitzgerald.

Analee backed away from the window but remained in its shadow, too fascinated not to watch.

'What is it?' Morella said, tugging at her dress.

'Sshh,' Analee held a finger to her lips and smiled, her hand reassuringly on her daughter's shoulder. 'This is a moment when no other should be present.'

'But *who* is he?'

'He is a friend of Emma's. Mr Fitzgerald.'

'Why does he look so happy?'

'Because I think he likes her. See . . .'

'She likes him, too,' Morella said firmly, clasping the window sill. 'She looks very happy, too.'

After their greeting Hugo stood back and pointed the way along the path for Emma. Briefly his hand encircled her waist and lingered a moment. She seemed to merge into him and as they began to walk slowly towards the copse by the side of the river, Analee thought how well suited they were. The spell had worked.

'Come, let us go down and see Aunt Susan.' She clasped Morella's hand tightly. 'This is very exciting . . .'

'Will they get married?'

Analee laughed, raising her head. 'Oh, it is too soon to say. They might.'

Downstairs Susan Delamain sat in her accustomed chair by the fireside, though the fire was unlit and a large bowl of flowers stood in the grate. The windows were open and a shaft of sunlight fell on the polished boards of the floor. She smiled at Analee.

'Did you see?'

'Mr Fitzgerald.'

'She likes him very much.'

'Then I'm glad.'

'But he never seemed to want to see her. He showed no interest in her. She spoke of him a great deal. I wonder what changed his mind?'

'He would be a very lucky man,' Analee said, sitting opposite Mrs Delamain and holding Morella round the waist. 'She is too good for him.'

'Who is to say?' Susan clasped her stick with her swollen fingers. 'He is better than nobody. I do not like the thought of the empty years which stretch out for Emma unwed. An unmarried woman has no place in our society as I, a widow, know. I know too well the loneliness and *I* had my children to comfort me.' She smiled at Analee and nodded to Morella. 'She likes you very much, too.'

'I'm glad,' Analee said, meeting the gaze of Emma's mother. 'I love her. She is very precious to me.'

'I know,' Susan Delamain said. 'I know she is.'

3

'A toast,' Sir George said, getting to his feet and raising his glass. 'A toast to Emma and Hugo.'

Everyone stood up except the newly betrothed couple.

'To Emma and Hugo.'

Analee looked over the rim of her glass towards the happy pair. Emma was transformed by her happiness; even the simple dress she wore seemed to enhance her looks, her gleaming chestnut hair, her face no longer pallid but with a roseate glow as though she spent a lot of time in healthy outdoor pursuits. Hugo could hardly take his eyes off her and then, at that moment, he turned and met Analee's glance. His smile vanished and his face went ashen as though he had had a sudden sharp shock. Analee dropped her gaze, the toast was drunk, and everyone sat down; but when she glanced at him again Hugo was still staring at her and Emma had a puzzled expression on her face and seemed to look at him for reassurance.

'I never thought when I went to Whitehaven that I would return with a fiancé for Emma,' Sir George said with satisfaction, turning to Analee who sat on his right. 'He is fair smitten with her as you can tell. 'Twas only his modesty that made him decide not to speak before, a feeling of unworthiness. He has had to make his own way in the world.'

'I know that,' Analee said. 'And I hear he is doing it very well.'

'Oh very well. Rigg has it in mind to make him a partner and now, with this good marriage, it will make him all the more acceptable. I'm delighted, I must say. The Fitzgeralds are good solid supporters of the King and Emma is marrying into a family of staunch Hanoverians, not like those Allonbys. In them no good lies.' Sir George lowered his voice so that his mother would not hear. 'Hugo is far better anyway than that worthless Stewart although we do hear he is prospering in America. It is not that he doesn't work hard. It is his loyalties which are suspect. Once a rogue always a rogue.'

'I hope not,' Analee murmured, thinking what a rogue Hugo Fitzgerald had been – flirting with her, pretending to be loyal both to the Hanoverians and the Stuarts. She wondered if she had been right in bringing this marriage about. But Sir George obviously had no doubts about the man who was to be his brother-in-law, and indeed Hugo, with his open good looks, his dark curly hair and blue eyes was an attractive man. There was an air of integrity, of honesty about him that was quite deceptive. He had once declared himself in love with Analee ; she hoped that infatuation had passed.

Gradually she saw Hugo's colour return and for the rest of the meal he carefully avoided looking at her, all his attention being reserved for his fiancée until the women left the table while the two men concluded the dinner with brandy and cigars.

Analee took Susan Delamain's arm as she made her way painfully along the corridor to the drawing room. She was as light as a bird but Analee was aware of her weight as she leaned against her for support.

'Thank you,' she murmured, looking gratefully up at Analee as she put her into a chair. 'It is a great effort for me to move about as I used to. How happy I am to know that Emma is to be wed. It is such a weight off my mind, Lady Falconer. But I have another worry . . .'

She gazed at Analee, who drew up a chair and sat next to her. Henrietta and Emma had gone up to Henrietta's room to freshen themselves.

'Sometimes I feel I do not have long to live. If I die what will become of Morella?' She looked earnestly at Analee, who once again met the older woman's eyes. 'I had thought Emma would always take care of her,' Susan Delamain went on, 'thinking that she would not marry. But now what will happen?'

'I thought Lady Delamain spoke very fondly of Morella,' Analee said slowly. 'Very different from the last time I was here. I am certain that in the unfortunate event of your death Morella will be well taken care of.'

'Are you *quite* sure about that?' Susan leaned forward, lowering her voice even though there was no one else present.

'Quite sure,' Analee said. 'I will give you my word.'

'I know Morella means a lot to you. There is an affinity between you.'

Analee nodded without speaking and pressed the older woman's hands. Some things did not need putting into words.

Analee listened sharply in the dark. Something, some noise had awoken her. The windows were wide open because the night was hot and a bough of a tree beat against an open window. But it was not the sound of the tree. Analee was sure of that. She stirred uneasily in her bed and then sat up. Someone was in the room. Her heart slowly began to thud against her ribs.

'Who's there?' she said, wishing she had put the catch on the door. A sudden draught sprang up and she knew the passage of air between the door and the window had been disturbed.

She quickly got out of bed and reached for her robe. Then she stole silently around the bed so as to put it between her and the intruder. 'I will scream if you do not speak,' she said. 'In a trice all the servants will rush in.'

'Do not scream,' a voice whispered. 'I wish you no harm.'

'Hugo!' She groped on the bedside table and struck a tinder to light the candle. Her hands trembled and she felt them encompassed by two large ones.

'There is no need for light, my Analee. We can do what we have to just as well in the dark.'

'Hugo, you are mad!'

His arms encircled her and brought her down on the bed. His breath came heavily and he began to pluck at her nightgown. She started to struggle and gasped: 'I will scream unless you stop at once. Your whole life will be ruined, Hugo, if you rape me.'

'It is not rape, my Analee. It is love. I want you to love me, too. I think you once did.'

'That is utter nonsense. I never loved you – in fact I despised you. Your cunning and duplicity made you contemptible in my eyes.'

'That was a long time ago. I am no longer interested in politics. The Hanoverians are safely entrenched; but I am interested in you. I feel I will love you forever.'

'But you have just this very day proposed to another. You had the air of one wildly, nay, passionately in love. Have you taken leave of your senses?'

'I thought I was in love until I saw the quality of your glance. My

654

heart seemed to dissolve. I knew I loved the wrong woman, that I had made a mistake. The Enchantress was enchanting me again. I have a hopeless passion for you, Analee, and I am sure that once you feel the impress of my ardour you will be the same.' He pulled again at her robe, his hand groping for her breasts. Analee felt half stifled with the weight of his body on hers. He put a knee between her legs and tried to prise them apart. She gritted her teeth.

'If you violate me, Hugo Fitzgerald, you will not live to see Whitehaven again. Lord Falconer returns home tomorrow and will hear of this.'

'Ah, but will you tell him? Will you *dare* confess? Will not his rage be directed against you, too?'

'You do not care for your life?' Analee struggled as he roughly lifted her nightgown above her waist and began to fumble at her groin.

'I care only to know you. After that I think I have no more desire in the world.'

With a swift movement he threw himself upon her, attempting to straddle her. Analee took a deep breath and, making a superhuman effort, bit deeply into his wrist. She felt the blood gush over her bared bosom and, with a cry, Hugo lurched off her and fell onto the floor. Quickly she left the bed and ran to the door. But with her hand on the hasp she waited. No sound came from behind her except a stifled sob of pain. She knew she had nearly bared the flesh to the bone.

'Shall I call for help?' she said in a low voice.

'No, I beg you. I pray do not. I am unmanned.'

'You are lucky you were not properly unmanned,' Analee said, creeping over to the bed and groping once more for the tinder.

'I think you would, too,' Hugo groaned bitterly. 'You are a vixen.'

Analee struck the tinder and lit the candle. The scene before her was quite appalling. The bed was covered with blood and Hugo lay on the floor, the flesh hanging from his wrist where Analee's sharp teeth had bitten into it. He looked a pathetic, comical figure and Analee smiled with contempt as she looked about her for something to bind his wound.

'How we shall explain this I do not know,' she said. 'Luckily the explanation will be up to you because I depart at first light. The maid will think my woman's flow overtook me to soil the bed, though to be sure it looks like a carnage.'

She went to her valise and tore some strips from her clean underlinen which she soaked in a jug of cool water. Then she knelt by his side and began to staunch the blood.

'I did not know my own strength,' she murmured pitilessly. 'You were fortunate I did not sever the hand. I hope this will cool your ardour for good, Mr Fitzgerald, at least so far as I am concerned. You will never get the best of me. Never.' She pressed the loose flesh back into place and swiftly bound the wound. 'I hope it does not become infected for then you might die. I do not think, though, that my spittle is poisonous.'

'*You* are poisonous,' Hugo snarled. 'You are a viper.'

'Oh come, may not a woman defend herself?'

'I did not intend rape, you knew that.'

'I know that your approach was violent, sir, too violent for my liking. Your gestures were violent and you would have taken me against my will. You are a deceitful man, sir, and this deceit follows you through life. You pretended to love Emma Delamain, doubtless for base motives of your own. I do not envy her having you for a husband.'

'It is not true,' Hugo gasped, sitting upright and nursing his aching wrist. 'I was suddenly overcome by a passionate desire for her. I bethought me that it was time I wed and Emma seemed the most suitable, the most desirable person imaginable. I wanted none other . . . until I saw you gaze at me over your glass this evening, those bewitching eyes haunting me. They will haunt me until I die.'

The first rays of dawn were glowing through the trees and Analee decided to pack so that she could be ready to leave when it broke. She had made her farewells the evening before, saying that she would break her fast on the way, for she had no idea when the Falcon would arrive and she wanted to be there to greet him. She threw back the sheets and stared down at Hugo who, crestfallen, still sat on the floor, his nightgown awry, his face a mask of self-pity. Knowing about the spell, Analee suddenly felt sorry for him and also troubled that her own peculiar fascination for men, of which she was not unaware, was stronger than gypsy magic.

She folded her arms and stared down at Hugo, prodding him with a foot. 'You must be off now to your bed.'

Pathetically, Hugo held out his arm towards her. 'What shall I say about this?'

Analee shrugged. 'You must say what comes into your mind. You are an expert at deception, so something should occur to you. And then, dear sir, permit me to give you some advice. Contrive to be married *soon* to Emma Delamain and to make her as good a husband as she will make you a wife. Work hard and diligently and put your liking for deception, for intrigue, as far from you as you can. For it will only cause you trouble as it has already. Moreover, forget me and never mention my name again.'

Analee gave him a final little shove with her foot and he struggled to his feet, clasping his injured hand. Without a word he tottered over to the door and Analee opened it for him, standing silently to one side as he passed her without glancing at her again. She shut the door and carefully put the catch on it. Then she went over to the basin and, despite the chill of early morning, stripped and washed herself all over with cold water as though to expunge the memory of his attempts to defile her.

Analee lay in her husband's arms, aware of the gentle, satisfied rhythm of his body as he slept deeply after making love. She felt imprisoned in his grasp; a willing prisoner. Lying in their large bed at Furness, the afternoon sunlight glinting on the panelled wood-work of the walls, she was suddenly reminded with amusement and also revulsion of her encounter weeks before with Hugo Fitzgerald. What would the Falcon have said if word of that had ever come to his ears? Would he be lying as contentedly as he was now with a smile on his lips even in sleep, the relaxed fulfilled expression of a man who has had his senses gratified as often and as satisfactorily as he could ever have wished?

The Falcon stirred and the hand that lay loosely over her breast suddenly grasped it. When she looked round his large brown eyes were open, staring at her.

'What time is it?'

'The sun is high, my dearest. It is late afternoon.'

The Falcon sank back and stared at the ceiling fingers caressing Analee.

'What enjoyable weeks we have had, Analee,' he said, glancing

657

at her. 'Full of tenderness and love; but it is time soon to return to London. I hear the King is already asking after me.'

Analee tried to conceal a spasm of dismay.

'So soon, Angus?'

His lordship raised himself up on an elbow and looked at her with amusement.

'*Soon*? My darling, it is almost a whole month that I have been here in the north. Do you not realize that a man with my many commitments and duties has no right to such protracted leisure?'

'And do you want me to come with you?'

He stared down at her, frowning.

'Of course I want you to come with me! Are you not my *wife*? Do you not have duties towards me – duties besides these which you so obviously enjoy fulfilling?'

'But I have duties to the children too, Angus. The life for them up here is so good, so fresh and wholesome after London.'

'Then leave them here, my dear,' the Falcon said testily. 'They will be well looked after.'

'But I miss them, Angus. Besides they see so little of you . . .'

'My dear Analee,' the Falcon swung himself off the bed and sat on the side scratching his chest. 'I assure you that I hardly ever saw my father when I was small and, as you know, my mother was dead; but for all that I came to little harm. Is it not so, my dearest?'

Analee avoided his eyes. Much as she adored her husband, she considered him remiss as a father. He was not one to play with his children or to take overt pleasure in their company. At times he hardly seemed aware they were there and was frequently irked by them, especially Duncan. The sight of Duncan invariably drew a frown from the Falcon. Consequently the boy avoided him. Analee sighed and got out of bed on the opposite side.

'I am waiting for an answer, Analee.'

She turned to him, her expression unsmiling. But still she said nothing.

'I said, "but for all that I came to little harm." Does your silence mean you disagree?'

Analee got up and put on her robe, shivering slightly as she fastened it about her person.

'I wish you cared more for the children, Angus.'

'But I *do* care for them!'

He got up angrily and put on his own robe, a heavy velvet affair embroidered with gold thread. 'How can you say I do not care?'

'You take so little notice of them. You would leave them here for months at a time.'

'And what is wrong with that, pray? My dearest Analee, I know not about children who are brought up in gypsy camps; but those of the aristocracy are taught to be rarely seen and never heard. Above all, and at all times, to be subservient to their parents – an attitude that a good wife should heed *too*.' He looked at her severely and stalked through to his dressing room, banging the communicating door sharply behind him.

Analee sighed. Sometimes she felt she could scarcely talk to the Falcon about anything serious at all. Except in bed he regarded her with an air of amused toleration as though to emphasize the degree of difference in their stations in life. In many ways she knew that to him she was indeed a chattel – a beloved precious one, perhaps, and much valued – but nevertheless still a possession.

Duncan stood trembling in front of his father, his chin quivering, his hands behind his back. Yet despite his fear there was, withal, an attitude of defiance and Analee knew this was what so enraged the Falcon: that Duncan was unimpressed by his father's anger. He wore blue trousers, blue stockings and a white shirt, the sleeves rolled up to show his strong young brown arms. Analee could see the fingers latching and unlatching behind his back, the only sign that he was nervous. In front of him stood Lord Falconer, six feet six and a half inches tall, his black brows gathered in a knot in the centre of his forehead, his eyes glinting with rage.

'The fact, sir, that you disappeared for over an hour and no one knowing where you were *is* a matter of the gravest concern. You were disobedient and defiant and your behaviour deserves a good whipping.'

It was only a trifle – he was found almost before he was missed – but Analee knew that the Falcon enjoyed finding fault with Duncan for the least thing while the other children could get away with murder.

'You are not even sorry, are you, sir? I can see the light of defiance in your eyes.'

'I did not think it a very grave matter, father. I wanted to look at

659

the traps Nat had set in the wood. I could see the house the whole time.'

'Yet when Nat called you did not come. Being in charge of you he was beside himself with worry.'

'I did not hear him, sir.'

'I don't believe you, Master Duncan. You must know that any brigand can make off with you if you are found unattended. They could demand a large ransom to restore you to your family. They could kill or maim you, you the heir to the great estates of Falconer.'

The Falcon's voice was bitter. Analee knew that the Falcon never ceased to grieve that Duncan, his least favoured son, was his heir. As he unfastened the belt on his waist Duncan visibly began to tremble. It was not the first time his father had administered a thrashing.

'Take down your trousers, sir, and arrange yourself over that chair.' The Falcon pointed an imperious finger at a wooden chair near where Analee sat, and flexed the strap in his hands with every sign of enjoyment.

Analee suddenly remembered how he had physically abused her when they were first lovers and how he had once nearly killed her, suspecting her of infidelity. He was a cruel man who enjoyed cruelty for its own sake. He enjoyed inflicting suffering. She put out a hand and got to her feet, but Angus turned to her snarling.

'Pray be seated Analee! I want you to witness the chastisement of this young man, the apple of your eye.'

'I beg you, sir . . .' Tears came into Analee's eyes and she looked at Duncan, whose piteous glances at his mother were more than she could bear.

'Beg nothing, my dear. Now bend over, sir.'

Duncan falteringly tugged at the buttons of his breeches but the Falcon, livid with impatience, strode over towards him, reached out a great fist and tore the breeches, exposing his son's backside. Then he pushed him over the chair and raised the thick belt, bringing it crashing down on the small bare rump.

With every stroke Analee felt nausea; the savagery with which her husband applied the lash showed her how he enjoyed it. His lips were drawn back in a rictus of pleasure and his eyes gleamed. Every time the strap came crashing on his buttocks Duncan quivered, but uttered not a sound, his small hands tightly grasping the side of his chair until his knuckles were white.

Three, four, five ... with every stroke Analee inwardly implored him to stop and then she saw Duncan sag and droop over the chair. Her hands to her mouth, she ran across to her husband and struck him on his broad back.

'Stop, stop . . . you are killing him! Stop!'

The Falcon turned angrily round looking as though he would start to belabour his wife, a fine bead of froth showing at his mouth. He shoved her unceremoniously to one side and turned round to resume his task on the practically senseless boy, but Analee dived in front of him and stood protectively over Duncan.

'My lord, I forbid you to touch this child again. You must thrash me first. You said your aim was to protect him from brigands and kidnappers. Do you protect him from them only to kill him yourself?'

She turned round and clasped Duncan, who remained inert over the chair, tenderly drawing up his torn breeches over his raw buttocks. Then she wrapped her arms around him and gently rocked him in her arms. His head lolled to one side and his eyes flickered. She sat on the chair and drew him close to her, her eyes wet with tears. She stroked his brow and kissed him, hugging him all the time. She didn't look at her husband at all, but was aware of him strapping the belt again round his waist.

'Well, 'tis enough,' he mumbled, a shade sheepishly, Analee thought.

''Tis more than enough,' Analee said, gazing at him with contempt. 'You ought to be ashamed of yourself hitting a young child with such force. Your own son. 'Tis as though you wished him dead.'

The Falcon looked at her and she met his gaze. His face was puzzled.

''Tis true I do not love him and I know not why. My own son, my heir . . .'

'Sshh,' Analee cautioned him as Duncan began to move. 'It would not do for him to hear you. You had best leave us now and I will see to him.'

Lord Falconer gazed once more at the inert boy as though at a stranger then, with a sigh, put on his coat and walked swiftly out of the room.

Analee waited for a while crooning over her child and then, when he was sufficiently recovered to walk, she helped him up to his room and laid him gently on the bed. She bathed his tender backside with cold water, rubbing a sweet smelling balm into it, and then she dressed him in his nightshirt and put him face downwards on the bed.

'My father hates me,' he said, his eyes blinking rapidly with tears. Because she could not lie, she put a hand on his shoulder and stroked him gently, nuzzling him with her cheek.

'*I* love you very much. Your father is a fierce, impatient man.'

'I hate him.'

'You must not say that, Duncan! You must try and understand him. One day you will be the great Lord Falconer and you will honour his memory.'

'I never shall. He loves the others but he hates me. His face changes when he looks at me. I want to love him but I cannot because of the hate I feel coming from him for me.'

Analee marvelled that such wise words came from such a young head. He was scarcely out of his baby clothes, yet he expressed himself so well. Instead of a child of six he was more like one of eight or nine. His precocity was remarkable and this, too, was resented by the Falcon.

'I hope he goes away soon,' Duncan continued, beginning to sob onto the sheet, kneading it with his hands. 'I hope he never comes back.'

Analee straightened up and looked out of the window. In the distance she could see the snow-capped mountains at the end of Borrowdale. It was a rainy day and there was a chill in the air. Somehow it seemed expressive of the concern she felt about her husband's behaviour since they had had their tiff in the bedroom two days before. Since then he had been moody and talked increasingly of returning to London. She deeply regretted now bringing up her concern about the children. Perhaps in his heart it made him feel guilty and this violence towards Duncan was a way of releasing his spleen. Better she had not spoken than to have caused this outrage.

Gradually Duncan's breathing grew heavier and he fell into a deep regular sleep. She covered him with a light blanket and tiptoed softly from the room, leaving the door ajar in case he called.

The house was quiet, the smaller children taking a walk with Nelly and her two-week-old baby who had been born while Analee was still at Falcon's Keep. It was another boy, Dermot after her husband's father. Nelly would stay at Furness to look after the children while she and Angus returned to London alone to take their place at the Court.

There were once again rumours of war. The French were trying to undermine the English in India and America and the continent of Europe was buzzing with rumours. Some said that the French were again paying court to Bonnie Prince Charlie, to offer him support for a rising at home to occupy the English forces. Analee knew that Angus was immersed in politics, growing increasingly uneasy with the Pelham brothers, the Duke of Newcastle and his brother Henry, and plotting with William Pitt, whom he considered more capable of running the country. At one time there was talk of the Falcon going to command the English forces in India; but the King was anxious to keep him at home. He was one of the few men he trusted. Some said he would like the Falcon to succeed the Duke of Newcastle as Prime Minister.

Analee went along the corridor to the bedroom which she shared with her husband at the end of the house. It overlooked the lake and the mountains and, for most of the day, was filled with sunshine when there was any. But this was a grey, dull day and Analee pushed open the door feeling tired and in need of a rest. The sight of her husband using such violence against her small son had shocked her deeply.

The Falcon lay on the bed in the middle of the large room. He still had on his boots and his jacket, but his eyes were closed. Analee was about to go out quietly again when he opened his eyes.

'I have been waiting for you. I have a need of you.'

He smiled at her and lifted a leg as though to have her remove his boots. His eyes were lazy and amorous, a smile played on his lips. The thought that his violent action against her son had aroused his desire sickened her.

'I have things to do in the house,' she said and went to the door.

'Come here.'

Analee stopped, but did not look back. Then slowly she advanced towards the door again.

'I said, come here – wife.'

She put her hand on the door knob and glanced behind her. Her husband still lay on his back, his face turned towards her. The smile had been replaced by a cruel grimace. Analee felt sudden fear striking her heart and closed the door. Reluctantly she stepped back into the room.

'Has your violence aroused your desires, my lord?'

The Falcon leapt off the bed and, seizing her, threw her down on to it. He stood over her, his hands on his hips.

'Now listen here, woman. I'll tolerate no impudence from you, just as I do not care for disobedience from my son. I am the complete master of this house and I want you to know it.'

'I have no doubt of that, my lord,' Analee said fearfully, remembering only too clearly the occasion when he had violated her in Paris, half killing her. Although he had never been so violent since, she knew what he was capable of. There was some demon lurking at the back of his heart ready to disperse the gentle tender part of his nature, of which she had seen much in the past five years, surrendering to his frequent demands, gladly bearing him two children. She loved Angus Falconer because she had willed herself to do so, to forget the past; but the past was always there, like a threatening shadow. She knew it and she was afraid of him, love continually warring with apprehension and unease.

Analee looked up at him, her eyes pleading for tenderness. She felt if he despatched her love again it would not easily come back.

'Get undressed,' the Falcon said, and started to remove his breeches, turning his back on her. There was no tenderness, no dallying, no love play that made the act such a delight.

Obediently she sat up and began to unfasten her bodice. She took it off and put it neatly on a chair, then her skirt; she only wore simple clothes while at home in Furness. She turned round and saw that Angus was lying on the bed, as naked as she was. But he didn't look at her, his head was cradled on his hands and his eyes rested on the ceiling. She lay down beside him and gently encircled his body with her arms. She felt him tremble and suddenly without any endearments, he took her roughly and discharged himself after a few short thrusts like a stallion. Then he fell off her and, pulling the bedclothes over himself, was immediately asleep. He had not even kissed her, as though she were some harlot, some doxy to be taken and thrust aside. The tears ran down her face and she turned her back on him, weeping silently.

She lay there for an hour, not daring to leave; she heard voices as the children returned from their outing and the smell of food as the dinner was served. Someone knocked on their door, but when there was no answer they went away again. Finally the Falcon woke, yawned and sat up, his head tousled. He looked at her good-humouredly.

'I am very hungry. Send a servant up with some dinner for me.'

'Yes, Angus.'

Analee got obediently out of bed and quickly dressed. Her husband didn't even look at her, but had turned on his side again, his face resting on his outstretched palm, his eyes closed. She wanted to give the door a good bang to shatter his complacency, but she closed it gently – she would keep the rage locked in her heart because she could not hope to win against the power of the Falcon.

Downstairs there was a bustle of humour and activity. The older children sat at table, Nelly presiding at their head. She glanced up as Analee came into the room and her face clouded.

'Is all not well, my lady? Where is Duncan?'

'He is resting. His father gave him a hiding for getting lost. I have come to get food for his lordship who would dine in his room. He is out of humour today. I will take food up for Duncan, too.'

'And yourself, my lady? Will you not eat?' Nelly looked at her anxiously. 'You do not look at all well. Let me send food up for you.'

'No, I prefer to eat with you, as much as I can for I am not hungry. I will go and see Betty and arrange for his lordship's food to be sent up. I will prepare something nourishing for Duncan myself.'

Analee went into the kitchen and busied herself with instructions. Then she took some egg custard and sweet-meats for Duncan, arranged on a tray with a little posy of flowers. Once she would have done it for her lord; but not now. Not ever again maybe.

She did not go near his room all day and at night would have had a bed made up for herself in a spare room had she dared.

The Falcon rose at dusk and went to his study. He said he would dine there alone and he did. Two bottles of wine were sent in and some brandy. Analee dreaded the night and she went to bed early although this was no protection. To her surprise she fell asleep and when she awoke it was dawn and the place by her side was empty. In alarm she got up and, putting on her robe, went downstairs to his study. A candle gleamed under the door. With trepidation she knocked, leaning against it, her heart hammering.

'Come in.' The Falcon was sitting at his desk writing. He looked haggard and his eyes were bloodshot. A glass of brandy, untouched, stood by his side. He didn't look up as Analee came in. She stood behind him and said timidly, 'Is all well, my lord?'

'Aye, it is well.' He stopped writing and looked up at her.

'I am altering my will. I do not believe Duncan is my child. In law he is, so he will inherit my title. That I can do nothing about; but I will leave him as little property and money as I can.'

Analee's hand flew to her mouth.

'What are you saying, Angus? Has your rage made you insane?'

He turned in his chair and looked at her gravely.

'Analee, you have not been faithful to me. You know it and I know it. All the men ogle you and you are slave to their desires. McNeath told me you had bedded with Brent Delamain and I wager he is the father of Duncan; he was in Paris at the same time as us. I cannot trust you, Analee, and, because of that, I cannot love you.'

The Falcon's face was sad and Analee went up to him trying to take his hand, but he withdrew it from her and put it on the desk, grasping his glass of brandy with the other and taking a large draught.

'Angus, how can you speak thus to me? Your affair with my half-sister, Lady Constance Craven, was the scandal of London. You are known as a womanizer and kindly do not trouble to deny it. How can you talk to *me* of infidelity?'

The Falcon got up from his chair with an oath and seized her roughly by the arm.

'Don't you dare to speak to me like that, Analee. *I* am the master of the house, the master of your body and your soul. You depend on me for everything you have, everything you are. I gave you my name, my love, my children. Without me you would be a vagrant gypsy, a wanderer in the fields, a prey to any man. As it is you have flaunted your wealth, *my* wealth, and your looks to ensnare men. Do not think I don't see how they observe you, lust for you. I know you too well, your love of the amorous arts, to think you capable of resisting them.'

'My lord,' Analee said in a trembling voice, 'you do me grave injustice. It is true I am yours in body and soul and love only you. I have been faithful only to you. All your children truly *are* your children, the fruit of your lordship's seed. You should know the power of my love for you, for I have given you proof of it countless times. You enrage yourself unnecessarily with this irrational jealousy. How could I look at another man when I have you for a husband?'

Analee stared boldly at him, her expression submissive but also defiant. If she knew that she lied to the Falcon she had good reason to do so. As long as his suspicions remainded suspicions she was safe; but if he knew the truth he would kill her. He would kill her and throw her body in the lake and, being such a powerful lord, no one would put him on trial. They would remember she was a mere gypsy, even though the natural daughter of an earl, and forget all about her. Looking at him she realized that her old fear of him was returning again to displace the love and rapture of the past few weeks. With a man of such uncertain moods how could she ever feel secure? She thought of their loveless love-making earlier on – the Falcon had not treated her like that, like a common doxy, since the early days of their relationship when to him she was just a passing fancy, a woman he had picked up in a gypsy camp, never divining how passionately and hopelessly he would shortly fall in love with her. Was he now falling out of love? She remembered Paris and she remembered Lady Constance. It was only too easy to recall these bad bitter memories with someone as volatile and unpredictable as her husband.

The Falcon looked momentarily uncomfortable after Analee's speech and took another draught of brandy, his hand rifling through the papers on his desk. He had a night's growth of beard and looked unkempt.

'Well, that's as maybe,' he murmured. 'I have only your word for it. How is it that Duncan is so unlike me, so stubborn, so unruly?'

Analee gave a faint smile.

'If I may say so, my lord, those are two of your very attributes. Are you not a stubborn, passionate man who takes not kindly to discipline? Your son is very like you, in temperament and in looks.'

The Falcon stared at her but she did not falter; she met his gaze unflinchingly, staying the panic in her heart.

'I like him not; but I will reconsider disinheriting him. Maybe he will improve as he grows older. He needs a stern tutor to discipline him. I will separate him from his brother and sisters upon whom he is a bad influence and send him to Falcon's Keep with a man of iron discipline and good learning. I will teach the young puppy to conform.'

Angus grimaced with satisfaction and rubbed his jowl. He scratched his chin and looked at Analee .

'So, you *do* love me, eh? You had best prove it again. Get you upstairs and be ready to receive me.'

Time was when he would have taken her in his arms and tenderly embraced her, gently undressing her with words of endearment. Now he ordered her upstairs like a strumpet to fulfil his desires.

Well, if that was what he wanted, a strumpet she would be, not the wife of his bosom, the mother of his children, not a marchioness, but a common whore who prostituted herself for gain. And, in this case, what she wanted to gain was not jewels or finery or title, but her life and the welfare of her children. For these objectives, particularly the latter, she would do anything.

4

The Falcon was restless to be gone from Lakeland. Having made his decision about Duncan he lost no time putting it into practice; but sent him back to Falcon's Keep with McNeath who would look after him until a tutor arrived from London. Analee was only allowed a brief, tearful farewell of her eldest son. Fearful of showing her emotions in public, she took her intimate farewell of him in her bedroom where she hugged him and kissed him, promising him that she would always look after him, protect him from his father's ire.

'For Papa is essentially *good*, Duncan. What he is doing is for your welfare. You must always remember that.'

Duncan had rubbed his behind, still sore from his thrashing, and looked at her distrustfully.

'Why is he sending me away, Mama?'

'Because he wants you to be taught. We are going to London and he thinks you will be distracted there. It is for your own good. I will write to you every day, my darling, every day . . .' Tears came into Analee's eyes as she knelt and kissed him. She felt his little body stiffen and knew that he distrusted her, too. In his small world there was no one he really trusted.

'Ma'am, his lordship . . .'

McNeath advanced, his face wrinkled with compassion, and held out his blunt strong hand towards Duncan.

Analee brushed away her tears and pushed Duncan gently forward. 'There, my darling, go with good McNeath. He will look after you. . .'

Analee turned away and buried her face in her hands. She did not watch them go out, but lay on her bed sobbing, hearing the sound of the coach as it went slowly up the drive towards the road at the foot of Catbells.

There was a movement in the room and she drew herself up in the bed, thinking it was her husband. She wanted to show him a brave face, for Duncan's sake. She had begged him not to send their son away, but he had refused to listen to her. Once his mind was made up on anything, nothing deflected him from it.

Analee tried to keep up a show of good spirits for the sake of the children and the household; but her heart was heavy especially because, since his whipping of Duncan, an estrangement had grown up between her and her husband that affected the tenderness of their marriage bed. Every time he took her in his arms she recalled a man to whom violence was no stranger, one who had once beaten the daylights out of her and left her near death. One who would thrash the tender flesh of a young boy until it bled. When he reached for her she trembled involuntarily, only hoping that he would think it was desire.

Now she trembled as a hand was laid on her shoulder. But the gesture was tender and womanly and she grasped the slight, familiar hand. 'Nell.'

'Oh, Analee, what has become of his lordship? His behaviour is so strange of late. Even McNeath comments on it.'

Analee struggled up, smiling bravely at her old friend.

'His lordship is restless, Nell, anxious to be back in London. I think I have detained him too long. You know he is much older than I and does not get the same pleasure from young children. They irritate him. He is a man used to action and the bustle of cities and I fear the country bores him. He will soon recover his old form when we are back in London. Of that I am sure.'

Analee turned her head away so that Nelly would not observe her expression. But she realized she could not withhold the truth from someone who knew her so well.

'There *is* something wrong, Analee, isn't there?' Nelly spoke softly and sat on the bed beside her mistress with the familiarity of one accustomed to taking such liberties. Analee suddenly leaned over to Nelly and buried her face in her matronly bosom, for Nelly had gained weight since, as young women, they had scrambled over the fells together.

'Oh Nell, I am so unhappy. You know it, you have sensed it. His lordship and I had words one day last week and nothing has been the same since. I accused him of not being fond of his children and he resents it bitterly. Of *course* he is fond of them Nell . . .'

'Not so as you'd notice,' Nelly sniffed and patted Analee's back. 'Sometimes he hardly seems to know they are there. He never seeks them out and they all go in fear of him, especially Duncan. My goodness how he blenches when his father passes. Runs and hides he does . . .'

'But Nell, my husband is an important man. An *older* man; a lord, a Marquess. We do not really understand such folk, you and I. His lordship says that the aristocracy are bred to ignore their children. He was. For all I know, he may be right.'

'Well,' Nelly said firmly. 'It is not *my* way and it is not *your* way, whatever his lordship may say. I consider it very strange behaviour. His lordship is a moody man, that we know. But things are alright . . . between you, Analee?' Nelly searched her face anxiously.

'They are not as good as they were; but I am sure they will be alright again. It is a temporary phase. That is all.' Analee wiped her eyes and, straightening up, blew her nose vigorously, leaving it shiny and pink. 'We have enjoyed such rapture in each other's arms that I cannot believe we will not again. At times I fear him remembering what he can be, what he can do. Seeing him hit Duncan . . . affected me. I tremble a little now when he embraces me; but it will pass. When we return to London all will be well. The only thing that really grieves me is his attitude to Duncan, the fact that he cannot abide him. Did one of the others offend him as much he would not feel the same.'

'But it is singular that he dislikes Duncan, for his young lordship resembles him so.'

'That is exactly what I say, Nell! It is very strange, as if he divines the truth. Of course I strenuously deny it.'

'Oh of course! You *must*. If he knew the father was his arch enemy the . . .'

Analee put a hand to her lips and looked anxiously at the door. 'Do not say it, Nell. Do not say the name. If he were to hear he would kill us both. There, kind, good Nell; go down and bring me some broth to restore my spirits. I must keep myself strong for the sake of my children. I must conceal my feelings.'

Nelly reached into her pocket and produced a large white envelope. 'I bring you this. It came by special messenger.'

Analee took the envelope and, examining the writing, saw the small crest on the pocket 'Mr Rigg has a crest?' she smiled. 'He too, will be ennobled next.'

'It is from him?

'It is from Sarah. I know the writing.' Analee tore it open and quickly perused the contents. 'They want us to visit for the wedding of Emma and Hugo. Oh I think we should not go.'

'But why not?'

'In case, on seeing me, Mr Fitzgerald declines to go to the altar! I dare not. The sight of him makes my lord so jealous. I tell you what, Nell, I will invite the Riggs before we go. They can come with their children for the day and we will contrive a happy family party.' Analee glanced at her slyly, her accustomed good spirits returning. ''Twill be a change, will it not, to see my good lord in his unaccustomed role of a family man?'

The Rigg family not to be outshone by the might of the Falcon, travelled to his home in Lakeland in style with three carriages, four outriders, numerous servants and a nursemaid for each of the youngest of their six children. When Analee saw the long procession wend its way along the road and through the gate she stared at it at first in amazement and then with laughter, muffling her giggles as Nelly put the finishing touches to her simple toilet.

'Perhaps they have come to stay for a week.'

'They are only here for a few hours, Analee.'

'*En route* to Delamain Castle perhaps, but still a formidable retinue.'

Analee decided to put rings on her fingers after all or the Riggs might feel insulted. Then she glanced at her face in the mirror and patted her thick luxuriant hair before going quickly downstairs to join the Falcon who was already standing at the main door, his mouth agape. He turned as he heard Analee.

'You did not tell me they were stopping.'

'They are not, Angus. It is only a visit. I think it is done to impress.'

'The carriages cannot all fit into the drive.' Angus gestured to an equally dumbfounded servant and told him to go and stop the third carriage from trying to approach the door.

'They will have to walk,' Angus said bad-temperedly. 'What a carry-on.' He put his hands behind his back, thrust out his jaw and stared aggressively at the interlopers as though at an invading army.

And, indeed, the scene had aspects of an invasion as the grooms reined the horses, postillions hurried down from their perches, carriage doors were flung open and a variety of people, old and young, descended to the ground. The number of servants from the Rigg household outnumbered those from that of the Marquess of Falconer by about three to one, and they scuttled about all attired in a gorgeous livery of emerald green and yellow that Mr Rigg had had designed by a tailor in Carlisle who also worked for Lord Lowther.

But almost all, male and female, were outshone by the corpulent figure of Ambrose Rigg himself as he carefully descended the small ladder let down from the carriage, clutching the hands of two stalwart servants who stood on either side.

Mr Rigg had chosen to be clad in purple from head to foot, or rather from the neck where his coat began to his knees where his breeches ended. It was not a gentle nostalgic purple such as adorns the persons of bishops, judges and others prominent in society's hierarchy. It was the colour of rich gentian accentuated by the high gloss of the silk imported from the Indies. His waistcoat was of a pinkish purple, more the tones of a foxglove, and heavily decorated with purple braid woven in the silk mills of Macclesfield. His high starched cravat, of pure Brussels lace, frothed at his throat, and his stockings were of the sheerest white silk fashioned in Leicestershire. His black shoes were adorned with gleaming brass buckles and from the sleeve of his frilly shirt flopped a large white handkerchief stained with snuff. His full bottomed wig was slightly awry, due to the bumpiness of the journey over the hills from Cockermouth. His red face was puffy with lack of sleep, such had been his excitment at the prospect of a meeting at last, as an equal, with the great Lord Falconer towards whom he now advanced trying unsuccessfully to bend his solid body deferentially at the waist.

The Falcon regarded this apparition with all the amazement of a general on the field surprised by an unanticipated attack. His mouth hung open and he slowly descended the steps towards the paved courtyard.

"Tis Mr Rigg, my lord,' Analee whispered, scarcely able to suppress a smile, but doing so quickly as she saw the neat, though ample, figure of Mrs Rigg encased in sensible brown buckram follow a few paces behind her spouse. She in turn had a trail of small Riggs behind her though Henry, who was thirteen, was taller than his parents. Elia, eleven, and no beauty, had something of the imperious look of her Allonby ancestors. Norman, nine, and Caspar, seven, were both smaller editions of their father. Augusta, who had looks unlike any of the other Riggs, was four and Joanna Rigg, whose looks it was difficult as yet to ascribe, was the baby.

As Ambrose seized the hand of the Falcon, his expression of delight akin to apoplexy, his wife came to his side and the junior Riggs formed a straight and respectful line behind their parents as though waiting to be presented.

'My lord!' gushed Ambrose Rigg, wringing the noble hand. 'You have no idea what an honour it is for my humble family to be received by your lordship.'

Ambrose Rigg bent so low over the hand that Analee thought at any moment he would kiss it. She hastily came forward smiling, while the Falcon remained dumbfounded, content to let his hand be wrung until it pained him.

'How very pleasant to see you again, Mr Rigg, Mrs Rigg,' Analee turned to Sarah and embraced her on the cheek. 'And all your children – my goodness! How you've grown, Henry, and Norman, I hardly recognized you. But, my dear little Elia, you are bound to be a beauty . . .' Analee leaned and kissed her cheeks, pinching them with her fingers while the children all registered their various degrees of pleasure at having their names remembered by their distinguished hostess who had not seen them for three years.

'May I present my wife Mrs Rigg, sir?' As Ambrose pompously brought Sarah forward the Falcon recovered his composure and thankfully took the hand of Mrs Rigg, perfunctorily bending his head to kiss it.

'Ma'am, I congratulate you on your progeny.'

'Oh, thank you, Lord Falconer.' Sarah Rigg, whose home Furness Grange had once been, found her tongue and smiled gratefully at his lordship. The past was still too full of sad memories for Sarah to have looked forward to the visit with any sense of pleasurable anticipation. Even though she knew that Analee had vowed to restore the estate to any of the Allonbys who lawfully returned from exile, it pained her to think the ancestral Allonby home was in the hands of strangers.

His lordship righted himself and was about to escort Mrs Rigg into the house when his eye was caught by a movement from the second carriage and a young woman stepped from the door to the ground, daintily picking up her skirt as she came down the small set of steps placed for her. Rigg hurried over as fast as his fat legs could carry him and took the elbow of the young woman, leading her back to the reception party. Analee raised her eyes and looked enquiringly at Sarah; but, before she could reply, Ambrose said:

'May I present to your lordship and your ladyship Miss Anna Cameron, my sister-in-law, who has lately come from America?'

The Falcon opened his eyes wide in admiration, his demeanour immediately and subtly changed by the appearance of this young woman. Analee observed how he squared his shoulders so that he appeared to advance his height an inch or two and brushed some imaginary specks of dust from the front of his coat. Analee having seen many times the effect of female beauty, not the least her own, on his lordship, knew that the Falcon was impressed, as indeed she was herself.

For Anna Cameron was no raw-boned red-faced American from the backwoods, but a beauty, with red gold hair and large turquoise eyes which gleamed with youth and excitement and, maybe, a suspicion of belladonna which Italian ladies used to make their eyes shine. She was small in stature but exquisitely proportioned, like a miniature figurine of Meissen porcelain with a narrow waist, a high full bosom and the whitest sloping shoulders which were only partly covered by her dress of white gingham dotted with small red and blue spots. Her bonnet of the same material partly framed her face into an attractive oval and her red mouth was elegantly formed yet relaxed and friendly as her brother-in-law, clearly relishing his role, led her over to their hosts. Miss Cameron dropped a low curtsey and the Falcon, still preening himself, bowed and bent low to take her hand and help raise her up.

'Charmed to meet you, Miss Cameron.' The Falcon's hooded eyes gazed into hers and lingered for a long moment.

'I am so honoured to make your acquaintance, Lord Falconer,' Miss Cameron said, blushing only slightly as she turned and dropped a similar curtsey to Analee, 'and your ladyship.'

'How do you do, Miss Cameron. You are the sister of Stewart Allonby's wife?'

'Yes, Elizabeth is my sister! 'Twas she who kindly arranged that I should come to this country and stay with Mr and Mrs Rigg before proceeding to London.'

'Ah you are going to London?' The Falcon said with undisguised interest in his voice.

'Yes, sir. I am staying with friends of my father, Mr and Mrs Peto of Cavendish Square.'

'Peto? Peto?' His lordship screwed up his nose, gazing at the sky as though for enlightenment. 'I know them not, I fear. Peto, Peto. Let me see. Know you anyone by the name of Peto, my dear?'

'I assure you, sir, they are not in the least well known or distinguished,' Miss Cameron said with another faint blush. 'They are wealthy merchants who came recently to this country from America where they were near neighbours of ours. Mrs Peto very much missed her family.'

'Ah, merchants . . .' the Falcon said as though dismissing the idea from his mind. 'No, we would not know such people.'

Analee saw Sarah turn red at the remark and the pleasant smile vanished abruptly from the face of Miss Cameron, a young lady whose own family fortune was founded on trade.

Rigg, however, appeared unperturbed and gestured towards the house with his small, plump hand. 'This was the Allonby estate, my dear; in your brother-in-law's family for generations.'

'Aye and like to be restored someday,' Analee said, the expression of rage at her husband's disparaging remarks being quickly dispersed by her anxiety to make their guests feel at ease.

'Stuff,' the Falcon said uncompromisingly. 'I have no intention of restoring it. The Allonbys are traitorous folk who betrayed this country, saving yourself, ma'am, always saving yourself.' The Falcon made an exaggerated gesture towards Sarah, who however did not appear altogether mollified by it. Her lips were drawn together in a straight, disapproving line expressive of irritation and unease.

'They were not traitors, my lord, but had their own points of view,' Analee said firmly. 'Had the Stuarts been successful, it is your lordship who would now be languishing in exile with your estates maybe in the hands of the Allonby family. It was a matter of loyalties. The Stuarts, after all, were once the legal kings of England.'

676

'Mistaken loyalties if I may say, ma'am,' the Falcon said with a display of good humour as unaccustomed as it was unexpected, winking broadly at Miss Cameron who appeared discomforted by the exchange. 'You see my wife *will* argue with me, Miss Cameron. I hope they bring up women to be more respectful of their spouses where you come from.'

Miss Cameron laughed with relief, showing dainty even teeth. 'Oh no, I assure you, Lord Falconer, quite the contrary. The women of the new world are very spirited in their attitudes towards their menfolk. Not *all* of them of course.'

'Not *you* I hope,' Angus said flirtatiously, drawing nearer to her.

'I am not wed, Lord Falconer. I cannot say what I will do.' Miss Cameron smiled at him archly and Analee felt a tremor of irritation which she was careful not to show. She knew that, but for the presence of this nubile young woman, Lord Falconer would have pounced on her spirited remark with his customary bullying attitude.

'The women in America are certainly different from us,' Sarah Rigg said, taking the hand of her youngest son. 'They have a much harder life. They have to become accustomed to being as strong as the men. Some of the tales Anna has told us you would not believe, Lady Falconer. Women besieged by marauding Indians, having to endure deprivation and starvation for weeks on end.'

'Indeed it is not only the Indians who behave like savages,' Angus said gruffly. 'You should have seen what some of the fleeing Stuart troops did. Why, I recall the slaughter in a camp of gypsies . . .' The Falcon paused and looked at Analee, who blenched and put her hands to her face.

'Oh do not, Angus. Even to recall that scene to this day . . .'

'Ah, you see!' his lordship said with satisfaction. 'So much for the Stuarts.'

'I assure you my brother-in-law is not like that,' Anna Cameron said defensively. 'He is a perfect gentleman, the very model of what we always imagined a well brought-up Englishman to be. He is kind, considerate, just to the slaves, beloved by everyone, adored by his wife and children . . .'

'Ah, there are children?' Analee said eagerly.

'Oh yes, Lady Falconer, three already.'

'My goodness, such a large family!'

''Tis our tradition, ma'am,' Ambrose said pompously, looking smugly at his brood. 'The Allonbys breed well.'

'Come and take some refreshment,' Analee began ushering them into the house before Sarah could protest at her husband's vulgarity. 'Our children await the arrival of yours with great anticipation though they are mostly younger, I fear. Your elder children might perhaps like to take a boat on the lake after they have eaten?'

'Oh, capital!' Norman said. 'May we, father?'

'Of course, my boy,' Ambrose purred, rubbing his hands together, delighting in such intimacy with the aristocracy. 'Her ladyship is too kind. Too kind.'

In many ways it was a successful day even if not quite the scene of family conviviality that Analee had anticipated, for the Falcon made no attempt to conceal his admiration for Miss Cameron. He insisted on personally showing her the house, especially the older parts that had come from the ancient Abbey of Furness when the house was part of the monastery lands, and the gardens that had been so lovingly laid out by John and Stewart Allonby before their defeat in the Rebellion.

He paid such court to Miss Cameron that from time to time Analee perceived Sarah or Ambrose Rigg steal a quick glance to see how she was taking it; but she pretended indifference, or ignorance, and kept a relaxed smile upon her face which was not easy for her to maintain. Sarah had informed her that Anna was just twenty-two – the age the Falcon liked, though older than her half-sister who he had seduced five years before. Doubtless Miss Cameron was also a virgin, and doubtless much taken by the attentions of the powerful Falcon. Doubtless too she would be unable to resist his charms, if forced upon her.

'Miss Cameron must visit us in London,' the Falcon declared as the sun began to sink over the hills and the time for departure drew near. 'Must she not, my dear? You could introduce her at court.'

'I would be delighted, Angus,' Analee said sweetly. 'Nothing would give me more pleasure.'

'I am sure the Princess of Wales would be much taken by her – well-bred young women from the new world are a rarity at court.'

'Her Royal Highness is a widow,' Analee said to Anna. 'But she has recovered remarkably from her bereavement and brings up her young son, George, to succeed his grandfather. She is a woman of much spirit.'

'Oh, what you say is so exciting!' Anna clasped her hands together and gazed starry-eyed at Analee. 'I cannot believe my good fortune. Ambrose, Sarah do you hear – I might be presented to Her Royal Highness the Princess of Wales?'

'Aye, and to His Majesty himself, why not?' the Falcon said idly, taking snuff and passing the box to Ambrose who grovelled once again – he had done little else all day – with gratitude and took too large a pinch, making himself sneeze. His wife gazed at him with her usual disapproval, and averted her eyes from the spectacle of his bulbous red nose, brown with snuff, being encased in his already stained handkerchief. The Falcon, of course, would never be caught in any such gaffe, delicately taking just the right amount between his finger and thumb and positioning it at just the right angle in his nostril. 'I am well in with the court,' he continued, dusting his nose with his spotless handkerchief and ignoring the antics of Ambrose. 'His Majesty would, I am sure, be delighted to receive Miss Cameron. He is old, of course, and feeble, but still the King of England. And Lady Yarmouth too, Queen in everything but name . . .'

Analee glanced at her husband, whom she knew rumour said had received the formidable countess's favours. Lady Yarmouth was known to have a weakness for him and to be able to refuse him nothing – not even her bed. The thought of her husband copulating with the King's mistress was beyond Analee's comprehension; but at least it was only for gain, to be privy to the inner secrets of the court and Cabinet. There could not be a spark of physical attraction. She much preferred that to his sharing a bed with such as Anna Cameron who was far more likely to ensnare his passions and cause untold mischief to her and her family.

'When shall you be in London?' the Falcon said with deliberate vagueness. 'Soon?'

'She will not stop for the wedding.' Ambrose quickly took his fourth glass of port. 'It would not do for Emma to find her with us.'

'Ah,' his lordship nodded wisely. 'Emma of course having been rejected by Stewart?'

'Exactly,' Ambrose agreed sagaciously and put the delicate glass to his thick lips.

'So when is the wedding?'

'Next month. Young Hugo is very uxorious, eager to be wed. He is building a fine house on some land I gave him outside Whitehaven. It will not be ready of course, so they will lodge with us for a time. But if your lordship and your ladyship would be good enough to take young Anna here under your protection in London I know she will be in the seventh heaven.'

Analee had no doubt at all that she would. She was glad to see them go, but sorry to think that, all too soon, she would see Anna Cameron again. She thought of Reyora and her warning, and somehow Anna Cameron seemed like the harbinger of misfortune.

5

Prince Charles Edward Stuart put down his tumbler full of whisky and stretched his legs in front of him. Brent observed how his hand shook as he placed the glass carefully on the table by his side. The Prince's appearance shocked Brent even though he had heard how much he had deteriorated since his long, fruitless ten years of exile began. Yet there was still a kingly quality about him, the air of a man used to command. Brent remembered how much he had revered and loved him. He looked at him sadly and shook his head.

'But I assure you, Delamain, there *will* be war in Europe. The French are eager to use me for their own ends and I them for mine. I have not waited all this time in vain.'

Charles picked up his glass and, downing its contents, held it out imperiously towards Brent. 'Pray fill my glass. This is the best whisky from Scotland. I still have my contacts, my loyal followers, whatever you may have heard.'

Brent assumed an expression of innocence, but the Prince wagged a finger at him. 'I can see you do not think so. You have heard rumours of me, false malicious rumours. I assure you I have many loyal followers. What kind of life do you think I lead here, hounded from pillar to post? Even now my residence in Basle is under perpetual surveillance. I come here to Paris – to the house of my friend and banker Waters – skulking through the night. But, Delamain, I promise you this time we shall triumph. We shall . . .'

Brent shook his head again. 'I beg your Royal Highness not to deceive yourself. The Hanoverians are too well established in England. The King is secure on the throne . . .'

The Prince's face, once so lean and handsome, now heavy and dissipated, glowered. 'Do not all that impostor "King" in my presence, Delamain! You should know better. They call my father the Pretender! It is *he*, Prince George of Hanover, who pretends. Kindly hand me my glass.'

Brent hastily refilled the glass and handed it to Charles, who sipped the contents eagerly. All that Brent had heard about his heavy drinking, his dissipation was true. The Prince had aged in the last few years and his once splendid figure had thickened. 'I beg your pardon, your Royal Highness. I am asking you to face reality . . .'

'Do not talk to *me* of reality, Delamain!' The Prince thumped his knee and some of the liquid spilled from the glass on to his crumpled, faded suit. There was even a patch on the pocket. Brent recalled how immaculate his old leader had once looked even in war, how brilliant his court in Edinburgh before the tide turned against him. Bonnie Prince Charlie, how the ladies loved him. Even his wig looked as though it was never combed and fitted him badly. 'I know all about reality. I live in it constantly. It is you who are in dreamland. Know you that King Louis of France has in mind to marry me to his daughter, Madame Adelaide? That he is full of plans to restore my father to his throne, and that I am to lead a fresh invasion of England? Know you that, Delamain? I see you still look disbelieving.'

'It is hard to credit, sir, with our own forces so dispersed.'

'I assure you it is true,' Charles said petulantly. 'Louis will do all he can to provoke cousin George. I have sent for you to offer you a place at my side, as my right-hand man. You will come to live at Basle so as to receive my orders daily. I want you to carry messages between Switzerland and France, and France and England. The Princess of Wales is at the heart of the English efforts to have me restored. I want you to go to London and make the acquaintance of Mrs Catherine Walkinshaw who is housekeeper to the Princess.'

'I cannot go to London, sir, I fear for my life. I cannot set foot in England. Lord Falconer in particular desires to hound me . . .'

'Ah, Lord Falconer,' the Prince said thoughtfully, emptying his glass yet again and handing it once more to Brent. 'You know that Lady Falconer to whom you once introduced me is sympathetic to our cause? May she not be of help?'

Brent's heart leapt. To see Analee again he would risk his neck. 'I believe Lady Falconer is an intimate of the Princess of Wales. I might contrive . . . Mistress Walkinshaw, you say?'

'Aye, she is the sister of . . . well I suppose you know all about Clementina Walkinshaw, my common-law wife?'

Brent gazed at the ground. 'I did hear rumours, sir . . .'

'Oh come, man, all the world knows it and that we have a child. Mistress Catherine is the sister of my good lady and would do all in her power to help our cause. Yes, you get Lady Falconer, the Enchantress, to come to your help once again. And give her my respects should you see her.' The Prince smiled, as though at a pleasant memory, his face transformed.

Sister Mary Gertrude sat in the convent parlour, her hands tucked in the sleeves of her habit. The black nun's veil had finally obscured any traces of beauty and her face had the pallor of those who enclose themselves for a long time indoors. Her luminous eyes gazed at Brent and she thought over his words. Then she shook her head. 'I would have naught to do with him, Brent. So many good people have deserted him. Why, last year even the devoted Goring left him to go into service with the Prussians.'

'I know, that was a blow to the cause. The Prince treated Goring so badly. It is because he is so short of real friends that I feel I cannot fail him, Mary.'

Brent looked at his former wife and found it impossible to recall the days when he had loved her, been under the spell of her golden beauty many years ago in Lakeland. The nun's black habit had come between them forever. But it had made her a friend, a confidante he badly needed. He had come for her counsel.

'But, Brent,' she said in her soft convent voice, cultivated through years of speaking in whispers, 'I thought you had left the service of the Prince? Did you not go to America to seek your fortune there?'

'I found the country too rough,' Brent replied, beginning to pace restlessly up and down the convent parlour. He stopped in front of a statue of St Scholastica, the sister of St Benedict, founder of the order to which Mary now belonged. The gentle ageless plaster face, illuminated by the soft glow of candles, gazed down at him. 'I liked not the life. I prefer the ways I know in Europe. The new Americans are crude, thrusting people. They think of nothing but money. The work I didn't mind; but the way of life . . . no. They cannot rest without news of the mother country. They ape France and English fashions in ridiculous ways. They have houses modelled on our styles and their servants wear liveries and white gloves. But their use of slavery is quite abhorrent to me. Scarcely a labourer in the fields is a free man. Many of those who are not black slaves, imported in vile conditions from Africa, are indentured men, like Stewart was, sent over there for crimes committed in England. The way they treat their servants and slaves is appalling. They do not think of them as human beings.'

'You are too kind, Brent,' Mary said gently, remembering how passionately and for how long she had loved him, a love that had now been sublimated in that higher duty that she owed towards God. 'You have too gentle a nature. I would to God that it could be used to some higher purpose.'

'Of what kind?' Brent turned from perusing the countenance of the statue, clothed, like Mary, in its black Benedictine robes, and looked at her.

'Did you ever think of offering yourself to God, too? I have found such happiness within these walls, Brent.'

'As a priest?' Brent looked at her incredulously.

'Why not? Or a monk. It is a tradition in both our families, the Allonbys and the Delamains. Don't forget your brother Tom who as a priest also died for the Stuart cause in the Rebellion.'

'I am not like to forget,' Brent said grimly. 'But I have no calling, no vocation. I am not attracted to the life, Mary.'

'Are you sure?'

'Quite sure.'

Brent thought of Analee and his conviction that one day, one precious day, she would be his. As long as she was alive, married to the detested Falcon or not, he would remain in the world.

'Is it still Lady Falconer for whom you pine, Brent?' Mary spoke quietly, but the tone of her voice was sad. But for Analee she and Brent would still be married, maybe the parents of the children Mary had always longed for. Analee the Enchantress had unwittingly intervened and crushed their love.

'Of course I pine not for Lady Falconer,' Brent said gruffly. 'I have not seen her for years. I hear she has borne more children to that, that . . .'

Mary held up a soft white hand. 'I can see that you *are* still enamoured. You can hardly bring yourself to say his name – the Falcon.'

684

'Ah, say not that wretched name.' Brent snarled. 'How I hate the man.'

'Then it *is* Analee . . .'

'You know I can never forget her.'

Mary got to her feet and went over to him in the gliding, unhurried steps of the nun. She seemed to have diminished in size since she had taken the habit and she gazed up at him placing a hand on his arm, even though convent rules forbade any contact with a man. 'That is why I suggested you should become a priest. Your closeness to God will help to put her out of your mind. She has enchanted you, Brent, and only God can undo so powerful a spell.'

'You believe she has enchanted me? You believe in magic?' He gazed down at her in amazement. 'You, a woman of prayer, believe all that?'

'Of course. There is good magic and bad magic. Good magic comes from God – that is the spiritual side of our nature. Prayer is magical, its power and the transformation it can bring to our lives, I know.' Mary permitted herself a brief, bitter smile. 'Who knows better than I the power of prayer? The balm that it can bring to the soul in trouble?'

As Brent's expression changed to compassion – for he knew that she referred to her love for him – she let go of his arm and turned away, a bent, rather aged figure though she was scarcely thirty years old. Although her convent life had given her the repose she so earnestly sought, it had both aged her and made her ageless. She was no longer a young woman but she would never be a very old one. The regularity of the life, the healthiness of the routine, would give her that white unlined skin that also deprived her of her femininity, her sex. Her shorn hair was hidden forever under the veil, her smooth brow obscured by the white wimple which almost hid her eyebrows. She had been such a beauty. Blue eyes, golden hair, a fresh, healthy complexion . . . only the blue eyes remained and their rich colour, almost sapphire, was fading because of so many hours spent in the dark, eyelids tightly closed in prayer.

'Aye, I *am* still enamoured of Analee,' Brent said quietly. 'I'll confess it. I no longer think of her as much, but when I do it gives me pain, physical pain here in my heart.' Brent touched his chest.

'I wandered throughout America trying to forget her, but to come back to France . . . ah!' Brent took a deep breath and looked at he ceiling. 'It means that only the Channel lies between us.'

'The Channel *and* Lord Falconer!'

'Aye,' Brent lowered his eyes dejectedly as though the vision he had just witnessed had faded. 'Aye, Lord Falconer. Child of Satan if ever there was one.'

'Only prayer can defeat a son of Satan,' Mary said, sitting down again and placidly crossing her hands. She momentarily close her eyes as if in prayer'

'Then you must pray, Mary,' Brent said urgently. 'You must pray that he may be overcome.'

'I will pray that the will of God will be done,' Mary said, opening her eyes and gazing at him. 'What it may be I know not, but that it will be done.'

'Amen,' Brent said. 'In the meantime what am I to do, Mary? You who are nearest to me of all women, nearer even than my sister Emma. What shall I do with my life since I do not feel the call of God to be a priest?'

'I do not think you should ally yourself with the Prince,' Mary said firmly. 'Even in the convent away from the world we hear all kinds of things about him.'

'That he has a mistress?'

'Not only that but that he treats her badly. He abuses her and fights with her in public, oh yes, even in the streets of Paris. He is always drunk and abusive to his friends, who desert him in droves. He will not visit that pathetic old man his father who languishes for sight of him in Rome, or reply to the letters of his brother, Cardinal York. He is dissolute, intemperate, vicious, trusted by no one, deserted by his friends.'

'Yet I remember him as he was. Ten years ago what a different tale we had to tell. Full of hope.'

'Aye, but a decade has passed and one must be reasonable.'

'Charles II, the Prince's illustrious ancestor, was restored to the throne after a longer period wandering in the wilderness.'

'Yes, but England did not have a lawful popular king on the throne. Cromwell was dead. We have had over forty years of the Hanoverians. They are there to stay, Brent. The Stuarts will never be restored and I speak as a faithful servant of His Majesty King

James III in Rome. Were his son more like that saintly man then I would have more hope for the Cause. As it is I have none.'

'I will do one last thing for him,' Brent said. 'Not be his henchman in Basle, but I will do as he asks and go to England.'

'Where you may be apprehended and hanged. Remember it is not so long since poor old Archibald Cameron met his end.'

'I do not think they will hang any more. They are granting pardons, restitutions of estates. As you say, they are very secure. But, Mary, there is a storm brewing not only in Europe but in India and America between the French and English. It was very evident when I was in America, the hostility between the English and French who are building a line of forts from St Lawrence to Mississippi in an effort to divide the country. The Prince says that King Louis has offered him assistance to conquer England. He is very buoyant, very optimistic. And there still are traitors at Court. The Princess of Wales perpetuates the hostility traditional between the heir to the throne and the monarch and is said to nurture known Jacobites among her suite. One of them is no less than the sister of the Prince's mistress, Catherine Walkinshaw.'

'Oh, but she has been there for years, maybe twenty or more.'

'Aye, but she is still a spy. She regularly sends messages to the Prince. Her family were all staunch supporters of the Stuarts. The Prince would have me meet her and find out how lies the land, and to meet her I must first approach the Princess, and to get near her I must seek the help of the only woman who can bring it about . . .'

'Analee,' Mary said sadly, looking at him. 'The Marchioness of Falconer. That is the real reason you wish to go to England. I knew that sooner or later she would have a part to play.'

'Mary, can you not arrange it for me?' Brent said urgently, going over to her and lowering his voice. 'Arrange a meeting with Lady Falconer in one of your convents, say somewhere in the country, not too far from Dover.'

'You know we have no convents there, Brent. The nuns were sent packing after the revolution of 1688. But stay, I do have a thought. One of our nuns is from an aristocratic family in Kent who are deeply divided over the Rebellion. Half of them joined the Prince but the other half strongly supported King George.'

'Rather like our own family.'

'Aye. Well, the equivalent of Sir George Delamain is Lord

Goodacre who lives not far from Folkestone. His wife is a loyal supporter of our cause – all the women favoured the Prince and the men the Hanoverians. Her sister came to France to become a nun. I am sure Lady Goodacre will gladly receive the Marchioness of Falconer, if she is willing, and will make arrangements to disguise you. There, it is all I can do.'

Brent bent down to embrace her, such was his gratitude, but Mary abruptly turned her face away, her eyes closed, her lips silently working in prayer to keep her from temptation.

Although acquainted with the name Goodacre, Analee could not think why she had received a letter from her ladyship urging her to visit Kent. The missive had been delivered with a good deal of secrecy, the bearer of the letter begging to be allowed to give it personally into her ladyship's hands and then waiting downstairs for a reply.

'*I am acting for someone*,' the letter stated cryptically.

'*If your ladyship will be so good as to make the journey an Important Person will be forever in your debt.*'

The Prince! The Important Person could only be he. Analee got up from her desk and paced the floor in agitation. The Prince had sent for her again. She knew about the rumours of war – all London was full of them and the wealthy were sending their riches to the country. She had sworn to abjure him and love only her husband; but her husband had betrayed that love yet again. She rang the bell and the servant who had brought her the message appeared.

'Is the messenger from Lady Goodacre here?'

'Yes, my lady.'

'Ask him to come up. Is his lordship at home?'

'No, my lady.'

Analee nodded with satisfaction and stood at the window looking into the formal garden of Falconer House, until there was a timid knock at the door and a young man stood awkwardly on the threshold, his hat in his hands.

'It is so good of Lady Goodacre to invite me,' she said. 'Tell her that I will accept. It is today week is it not?'

'Her ladyship begs you will stay a night or two.'

'I am not quite sure, because I know not my husband's movements. He may make it impossible for me to accept.'

'I understand, my lady,' the servant bowed.

'But tell Lady Goodacre I will contrive it somehow. See, I will pen her a short note.' Analee sat at her escritoire and began to write rapidly, dipping her quill several times in the ink. Then she sanded the paper, sealed it in a crested envelope and gave it to the servant, together with a sovereign. 'All being well I shall see Lady Goodacre today week and stop a day or two.'

The servant bowed and withdrew, putting the sovereign safely in a deep pocket.

'Goodacre,' the Falcon said, looking suspiciously at Analee. 'How came you to know Lady Goodacre?'

'I met her at court, Angus.'

'But why should she want us to stay for no reason?'

Analee recoiled at the word 'us'. 'I think she is being hospitable. We liked each other.'

Angus yawned. 'Lord Goodacre is a profound bore. He can talk of nothing but his gun dogs. Well, you may go if you like, but I shan't.' Angus looked shrewdly at Analee, calculating that his chances of making a conquest of Miss Cameron in her absence were good. She had so far shown not the least inclination to respond to his amorous advances and seemed determined to remain in the good books of Lady Falconer, whom she appeared to admire. Well, he would see. Few women could resist his charms if he was determined.

'No, Angus, I feel my place is by your side,' Analee said without a hint of sarcasm.

Since her arrival in London the previous month, Analee had befriended Anna Cameron and to her surprise found that her company was invigorating and refreshing. Not only was she eager to learn, but her stories of life in Maryland were a source of endless interest to one who enjoyed travel and new experiences as Analee did. Although Miss Cameron could not have remained ignorant of the Falcon's interest in her she did nothing to respond to him by the slightest alteration in her behaviour. Analee supposed her indifferent to his advances, indeed shocked by them, as any well brought-up girl should be.

For her part however, she wished that Miss Cameron would soon return home so as to retain the purity of her state.

'Why no, I insist that you see your friend Lady Goodacre,' Angus said ingratiatingly. ''Twill do you good to visit the country again.'

'Oh, I am touched that you should think of me,' Analee replied unemotionally. 'I would not have thought that my comfort was your lordship's paramount concern of recent weeks.'

Angus looked sharply at her and raised a threatening finger, shaking it in front of her face. 'Now listen here, my dear Analee. I am a patient man, I trust, but I will not continue to endure these snide remarks on your part. How mean you that I have not had *your* comfort in mind?'

Analee gazed steadfastly at him, as she played with the emblem made of Falcon Gold which hung round her neck.

'I fear your lordship has grown indifferent towards me. Your embraces are not as tender as they used to be nor, alas, as frequent. Do I displease you, my lord? Your absences are both many and prolonged. If I have aught to say you do not appear to listen. Have you grown tired of me, sir? Is there perhaps another fortunate lady vying with me for your affections?'

The Falcon reddened and turned sharply on his heels as though wishing to avoid the omniscient, penetrating light in those fiery dark eyes.

'What you say is tosh, my good woman. Of course you do not displease me! But you must remember I am not as young as I was. Perhaps my vigour has diminished – though I hope not. I am a busy man with onerous demands made on my time from all quarters. This fact alone should be enough to explain my frequent absences from home. Alas, I cannot always take you with me because these are occasions of concern only to men, those of us who by our station in life are entrusted with the governance of the nation . . .'

'What you say is doubtless all very true, my lord,' Analee said evenly. 'However I cannot help hearing gossip – people delight in tittle-tittle you know – that would have you gracing *as a single man* the tables of many illustrious hostesses in London. Why is it that these ladies are privy to such august counsels and I am not?'

The Falcon stared moodily out of the window, still avoiding her gaze, his hands thrust behind his back in his customary attitude of defiance.

690

'Some things are hard to explain, my dear. There are certain women in London who are both well-born *and* well-educated. You alas, through no fault of your own, are neither. These matters we discuss would be quite beyond you.'

The flush on Analee's face grew deeper, suffusing her neck and the swell of her bosom. She clenched one of her hands and angrily kneaded it into the palm of the other.

'The rumours that get around, my lord, do not concern weighty matters discussed at the dinner table; but what happens *afterwards* . . . Besides *I* am the daughter of a lord, as well-born as your lordship, almost.'

The Falcon threw his head back and laughed cruelly. 'Nay, conceived in a haystack and born in a gutter, the daughter of a common gypsy. It was just St March's fanciful idea that you were his daughter. Maybe he wanted to get nearer to you for base ideas of his own. Eh? Has he tried to fondle you while pretending to have sired you? Eh? Eh?' The Falcon turned towards Analee, his handsome countenance spoiled by an ugly leer.

Analee was suddenly seized with such contempt for her husband that for all the world she would have picked up the iron poker that lay in the grate and hit it about his head. She felt the sweat spring to her brow and clenched and unclenched her fists. 'How can you talk so evilly, Lord Falconer? Surely the Devil himself is with you. You have made the land so fallow that he has embedded himself deep inside you. To entertain such a notion when you so welcomed the news, told me you had always known I was well-born . . .'

'Ah, that was different,' the Falcon said, continuing to smirk. 'I would say anything in those days, besotted with love of you, anything to please you. I thought it most unlikely the whole time, I must say. What proof does he have?'

'My mother's name was Morella. The circumstances were just as he said . . .'

'But *you* did not know that.'

'But I did. I knew one part of the story and he the rest.'

'You put the words in his mouth.'

'I did not.'

'The idea in his head.'

''Tis not true!' Analee's breathing quickened.

'Ah, yes. No doubt he had it in mind to lie with you. One day he would . . .'

'Stop, my lord! How can you be so base? You think I would lie with my own father?'

'I think you would do anything, Analee,' his lordship said loftily, taking his snuff box from the pocket of his vest. 'At heart you are a whore; the profligate way you have behaved with me has been disgusting. You flaunt and display yourself in a way one would not expect from a well-born woman. She would not have the instincts you have. That is how I know you are the daughter of common gypsy folk – aye, mother *and* father – and not a lord.'

'Because I enjoy the arts of love, sir, you wish to make me feel ashamed?' There were tears in Analee's eyes, but tears of rage, not regret.

'You have no modesty, Analee. No real lady would enjoy the carnal act so much. That is the prerogative of men, whose playthings women are. However roughly I launch myself upon you you are always ready to accommodate me, as though you enjoyed it.'

'So that I will not be hurt, sir! If I refused you, you would tear me apart as you once did. I have never forgotten that you nearly killed me.'

'You enjoyed even that, you slut. Rape in the gutter is really what you desire . . .'

The sting of Analee's hand across his face took the Falcon by suprise. He staggered momentarily and then put his hand to his cheek, staring at her. 'How *dare* you!' He raised his free hand as though to hit her.

'I will do it again though you tear me limb from limb. I am your wife, Lord Falconer, a peeress of the realm. Yes, you have given me your name and raised me to the peerage of England. As such I am known to the King, to the Princess of Wales, who has given me the privilege of treating me as a familiar. I am the mother of your children, lords and ladies all. Nothing can undo that even though you divorce me and put me in a convent, or confine me in a dungeon. Maybe you have one in Falcon's Keep in mind for me? Nothing can undo what you have done. I am your wife and as such I will not submit to your insults and abuse.'

'You have no rights . . .' The Falcon's hand still lay against his painful cheek, but he seemed to change his mind about striking her.

'Oh yes, I have.'

'You are subject to me, body and soul.'

'The law would not allow you to kill me; but I am not your concubine. I pity you, Lord Falconer, that you hold womenkind in such small regard. Maybe had your mother lived, had you known the gentleness of her love, you would not treat me, or women, thus. It is because I know how capable of tenderness and affection you are that I grieve to see you behave like an animal. Now you would make my son, Duncan, grow up like you, deprived of a mother's love. Send me away by all means, Angus; but let me be with Duncan. Let me give to him all the love that you will not permit me to give you.'

Angus took his hand away from his cheek and slumped in a chair, his long legs spread out before him. His head hung on his breast and he gave a deep sigh. 'You talk so well, Analee, that sometimes I feel you must be of noble birth. Yes, you have the temperament of a lady, but the morals of a whore.'

'I have never been ashamed of liking the amorous arts, sir, of knowing how to please your lordship in bed. As a woman I have had my full satisfaction, and the privilege of breeding your lordship's children. I know not why you have turned against me, nor what I have done. Whatever happens in my life, Angus, I will always treasure the memory of these past five years and the good times that preceded them, when we were first lovers, first wed, had our first child.

'You are a powerful man, easily bored. You seek perpetually for fresh entertainment, new things to do. It seems to me that you need another war, my lord, and no doubt you have taken your share of other women although I would that you would not seduce young Anna, much as you may wish to. She is a gently reared girl and 'twould ruin her for life; moreover she does not appear brazen, from what I have observed, as that hussy my half-sister, Lady Constance Craven, did.'

A sparkle came into the Falcon's tired eyes. 'What you say about Anna Cameron is rubbish, but about Lady Constance you are correct. Yes, she had your dispositions all right, your whorish inclinations. Maybe St March sired you after all. Constance

693

certainly delighted in being bedded by me. I hope she gives her husband such pleasure.'

'And I hope he approves if she does,' Analee said with asperity, 'seeing he is a grandee of Spain and you consider it unladylike to enjoy the pleasures of the bed.'

'Lucky man,' Angus sighed. 'Lady Constance Craven now a Spanish duchess. I think she will be stifled by the court of Spain. Maybe a little of the formality of it would suit you. Do you care to visit her?'

'No, thank you, I do not care to see Lady Constance again. I am of a jealous disposition, my lord, even of someone who no longer cares for me and affects to despise me. She caused me such suffering and heartache. I would not be a woman if I were not jealous.'

The Falcon laughed and rubbed his knee. 'There are things I still like about you, Analee. You have spirit. You . . .'

From the look in his eye Analee knew that the conversation had bred lewd thoughts in his mind. In a moment he would order her upstairs to perform the marital duty that he affected to despise her for. She felt such rebellion in her heart that she decided to refuse, whatever that would precipitate, when the door opened and a servant, bowing very low, said: 'Miss Anna Cameron begs your ladyship to receive her. She is waiting downstairs.'

'Oh, I had forgotten that she was coming,' Analee said with relief. 'The Princess of Wales has graciously asked us to take tea with her.'

'Ah, Leicester House again, eh?' the Falcon said, eyeing her suspiciously. 'You are still hob-nobbing with that old Jacobite crowd?'

'We never discuss politics, sir, Her Royal Highness is much more interested in the arts and related matters, as well as the welfare of her children and hopes for the marital happiness of the Prince of Wales. Pray show in Miss Cameron.' Analee concluded, turning to the footman who had announced her. As she said this she noticed the Falcon get up and start to preen himself with sly glances in the mirror, his hands on his cravat, straightening his wig. Then he turned with an eager expression to stare at the door.

Analee held out her hands to Anna in greeting as she came through the door, noting the freshness of her looks, the eager smile on her face. She wore an enchanting gown of patterned orange silk, with a round décolletage and a broad collar of chiffon edged with lace. On her head she had a close fitting cap of white muslin under a natural straw 'bergère' hat with a turned-up back. She responded to Analee's embrace with her usual warm affection and then curtsied without a trace of flirtatiousness to the Falcon.

'My lord.'

Angus took her hand and kissed it, bowing low. He held it in his for a second longer than necessary, gazing into her eyes. 'My dear Miss Cameron, you look exceptionally ravishing today. You are sure to find a beau in London who will throw all he has at your feet. I wager you have one already. Eh?'

'Lord Falconer, you are too kind,' Anna said unaffectedly, smiling at Analee. 'Indeed it was not my intention to find a husband over here, but to enjoy myself and that I am doing thanks to you and her ladyship.'

'But why not?' the Falcon said, reluctantly letting her hand fall. 'There are many young noblemen who would feel honoured to give you their name. Indeed were I younger and, of course, free, I would not hesitate.'

Miss Cameron's smile vanished and she looked at Analee with embarrassment. 'Your lordship is so kind; but the charms and accomplishments of Lady Falconer are the talk of London. I hear nothing but praise wherever I go.'

'Ah, but you have an advantage over Lady Falconer, my dear, and one she would not deny,' the Falcon said waggishly. 'You are educated. She never had any learning and you I understand, are familiar with the classics. Nor can she play a note, while I have heard you perform, to my considerable delight, on the pianoforte. Your voice also is divine. Whatever else Lady Falconer was when I married her she would not deny that she was singularly ill-accomplished. She could neither read nor write.'

A silence fell in the room and the colour of Analee's face heightened. 'It is true, my lord,' she acknowledged with a slight smile, 'that I was a common gypsy, as your lordship has not infrequently pointed out, when you did me the honour of giving me your name; but I believe that you were not displeased then, and that since that time I have done much to make up for my lack of education. It is true that I do not read Latin and Greek or speak

695

French like your lordship, but I can now read and write. I have mastered the household accounts. I am a good breeder of children and, I believe, not clumsy on the dance floor. I have made the best uses I could of what little nature has given me.'

'Oh, Lady Falconer, you have!' Miss Cameron said admiringly, turning away from the Falcon as if to indicate her displeasure. 'What would *I* not give for your beauty and accomplishments. *You* are the talk of London.'

'We must go,' Analee said, glancing at the clock on the mantelpiece. 'It would not do to keep the Princess of Wales waiting. She is yearning to hear about your adventures in America, and I believe the young princesses will be at her tea today.'

Miss Cameron clasped her hands with excitement and stared at Analee with delight. 'Oh, I can hardly believe it! What will my parents say when they hear this?'

'Ah, but what would they say if you were presented to the King?' Angus said, circling her and, like a stag scenting a doe, endeavouring to catch her eyes again.

'The King, my lord? Would Lady Falconer arrange it?'

'I can get someone *far* more important to arrange it,' the Falcon said dismissively. 'Lady Yarmouth *herself* is prepared to present you to the King.'

Analee looked sharply at Anna and then at her husband, her eyes smouldering. 'But I could present Miss Cameron, Angus, as I myself have been presented at court.'

'Oh, my dear, do not bother yourself. Besides I know you mean to go away for a few days. Take a week, as much as you like, with Lady Goodacre,' the Falcon waved a hand at her, as though desiring to spirit her away, while edging nearer to Anna. 'Take two. I assure you it will give Lady Yarmouth much pleasure to act in your absence. Much pleasure – almost as much as it will me.'

The expression of excitement in Miss Cameron's eyes turned to apprehension, but, as she tried to look for help to Analee, the huge frame of the Falcon came between her and his wife and all she perceived was the look of naked desire on his face.

6

The journey to Folkestone was accomplished at a leisurely pace in one of the Falcon's comfortable carriages with two postillions and an outrider. They took the Dover road, which was considered safer because it was busier and there was less chance of apprehension by highwaymen. Analee was familiar with the route until Dover because she had travelled on it so much when she and the Falcon went to France at the end of the previous war. It was, on the whole, a happy time and she sat back in her seat thinking on those days, surely never to be recaptured? She sighed and glanced at her maid, but she was asleep. How Analee missed the companionship of Nelly, who was at Furness looking after the children. She wished she could join them.

At Dover the carriage took the coast road through Folkestone to the ancient Cinque Port of Hythe, and then climbed a steep hill to the imposing castle that stood on its brow with a magnificent view of the Romney marshes. Indeed on a clear day the coast of France could easily be seen.

They had stopped at an inn near Canterbury over night, but still Analee was tired and glad of the glass of Madeira that her hostess offered her as soon as she had greeted her in the courtyard and taken her into the long drawing room.

'It is so kind of your ladyship to come,' Lady Goodacre said, fussing around Analee. 'As you can imagine it is an important mission.'

'I am intrigued, I must say,' Analee said, loosening her travelling cloak and sipping the wine. 'You took a risk, did you not?

Lady Goodacre looked at her proudly. 'I would do anything for the cause, Lady Falconer. I am of Scottish descent; Annabel McCleod was my maiden name, and our branch of the McCleod family has always been loyal to the Stuarts. Alas, the Goodacres have been the other way and during the Rebellion my husband and I were at loggerheads. Our immediate family are split, too, but of course time has done much to heal that. We have little doubt that the Hanoverians will remain on the throne – alas!' Annabel Goodacre wrung her hands, pacing up and down.

'You would still like the Stuarts to be restored?' Analee looked at her over the rim of her glass.

'Of course, Lady Falconer! They are the Lord's anointed, appointed by God, upholders of our Holy Catholic Faith. Of course I would like them to be restored. I pray for it daily. Do you not?'

Analee looked into the fire that had been lit against the September chill. 'I would like it above all things but, like you, I do not think it will happen.'

'And like mine, too, Lady Falconer, your husband is not only a committed Hanoverian but a general in the army of the King!'

'Aye, it is a difference that has often come between us,' Analee said sadly, gazing at her hostess. She was a pretty woman about ten years older than Analee, but her face seemed prematurely lined as though from the tension and suffering she had undergone, and her black hair was flecked with grey. 'We have not met before, Lady Goodacre, have we?

'No, Lady Falconer. My husband, though a good man in many ways, does not allow me to go to London, where he is sure I will scheme and plot with those that gather round the Princess of Wales at Leicester House. Of course I would not. I am so unimportant no one would listen to me. But my Stuart loyalty is unquestioned, and when my sister, who is a nun in France, made this request I was delighted and honoured to be of service.'

'Is he here?' Analee said breathlessly.

'Yes,' Lady Goodacre lowered her voice to a whisper. 'He is asleep. He came into Rye by the night tide and only went to sleep this morning. He is weary from his journey.'

'Oh, how I long to see him,' Analee looked yearningly out of the window. 'To think he is in this very house. No wonder you feel honoured.'

Lady Goodacre looked at Analee with a slight frown but continued, 'It is always an honour to serve the cause, Lady Falconer. Alas, how many of the Prince's previously loyal followers are defecting. Even Lady Primrose, an erstwhile friend of mine, talks against the Prince whom she formerly so admired. I often feel that he is like Our Lord, betrayed by those who once loved him the most.'

'And does he plan to see others here?'

'*He*?' Lady Goodacre looked at her with surprise, when the door slowly swung open and in its shadow stood a tall man gazing at Analee. She got to her feet and sank to her knees in a deep curtsey.

'Sire,' she said and held up her head as the figure by the door came into the room.

'Analee.'

Analee stared up at him, and a feeling of such faintness overcame her that even on her knees she swayed and would have fallen to the ground if Brent had not quickly knelt beside her and supported her under the arms.

'My Analee.' He rested his head against hers and clasped her gently to him. Analee heard the door shut and realized they were alone.

'Brent.' She could hardly utter his name. All her love for him came sweeping over her, flooding her heart and banishing the memories of past unhappiness. She leaned against him and her eyes misted with tears. She could feel the swift thud of his heart and knew that he felt the same. His lips brushed her face, his body against hers trembling.

'Analee, my Analee. Always my Analee whatever happens, whatever you say.'

He held her away from him and looked at her, smoothing her hair back from her brow. Then he kissed her wet eyelids, her cheeks and when his lips met hers he found them ready for him, merging with his, her passion as demanding as his own.

Finally they broke apart and, still panting, he sat beside her on the floor and took her hands between his, looking into her eyes. 'I hardly dared hope you would still feel the same. It has been five years.'

'I feel I love you more,' she said simply. 'We are never parted in spirit, Brent.'

'Never a day passes but I think of you, wherever I am, whatever I am doing – on the seas or in America or France, and last thing at night I always call your name to waft me on the tide of sleep.'

'I thought you were the Prince.'

'I realized that when I saw you curtsey.'

'Lady Goodacre said it was an Important Personage.'

'Am I not an Important Personage?'

'Oh you are, you are.' She touched his chest, her hand lingering over his heart. 'I hope we have not shocked her ladyship. She left the room right quickly I see.'

'I am sure she will be discreet. She is a good person.'

'I hope not too good to disapprove of us. Have you not noticed sometimes that the closer people are to God, the more distant and the more critical of their fellows they become?'

Brent laughed and, helping her up, led her to a sofa which looked on to the fine view of the marshes and the sea. A terrace ran along the front of the house and the door leading on to it was open so that they could see the golden-pink band of sun that settled beneath the western horizon.

'How long are you are here for, Brent?' She took his hand again. 'And what is your mission?'

'The Prince has asked me to be his right-hand man.'

Analee stared at him, not knowing whether to be sorry or glad. 'And will you?'

'No.' Brent shook his head. 'No. It is ten years since the Rebellion and I am weary of wandering, of being an outlaw. His cause is lost and everyone knows it but he. But because of the love I once had for him I agreed to come to England to try and see Mistress Walkinshaw, the sister of the Prince's mistress. But it is too dangerous for me to go to London. Even here I imperil Lady Goodacre by my presence. So I thought of you. You must see Mistress Walkinshaw for me.'

'Then it is true that Clementina is his mistress?'

'He lives with her. They have a daughter, Charlotte. They travel around like fugitives from justice and the Prince is reputed to treat her badly. Even by not marrying her he dishonours her. No one respects him for it, but he still hopes to wed a Daughter of France.'

'Poor woman,' Analee said sadly. 'Of course I know Catherine Walkinshaw. She has been in the household of Princess Augusta for many years. She is now her housekeeper.'

'You know her well then?'

'Yes, we are acquainted. I am one of the few the Princess allows into her private apartments.'

'And is she still a Jacobite?'

'We never talk of politics. We never have. The Princess is too aware of my relationship to the Falcon. She was very kind to me the other day when I introduced a young American friend to her, the sister-in-law of Stewart.'

'Anna Cameron!' Brent said with amazement.

'You know her?'

'Of course. I stayed with Stewart in Maryland and the Camerons gave a ball for me. Anna is a beautiful young girl.'

'It is a wonder you did not fall in love with her.' Analee looked at him slyly and his grasp on her hand tightened.

'Do not mock me. With your face etched in my mind how can I ever look at another? I will never marry unless it be to you.'

Analee lowered her head and brushed yet another tear from her eye. 'You know it can never be. Though the Falcon's feelings towards me have cooled yet again I still do not think he wishes to divorce me. Even if only to goad me he will keep me. He has already sent my eldest son Duncan away from me because I love him so much.'

'That swine has had made you terrible unhappy,' Brent said angrily. 'He treats you like a plaything. How you tolerate it I do not know.'

Analee looked at him, her eyes clear and untroubled. 'I loved him. I never hid that from you. He spoke to me with a strange magic . . .'

'Loved. You said *loved*!' Brent rose to his feet with an exclamation. 'Is it possible that you could be finally out of love with him?'

Analee gazed sombrely at his excited face.

'I cannot be certain, Brent. He arouses such a conflict of emotions within me. When I am away from him I see him in a different light from when we are together. Yet recently I nearly came to hate him as he taunted me in London about my birth and lack of education and indirectly accused my father of desiring carnal relations with me.'

'The man is a monster!'

'He is also jealous of me, as I am of him. He is much talked about in London for the attention he pays to women. Yet he denies this to me and says his powers are waning on account of his age. He is no longer as . . . attentive to me as he was.'

'Good! Would he could withdraw his cursed attentions altogether.'

'Maybe he will, but even then I cannot leave him. My children

701

are too important to me, Brent. And I cannot forget that for many years I have lived with the Falcon in the greatest harmony and bliss. For that at least I am grateful.'

'Do not speak to me of bliss,' Brent said ferociously. 'Even to imagine you in his arms makes me want to throw myself over that cliff.'

'You must accept it, Brent,' Analee said quietly. 'You know that I always loved the Falcon. I fell in love with him when I never thought to see you again, and in his love I was ready to remain until I died had he not mistreated me so. I told you I loved him but I also told you he was a hard man, a difficult man to know.'

'How *could* you after he nearly killed you in Paris, raping you and half strangling you? How *could* you?'

'Because I was nothing,' Analee said simply. 'Women have no rights in this world, as you know, Brent. I was his wife, his possession. I had nothing of my own, nowhere to go. And I loved my children though wealth meant nothing to me. It never has, of that I can assure you.'

'I believe you,' Brent said grudgingly, sitting by her side again. 'You are too honest and noble a woman to desire a person's wealth.'

Analee gazed at him and took his hand.

'You are my great love, Brent, because you are steadfast, honourable and true. But the Falcon is my passion. I can only ask your understanding and forgiveness, even if I do not deserve it.'

'You do deserve it, Analee.' Brent gazed tenderly into her eyes. 'Yet I do not believe that we did not have passion. We *did* and we could do again. I would do anything to have you, Analee. Anything.'

Analee looked into the eyes of the man who had loved her with such devotion for so long. How happy they would have been; of that she had no doubt. He would not have given her the fame and fortune of the Falcon, but of what use was that from a man whose passion so quickly turned to scorn? They would have lived abroad perhaps, in exile, but their love would never have wavered. How much had she sacrificed to become Marchioness of Falconer?

'Well, maybe my lord will one day put me aside in favour of a younger and more educated woman to preside at his table. He certainly has an eye for young Miss Cameron. He was *most* anxious to encourage my visit here. To get me out of the way, I suspect.'

'Oh, she turns many a head,' Brent said. 'She was much sought after when I was in Chesapeake, but not by me I assure you. Besides, I fancy she too would have an eye for a fortune but, even more, a title because her family has wealth. Titles are very popular with Americans who have foresworn them to live in their new country.'

'I like her,' Analee said firmly. 'She is an unaffected girl, spirited. The Princess of Wales was taken with her and I believe she is to be presented to His Majesty while I am here.'

'*You* will not present her to the King?'

'His lordship, my husband, thought the Countess of Yarmouth more suitable. I even understand there is to be a little supper given by her ladyship, with the King and my husband as the only male guests.'

'That dreadful old whore,' Brent said with disgust. 'That disgusting crab . . .'

'Tush, Brent,' Analee said with pretended indignation. 'You are talking of the mistress of the King.'

'Frau Wallmoden. That's what she was when he brought her here just to be his whore. Countess of Yarmouth indeed! What an ordeal for Anna, three old drones drivelling over her beauty.'

'You do not talk of my husband, I trust, as an "old drone"?' Analee looked at him wickedly.

'He is certainly twice her age, is he not?'

'He is,' Analee nodded. 'But he is a well-preserved man, certainly not an "old drone". Had he desired my love he would have retained it.'

'And has he lost it, Analee? I must know.' Brent sat beside her again, looking earnestly into her eyes. 'I *have* to know. Has he lost it forever?'

For a long while Analee looked out at the scene before them, then she got up and went to the door. A mist was rising from the marshes and the sun on the horizon had changed into a red ball of fire which would suddenly disappear, causing night to fall. She thought of Brent's dangerous journey over the marshes and shivered.

'I cannot be sure, Brent, that it has gone forever. He has

certainly tired of me as men do tire of women, whether temporarily or for good I know not. It is well known. He has had what he would of me, enjoyed my best years and perhaps he now would take another wife. He is not content with injuring my pride by parading his mistresses although in London he takes care not to do it in front of me. Knowing my temper he doubtless fears I would tear out their eyes, and he would not be wrong. I think he would marry someone more worthy of bearing his illustrious name – maybe a German princess or a member of the high English nobility. I doubt whether even Miss Anna Cameron, beauty as she is, would do, as he has no need of her money, and her family, besides being Jacobite, is not noble. No, he will toy with her and try and seduce her; but he will not wed her.'

'You think he really will divorce you?'

As Brent continued to look at her incredulously, Analee considered her reply.

'I am *not* sure about divorce. I have given him no grounds. I am a faithful wife, a good mother. Besides I too have my friends at court and my father, you know, is the Earl of St March, even though he lives most of the year in Spain. I am not a complete nobody as his lordship likes to pretend. He will have to take care. Very great care. Besides,' Analee turned her enchanting smile on him, 'I have my spells. I have not forgotten my old gypsy magic entirely.'

'I would wed you, Analee.'

'Alas,' Analee turned to him sadly, drawing him to her so that they both stood in the doorway of the terrace, arms around each other. 'It is not to be. You cannot return to England and I cannot leave my children. I would die if I were parted from them, and his lordship knows that full well. I would never sacrifice my children to my love, even to you, Brent. Even to you. Now you must tell me what it is I must do, for our hostess will think us rude if we do not go and see her.'

'I want you to talk to Mistress Walkinshaw and report to me. Ask her what is the extent of Jacobite support in London, who would rally to the Prince and so on. She will know everything. She will have all the facts at her fingertips.'

'And then?'

'You will send a letter through Lady Goodacre to her sister in the convent. Mary will give it me.'

'Ah, Mary,' Analee's eyes clouded. 'You see her?'

'I visit her in the convent.'

'And is she happy, Brent? Has she any regrets ?'

Brent swallowed and grasped Analee's hands. 'She has accepted the Will of God. She thinks He wanted her to be a nun and she has found peace. She says you were His instrument in this because her love for me was very powerful. God works in mysterious ways. She is like a sister to me, a close friend.'

'I am glad. And the Allonbys – John and his wife? Are they happy?'

'I think so. He pines for England and no longer believes in the cause. His wife is a Frenchwoman, Thérèse. She is a good Catholic and a good wife to John and mother to his children. They have three babies.'

'I'm glad. I have always said I will restore Furness to him if he is pardoned.'

'He says he will never seek a pardon. He will never live under the Hanoverians. He is content to spend the rest of his life in France, and Stewart is now an American. Furness is yours forever, Analee.'

'Unless the Falcon takes it away,' Analee said. 'Who knows where his wrath will lead him?'

Brent turned to her and enfolded his arms about her again. She remembered the moonlit night when they had first loved each other. How long ago it was. She longed to melt in his arms, to spend a night of love with him. Her loins ached for him. She looked up into his eyes. He was still her *gadjo*, more beloved now than before. He had lines now on his face that made him look older but also stronger, and his once gold-blond hair was ashen-coloured. But his deep blue eyes were still vivid and as she looked at them all she could see mirrored was herself, his eyes blazing with love for her.

'When must you go?' she whispered.

'Tonight.'

'Tonight? Oh, Brent, *not* tonight!'

'I came in on the tide and I'm going out on the tide. We can trust no one and I dare not linger here. Lord Goodacre's servants are loyal to him and might betray me. I wanted to take this risk just to see you again.'

'Then we must kiss and part,' Analee said, her heart heavy with grief. 'Until we meet again. When will that be?'

'We are never parted,' Brent said, pressing her to him. 'But one day we will be together forever. It is only a matter of time. The gypsy promised me. She promised.'

'I did not know I was assisting at a lover's tryst, Lady Falconer.' Annabel Goodacre said the next morning as Analee, heavy-eyed because of lack of sleep, sat facing her at breakfast. She had watched Brent by the light of the moon as his horse, escorted by one other, made its lonely way down the path from the castle and struck out across the misty marsh lands. She felt that with him went the only man who had ever really loved her not only for her body, as others did, but for herself. He would not toss her aside as the Falcon had done because he sought new pastures in which to take his pleasure. He would love her when she was old, no longer the object of women's envy and men's desire.

'You misunderstand, Lady Goodacre,' Analee said with dignity. 'It was no tryst. You must know I was expecting the Prince.'

'But when you saw Mr Delamain, you almost fell into a swoon.' Lady Goodacre sat upright in her chair as though she were reprimanding a recalcitrant child.

'Mr Delamain is a *very* old friend. All his family sacrificed themselves for the Cause. One brother was killed. He himself was sentenced to death and his cousin, Stewart, deported to America. The whole family was dispersed. Of course I swooned when I saw Mr Delamain. I thought he, too, was dead.'

'Oh.' Lady Goodacre primly wiped her mouth with a starched napkin and broke a piece of freshly baked bread. 'I am sorry if I misunderstood.'

'Indeed you did misunderstand,' Analee said with asperity. 'Though you can be forgiven in the circumstances. I did not come here to deceive my husband.'

Lady Goodacre, who had heard all the rumours about the amorous exploits of the Falcon, would not have been all that surprised if she had; but as a good Catholic she could not tolerate infidelity, however justified. Her face broke into a smile. 'Let us be friends, Lady Falconer. I assure you I have need of them, exiled as I am in this remote part of Kent. My husband and I have never really become reconciled because of our differences in the war. Of course I have been an obedient and docile wife and borne him children, but even they divide us. The girls are still all very partisan for Bonnie Prince Charlie, even little Amelia who is only seven.'

'Oh, I would *love* to see your children,' Analee said. 'I have heard them running about, but in this great house I could not find them. My own children are at our house on Derwentwater. I miss them every day.'

'You should bring them to visit,' Annabel Goodacre said. 'We should like nothing better.' She leaned over and said earnestly, 'I hope you will forgive what I said earlier, Lady Falconer. I am, you know, a pious woman, and I misunderstood what I saw. I believe a woman should be true to her husband whatever justification she may have to be otherwise. The marriage bond is for life, is it not? I know that Sister Mary Gertrude, my sister's companion in the religious life, and Mr Delamain were once wed; but even then he is not free to marry again, not in my eyes. God has joined them together and only God can put them asunder.'

Analee gave a delicate cough and finished her coffee, pushing the cup from her. 'I believe they were never joined in the physical sense, Lady Goodacre. The marriage was not consummated.'

'Oh!' Lady Goodacre looked embarrassed and found something very interesting to stare at on the floor. 'I am sorry. I did not know.'

'I feel we should not judge other people when we do not know their circumstances. Is it not so?' Analee gazed at her hostess, who looked past her to hide her confusion.

'I do agree, Lady Falconer. I seem to be doing everything wrong this morning. Oh I do hope you will stay a few days. I can't tell you how much having a friend here will cheer me up. Will you stay? Can you? *Please.*'

Analee thought of the misery of her life at their house in Piccadilly, her jealousy as the Falcon went about making amorous conquests. She was tired and felt rather ill. The bracing sea air would do her good. Besides, the Falcon did not want her back. He had told her.

'I would love to stop a few days, Lady Goodacre. But you must promise to call me Analee. Then we can really be friends.'

* * *

King George II was an old and feeble man and his passion for routine was as meticulous as ever whether he was at his palace in St James's, or his beloved home Herrenhausen in Hanover. The Falcon found court life stifling and the men around the King were as old and stuffy as His Majesty.

But it was obligatory to be seen a lot at the court. Especially now with the political uncertainty at home and the threat of trouble abroad. The Falcon was an intimate of William Pitt who had been in the government since 1754 and was known to be anxious to hold the reins of command tightly in his own hands. The Falcon could sense a greatness in Pitt that he had never seen in the Pelham brothers, but he feared that he was too unstable to govern the nation. He was excessively preoccupied with his health and was thought to have periods of madness when he did not move from his home.

The Falcon was restless. Part of what Analee had said was true. War and battles suited him. He was always at his happiest when chasing the enemies of the King. He was fond of feminine company to soothe him after hours of political discussions in the corridors of power at St James's or Hampton Court, and there were several beds in London where he was welcome so long as the husbands of the women in question were not in them too. It was a world of subterfuge and deception that he enjoyed – providing he was not cuckolded in turn, which was why he guarded Analee so jealously.

The supper given by Lady Yarmouth, ostensibly for him but really to present his new attachment Miss Cameron to the King, had been an outstanding success. She had looked ravishing in a gown of turquoise blue that matched the radiant colour of her eyes, and her flame gold hair was twisted around a velvet bandeau of the same colour, while she wore turquoises at her throat and on her wrists. The King was palpably charmed and seemed to recover some of his former zest for life.

The Falcon had collected Anna himself in his carriage, but had not deigned to enter the home of the Peto family in Cavendish Square in case they saw it as a sign of approval. He did not mix with trade. It was all he could do to stomach the dreadful family of Rigg, and that was only because there were family connections that he could not ignore, much as he deplored them.

After the supper the Falcon also took her back; but he did not touch her or do other than kiss her hand before his servant saw her into the house where the candles were still ablaze and the doors open in welcome. The Peto family had even put on a large supper in the hope that the Falcon would honour their home; but he did not. He knew how to play his cards, and women found men irresistible who did not pursue them too obviously – at first anyway.

The Falcon felt a commotion in his breast regarding Anna Cameron that he could not recall experiencing for many years. Maybe Lady Constance Craven had been the last one to move him thus, but she was only seventeen and he knew that, whatever her hopes, it could only ever be an affair. He had wanted to bed her, but not to take her as his wife. Besides, then, he was still in love with Analee. They called her the Enchantress and for long she had enchanted him. He never thought he would tire of her, but he had. He was of an age when he needed something big and important in his life. He was not of that mould of men who are made for a lifetime of selfless, mature love. He had not married until he was in his late thirties, and now he was only a few years off fifty. Who knew how many years were left to him to have one last passionate fling, especially with rumours of a new war in the offing?

The day after the King's supper he sent Miss Cameron roses and the day after that a brooch made of gold filigree surmounted by exquisite diamonds and rare pearls. The day after that he sent a note to ask her to another small supper given by a friend of his at his house in Mayfair. The friend, a major in the Falcon's regiment, and his wife had been well instructed and withdrew after supper was served to the amazement of Miss Cameron, who had found them good company.

'But we are alone!' she exclaimed, looking at the Falcon in surprise. The Falcon put a large hand over hers and pressed it.

''Twas what I intended.'

'You *planned* this, Lord Falconer?'

'Aye.' The Falcon gazed into her eyes and withdrew his hand. He knew exactly how to deal with women, even reluctant ones. He could never recall not making a conquest.

Miss Cameron looked flustered but reassured by his apparent calm. She had not known how to deal with the brooch, thinking it too rude to send it back. She was not altogether accustomed to the ways of the English aristocracy. So she hid it beneath her underlinen away from the prying eyes of Mrs Peto.

'Have some lobster,' Lord Falconer said. 'I hear it is excellent.' He poured a glass of fine white Burgundy wine, and gazed into her eyes again as he toasted her. 'To us,' he said.

She blushed and sipped at her glass. Then she raised her eyes and stared him in her frank American way, placing the glass by her side. 'I think I misunderstand you, Lord Falconer. I am *very* friendly with your wife.'

'Exactly,' Angus said with equanimity, gnawing at the claw of a lobster. 'I am looking after you while she is away. She asked me to.'

'Oh! Oh, pardon.' Miss Cameron smiled and relaxed visibly with relief. His lordship also smiled, but inwardly. She would be hard to get, but he would get her.

The next night he took her to the theatre, again in a crowd of friends so as to avoid scandal at being seen with her in public, and the night after he contrived for a handsome unattached equerry of his to escort her to a ball at court. Once there, the equerry pleaded the call of unexpected duty and hurried away and the Falcon, conveniently at hand, stepped into the breech. He took care not to dance every dance with her, but again he took her home.

'When will your wife be back, Lord Falconer?'

'Very soon, ' he said, kissing her hand, as she was helped down from the carriage. 'She will be so grateful to me for looking after you.'

The Falcon felt he was head over heels in love. The titillation had worked as much on him as he hoped it had on her. He passionately desired her. She obsessed his thoughts and he dreamt of her at night, seeing those deliciously sparkling eyes, that minx-like mouth, the surprisingly direct air, that taut virginal bosom so prominent and white in her low-cut evening gowns.

Analee wrote that she was enjoying herself and he sent a personal messenger to say he was immersed in affairs of state and she should stay as long as she liked. Not a day passed but he did not arrange to see Miss Cameron, and as yet he had not even kissed her lips. He was an ardent but patient wooer. He had arranged for her to be escorted to a ball given for the young Prince of Wales who would succeed his grandfather in the event of his death – which some thought would not be too long delayed. The ball was at Hampton Court and the Falcon, though restraining his impatience to bring her there, looked forward to the long drive back to the city when it was over. He would contrive to stop in order for her to admire some part of the river and there . . . His lordship shivered with expectation as he eagerly surveyed the couples who came in through the huge doors.

She was late. He cursed and looked at his watch, aware of the many flattering female glances that alighted on him. In his general's uniform, scarlet coat, buff breeches and black boots, he knew he looked particularly fine. Really he could have any woman he chose. He held himself up and squared his shoulders. Why, then, should he choose this snippet, this daughter of tradespeople from the new country? In every way she was unsuitable, but she enticed him. He was in love.

'Ah, Falconer,' an unfamiliar head bowed, and he glanced curiously at the newcomer. 'Edward Goodacre, Lord Falconer. We have met before.'

Angus surveyed him through his quizzing glass and smiled. 'Why, Lord Goodacre. What an unexpected pleasure to see you. I would have expected you to be in Kent entertaining my wife.'

'Alas,' Lord Goodacre said, accepting a glass of champagne from a passing servant, 'I have not had that pleasure. I seldom go to the country and my wife never comes to town.' He glanced at the Falcon as though expecting that, as a man of the world himself, he would understand this state of affairs.

'Your wife never comes to London?' The Falcon exclaimed with surprise.

'*Never*.' His lordship shook his head vigorously. 'Confidentially, Lord Falconer – I know I *can* tell you this in confidence – I never trusted my wife.'

'Ah?' The Falcon smiled understandingly. He felt he should take a look at Lady Goodacre if she was a person of the kind her husband seemed to be suggesting.

'Oh not in the way you imply, Lord Falconer,' Lord Goodacre said hurriedly, frowning with displeasure. 'The virtue of my wife is unquestioned. She is a devout member of the Roman Catholic Church, alas. Also, I am sorry to say, she is a convinced Jacobite.

That is why I never allow her to come to London. I do not want her to fall into any intrigues that may be still afoot – not that I think many are. God bless his royal Majesty.' Lord Goodacre raised his glass and turned towards that part of the room where the old King was making his arthritic way among a group of courtiers with Lady Yarmouth on one side and George, Prince of Wales, on the other.

The Falcon meanwhile gazed, thunderstruck, at Lord Goodacre. 'Your wife is a *Jacobite*?'

'Aye, I am sorry to say, Lord Falconer. I can assure you that my own sympathies never . . .'

'Oh I know that, I know that,' the Falcon said impatiently with a dismissive flourish of his hand. 'I know quite well you are a loyal subject, etcetera, Goodacre. Alas, in quite a few families, my own as well I regret to say, there are these divisions of loyalty. However, what intrigues me is, if your lady never comes to London – *never* you say . . .'

'Oh never, never, Lord Falconer. I have not allowed it since the Rebellion. She has come no further north than Maidstone and only visited *there* once.'

'Then,' said Lord Falconer, lowering his voice menacingly, 'how comes she to be so well acquainted with Lady Falconer?'

'Ah!' Lord Goodacre put down his glass and scratched the side of his wig. 'That's a point.'

'My wife mentioned she was particularly friendly with Lady Goodacre.'

'Yes, my wife told me the same.'

'Then how did they meet? Lady Falconer has never travelled in Kent that I know except to go to France, and always with me. I have never met your lady wife, to my regret,' the Falcon added insincerely.

'That is very strange, Lord Falconer. Your wife is not Scots by any chance? Mine comes of a branch of the McCleods.'

'She is certainly not Scots,' Lord Falconer said with exasperation, his opinion of Lord Goodacre's acumen sinking fast.

'I did not think she was. Then it cannot be that, that they knew each other as girls for instance.' Lord Goodacre trailed off helplessly.

'*I* think they have never met,' Angus said, his suspicions

growing to enormous proportions. 'I am beginning to suspect some dreadful plot is being hatched in the quiet countryside of Kent.'

'Oh, my goodness gracious!' Lord Goodacre exclaimed nervously. 'My wife would never lend herself . . .'

'It is what *my* wife would do that worries me,' Angus said. 'You do not know Lady Falconer.'

7

Although she trembled inwardly, Analee gazed at her husband with composure, her head proudly raised, her hands neatly folded and relaxed in her lap. She had never once avoided the Falcon's eyes all during their long and painful interview, for she knew that would be her undoing. She still wore her travelling dress, having been summarily sent for from Kent and escorted by a lieutenant of the Falcon's troop. She felt like a prisoner being led to her doom.

The Falcon had started politely enough, the cat teasing the mouse, enquiring as to how she had enjoyed herself, the state of the weather in Kent and so on. At first she thought he knew about Brent's visit, that somehow his spies had discovered even that fact; but then she realized it was her relationship with Lady Goodacre which interested him. How came she to know her? The reason for the sudden visit? Analee thought very rapidly, as she had all during the long journey to London, what explanations she could give, trying to anticipate his questions. In some things she had been right; but in how she came to know Lady Goodacre, seeing that worthy woman was known not to be allowed to visit London . . . She wrestled inside herself for an explanation, seeking desperately for a solution.

'You had never been to that part of Kent, Analee, had you?'

'No, my lord.'

'Not even when you were a wandering gypsy?'

'That was in the West Country, sir, before we came north.'

'Then my question remains to be answered, Analee. How *came* you to know Lady Goodacre, that she could address you in terms of such intimacy? You lied to me didn't you?'

Analee met his gaze unflinchingly: 'I told you a white lie, sir, because of your hostility to Jacobites. I am acquainted with Lady Goodacre through the Allonbys, sir. She is a friend of that family of many years standing. Despite my devotion to the Hanoverian cause, and loyalty to his Majesty King George, sir, I do retain friendship for those who were so good to me; you know that.

They once saved me from cold and starvation and, indirectly, led to my reacquaintance with your lordship – though whether the memory of that pleases you now or not I am not bold enough to say.'

Analee lowered her head but her eyes were glinting in a manner very far from humility. She still did not know what this was leading to – whether he knew about Brent. If he did she might as well go to her room and take poison; he would never forgive her. She rather felt though that if he knew about Brent he would have been more violent; this was more in the manner of an interrogator bent on discovering the truth. He might well come to the use of the rack, but not yet.

'Ah, the Allonbys,' the Falcon said, straightening himself and leaning an elegant elbow against the mantelpiece. 'There *is* a Jacobite connection. I thought so. Lord Goodacre hinted as much when he told me the reason he refused to let his wife visit London. I have *unmasked* you, Analee!'

'Not at all, my lord.' Analee raised her head again, meeting his gaze. 'Your lordship is wrong to insinuate a political motive in this meeting of two poor women. After all what power have such as we, Lady Goodacre and myself, compared to the might of men? Lady Goodacre has never had any political dealings, being a loyal wife and devoted mother. Her family, it is true, supported the Stuarts, but how many others did the same? Is loyalty a sin, sir?'

'Yes it is, in some cases,' the Falcon snapped.

'Well I beg to differ. I think you would value it highly, my lord, if you were on the defeated side. Supposing the Stuarts had won – would you have deserted the cause of Hanover? No, my lord, I know you too well. You would not.' Analee took a deep breath and crossed her fingers before she went on. ''Twas Miss Cameron who brought me news of Lady Goodacre, through Stewart Allonby. His sister Mary was her friend and I wished for news of Mary.'

'Ah, I see. It was Miss Cameron, was it? Is *she* come among us as a Jacobite spy?' The Falcon's pulse quickened. Had that vixen . . . but no, if she had wanted to spy on him she would have been nicer to him, she would have responded to his overtures. After all, she was not a young girl, but a woman of twenty-two years. He had had a very hard time with her in the carriage after

715

the ball at Hampton Court. She had threatened to leave the coach and find her own way home if he did not order his driver to recommence the journey. She had looked as though she meant it. He had felt very disgruntled and full of chagrin. But it only whetted his desire. He wanted her more than ever. What a chance, now, to see her again.

'Of course not, Angus,' Analee said impatiently. 'She has no connection at all with the Jacobites.'

'And why should *you* want to know about Mary Allonby? To find out where the scallywag of a husband is, is that it? Eh? Eh?'

'Why should I wish to know where he is, sir?' Analee said trying to keep the relief out of her voice. So the Falcon did not know. Inwardly she thanked God. 'I am married to you, a faithful wife, the mother of your . . .'

'Oh yes, yes I know the mother of my children, all that sort of twaddle,' the Falcon interrupted her rudely, waving his hands. 'I have heard it all before.'

'It is true. I have not seen Brent Delamain for years. It is said he is in America, so Lady Goodacre thought.' Analee decided that it might be judicious to put two thousand miles between herself and Brent and then she regretted it. Anna Cameron! The Falcon would question her! She began to be afraid of the web that, subtly, was being woven round her – a web of lies and deceit, partly fabricated by herself. The Falcon, like a great spider, sat in the middle.

'I think I will question Miss Cameron,' the Falcon said in silky tones. 'I will summon her here before you have time to see her privately and fill her with your lies. *I* will observe her reaction for myself. I think she is still in London.'

'Do you not *know*, my lord?' Analee said with heavy sarcasm. 'Surely she has been under your protection?'

'I have scarcely seen the girl,' the Falcon said tersely, 'except at court of course. She seems well enough taken care of by the younger generation. I said I would introduce her at court and I have done my duty. 'Tis all.'

He turned away abruptly, whether to disguise his confusion or not Analee was unable to tell, and pulled the bellrope. He ordered a servant to go directly and fetch Miss Cameron from Cavendish Square and take no excuses, and then he abruptly left the room.

There was nothing she could do. Analee went upstairs to her bedroom and slowly changed from her travelling clothes; then she lay on her bed for a few minutes feeling utterly dejected. They had travelled all the way from the castle without stopping and she was exhausted; she was also frightened and unsure of herself. For once she was in the wrong; her husband was right to be suspicous, he had every cause. She only felt really secure when she knew she was not to blame. Now she was not only lying but endangering those she would give her life to protect. Well, if necessary she must give her life; it would be worth little, anyway, if he found out. Then she thought of her children, and her eyes brimmed over with tears.

It seemed a very short time before a servant knocked on her door and announced the arrival of Miss Cameron.

As a contrast to the previous encounter with her husband, now he was all smiles. He, too, had changed into a royal blue *justaucorps*, a coat that hung loosely fom the chest, the long skirts stiffened with buckram. Under this he wore a long sleeveless waistcoat of oyster-coloured silk with matching breeches fastened at the knee and round-toed black leather shoes fitted with metal buckles. Around his stock he wore the solitaire, a black ribbon tied into a bow under the chin, which was considered extremely smart. His wig was short, its queue tied with a black ribbon. He seemed to have made every effort to look like a young blade without appearing ridiculous; and he had succeeded. She thought he must have spent all the time since they parted grooming himself for the occasion. In a way it amused her as she stood by his side ready to receive Anna Cameron.

Miss Cameron, when announced, sped into Analee's arms and kissed her. 'Oh, Lady Falconer, I have missed you so much! Did you enjoy your visit?'

Analee returned her embrace and then kept her hands on her shoulders while she studied her face. She had to be careful not to try and convey any message either with her eyes or by pressure from her hands. The Falcon would be observing her closely. She merely *willed* Anna to be receptive to her gypsy vibrations, those mysterious messages she was able to send by almost magical means.

'I have missed you, too. I hope his lordship took care of you?'

'His lordship was very kind,' Anna said guardedly and Analee

717

was aware of the shifty, guilty look she gave the Falcon. Her heart sank.

'We scarcely met at all,' the Falcon said airily. 'I told you I was busy with affairs of state. But I saw to it that Miss Cameron was well looked after.'

Anna glanced at him again and Analee saw a faint blush steal up her cheeks. If the Falcon had offended her maidenly susceptibilities there was hope. She doubted if this well-controlled miss from the new world would be as ready to yield the priceless jewel of her virtue as her wanton sister Constance had years before.

'And what is the reason for you sending for me?' Anna said disarmingly, accepting the chair the Falcon held out for her. She gave Analee that frank open smile that seemed incapable of deception.

'I wish to bring you Lady Goodacre's greetings.' Analee willed in her heart for Anna to understand. Miss Cameron however gazed at her with some surprise.

'I understand you are acquainted with Lady Goodacre,' the Falcon's tone of voice changed so as to sound slightly menacing.

For an instant Anna looked from him to Analee and then, her own expression unchanged, she said brightly, 'Why yes, but only indirectly.'

Analee felt that, for a girl of twenty-two, she was of a marvellously perceptive and diplomatic disposition. Her gypsy spells had undoubtedly helped. Anna was saying things without really knowing why. Analee knew she had her in her power. She intervened quickly.

'I was saying to his lordship that I sought news of Mary and John Allonby, and that, through Stewart, you directed me to Lady Goodacre whose sister is a nun in the same convent as Mary.'

The Falcon looked annoyed and tried to interrupt, but Miss Cameron said with great naturalness and ease, 'Yes. Stewart was very anxious to have news of his brother and sister. He wants me to visit them when I go to France. I shall hope to stay with Lady Goodacre on the way.' She smiled with the greatest naturalness at Analee who thought that she would never know what she had done. Or perhaps she did. There was nothing the Falcon could do now.

'I like not my wife having truck with Jacobites,' the Falcon said

718

sulkily, like a bad loser who has lost at cards. 'You would do well to steer clear of them, too.'

'But, Lord Falconer, is not His Majesty, gracious King George, securely on the throne of England?' Anna raised her well-shaped eyebrows in some surprise. 'Does he not have an heir and numerous progeny to secure the throne? I believe the only heir to the Pretender James in Rome is his son who is unmarried and childless. Another is a Cardinal and celibate. What danger is there to the well-established and much beloved English monarch we have today?'

'Unmarried but *not* childless,' the Falcon said viciously. 'He has a natural daughter and drags her around like the millstone she undoubtedly is.'

'But she is surely no threat to the throne?'

'Oh none at all,' the Falcon said, roaring with laughter. 'A bastard *and* a girl. What chance has she?'

'Oh I don't know,' Analee said, her eyes glinting dangerously. 'Was not I *myself* a bastard *and* a girl? What is more I was also a common gypsy. Who would ever have thought I would become Marchioness of Falconer – bastard, a girl *and* a gypsy? Would *you* have thought it, my lord?' She stared haughtily at her husband whose complexion grew mottled with rage.

'This is where your raw, humble origins show, Analee. No real lady would talk like that in front of one of such refinement as Miss Cameron.'

'Oh, I assure you I am not offended.' Anna Cameron nervously clapped her hands together. 'I heard Lady Falconer was a gypsy, but I never . . .'

'Thought to hear such a tale?' Analee looked at her. 'Quite. So you see the daughter of Prince Charles may find herself one day on the throne of England, or maybe his son if he had one . . .' She gazed innocently at the Falcon who looked as though he was about to have an apoplectic attack.

'I could have you in prison for treason the way you are talking! Let me hear no more of it.' The Falcon looked angrily at the fob watch at his waistband and clicked his fingers. 'I have an appointment with Mr Pitt and Lord Ligonier. Both are convinced we shall have war before a twelvemonth is out; although all this frenzy about the threat of a French invasion is ridiculous. 'Tis started by the French – and fanned by the Jacobites, the few there are. May I escort you home, Miss Cameron?'

Every time he talked to her his voice became softer and his expression gentle, even amorous, Analee thought. Yet she liked the girl; her open good nature was appealing.

'Do stay and take tea with me,' Analee said. 'I am sure we have a lot to say to each other. I can tell you all about Lady Goodacre!'

Analee looked brightly at the Falcon whose face was now purple with irritation. He plucked at the braid on his handsome new coat and seemed about to crush the delicate face of his timepiece in his hands. Through trying to be too clever he had got himself into a thoroughly awkward situation. But, looking at them both, he knew there was nothing he could do. He must rely on Anna's discretion. If Analee heard about the scene in the carriage he would never hear the end of it. But it was not a thing that Miss Cameron should want noised abroad either. How he had managed to raise her skirts and fondle her thighs – alas, only too briefly – before she slapped him hard. He glowered at Analee, smiled at Miss Cameron, kissing her hand and then glanced at himself in the mirror, straightening the black band at his throat.

'Do not keep Mr Pitt waiting, my lord,' Analee said pointedly. 'He may keep you out of the government if he ever forms one.'

Neither woman spoke as they heard Angus's heavy footsteps run down the stairs. Then Analee sighed and rose to pull the bellrope. They went to the window and looked out on the bleak landscape. The October weather was cold, a freezing wind blowing endlessly from the east. Analee shivered.

'Thank you,' she said, turning to her guest.

'I know not what I did. The whole thing bewildered me.'

'I could see that. Yet your replies helped me enormously. Thank you again.'

'I hope I have not been guilty of assisting in a deception, Lady Falconer!'

'No. Perhaps of saving my life.'

'It is as grave as that?'

'It is very grave.'

'It *is* to do with the Jacobite cause?'

Analee stared at the young girl, wondering if she had got herself into a worse situation than before. 'It is in a way.'

'Oh, how thrilling! 'Anna clapped her hands together and came over to Analee. 'I am devoted to Bonnie Prince Charlie, Lady Falconer! What tales Stewart has told of him, and Brent Delamain his cousin who visited him last year. His landing at Eriskay, his swift victories, his charm and ease in command. My family of course have always supported the Stuarts.'

'But from afar, 'tis not the same thing. So you met Mr Delamain?'

'Yes. He was there for about six months. He was very restless.'

'Did you . . . like him?' Analee tried to control the jealousy in her voice.

'Oh, very much.'

'He is a very personable young man, is he not?'

'Oh he is not *young*, Lady Falconer! He is well over thirty! But he was personable enough. Quite a few of the unattached women set their caps at him. But Stewart told me he was in the grip of a strange enchantment – a permanent love for a woman who was now married with children; but he had vowed never to marry anyone else. Knew you this tale?'

'I heard something of it,' Analee said lightly, her heart leaping with joy. 'It happened before the Rebellion.'

'I never saw him so much as glance with interest at another woman. Yet he was always very polite and a good dancer. It was rather romatic, this tale of his faithful love.'

'And have *you* ever had an attachment?'

'Oh, one or two flirtations, nothing more. I am not of a mind to marry until I have travelled and seen something of the world. You have no idea how tedious life in Chesapeake can be.'

'But *will* you settle in Chesapeake?'

Anna looked at her in surprise. 'Why, I suppose so, Lady Falconer. I never thought any different. My two sisters have.'

'Would you not like to stay in England maybe? Marry a man of title and wealth here?'

Anna Cameron appeared never seriously to have considered the matter. She looked at Analee with wide-eyed surprise that made Analee wonder whether a girl of her age could really be quite *so* innocent.

'I had not given thought to the matter, Lady Falconer. It is true there are one or two men kind enough to pay me attention.'

'One or two! I heard that you were quite a sensation at court.'

'Oh, how kind!'

'And the Princess of Wales took to you most kindly. You are a great success.'

'Her Royal Highness was most gracious. What a tragic loss her husband must have been. Now she will never be Queen.'

So Miss Cameron *was* ambitious Analee thought – the main thing in her mind being that Princess Augusta would never be Queen, not that she had lost a husband. She wondered just how open and simple her new young friend was.

A footman entered and Analee gave the order for tea then, when he had left, she moved her chair nearer that of Anna Cameron.

'To return to Lady Goodacre.'

'Yes, Lady Falconer?' Miss Cameron opened those dazzling turquoise eyes very wide. Her prominent lids were almost opaque and her face had a sculptured, classical quality.

'I did want to see her in connection with the Allonbys. That was quite true.'

'I see.'

'The trouble is we had never met and Lord Falconer thought we had.'

'Oh.' Miss Cameron appeared to think this a very grave matter.

'I knew he was very suspicious of the Allonbys because he has always suspected me of harbouring Jacobite sympathies on account of my friendship for them.'

'And have you, Lady Falconer?'

'Shall we say I am . . . sympathetic.'Analee hesitated in choosing the correct word.'But I am not a traitor. My husband, as a senior general in the army of the King, always has my first loyalty, my undying devotion.'

'Oh, quite.' Miss Cameron's thoughts flew to the Falcon's behaviour during his wife's absence, the scene in the carriage by the river. She had had to fight him off, fearing for her virtue. She suddenly felt sorry for Analee who was such a beautiful woman; who did not deserve to be made cuckold in this matter. But the Marquess was a very attractive man. Miss Cameron was flattered by his attentions even though she disapproved of him, and never expected to respond to someone who was at least as old as her father, if not older. She found her thoughts straying to him more and more and she would look every day at the little jewel under her linen in her drawer He must think very highly of her to have selected such an expensive present. She would put it on her bosom and imagine being seen in company with him, smothered with jewels, all eyes turned to admire her . . . as they did now; but there were, she knew, also whispers. The Falcon had a reputation. It made her slightly ashamed of being seen in his company for fear of what people would say, the tongues that would wag, sullying her good name.

But she thought of him a great deal; he aroused feelings in her that no man had before. To be a Marchioness . . . she looked at Analee and suddenly reddened. She felt so disloyal and faithless to this good friend. She had helped her by lying because she felt guilty. Anyone could see that husband and wife didn't get on. He obviously wanted some excuse to get rid of her and she, Anna Cameron, would not sully her conscience, disrupt her peace with God by assisting in such a foul deed.

But she had put Analee on her side. Now they both liked her . . . very much.

'You are very thoughtful, Anna,' Analee said, gazing at her with some consternation. Her guest had fallen into a brown study and the leaping flames in the grate were reflected in her large translucent eyes. What a colour they were, like the sun on some dappled lagoon the like of which Analee had only ever heard about from people who returned from the West Indies.

'I was just thinking,' Anna said guiltily, 'how unfortunate it is that families had to be divided by this sad affair.'

'You mean Stuarts versus Hanoverians?' Analee enquired, not altogether convinced by Miss Cameron's explanation and then, as she nodded, 'It has been the same for generations. It has gone on since James II, the father of the present exile in Rome and grandfather of Prince Charles, was expelled in 1688 from England. It was right that he was the true King and his son, the heir of his body, his successor. But people tried to pretend he was not his real son. The Hanoverians were only very distantly related to the English royal family, through a daughter of James I, the Queen of Bohemia. It was such a tenuous connection that few thought it would ever be realized; but then religion came into it and religion is a very strong emotion. The Whigs were determined to keep the Catholic Jacobites out. They succeeded. 'Twas from Mary Allonby I learned all this, and I have studied more since. I remember the day she told me – oh, before the war in far-off Lakeland and I a gypsy to whom she had given refuge. She was the mistress of the house . . . 'Analee shook her head. ''Tis a sad, sad tale.'

'I know you have been very good to the Allonbys,' Anna said gently. 'Stewart is very grateful for it.'

'Is he happy?'

'Oh yes. Very. He and Elizabeth are well-matched, although she is very strong-willed. But she loves him so much because he is so handsome that he can do what he likes with her. They have three lovely babies, two boys and a girl.'

'Will he ever come home, do you think?'

'Never. He says his place is in America. And, because he is pro-Stuart, he is against the English government and thinks it should not have so big a say in the colonies' affairs. Many Americans think the colonies should rule themselves and are pressing for the right of self-determination, to have their own houses of assembly and make their own laws.'

'Really?' Analee looked rather shocked. 'You mean there is rebellion?'

'Oh not yet. The French are the problem at the moment. They want to try and drive the English colonists into the sea; but once we have got rid of the French then we shall set about ruling ourselves. It is only a matter of time and Stewart is prominent among those who think this way. He would love to get even with the English government for dispossessing him of his lands and birthright.'

'Take care not to let the Falcon hear you talk like that,' Analee said, moving to one side as the footman, followed by a succession of lesser menials and maids, brought in the tea things. 'Or he will have you shipped back to America . . . or even clapped in irons.'

Miss Cameron's face grew round with pretended apprehension and Analee, liking her more than ever, burst out laughing and impulsively kissed her cheeks, relief in her heart once more.

* * *

Miss Catherine Walkinshaw, Housekeeper to Her Royal Highness the Princess of Wales, looked severely at Lady Falconer, her sensible mouth pursed in a disapproving rosebud. She was a stout woman, not remotely good-looking. It intrigued Analee to wonder what her younger sister looked like to have captured the heart of the man who, at one time, most women in England or Scotland would have given their lives for, to say nothing of their virtue. Although she had lived for many years in England, Mistress Walkinshaw retained her strong Scots accent and her hair was plainly dressed and sensible, like the rest of her.

'Your ladyship is greatly mistaken if you think I have any truck with the Jacobites,' Miss Walkinshaw continued, scarcely opening that prim mouth. 'Whatever my family thought or may think, *I* am a loyal supporter of His gracious Majesty King George. And, moreover, since my unfortunate sister dishonoured our family, many more of us have gone over to the other side, so shocked were we all by the way she openly disported herself.'

Miss Walkinshaw clamped her mouth shut and produced a gold snuff box from the pocket of her capacious gown. 'Do you take snuff, Lady Falconer?'

'No thank you, Miss Walkinshaw.' Analee looked on with interest as Miss Walkinshaw expertly put a pinch in each nostril and gave a large sniff, her eyes suddenly watering.

'Do you not think it is the Prince who has behaved dishonourably in not marrying your sister? She must love him very much and has borne him a child.' She saw Miss Walkinshaw wince and hurried on. 'I think that is very praiseworthy, very noble and loving. Do you not think so?'

'I do not indeed,' Miss Walkinshaw said, her mouth rounder than ever, 'and I am surprised that you do. She is living is sin and her child is a child of sin. We acknowledge her as no relation of ours. My family has suffered severe hardships for the Jacobite cause, as you may know, Lady Falconer; my parents went into exile and endured great poverty. But for my sister to have behaved the way she has, has brought shame on our family name. My mother has sworn that she will never speak to her again and means to keep to this, I know.'

'I am sorry to hear you speak thus,' Analee said quietly. 'I know not your sister; but when a woman gives her heart to a man as she has done I think she is to be admired, not scorned.'

'You can think what you like, Lady Falconer,' Miss Walkinshaw said firmly, agitatedly tapping her snuff box. Clearly she was suffering from emotion and the strong pungent powder helped to calm her. 'Your opinions are your own affair; but I do not wish to hear my sister's name mentioned again. It is no concern of mine. I would never scheme or plot against this beloved monarch. Believe me.'

'I do,' Analee said with conviction. 'I do not know how I came to be so misinformed. Please forget we have ever spoken.'

'I would like to know how you did come to be so informed,' Catherine Walkinshaw said 'as aspersions are obviously cast on my loyalty. I shall speak to the Princess about this.'

'Oh pray do not, Miss Walkinshaw,' Analee said quickly. 'It could lead to too much trouble. I was simply told that you . . . kept in touch, that is all.'

'Well you were misinformed and I am not in touch. I am surprised at you, Lady Falconer, with your husband having the high position he has, the ear of the King at all times.'

'I assure you I am no traitor,' Analee spoke softly. 'But, like you, I have been well acquainted with those who, for reasons of their own, were loyal to the Stuarts. I am simply assisting them, and him . . . the Prince.'

'He has no chance at all, you know,' Miss Walkinshaw said, modifying her tone from one of strict disapproval into chattiness. Despite the sobriety of her ways she was known to enjoy a gossip. 'Princess Augusta used to talk of him kindly, but no more. She is too dependent on the goodwill of the King. Before she was loyal to her husband who was forever plotting against his father, as these Hanoverians do. The present King plotted before that against his father George I. I think the late Prince Frederick thought he might conspire with the Stuarts to topple his own father; but God punished him for his disloyalty and struck him down in his prime.' Miss Walkinshaw's eyes glinted with satisfaction at the thought of divine intervention on such a massive scale. 'Aye, in his prime. 'Twas the wrath of God. And if you take my advice, your ladyship will keep well away from such treasonable activities in case God should wreak his vengeance against *you*, too.'

Miss Walkinshaw clamped her mouth tight shut again like a trap and folded her hands firmly on her lap sitting up straight as a ramrod, bristling with righteous indignation.

And, indeed, Analee felt she had fallen into a trap. By asking her to speak so openly to one as close to the court as this woman, had her beloved Brent unwittingly betrayed her?

8

The casual gardener was a tall powerful man and Dulcie, one of the parlour maids at the Castle, had her eyes on him from the moment he came to help cut down the dead wood in the park surrounding Goodacre Castle. She would spy at him out of the window and when the gardeners and the woodsmen gathered together for food, she made sure that she was around, too.

In no time at all Dulcie and the gardener were trysting in the outbuildings and it was not long after the first encounters, the first gropings and kissings and squeezings, that he bedded her in the hayloft in the far barn on the estate.

She was a lovely piece of comely flesh and, knowing that as soon as he had what he wanted he would have to go back and report to his master and never see her again, Gwyn Dyffed took his time in finding out what he wanted to know.

'I liked ye since I first set eyes on ye,' Dulcie said to him one day after they had completed their love-making and were resting comfortably in the warm hay that had only been gathered in that summer. From the slats in the pigeon loft high in the barn, the sun shone on the dried golden grass and the soft cooing of pigeons enhanced the idyllic nature of the late afternoon. 'Will ye be stopping 'ere long?'

Gwyn looked at her slyly. The work in the woods was hard but, as a trooper in the Falcon's regiment, he was used to hard work and Dulcie was different from the usual run of soldiers' doxies. She was clean and well spoken, a local girl, and the hunger with which she returned his embraces made him hopeful that she was choosey about whom she lay with.

'I can't stop long,' Gwyn said, kissing her pink, rounded breast only partly covered by the hay. 'But I'll be back. I like it in these parts – especially your parts,' he said drawing back the hay to inspect her thighs.

'Do you wander about then?'

'Aye, seeking work, casual.'

'And do you always have a good time like this?' She winked at him and stuck out her saucy pink tongue.

'I *try*, but I don't always succeed. Do you get many strangers in these parts? Many visitors?'

'What do you mean?' Dulcie partially sat up and stared at him. 'What are you after?'

'Nothing. I just wondered.'

He put his mouth firmly down on hers so as to replace the suspicious gleam he saw in her eyes with the lights of love. He was a big man and she squealed as he positioned himself upon her again and recommenced the timeless ritual of mating.

'You aren't half strong,' she said after it was over. 'I never knew anyone do it as many times as you.'

'It's practice,' he said, laughing.

'Oh you're *that* practised then, are you?'

'You wouldn't like a man that wasn't, would you now?' He looked down at her pink flushed face and kissed her pert nose.

'I'd like a man vigorous like you, but faithful. Would you think of settling here?'

'I might, and I might not. You must be nice to me.'

'Like what? Aren't I nice enough?' She wriggled her hips and he covered her with his arms and gazed into her eyes.

'I'm looking for someone, a man who owes me money. He didn't pay me and I want to find him. Until I do I shan't settle.'

'Oh, *that's* why you ask them questions,' Dulcie said smiling. 'Everyone says you asks a lot of questions. I can see you mean to 'ave him.'

'I do.' Gwyn said. 'He cheated me.'

'What was his name?'

'I can't tell ye; but he was a landowner, a nob. He employed me for three months without pay. I thought he might have been here, visiting.'

'Visiting here? No one ever visits here.'

'No one?'

Dulcie screwed up her fetching amber eyes and Gwyn's heart began to beat more quickly. The Falcon had promised a large reward as well as promotion if he got the information he was after.

'Nay. Lord and Lady Goodacre don't get on. He stops in

London and she is alone here with the children. There are only two in the schoolroom now, the rest grown up.'

'And she never sees *no* one?' The dismay showed on Gwyn's face and he leaned back in the hay resting his head on his hands.

'I only recall one visitor in the past month – a beautiful lady from London, ever so elegant. She stayed about a week and they spent all their time walking and riding, playing with the younger children. She was the wife of some very big nob in London, gentry.'

'And she was here all by herself?'

'Oh aye, except for her maid, and the servants who had ridden with her. One of them was not bad-looking, but not like you.' Dulcie stared at him archly. Gwyn felt disappointed and defeated. He would have to go back only to report that Lady Falconer had been here alone. He felt privileged to have enjoyed the confidence of his commander, to be given such an important mission; but there was nothing to tell.

'I'm *very* choosey.' Dulcie said quickly. 'The last man I had was a sailor from France . . . Oh, that reminds me,' she put a hand to her mouth and sat up. 'There was somebody else here, but I never saw him, only in the distance.'

'Yes?' Gwyn was seized by a feeling of excitement.

'He came with the sailor but only stopped twenty-four hours, then he left.'

'When did he come?'

'The day that grand lady came from London. I recall it because the sailor was a lusty man like you and made eyes at me in the servants' hall over dinner. We tumbled in the woodshed at night. He had to leave soon after that.'

'Those Frenchmen carry the pox, they say,' Gwyn said, feeling a little less enthusiastic about his paramour. Little bawd, going with Frenchmen, not as selective as he thought.

'This one didn't,' Dulcie said indignantly. 'He wasn't just an ordinary sailor.'

'I thought you were more choosey!'

'I am.' Dulcie looked at him indignantly. 'You're jealous.'

'Who did he come over with?'

'Someone to see Lady Goodacre. I know no more. I didn't wait on that day so I never saw him. It was all very secret; none of us were allowed near him. In fact very few knew he was there; I heard him speak though, and he had an English voice; he wasn't a foreigner.'

'You couldn't say at all what he looked like?'

'No. But he couldn't have been your man.'

'Why not ?'

'Because he came from overseas with the Frenchie.'

'He came from France?'

'Oh yes. You're sure you're not a government spy or something like that?'

'Course I'm not,' Gwyn said, closing his eyes at the thought of the reward he would get. 'Do I look like one?'

'Yes and no. You look like a soldier to me.'

'I was in the war but I left it because the pay was awful. We must go, Dulcie.' We shall be missed.'

'I'm cold, too,' she said, shivering. 'I wish I had your body to warm me every night.'

'Maybe you will,' he said, kissing her lightly. 'Go on back to your duties at the house; and take care you tell no one about our talk.'

'Who could I tell?' she said.

She ran back to the house while he set off towards the wood. She felt almost in love with him and made plans as to how she would try and ensnare him to stay. Maybe Lady Goodacre would give him a permanent job on the estate if only he could find the man who owed him money.

But the next day, when she slipped away to keep their tryst, no welcoming lover rose up from the straw. The barn was empty, and the day after that the same, and the day after that. The temporary gardener had gone.

The Falcon had never really known torment like this; it was as though he had a sickness. Every other woman he had been sure of, even Analee, but not this one. She pretended she didn't care, and did it very convincingly. He would do anything just for a glimpse of her because, now that Analee was around, he had to be even more circumspect than before. What was more, Anna and his wife got on so well. They went for drives together, rode in Richmond Park or attended little tea parties given by various ladies of title.

731

Anna even called the Marchioness by her Christian name; their friendship was very galling to the husband of one and would-be suitor to the other.

She was very, very reserved with him – he'd hardly spoken to her since the encounter in the carriage on the way back from Hampton Court. His only hope was that she didn't return the jewel. Surely she knew the meaning of a present like that? As long as she kept the jewel he felt some hope.

Then Gwyn Dyffed returned with his report and the Falcon's whole outlook on life changed. His unerring instinct for trouble had proved correct.

Analee was sewing in her sitting-room when he burst in, flinging back the door and shouting at the top of his voice. He had felt such pleasure that it was difficult to contrive to appear angry; but he managed it. His veins bulged at his neck and his eyes were like forks of lightning. She put down her sewing and gazed at him.

'What is it now?' she said calmly. Knowing how much she irritated him she had been prepared for some outburst; he would contrive something, she knew.

'You outrageous slut,' he said. 'You *did* go to a rendezvous at Castle Goodacre.'

'I know not what you mean,' she said, her hands suddenly starting to tremble.

'You, did, you did, you *did*! I have had a spy there and he reported to me today. He did his work well. You received a man who came from France. Who was it?'

'I must deny all knowledge,' Analee said with a calm she did not feel. 'I received no one.'

'Someone came there when you were there, accompanied by a French sailor.'

'What makes you think he came to see me?'

'Then he did *not* come to see you?'

'I saw no one.' Analee looked into his face, knowing well how to lie to save others including herself. She should have known that her husband would be thorough. Oh, would she had never gone! But it was no use now.

'Was it the Prince?'

'What an absurd thing to say! Why should the Prince – I

assume you mean Prince Charles, knowing how your mind works – come to see me?'

'No, it would not be him. Besides I know where he is. We have him constantly under surveillance. You know I shall have Lady Goodacre on the rack for this, don't you?'

Now the panic she felt almost overwhelmed her. She could stand torture. But Lady Goodacre . . . and what for? Maybe he was bluffing. She tried conciliation. She got up and smoothed her skirt, put a hand to her hair, composed her features. 'Angus, my lord, if you would send me away, send me; but do not contrive artificial circumstances, do not involve good and innocent people. Will you never cease your Jacobite witch hunt, cease your suspicions? Because your nature *is* suspicious, Angus Falconer. You thrive on intrigue and suspicion as some need light and air. The Rebellion is past these ten years, the Prince is undone, he has lost all his suport, his followers have dispersed. The second Hanoverian King is a feeble man and the third, a strapping young Prince, prepared to succeed him – who knows when, any day now.

'If you wish to put me away, put me away – I find this life intolerable, existing with a man I loved but who no longer loves me, who is vexed by my very presence. Let us separate, Angus. I will go . . .'

'You will go where *I* put you,' Angus said, seizing her arm and snarling into her face. 'I'll have you sent to the Tower for high treason.'

'Everyone would laugh at you. Known Jacobites are having their estates restored. I believe one or two are even at the court. They would mock you. You are making plots where none exist. You are becoming a foolish man, in your dotage . . .'

The wrath on Angus's face increased and he twisted Analee's arm behind her, his face an inch away from hers.

'You are a traitor, you are consorting with traitors, you try only to injure me, sully my name. You think I am easily misled but I am not . . .'

'*I* think that, Angus? Oh, fie!' Analee said, her face beginning to pale with pain. 'Leave off my arm, I beg you . . .'

'You're a whore, you cuckold me; you're a Jacobite, you deceive me; you're a necromancer, a . . .' With every word

733

Angus twisted her arm a little more behind her back and the tears started down Analee's cheeks.

'Angus, if you do not let me go you will . . .'

The Falcon brought Analee's arm right up to behind her back and, as her face contorted with agony, he gave it a savage twist and there was a loud snap. She closed her eyes and swayed and, surprised by his own strength, Angus stepped back and gazed at her with consternation as she fell senseless to the floor, her arm at an awkward angle beneath her body.

He stood and looked at her and wished he had killed her. He hated her so much and she would always be a thorn in his flesh, a hindrance to his ambitions.

He pulled the bellrope and went to the door shouting to the servant who ran quickly up the stairs.

'Fetch a doctor! Lady Falconer has fallen and broken her arm. Hurry up man, or I'll have you whipped.'

Analee knew it was the end; but she felt no remorse. Not even the broken arm was as painful as the bruise to her heart. The last time he had injured her he had been full of anguish, but not this time. He didn't even come and see her as she lay in bed, but sent instructions that as soon as she was fit she was to travel north. Then he went on manoeuvres to Somerset with his regiment without saying goodbye.

She made no farewells except to send a note to the Princess of Wales saying she was leaving to visit her children. She sent the same note to Anna Cameron, who had tried to see her; but Analee wanted to see no one. Now that her marriage to a man, once so beloved, was finished, she felt empty and hopeless inside – much, much sadder than she had imagined.

She was also frightened. Having gone so far, she wondered how much further the Falcon would go. She felt he would go to the bitter end to find out the truth and she feared for her innocent friend, Lady Goodacre.

Usually when she travelled north, Analee broke her journey at Delamain Castle, but this time she felt no such desire. She wanted to recover, to regain her strength; to mend both her broken arm and her broken heart. She went straight to her beloved home on Derwentwater, the refuge she always sought when in pain. As she came over the water and the familiar outlines of the house appeared through the mist on the lake, she began to weep and when she saw Nelly and her children lined up to receive her on the jetty, she broke down completely and had to be helped from the boat. By night she had a fever and the following day she was delirious.

'Is her ladyship dying?' Nelly said to the doctor who had been hastily summoned from Keswick.

The doctor shrugged. 'She should not have travelled with that arm. How came she to break it? She must have been in great pain. 'Tis swollen to such a size.'

'I know not, sir. I have scarcely got two sensible words out of her since she arrived.'

'The pain caused by the jogging of the carriage over five days must have been considerable. I am shocked his lordship let her travel thus.'

'I believe he is away, sir.'

'Ah, that explains it. It will be her ladyship's impulsiveness because I know his lordship to be a kind and compassionate man.'

Nelly grimaced behind the doctor's back; then saw him out of the house.

'We shall have to send for his lordship if she gets any worse,' he said, getting onto his horse and looking down at Nelly. 'I fear those poor children will soon be motherless.'

Nelly ran upstairs weeping, and flung herself across Analee's hot and restless body as she lay on the large bed she had once shared in such love with the Falcon.

As Nelly wept she felt a hand on her back and looked in surprise to see that Analee's eyes, though bright with fever, were open.

'You must fetch Reyora, Nell. Fetch her quick.' Then she lost consciousness again and her breathing became harsh and more rapid.

Nelly rushed down the stairs and sent two servants, each to take different routes, to fetch Reyora and bring her back at once. They were not to stop for a single moment on their way there or on their way back, whoever brought her.

All that day Analee's hot body twisted in the bed and Nelly tenderly bathed her, frequently changing her chemise and sheets. Analee would call out and clutch Nelly, but did not appear to

735

recognize her. Then at about five in the afternoon she grew calmer and a steady rattle began in her throat. She opened her eyes but she did not see. She was dying.

Nelly dried her eyes and went downstairs to fetch the children. Even though she could not recognize them they must take farewell of their mother. Clare led the others into the room, clasping Beyrick by the hand, and bade them all kneel by their mother's bed. The awful rattle continued and Nelly knew it was just a matter of time.

'You must kiss your mama,' she said brokenly. 'She is very ill.'

'Is she dying?' Clare said in her grown-up voice.

Nelly couldn't reply. Her heart was too full and she knelt down and lifted little Charlotte onto the bed.

'I will kiss Mama and make her well,' Charlotte said and put her little rosebud mouth against Analee's hot cheek. Then Beyrick followed and finally Clare took her mother's hand and held it against her heart. Then she burst into tears and Nelly bade the servant, who was with them in the room, take the children out again.

'I cannot leave Mama. I will not!' Clare sobbed and tried to get on to the bed with her mother. 'Oh Mama. Mama. Do not leave us.'

'Your mama will not leave you,' Reyora said, still breathing hard from the journey and putting her firm hand on Clare's shoulder. 'I promise you that, little one. It is not her time. Now go, and good old Reyora will make her better.' Reyora smiled at the child, already glancing anxiously but with practised skill at Analee and reaching into her bag for her lotions and unguents. 'Take them out, Nelly, and then come back to assist me.'

Nelly did as she was bid and when she came back Reyora had taken the bedclothes off Analee and was running her capable hands carefully over her body, lingering on her arm.

'It is this where the poison comes from. I suppose *he* did it . . .'

'I know nothing,' Nelly said, still too distressed to speak logically. 'I only heard Analee was coming home; when she arrived she already had the fever.'

'He did it. I know. He is a violent man and she is in the most terrible danger from him. Would that we had not saved him when he lay so near death in Germany. I thought then that it was a

736

mistake, but what could I do? She loved him and as long as love is left one is powerless against evil. When her love for him is dead it will no longer be necessary to save him.'

'And is it dead?' Nelly asked, marvelling at the way Reyora's skilled hands were tending the wounded arm, rubbing soft unguents into it and binding it with leaves impregnated with creams and herbs until a gorgeous fragrance filled the room replacing the smell of sweat and the fear of death.

'I hope so,' Reyora said, looking at her patient. 'I think so. I knew she was ill, you know. The messenger was no surprise. I felt uneasy and kept on seeing her in my mind, except that I did not know where she was. I thought that perhaps she was in London.'

'Would she have died without you?'

Reyora shook her head. 'I think not. It is not her time. We all have a time you know, Nelly, though one can postpone it as I did with the Falcon in Germany. Next time I will make sure it is not postponed.'

'She loved him so much . . . and he her.'

'But he is not a good man. He was momentarily redeemed by her love; but he is bad. The badness will come out as it has now. She is surrounded by his evil desire to do her harm.' Reyora's hands wove an imaginary aura around Analee, describing a large arc. 'There.' She patted Analee's arm gently and laid it by her side. 'It will heal and the poison will slowly ebb from her body. You go and rest now, Nell, and I will stay with her. Tell the children that next time they come to see their mama she will greet them with a loving smile.'

Nelly burst into tears and, kneeling, kissed Reyora's hand. 'Oh, Reyora, without you . . .'

'Without me neither of you would be here,' Reyora said, smiling, and patted her shoulder. 'Go now and I will tell you when Analee is ready for some warm broth.'

Reyora sat with Analee through the night, watching the fever ebb and the swelling in the arm go down. Occasionally she replaced the herbs that bound it and at dawn she went into the garden and gathered fresh ones and fresh leaves from the coniferous trees and laurel bushes. She sluiced her face in the icy waters of the lake and watched the sun break over the hills. She was very tired, but happy. When she returned to Analee's room the first beams of the sun bathed the room in a rosy radiance and Analee lay quiet and breathing normally, her eyes clear and free from fever, wide open.

'Reyora,' she said simply. 'How did you know?'

'You sent for me. Even when near death you murmured my name. But I knew,' Reyora said, sitting by her side and taking her hand. 'I knew you were unwell because you were distressed.'

'It is as though I waited to be home to be ill,' Analee said, still speaking in a feeble voice, 'so that you could be with me. Home, my Lakeland, my only home – not Falconer House, not Falcon's Keep, but here, Furness Grange. I would he would leave me here all my life.'

'Perhaps he will.'

Analee shook her head. 'He hates me, Reyora. He has such a hatred for me that breaking my arm was only a symbol of breaking me. He wants to do me great harm.'

'I will not let him,' Reyora said. 'I will stop him.'

Analee shook her head wearily and the sweat broke again on her forehead. Reyora wiped it with her hand and stroked Analee's brow.

'There, there, you must remain calm.'

'I have done so many foolish things,' Analee said 'So very foolish, endangering others.'

'You have lain with another man?'

'Oh no!' Analee managed a weak laugh. 'But I saw Brent again briefly, and took a message from him to a servant of the Princess of Wales. I have endangered myself and other good people, and for what? The Rebellion is dead.'

'I will never forget what they did to our people,' Reyora said bitterly. 'I recall the destruction of the Buckland gypsies by the Prince's men. Now he has his punishment. I am glad.'

'But it was not he! He was not there! They were savages, disappointed with defeat and gone amuck.'

'But the Hanoverians slew no one when they came to power. They have given this country peace.'

Analee looked at Reyora and weakly returned the pressure of her hand. 'My dear Reyora, much of what you say is true. Were the Falcon not such a cruel man and on the Hanoverian side, I would love them more. But the Prince once held me in his arms,

738

he gave me a child. He comes from a long line of kings. I honour his memory. For Duncan's sake I do all I can for his father.'

'Ah,' Reyora said. 'Now I understand. You do it for love, not power.'

'You once said Duncan was the child of a great man. It was he.'

'I understand,' Reyora said gently. 'You are always governed by your passions, Analee.'

'The Falcon knows I saw someone at a house in Kent. If he finds it is Brent Delamain God knows what he will do. He will divorce me, but he will not let me stay here. I shall be universally disgraced. He will order me to some barren place away from my children, my friends. He will leave me there for life like I heard tell the father of King George II left his mother. For thirty years she languished in prison for love.'

'I will not let it happen to you, Analee. The days of the Falcon are numbered.'

'Oh no!' Analee looked at her in alarm. 'You *must* not harm him. My children, what will they do . . .'

'I do not say *when*,' Reyora replied calmly. 'The days of all of us are numbered, after all. *I* certainly will do nothing to harm him . . . but nothing to save him either. He is already on borrowed time.'

'I wish you had not told me that,'Analee said brokenly. 'I have some lingering love for him.'

'Then you are foolish.' Reyora replied, stroking her hand. 'You must try and put him from your heart – you must, you must or he will only cause you more unhappiness than you are able to bear. I have not supernatural powers, Analee. I cannot alter the future, only influence the way things happen. Believe me you are in great danger – not physically, but for your own peace of mind. Great events are going to happen that will affect us all, but you in particular. Did I not promise you bad and good, bad and good for several years?'

Analee nooded, blinking through fresh tears. 'If I had known I would have preferred death. To lose the Falcon's love . . .'

'For a time it will continue, but one day you will find a greater love. I also promised you lasting happiness. And that will come to pass too . . . sooner than you think. Now send for your children, my dear friend, so that they can be reassured their mother is not dead.'

And as the children were brought in and ran to her bedside crying with joy, Reyora stood in the shadows at the back of the room looking at the happy scene, her eyes hooded with the wisdom of one who can see not only the past, but the future too.

9

All London was beginning to talk – or rather, not *all*; but that small, fashionable, select portion of the population that mattered: those who had both wealth and breeding and who frequented the courts and the upper echelons of high society. In short this small, but very powerful section of society was talking about Miss Anna Cameron and her relationship with the Marquess of Falconer.

By the spring the gossip was such that Mrs Peto, in whose house Lord Falconer had still not put one foot, was thinking of writing to Anna's mother appraising her of this very distressing situation regarding her daughter and a man not only married, but a premier Marquess of England. Mrs Peto was both titillated and shocked by it; but one thing was certain, she could not get a word out of Anna, not one single word other than an exclamation accompanied by a look of shocked surprise equal to Mrs Peto's own.

'Lord Falconer is like a guardian to me, Mrs Peto!'

'But Mr Peto is your guardian,' Mrs Peto averred, flustered.

Anna gave her that look of disdain which now came easily to one who, though of democratic upbringing, knew that she was desired by a famous nobleman.

'Alas, Mr Peto is not, I believe, accustomed to those reaches of society to which Lord and Lady Falconer have access. Is he?'

No. He was not. Mrs Peto looked at her feet; they had never even been inside the court, never mind seen the King or the Princess of Wales.

'I still think it is wrong, Anna. People are talking. I know. I may not move in the very highest reaches of society, but we are well enough placed to know what people are saying.'

'And what *are* they saying?' Miss Cameron said, shaking her pretty head, the well-dressed curls bobbing up and down.

'Well, that you and Lord Falconer . . .'

'Yes?' She raised her head, showing the delicious dimple in her determined chin.

'That you and he . . .'

741

'Come to the point, Mrs Peto.'

Mrs Peto hung her head. 'I know not how to put it delicately.'

'We are not lovers, Mrs Peto. I am not his lordship's mistress, if that is what you are suggesting.'

Mrs Peto went crimson and raised her hands to try and hide her face. 'Oh, my dear, never was such a thing even *remotely* suggested.'

'Then what *is* being suggested?'

Those clear turquoise eyes began to sparkle with interest. How the Falcon would have enjoyed this exchange, Anna thought. How he would have loved crushing Mrs Peto and her absurd, middle-class insinuations.

'I think the suggestion is, that is to say people *think*, the relationship is too close. Lady Falconer after all is . . . his lawful wife.' Mrs Peto finished lamely and felt her hot cheeks. This little miss was making a fool of her. Mrs Peto had seldom known a girl change as much as Anna Cameron had in the six months since she came to London. Not only physically but in every way. She was more beautiful, more poised, more elegant, more sure of herself, and . . . Mrs Peto, with her natural modesty, would not have known exactly how to put into words the next thought that came to her mind. There was a quality about young Anna Cameron that a woman had when she felt fulfilled as a woman, when she was beloved and loved in return. Mrs Peto knew quite well that the only person who could have brought that about was Lord Falconer because, to her certain knowledge, Anna had eyes for no other more eligible and younger men.

Not that there were not a lot of them about. They were mostly dashing young officers acquainted with Lord Falconer and ambitious for promotion and preferment with all the talk about war. They escorted Anna everywhere, picked her up, brought her home, danced with her . . . but when the Marquess appeared, and invariably he did, they melted away like ripples on a pool, only to converge when their presence was required again and his lordship exited discreetly from the scene.

'Lady Falconer knows full well what his lordship is about,' Anna said, studying the toe of her delicately shaped silk slipper. 'She is detained in Lakeland through ill health. Besides, his lordship is often abroad at the court of King Frederick. When he is here he is kind enough to keep a *paternal* eye on me. I'll thank you not to listen to gossip, Mrs Peto.'

And Anna flounced upstairs and sat on her bed wondering how she could get away from this place. She was nearly twenty-three. She knew she was at her peak. She was beautiful, accomplished and desirable. How much longer would she remain like this? How long would the Falcon's infatuation last, when his own wife was considered such a beauty, a woman who, though past thirty, had never lost her looks. Indeed, some said she was more lovely than when he had married her. Anna was aware, as well as gratified, that the Falcon had sent his wife away because of her. She admired Analee, she was a little afraid of her; but now that she felt her position more secure she no longer liked her so much, because how could you continue to like the woman whose place you eventually hoped to take?

Anna knew that the lecherous Falcon really only wanted her youthful body, and would be content to make her his mistress; but as soon as she took that step she was finished. Having possessed her, his ardour would cool. She knew enough about his reputation in particular, and men in general, to be sure of this. She didn't want merely to be his mistress – to be taken up and discarded when he was replete, like so many before her. She wanted to be his wife.

There was no doubt, as the year 1756 got into its stride, that there was going to be a war. In Europe the continental powers were openly preparing for it – France, Austria and Russia against Prussia and England – and in India and America the first salvos had already been fired. The fear of the invasion of England died down, but troops from Hanover and Hesse still remained to protect the kingdom. They had been hastily summoned by George II because of the poor state of the English army.

The Falcon was excited at the prospect of war. He trained his men unmercifully and plotted to get rid of the hopeless Newcastle (his brother Henry Pelham was dead) and put William Pitt in charge of the country. But the King couldn't abide Pitt and many thought that he would have to wait until the old man died. Pitt and the Falcon were alike, they were both vain men and thought they could do things that no one else could. Their mutual admiration was equally based on mutual self-interest.

The Falcon thought most about war, but he gave almost an equal amount of time to thinking about Miss Cameron. He arranged their meetings with all the strategic skill of the great commander he was. He took delight in deploying his forces here, withdrawing them there and entering himself to make the assault. He tried to make the encounters casual and always delightful. Sometimes when he was expected he did not turn up at all. He knew that this was still the best way to get a woman. He thought it was the only way to get Anna Cameron. He had never known such a wilful filly in his life; she had the bare bit between her teeth and would not let go. She was altogether fresh and delightful.

He was wildly, madly in love with her.

The Falcon only ever managed really to get her to himself at the intimate little suppers he got his subordinates to organize. Over an exquisite meal in elegant surroundings with a warm fire in the grate and the candles glittering on the table, he felt he was at his best; witty, light-hearted and amorous.

On this particular evening in March he had taken special care with his always meticulous toilette. Though his darling did not know it, the house in which they were going to have supper after the theatre would be available for him all night.

This was the night he was determined to bring to fruition all his plans. The thought of the carefully planned – oh, planned for how long! – seduction being achieved at last filled him with an almost unquenchable burning in his loins. He had been careful not to lie with a woman for a whole week so as to savour the moment of rapture to the full. Once *she* became his mistress he would totally discard all the others and be faithful only to her. He had every hope of taking her to Potsdam in the spring. He remembered the delicious seduction of Lady Constance and had recourse to a large glass of water to cool himself down.

The Falcon scarcely knew what the play was about; he certainly never recalled its name or who was there. He didn't even sit next to Miss Cameron, but some distance away with a bevy of young officers and their ladies in between. But he sat in his seat in the box just behind and to one side of her, so that he could observe her profile, the lovely classical lines of her bosom, the sculptural curve of her neck. In the light from the stage she half turned to him and, briefly, their eyes met. Then she turned away again, a little smile playing on her mouth. A mist arose in front of the Falcon's eyes and his head swam. He was sick with desire.

The supper was pregnant with emotion. The atmosphere was so right. He had taken Miss Cameron into the house in Half Moon Street and bade goodbye to the other guests even before she realized they were to be alone.

When she did she stood at the foot of the staircase and looked at him with a wondering eye. He seized her arm and hurried her upstairs. All the servants were from his household and his regiment; his own picked men. There was even a maid waiting for her in the dressing-room so as to give her a feeling of confidence, that she was not alone in a house full of men.

She smiled at him playfully across the table and he leaned over and took her hand. Oh, the exquisite turn of the lips, the provocative dent at each side of her mouth – how sensual! He had not even kissed her. He almost groaned at the thought and poured some more wine with a hand that shook.

'It has been a lovely evening, my lord, but then every evening with you is.' She returned the pressure of his hand with a slight, very slight squeeze. 'I know not what I shall do when I return home.'

'Home?' the Falcon said, sitting bolt upright. 'What do you mean, return home?'

'I have to go back to Maryland, my lord,' Miss Cameron said with feigned surprise, batting her long black lashes against her very clear ivory cheeks. 'I cannot stay here forever.'

'But you can't go now!'

'But why not? Your lordship and her ladyship have been kindness itself. You have *both* given me the sort of life I never dreamed to aspire to. In fact, it will be hard for me to settle down in Chesapeake!'

'You don't need to settle down in Chesapeake,' his lordship said thickly. 'You can stay here.'

'Oh, but my lord, I cannot. You know that. You must know that people are talking, sir.'

'Talking?' his lordship barked imperiously.

'About us.'

'Ah. Huh.' The Falcon got up and strode from the table, his

hands behind his back; but he couldn't take his eyes off her. How bewitching she looked tonight in a gown of primrose yellow, the petticoat flounced and furbelowed, the overskirt edged with ribbon and bows and worn over an oval hoop. Her décolletage was edged with ruching and, in the centre of her bosom just at the V of her deep cleavage, was a saucy little bow as if to focus the eyes of her admirer on that crucial and important part of the anatomy.

There was a becoming flush on her cheeks and, in his mind's eyes, he saw it spread down her neck and over her bosom as when a woman is engaged in the ecstatic emotions of love. He shut his eyes, the vision almost overpowering him. 'Ah, they talk about us, eh? What do they talk about?'

'That is just what I said to Mrs Peto, sir; but she said she would write to my mama.'

'Oh, that common trollop!'

'Exactly, sir. She is not a trollop, that I do know, but she is certainly excessively common. I regret that I have associated far below the station enjoyed by your lordship in society.'

'But 'tis no fault of yours!' The Falcon exclaimed coming to her side and looking down at her. 'And believe me, you are far above them in every way, a jewel, an adornment to the social life of London.'

'Alas, Lord Falconer, you are too kind.' Miss Cameron lowered her eyes modestly. 'I know quite well that I must seem very raw and gauche to you, a rude product of the open classless society of America . . .'

'Oh, my dear, do not say that.' The Falcon impulsively threw himself on a knee beside her and, taking her hand, pressed it to his mouth. 'You are unique, without equal, no one can match you for attainment, beauty, dignity. You are in every way a perfect specimen of womanhood and I yearn only . . .' The Falcon paused, his heart beating wildly, and looked at her.

'Yes?' She scarcely spoke above a whisper, her own heart undergoing some slight commotion, the meal forgotten.

'I yearn only to make you mine.' He raised himself and took her with him into his arms as he regained his full height. Then he crushed her to him, kissing her lips, whose firm yet silky texture he had so much imagined in his tormented waking dreams. He could feel the quick swell of her bosom and he tried delicately to reach

746

down inside her décolletage, but suddenly a vice-like hand grasped his wrist and he jerked back his head and looked at her in surprise.

'Stay, my lord! I am not to be fondled like a doxy.' She swiftly resumed her seat and put her glass of wine to the lips he had so freshly kissed.

'Oh, my darling Anna,' he pleaded, again on his knees. 'Do not torment me. If you knew how I desired you. I will be a very tender lover, my sweetest. I will not hurt you when I introduce you to the delights of love. For you are made for love, Anna. Your body proclaims it. Come.' His lordship, his confidence apparently recovered, got up again and took her hand. 'Come see what I have for you.'

Miss Cameron looked at him in surprise and, since she had no appetite, allowed him to lead her from the room. He took her along a deserted corridor, up another flight of stairs and along another corridor. Then at the end he opened a door and, standing back, propelled her gently inside. 'See?'

Anna Cameron gaped at what she saw. An enormous four-poster bed, with sheets turned back, stood in the centre of the room. Candles burned on tables at either side and on a dressing table on which also stood a mirror, an assortment of boxes, and brushes and combs. On one side of the bed there was a freshly laundered nightshirt and cap and on the other a long flimsy chemise. A fire roared in the grate and on yet another table there stood wine in a cooler, two long-stemmed glasses and a variety of fruits and sweetmeats. She heard the door close behind her and she stared back in panic. The Falcon leaned against the door, his face simpering with adoration.

Anna took a deep breath and walked into the centre of the room before turning to face him. 'Lord Falconer, may I ask the meaning of this . . . this outrage!'

'Outrage?' said the Falcon, nearly choking with surprise. He came over to her and quickly took one of her trembling hands. 'My darling, this is no outrage. I thought you wanted it, too.' He tried to take her again in his arms. 'Oh if you knew, my Anna, how I have waited for this moment. How I have longed . . .'

She shook herself free and stationed herself near the door, her eye on the key which, she perceived, he had not turned. 'Lord Falconer, you greatly misunderstand if you think that, raw and naïve though I am, without the benefit of high birth or a noble family, I would give myself to you as a common whore.'

'Oh, not a *whore*, my heart,' the Falcon said, once again rushing over to her. 'No common whore. Oh, God forbid, my darling, for you to imagine I would ever think of you like that . . .'

He tried to take her hand, but she snatched it away. The expression on her face was furious and her breath came in short sharp gasps as though she were in desperate need of air. In another age, in another place, Miss Anna Cameron would have made a fortune as an actress.

'Do I understand that you are asking *me* to go to bed with you, my lord?' Miss Cameron put another inch on her height as his lordship's seemed to diminish. 'That I would allow you to dishonour me, *me*, Anna Cameron whose father Hector Cameron of Chesapeake, though not of noble birth, has a family at least as old as that of Falconer? Moreover, my father is one of the wealthiest men in Maryland and I have been brought up as the daughter of a gentleman and a landowner. If you think I would lightly part with my prized virginity to a man who, however distinguished and noble, is *twice* my age, *married* and the father of numerous children . . .' Anna Cameron threw back her head and laughed at him mockingly, then turned and swiftly unlocked the door, stalking down the corridor the way they had come.

Lord Falconer whose carefully laid plans had anticipated this possible outcome – after all, had he not tried to dally with her before? – knew she would be met in the hall and escorted home. He lay on the bed and stared at the ceiling. Then he sent for his valet and told him to get him a woman with all despatch. Any woman would do. Any woman at all.

The next day, Anna Cameron received another jewel. It was a rope of pearls with small equally matched diamonds at every fifth place. Inside was a card on which was scrawled in his lordship's bold hand, '*I will not be deterred.*'

Anna smiled to herself and put the card to her lips. Then she placed the precious necklace next to the brooch in her bottom drawer after holding it for some time round her neck, admiring her reflection in the glass, liking what she saw.

* * *

748

Mrs Peto was quite overcome at seeing the Marquess of Falconer step out of his carriage and walk up to the door. She nearly fell over herself as she received him in the hall. He took care not to take her hand, but bowed slightly and she led him into the immaculate parlour apologizing for the state it was in and for the absence of her husband who had gone to Plymouth.

'Plymouth?' boomed his lordship.

'He is looking for passages for us to return to America.'

'Return to America?'

'Why yes, sir.' Mrs Peto curtsied. 'We are to escort Miss Cameron home.'

The Falcon looked at the ceiling and groaned inwardly. 'Is she here?' he said.

'I will fetch her to your lordship this instant.'

Mrs Peto curtsied again and went out of the room backwards, as one who is in the presence of royalty.

Anna had seen the Marquess arrive; but kept him waiting a further fifteen minutes despite the pleas of Mrs Peto. Then, when she was ready, she slowly made her way downstairs, telling Mrs Peto she should take care not to listen at the door or his lordship would have her deported to the colonies. Mrs Peto, who had had every intention of doing just this, fled upstairs to her sitting-room. Who had not heard of the awful power of the Falcon?

Anna Cameron curtsied low and the Falcon bowed. Then he kissed her hand and raised it to his lips.

'What is it you want?' he said.

She didn't reply but gazed into his eyes. There was enough laughter in her own to give him hope. 'You know I cannot be your mistress,' she said. 'I cannot permit it. Whatever else other women may do, I am not like them.'

'Of course not.'

'I have heard of Lady Constance Craven and others. I know they were young, too, even younger than I; but they ruined their reputations irretrievably.'

'Lady Constance subsequently married a Spanish duke,' the Falcon said placatingly.

'Yes, but I believe she had advantages that I have not,' Anna raised her eyes to him and fluttered her long black lashes. 'Powerful connections, important friends, an aristocratic birth.

When one has all these things, little peccadilloes are easily forgiven; indeed they are sometimes expected of those of high birth. For a girl like myself, whatever I may say about my father, it would be ruin. When your lordship tired of me I would be sent home in disgrace. Even in America no man would look at me for all would know of my reputation. I might be married to a woodsman and live in a hut; but no one else would touch me. My father might even disinherit me, for I would bring shame on his name. My sisters are married respectably and well. I would share his fortune with them as we have no brothers.

'What is there for me, Lord Falconer, if I do what you wish? And believe me, I am honoured that you should desire me so much.' She gave a little curtsey which his lordship found enchanting. He felt his heart would snap in two. He bowed his head and then took his seat in a large chair, spreading his long legs before him. She stood by his side and looked at him. He took her hand and gazed up into her eyes.

'You are quite right, Anna. You are absolutely right. If I had not been so besotted with love, so blinded with desire, I would have seen it for myself, a selfish whim that would ruin you; but I would never tire of you, my darling, never have given you up.'

'Ah, you say that now, sir.'

'It is true, Have I not courted you for months, with what reward? Only one kiss. Have I not been rebuffed by you, my plans set awry? As you are kind enough to say, I am not without attractions and I know it. Women do not seem to experience difficulty in acceding to my demands. I know not why, but there it is. Only you, Anna; only you have refused me for so long. And I believe you mean it. So, what is it you want?'

'I want to go home, sir; because I cannot stand the torment of this life with you.'

The Falcon let go her hand and jumped up. 'It torments you, too? You desire me as well?'

'I love you, my lord. Surely you know that?'

The Falcon groaned openly and fell to his knees clasping both her hands and kissing them. 'Oh, why did you not say it before? Why did you leave me in such misery? Why did you make me think you did not want me?'

'Surely you knew I wanted you, my lord, because I did not

refuse your advances, your many, many invitations? Surely you knew what I felt?'

'But how could you love a man like me? As you say, I am so old. I did not dare hope.'

Anna put a hand on his head and stroked his brow with her thumb. 'To be loved by the Falcon. Is it possible? But to love the Falcon, yes, that *is* very possible. It is not merely that I am flattered, but I am overwhelmed by your attraction. And if you are as old as my father, that was said in pique. You are a very handsome, attractive man, my lord.'

'Then what shall we do? What shall we do?' The Falcon closed his eyes and kissed both her hands, pressing them against his heart.

'I know not what to do, sir. It is not in my power.' She lingered on her words and the Falcon opened his eyes and looked up at her. Then he rose, dusted his knees and took her to a sofa where he sat beside her, still holding her hands.

'Power?'

'There is nothing I can do, my lord. It is something only you can do about . . . your wife.' She gazed at him and from the expression in his eyes she could see the thoughts that flashed through his mind.

'Analee?'

'Well yes, sir, she is your wife. But as long as she remains so, we cannot proceed any further.'

The Falcon was silent and Anna's heart sank. She had over-played her hand.

'Analee,' the Falcon said quietly to himself over and over again. 'Why did I never think of it?'

'Think of what, sir?'

He looked at her, his eyes very grave, his expression solemn. 'Getting rid of her. Isn't that what you mean?'

'Getting rid . . .' For a moment she panicked, thinking of his violent reputation.

'Divorcing her, you idiot girl! Divorce! Aye, I'll divorce Analee and . . .' He put an arm round her waist. 'Marry you. *That* is what you want, isn't it? Why didn't I realize it?'

Anna Cameron licked her lips and felt a fresh tremor of fear. 'I do not want it; but if you want me . . .'

'It is the only way to have you, you little minx – and, by God, I'll get you!' The Falcon laughed and slapped his thigh. 'You want to be a marchioness? Then you shall. I will divorce Analee and we shall be wed. Aye, wedded, and *then* I'll bed you, you little . . .' The Falcon's black eyes turned almost red with desire.

'But first the ring,' Anna said. 'If you think it can be done. Divorce is, I believe, not very easy, my lord.'

'No, it is not easy; but it can be done, especially for someone in my position. It requires an act of Parliament.' The Falcon stood up and went to the window, rubbing his chin. 'I could divorce her on the grounds of adultery, but better of treason . . . *if* I could find out whom she saw in Kent before I sent her north. *If* I knew she consorted with Jacobites. *If* I had proof.'

'Treason? Not adultery?'

'Aye, maybe that, too; 'tis harder to prove, but I suspect she went to Lady Goodacre to meet an emissary of Prince Charles. Analee was always thick with those Jacobite rascals. Now if I could find out . . .' he slapped his forehead and came back to the sofa, sitting next to her again.

'You know Lady Goodacre, do you not?'

Anna remembered the lie. Oh how foolish she was; but then she had not thought that one day she would be within an inch of being a marchioness. 'Yes, of course, sir.'

'Aye, because 'twas through you that my wife went to see her.'

'I only know *of* her, sir.'

'Aye, aye. *Of*. It makes no difference. I will *send* you as my emissary. Ingratiate yourself with Lady Goodacre and find out who this person was. And take care you don't dally with any of the servants there as my last spy did!' Angus threw back his head and laughed but Anna Cameron was not amused.

'My lord, if coarseness comes into this I shall think again.'

'Oh, my darling, my angel.' Angus threw his arms around her and kissed her cheek. 'I cannot *wait* for you to be my marchioness, and make a real gentleman out of me. And I am sure you will. Everything will be very correct and above board in our household.'

'Was it not before?' Anna smiled, a quiet mysterious smile.

'Well, it certainly will be now.'

'And no straying, my lord, *if* I am to be your wife. I shall keep a careful eye on you.' She gave him a warning look and his heart turned to jelly.

'Oh, my darling, as *if* I would ever need to.'

If Anna Cameron felt like a traitor she was careful not to let it trouble her. After all, bringing about a divorce – hardly ever heard of – in order to be a marchioness, was playing for high stakes. One had no longer to think about one's orderly upbringing, one's religious training and code of conduct. Marchionesses in this world were few. There were certainly none in Chesapeake, Maryland, or Baltimore for that matter.

She felt she had changed; that she had risen to a different plane. She had not only captured the love of an important man. He was willing to put off a very beautiful and powerful wife for her. Surely she, Anna Cameron, must be something exceptional to accomplish this? Surely she was rather apart from ordinary mortals, in another realm altogether? She no longer thought as she used to. She *was* different.

The thought of this difference, this new apartness, stayed with her during her journey to Kent; the knowledge, too, that she was going to deceive a woman she didn't know and, possibly, bring danger upon the followers of the Prince she admired. Had she not been brought up as a Jacobite? To detest all things Hanoverian? Ah yes, but that was before she had fallen in love with a Hanoverian general – or rather not so much fallen in love with him (after all he was so much older and it really was difficult to feel passionately about a father-like figure) – as wished to marry him. And the more she thought about it the more she determined to marry him; to be the Marchioness of Falconer. She decided that nothing, family loyalties or political allegiance, would be allowed to stand in her way.

Lady Goodacre adored company, and what else could she say to a friend of Lady Falconer's other than how glad she was to see her? She hoped she would stay a few days and explore with her this lovely part of Kent. Anna Cameron was not yet a hardened practiced deceiver and even *she* felt ashamed at the extent of Lady Goodacre's hospitality. She was really only passing through, she said; she couldn't stay long.

At least she agreed to stay the night and over dinner she entertained her ladyship with an account of the developments in Maryland, the fears of war and yet the hopes of getting rid of the French. Annabel Goodacre kept on looking carefully at the beautiful girl opposite her wondering which side she was on, how much she could be trusted.

'Stewart Allonby is the brother of a nun who is in a convent in France,' Lady Goodacre said cautiously, after telling the servants to leave them alone. 'In religion she is Sister Mary Gertrude. My own sister Felicity is a nun in the same house. That is how I know the Allonby family . . . and the Delamains.'

'And that of course is the connection with Lady Falconer,' Anna said, her beautiful turquoise orbs seeming to understand for the first time. 'Of course I see it now!'

'I understand Lady Falconer is unwell.'

'Alas.' Anna Cameron's features suitably composed themselves into an expression of distress. 'But I understand she is a prey to ill health.'

'Oh?' Lady Goodacre said sipping her wine. 'She looked extremely healthy to me. Rumour has it that she is of gypsy stock.'

'Oh yes, she is. There is no doubt of that.'

'Then I would have thought her very strong.'

'I believe it is partly a nervous indisposition.'

'Really?' Annabel Goodacre looked unconvinced. 'A pity. I liked her so much. She was here in the autumn. I hope she will come again.'

Anna Cameron was beginning to feel her visit was pointless, for at that moment her ladyship signalled for the servants to re-enter and all personal conversation ceased. She felt she had not really established a rapport with her hostess and the next day she had said she would go.

But because she was lonely and, a good deal of the time, rather sad, Lady Goodacre enjoyed a glass or two of Madeira or port after dinner and on this evening she threw back the doors that led onto the terrace, her face rather flushed. 'I really feel I need air,' she said. 'See, it is such a lovely evening. So mild for this time of the year. Come, let us take a turn on the terrace.'

She turned to Anna Cameron, who thought the evening was distinctly chilly and wrapped her shawl closely around her.

However she accepted Lady Goodacre's arm and went with her onto the terrace.

'Oh, the view is marvellous!' she said. 'Quite breathtaking. Is that the sea?' She pointed to a ribbon of silver gleaming in the distance ahead of them.

'Yes, it is the Channel and when the weather is clear you can see France.'

'Really?' Anna caught her breath and was glad she had come outside. She pulled her shawl more tightly round her, aware of Lady Goodacre's arm closely linked in hers. 'I long to go to France.'

'You must have friends there?'

'Oh, yes.'

'I suppose your family support . . .'

'Of course.' Anna gave her arm a comforting squeeze. 'Cameron, you know.'

'No doubt related to poor Archie Cameron who was executed long after the Rebellion?'

'I think there was a connection,' Anna said cautiously, knowing there was not.

'Do you think they will ever return?'

Anna felt she had to be careful. Because she was here on a secret, devious mission she could not be sure that Lady Goodacre was not devious too. 'I don't know.'

'But you hope so?'

'Of course.'

'And Brent Delamain, would you see him in France?'

'I think he is in America. We saw him in Maryland last year.'

'Oh no. He is here.'

Anna stopped and a little *frisson* passed along her spine. 'Here?'

'Well he *was* here; he is not here now.'

'You mean he was *here* . . . at Castle Goodacre?'

'Yes.'

'Oh I wish I could have seen him!' Anna felt her heart skip a beat.

'He was here only very briefly; then he went to France. I don't suppose I should tell you this, but I know you are a friend. He came to see Lady Falconer. But of course you must not tell anyone, never breathe a word.'

Suddenly Anna wished she hadn't come; she wished she had said 'no' and let the Falcon do his own spying. She wished she were not ensnared by him, not so desirous of becoming a marchioness. She remembered her brother-in-law Stewart, that implacable foe of the Hanoverians, her friendship for Brent . . . what could she tell Lord Falconer now?

'I think we should go in,' she said, starting to tremble. 'It is getting cold.'

'Oh, I do wish you would stay on,' Lady Goodacre said pressing her arm. 'I am so glad you came.'

10

Analee saw the small troop of soldiers riding swiftly along the road below her as she walked over Manesty Moor, arm in arm with Nelly, on her way back to the Grange. She stopped and, shielding her eyes against the strong spring sunshine, pointed with her finger.

'I think we are being occupied by the militia, Nell! Or maybe we are at war!'

The two women looked at each other in surmise and began to run down the moorland laughing like girls, their hair flying in the wind. Analee felt that nothing could detract from her happiness now, after these months surrounded by the love of her children and servants in her Lakeland home. Except that she knew the Falcon was alive she never heard from him. He made no communication and sent no instructions. But at last she was content and at peace. She no longer sought to identify her life with his.

They reached the house just as a servant was issuing forth towards the way they had come. When he saw Analee he was already breathless and, stopping, bowed. 'My lady, there is an officer to see you.'

'To see me?' Analee's hand flew to her breast. 'Oh, I hope nothing untoward has happened to the Falcon!'

At the back of the house she could see the men who made up the troop watering their horses and quickly she ran inside, along the passage to the front drawing room. An officer she did not know stood at attention and saluted her. Then he bowed.

'Lady Falconer, Colonel Middleton, madam, of the garrison stationed at Carlisle. Your obedient servant, Lady Falconer.'

'How do you do, Colonel?' Analee was still panting from her run and her cheeks were flushed. Colonel Middleton had heard of the legendary beauty of her ladyship, but even he was unprepared for what he saw – her black hair tumbled about her face, her bewitching eyes gleaming with health and vitality, her enticing chin tilted at a provocative angle. 'I hope there is nothing wrong with my husband?'

The colonel swallowed and lowered his gaze reluctantly from the vision of female beauty to a piece of paper he held in his hand. 'No, madam. Lady Falconer,' he cleared his throat and his fingers tugged at his tight, stiff collar, 'Lady Falconer, I regret, ma'am, that I have orders to apprehend you and convey you to Carlisle Castle.'

'Apprehend *me*, sir?'

'For treason, ma'am.'

The Colonel's face was as scarlet as his uniform and his collar seemed to have become unbearably tight.

'That is what is writ on this paper, ma'am.' The Colonel made a pretence of studying it carefully to hide his embarrassment.

'*Treason*?' Analee threw back her head and laughed heartily, then good-naturedly pointed to a chair. 'Pray, Colonel, do sit down and loosen your collar. I will send for refreshment for you. You will find there is some error.'

'There is no error, ma'am, alas, though I confess I do not understand it; but these were my instructions given to me by the governor of the castle himself. And it has the stamp of a very high authority in London.'

'The King's I hope,' Analee said loftily, 'for nothing less will do for me.'

'I am sure the governor will show you the document, ma'am. I am come to take you there, Lady Falconer.'

'To Carlisle Prison?'

'Yes, ma'am. Those are my instructions and I have no alternative but to obey them. I am sure everything will be sorted out there and your ladyship will soon be restored to your freedom and your estates.'

'I see.' Analee went over to the bellrope and gave it a sharp tug. When a servant entered she asked him to send Nelly to her quickly and then she turned to the Colonel.

'I must bid farewell to my servants and children, sir, for who knows when I may see them again?'

'Oh, very soon, Lady Falconer, I am sure of that. I daresay there is some muddle that will soon be sorted out. I am distressed to bring you this news, my lady. I . . .'

'Do not distress yourself any further, sir, but enjoy your refreshment. I may bring my maid with me, may I not?'

'Of course, ma'am.'

Analee went swiftly from the room greeting Nelly as she approached the door and, taking her upstairs, told her what had happened. Nelly clasped her face in her hands and burst into tears.

'Oh, Analee, how could this be?'

'It is his lordship who is behind it, never fear. This is some devious plan of his to get rid of me. Well, I have good and powerful friends, Nell. I do not believe that they will let this happen. I will demand to be sent to London, to the Tower if need be, and then I can set things happening. Now, Nelly, I want you to come with me because I need you; but I want you to send two messengers. One for Reyora who must come and look after the household in our absence and one to Sir George Delamain who, whatever his faults, will I believe be aghast at this news and will do what he can to help me. Run quick, Nell, and organize this and then hasten back to help me pack my things.'

The Governor of Carlisle Castle bent low in the presence of his distinguished prisoner and put the piece of paper in her hands almost supplicatingly. 'See for yourself, Lady Falconer. It is signed by the Duke of Newcastle.'

And indeed it was, with a mighty flourish, too, as though by someone pleased with his work.

'My husband's close friend,' Lady Falconer murmured. 'I wager His Majesty would not have put his hand to a document like this.'

'It says you are arraigned on a charge of high treason, ma'am, and are to be held here until a trial is arranged.'

'I desire to be tried in London where all may hear of it, sir, and not skulking up here out of the way where I may be condemned unheard. Is the dungeon ready, sir?'

'Oh, ma'am, no *dungeon*,' the governor said, attempting a nervous laugh. 'A suite of rooms has been prepared for your ladyship where you shall have all the comfort you can desire, and what food you order shall be put before you. I assure you, ma'am, I am only doing my duty.'

'I am quite certain of that, governor,' Analee said bestowing on him the smile that would ensure he would forever be her slave. 'I am certain you are.'

* * *

759

The Falcon looked pale but triumphant. The deed had been done. He had bullied his pusillanimous friend into signing the document that committed Analee for high treason. All he had to do now was to bring this information to the ears of the King. This was the part he least liked; Analee was a favourite with the old monarch.

Anna Cameron looked pale, too, and not so joyful. She felt that the consequences of accusing and arresting his wife would be far more serious than her swain seemed to think. As she stared at the paper that brought news of Analee's arrest her hand trembled.

'Oh, Angus, do you not think you go too far? Would adultery not have been less serious?'

'Aye, and harder to prove. I do not know she has lain with other men, for sure; but I do know she met the perfidious traitor Brent Delamain at Castle Goodacre and if necessary Lady Goodacre will be prepared to swear it.'

'You have asked her?' Anna felt herself blushing, knowing that her treachery was responsible for having brought this about.

'I have told Lord Goodacre what transpired. He was horrified. I said if his wife did not testify against Analee I should have her clapped in irons and committed to prison for treachery too.'

Anna thought of the timid, gentle person who had given her hospitality and she blushed even more. The Falcon put an arm round her waist and drew her to him pressing his lips against her cheek. Even though they were betrothed she permitted him no liberties, no intimacies other than a chaste peck on the cheek. He yearned for her more than ever, this delicious nubile person who made herself so inaccessible. What a jewel to be prized!

'There, my love, do not worry your pretty little head. Now I have a surprise for you which I hope will please you. I have in mind to purchase a house for you where you will have your own servants and not the surveillance of that remarkably common Mrs Peto.'

'Oh, Angus. Is it possible!' Anna forgot about her treachery and, clasping his hands, looked into his eyes.

'Of course it is possible! You will be chaperoned by an old friend of mine, Lady McKeith, a lady of the greatest respectability. For all anyone knows it will be her house, for I feel we must maintain the greatest discretion until this difficult time is over. I must appear to be grief-stricken that my wife is apprehended for treason. I shall wear a black band.'

The Falcon roared with laughter and poured two glasses of Madeira, one for his darling and one for himself. He carried them over and, putting a glass into her hand, raised the other in a toast. 'To us, my dearest.'

'To us, Angus.' Anna Cameron raised her glass, and only the look in his eyes gave her any confidence or strength to face the future. There were certain things that even a young lady of determination and character from Chesapeake found somewhat daunting.

The Falcon put down his glass and stood with his back to the fire rubbing his hands. It was cold even for April. He gazed at his bride-to-be relishing his power over women, even a woman of such spirit as this. To think he had never sampled the delights of her body. No woman had ever resisted him for so long, certainly not that wanton Analee, who had given her body to him even before her husband was cold in his grave. What a disgusting whore she was! He wrinkled his nose with distaste at the memory, forgetting how he had adored her. As soon as he had his divorce he would set about disinheriting all her children on the grounds that they were bastards. He would breed afresh from the delicious body of Anna and oh, how he would relish doing that! What a girl of spirit and daring she was, what a companion. As he gazed at her an idea came to him and his look changed from simpering adoration to thoughtful calculation.

'I have just thought of something, my dear.'

'And what is that, my lord?' She came shyly up to him and stood by his side, an arm timidly stealing about his waist. Even her touch on his thick coat made him tremble.

'If we could get that traitor here to stand trial, *too*, then we would despatch the business all the more quickly.'

'Which traitor, Angus?'

'Why, Brent Delamain, my darling. He and Analee together in the dock. Oh, how I should like that!' The Falcon gave a fiendish chuckle, going over to fill his glass with more wine.

'Oh, Angus, can you not leave well alone? Is it not sufficient to have her languishing in gaol?'

'Languishing!' Angus gave a snort. 'My dear, you know not what you say. My wife is not one to languish. Oh, no! She will have her gaolers all eating from the palms of her traitorous hands; she will be lying with them each in turn at night, strumpet that she is. Oh, compared to your sublime virtue, my darling, your maidenly chastity, you have no idea what a whore Analee is. That I could permit her to bear my children fills me with nausea.' The Falcon passed a hand across his head and closed his eyes as though sickened by the vision.

Anna Cameron gave her betrothed a shrewd look. If chastity was the way to retain the respect of the Falcon perhaps she would do well to remain a virgin forever.

'Now to business.' Angus opened his eyes and went briskly to his desk. He sat down and began writing. 'I am going to use you again, my treasure.'

'In what way, sir?'

'I am going to send you to Paris to seek out Delamain.'

'Oh, Angus, I cannot do that,' Anna cried in alarm. 'I have done enough harm.'

Angus turned round and looked at her. 'Harm? You silly goose, what harm?'

'I have been . . . very disloyal to a friend already. Have I not done enough?'

'You have not been disloyal, my poppet. You have been very *loyal*. Loyal to our Hanoverian King. You have made yourself worthy to be my Marchioness. When His Majesty hears how we have apprehended the traitors together he will undoubtedly make me a duke and then, my angel, you will become a duchess!'

A duchess! Anna closed her eyes and swayed slightly. A duchess. However would they react in Chesapeake to *that*? 'What must I do?' she said.

Sir George Delamain did not look well. His face was always rather pale, as of one who spends a lot of time poring over figures, but his skin now was positively translucent and he had lost weight. He gazed at Analee piteously and she put a hand on his arm.

'Pray sit down, good Sir George, and I will have a glass of wine sent in to us.'

'Thank you, my lady.' Sir George sat heavily down in the chair indicated by Analee and passed a hand across his brow. 'Believe me, Lady Falconer, this has been a severe shock to my family.'

'And mine, Sir George,' Analee said, sitting in a chair by his side. From the windows of her suite she had views over the flat countryside, but in the distance she could see, on a good day, the hazy peaks of her beloved Lakeland.

Except for the fact that she was not allowed to leave the precincts, she did not feel contained in any way. She could walk in the pleasant grounds, eat and drink what she liked, see whom she pleased and generally behave like the lady of distinction she was, rather than a common prisoner. The governor was never less than extremely deferential and her letters, the many that she wrote, were uncensored and sent to London by special messenger.

And Analee had not been idle. Her quill had flown swiftly over paper and one of the first letters she had sent had been to the friend and patron who had once offered her a position in her suite – the Princess of Wales. She knew that at the moment it was useless petitioning the King; the influence of Lady Yarmouth would not be in her favour. In fact it was doubtful whether a letter would get to him that Lady Yarmouth had not seen first. Even ministers of the crown had to seek an interview of the monarch through his powerful mistress. But she did write to a lord who, besides being a close friend and ally of Princess Augusta, was an influence on the young Prince George, and who knew how soon he would succeed his grandfather?

'Lady Delamain took to her bed for several days when she first heard the news of your apprehension and incarceration.'

'How sorry I am to hear that,' Analee said, thankful for her own robust good health. 'And you look none too well, Sir George.'

'Ah, I have found it a hard winter. I have had many fevers and indispositions and am in a weakened state; and now this news . . .' Sir George blew his nose vigorously in his large handkerchief and Analee perceived that his eyes had filled with tears. 'There is of course no *doubt* that Brent did come to Kent?'

'None at all, I'm afraid; but he did not come to plot treason. I think he has hopes of a pardon from the King.'

'Oh?' Sir George looked at her with consternation. 'Without grounds, I trust?'

'You would not like him back, Sir George? After all, is he not your heir?' Analee looked at him sadly thinking of the irrational force of family feuds; but the brothers had never been close.

'No, I would *not* like him back, Lady Falconer.' Sir George thumped the floor with his stick. 'He was always a ne'er-do-well. The bulk of my estates and fortune will pass to my daughters, the title and castle to a cousin. I have it all arranged. I never want to set my sights on Brent Delamain again and this latest incident . . .' Sir George wiped his eyes. 'What will it do but bring fresh dishonour on my family? Have we not had enough? Must we go through it all again? Did I not speak for Stewart at his trial? Must we go on suffering, we of the family who have always been loyal to His Majesty?'

'I think you owe it to your family and yourself to speak for your brother, Sir George,' Analee interjected gently. 'I know he wants to give up the life of a wanderer and settle down. If you could say that your brother had made approaches to you through me for a reconciliation, that would put a completely different complexion on things, would it not? There might never even be a trial. Surely you would wish to avoid *that* scandal, Sir George? A trial in London for high treason? I assure you I will make the biggest splash I can. The trial of Catherine of Aragon before King Henry would pale in comparison to mine.'

Looking at her Sir George believed her; but suddenly the dark in his mind was illumined by an unlooked-for, a completely unexpected ray of hope. 'There would be *no* trial? No scandal?'

'None. You would go direct to a source near the King – I have one in mind – and say that Lord Falconer is quite mistaken in his suspicions. That Brent wants to make amends and return to England. That he met me for this purpose hoping I could influence his lordship; but I knew it was useless. However I have spoken to you about the matter, and Brent has been in touch with you again . . .'

'But it is all lies, Lady Falconer.' That honest baronet looked perplexed and the Marchioness got up and walked with stately splendour, as only she knew how, over to the fireplace. She warmed her long fingers on the flames; she closed her eyes and made a wish – she wished as only she could, willed as only she knew how.

She willed him to do her bidding. She willed it with all her heart.

'It is the *only* way, Sir George, to save your family. You wish that, do you not? I am sure the scandal will kill her ladyship and bring the name of Delamain into infinite disrepute – such that you never suffered before. And I assure you Brent will always be grateful, and so shall I.'

He looked into her eyes and knew he had to do as he was bid; he had no alternative. 'I will do it, my lady.' He bowed his head and suddenly he felt a little better. He did not feel so cold and the arthritic pains left his limbs. He looked at her and smiled. She really was an enchantress, there was no doubt of it at all.

'I knew you would, good Sir George. You are very wise. Now we must send an emissary to Brent, someone we can trust. Someone who will say what is afoot.'

'But who can we trust to do such a thing?'

'There is a young girl in London who is very close to the Allonby family. Her name is Anna Cameron. Her brother-in-law is Stewart.'

'Miss Cameron? I know of her,' Sir George said, avoiding Analee's eyes.

'Of course you know of her. She stopped with the Riggs, did she not? Now if you could see her . . . why pray, what is it, Sir George?' Sir George had gone ashen again and avoided her eyes. 'Are you not well? Let me send . . .'

'No, Lady Falconer,' Sir George held out his hand as she got up to pull the bellrope. 'I had hoped to spare you this.'

'Spare me what, Sir George? Speak.'

'This Anna Cameron, the one you mentioned, the sister-in-law of . . .'

'Yes, yes, pray go on, sir.'

'Rumour has only just reached me, my lady, and rumour it is I assure you, that it is on her account that you are in this gaol.'

Analee sat down abruptly and tried to compose her features. '*My* account? Pray explain, Sir George.'

'It distresses me to say it, Lady Falconer.'

'But say it nevertheless.'

'It is said, my lady, only rumour mark you, that by bringing this trumped-up charge of treason his lordship wishes to divorce you and put Miss Cameron in your place.'

Analee felt her head reel and steadied herself on the arms of her chair. Why had she not known it or guessed it? Why had her powers not told her about this? Were they deserting her? Was she too much a lady and less a gypsy? Why had she put Miss Cameron so firmly out of her mind? She remembered those turquoise eyes and she thought they would haunt her for the rest of her life.

'Then it must be Emma,' she said without emotion – Sir George was afterwards to relate how uncannily calm she was – 'for who else can we trust?'

Emma Fitzgerald, scarcely six months married, listened to her brother with amazement. Fortunately her husband was in White-haven and not privy to this extraordinary story.

'But you expect *me* to go to France?'

'There is none other.'

'What about yourself?'

'They would never receive me. At least you owe Brent some loyalty, for he helped you.'

'And what do I owe Lady Falconer? Nothing.'

And then she remembered the spell. But had the spell really worked? It had brought Hugo to ask her to marry him; but it had not brought to their marriage the love and rapture she had hoped for, nay expected. Her husband was a cold lover, an indifferent spouse. He spent most of his time at his bachelor quarters in Whitehaven and buried himself more in his work than ever before. She lived with the Riggs and went every day to supervise the building of her own home. She hoped that when it was ready Hugo would give her the love she desired and, with it, children.

'It is not what you owe or do not owe Lady Falconer, my dear – though, poor woman, I feel sorry enough for her; her husband has some plan to put her away and marry another.'

'Oh?' Emma looked at him with interest.

'Aye, Anna Cameron has caused any amount of mischief in that household.'

'Anna Cameron? You do not mean the sister-in-law of Stewart? The one that stopped here?'

'The very same. The Falcon is enamoured of her and desires to divorce his wife and make her his marchioness.'

'Anna Cameron,' Emma said wonderingly. The sister of the woman she had the greatest cause in the world to hate – Elizabeth Cameron, whom Stewart had preferred to her. 'Then perhaps I *do* owe something to Lady Falconer?'

'How is that, Emma?'

766

'I would not like to help Miss Cameron's advancement one jot. I would do all I can to prevent it.'

'Well, that is capital,' her brother said, wriggling in his seat uncomfortably. 'I had no idea you felt so strongly, especially as you are well and happily married. At least, I trust you are happy?' George looked at her doubtfully. 'Are you?'

'Of course I am, dear brother. It is true my husband is excessively devoted to his work and I am often on my own; but I see to the building of our house and I help Sarah with the new baby, and . . .' she gestured lamely, 'there is plenty for me to do.'

'You know that Hugo has no love for our brother, my dear?'

'Of course I know it. His name is never mentioned here.'

'Then how shall you explain your journey?'

Emma looked at him thoughtfully. 'I shall have to take Sarah and Ambrose into my confidence. They will think of something. They are the only people we can trust.'

But Ambrose was doubtful as to the wisdom of the venture. He picked his nose thoughtfully and then surveyed the contents with interest before popping them into his mouth. His wife grimaced with disgust and looked down at the new infant asleep in her arms – the most beautiful of her children yet. She hoped the last. Oh, how she hoped. She was forty and felt past child-bearing. Someone had told her that if she suckled the baby for a long time she could not conceive while she was doing so. In that case, she felt, she was prepared to suckle it forever. Before, she had employed a wet nurse; but not now. The trouble was that as she grew older her milk seemed to get less plentiful. She sometimes felt the baby did not have enough to eat.

'I have small regard for your brother as you know,' Sarah said to Emma, rocking the baby in her arms. 'He has always been irresponsible. 'Twas he who sent you on that perilous journey to America, that ended in such unhappiness. Why should you risk your life for him?'

'I am not risking my life!' Emma expostulated, regretting she had decided to tell the Riggs. Ambrose, after all, thought a great deal of Hugo.

'How do you know you are not?' Sarah said quietly. 'Getting involved in spying and plotting. It is neither safe nor wise.'

'I agree,' Ambrose said, beginning to excavate the other nostril.

'Oh, I agree.' Then he looked at the frown on Sir George's face and remembered the amount of business they did together. It would not do to annoy the baronet. On the other hand he did not wish to anger those who might advance him in the future. With his entry into civic affairs he hoped one day to join the ranks of the gentry himself, at least as a knight. It was difficult to know what to do.

'It is our family name,' Sir George said with an air of desperation. 'Emma's as well as mine. Lady Falconer prophesies a scandal the like of which will completely undo our family. She swears that as a peeress she can demand trial in the House of Lords and . . .'

'Oh dear,' Ambrose shook his head nervously. 'Scandal on that scale . . . oh dear.'

'And I can see her doing it,' Emma said.

'And I.' The baby burped in its sleep and Sarah rubbed its back. 'You will have to go to see Mary,' Sarah said after a while, nestling the baby in her arms again. 'You can tell your husband that you wished to see her on my behalf. We are anxious about her welfare and I cannot go because I am suckling my baby. You can stay in the convent with her; you will be perfectly safe, *and* she remains on good terms with Brent. She will know where he is to be found.'

Ambrose sat back with a sigh of satisfaction. The security of his trade with Sir George was assured. That was really all that mattered – trade and the making of money and, he thought, looking at his latest progeny with satisfaction, the siring of children to whom to pass on his fortune. But perhaps they now had enough. Seven lusty children, four boys and three girls. Besides, he didn't want to wear Sarah out so that she could not bring them up. That was her job now, to look after his home and rear his children. His needs were perfectly well satisfied by a beautiful young mistress he had recently set up in Whitehaven in a little house at the back of the town. She was only twenty-two, the widow of a sailor, grateful for his patronage and experienced in the amorous arts. She was absolutely ideal – clean, wholesome and rather naughty. The sailor had taught her some most interesting ways in bed that he himself had learned in foreign parts.

Ambrose Rigg wriggled in his seat with satisfaction, his mind on carnal delights and the satisfaction of knowing that he led an industrious, successful and most rewarding life. Let others do as they liked, he thought, let others do as they liked.

Sister Mary Gertrude was surprised at the unexpected visit of her brother Stewart's sister-in-law. She had had no word of her coming and was in retreat. The Reverend Mother gave her permission to see her and Sister Mary Gertrude broke her silence with reluctance as the devotions before Easter were important to her. She was surprised by the beauty of Stewart's sister-in-law and wondered if she resembled her sister Elizabeth. If so her brother was a lucky man; but earthly beauty no longer mattered to Mary. The only beauty now for her was the cross of Christ.

'It is dangerous for you in Paris,' Sister Mary Gertrude whispered, gazing at the lovely girl opposite her. 'France and England are on the verge of war. Did you not know?'

'Oh, I know,' Anna Cameron said. 'The French and the English have been openly skirmishing in my country for a long time. Two years ago, in 1754, Colonel Washington was routed by the French at Fort Duquesne and is itching to have his revenge. No, I am not afraid of war.'

'But why have you come?'

'Because I wished to see the Allonby family, you, your brother and, if possible, Brent Delamain before I return to America. Stewart will wish to have first-hand news of them. I daren't go back without seeing you all. I shall probably never cross the waters again, but settle down as a good housewife in Chesapeake.' Anna Cameron lowered her eyes modestly, not even having the grace to blush, despite the perfidy of lying in this holy place.

'I wonder you have not wed already,' Mary said. 'You have such beauty; but you must not stay here long. Any enemy of France will be in danger here.'

'*I* am no enemy of France!'

'Are you not?' Mary looked at her gravely and smiled. 'Good. The English are welcome here so long as they do not support the Hanoverian government. You can come and go safely if you are a Jacobite. Are you one?'

'Yes,' Anna whispered, but this time she did blush.

'I thought as much. You would hardly be Stewart's sister-in-law were you not. You can stay in the convent for a few days while I arrange a meeting for you. John and his family live at Plessy just outside Paris.'

'And shall I see Brent?' Anna's voice faltered and she coughed as though from an obstruction in the throat.

'Alas, I do not think so. I do not even know where he is. Somewhere on the Prince's business doubtless. He grew very excited a few months ago when there was the prospect of a French invasion of England.'

'I know, the English were in a ferment about it.'

'Then, as you know, plans miscarried. Some say the Prince was too timorous.'

'Then I shall not see Brent?' Anna could scarcely conceal her disappointment.

'Did you particularly wish to see him?' Mary smiled at her, thinking how attractive this lovely girl would find her former husband. But would he look at her, with his obsessive love for Analee? Hardly. Mary wished that Brent would find someone he could love and settle down with. Maybe Anna Cameron *would* do after all; she was certainly very lovely. Then he would go back to America with her and live in harmony away from the Prince's influence and the proximity of Analee Falconer only a few miles across the water. 'It will not be easy; but I think I can arrange it. You will have to be patient. But we have our Lenten services all this week in the convent chapel. You are welcome to share our devotions.'

'I should like nothing better,' Anna Cameron said, clasping her hands piously and raising her eyes to heaven.

The Good Friday devotions seemed endless, the chanting went on interminably and the beautiful singing of the nuns, though pleasing to the ear, did nothing to ease the feeling of hard wood on delicate knees. Anna Cameron rested her bottom on the bench of the pew behind her and listened to the craving of her stomach. It seemed hours since she had eaten. She glanced at her maid but she was asleep, her chin resting on her hands.

A week had passed and Anna was fretting. The streets were judged so unsafe that the Reverend Mother would not let her go out, even with her maid and a convent servant. Troops were roaming the streets at all hours and no young woman was safe in them unless she had the protection of the veil. Not even soldiers molested nuns – French nuns anyway. It was a different story in foreign countries where they raped and pillaged at will.

Entering the convent chapel Emma saw the beautiful girl immediately and wondered who she was. With her black veil and subdued clothing obviously some postulant come to see if she had a vocation.

Emma was a loyal member of the English Protestant Church and all this popery was offensive to her – the Allonbys and the Delamains had been split in religious matters as much as in political ones, although Emma's mother was a Catholic and her eldest brother Tom had been a monk. Like her brother George, Emma had chosen the Protestant faith. Had she married Stewart Allonby she would gladly have embraced Catholicism; but Hugo, too, was a Protestant and so was Sarah Rigg.

The beautiful girl glanced at Emma standing at the back of the chapel and then she turned her head and pretended to be absorbed in her devotions. Emma could not make out any of the nuns in the choir. She had been told that Sister Mary Gertrude would still be many hours in the chapel during this long Good Friday service. Emma decided to leave her bags at the convent and go straight to her cousin John Allonby. It was vital to find Brent and tell him what had happened to Analee. To try and get him to petition the King and return home.

Emma slipped out of the chapel and gave quick instructions to her maid and the sister porteress at the convent door, together with a message for Sister Mary Gertrude. The hired carriage that had brought her here from Boulogne was waiting outside together with the servants she had engaged. She had been warned not to travel without male protection.

She got into the carriage with her maid and gave directions to the driver, then she leaned back and closed her eyes, the steady jogging of the carriage making her sleep again.

John Allonby stared incredulously at Emma as his wife, Thérèse, led her in through the door of his study.

'You do not recognize me?' she said, smiling and letting her hood fall back.

'My dear Emma . . . of course.' John went over to her and took her in his arms. 'Of course; but you are a woman, no longer a maid.'

'Aye, a married woman.' Emma stepped back and gazed at him.

'So I heard.' The smile left John's face. 'So I heard.'

'Doubtless from Brent. He and my husband are old enemies.'

'I'm sure it is in the past,' John said quickly. ''Twas all a long time ago. I am sure Brent wishes you every happiness.'

'Then he can tell me himself for I have come to speak to him. Do you know where he is?'

John went over to his desk and taking up his long clay pipe filled it slowly with rich Virginian tobacco. He indicated a chair to Emma and smiled at his wife. 'Would you bring us coffee, my dear?'

Thérèse gave a little bob and nodded her head, smiling at Emma.

'She speaks no English, alas.'

'She seems very nice. I long to see your babies.'

'You must tell me about Sarah – seven now! Somehow I never saw Sarah as the mother of seven.'

'I think she will be the mother of twenty if she does not take care! Mr Rigg is very uxorious, very keen on establishing a dynasty.'

John wrinkled his nose and put a spill from the fire to his pipe. 'I found it very hard to be fond of my brother-in-law.'

'His personal habits are disgusting; but his heart is good. He is a kind man; he sent the money for me to return from America, and did not reproach me for my folly as Sarah did. He gets on well with my husband. I like him.'

'Good.' John nodded, getting his pipe to draw satisfactorily. 'After all, that is the most important thing. You have your priorities right, Emma. I am glad. You must tell me all about . . .'

'In time, John, in time. But I want to hear all about Brent. It is very important that I see him. Please tell me how I can find him.'

'That is very simple,' John said. 'He is upstairs playing with my children. He arrived here only an hour ago; in Paris only yesterday. He is always very mysterious about his movements. He will be so excited when he knows you are here.' John beckoned and, her heart beating with excitement, Emma followed him from the room.

11

Emma scarcely recognized Brent romping on the floor with his nieces and nephew, laughing, his clothes awry, his hair tousled. She had been so used to seeing him serious and grave in the years of the Rebellion and after, in his years as a refugee. As she opened the door he clutched at three-year-old Hélène who fell on top of him giggling with laughter, and then he gazed at her and she saw that his eyes immediately went to the place he had left his sword.

'No, Brent. 'Tis I.' She held out her hands and he took them, using them to lever himself up from the floor. He looked as though he did not know whether to be glad or sorry to see her.

'Emma.' He clasped her hands and kissed her cheek; but she could feel no warmth emanating from him. He didn't know whether or not to trust her, so much was clear.

'I come as a friend, Brent, your sister.'

His expression relaxed. 'Of course, what else, Emma?'

'I know you do not like my husband.'

'Ah, but I am not married to him,' Brent said lightly. 'For which I thank God.' He put on his sword belt and, turning, introduced the children to her. There was only a year between them all – Hélène, the eldest, three, Eustace, two and the baby, Marie, still in the arms of her nursemaid who sat on a nearby chair. Emma hugged them all and murmured endearments but they looked at her uncomprehendingly. 'They know not a word of English,' Brent said.

'Of course not. But you speak French very well.'

'I have to pass as a native at times,' Brent said, waving to the children as he closed the door behind Emma and himself. 'Or I will be killed for an English dog. It is not safe here for you, Emma. Were you stopped on the way?'

'No. My coachman and servants are French. I came by boat to Boulogne and Rigg's agent had arranged for me to hire them there.'

'You came *all* the way by boat?'

'Yes, from Whitehaven. Ambrose thought it was quicker. I was very sick!'

'The seas around our coast are treacherous. It is what has kept the English safe – so far anyway.'

'So far?'

'The Prince is very hopeful of a successful invasion.'

'And you, Brent?'

They had reached John's room and he stood up to greet them as they came in, looking anxiously from one to the other.

'Oh, we are speaking, John. Never fear!' Brent said laughing and putting an arm lightly round his sister's shoulders. 'Even though she is married to a traitor.'

Emma shook herself away and looked at him furiously. 'My husband is no traitor, Brent, but a good and honest business man. He has no truck with politics now.'

'I wish I had not either,' Brent said, sitting in a chair and accepting a glass of wine from John. He gazed at Emma and nodded his head. 'Aye, truly. I wish I were a free man able to live in England.'

'You are no longer loyal to the Prince?' Emma looked at him sharply.

'I am as loyal to him as I can be. That is, I would not betray him; but I cannot trust him. The Prince I loved, for whom our brother gave his life, is not the man he was. No one trusts him any more. He drinks too much, makes too many enemies and takes too many chances. He is always moving around in disguise – and some think him ridiculous. He was recently seen wearing a false nose to resemble Marshal Saxe! He sent me to England on a fool's scheme and nearly had me arrested; but for Analee I would have been.'

'Analee? How came she into that?'

'I knew it was folly for me to risk being seen in London so I came only to Kent and asked her to approach the sister of the Prince's mistress, Clementina Walkinshaw, who he said was loyal to the cause. The sister, Catherine, would have no truck with it at all, or conversation with Analee. She said that her family had completely rejected Clementina. Analee endangered herself even by mentioning it and had it been I, I should have been apprehended and sent to the Tower. Even the Prince's mistress is not loyal to him and old friends like Lady Primrose, Goring and others speak against him loudly. He asked me to be his right-hand man, and when I went to see him in Basle to tell him about Analee's visit he castigated me for not going myself and said *she* was a traitor! He was so drunk he almost threw me out of the house and had it not been for the intervention of Clementina I should have had nowhere to stay.

'I am finished with the Prince. I tell you that.'

'I am glad to hear it,' Emma said and quietly, quickly told him what she had come for.

For a long time Brent sat with his head bent on his chest and his eyes closed. After a while Emma perceived that tears were stealing down his cheeks and when he opened his eyes they were red and full of suffering. 'She is in gaol, for me?'

'Accused of high treason – treason against the monarch and punishable by death.'

'I must go to her at once!'

'That is folly, Brent,' John said, putting his glass to his lips. 'Emma has a plan.'

'You are to approach the ambassador here and ask for a pardon. You will swear that you will have no more to do with the Prince and that you wish to return to England. The King is granting clemency to many people now because the throne is so safe.'

'But what about the invasion scare at the end of last year? I hear there had been nothing like it for years.'

'It died down. Pitt did not believe there would be an invasion and people are listening to his views more and more. Some say he will be asked to form a ministry and run the country.'

'He is detested by the King,' John said.

'No matter. That is what we hear, although in Cumbria we are not exactly at the heart of affairs; but Mr Rigg is keenly interested in politics and one day hopes to be mayor of Whitehaven.'

'Indeed?' Brent tried to look grave, but could hardly keep himself from laughing. 'Perhaps they will ask *him* to run the country. I can just see old Rigg at the helm.'

'Do not mock him, Brent.'

'I do not mock him. I *respect* him. If it were not for your husband I should still be working for him. Anyway I have to see the ambassador. Go on.'

'George is going to London, maybe he is there already. He is to see Lord Bute who, he thinks, will be sympathetic to you. Lord Bute is a close friend of Princess Augusta who loves Analee. Everyone in London is aghast at what has happened. They think for Analee's sake the King will listen kindly to you and grant a pardon.'

'And what about the powerful Falcon?'

'The Falcon is still powerful, but not as much as he thinks. He is very friendly with Mr Pitt who is disliked by the King, and people also disapprove of a liaison he has formed with a young woman. They think he wants to put away Analee and take her for his wife.'

Brent shot out of his chair and clasped his sister by the shoulder, staring into her eyes. 'Say that again? He wants to marry another?'

'So it is said – to Miss Anna Cameron, who is distantly related to us through marriage.'

'*Anna Cameron*.' Brent sat down heavily and took a gulp of his wine. 'Miss Anna Cameron of Chesapeake?'

'The same. The Falcon has become infatuated with her.'

'Well, she *is* very beautiful,' Brent said as though dubious about the whole thing. 'But compared to Analee, how could any man desire . . .'

'Oh, other men *do* find other women desirable, too, you know, Brent,' John said lightly.

'Yes, but the fiend has wed her; she loved him! What greater joy can any man wish for? She has borne him children – oh, would she had borne *me* children.' Brent gazed at the ceiling, his hands clasped as though in prayer.

'Your chance of wedding Analee may not be as remote as all that if the Falcon divorces her,' John said quietly. 'All the more reason to try and legalize your right to be in England, to plead for a pardon.'

'I will do it. I will do it,' Brent said, jumping up. 'Oh, the very thought . . . quick, how soon can I see the ambassador?'

He looked eagerly at Emma who smiled.

'It will not be as simple as that; but plans are afoot. We shall go back to Paris together where there should be a message for me at the convent. Mary was at prayer and I did not see her. Come, I will take you to see Mary and try to discover what news, if any, there is from London.'

* * *

On the way back to Paris from Plessy, on the outskirts, brother and sister talked as they had not had the chance to for a long time. Emma was more reserved, saying little about her marriage; but Brent, in the presence of so close a relation, let all pour forth – his disillusion, the unsatisfactory nature of his wandering life, his pent-up longings for Analee.

'She has ruined your life,' Emma said grimly, staring out of the window.

'Oh no. Since I realized the cause was lost, 'tis the only hope I have had for the future. I knew her marriage with that tyrant would not endure. She was bewitched by him, impressed by his position. If the war had not intervened to part us *I* would have married her . . .'

'And been disinherited by *your* family,' Emma said tartly. 'You never had anything to offer her, Brent. Lord Falconer had everything.'

'She did not want riches or title. I know that. With me she would have had happiness. With him she has had nothing but misery, sadness and abuse. Yes, I would like to go back to England, to get work and become respectable again. *Then* I shall be worthy of Analee.'

Brent sat back with a deep sigh of satisfaction; but Emma wondered if he really found self-deception so easy. He had no fortune, and what sort of work could he get? He could not work with Rigg now that Hugo had his place; and even if he could get some work like this, would the Marchioness of Falconer, used to great estates and many servants, settle down to such a life? Would she want to?

'Let us go first to my lodgings,' Brent said, sitting up as the carriage entered the narrow streets of Paris clustered with buildings. 'Mary may have left a message for me there. I doubt whether we can disturb her devotions before Easter Day is out.'

'Mary knew you were here?'

'Yes, I sent a message round yesterday. I am stopping in the house of friends just near the convent. I told her I was going to see John first because I knew she would be at her devotions.'

'Mary at least will be glad to see the end of your life as a wanderer.'

'Aye. She will have peace at last.'

'It is what she wants?' Emma looked at him in the gloom of the carriage.

'Yes. She said she never doubted now that she had a vocation. It was the will of God that our marriage should founder.'

'I see.' Emma pursed her lips and thought not of the will of God, but of the almost frightening power of the Enchantress. Did she not make Hugo fall in love with her? He told her that he had had a sudden vision of her, Emma, after not thinking of her for years. Then why, *why* was their marriage less than satisfactory, his devotion less than total? She yearned to have a home and a child. Yet although they lay together often enough, when he was home, his love-making lacked passion. She always had a feeling of dissatisfaction, of disappointment afterwards. Was this why she did not conceive? She thought again of Analee; the one person who, with her uncanny instincts, would be sure to know.

'Ah, here we are,' Brent said, looking out of the window and tapping on the roof for the driver to stop. Emma peered at the narrow grey buildings closely huddled together. It was a poor, mean part of Paris. The streets were filled with rubbish and horse manure, and stray cats and dogs picked among the litter. She held a finger to her nose.

'Aye, it stinks, does it not?' Brent said cheerfully, helping her down. 'But a vagabond such as I must lay his head where best he can. Few Jacobites have money to spend on fine houses.' Brent took her arm and knocked gently on the door looking to right and left up the street, his hand on his sword. 'One must always be prepared,' he said. 'Newcastle has the Prince followed every-where; so why not me?'

'Maybe because you are not the Prince,' Emma said, and then smiled as the door opened and a timid-looking servant stepped back and bowed the way inside. She spoke rapidly in French to Brent who finally turned with a puzzled frown to Emma.

'There is someone waiting for me upstairs. She did not know whether or not to let her in and then thought she looked such a fine lady that she could not refuse.' A sudden light came to Brent's eyes. 'A *fine* lady! Maybe it is Analee?' He leapt towards the stairs but Emma restrained him.

'Do not be so hopeful, Brent. Analee is in Carlisle gaol. Take care.'

The smile vanished from Brent's face and he put a hand on his sword. 'You had better stay here,' he whispered.

'I shall come with you. I doubt a woman would carry a sword.'

They went slowly up the stairs and as they did a door at the top opened and a face peeped out. The face looked rather fearful and apprehensive, but still recognizable as the door opened further and the person revealed herself, smiling shyly.

It was the girl Emma had last seen in the convent chapel at her devotions. Emma gave a sigh of relief. ''Tis an emissary of Mary,' she said. 'I saw her in the convent chapel.'

''Tis Anna Cameron,' Brent exclaimed, going up to her and taking her hand.

'Do you remember me?' Anna looked past him at Emma.

'Of course I do. Anna, this is my sister, Emma Fitzgerald.'

Anna blushed and gave a timid smile. 'How do you do. I saw you in the convent.'

'And I you.' Emma did not smile. 'How come you to be here?'

'Sister Mary Gertrude gave me Brent's address. I waited a whole week before she knew it. I have come to bid farewell to him, Mary and John Allonby before I return to America.'

'You are returning to America?'

'Yes. I was only here for a visit.'

'Come in, come in,' Brent said cheerfully. 'Do not let us talk in the passage! Ah, good, I see there is a fire lit.' He rubbed his hands. ''Tis cold for spring. Well I am delighted to see you, Miss Cameron, though, I confess, surprised by your news.'

'Oh?' Anna paused in the act of divesting herself of her cloak and glanced at him curiously. She was indeed beautiful, Emma thought. She had not met her during her own brief visit to Maryland. She would have been too young to attend the ball where Emma saw Stewart dancing with Elizabeth Cameron. She had hoped she would be plain like her sister, but she was not. No wonder the Falcon was rumoured to be enamoured of her. 'What news?' Anna continued after a pause, taking the seat Brent held out for her.

'That you are returning to America.'

'But why should you be surprised?'

Emma looked at Brent and shook her head in warning; but there was a reckless light in Brent's eyes and he ignored her.

'It is rumoured, or so I understand, that Lord Falconer would have you for his second wife.'

'Rumours travel quickly, do they not?' Anna said angrily. 'It is, I assure you, quite a false and malicious rumour. Lady Falconer is a friend of mine. The fact that she and her husband are at loggerheads has naught to do with me.' She shook her head and made to put her cloak round her slim shoulders again. 'I see I am not welcome here.'

'You are *very* welcome,' Brent said placatingly. 'Do not misunderstand me, and I apologize if I have believed something false and malicious.'

'Nevertheless, I feel I must go,' Anna said standing up. 'I do not *feel* welcome. Thank you for receiving me.'

'There is no need,' Brent tried to bar her way, but Emma spoke quietly from behind.

'Let her go. You know she is lying. Why is she here at all?'

'Because, as I said . . .' Anna was beginning to be afraid. The mission that she had never wanted to embark on was proving a disaster.

'I, for one, do not believe your tale,' Emma gazed at her with dislike. 'It is well known that the Falcon has brought this charge against his wife, and Brent, because he is tired of her. The rumour is all over London that you and he are constantly together. I wonder what business you have here when the Falcon is well-known to be desirous of apprehending my brother? You found out where he lived by subterfuge. What is your *true* purpose here, Miss Cameron?'

Anna's face flamed and she wrapped her cloak securely round her, turning her back on Emma, and trod daintily down the stairs. Brent hurried after her.

'Leave her!' Emma commanded, and Brent called back.

'At least I must see her home. The streets are dangerous.'

'Then how did she get here? Brent!'

But Anna was by the door downstairs and Brent close behind her.

'Pray forgive my sister, Miss Cameron. I am sure there is an explanation. It is just that we have to be so careful . . .'

Anna glanced back at him scornfully and stepped out onto the road looking to right and left for the escort sent with her by the

Falcon. There was no sign of him. Her apprehension returned. She turned to Brent. 'Perhaps, if you would. As far as the convent.'

'It is no distance. You came with a servant?'

'Yes; but I know not where he is.'

Emma stood at the door of the house watching them walk away together. It was a quiet street and dark in the late afternoon. No wonder people were frightened to walk abroad.

It was she who saw a tall man detach himself from the shadow of a nearby house and stride quickly after Brent. She started to run up the street and, just as the man closed in on Brent and drew something from his cloak, she screamed.

Brent heard the scream and felt the movement almost simultaneously. He spun round and saw a dagger coming down at him from a sharp angle. His strong wrist, aided by the quick reflex of one who had been a fugitive for so long, grasped the wrist that held the dagger and with the same movement he took his own short dagger from his belt and drove it into the chest of his attacker. The man gazed at him with an expression of astonishment and then, staggering, fell to the ground without a sound, Brent still clasping his wrist. The dagger that was meant to kill Brent clattered to the ground. A mangy dog with only three legs, which had been inspecting a pile of foetid rubbish, limped up and smelled it. Then, looking disappointed, it limped away again. Brent turned the man on his back and bent to put a hand on the pulse on the side of his neck. 'He is dead,' he said.

As Anna stared at the face of the attacker a scream rose to her throat, her eyes wide with fear. By this time Emma had reached them.

'Are you all right? Are you all right?' Her hands frantically grasped at Brent's clothing.

'Yes, quite all right. Just. If you had not screamed it would have been a different tale. This rogue was just about to plunge a knife in my back.'

Emma looked up. The street remained deserted. Screams were common enough in the streets of Paris without people so much as turning a hair, never mind coming to a door or window to discover what was amiss.

'You must go quickly. Go to the convent and wait there. I will get your things from your lodgings and bring them with me. You must not go back.'

'But why not? This was a footpad.'

'How do you know? More like an assassin. I saw the way he came from the shadows of the house and strode purposefully after you. He had been awaiting you, Brent. It was you he wanted, not money.' She turned and gazed at Anna whose ashen face was now stained with tears as she stared with helpless fascination at the face of the dead man.

The Falcon, still in his nightshirt, gazed with distress at the stricken woman as she slumped in the chair by the hastily-lit fire. He tried to press some brandy past her lips to stop them chattering.

'I will call for a doctor,' he said anxiously, turning to the servant assisting him. 'Go and fet . . .'.

'I need no doctor,' Anna Cameron said, looking at him. 'I need a priest.'

'But my darling, we cannot be wed until I am divorced.'

'I am not talking of marriage, my lord. I am talking of saving my soul. What you have done is to cast me into the depths of perdition.'

The Falcon knelt by the side of the chair and put his hands on Anna's cold ones. He nodded briefly to the door and the servant, understanding, bowed. 'Leave us now. Now, my darling, tell me what has happened, why you are in this state. Where is Gwyn?'

'Dead.' Anna shivered and burst again into uncontrollable sobbing.

'Dead?' The Falcon felt suddenly cold and moved nearer the fire. 'You came home alone?'

'All alone, except for my maid. 'Twas a frightful journey.'

'Tell me what happened.' The Falcon rubbed his own cold hands.

'You did not say you wanted to kill Brent Delamain.' Anna was stricken by a renewed spasm of sobbing. 'You said you had looked for him for years, and I had only to mark the place where he lived. I would not be involved.'

''Twas true,' the Falcon said stoutly, hoping she would believe him.

'Gwyn came after him with a dagger and, were it not for Emma Fitzgerald screaming behind him, Brent would be dead, not Gwyn.'

'The fool.' The Falcon got up and stared moodily into the fire. 'The clumsy, idiotic fool. I thought he knew better.'

'Better than what?' Anna's voice grew sharp with renewed terror.

'Than to make a *fracas* in the middle of the street. He was to do it by stealth; certainly not when *you* were there.'

'You mean he *was* to kill him?' Anna sat upright in her chair, her body seized by a fresh fit of trembling.

'No, no,' the Falcon said hastily, seeing her face. 'To bring him here as I said.'

'I find it hard to believe you, my lord. I think Gwyn was sent as an assassin and I merely to mark Brent. Like Judas I was to identify him; your henchman to complete the work. Had I known that, my lord, I would never have agreed to assist you in this treachery.'

'My little darling,' the Falcon said anxiously, putting his arms about her. 'I fear for your health. Your mind must be deranged if you think I would do such a thing. I wanted Brent to be tried alongside Analee.'

'Then why did Gwyn come after him with a dagger? I saw it myself, a long, ugly thing with a sharp curved blade.'

'I should think to frighten him,' the Falcon said, inwardly cursing. 'He was too inexperienced to have been sent with you. Oh, my darling, please forgive me? *Forgive* me?' He tilted her head and looked into her eyes; but Anna only saw treachery in their dark depths. She longed to believe him; she had already done so much for him. She had betrayed her friends and espoused a cause she despised. What would her father say if he knew?

She shuddered to think. The Falcon enclosed her in his arms; she could feel the heat of his tall, strong body and she leaned her head against it.

She could never go home now. She felt she bore the mark of Judas on her soul.

Lady Yarmouth was very busy indeed; she practically ran the country and at a time of political crisis ministers and potential ministers were forever making their way to the backstairs of St James's Palace and seeking an interview.

But it was not the Falcon who sought the interview with the most important woman in the country. He was abruptly summoned at short notice and ordered to present himself forthwith.

Even the Falcon dared not disobey.

Lady Yarmouth had always had a soft spot for the Falcon. She admired his combination of manly vigour, cunning, shrewdness and downright aggression. Moreover he had flattered her when she had first come to the country as the King's mistress and many, not realizing the power she was to wield – for the King had had mistresses before – did not pay her sufficient respect. Some were even inclined to laugh at her behind her back. But the Falcon seemed to have perceived that the newly widowed King wanted not so much a mistress as a wife and Amalie Wallmoden seemed very suitable, a queen with the power but without the title. In time she grew very powerful indeed.

The Countess was not yet forty, but she appeared to have aged as the King advanced in years, and she had grown fat. She gazed at him forbiddingly as Lord Falconer was led into her presence, bowing low.

'Pray take a seat, Lord Falconer.'

'To what do I owe the honour, Madam?' The Falcon gazed at her, uneasily aware that his chair was lower than hers and that the expression on her face was far from gracious. She was really the only woman of whom he felt just slightly afraid.

The Countess, whose time was at a premium, tapped a document before her. 'We have here a petition for clemency, Lord Falconer.'

The Falcon noted the royal 'we' and bent forward to inspect the document. 'Doubtless from my wife, Lady Yarmouth.'

'No, *not* your wife, my lord. It is from Mr Delamain whom you have accused of treason *with* your wife.'

'Ah, perfidious rogue!' the Falcon growled. Would that Gwyn's dagger had penetrated his heart as was intended! That bungle had caused no end of aggravation, as he knew it would. Anna Cameron was once again making arrangements to return to her native land and the wife of Gwyn Dyffed was making trouble, wanting to know where he was. In truth the Falcon could say he did not know. Probably lying in some pauper's grave in a Parisian burial yard. Bodies unclaimed in Paris streets were not so very uncommon. He didn't have a pang of remorse for the man he had sent to his death; just irritation that the plot had failed.

'He wishes to return to this country, sir. This is a plea to His Majesty for pardon. He renounces the Jacobite cause entirely and begs forgiveness. He says it was for this reason that he met Lady Falconer in Kent.'

'Lies, ma'am, all lies,' the Falcon blustered, swinging back on his chair and wishing that he were at least on the same level, if not higher than Lady Yarmouth.

'It is supported, sir, by documents I have here.' Lady Yarmouth turned to the table at her side. 'One is a deposition from Lady Goodacre which confirms this; the other from Sir George Delamain who says that his brother has long importuned him to intercede with the King. It is *this* document, my lord, that has impressed His Majesty most. Sir George has always been devoted to the cause of Hanover, investing time and huge sums of money for arms in support of the King. You do not dispute that, I think.'

'Why no, ma'am,' the Falcon said sulkily. 'Except that the news surprises me. I had thought there was no love lost between the brothers.'

'Exactly. That is why it has surprised the King. Sir George has no heir, you know.'

'Is he like to die?'

'We pray God that he is not; but it weighs heavily on his mind. The heir to his title is a distant cousin. He has two daughters and we understand Lady Delamain is unlike to conceive again. For this reason Sir George would forgive his brother and entreat the same of the King.'

'His Majesty will refuse it, of course,' the Falcon said loftily. 'Brent Delamain is an unrepentant rogue.'

'He seems to *be* repentant though, sir.'

''Tis the first I hear of it. He was near hanged just after the Rebellion.'

'But *escaped*, sir.' The Countess looked strangely at Lord Falconer and he was suddenly visited by an unsettling thought. It was he who, at the behest of his wife, had masterminded the plan for Brent's escape. Supposing this ever came to the ears of the

King? Supposing it had come already? Then he, the Falcon, would be tarred with the traitor's brush, too. Maybe he was being warned.

It was a most distressing thought; but, looking into those knowing eyes, that impassive Teutonic face, he could not divine the answer. He wriggled uncomfortably in his chair.

'His Majesty, as you know,' the Countess sighed, 'feels he is coming to the end of his long and illustrious life. He is no longer young. He would leave the throne as strong for his grandson as he can.'

'But it *is* very strong, ma'am,' the Falcon said indignantly.

'Aye, but can it ever be strong enough? The more who renounce Jacobitism, and are seen to do it, the fewer there will be to plague the new king. This public act of Brent Delamain's, coming when so many others have recently been granted permission to return, will be one more nail in the coffin of that wretched cause.'

'So His Majesty is of a mind to grant it?' the Falcon said dejectedly.

'Aye, he is. If not for your sake or that of Mr Delamain, for that of your wife of whom His Majesty is fond and whom he feels you have sadly abused.'

'I, abused?' The Falcon looked at her with surprise.

'Yes, abused, Lord Falconer. His Majesty is very grieved that you should have brought an accusation of treason against her without consulting him . . . or me,' her ladyship concluded pointedly. 'Lady Falconer is highly thought of at court. Her virtue and devotion to your lordship – in the face of your lordship's many blatant peccadilloes – are much admired. The Princess of Wales has even made entreaties to us on Lady Falconer's behalf. We have had scores of people approach us to condemn you. In fact, my lord,' Lady Yarmouth replaced the papers on the table and folded her hands, looking at him severely, 'His Majesty feels that your unpopularity is such that you would be best out of the country.'

'Out of the country! Why . . . ?' The Falcon half rose from his chair, his face scarlet with rage.

'For your own sake, sir, so that you are not mobbed when Lady Falconer is released.'

'I can take care of myself, ma'am.' The Falcon bit his lip with chagrin.

'It is *not* to be banishment, my lord,' the Countess smiled at him at last with some of her former affection. 'His Majesty is very sensible of your many good qualities.'

'Gratified, ma'am, I'm sure.'

'He values you highly as a diplomat, a soldier, a statesman. He would have you go to the court of King Frederick and consult with him on strategies in the forthcoming war. Since the French signed the Treaty in Versailles with the Russians and Austrians in May, there is no doubt that there will be a war. Here we are very exercised as to who is to run the country. Newcastle is weak, Fox vacillates too much and the Duke of Devonshire is not sufficiently experienced. We may have to turn to Pitt.'

'You could do worse, ma'am.'

'I agree with you; but so far the King does *not*. However, Lord Falconer, what say you to this suggestion, which I may say came from the King of Prussia himself?'

The Falcon preened himself and leaned back again in his chair, his legs stretched out before him. 'The King was good enough to say he admired my qualities when I was in Potsdam last.'

'He thinks *very* highly of them. He would value your counsels and it would be a chance to be out of the way, would it not, for a while? Might not that be a good thing? You have accused your wife of treason on insufficient grounds. You must give her time to recover from the wounds you have caused her. Then maybe when she sees you again she will be in a better frame of mind. I would also advise you to get Miss Cameron out of the way . . . *well* out of the way. After what has happened to Lady Falconer, the King does not approve of *her* at all.'

The Falcon looked at her and knew that he was beaten. How could he now say that he wished to divorce Analee and marry Anna? The King would never grant permission, never allow a bill to be laid before Parliament. The Falcon knew he was in a weaker position than he had ever been before. Now he had no wife and the woman he loved would leave him when she heard this news. The King did not even *like* Anna? What chance of her being a duchess now? He groaned inwardly.

Once again the spell of the Enchantress had succeeded.

12

Brent Delamain, pale and tired from lack of sleep, stood facing his brother. He had not been asked to sit. Sir George leaned heavily on a stick, his frame trembling slightly. Brent was as much shocked by how old and feeble he looked as by what he had to say to him.

'I have done all I can for you, brother, to avoid a scandal . . .'

'I am grateful . . .' Brent began, but George held up a hand.

'I want none of your gratitude. What I did was for the family and not for you. I did not want our name dragged yet again through the mire. Through the goodness of the King you have received a full pardon. He may forgive you, but I never can. I hope not to see your face again before I die.'

Sir George staggered and collapsed into a chair. Brent wanted to go over to him, but dared not, besides being frozen into immobility by his brother's words. Sir George breathed heavily and took a sip of water.

'Then what am I to do?' Brent said when his brother had sufficiently recovered to listen to him. 'I have no home, no money, no work.'

George shrugged. 'You have managed before; you must contrive to do so again. I am sure your wits will sustain you; they always have. But pray do not take up with your Jacobite friends again, or the next time it will be the gallows, I myself standing underneath to enjoy your last.'

'You sound as though you hate me,' Brent said bitterly.

'Well, I have little love for you, I'll confess. I have no reason to feel otherwise. You and your brother Tom, to say nothing of the Allonby cousins, have brought only shame and disgrace on this family. It has been an intolerable burden and has made me a sick man. Oh, do not look so hopeful, I am not like to die yet.' Sir George coughed painfully. 'Nor for many a long day. I would not have this estate fall into your hands for all the world, nor *my* hard-earned money. I hope it will be to your children that it will go and not you. You have done nothing to deserve it. So that is your first duty, Brent – to marry and raise children . . . a son must be sired quickly.'

'I have no plans to wed,' Brent said quietly.

'Then you'd best make some. If you bring a wife here I may receive her and if you produce an heir I will have him educated at my expense. Henrietta is barren,' Sir George paused and looked in front of him as though without seeing. 'I had in mind to divorce her and take another. But I cannot. In my way I love her. I could not do it. I am not such a hard man, am I, Brent?'

'No.' Brent looked at his brother and thought how different they were; they looked different and their natures had never been complementary. Theirs had always been a rivalry, a mutual distrust. George always careful, thoughtful, parsimonious – Brent the very opposite: impetuous, careless, generous. 'Not as far as others are concerned; but to me, yes.'

'Did I not go to the court and plead for you? Lie for you? Humiliate myself for you? What more did you want me to do? Embrace you?'

'I hoped you might forgive me and take me to your heart.'

'Well, I cannot. You are not welcome here. I have thrown you out before and I do so again. You must pay your respects to our mother, who is ageing fast, and then you must go from hence. I daresay Rigg will be able to give you some kind of employment. He is growing very rich. He is a good fellow. Maybe you can lodge with our sister. I hear her house is finished.'

'You know I cannot!'

'Because of Hugo? I thought that was all in the past?'

'I detest the fellow!' Brent glowered at his brother who got slowly to his feet and came over to him until he was within an inch or two of his face. Then he grasped the lapel of his coat and shook him.

'It is time you dropped these likes and dislikes, my good man. You are over thirty years of age and have not a penny to your name. It will take you a lifetime to restore yourself with society – to repay your country for the harm you have done.'

Sir George let go his lapel and staggered back, his face working with emotion. He raised a trembling hand and shook his finger at his brother. 'And take care to keep away from that woman, that witch who has brought so much disaster in her wake. You know who I mean, don't you? You *know*?'

Brent nodded his head and his heart began to beat more quickly. He knew, but he said nothing.

Morella gazed with interest at the uncle she had never seen. She sat with a docility unusual for her, her hands gripping the edge of her chair. She had on her best dress with a long bow hanging down the front and her fair, almost white hair was carefully arranged in neat ringlets which clustered at the base of her neck. Her clear cornflower-blue eyes looked out at him unsmilingly; but she did not trouble to conceal her admiration. This tall, blond, good-looking man was so unlike Uncle George with his choleric temper and his mean-mindedness.

Looking at them, comparing them, Brent's mother was sure her suspicions were right. Years ago, before the Rebellion, her son was rumoured to have become hopelessly enamoured of a gypsy – and Morella was a gypsy's child. Yet what gypsy would acknowledge that white skin, that straw coloured hair, those very deep blue eyes? Besides, there was so much of Brent in Morella – she was impulsive, carefree and warm-hearted. She made friends easily and people loved her; she was a madcap, always courting trouble. How like the young Brent who had grown up in this very castle. How unlike his brother George. She had no proof and she dared not ask; but, putting two and two together, she had long ago reached the opinion that Morella was the daughter of her son and Lady Falconer, erstwhile gypsy; that Morella was her granddaughter, her very own blood.

Susan sighed sadly as she looked at the son she had not seen for over ten years. The weeping was over; just to know that he was safe and at home was enough, though there was still a long way to go . . . a very long way to go, it seemed.

'Then you must live here.'

'I cannot, mother. My only hope really is with Rigg. I am sure he will give me a job on one of his boats. I do not necessarily want my old position. Hugo has that! I am a good sailor, an expert fisherman.'

'Oh, Brent, you will not be tempted to . . .' His mother looked at him anxiously, glancing at Morella. 'My dear, will you leave us for a moment and go and play? I want to talk privately with Uncle Brent.'

791

'I want to hear,' Morella said in her clear voice.

'But you can't.'

'But I can!' Morella's eyes sparkled and she banged her fists on her lap.

Mrs Delamain stood up and gently took hold of the child, propelling her towards the door and giving her a playful slap on her little behind. 'Now off you go and do as you are told.'

Brent watched her, laughing; he leaned against the window sill with his arms folded. 'She is a scamp. She is the gypsy child I sent you?'

'Yes, all those years ago.' His mother looked at him solemnly. 'You remember it?'

'Aye, very well.' Brent scratched the back of his head. 'I was riding along after the skirmish at Clifton and all our men were in disarray. Then a gypsy troupe came along, and a woman carrying the sick baby. I told her to seek you out and you would give her refuge. She made me a promise that has sustained me through my life.'

'And it is?'

'She said I would endure much suffering but that in the end all would be well. I would have my heart's desire.'

'And what is your heart's desire, Brent?' His mother dropped her voice and looked searchingly at him.

'I cannot tell you, mother; not yet. But when I have it, I shall; and that day will come. It will.'

'I hope it will, my son, for you.' His mother bowed her head and sat heavily in a chair. 'Oh, I hope so; you have endured so much and now you have humiliated yourself by begging the Hanoverian King for pardon.'

He looked up at the bitterness in her voice and came over to her, squatting by her side. 'You are angry with me, mother? You think I should not have done?'

'I am not angry with you; I know the circumstances. I am sorry it had to happen, that is all. All my life I have hoped for the return of the Stuarts. Your father and I were exiled for years for the cause and he died a broken man because of it.'

'Would you have had *me* die in exile, mother? Would it have been better?'

'I don't know,' Susan said brokenly. 'I really don't know. But what I was going to say to you before I sent Morella out, was to beg you not to jeopardize your life again. Leave the Stuart cause to others. Is there, do you think, any hope?'

He took her hand and brought it to his lips. 'Mother, in your day there was still hope. The Hanoverians were newly on the throne. There was King James with his two lusty sons and everyone full of hope. But now there is none, mother. The Prince is unfit to be a King; *he* has lost the loyalty of all who loved him in a way his old father never has. The King in Rome is still our King; but he is the last of the line. All our people are bitter and in disarray, Mother; there was even an attempt to have me assassinated in Paris.'

'By one of *your* people?'

'Who else? I was staying at a Jacobite house. No one else knew I was there. The Prince felt I had failed him in England and tried to throw me out of his house. It is my suspicion that he then sent someone to try and kill me with a dagger. 'Twas Emma saved me.'

'Oh! She never told me!' His mother put her hands to her face.

'She would not want to worry you; but that is what made me decide to ask for pardon. I could trust no one, mother. I knew not where to turn.'

'I understand, Brent,' his mother said slowly. 'Now I do understand why you came home. I did not know things had come to such a pass.'

'It was not easy for me to recant, mother; to sign the paper and swear the oath of loyalty to King George. I shed bitter tears; but I had no option.'

'I know you didn't,' his mother said, 'and thank God you are safe. But where will you go if you will not stay here?'

'I am going to see Rigg. George thinks he will give me work. I will do all I can to make my fortune, mother, and to bring you happiness. You have suffered so much for all of us.'

'But you have suffered, too. George hopes you will marry and provide . . . an heir.' His mother turned away with embarrassment and he saw her lips tremble. 'There is a lot I do not know, Brent, about the past; but some of it I have guessed. I hope you will be able to make a new life and do as George bids?'

But Brent's heart was too full to answer. Analee, his precious Analee, was only a few miles away resting at her home in Lakeland after her release from Carlisle Castle with a full apology from the King on the part of her husband, now disgraced and sent abroad.

'I shall be happy one day, mother,' he said at last. 'And you will be happy too.'

Lady McKeith had seen better days, both with regard to her face and to her fortune. The passage of time had not been kind to her once-fabled beauty, and her considerable fortune had been gambled and fritted away by her husband Sir Keith McKeith. What little was left had gone to the coffers of the Young Pretender whom Sir Keith followed to France, after the failure of the Rebellion, together with his unwilling lady.

As fond of the bottle as his master the Prince, Sir Keith had succumbed to its effects sooner, not being such a young man, and was laid to rest in the soil of France. Lady McKeith promptly abjured her husband's views and, obtaining a pardon, returned to England, one of the first to do so. She had always been an indifferent supporter of the Jacobites because early on she had seen quite clearly what others had merely sensed: that they would lose.

Isobel McKeith cared too much about fun and fashion to be on the losing side. For a time, when the Prince had appeared to be winning, she had worn the white cockade and even danced with him at a ball in Edinburgh; but after the retreat from Derby she knew quite well which way the wind would blow. She followed her spouse reluctantly into exile, and came joyfully home again after his death. She was still relatively young and a very merry widow indeed. One of the first to help her warm her lonely bed had been the Marquess of Falconer and from time to time he had returned to it until he met the latest object of his desires, a woman with whom he had fallen head over heels in love, for whom he had risked disgrace and finally exile – Anna Cameron.

Shortly after his interview with Lady Yarmouth in the spring, the Falcon had received his orders to proceed to Potsdam or Berlin, wherever King Frederick should be found. He was not to take leave of Lady Falconer who, understandably, was not anxious to receive him, and he was to arrange for the passage of Miss Cameron to her home in America forthwith. He was not even allowed to take leave of the King. It was indeed a kind of exile.

The Falcon did everything he was bid, except for one thing. Under the guise of leaving for America, Anna Cameron left instead for the continent of Europe where, in the company of Lady McKeith, she travelled from one capital to another, doing a kind of grand tour until such time as the Falcon should send for her.

Lady McKeith found it hard to credit that Miss Cameron had so far resisted the considerable charms of the Falcon and that her virtue remained intact. But his lordship assured her it did and that he would be the first, the only man to break it. Until such time, Lady McKeith was paid a comfortable sum to entertain Miss Cameron and keep a very firm eye on her. Lady McKeith did not find this a difficult task: her charge appeared immune to the attentions of other men. Lady McKeith did not know that Anna Cameron still felt the mark of Judas on her soul – that, but for the merest accident, Brent Delamain would be dead and she responsible.

In August 1756 King Frederick invaded Saxony on the advice of the Falcon, who was anxious to see battle. It was put about that the Austrians were preparing to mobilize against him anyway, so he decided to strike first. By October the Saxons had surrendered and their troops had been incorporated into the Prussian army. The victory of Frederick made up for the loss to Britain of Minorca the previous spring and the humiliating disarray of her government.

Under the terms of the Treaty of Versailles, France was obliged to provide Austria with troops if she was attacked, which she did. She also decided to invade Hanover and began assembling an army preparatory to the commencement of operations the following spring.

Lord Falconer threw himself with vigour into the preparations for war; he was the main liaison with the British Ambassador to Berlin, Sir Andrew Mitchell, and it was also through this old friend of his that he managed to send messages to his beloved, hoping for the time when she would be able to join him. Knowing that, by the spring Europe would probably be into a full and bloody war, the Falcon felt he had not much time in which to make her his. But though he was an expert military strategist he could not find a way to disburden himself of his wife; everything he had tried had failed. For a while he thought of having her murdered; but

795

something like that was too risky. The finger of suspicion would immediately be pointed at him, and the way that the attempt on the life of Brent Delamain had been bungled gave him fair warning of what to expect when something delicate was undertaken by one of his underlings. It was a chance he could not take.

Gloomily, the Falcon, when he had time from momentous affairs, pondered the future. The war would be a long and bitter one, of that he was sure. Maybe he could go to India or America and not return to England for years. In that case who would know?

The plan that he finally made was risky; but the Falcon was a man who thrived on risks . . . and, besides, for a few years, months or even days, of delight, was it not worth it?

He sent a message to Lady McKeith, temporarily lodged in Geneva with her charge. One day she came flying into Anna's bedroom waving the paper.

'Oh, it has come, Anna, it has come.'

Anna, who was penning a letter to her mother, jumped up from her desk. 'What has come, Isobel?'

'The divorce! His lordship has just written. The divorce is made final. He is free to marry. Oh, Anna, I am so happy for you.'

She threw her arms round Anna and hugged her. She hugged her tightly and tenderly because she had become fond of her and was sorry for her part in his deception; but how could she disagree with the Falcon? Besides, he kept her alive and in the style to which she was accustomed. She was privy to his plans and he paid her well to keep Anna circulating far away from people who might know more about what was going on in London, who might know that the Marquess and his Marchioness were as wedded as they had ever been, in the eyes of both the law and the church.

'He said he would do it!' Anna gasped, looking at the letter the Falcon had written. The one with the fuller explanation was carefully locked away. 'Oh, I did not believe he could do it. Did you?'

'I believe the Falcon can do anything,' Lady McKeith said diplomatically, thinking how much had been hidden from the poor girl; she had seldom known such a victim of deception.

'But Lady Falconer *agreeing* to the divorce – and so quickly.'

''Twas she asked for it, I believe,' Lady McKeith said, lies springing as naturally to her lips, due to her many years of political intrigue, as to her paymaster's. 'To be accused of treachery was the final straw. Quick now, we must pack. The Falcon awaits us in Berlin.'

Anna ran to the wardrobe and flung her clothes on the bed. 'Oh, send me my maid quickly, Isobel. I cannot believe I shall soon be a marchioness.'

Action suited his lordship. Although there were as yet no English troops engaged in hostilities he had managed a skirmish or two against the Saxons. His only dread was that the Duke of Cumberland would be sent out in command of the Hanoverians and his bigamy would be discovered. There were few English in Berlin. His beloved would be effectively cut off from sources of gossip. Yes, it was worth it. She was lovelier than ever. As his eyes alighted on her he trembled at the thought that he would soon hold her in his arms.

Anna's first glimpse of the Falcon in his magnificent uniform made her feel shy. She had not seen him for over six months, his letters was cursory, few and far between. He was not a man used to pouring out his heart on paper. Lady McKeith discreetly left them alone and for a moment they gazed at each other. Then he went swiftly over to her and folded her in his arms.

'Oh, my beloved.' She was trembling. He lifted her chin and looked into her turquoise eyes brimming now with tears. 'Why, darling, are you not happy?'

'Terribly, terribly happy,' Anna brushed her eyes and tried to smile but her chin still trembled. 'I cannot believe it. 'Twas so easy.'

'Oh, 'twas not *easy*,' the Falcon said, mentally banishing his own misgivings. 'But the King was anxious to please me.'

'Does he know that we are to be wed?'

The Falcon held her away from him and looked at her gravely. 'Oh no, my dear, and nor must anyone for the time being.'

'But why if . . .' A shadow had fallen over her face and he quickly kissed her cheek.

'It would not be seemly. You understand, when the divorce is only just granted, it would not help my reputation to marry again in such haste.'

'Then we have to wait?'

'Oh no, my dearest . . . What! do I see desire in your chaste eyes, you saucy girl? No, no, we can marry at once, but we must be discreet. You see that, don't you?'

Anna Cameron looked over his shoulder and the expression on her face relaxed. It was not lust he had seen in her eyes – far from it. He had been mistaken for thinking the desire in her eyes was for his embraces. It was simply her longing to be made respectable after all these months of doubt and waiting; to be a marchioness and secure in the strength of his name.

Lady McKeith sobbed all during the short ceremony performed, in a room of the house the Falcon had rented in Berlin, by a Prostestant minister who had not been alerted as to the circumstances of the marriage. If he had his suspicions he kept them to himself. He was receiving a most generous fee and a case of brandy to boot. Besides, he neither spoke nor understood a word of English and what papers he was offered were passed by him unread.

The Falcon looked nervous and kept on glancing over his shoulder as though at any moment he expected the door to fly open and his wife to appear on a broomstick. But if Analee divined his intentions she gave no sign. He was well and truly, if bigamously, married. There was now nothing to prevent him claiming his prize.

Anna was the most calm of those present; besides herself there was her groom and the parson, Lady McKeith and two members of her husband's entourage. She felt serene in the knowledge that she had attained her goal – the goal for which she had lied, cheated, betrayed and nearly murdered.

She now thought herself a marchioness. When they were pronounced man and wife she gave the Falcon a brilliant smile of gratitude. He misinterpreted its meaning and his loins burned with renewed desire.

The new Marchioness of Falconer lay nervously in bed. The time had come. She tried to calm her misgivings by thinking that her virginity was no sacrifice; she had kept it long enough, and for good reason. It had not been difficult. She had never experienced the slightest desire to divest herself of it. Lady McKeith, who had helped her change from her wedding clothes into night attire, murmured a few words but received no answer. She was surprised by the state of the young woman's ignorance. However, it was no concern of hers. The Falcon was quite used to this situation, he would know what he was about. She thought rather wistfully of the times he used to take advantage of her favours, and went sadly to her lonely bed.

The door from the adjoining room opened and the Falcon, magnificently attired in a crisp white nightshirt and an embroidered gown, entered. Anna sat up in bed with her hair brushed back; he could see the swell of her breasts beneath her lawn chemise. He took a deep breath and went up to the bed. Anna raised her lovely eyes and looked trustfully at him. He sat on the bed and leaned over towards her, gently brushing her lips. They were cold and did not give easily under his pressure. He straightened up and looked at her. 'Would you like some wine, my darling, to relax you a little?'

'I am quite relaxed, my lord,' she said nervously. 'I had plenty of wine at supper. It has made me sleepy.'

A doubt came into the Falcon's mind but he put it aside. He would have hoped that, after all these months, she would have been a trifle more willing even if her desire was, understandably, not equal to his. He took her in his arms again and crushed his mouth more firmly against hers. She still didn't yield but remained wooden and upright; her mouth tight shut, cold as ice.

He put a hand down her bodice and tried to fondle a breast. She began to struggle and he sat up again. 'What is it, my beloved? I have come to love you. You must not resist me. I am your husband.'

'Could we not wait until morning?' Anna gave a yawn. 'I am so tired. The excitement of the day, the wine . . .'

A red cloud came over the Falcon's eyes, momentarily obscuring his vision of the beloved. His heart throbbed so painfully that he felt short of breath. The sight of her loveliness, her bewitching mouth, her enticing breasts . . . He leaned down and, seizing the sheets, threw them back.

Anna immediately curled up and put one hand protectively across her bosom, the other at her groin even though it was fully covered by her night attire. Her youthful form made him sick with desire; he could just see her trim bare ankle beneath her chemise. Anna looked frightened and a lock of her red hair fell over her face.

The Falcon delicately touched an ankle and let his hand slowly travel up her leg. 'My darling, do not tremble. Anna, I am your husband. I want you. I need you so much.'

'Could we not wait until morning?'

He slowly eased her chemise her legs, resisting her attempts to lower it again. He made soothing noises and then leaned over to nuzzle her cheeks, his tongue gently trying to prise open the aperture of her lips. Surely she must at least *begin* to experience some desire now? He grasped her thighs and eased his hand into her groin, trying to part her tightly-closed legs.

Anna gave a little cry and started to struggle once more, resisting him. The Falcon inserted his hand more firmly, the other clasping her behind the back, his lips pressing on hers. But everything remained tight. The legs, the lips; her whole person was barricaded against him. He felt a wetness on her cheeks and reluctantly raised his head.

His bride was weeping. He took his hand away and pulled down the chemise. Then he got off the bed and went and poured himself some wine from the cooler by the side of the bed. If she did not need a drink he did. When he turned round she had drawn up the sheets over her shoulders and was pretending to sleep. The Falcon gave a deep sigh and went and stood by the fire, warming himself as he slowly sipped the wine, wondering what to do. The cold in the room was causing his desire to ebb. Perhaps he should get into bed and snuggle up against her? He would at least be warmer.

He finished his wine and removed his gown. He then went to his side of the great bed and slipped under the sheets. Anna moved as far away from him as she could, her back towards him. She was curled up in an attitude of self-protection, as though against attack.

Angus lay for a while and stared at the ceiling. This was very different from his last wedding night. He thought of Analee and her wicked wanton ways. He thought of her lovely luscious body and her beguiling brown eyes. He tried to put away the image and replace it with that of Anna. It was very difficult.

He put out a hand and touched Anna's back; he felt her recoil.

He edged up to her until he could feel the warmth of her body. He put a hand gently on her shoulder. 'My beloved, let me lie against you and warm myself?'

'I am *very* sleepy.'

'If I let you sleep, will you love me a little in the morning?'

'Yes.'

He lay silently beside her, feeling her trembling. He blew out the candle and moved away from her. The trembling ceased and her breathing became deep and regular. She was certainly exhausted, but he had never had such failure with a virgin. By the time he reached the supreme moment, usually they were eager to yield. His technique was legendary. He turned on his side and fell into a fretful sleep.

When he awoke the bed was empty. He sat up and adjusted his eyes to the gloom. He could hear the birds singing and knew it was dawn. With a curse he leapt out of bed and looked for his robe. It was bitterly cold. He found a tinder and lit the candle and went over to stoke the fire. His bride sat huddled in a chair, fast asleep. She looked so pale and pathetic that his heart went out to her. The tears were hardly dry on her cheeks. The Falcon put down the candle and knelt beside her. She opened her eyes and stared at him.

'You look scared half to death.'

'I did not know it would be like this.'

'But I did *nothing*. My darling, it is the most delicious . . .'

'But I *am* frightened.'

He took her hand and kissed it, holding it to his face. 'Anna, you have to know some day. 'Tis the lot of women.'

'I know, but must it be yet?'

'Well, when can it be then?'

'When I am ready.' She started to shiver.

'My darling, you will freeze to death before you lose your maidenhead. Come, let me take you to bed.'

'Oh no, please!' She curled herself up in the chair like a very frightened little girl.

The Falcon got up and, bending down, put one hand under her knees, the other firmly round her neck. She gave a little cry and started to kick, but he carried her to the bed and gently laid her down. 'There.' He covered her with the bedclothes and looked at her. 'Now I will get in with you and lie with you, just to keep you warm.'

'Only that?'

'Yes.'

Angus took off his robe, blew out the candle and climbed into bed beside his beloved. It was almost daylight. Anna was as near the far edge of the bed as she could get, but he moved over towards her, his arm encircling her. She put a hand on it and tried to move it away.

He kissed her ear and moved his face over hers. She tried to turn it into the bed. The Falcon felt he would burst. He had never had such a recalcitrant female, never mind one to whom he was supposed to be married. He had a right. How long would she expect him to be patient? It could last for days, weeks.

The Falcon threw back the clothes and got out of bed. He went over to the fire and tried to rekindle it with the tinder with which he had lit the candle. He was not used to this menial work and he was not very good at it; but at last he managed it. Then he went to the wash-basin and washed his hands in the freezing cold water. He poured himself more wine, left over from the night before, and drank it at a gulp. Then he went and stood by Anna. She was gazing at him with one eye, the other firmly shut. He suddenly reached for the hem of his nightshirt and, in one movement, pulled it off. Anna shut both eyes and her mouth opened to scream. The Falcon swiftly threw back the bedclothes and jerked her chemise over her hips exposing the beautiful thighs he had never seen, her delicious mound covered quite thickly with red-gold hair. He stared lustfully at it, his desire knowing no bounds, and as she began to scream he put a large hand over her mouth, and with the other he roughly prised open her legs.

'I didn't mean to do it this way,' he said at last, gazing at her, feeling slightly abashed now that it was over and the desire was spent. She didn't reply and her eyes were closed, her face as white as the sheets. He gently eased himself out of her and the place where he had entered was like a wound, red with blood. He had been very savage and harsh and he felt ashamed. He had never defiled anyone against their will; it had never been necessary.

He would spare her more shame and let Lady McKeith attend her. He drew down her chemise and covered her gently with the bedclothes. Then he pulled on his nightshirt, put on his robe and sat beside her his hand on her shoulder. 'It is over now. It will never be like that again. I'm sorry, Anna. I have desired you for so long. I could not contain myself. I'm truly sorry.'

He gazed at her face, but her lids remained shut though he could see her eyes moving rapidly beneath them. The colour was returning to her face. He leaned down and kissed her cheek, patting her shoulder, once again feeling inadequate.

Then he went slowly and quietly out of the room.

The Falcon had appointments all day. There was a lot to be done in the winter to prepare for the war in the spring. He wished his mind could linger happily on his bride, but it could not. Every time he thought of her he felt deeply ashamed. She was not even his bride, his wife. He had wished to deflower her sweetly, to make it an occasion to remember. She would certainly never forget it.

He bought her a jewel; but he knew he delayed going home and was late. Lady McKeith received him with reserve and glanced at him reproachfully.

'Is she all right?' he whispered in the hall.

'She had a terrible shock.'

'I tried to do it gently. She would not let me.'

'You should have left her a while to get used to the feel of a man beside her in bed. It is a strange experience for a maid.'

'But she is twenty-three!'

'It does not make it any easier being older. You should have been more gentle. You owed it to her to be more patient. I am surprised at you, my lord.'

'Is she in bed yet?'

'No, she awaits you in the drawingroom. I have talked to her gently all day, explaining to her the ways of men. I *think* she will be more compliant; but take care to be gentle with her, sir.'

The Falcon lowered his eyes and fingered the box with the jewel in his pocket.

'If you could not have restrained yourself last night, if your need was so urgent you should have waited until she slept and come to me. I would have accommodated you quite willingly.' She glanced at him archly.

The Falcon raised his eyes to the ceiling and then looked at her.

'I didn't know you could have a surrogate bride on a wedding night. But it may come to that yet.' He patted her arm and went upstairs to the drawingroom.

Anna had taken a lot of care with her appearance and greeted her lord with a brave smile, her lower lip trembling. The Falcon went over to her and pressed the box into her hand. Then he kissed her cheek. 'Am I forgiven?'

'I was very ignorant. I did not know what to do.'

'I should have had Lady McKeith instruct you in the absence of your mama.'

'She tried, but I would not listen. I couldn't believe it when it happened.'

'The trouble is you *seem* so grown-up, so assured. 'Twas hard to believe you were not.' He kissed her cheek and she trembled. During the meal, which was served *à deux*, he talked about the day he had had and the war that was to come.

'Oh, I *wish* we could go back to England,' she said, 'that the war could be averted!'

'My dear, we shall not be able to go back to England for a long time. I have much to do here.'

'But we can't stay forever on the continent. I wish to be properly presented at court as your Marchioness.'

The Falcon poured some wine into her glass with a hand that shook slightly. 'We shall have to be patient, my dear.'

Despite her determination to be different, Anna felt herself tremble involuntarily later on as her spouse got into bed beside her. Lady McKeith had spoken to her with great tact but great frankness for the best part of the day. The more she relaxed in her husband's arms the more pleasant it would be, she was told. She should respond to his advances in order to enjoy herself. But when she felt the Falcon reach for her, inwardly she shrank into herself and put her legs tightly together.

'I will only embrace you and kiss you tonight, my darling,' the Falcon murmured, 'so that the tear I made can heal. It is quite natural and will soon be better. I promise you, you will love this act like most women do. In time. In time.'

Still the bed continued to shake beneath her.

The Falcon tried again. 'See, if I caress your breast it will give you pleasure, like this.' The Falcon eased his forefinger over her bare nipple but he could feel the gooseflesh of her cold skin. She was as cold as a corpse, as taut as the string of a bow. After some more attempts he gave up and turned his back on her, lying with his eyes open until he heard the long, slow regular breathing of sleep.

Then, when he was sure she would not wake, he crept out of bed and went quietly along the corridor, knocking gently at the door of Lady McKeith.

Her bed was warm and enticing, snug and inviting. Her body pliant and sweet-smelling. She encircled him with her arms and drew his body hungrily against hers. 'I knew you would come,' she said. 'I don't think Miss Cameron is made for love.'

'*Never*?' The Falcon looked at her with anguish, rubbing his suffering loins against her eager, receptive thighs.

'I have the feeling that she does not take kindly to the art and never will.'

The Falcon groaned and buried his head in the rounded, ample, willing bosom of Isobel McKeith.

'If you had asked me before I would have told you.'

'Why did you not say?'

'Would you have listened? I never saw or heard a man so besotted with love.'

'No, I would not have listened. I could not believe it. She is so nubile, so beautiful.'

'Alas, beauty of form is not always accompanied by a passionate nature. Beauty is deceptive,' Isobel said. 'I knew at a glance she was cold. How could she have refused *you* for all this time; for you attempted before, of course, did you not?'

'Of course. She resisted me most virtuously. She wanted marriage. It made her only more desirable to me. I never dreamt of this. Who would?'

'Men are fools,' Isobel thought but she did not say it. Unlike Miss Anna Cameron she could never get enough of the attentions of a man and was grateful for them when she did.

13

Analee found that the bruise to her soul caused by the perfidy of her husband took longer to heal than any physical wound. Despite the apology from the King himself, despite the many letters of support and sympathy from friends, despite the knowledge that she was respected and loved on a scale she never dreamed possible, it was still the knowledge that her husband had wanted to destroy her that seemed so hard to bear.

For many weeks after her release from Carlisle she was languid and depressed. She found that even her beautiful Lakeland home in the spring and summer, and the presence of those who loved her, were insufficient to lift it.

But in time Analee grew better, maybe because she realized that this really was the end of her life with the Falcon. Whatever happened now, whatever he did or said, nothing could ever be the same as it was. She came to accept her status as a woman without a husband and her thoughts went to building a new life around her family.

Her first joy was getting Duncan back from Falcon's Keep. With the Falcon abroad no one dared disobey her command. She was even more powerful now than she had been before her imprisonment. So Duncan was returned to her from that gloomy fortress, little worse for his banishment. He was such a bright and attractive boy that he had completely won the heart of his stern tutor who came with him to Furness to continue his education.

So the spring passed into summer and summer into autumn. When the winter came the news from abroad was worse than before, but by the beginning of the new year Mr Pitt was firmly in command of the government. Admiral Byng was shot on his quarter deck for his failure to hold Minorca and the spirits of the country rose.

Analee thought frequently of Brent and their daughter Morella. He was in Laxey in the Isle of Man operating the bulk of Rigg's extensive fishing fleet. He had begged her to see him but she refused, saying that, their names having been brought together, it would be folly to meet until the business was forgotten. Any word of it back to the King or the Falcon could destroy all that had been done . . . and one must not forget that their release was based on an untruth. She had always felt worried about what Catherine Walkinshaw might say; but, doubtless for reasons of her own, that good woman had decided to keep her knowledge to herself.

One day Analee was working at her embroidery listening to a story read by Clare. Beyrick and Charlotte sat at her feet, their mouths open, their eyes wide with interest as their sister took them through the mysteries of Aladdin's cave. It was a peaceful scene: a large fire was in the grate, the smell of burning logs, the dogs asleep on the floor, a cat sitting on the low bench that ran along by the window. Outside the skeletal branches of the tree beat against the mullioned window panes and the haze of winter obscured the distant hills. Except for the crackle of the logs and the piping voice of Clare, no sound disturbed the tranquillity. Analee snipped a piece of wool from her tapestry and prepared to thread a needle with a fresh colour. She had been aware of the thud of hooves along the lonely road that led to the Grange in the recesses of her mind, but it was not until they grew louder and entered the courtyard that she raised her head and glanced out of the window. A dust-covered stranger descended from his horse and passed rapidly out of sight into the house. She wondered who it could be. Few people passed this way in winter and most provisions and the post came from Keswick by boat.

There was a flurry outside the door and a servant stood back as the stranger she had observed on the horse entered and bowed low. Analee put down her sewing and bade Clare stop reading.

'My lady,' the messenger produced a letter from beneath his cloak, 'I bring very sad news.'

'The Falcon!' Analee gasped. 'There is something wrong with my husband?'

'I am from Delamain Castle, ma'am, Sir George Delamain is dead.'

Analee felt a *frisson* run through her body. Nelly, hovering in the background anxiously, having been as disturbed by the presence of the stranger as Analee, hurried forward and dropped a curtsey. 'Shall I take the children, my lady?'

'Would you, Nelly? I am so shocked I must have time to recover my wits.' She managed to smile at her children and bade the messenger take a seat.

'Thank you, my lady, but I will not sit in your presence. I am but a servant of the late Sir George.'

The *late* Sir George. Was it possible?

'Then you must have something to eat and drink in the servants' quarters before you leave. Pray tell me, how did this distressing event occur?'

'Sir George had been ailing all winter, ma'am, prey to one bout of ill health after another; but there was nothing serious or untoward until three days ago when he was suddenly struck with the smallpox. Such was his weakened state that he died within twenty-four hours.'

'Oh! I am appalled,' Analee put her hands to her spinning head. 'Oh, and how is poor Lady Delamain?'

'She has taken it very badly, ma'am.'

'I must go to her.'

'I think her sister is coming, your ladyship. There is also Sir George's mother and his brother, now Sir Brent, has been summoned. The funeral has already taken place because of the risk of infection.'

Infection. Morella! Analee's heart raced and she sat down quickly. The dreaded smallpox could spread like fire.

'I simply came to tell you, ma'am, and I am on my way to inform others who knew Sir George, including Mr Rigg and Mr Fitzgerald. I am bound to Whitehaven and Cockermouth now.'

'I will write to her ladyship before you go,' Analee said, rising from her chair. 'Pray go now and take nourishment before you proceed on your journey.'

The servant bowed and withdrew and, for a long time, Analee stood by the window gazing onto the lake.

Sir Brent. Sir Brent Delamain. Far, far before anyone could have dreamed it, he had come into his own. He was now the owner of Delamain Castle. It was almost as though George had foreseen his untimely death. If this had happened but a year before Brent would have been an exile, a renegade, a traitor and the title would have passed to a remote cousin who lived in Wiltshire.

Analee put her face in her hands and sobbed – whether through grief for Sir George or relief for Brent she could not tell.

Anna Cameron was very bored. She was bored with embroidery, bored with reading, bored with the sights of Berlin, bored with the company of Lady McKeith who sometimes seemed like a gaoler. They couldn't do this and they couldn't do that. They went nowhere in society, neither to the court of the King nor even the British Embassy.

'You must consider it as though the Falcon was in mourning,' Lady McKeith had said, trying to temper her impetuosity. 'It would never do for him to parade his new wife so soon after getting rid of the last.'

'I don't see why. She wanted to divorce him. She *asked* for a divorce.'

'Yes, but among the nobility such things are done with delicacy. You do not just put off your old wife and take another.'

'I think his lordship is ashamed of me.'

'Of course he is not! You know he adores you.'

'Does he?' Anna Cameron had looked at her chaperone; but Lady McKeith had lowered her eyes, refusing to meet her gaze.

That was a few months ago. Now the spring had come and the plans that King Frederick had been working on all winter were on their way to maturity. He had prevailed upon the English to return all the Hanoverian and Hessian soldiers who had been hastily summoned to meet the threat of a French invasion. They were also to subsidize Brunswick and Saxe-Gotha to provide troops to swell Frederick's army. The new army was to be called the Army of Observation and King Frederick hoped the British would send a contingent of cavalry. But England was too committed elsewhere to send any troops; and, moreover, she was busy raising more regular regiments to send to India and America.

The Falcon was often away. He went with Sir Andrew Mitchell to arrange for the subsidy to Brunswick and inspected the Brunswick troops. He met Lieutenant General von Schmettau who had been sent as an emissary by Frederick to Hanover and discussed tactics with him there. In February it was rumoured that the Hanoverian government was trying to arrange neutrality with Austria. But, also in February, Pitt convinced the nation of the importance of the alliance with Prussia and began to put England on a proper warlike footing.

Then the one thing the Falcon dreaded happened. The Duke of Cumberland was appointed to command the Army of Observation. This meant that the British would start to flock to the Continent and his awful secret would be out. What would the King have to say to a bigamist? The Falcon had tried to get Prince Henry, brother to King Frederick, as commander; but the King wanted the son of the English monarch who was also Elector of Hanover. In April the Duke of Cumberland was due to arrive at Stade on the mouth of the Elbe and the Falcon was to be sent with others to welcome him.

He left his new 'wife' behind. He only wished that when he returned she would have gone forever, disappeared from the face of the earth. His bigamous marriage had been a terrible failure. In all his considerable experience he had never known a woman so bad in bed as Anna Cameron. He was now able to claim his rights with a fair amount of ease, but without any pleasure. Had he not taken her in the circumstances he had he would have left her long ago. Not only did she afford him little pleasure, she clearly took none herself; she never relaxed or unwound but was always on the verge of fear as though in dread of the act. Her body was always cold and her limbs always stiff.

He could not summon up the courage to tell her about his deception. She would surely go back to England and delight in exposing him, just to extract the maximum revenge.

'May I not come with you to greet His Royal Highness, my lord?' She hardly ever called him Angus as though out of fear or exaggerated respect. It emphasized their lack of intimacy.

''Tis out of the question,' he said briefly, looking up from his papers. It was the night before he was due to depart.

'But *why*?'

'Because it is a military occasion. Europe is no place for a woman to travel through now the French army has moved towards the Rhine. We have evacuated Wesel. Hostilities have begun.'

'But shall I be safe in Berlin, sir?'

'As safe as anywhere.'

'Could I not go back to England?'

'No.'

810

'But why?'

'Because I say so.'

'That is not sufficient reason, my lord.'

He looked sharply up at her, aware of the bright flush on her cheeks, the light in her eyes. When she was not being unduly submissive she was bad-tempered. She was like a child, capricious, veering between moods. He would treat her like one.

'It is quite sufficient for me,' Angus said, returning to his papers.

Anna came over and stood by the table on which he was writing. 'I *demand* to go back to England! I shall go when you are gone, whether you wish it or not, and take my rightful place at Falconer House.'

'*Your* rightful place!' The Falcon glared at her and put down his quill. He stood up and towered over her menacingly. '*Your* rightful place is where I command it. And I command that you stay in Berlin.'

'You are a tyrant, Lord Falconer.'

He raised a hand and hit her across the mouth. She stared at him and staggered back as the tears sprang to her eyes. A little blood trickled from the corner of her mouth. Even looking at her disgusted him. He had never fallen out of love so quickly, or with such cause. How had he ever considered her beautiful? Why had he been unable to sleep at nights for thinking of her? Why had he plotted and worked for months – for this? She was superficial, silly and unbedworthy. The Falcon went back to his chair and sat down, taking up his quill again; but the sound of her weeping was too distracting. He gazed at her and tried to summon up some pity. On the other hand he felt she had trapped him. He was saddled with her; he could neither send her to England nor to her mother in America. They could not stay here forever. He wanted to go now neither to India nor America, but to bring his own troops over from England and join in this exciting continental fray. The only feasible thing to do was to have her killed; but Isobel McKeith seemed to be fond of the girl. He knew he could not count on her loyalty.

'I am sorry,' he said at last, 'that I struck you. I find you excessively vexatious at times. You seem to have no interests, no occupations. I know not what to do with you.'

'Send me to England.'

811

The Falcon banged the table. 'I have told you I cannot! 'Tis out of the question. I pray you now desist. Desist, I tell you.'

'I am not allowed to go abroad, to mix with the Prussians nor visit the British Embassy. I, the Marchioness of Falconer, am treated like a prisoner.'

'It is for your own protection. Berlin is full of spies, the country is at war.'

'I fear you no longer love me, my lord?'

The Falcon looked at her and went over to her. He touched her shoulder and kissed the top of her head. 'You are a silly goose. You know I am preoccupied with affairs. It does not mean I do not love you.'

She gazed up at him trying to smile, but her cheeks were stained with tears. 'I am glad of that, sir, because I am to have our child. I hoped that it would give you pleasure and, if you still love me, I know it will.'

The Falcon shut his eyes and hoped that when he opened them she would have gone; but no, she was still there, gazing at him with an expression of trust, even hope.

'You see why I want so much to go back to England, sir? To give birth in your lordship's home. Would you reconsider now?'

'A child?' the Falcon echoed lifelessly.

'Your lordship is not pleased?' Her face clouded with anxiety.

'Why should I be pleased? I am certainly not delighted.'

'But why not, sir?'

'Because this is no time to be having children.' Lord Falconer got up and began restlessly to pace the room. 'What with war, and . . . uncertainty.' He looked at her and wondered if he could have her killed and put away without anyone knowing, and the bastard child with her.

'But did not your lordship think I might bear a child?'

No, he hadn't. He thought children came from pleasure, and he had had very little and she none. He had told her to use the sponge but she did not like to have such intimate contact with her body. Such was her prudery, her shame, that her flesh, and his, seemed to disgust her.

'I thought that, as you had not up to now, you might not. I thought you might be barren.'

'Your lordship sounds as though you wished it.'

'Of course I do not wish it. I simply feel it is not the right time.'

The Falcon strode out of the room, banging the door behind him, and sought out Lady McKeith in her room.

'I told her she should not tell you yet. I knew you would not be pleased.' Her ladyship shrugged her shoulders. She too hated Berlin and wished to be back in London. She had tired of the whole game, the indifference of the Falcon and the fear and insecurity of his pathetic, unlawful wife.

'Can she not get rid of it?'

Lady McKeith looked at him in surprise. 'But why should she? She thinks she is a marchioness and the child will be a lord or lady. She is proud of it. In her opinion it is the only good thing that has come out of lying with your lordship.'

'She says that?'

'No, but I know it. You are in a pretty pickle, Angus Falconer, and I know not what you can do.' Lady McKeith looked at him with a smirk, as though pleased at his discomfiture.

'I should never have put away my wife, Analee.'

'A lot of people said that at the time, my lord.'

'They were right.' The Falcon looked wistful. 'I think of her a lot, comparing her to . . . that!' He glanced towards the door. 'I must have been deranged to prefer her to Analee. I was an old fool, bewitched by young flesh. Well, 'tis no use moaning. Not now.

'Look, I am leaving tomorrow for Stade. I will think of a plan and write to you. Meanwhile if you can endeavour to procure an abortion, pray do. I care not how you bring it about, drug her if you like. I will pay you well if you succeed.'

Lady McKeith shook her head, still with the same mirthless smile. 'It is no use, my lord. She is determined to have that child. You know her prudery. She will let none touch her. Even the doctor who confirmed what I already knew, that she was with child, could scarce get near her. All he was allowed to examine was her belly, which has begun to swell. Were you not so preoccupied you would have noticed it yourself!'

'Even *I* scarce get to see her belly,' the Falcon snorted. ''Tis a rare privilege indeed to see under her nightdress.'

'Well,' Lady McKeith continued, 'it is the one thing in her dreary life to which she now looks forward. She knows she has lost your love, that she cannot please you in bed or share your interests. She feels you despise her. Going back to England and having your child have become obsessions with her and, believe me, she will bring them both about.'

The Falcon hit the wall with his stick, swore savagely and walked out of the room banging the door behind him with such force that two pictures in the hall fell off the wall, and the glass broke into tiny fragments.

14

Lord Falconer didn't know with whom his irritation was the most profound; whether it was with the French, who had already crossed the Rhine and were continuing to advance; with the Erbprinz of Hesse Kassel, commanding the Prussian and allied troops, who was perpetually retreating; or with the vacillations of his own master the Duke of Cumberland, who clearly wished the war to stop altogether.

The Duke kept on writing effusive letters to the enemy commander Marshal d'Estrées signed *votre ami affectionné*, and doubtless getting the same back. Yet all the time the French gained ground, pouring troops into their advanced positions. By 12 June d'Estrées had occupied Wiedenbruck and then Rietburg. Cumberland, at last, decided to stand and fight – to turn his Army of Observation into one of action – although he was without any clear information about the strength or intentions of the enemy. He himself had thirty-eight squadrons and fifty-two battalions, almost the whole of his army.

On the morning of 13 June, d'Estrées sent his light troops round both flanks of Cumberland's position. Cumberland immediately decided to retire despite the entreaties of Lord Falconer.

'I would remind your lordship,' he said haughtily, 'that *I* command this army, not yourself. What is more you are merely here as an *adviser*, Lord Falconer, and have no official position at all.'

The Duke swept out of his tent and went to consult with officers who were more keen on ingratiating themselves with him.

Angus looked at McNeath and shook his head. 'This is not the man I heard tell of at Culloden. He has gone soft, McNeath. He is totally uninterested in waging this war. He only desires peace. 'Tis because, he says, the Hanoverians have no argument with the King of France or the Empress of Austria. He fears Hanover will be too easily overcome. I know not where it will end.'

But during the night, to the Falcon's fury, the command came to withdraw. Immediately there was chaos as the order did not reach all the troops, and some began to retire through others who thought they should stay where they were. The result was that they fired on one another.

In the dawn the Falcon tried to take command, riding among the disaffected troops and doing what he could to restore order. As the troops slunk back to Bielefeld the French were at their heels and fighting recommenced. The Duke of Cumberland was nowhere to be seen, having moved off at first light to be sure of safety.

'It is useless, my lord. You must retreat,' McNeath urged, gazing anxiously into the gloom. 'See, there are the flags of the French.'

The Falcon put his telescope to his eye. Sure enough they were advancing in disciplined and orderly ranks whereas all around him the Prussian rear guard was in a state of chaos. He suddenly felt ashamed of himself and the men. He was only here as an observer, it was true. Officially he had no part in the war at all; but to see such craven behaviour was a sight so distasteful to him that he could not stomach it.

'Come, McNeath,' he said peremptorily. 'Gather a body of troops and let us charge them.'

'My lord,' McNeath looked around in consternation, 'all the troops have their backs to us.'

'Then we alone will face the French.'

'I beg you, my lord . . .'

It was too late. The Falcon drew his sword and charged towards the oncoming French ranks. It was such an astonishing sight that those in the front row of the advancing troops paused, and those behind almost fell on top of them. Then, quickly recovering his composure, a solitary infantryman from the French ranks raised his arm, put his musket to his shoulder and fired. The Falcon fell immediately, his horse charging on without him until it too was brought to the ground.

For a moment there was an eerie silence in the dawn as McNeath flung himself off his horse and knelt beside his master. He was not dead; but a great mass of blood belched from a huge wound in his side. His eyes were closed and his face pale as death. Two French officers came up and gazed with astonishment at the stricken Falcon.

'He rode like a madman.'

'To his death. He was bent on self-slaughter.'

McNeath looked at them with resignation, expecting any moment the bullet that would finish off his master and then another for him, too. That was how they had despatched the Jacobites at Culloden, without mercy. He was prepared. He would not plead. But the French were standing around in a state of great consternation, as though it was something they had not seen before and could not understand. Suddenly there was a small commotion at the rear and the body of troops sprang hastily to attention. The two officers bowed and gestured helplessly at the fallen soldier.

Marshal d'Estrées peered to the ground and then looked incredulously at McNeath. 'It *looks* like Lord Falconer.'

'It is, sir.'

'It is impossible. What is his lordship doing here?'

'He was adviser to the Duke of Cumberland on behalf of the King of Prussia, sir.'

'Of course.' The Marshal straightened up and shook his head sadly. 'The retreat of the Prussians and their allies will have sickened a man of such valour. Take him up gently and carry him to my tent. He will be treated not as a prisoner but as an honoured guest – and send immediately for the doctors. Come!' He gestured to McNeath whose eyes filled with tears of gratitude. 'Lord Falconer may be mortally wounded, but he will die as the hero he is. How *Le Faucon* must hate this sort of timidity!'

By nightfall Angus had recovered consciousness, but the wound in his side was a terrible one and the French doctors had had to operate on it to remove pieces of shot. McNeath had stood with him administering brandy during the agonizing process, during which the Falcon fainted anew several times. Now the wound was dressed and bandaged and the Falcon seemed peaceful. As he lay in his tent the flap was drawn back and Marshal d'Estrées entered quietly and looked at his prisoner.

'Well, my lord, do you recognize me?' he said in French.

The Falcon stared at him, tried to raise his head and then smiled replying in the same language. 'Louis. Louis-César. We meet again on the battlefield. How are you, my old friend?'

The Marshal put a hand out and smiled. 'Better than you, my dear Angus. Never did I think to see such a sorry sight.'

'Those Prussians have no stomachs,' the Falcon growled. 'I urged them to advance and they all fled.'

'I have not seen you since you were in Paris to discuss the peace in '48, Angus.'

'Oh come, have we not met since then? No? Maybe you were too busy plotting with those Jacobites. They . . .' The Falcon paused and gasped with pain. McNeath bent forward and put a glass of brandy to his lips. 'Ah, I think I am done for, Louis-César. At least I died with my face to the enemy and not my rump.'

'You will not die. We have the best surgeons here with us. I have told them that if you go to the grave they follow you. No, Angus, your wound is grave but not fatal. We will get you to your own lines, unless you prefer to go to Paris?'

Angus managed a weak smile. 'There I think I *will* be despatched to my Maker – by the Jacobite renegades if not by King Louis. No, send me to Cumberland. Thank you, my old friend. I hope you lose!'

The Marshal bent over and kissed both his cheeks. 'I hope your force loses, but not you, Angus. I hope to see you in Paris as an honoured guest at the court when we are at peace again.'

The Falcon shook his head. 'Not for a long time, Louis-César. This will be a very bitter war. But thank you, my old friend. You have saved my life.'

'Do not forget to give my regards to – Lady Falconer.' The Marshal raised his right hand to the sky and kissed the tips of his fingers. 'Ah, the Enchantress. Is she here with you?'

'No.'

'Then have them send for her. She will restore you to health in no time.'

'Sir Brent Delamain, ma'am.'

Nelly looked anxiously at Analee and then glanced behind her shoulder.

'Sir Brent . . .' Analee rose to her feet and put a hand to her breast in a futile attempt to quell the rapid beating of her heart. 'He is *here*, Nell?'

Nelly nodded excitedly and then stood back, stifling a gasp as Brent gently edged her to one side and came slowly into the room.

'You cannot throw me out,' he said with pretended solemnity and then he smiled and held out his arms.

With a cry Analee rushed into them, flinging her head against his chest. He didn't attempt to kiss her, but put his arms around her protectively, hugging her to him.

'I knew if I asked you would not let me; but this agony has gone on for long enough. I have come to claim you, Analee.'

Analee leaned her head against his chest aware of his strength and power, his gentleness. She seemed to hear his words from a long way off and the echo reverberated through the room.

'*Claim* me?'

'Aye. I am determined on't. How long is it since you saw that ruffian of a husband of yours?'

Analee didn't reply and a hand lingered on his chest before she left him with reluctance. 'I have not seen my lord for eighteen months; but he is still my lord, my husband, Brent. Now he is with the Duke of Cumberland in Germany.'

'Aye, and badly the war is going, too from all I hear.'

'It makes no difference, Brent.'

He strode over to her and seized her shoulders, drawing her close to him once more. With unaccustomed delicacy Nelly quietly withdrew and closed the door, staying outside in case anyone should try to venture in. Analee heard the door click and smiled to herself. She put her face up to Brent and he gazed at her lips. Then he gently kissed her. For a moment the desire she felt for him was overpowering. To feel the impress of his lips, the warmth and strength of his body was almost too much for a passionate woman like herself who had been for so long without a man. He felt her trembling and his hands tightened round her.

'Take me here, Brent, if you want.'

She felt him quiver, but he gently eased his mouth away, keeping his arms about her. 'I want, but I will not. I want to wed you, Analee. I have thought long about it; debated within myself, sought advice from those I trusted.'

'But how can we be wed when I am wed to another?'

'There is such a thing as divorce. It is not easy, but I am sure the King will grant it, having in mind the way the Falcon has treated you.'

'I am sure His Majesty will do no such thing. There are many husbands who abuse or ignore their wives. If they were all allowed divorce where would it end? A woman is meant to be resigned – and chaste. I find both a burden, being tempestuous and hot-blooded by nature. Maybe if in ten years I neither saw nor heard from my lord he might be prepared to consider the matter. But what is eighteen months in a lifetime?'

'It is not only eighteen months separation, Analee! You know that full well. It is what he has done; having you put in gaol, humiliating you.'

Analee kissed his cheek and moved away. His proximity was too much for her; she felt too weak. 'Brent, although to you the time seems unendurable – and it is, aye, for me as well as you – it is not such a very long time for others. Do not you think the King would immediately be suspicious if I petitioned for divorce? He would ask why and I would have to say to marry you. He would recall that we were accused together of treason and all my friends would disperse, like the waves receding from the shore. People, alas, are all too fickle and there are many who know I was born of a gypsy – not that I am ashamed of it, as well you know; but they would soon start to talk and mock, pointing a finger and saying I had the morals of a whore. I have my children, Brent; they come first. I would never bring shame on my children.'

Analee felt more in possession of herself and turned to Brent her colour high, her bosom quickly rising and falling 'My children are very precious to me, Brent; more important to me than my own happiness. As long as their father lives – and God grant that will be for many years – I would do nothing to make them ashamed of me; even if I have to live in this way, like a nun, for the rest of my life.'

Brent squeezed his hands together and his whole frame shook with anguish. 'I wish I had taken you when you asked.'

'You thought it was nobler to ask me to marry you than to lie with me? You did not used to be like that, Brent. I think inheriting a title has made you more aware of your responsibilites. Or is it that, now you are a baronet, making love on the floor is undignified?' She smiled at him mockingly. The old Analee coming to life.

'Oh, Analee, do not talk like that! I only wanted you to know I had not just come for that one thing – your precious body. Of *course* I want to lie with you and love you. Every occasion has been exquisite to me and lingers forever in my memory. Have we not lain on a forest floor as well as in a soft bed? But you have told me not to come and see you. You forbade it. I obeyed your command because I saw the sense of it; but I think of you every day, not once but many, many times. Without you my life will never be complete, never be happy. I am a lost man without you, Analee. Without you I cannot function.'

'I am only half a woman, too,' Analee murmured, her hand stealing into his. 'And that half is broken. I have given such love to the Falcon, to have him smash it in my face. For months someone tasted my food in case he tried to send poison to me. If there were noises in the night I feared that an assassin had been sent to kill me. I felt such waves of evil from that man. I cannot tell you.'

Analee put her face in her hands, her eyes shut as though with horror at the memory. 'Oh, do not think that I would have risked the life of my servants by getting them to taste poisoned food! 'Twas *they* who did it without my knowledge. Nelly told me. They all feared the Falcon, even those who had once loved him, as I did. Oh, not as I did. No one could have loved him as I did.'

'Do not talk to me of your passion for him!' Brent wrenched his hand away and went to stand by the window. How well he looked in his suit of brown alpaca, Analee thought, a full white cravat at his throat and lace at his wrists. He wore his own hair unpowdered, tied back with a brown velvet ribbon. He looked like the elegant *gadjo* she had known all those years ago, as he stood at the back of the tavern outside Penrith watching her dance. Now, twelve years on, the lines on his face had deepened, his hair was darker; but age had given him an air of distinction that he had lacked as an impetuous youth. His frame was still powerful and muscular, no surplus fat anywhere, and there was an ascetic quality about his eyes and lips that told her he was not a profligate like her husband. The Falcon had grown sensual and a dissolute look had replaced the once disciplined fervour in his eyes. She knew that Brent saved himself only for her.

'It is no longer a passion, Brent,' Analee said quietly. 'I fear him. When he comes back from the war I know not what he will do; for I think he hates me and would do all he could to endanger me.'

'Let him try!' Brent said, shaking a fist at the ceiling.

'What could you do? We are both powerless. Maybe he will stop in London, contenting himself with his amours, the younger women he likes increasingly to disport himself with, trying doubtless to recapture his own youth. But, Brent, I live only for today. I never know what tomorrow will bring, or the day after. I have all my children in good health and vigour, for which I thank God. My servants protect me and love me and I grow increasingly enchanted with this lovely country, this Lakeland. I have the pleasure of watching the seasons day by day as they change the character of the woods and meadows, the hills and pasturelands, even the water itself. I am become resigned, nay, content.'

'I want you more than ever,' Brent whispered, closing his eyes. 'Merely to hear your voice is a torture to me.'

'Then you should not have come to torture yourself,' she said gently and she leaned her head on his shoulder and placed an arm lightly around his waist. He bent to kiss her when they were disturbed by a hammering at the door and sprang apart.

'Madam, it is I, Nelly. Oh, may I enter?'

'Of course, Nell.' Analee went quickly to the door and opened it. By Nelly's side was a stranger, covered with mud, his face caked with dust and dirt. He breathed quickly as one who had ridden for a long time without stopping.

'Who is this, Nell?' she said in alarm, drawing back and looking at Brent.

'I am come from the Duke of Cumberland, Madam. He bade me ride as I have never ridden before, and I obeyed his Grace's command, one horse even dying beneath me.'

'Yes, yes?' Analee said, trying to stifle the panic in her breast.

'It is your lord, Madam. Lord Falconer is gravely ill.'

As she swayed, Nelly put an arm round her to support her. Brent didn't move from where he stood, transfixed, by the window. Nelly took Analee to a chair and helped her sit down. Analee stared in front of her, strangely unaware of anything or anyone. Then she said slowly, 'The Falcon, gravely ill?' Her eyes focused on the stranger, and she struggled to rise, but Nelly held her back. 'Where? I must go to him.'

'He is on his way home, ma'am, slowly by coach. He was wounded near Minden and appeared to make a good recovery as he was well taken care of by the French. But his condition deteriorated once he was brought to Hanover and his Royal Highness wished to send for you, as his lordship cried for you continuously. His Royal Highness then thought that he could not possibly reach you in time and the Falcon said he wished to go home. But the journey is slow and painful and I do not know if he will die on the way.'

'But where, where, *where* is he now?'

'Last time he was on the Dutch coast, ma'am, ready to cross the sea. For all I know he may now be in England. They will send fresh word to you as soon as he is.'

The man staggered and Analee looked at him with concern. 'Nelly, you must see this good man has food and rest. Go now and then return to me when I have recovered my wits.'

Nelly led the messenger to the door and Analee stared after him as though she had seen a ghost. Brent went to the door and closed it then came over to her and knelt by her side.

'I know not what to say.'

'Why did I not know something was wrong?' Analee said. 'In the old days my powers would have alerted me. Yet I have slept like a baby, my dreams were sweet and happy. How did I not *know*?'

'Because you no longer love him.' Brent gently took her hand and brought it to his lips.

'No, it is because my powers are no longer with me. I cannot see things as I did. I am mortal, after all, Brent.' She tried to smile. 'No longer an enchantress.'

'For me you are *always* an enchantress. Oh, Analee, what will happen now? If he dies . . .'

She quickly put a finger on his lips and pressed them firmly. 'Shhh, do not say it. I would never wish that Lord Falconer should die if I could do aught to prevent it. And did you hear? He asked continually after me. If he is well enough to travel there is hope. Go now, Brent. I know you are a Christian, so pray for me. Pray for us both, Angus and myself – for if he dies what will become of us all, his children orphaned and me, a widow?'

'If he lives it will be worse,' Brent began but Analee put her hand across his mouth and stared at him, fear and distress obliterating the customary light in her eyes.

* * *

As the boat came over the water Analee stood on the jetty shielding her eyes. Although the sun was behind and above her it cast a glare upon the water, and the harsh reflections of the surrounding mountains made it more difficult to see the slim outline of the skiff that bore the Falcon home.

No sooner had the messenger left than Analee received fresh word that her husband was stronger and would make the rest of the journey to Lakeland. Every day brought news of him, where he was, the state of his health and how much he longed to see her.

The Falcon, she thought ruefully, was like a child. Whenever he was ill he needed her. This time she would harden her heart to his need; she would be a good and dutiful wife and nurse but nothing more. She would never allow him to tear her heart again. But as soon as she saw his battered body being carried out of the boat she experienced such waves of shock, tenderness and compassion that her stern resolutions fled from her as she ran to his side and gazed at his stricken face.

He did not speak, but from the deep recesses of his sunken sockets his eyes blazed out at her, full of love and the desperation that had forced him to make a journey many would have given up long ago. For every tilt of the carriage, every lurch of the boat had been agony; but his spirit was borne aloft by one thing: to see Analee again.

As she looked upon him and smiled, stroking his brow, the expression of desperation was replaced by contentment, and he closed his eyes as they bore him into the house and up the stairs to the bedroom that overlooked the lake and, in the far distance, the jaws of Borrowdale looming like sentinels.

He had shrunk to half his size; his frame was like that of an old man. His hair was almost white and his growth of beard grizzled and grey. She helped to strip his body and then she washed it down, dressing and bandaging the terrible wound herself and noticing how it still bled and festered; a huge suppurating sore. The Falcon opened his eyes, following her as she moved quietly around him assisted only by a weary McNeath and Nelly. He seemed either too exhausted to speak or incapable of speech. She did not know. The bowl of water to bathe him was refreshed time and time again and finally she put a clean nightshirt on him and, between them, she and McNeath gently pulled the bedclothes over him and tucked them tenderly around him as though he were a baby. He then closed his eyes and, sighing deeply, fell into a deep sleep, a slight smile hovering on his mouth.

Analee, pale and distressed, stared at McNeath. 'He did not utter a word. Can he still talk?'

'He is worn out, ma'am. He has scarce spoken since Derby. Only every now and then he called your ladyship's name, repeating it to himself, "Analee, Analee", but every time we wanted him to rest he forced us to go forward. I have hardly stood the journey and I don't know how his lordship has. Some demon drove him on.' McNeath looked sadly at the Falcon and swayed slightly, passing his hand over his brow. Nelly took his arm, supporting him as Analee said:

'McNeath, you too must go straight to bed and Nelly will bring you refreshment. First you must tell me how my lord came by this terrible wound; but before you do that I must send for Reyora. She is the only one who can help him now.'

After McNeath had told his story and two messengers had been sent for Reyora, Analee went slowly up to the bedroom and sat by the bed where the Falcon still slept peacefully, breathing gently, never turning once, the expression on his face serene. Analee took his hand and at her touch he trembled and his eyelids flickered. The late afternoon sun stole through the window and the gentle lapping of water, the sighing of the wind in the trees were the only sounds, apart from his deep regular breathing, that could be heard.

Maybe he would recover . . . Surely he should be dead by now from that wound? Already the colour of his face had improved. In her care his wound would heal and he would put on weight, recover his strength. Maybe once again . . .

'Analee . . .'

'Yes, my lord. Angus?'

''Tis you then and not a vision?'

'I think you have a vision, sir, for your eyes are still closed.'

'I am dreaming of you then. I am still in Hanover in the palace of Herrenhausen and a little bird taps at the window.'

'No, no Angus, that was many years ago. Then you were also healed and came back to me. You will be again. I have sent for Reyora and I am here. It *is* real.'

825

His eyelids flickered but still they did not open. Once again he smiled and slept, Analee continuing to hold his hand. How could she *not* love him, this man she had married in the midst of war, who had given her his powerful name and three beautiful children? How could she *not* love him when, although he was not true to her, she was the one he needed when in pain and distress, when only the thought of seeing her kept him alive? All her old love for him returned, flooding her, suffusing her being as though he had never caused her such heartbreak and pain. McNeath said that many were the times he thought the Falcon was on the verge of death, but he had only to say her name to gain the strength to continue.

Perhaps she still had her magical powers. She closed her eyes as she pressed his hand, willing all her strength into the Falcon to restore him to life. She had done it once before, after Falkirk. She would save him yet again.

The sun sank below the hills and a mist rose on the lake. The sighing through the trees became a soft breeze and night slowly fell. Nelly entered with candles and stood by Analee's side gazing at her master.

'How does he, Analee?'

'He sleeps very peacefully. He has spoken to me, but I think in his sleep. He thought he was in Hanover. But I do not like his weakness, Nelly. I wish Reyora would come.'

'Are you sure Reyora *will* come?' Nelly said gently, a hand on Analee's shoulder.

Analee looked at her, startled. 'Of course I am sure Reyora will come! Why should she not come? She has never failed me yet.'

The expression in Nelly's eyes was enigmatic and Analee grasped her hand and shook her. 'Why do you look at me like that, Nell?'

Nelly avoided Analee's eyes. 'I have no reason, I merely wondered, 'tis all.'

'Then if you have doubts we must send another messenger. He must command her to come. If she does not come I will go and get her myself and drag her here!' Analee bit her lip savagely, looking at the sleeping Falcon; but her heart now was troubled. Supposing Reyora would not come. What then?

'Calm yourself, ma'am,' Nelly said. 'I am sure she will come if you think so. I will get you some food. The children are anxious to see their papa.'

'Not yet. Not until he is better. Tell them they will see him in good time.'

That night Analee got into bed beside her husband willing him life. His breathing was shallower and a feverish sweat had broken out on his forehead. As she moulded herself to him she gently stroked his body trying to infuse him with life, the life that had given life and brought life. Then she put her arm about him and the tears started to flow as she thought back on the happy times they had shared. Her memory kindly obliterated the many bad moments that had intervened, the times when he had neglected her, cast her into prison, undoubtedly wished her dead. She remembered only the great love they bore each other for so long.

During the night his fever rose and at dawn she got out of bed and went to summon Nelly who clung to McNeath as though she never wanted to be parted from him again.

'Nelly, the Falcon is worse! You must get up. Reyora should be here by now.'

McNeath stirred as Nelly left his side, but she kissed his cheek and bade him stay where he was.

'I will go send another messenger,' she said, dressing quickly. 'Do you wish me to send McNeath?'

'No, let him sleep. We will now have sent three messengers. *Why* is Reyora not here?'

Nelly ran down to despatch yet another servant on horseback and Analee returned to her bedroom, clasping her gown around her in the cold morning. The Falcon now tossed in his bed and the moaning he made filled Analee with fear. When Nelly came back they bathed him again, but saw that the yellow pus round the wound was turning green and an evil, sickly-looking slime was oozing from it together with fresh blood. The smell was vile.

'Oh, I *would* I had the potions and herbs I used to have. I *would* I remembered the spells.' Analee clasped her head, her face stricken with anguish. Just then they heard the sound of hoofbeats and Analee ran to the window, flinging it open and looking out.

A solitary rider climbed wearily off his horse and ran into the house.

'Tis Gilbert. The one we sent first. Quick, bring him up here.'

Gilbert, sodden with the dew and pale with weariness, was

brought into Analee's room and sank to his knees in front of her.
'She is gone, ma'am.'

'Gone? Reyora?'

'She has gone from the tribe.'

'I do not believe it!'

'They were all very *silent*, ma'am, and acted peculiar. I had the feeling she was somewhere in the camp but would not come out.'

'But did you look? Did you look?'

'I looked everywhere and besought them to find her for your sake. Tom has stayed on to scour the neighbourhood.'

Analee reached out and gently drew him up. 'Do not distress yourself, Gilbert. You have done well. If Reyora does not come I myself will go and fetch her. She is there, I know. Is she not, Nelly?' She motioned Gilbert out of the room and then turned to Nelly. 'Is she not? You *knew* she would not come?'

'Did she not say, Analee, that she would not help him again? Did she not say it because of the way he has treated you?'

Analee nodded, her eyes haunted. 'Aye, she did, and she has no right! I want him well. I *love* him. I will have him better. I will go and fetch Reyora myself.'

Nelly took Analee's hand and pressed it. 'Do not go, Analee. If the Falcon should die while you were away you would not forgive yourself. Perhaps it is his time,' she looked over towards him, gravely shaking her head, 'and Reyora knows it.'

'But Reyora could stop it. You know she could . . .'

'Did she not say he was on borrowed time? Once you saved him, once she saved him and now . . .'

The Falcon cried out and Analee ran to him. His body was hot, his face flushed. He gazed at her in agony. 'Oh, Analee, I hurt so much. My body is burning. Pray give me water . . .'

Nelly filled a glass and gave it to Analee who held it to the Falcon's lips supporting his head with her arm. He sipped greedily and then leaned against her breathing harshly. 'I am going, Analee. I have seen death in the night beckoning to me. Oh God, I would not leave you now! How I repent of all the follies of my life . . .' He lay against her, too weak to continue and his harsh stertorous breathing frightened her. She bathed his body again, covering him lightly with the sheet, and his pulse grew less rapid, his breathing easier. He took her hand and smiled at her.

'I repent all the follies of my life, my injustice to you . . .'

'Do not speak of it, Angus.' Analee sat by his pillow and took his head on her breast. He snuggled up to her and clutched her as a small child does when it is frightened.

'But I have always loved you, Analee. Always. You might not believe me, might not think it possible, but 'tis true.'

'I know it is true, Angus, and when you are well we shall enjoy life together as we did before.'

'Oh, would that we could.' Tears ran down the Falcon's face and Analee gently stroked his cheek with her hand, brushing away the wetness. 'But I think God will not give me another chance. I am a cruel man, bent on having my way and prone to do injustice. I loved you so passionately and yet I abused you most vilely; but all the time, Analee, even in Berlin, my thoughts turned to you.'

He looked up at her and Analee saw shame stealing over his face; he averted his eyes.

'Berlin . . .'

'Yes, even in Berlin. Oh, how I do repent . . . oh.' The Falcon gave a convulsive shudder and his head fell from Analee's bosom. His eyes stared in front of him and he seemed in the grip of some seizure.

Nelly, who had been standing in the shadows by the window, rushed up and together they straightened his body, terribly twisted and tormented by spasms, while froth ran out of the corner of his mouth and his eyeballs swivelled in his sockets.

''Tis a fit,' Nelly said. ''Tis the fever. Oh, pray God . . .'

McNeath came into the room and went quickly to his master's side, his face contorted with grief. He seized him and held him down and after a while the spasms ceased and the Falcon's eyes closed, and once more he went into a deep, weary sleep.

'McNeath, *you* must go for Reyora. Tell her I command her; that if she does not come I will never speak to her again; that I will have no love for her and wish her only harm.'

'The second messenger has come back, my lady. He cannot find her.'

'Then you must go. She is there. Speak to the head of the tribe.'

'Aye, ma'am, I will.'

'Take another servant with you to show you the way. Only *you* can bring her back, McNeath.'

McNeath turned and, kneeling by the side of the bed, brought his master's hand to his lips. As he kissed it the tears poured down his face and he leaned his head against the bed, sobbing. 'Oh, I cannot go. I cannot leave him. I have loved him and served him all these years, my lady. How can I leave him now?'

'It is the only way to save him, McNeath. The only way.'

Analee gently helped him to rise and turned her head away, her own eyes filled with tears, as McNeath bent once more and kissed the Falcon's face. Then he turned abruptly and left the room. Nelly followed him.

Analee could hear the preparations for departure downstairs, but it only seemed to enhance the silence in the room. She sat on the bed and put her hand on the Falcon's heart. The beat, at first unnaturally fast, was now very feeble and his breathing was light and jerky. She thought for a moment that he had overcome his crisis and would recover, but the pallor of his face told her otherwise and there was a strange rasping in his throat like the prelude to the death rattle. She threw herself across his body and clasped it, willing her life to flow through him, willing him to live, but she felt no force go from herself to him. She kissed his cheeks and his lips, tenderly stroking his brow, and all the time that urgent summons was going from her body to his until she felt almost weak with exhaustion. But she knew there was no response. Her powers had failed.

'Analee.' His voice surprised her by its calm and strength. Her heart leapt and she sat upright and gazed at him.

'Angus. You are better?'

'I feel better. Suddenly I feel better,' he said and gazed at her lovingly. 'You enchantress, you are at work again, are you not? Healing me? Making me strong?'

'Yes. Oh yes.' She leaned her cheek against his breast but still the heart beat was very faint, almost a flicker. With difficulty he drew his arm from beneath the bedclothes and put it around her, his fingers on her bosom.

'I still desire you, enfeebled though I am.'

'But soon we will lie together, Angus, as we used to. I know it.'

'I do not think so, Analee.' The Falcon shook his head.

'But I am making you strong. You said.'

'It is pretence, is it not?' the Falcon whispered, his eyes clouded with grief and pain. 'You and I are deceiving each other. It is too late. I feel my life ebbing away. Oh, would I could stay here with you; but it was here I wished to die, Analee, if God wills that I die. Once here with you, in our beloved home, among our children, I felt I could die in peace. Now will you bring the children to me?'

'Oh, Angus, no, no!' Analee put her arms around him but Nelly, always hovering in the background, came forward and leaned over her.

'The children are outside, my lady. I told them to expect a call to see their papa. You must be strong for them.'

She opened the door and, preceded by Duncan, the children trooped in, Clare taking Beyrick and Charlotte by their hands. Timidly they approached their father's bed, the youngest scarcely able to peep over the top. Between them Analee and Nelly propped him up on his pillows and he gazed at his children from his sunken pain-wracked eyes. Then he put out a hand and drew Duncan to him.

'You will be the head of a great house, Duncan.'

'Yes, sir.' Duncan looked at him solemnly.

'But your first duty is to your mother. You must always look after her and protect her. I charge you with that. Is it clear?'

'Yes, sir.' Duncan gazed impassively at his father, showing no emotion.

'Good. The rest is taken care of.' For a while the Falcon gazed at him and then sighed and patted him on the cheek. 'Give me a kiss, then.'

Woodenly Duncan bent down, pecked his father's cheek and turned away. His eyes were quite dry. But Clare, as she approached, was already weeping. As her hands left those of the younger ones they tried to scramble on the bed but Nelly stopped them.

'Now then. You must not disturb your papa. He cannot romp with you until he is better.'

'But will papa get better?' Beyrick said, looking at him with interest.

The Falcon smiled. 'Of *course* I will, you rogue. My Beyrick.' He ruffled his tousled head fondly and put a finger playfully on his nose. 'My favourite son,' he murmured.

'But why must Duncan look after Mama?'

'Because I may not see her for some time. I am going away.'

'To the war?'

'A sort of war.' The Falcon's voice sunk to a whisper and he kissed Beyrick and Charlotte holding them both briefly, seeming to grow feeble with the effort. As Clare bent to kiss him she threw herself across her father in a torrent of weeping.

'Oh, Papa, Papa, do not go. I beg you.'

'There, my little Clare.' The Falcon held her tenderly. 'You will be like your mama, I know, a beauty. You could do worse than try and emulate her for the rest of your life. She is not only beautiful, but wise and faithful, virtuous – a good and loving wife and mother, a woman to admire. Hold her always before you as an example.' He kissed the top of Clare's head and, as his eyes closed with exhaustion, Nelly shepherded the children away, the younger ones running before her, Clare still weeping, trying to cling to her father. Only Duncan remained unaffected, solemn and detached. He was the last to leave the room and, as he stood on the threshold, he turned and stared thoughtfully at the dying man before closing the door behind him.

The Falcon gazed at the door for a long time. 'Yes, he is my son without doubt. I still do not like him, but he has all my ways. He will be a very ruthless man, Analee. You will have to bring him up strictly. And now you, my sweet wife.' He beckoned to her, and she came over to him dragging her feet, her heart so heavy she thought that it, too, would stop. Watching the children make their farewells had been a terrible trial to her. She sat by him and he stroked her hair, caressing the tresses which fell onto her swelling bosom.

'My Analee,' he said, looking into her eyes 'there is something I would tell you now that I am dying; for the thought fills me with grief and remorse.'

'What is it, Angus?'

'It may cause you pain.'

'Even then, tell it me.'

'You remember Anna Cameron?'

Analee felt her heart give a little leap. 'Yes.'

'Of course you remember her. Well, you know I was an old fool, having my last fling, but I mistakenly became attached to her.'

'I thought as much, Angus.'

'In fact,' the Falcon paused and seemed to be fighting for breath, 'she was with me in Berlin. I want you to look after her, Analee. I did not treat her well. Look after her for me. Go and fetch her when I am gone. Will you do that?'

Analee swallowed and nodded; but the tears rushed to her eyes, making her choke. That, on his deathbed, he could think of another woman!

He pressed her hand. 'Be brave, Analee, be generous. Compared to you Anna Cameron was nothing to me, but I regret the incident. She has to be looked after. Do not reproach me. Retain in your heart only love for me; because that was all I ever had for you. Analee . . .'

He gazed at her as though wanting to continue and he opened his mouth, but no words came. He clutched at her arm and half drew himself up, his face illumined by a brilliant smile. But suddenly his grasp on her arm slackened and he fell back on the pillows, his eyes still open, the smile remaining on his face.

For a long while she looked at him, her hand on his still heart. She leaned forward and, drawing his lids over his eyes, imprinted on each of them a silent lingering kiss. She continued to sit by his side until darkness came, holding his hand as it grew cold, its lifeless fingers in hers.

When Nelly gently tiptoed in Analee did not know how long he had been dead, or how much time had passed. For a long time Nelly gazed at him, then she turned and kissed Analee.

'Reyora is here. She came with McNeath.'

Analee turned and behind Nelly stood her old friend, with her wrinkled face and wise eyes, her bag of potions and unguents in her hand. Analee stared at Reyora who returned her gaze unblinkingly.

'You are too late,' she said.

'I know.'

'Why did you not come before?'

'It was his time.'

'But, oh, Reyora, you could have . . .' Analee burst into tears and threw herself against Reyora who put down her bag and enfolded her in her arms, hugging her.

'No, my dear. I could not. There was nothing I could do. He was on borrowed time as it was. And look how he misused it. Have you forgotten that?'

'Oh, but he would have changed. I know. We should have been as we used to. Happy, this time, forever.'

Reyora shook her head slowly, her face resigned and sad. 'He would never have changed, Analee. I knew that.'

'And *that* was why you did not come?' Analee still shook with sobs and Reyora stroked her shoulders tenderly.

'I knew that it was his time. There was no point. No point at all.'

She continued to hold Analee until her wild sobbing ceased and a feeling of calm pervaded her. Analee took a handkerchief and, wiping her eyes, straightened up, looking at Reyora whose calm enigmatic face gazed back at her.

She would never know the truth.

15

The journey had done much to assuage her grief in those awful days after the death of the Falcon, his burial in the family tomb at Falcon's Keep and the legal and civil complexities connected with the death of a great nobleman and the accession to his title and estates of his eldest son, the eight-year-old Duncan. Many people journeyed up from London for the funeral including Mr Pitt and the Duke of Newcastle. The King send a personal representative, his mistress the Countess of Yarmouth. No higher honour could have been given, but perhaps her ladyship had her own, more intimate reasons for wishing to bid farewell to the remains of the mighty warrior. For a hero he was. The King was increasingly displeased with his son's reverses abroad and the brave, though futile, act of the Falcon had restored him to the nation's favour.

Analee bore it all with calm, good humour and dignity. She was supported by her father who had hurried over from Spain on hearing of the Falcon's illness and now accompanied her to Berlin where they had arranged, in advance, for a house to be rented for the short time they were there.

Berlin was a frenzied place in which to be, with troops passing through it and much of the civilian population packing up ready to leave in case of a French invasion. Apart from being with his beloved daughter the Earl of St March had not enjoyed journeying through embattled Europe.

'I shall be pleased to be home,' he said, looking out into the deserted streets – a curfew of sorts had been imposed. 'You should have sent for this woman, Analee.'

'He asked me to go myself; it was his last wish.'

'But *why*?' The Earl of St March gazed at Analee, noting with concern her weariness and dejection.

'I felt I owed it to him.'

'You owe him *nothing*. To fetch his mistress! 'Tis a monstrous thing to ask.'

'Then perhaps I wanted to get away. I must say I do not relish the thought of seeing my husband's last mistress – the last of many. Maybe he felt an especial affection for the girl.'

'But he came back to you.'

'Yes, and I know he loved me. He had such flights of fancy and I suppose he would have continued to have them.' Analee got restlessly up from her chair and began to pace up and down. 'I know not. However what is done is done and he is gone.' She got out her handkerchief and removed a tear from her eye. 'And I miss him. I always will. I would always have forgiven him and loved him again. I know that now, Father. The Falcon was something so special to me that I cannot replace him. Ever. I will never try.'

The Earl bowed his head and took his daughter's hands between his. 'Aye. There was a chemistry between you, and only you knew it. Only you and he, and he can feel it no more. Now, my dear, if you will see this woman, let us get it over. I detest this place. Will you take her back to London?'

'Yes, and see that she is shipped off to her home in America. I must say I thought she had gone there long since. I did not know he had taken her with him. Maybe I would not have welcomed him back so kindly if I had.'

'You have a generous heart, my dearest Analee. What other woman would have done this – gone and fetched her late husband's paramour?'

'The Falcon was no ordinary man and I am no ordinary woman. That is why,' Analee said, riffling through a notebook that she had taken from her bag. 'Now let me see, McNeath gave me the address. Yes, here it is . . .'

'I will call the coach. Let us . . .'

'I must go alone, Papa.'

'But, my dear . . .'

Analee held up a hand and shook her head. 'No, I must go alone. It will not be pleasant for me; but 'twill not be pleasant for her either. The last legacy of the Falcon was typical of him – guaranteed to cause a lot of distress all round. I will greet Miss Cameron, talk to her and then arrange for the lease of the house to be surrendered. Of course, I also wish to see if my husband left any effects, jewels, notes and such like. That is another reason I came. I have to leave his affairs in order, Papa, you know that.'

'And then what will *you* do, my Analee, have you thought of *that*?'

'It is early days, Papas. The children are still grieving their father – all except Duncan who mourns his passing not at all. It is very strange.'

'But his father was so stern with him.'

'Yes, but nevertheless you would have thought some spasm of grief would have touched him, for he is a sensitive, gentle boy. No, they disliked each other. My lord even showed that on his deathbed. Ah well, Duncan now as the Marquess of Falconer has his own important way to make in the world. And I must be by his side to help him. That is my duty now.'

'And Morella?' The grandchild he had never seen. There was a question in the Earl's eyes as he looked at Analee.

'Ah, Morella,' Analee sighed. 'I would like very much to set that situation to rights; but I do not know what to do.'

'But Sir Brent Delamain is her father, living in the same place as she and not knowing of the relationship.'

'I know,' Analee agreed, passing her hand wearily across her forehead. 'There are some things that one does in life, Father, that are a permanent source of sorrow and regret. Yet, at the time, one did not know what to do for the best. That is how it was with me. Two things have happened that I could never have predicted: Brent Delamain has succeeded his brother and Lord Falconer is dead. You are right, once I have sorted out these various affairs to do with the Falcon's death, I must turn my attention to the problem of Morella. Now would you kindly call the coach for me, Father, and direct the coachman as to the route he must take?'

The house near to the Royal Palace in Berlin was larger than the kind of establishment Analee expected the Falcon would have taken for such a short sojourn. Maybe he had wanted to impress his mistress! The door was opened by a footman and yet two others greeted her in the large paved reception hall. She did not give her name but said she wished to see the mistress of the house. She kept her cloak on and her face hidden by a hat with a large low brim.

Analee felt apprehensive as she awaited Anna Cameron. Did she, for instance, know of the Falcon's death? What would she say? What would they both do? Now it *did* seem unfair of her husband to have given her this task. Only now did she regret she had not ignored his last wishes. What had made her come? Curiosity? Duty? Or maybe a mixture of the two, combined with a desire to get away from England, to travel abroad in the company of her father who would leave her after this and return to his home in Spain.

The ornate clock on the marble mantelpiece struck three. She was being kept waiting, perhaps deliberately. Had Anna Cameron spied her arrival from some hidden vantage point? She began to tap a foot impatiently when the door opened and a servant, stepping back to hold the door open, bowed at Analee announcing: 'The Marchioness of Falconer, madam.'

Analee rose to her feet with a smile, only realizing a moment later that it was not she who had been announced as the Marchioness of Falconer! She stared as Anna Cameron came slowly and haughtily into the room preceded by a second servant and followed by a third. Behind her was a gentlewoman some years older, probably a companion. The surprise at the style of announcement was nothing to the shock Analee got when that lady advanced, her large belly thrust out before her, obviously in a fairly advanced state of pregnancy. Analee closed her eyes momentarily, her senses reeling. *This* was why the Falcon had wanted her to look after Anna! She was carrying his child.

Analee, rapidly trying to recover her wits, held out a hand as Anna stopped her stately progress and gazed imperiously at her.

'Why, 'tis Lady Falconer.'

'Indeed, Miss Cameron.'

'*Lady Falconer*, too, if you do not mind. Although it is confusing I understand that both past and present wives bear the same title.'

'Past and *present* wives,' Analee said with amazement, the light at last beginning to dawn. 'Am I to understand that you consider yourself *married*, Miss Cameron?'

Anna Cameron flushed and the woman beside her came forward. 'May I introduce myself, Lady Falconer? Lady McKeith. I think we met briefly in Paris in 1748.'

'How do you do, Lady McKeith?' Analee took her hand with her usual friendly smile, though she had not the faintest recollection of ever seeing her before. 'Of course we did.'

'I am afraid something very untoward has occurred, your

838

ladyship,' Lady McKeith said, glancing nervously at her companion whose air of haughtiness was gradually yielding to one of bewilderment. 'Lady Falconer . . . er, Miss Cameron, that is to say, has undergone a ceremony of marriage with Lord Falconer. As you see, she is shortly to bear his child.'

'I see that quite clearly,' Analee said, unfastening her cloak with a grimace. 'Getting her with child was one thing and, I regret to say, not such an uncommon one; but his lordship was in no position to marry Miss Cameron being, at the time, married to myself.'

'There was no divorce?' Anna cried shrilly.

'None of which I am aware and, even with one so unpredictable as his lordship, I think that even I should have heard of that.'

'You never petitioned for a divorce?'

'Never. His lordship was married to me until the day he died.'

At this Anna, who had been growing visibly paler, fell to the ground. Lady McKeith rushed up to her kneeling by her side and taking her pulse. She too had gone white and gazed at Analee.

'Until he *died*, Lady Falconer?'

'Alas, his lordship died over a month ago from wounds sustained during the fracas in June against the French. How far gone is Miss Cameron?'

'Seven months, your ladyship.'

'I see. And no word of him reached you?'

'No word at all. Berlin is in absolute chaos with a French invasion expected any moment. The court is in a turmoil, preparing to move to Magdeburg. In any event I was under instructions from his lordship not to allow Miss Cameron to go near the British Embassy.'

'You knew why?'

Analee gazed at her severely from under the brim of her wide hat, a large ostrich feather concealing the steely glint in her eyes.

Lady McKeith was very busy fanning Anna's face, and avoided her gaze. 'Yes.'

'Then you were a party to the deception? How cruel of you, Lady McKeith.'

'Believe me, Lady Falconer, I had no alternative. You know how determined his lordship can be . . . I'm sorry – could be.'

'Indeed I do know. You had best see that Miss Cameron gets up

839

to bed and rests. Poor child, she has had a double shock. She is not married, and her paramour is dead. Then come down and attend me, Lady McKeith, and we shall decide what is best to be done. Why he could not bed her without pretending to marry her I do not know.'

'She would not do it, my lady. She was adamant.'

Analee raised her eyebrows and permitted herself a wry smile, 'Undoubtedly a challenge to his lordship.'

'I am afraid so. He was obsessed with her and then when he had got her there, it was not the paradise he thought it would be.'

Analee held up a hand and glanced at Anna. 'Pray spare me details, Lady McKeith. It is, I assure you, of not the *slightest* interest to me. Now do as I say.'

A week later Analee said goodbye to her father and, accompanied by Lady McKeith, set off for home travelling through a continent ravaged by battle, and arriving in London after a long and wearisome journey undertaken by stealth and at great speed. Analee installed Miss Cameron at Falconer House, dismissed Lady McKeith to whom she had taken a dislike for her obvious duplicity, and set about deciding what to do with the woman who would shortly bear her late husband's child.

After two days, when she thought Anna would be rested, Analee went into her room to find her sitting comfortably in a chair, looking out of the window. Her colour was better but she still looked pale. The shock about Angus's deception and subsequent death had been so profound that she had scarcely spoken at all during the journey home. She looked at Analee as she came in, but did not smile.

'May I sit down, Anna?'

'Of course, it is your home.'

Analee drew a chair up as close to her guest as she dared. 'Anna, his lordship's final charge to me was that I should befriend and look after you. This I want to do.'

'How can you be friends with me? We are rivals.'

Analee sadly shook her head. 'Not for a man who is dead. We are his widows.'

'He cared nothing for you. He adored me.' Anna shut her eyes, the tears rolling down her cheeks.

Analee swallowed hard, summoning to her aid the best of her

nature, banishing jealousy and bitterness. 'I am sure he adored you, Anna; after all what he did was no light thing. A bigamous marriage is a very grave offence; but I feel that I must point out to you the fact that, when mortally wounded, he came all the way back to me. He wanted to die with me at our home in Lakeland. That is the final test of fidelity, is it not? In marriage and out of it.'

'He knew not what he was doing. They brought him home.'

'No. He *asked* to be taken home. The pain of the journey undoubtedly hastened his death. I was his wife, Anna, in spirit and in body, and it was with me he wished to die.' Analee got up and slowly began to pace the room. 'Now, having said that, I do not desire rivalry or jealousy between us. What is done is done. On his deathbed his lordship asked me to look after you. He did not tell me you were with child, although I should have guessed it. He certainly did not tell me he had bigamously wed you, and that must remain a secret. I hope I have paid Lady McKeith enough to keep her mouth shut. No one but you and I know about all this, and I am going to take you to Lakeland to have your baby. If we summon a doctor or midwife in London all the world will share the secret.'

'I am not ashamed,' Anna said, raising her chin and gazing at Analee with dislike.

'Good. You should indeed be proud to bear his lordship's child, a lasting momento of him. Then what will you do, Anna?'

'*Do?*' Anna gazed at Analee. 'I have never thought what I should *do*. I thought I was his wife, a marchioness, well provided for, secure for the rest of my life, whatever happened to Lord Falconer. Now I know that I have no title, no wealth and my child will be a bastard. What do you *expect* me to do?'

Anna's voice rose almost to a scream and Analee knelt by her, taking her hand. 'Hush, my dear. There, you have got it out and it is over.'

Anna put her head in her hands and sobbed. 'I thought my child would be a lord or a lady. It will be nothing. A bastard.'

'It will be a child, boy or girl,' Analee said with calm practicality, continuing to stroke Anna's head. 'I myself was born, as they say, on the wrong side of the sheets. I find it no disadvantage to have parents who were not wed. Indeed, sometimes it is an advantage. My father loves me dearly and I only have beautiful memories of my mother. Your child will have had a distinguished man for a father, and a beautiful, brave-spirited girl for a mother. I think that a fine inheritance.'

'*Fine*?' Anna stared at her, her lips curling. 'But what shall I tell my family?'

'Tell them that your husband died. We shall invent one for you; maybe a soldier you married in Berlin. Maybe . . .'

'Oh, I cannot. I cannot return to my home unwed and with a child.'

'But no one will know.'

'I told my mother that I had married the Marquess of Falconer, that we were blissfully happy and expecting a child.'

'Oh.' This was a complication Analee had not thought of. Of course the girl would tell her mother.

'I told my mother that I would bring his lordship to America and . . .'

'Oh dear, oh dear,' Analee said. 'Well, I will assist in any lie except that of deceiving people into thinking my husband had divorced me. That I will not do. It would be a slur on myself and my children; also to his name because I know he did not *wish* to divorce me. Now, Anna, let us be practical. Even though you are not ashamed of your condition – an attitude I fully applaud – it would be wiser, would it not, to move out of London?'

Anna hung her head and gnawed at one of her finger nails. 'Maybe.'

'Good, that is what I think.' Analee got up and shook her skirt.

'But after that, after the child is born?'

'Well, we have to go one step at a time,' Analee said. 'I will always protect you because that was what his lordship asked of me. You and your child will always enjoy the protection of the Falconer family. That I promise you. If you wish to return home there will be money for the journey. If you wish to stay here we will devise some plan. I will protect you. Never fear. Your child will always be provided for. It is what the Falcon would have wished.' Analee smiled and turned to the door, not seeing the look of hatred that Anna Cameron cast at her back.

'I can't think why you did not warn me,' Analee said to McNeath, who hung his head and shuffled his feet. Behind him stood his wife, her arms akimbo, face flushed. She looked as though, as soon as she had her husband to herself, she would give him a good hiding.

'I did not *dare* say anything, my lady.'

'You did not even tell Nell!'

'No, ma'am.' McNeath stole a guilty look at his wife. 'I thought it best your ladyship should find out yourself. I couldn't find the words, ma'am.'

'You could have found them for *me*, you nincompoop!' Nelly screamed. 'I would have spared her ladyship such an encounter.'

'Perhaps 'twas as well,' Analee said, shrugging her shoulders and gazing thoughtfully at the lake. 'I might have lacked the courage to go at all.'

'But what will you do with her, my lady?' Nelly said in a hoarse whisper, looking over her shoulder although Anna Cameron was safely in her room resting from the journey.

''Tis a bitter legacy from the Falcon. She is not a pleasant person, such as I remember her, but has become brittle and hard. She is greatly embittered and resents anything I do for her. I do not know what will become of her. I cannot bear to think about it. But she will be the mother of a child by his lordship. I cannot reject her, and she does not wish to go home, having told her family that she is married to him. When they learn of his death they will think she is a widow, but eventually they must learn the truth.

'My father thought she would be best off abroad, posing as some widowed, respectable lady with a child. Of course, I would provide the money for her to live in a suitable state. But she rejects the idea. I think she prefers to be a thorn in the side of his wife, seeing that she cannot have my husband. Anyway, Europe is no fit place in which to reside at the moment though my father says Spain is quite safe. However, he does not want her there! We shall see, Nelly. Maybe she will be of a more pleasant disposition when her child is born.'

Anna Cameron resented Analee, disliked her children and made herself generally unpleasant about the house. She also gave herself the airs of a marchioness even if she had no right to the title. Sometimes Analee thought that Anna was indeed the owner of the house and not her; her little bell rang imperiously all day long to summon servants to fetch this and bring that. Gradually Analee felt that she had a rival in her own home and her resentment of Anna grew as her attempts at friendship were continually firmly rejected.

'I do not see how we can live together if you persist in this attitude,' Analee said, confronting Anna one day after a bout of unpleasantness involving Nelly. 'Nelly McNeath is a very old friend of mine, not a mere servant.'

'But I will not have her children near me!' Anna said, wrinkling her nose with disgust. 'They ran alongside me as I walked by the lake, as though I were not a person of quality.'

'But they run alongside *me*! They play with my children all the time. They are all like brothers and sisters together.'

Anna looked down her nose and pursed her mouth in an expression of contempt.

'It seems to point to your own humble origins, Lady Falconer, does it not? It must have been *very* difficult for you to slough off your gypsy past and play the marchioness. I, of course, was born to parents who were legally married and in possession of a considerable fortune. The children of our servants are never allowed anywhere *near* us!'

'I am surprised to hear you talk like that, Anna,' Analee said, her voice rising. 'Take care you do not go too far with me! I am obeying my lord's wishes with regard to you, but not my own inclinations. Yes, out of compassion I was at first prepared to welcome you and treat you as a sister, despite my distress at learning of your close relationship to my husband. I was prepared to overlook all this in honour of his memory; but you are making it *very* hard for me. I cannot endure endless abuse.'

'His lordship was married in spirit to me,' Anna said contemptuously. 'I regard myself in fact as his lawful wife, his widow. He loved me passionately, desired me . . .'

'Oh, pray do not bore me with the details of your intimacy,' Analee said, putting down the embroidery she had been unsuccessfully trying to work. 'I am glad you gave him pleasure in his last days; but when he wanted comfort in his extremity and dire need, he knew to whom to come. *Me*, not you!' Analee thrust an imperious finger at her own breast and, gathering up her work, marched out of the door, cannoning into Nelly as she did.

'That girl, she is intolerable! She will make my life a misery. What did I do to deserve this?'

'Analee, Reyora is here.'

'Reyora?'

'She knows not if you will receive her.'

'Of course I will . . .' Analee paused and gazed at Nelly. 'Because of the Falcon?'

Nelly nodded. 'She is very upset about it. McNeath found her skulking in a tent that day and dragged her here. He has told me I should send her packing; but, as she is such an old friend of yours, of course I could not.'

'Of course.' Analee took a deep breath and squared her shoulders. 'How many things have been sent to try me in these days. Will there be no end to it?' She smiled at Nelly and opened the door of the small parlour where Reyora was sitting hunched over her special bag. As Analee came in she got to her feet and looked at her humbly.

'Oh, Reyora!' Analee felt a surge of emotion and clasped her friend to her bosom.

'I am forgiven, Analee?'

Analee stood back and looked at her. 'You did what you thought was right.'

'I was right. My powers are not limitless, you know. I could not have saved him.'

'But why did you hide?'

'Because I knew I could not help and you would blame me. The forces that wanted to take him into the other world were too strong. They had been pulling at him for some time, summoning him . . .'

Analee shuddered and clasped her hands about her arms in an attempt to warm herself. 'Oh, do not speak thus. It is as though a ghost is walking on my grave. So why have you come now, dear Reyora?'

'Because you need me.'

'I need you?'

'Yes. You are still surrounded by evil forces, Analee. Someone in this house hates you.'

'Oh no!'

'They would do you harm.'

'Harm *me*?'

'Push you out of the window or into the lake. Drug you at night. Someone who would benefit by your death.'

Analee sat down, too shocked to speak. 'But who would benefit . . . Oh no!' She clasped her head in her hands and rocked back and forwards.

'You know who it is?'

'My husband had a mistress. She is to bear his child. They entered a bigamous form of marriage.'

'And she is *here*?'

'Yes.'

'Then she must be got away. She is too dangerous. I cannot control her from afar.'

'But what can she do? She is large with child.'

'I know not how she will do it, but she will. She wishes you dead. Maybe then she can say she is legally married to his lordship. Is that a possibility?'

'I do not know; but she does hate me. I wanted to be friendly towards her and put myself out; but it is of no use.'

'You must send her away.'

'I cannot! She is very near her time. Any day.'

'You must be protected night and day . . .'

Reyora looked up as Nelly came in carrying a parcel, holding it out before her, looking at the card with it. 'Analee! Someone has sent you a present. See, a parcel came all the way from London. It just arrived on the boat with the mail.'

'Who would send me a parcel?' Analee gazed at the card. "From a well-wisher". I seem to recognize the writing. Do you not, Nell?' She handed it to Nelly who laughed and gave it back to her.

'Analee, you know I have not your accomplishments. I can neither read nor write.'

Analee smiled and began to open the parcel. 'I must have you taught, Nell; so that you can be a fine lady like me. Oh look! Chocolates and bonbons – all beautifully wrapped. I wonder who could be the well-wisher?' Analee raised a large nut to her lips. offering the box to Nelly and Reyora; but Reyora suddenly was seized by a spasm, stared at the ceiling and dashed the chocolate from Analee's fingers.

'Do not eat it. It is poisoned!'

Analee jumped and the box fell from her hand, the chocolates and bonbons scattering on the floor.

'Really, Reyora . . .'

'This is the danger I spoke to you about.' Reyora surveyed the scattered confectionery. 'You said you recognized the writing? Try again.'

Analee picked up the card and scrutinized the writing. '"From a well-wisher",' she murmured slowly. 'I know. I think it is Lady McKeith. She wrote me a letter of thanks before she left. I am sure it is her writing, a fine, bold hand. Why should she send me poisoned chocolates?'

'Who is Lady McKeith?' demanded Reyora gravely.

'She was the companion to . . . Oh!' Analee paused and stared at her friend. 'The companion to Anna Cameron, the mistress of my husband.'

'Then that explains it, does it not? It is a plot to get rid of you and say she is the legitimate widow of the Falcon.'

'But it is an *absurd* notion.'

'No matter. Two stupid, greedy, ambitious women are hardly likely to think of anything very profound. Maybe they thought there was a chance.'

'But how can we prove it?'

'Offer her the chocolates.' Reyora began picking them up from the floor with a smile. 'See what she does.'

Anna Cameron was resting in her room when Analee walked in bearing the box of chocolates, an anticipatory smile on her face. 'See! Someone has sent me a delicious present of bonbons from London! I must have a secret admirer.' Analee selected a luscious chocolate and held it to her mouth, holding the box to Anna. 'Try one, Anna, please.'

Anna Cameron changed colour and clutched her stomach. 'Oh, no thank you, Lady Falconer! I am not well enough.'

Analee paused in the act of pretending to put the chocolate to her rounded mouth and stared at her guest in feigned surprise. 'Oh? Are you unwell?'

'It may not be good for my stomach.'

'But you ate such a huge dinner.'

'That is why. Maybe I ate too much.' Anna heaved her

cumbersome form from the bed and propped herself on her arms. Her face was quite ashen and her lower lip trembled. She stared at Analee as though transfixed by a shocking sight.

'Anna, you look most *unwell*,' Analee said with concern, putting the box by her bedside. 'Maybe it is your time?'

Anna clutched her stomach and wriggled uncomfortably. 'Yes, I have had cramps all afternoon in the belly.'

'Well, I will just eat my chocolate and then go and fetch some help.'

Analee very deliberately selected a fresh chocolate, slowly took the wrapping from it and then made as if to pop it into her mouth, glancing at Anna from the corner of her eye as she did so. She saw Anna close her eyes, clutch once more at her distended stomach and then, lurching up, she grasped Analee's hand and the chocolate fell to the ground.

'Do not eat that!'

Analee raised her eyebrows in mock surprise and gazed at the chocolate on the floor. 'Why, Anna, whatever made you do that?'

'There may be something wrong with it.'

'But why should there be?'

'You never know.'

Anna burst into tears and Analee picked up the discarded chocolate and placed it with the others, putting the box safely out of the way. Then she sat on the bed and placed her hand on the shoulders of the weeping girl.

'Is there something *wrong* with them, Anna?'

Anna nodded her head, weeping violently.

'Are they poisoned?' Analee said sadly. 'Did you want to kill me so badly then?'

Anna first shook her head and then nodded, as though unable to make up her mind. 'I hate you!' she sobbed. 'But I do not want to see you die. I couldn't lie there and watch.'

'I should have done it quietly, out of the way, was that it? Indeed I would have, had not a friend warned me in a most uncanny way.'

'They say you are a witch,' Anna blubbered. 'I should have known it would not succeed.'

'But how could it? You would have been accused of poisoning me. 'Twas Lady McKeith sent them was it not?'

'She said I would then be Lady Falconer because I had married his lordship.'

'But your bogus marriage to him was while I was alive, Anna! You could never have been Lady Falconer, even with me dead.'

'I did not know. She said it, not I. She said, anyway, that with you dead I would have a claim on the Falcon's vast fortune on behalf of the child I would bear him.'

'I see.' Analee sat back. She felt very sad and dejected. 'I am sorry that you hated me so much, rejected my friendship.'

'How could I *like* you? I hated you! You were so condescending, so grand. I had nothing in the world and you . . . everything!' Anna made a gesture and then her face crumpled with pain.

'I did not mean to be condescending or grand,' Analee went on. 'It was a difficult position for me, but I wanted to do my best. I see I failed.'

'What will become of me now?' Anna cried again, her face grimaced in a spasm. 'I think my time has come, Lady Falconer. The agony in the belly grows greater.'

Anna laboured all that day and part of the next. Forgetting that she had wanted to kill her, Analee waited on her tirelessly, holding her hand, bathing her face, changing her chemises soaked with perspiration, talking to her with soft words of encouragement. Reyora sat by the bed massaging her belly, deftly probing in the birth passage with her skilled hands, but by late morning on the following day she shook her head.

'The child is lodged in the womb, Analee. You can only take it out by cutting open the stomach and I cannot do that.'

'But you helped me when Morella was born. You cast a spell.'

'This is different. The passage has not opened as much as it should. You must call the doctor immediately and tell him to bring his instruments with him. It is the only way the child and the mother can be saved.'

A messenger was sent swiftly to Keswick and within the hour the doctor and the midwife were on their way by boat. All the time Analee talked to Anna bringing her words of comfort.

'I will die, I will die, I will die,' Anna screamed. 'I can stand the pain no longer.'

'No, you will not die. The doctor is on his way. Because the

Falcon has given you such a fine, lusty child he will need instruments to deliver you. But do not be afraid, he is skilled in *accouchements*.'

'I will die,' Anna said, looking distractedly at the ceiling. 'I will die for my crimes against you and God.'

'No,' Analee smiled, stroking the hair back from her feverish brow. 'I forgive you and I am sure God will, too. When you are well, Anna, you will go with your baby maybe to Spain or Italy where there is no war, to rest and ponder on the future.'

'I will die,' Anna repeated tearfully. 'I will never live to see another day.'

'No, you are young and strong; but tired. The baby will be delivered before dark.'

Analee went to the window and for the tenth time looked out onto the lake. She was worried about Anna, who was showing signs of weakening. Reyora squatted beside her massaging her belly and murmuring soft incantations; but her eyes looked troubled as she gazed at Analee and from time to time she shook her head.

'Look, there is the doctor!' Analee cried. 'Nat is rowing him in the boat. Soon your troubles will be over.'

Anna began to cry and Analee went and sat with her again, telling Nelly to go down and welcome the doctor. She took her hand and squeezed it. Anna's eyes were tired and her face pinched and drawn. She beckoned to Analee, who put her head close to that of the suffering woman.

'He *did* love you. He murmured your name in his sleep. I was no use to him as a woman. I was fearful of the marital act. I hated him to touch me. I never made him happy and he despised me. I wanted to be a marchioness for the happiness it would give my family. I was too vain, too ambitious. Now I am paying for it all. I am cursed.'

Analee's eyes filled with tears and she found it hard to swallow. She grasped Anna's hand and turned away, trying to compose herself before the doctor came.

An hour later the baby was delivered, cut expertly from its mother's belly; a fine healthy girl who cried lustily as the doctor drew her out of the womb. But despite the undoubted skill of the surgeon, Anna Cameron, exhausted and frightened after her

850

protracted labour, too frail to stand the pain of the operation, only lived long enough to see the child she had endured so much to bear. She seemed to make a supreme effort to gather up her strength and smile at the child as if in farewell before she sank back, her eyes closed.

A few minutes later she died, her head resting in the arms of Analee who, throughout the terrible ordeal, had nursed her with such tender care, never leaving the side of the woman who had done so much to wrong her.

16

Catherine Walkinshaw tapped her snuff box and looked shrewdly at Isobel McKeith before opening the lid and delicately putting a pinch in her right nostril.

'Do you take snuff?' she said, holding out the box.

Isobel shook her head. She thought women taking snuff was a revolting habit but, unfortunately, a common one. Catherine Walkinshaw managed it very deftly, there was only a tiny trace of the brown powder at the base of her nostril. She repeated the process with the left nostril and then shut the box and stowed it away in the pockets of her capacious skirt.

'So,' she said. 'What you have to say is a very grave matter.'

'I have had it on my conscience, Catherine. I did not dare approach her Royal Highness with it; but thought first to discuss it with you.' Isobel shifted uneasily in her chair, her bright, artificially coloured golden curls bobbing about beneath her lace cap. She was really raddled now, rouged, powdered and patched but with an artifice that managed to bestow on her a semblance of past beauty.

'But what you are saying is that Lady Falconer murdered first her husband and then his mistress.'

Isobel lowered her eyes. 'I can see no other explanation. They both died within weeks of each other. Lord Falconer was considered fit enough to make the long journey from Hanover, only to die shortly after reaching home. As for Miss Cameron, I know how well she withstood the journey because did I not travel with her? She was a fine healthy girl, fit to bear many babies. But what happens? When we got to London I was curtly dismissed by Lady Falconer, without so much as a "thank you" or "call again", and Miss Cameron is whisked up to the cold north of England, away from the best obstetric surgeons, where she dies in childbirth – supposedly.' Lady McKeith lingered heavily on the word 'supposedly'.

'But what was Lady Falconer's *motive*?' Miss Walkinshaw murmured. 'What had she to gain?'

'To rid herself of a rival. I know the Falcon was bent on divorcing her and marrying Miss Cameron. 'Twas but a matter of time.'

''Tis a very serious charge.' Miss Walkinshaw looked thoughtfully at Lady McKeith, whom she had known since a girl. She did not really trust her but then she trusted no one, living in the same twilight world of truths and half-truths, loyalties and divided loyalties as others whose sympathies were or had been part Jacobite, part Hanoverian. For many years she had just tried to do her work as a lady in the service of the Princess of Wales; latterly endeavouring to forget the shame of the liaison of her youngest sister with Prince Charles Stuart, but people kept dragging her in. 'How would you propose to go about making it public, if that is what you wish?'

'I thought if you had a word with the Princess, expressing your own doubts.'

'You expect *me* to stand in a court of law and accuse Lady Falconer of murder?'

'Oh no, Catherine, nothing like that; but I do not think she should go unpunished. I feel very strongly about it.'

'Lady Falconer has but recently emerged from Carlisle gaol on suspicion of high treason. She was so clearly vindicated – do you think the King would listen to fresh rumours?'

'He might, if there were more substance. Lady Falconer had a very strong motive for getting rid of her husband. Very strong indeed. And was he not a hero? Do you think the King would condone *that*?'

'I will see what I can do,' Catherine Walkinshaw said reluctantly after a while. 'I do not like to see wrong go unpunished, but neither do I like to interfere where matters of such gravity are concerned. Now tell me, Isobel, what are you doing with yourself these days?'

She picked up her embroidery and leaned forward, indicating that the subject was at an end.

Princess Augusta's plain pock-marked face remained impassive as she listened to the story told by her friend of many years standing, one of the few members of her household whom she felt she could completely trust. Since the death of her husband and the knowledge that she would never wear the crown of England as its queen, she had become more settled in her ways. She was, for instance, on better terms with the King because she was anxious that her son George should get on well with his grandfather. She had been very careful to divest herself of Jacobite sympathies; but even then the factions in the two courts continued – some politicians, such as Pitt, favoured by Leicester House, others by St James's Palace. Her special friend and confidant was Lord Bute who had enhanced his power by supporting Pitt and Newcastle to form a ministry in the summer, shortly after the death of Lord Falconer.

When Catherine Walkinshaw had finished speaking the Princess did not at first say anything, but smoothed the tapestry that she was working on, regarding it from a distance with a critical eye. 'Do you think the colour of that rose is too loud, Catherine?'

Miss Walkinshaw bent forward, inspected the work and shook her head. 'It will tone down, Your Royal Highness. Maybe a paler shade for the flower on the right?'

'I think you are correct.' Princess Augusta nodded and, removing her spectacles, placed them on top of her work which she put on a table at her elbow.

'Catherine, why are you telling me all this?'

'Because I feel an injustice may have been done, Your Royal Highness.'

'To whom?'

'To Lord Falconer and his unfortunate mistress.'

'Yes, a pretty girl.' The Princess looked wistful. 'He used to parade her in a very unsubtle manner at court. The King was quite taken by her, but of course his loyalty was for Lady Falconer, as it will be again. If I were you I would forget all this tittle-tattle, Catherine. I would put it out of your mind.'

'But I have known Isobel McKeith since we were girls in Scotland, ma'am.'

'But she is flighty, is she not? As soon as Prince Charles Edward fled to France she tried to get her husband to petition for clemency to the King of England on the grounds that he had never taken up arms against him.'

Catherine shrugged. 'Ma'am, were there not many people with a duality of purpose? Even Lady Falconer herself . . . Why, it was

854

not so long ago, I hesitate to say this, ma'am, that her ladyship came with a message from the Prince wanting to know the dispersion of those Jacobites with sympathies in the English court.'

The Princess's face puckered with horror. 'Lady Falconer! An emissary of the Prince?'

Catherine spread her thick fingers on her skirt and regarded them gravely. 'I told her ladyship that I had no dealings at all with Jacobites, and disapproved of my unfortunate sister's connection with the Prince. She apologized for having misunderstood the situation.'

'I am dumbfounded,' the Princess said. 'I am horror-struck, for it would be after that that the Falcon accused her of treachery. He knew the truth.'

'Yes, ma'am.'

'Then she *was* a traitor?'

'It would appear so, ma'am, a *kind* of treachery.'

'I am amazed to hear it had gone so far. And her own husband a trusted counsellor of the King! Maybe she did have cause to murder him. Oh dear, I wish I had not this information, Catherine.'

'I too, ma'am. Believe me, I spent a very troubled night, tossing and turning, wondering whether or not to approach Your Royal Highness. You see, I feel that if I do nothing Isobel McKeith might noise it abroad until she has some vindication. There is no doubt that she nurses a bitter vindictiveness towards the Marchioness of Falconer. Very bitter indeed.'

The Earl of Bute, when consulted, was equally appalled. Like the Princess and, before her, Miss Walkinshaw, his immediate instinct was to do nothing; but the Earl knew that the King's memory of the Falcon was tainted by the knowledge that he had falsely accused his wife of treachery. That he might have been done to death by this same wife was a monstrous state of affairs.

'She was but a mere gypsy after all,' he said, gazing at the Princess. 'She has no real breeding as a lady.'

'She is very much loved by many people,' the Princess said defensively. 'I have always been very fond of Lady Falconer and there is no doubt her husband treated her shamefully . . .'

'All the more reason to kill him.'

'But he was very badly wounded.'

'Yet well enough to travel such a distance.'

Lord Bute put his hands under the tails of his coat and walked to the windows that overlooked the formal gardens of Leicester House. 'I will talk to Mr Pitt,' he said. 'He may be more objective, although he had a high regard for the ability of Lord Falconer and was dismayed when the King sent him abroad. He will know what it is best to do.'

Hector Cameron stared at Isobel McKeith, his eyes puckering with tears. She drew him to a chair and bade him sit down. She then went to the sideboard and poured from a decanter of brandy into two glasses. She needed to give herself courage as well as him. 'There, sir. Pray drink it at a gulp. It will steady your nerves.'

With a trembling hand Hector raised the glass to his lips and did as Lady McKeith had bid him. But his hand was still shaking as he replaced the glass on the table. 'My daughter, *murdered* by Lady Falconer?'

'What else can I deduce, Mr Cameron?' Isobel McKeith shook her head. 'She was a strong girl, the pregnancy uncomplicated.'

'But have you any *proof*, Lady McKeith?'

'Who can get proof, sir, from the wilds of Lakeland? It is as though Lady Falconer rules over her own domain there. Who would bear witness against her ladyship? No one, I am sure.'

'But there is a child, my grand-daughter. Lady Falconer wrote to me of her when she told me about the whole sad business. My wife, who has been made ill by the whole affair, bade me travel here at once. That our daughter should bigamously marry a man, thinking herself a marchioness, give birth to his daughter and then die . . . 'Twas too much for the poor lady, who has never enjoyed good health. The last we had heard from her was of her marriage in Berlin and that she was expecting this child and ecstatically happy. The next that she was dead, and the marriage had been illegal.'

'I can imagine the shock,' Lady McKeith sighed sympathetically. 'And how did Lady Falconer speak of your grand-daughter?'

'That she is a beautiful girl; that she is taking good care of her.'

'Well, that's a wonder,' Lady McKeith sniggered. 'I suppose even *she* balked at the thought of three murders. Though 'tis a wonder she did not bury her alongside her mother, and consider the task well done.'

Hector Cameron held up a hand, his lips trembling. 'I cannot bear to entertain such a suspicion, Lady McKeith. Lady Falconer seemed a much abused woman, by her husband, by my daughter. She seemed to have shown nothing but goodness and consideration in return.'

'Ha!' Isobel McKeith threw up her head in a gesture of scorn. 'Do you really suppose *that*? Her ladyship is a gypsy, and gypsy ways are evil – everyone knows that. It was not for nothing that she was known as the Enchantress. She is a witch. She should be burnt at the stake for witchcraft; I hear it is still done in some parts of Lancashire.'

'Oh I hope not, Lady McKeith! It was a common practice in my country in the early settler days, but is now stamped out. I would not like to see such a thing happen to Lady Falconer. If she is a murderess the law should take its due course; but burnt at the stake . . . no!'

'And do you think the law will take its due course?' Lady McKeith said mockingly, 'or do you not suppose her ladyship to be above it? I do. There is only one way to touch her.'

'And that is?' Hector Cameron got out a handkerchief and rubbed his watery eyes hard.

'She must be accused in public. You sir, you must vindicate the foul murder of your daughter and point the finger of suspicion directly at the Marchioness of Falconer, so that all may know the truth.'

Analee looked from the Princess of Wales to Lord Bute, the amazement on her face more telling than any expression of indignation. 'I know not whether to laugh or cry,' she said at last. 'That *I* should murder first my husband, then his mistress? Is it possible anyone would believe it? Do you not know, does not everyone know, that the Falcon should have died of his terrible wound in Hanover, and was only supported by his longing to die in my arms?'

'That *is* what I heard,' the Princess said looking at Lord Bute doubtfully.

'His lordship's wound was green and riddled with maggots. He

857

was like a corpse when he came home, as any number of witnesses will tell you. It was only his love for me that sustained him.'

'But his mistress . . .'

'I knew naught of Miss Cameron's position until after his death. I only discovered that she was his mistress, *and* with child *and* thinking herself Marchioness of Falconer, when I went to Berlin on his lordship's instructions. You think that I then plotted to bring her back and *murder* her? Oh, 'tis monstrous!'

Lord Bute gazed at her with admiration. She was a beautiful woman, a forceful character, there was no doubt of that; but was she telling the truth? He swivelled his eyes round to look at the Princess who appeared to be having her confidence in Lady Falconer vindicated. She smiled with relief.

'I agree it is monstrous,' Princess Augusta said at last. 'And I for one am satisfied. Are you not, Lord Bute?'

'I never doubted for a moment that the story was without foundation,' the Earl said ingratiatingly. 'But I knew it would spread further if we did not stop it.'

'By whom, may I ask?' Analee gazed fearlessly at them. 'May I not know the name of my accuser, or accusers?'

'I am afraid not,' Lord Bute said diplomatically. 'We gave our word . . .'

'Then how can I be satisfied unless I confront him, or them, or is it *her*, myself?'

The Earl shrugged and glanced at the Princess. 'We will see that it gets no further.'

'I am *not* satisfied,' Analee said, her eyes smouldering with anger. 'I demand justice!'

'Oh, please, Lady Falconer.' The Princess gazed at her pleadingly. 'Leave it here; let it drop. Catherine Walkinshaw . . .'

'Ah,' Analee said, looking at Lord Bute. 'It was Mistress Walkinshaw. I thought her a good friend of mine. Why should she spread such a lie?'

''Twas not Catherine Walkinshaw in the first place,' Princess Augusta said cautiously, fanning herself despite the cold of the room. 'But she told me of the rumour. I told Lord Bute. That is as far as it has gone.'

Except for Mr Pitt, Lord Bute thought, who undoubtedly had

told half the Cabinet by now. He shuddered at the idea of what they had put in motion.

'But why should Miss Walkinshaw believe such a scandal?'

As Lord Bute gazed at his feet, Analee knew. The one weakness; the misguided deed she had done out of pity for the Prince. Such a little thing, a stupid error that might ruin her whole life.

''Twas because I went to her,' she said without waiting for an answer, 'and told her of the Prince's request. She thought I was a traitor?'

'No, she didn't think you were a traitor,' Princess Augusta said earnestly. 'She was disquieted enough to speak to me about what she had heard. It was thought there might be ample reason for you to kill your husband – because he had caused you unsupportable pain.'

'I am, I was no traitor,' Analee said quietly, her hand on the medal of Falcon gold she wore round her neck. 'But I admit I *was* unwise. I was merely an emissary between the Prince and Miss Walkinshaw, the sister of his mistress. His Royal Highness mistakenly thought . . .'

'But how could he *think* such a thing? He must know that her family abhors the action of Clementina Walkinshaw?'

Analee shrugged her shoulders. 'That is what I do not understand. Believe me, Your Royal Highness, it was never my intention to help plot the restoration of the Stuarts; but I was torn between two allegiances – between loyalty to my husband and pity for my many friends who were in exile. I thought it innocent enough a request and I obeyed it. I was very foolish and repent of doing it. I can see now that it was open to misinterpretation. I deserve to be chastised, maybe; but not to be accused of murder.'

The Princess rose and Analee rose with her. Her chin was tilted proudly, but her eyes were downcast. Her lustrous black hair was set in modest ringlets which gleamed against the exposed skin of her shoulders. Her bodice and skirt were of a dark blue that enhanced her colouring, and her stomacher was of delicate lace, matching the lace flounces at her elbows. The Princess thought that if ever Lady Falconer were in the dock, the court would have to be composed of women if its judgment was not to be influenced by her beauty – and maybe even her own sex would be susceptible to her charm.

'I think many of us have mixed loyalties which we have

subsequently had reason to repent of,' the Princess said lightly. 'Even my husband was accused of Jacobite dealings and nothing could have been further from the truth. Happily those times are in the past and our nation is no longer divided. I am sure your ladyship will be very discreet in future. As for this matter,' the Princess gestured towards Lord Bute, 'I think we should all let it drop. It will soon be forgotten . . .'

'But my accuser . . .' Analee stammered.

'Your accuser will be dealt with, will be spoken to. Have no fear. Put the matter out of your mind and go back to your Lakeland home; but before you do, promise to take tea with me and tell me about your family, the new Marquess who I hear is such a handsome child, and so on.'

Analee dropped a deep curtsey. She did not feel satisfied but she did not know what she could do. She intimated that she would be honoured to take tea with her Royal Highness and then accepted Lord Bute's arm as the doors were opened and he led her into the small ante-chamber of the Princess's apartments. A way was being cleared for them by many who were curious to gaze upon the widowed Marchioness who was said to mourn her husband so much that she shunned the pleasures of the court, despite his blatant infidelities.

'I assure you, Lady Falconer,' Lord Bute patted her hand, 'the Princess only brought this matter up with the greatest reluctance, in your own interests . . .'

'I appreciate that fully,' Analee murmured quietly so that those around should not hear. 'But it has been an ordeal for me, my lord, and I have had so many sorrows in past years. Sometimes I wonder what I have done to deserve them.'

Suddenly she looked up as a small commotion started by the door towards which they were walking. A figure unfamiliar to Analee advanced slowly towards her, his arm outstretched, his finger pointing accusingly; but next to him was someone Analee knew very well indeed. She grasped Lord Bute's arm and he too stopped talking and gazed at the stranger who, obviously in the grip of strong emotion, shouted:

'She is a murderess! There! She murdered her husband and my daughter. She is a traitor to her country and a murderess! There, behold her: Lady Falconer!'

Even Lady McKeith, who had instigated the scene, looked momentarily dismayed by its effects; for no sooner had Mr Cameron stopped speaking than he was seized by liveried servants and pushed to the floor while shocked and amazed courtiers buzzed and hummed a ceaseless undercurrent of comment and conversation.

While Mr Cameron struggled on the floor with the servants who were reinforced by others, Lady McKeith held her hands to her mouth as if in horror. She looked up and her eyes met Analee's.

'I know now who has caused all this,' Analee said slowly. 'It is all clear to me now, my lord. Lady McKeith is the fount of this malicious gossip that threatens to destroy an innocent woman. I might have known.'

She gazed witheringly at Isobel McKeith, who lowered her eyes while the already high colour on her cheeks grew hectic. Mr Cameron, however, would not be silent and kept on shouting, 'Murderess!' whenever he had the chance, until the large hand of one of the servants was firmly clamped around his mouth and he was dragged into an adjoining room.

Lord Bute raised his eyes to heaven, wishing he were in the safe confines of his club drinking porter with his cronies.

'Come, Lady Falconer,' he said, taking her arm. 'I will have you escorted home.'

But Analee shook her arm free and smiled at him. 'I am afraid we cannot ignore this, Lord Bute. Now that I know the source of the mischief it is important to extinguish it, for I know it comes from the mouth of one who is indeed a genuine would-be murderess: Lady McKeith herself!'

Analee raised her voice for everyone to hear it and Isobel, who had begun to have doubts about the affair when they set out, now bitterly regretted it. She swayed and clutched the arm of a nearby courtier who moved quickly out of the way, not wishing to be tainted by one who had been instrumental in causing such an unseemly and unprecedented commotion in the apartments of the Princess of Wales. Lord Bute, looking increasingly agitated, demanded the room should be cleared as the door to the Princess's chamber opened and she came out to see what had caused the uproar.

'Why, Lady Falconer!'

'I know who my accuser is, ma'am.' Analee pointed a finger at Isobel McKeith, by now cowering in shame. 'And glad I am of the chance to rebut her charge in public.'

By this time the room had been cleared of all but a handful of spectators, those who were close to the Princess or court functionaries. It was, however, sufficient as far as Analee was concerned to constitute a small court. She curtsied to the Princess and pointed to the room where Mr Cameron had been taken.

'I hazard a guess that the poor man yonder is the father of Anna Cameron. He has doubtless been told wicked lies about his daughter. If Your Royal Highness will permit it, may he be brought back here?'

Princess Augusta looked helplessly at the hapless Lord Bute as though to imply that this business was all his fault.

'I think the matter had best be cleared up, ma'am,' he said.

'If you say so, Lord Bute, though I never did think that even my exalted position constituted a court of law.'

'I hope it does not come to that, ma'am,' Analee said firmly. 'But if it does, I am prepared to face trial, and we shall then see who ends on the gallows.'

Mr Cameron, still shaking, but a little recovered from his ordeal, was led into the chamber and a chair placed for him opposite that of the Princess to whom he bowed very deeply before taking his seat, mopping his brow. Analee, Lord Bute and Lady McKeith remained standing. Everyone stopped chattering and the air grew tense with expectation.

'Now,' Lord Bute said, bowing to the Princess. 'What is it you wish to say, Mr Cameron, against Lady Falconer?'

Mr Cameron again took out his handkerchief and nervously wiped the sweat off his face, after glancing at Isobel McKeith who stood agitatedly fiddling with the large yellow bows on her petticoat. 'I was informed that Lady Falconer killed my daughter, sir, after murdering her own husband.'

A gasp ran round those assembled who edged away from the chief participants as though fearful of contagion.

'We *have* heard this rumour,' Lord Bute said pompously, 'and have decided it was completely without foundation. *If* you thought this, sir, why did you not not take it to the proper authorities? The court of the Princess of Wales is not a place in which to make accusations of this nature, as you should know, even if you are from the colonies.'

'Lady McKeith told me that, because of the eminence of Lady Falconer, no one would listen to me, so I should make it in public.'

'I see.' The Earl turned to Isobel McKeith: 'And do you stick by these accusations, Lady McKeith?'

'I do.' Trembling inwardly Isobel McKeith drew herself up and stared defiantly at Analee.

'Do you have proof?'

'*Proof*?' Isobel McKeith looked at him with concern.

'Proof of the very grave charges you are making. Proof that Lord Falconer and Miss Cameron were murdered.'

'The proof, sir, is that they were both well before they set foot in Lady Falconer's house.'

'That does not constitute proof of murder, ma'am.'

'Besides, it is not true,' Analee intervened. 'The Falcon was near death and Miss Cameron was delivered by caesarian section of a baby after a long and painful labour. The shock of the operation coming after such an ordeal killed her. You have only to ask the doctor who performed it.'

'But Lady McKeith has said that all those who live near you are in your pay.' Mr Cameron objected.

'*Has* she?' Analee looked scathingly at Isobel McKeith. 'Does she doubt the probity of Dr Elmbeck who performed the operation, his midwife or the many servants loyal to the memory of my husband who were in the house at the time? Has she questioned *them*, for instance? I doubt it. Has she inspected the scar across the abdomen of poor Miss Cameron to see that the birth was not a natural one? I think not. And, as for his lordship, did she see the maggots crawling on the gangrenous wound from which he died? Did she question the many who attended him on his arduous journey? Did she?'

'Did you, Lady McKeith?' Lord Bute stared at her censoriously.

'How could I, my lord?' she complained querulously. 'I'm only saying what I *suspected*.'

'*Suspected*, Lady McKeith!' Lord Bute thundered. 'Did you say *suspected*? When you make charges of such gravity against a person of such eminence as the Marchioness of Falconer, do you not think you should do more than *suspect*? You should have proof; and when the Princess and I heard the facts we dismissed the story immediately, as I am sure all those who are here will, too.'

Many heads were nodded vigorously in agreement.

'I think such suspicions spring naturally to the mind of one who herself has entertained thoughts of murder,' Analee said quietly. 'And for the charges I make I *do* have proof and *can* call witnesses. Lady McKeith was instrumental in sending me a box of poisoned chocolates from which I should surely have died but for the timely intervention of a friend staying in the house, who, with uncanny prescience, suspected them.'

'Poisoned chocolates, poisoned chocolates,' the scandalous words ran round the room.

'*Poisoned chocolates*?' Lord Bute boomed. 'And you have evidence, Lady Falconer?'

'I have the chocolates, sir. They were kept in my cellar to preserve them in good condition should it ever be necessary to produce them in evidence against Lady McKeith.'

'This . . . this is monstrous,' Isobel McKeith spluttered. 'Something I heartily deny . . .'

'Do you deny the evidence of your own handwriting?' Analee demanded. '"From an admirer" or some such words were written on the card. I have it still. I recognized your writing instantly; but more important than that, and said in front of witnesses who I daresay would swear to it on the Bible, Miss Cameron confirmed it before her labour commenced. From her own mouth I have the evidence of Lady McKeith's foul deed.'

'But what could Lady McKeith gain by this?' Lord Bute looked across at Princess Augusta who was clearly transfixed by the whole proceedings.

'Believe it or not, my lord, she suggested to this innocent but troubled girl that if I were dead her bigamous marriage to the Falcon would be validated. That she would become Lady Falconer . . .'

'Lord Falconer entered into a bigamous marriage with this girl?' Princess Augusta understandably found it impossible to maintain the regal silence expected of one in her station.

'I'm afraid so, ma'am,' Analee said quietly. 'With the connivance of Lady McKeith who, one would think, should have known better. She assisted at this deception, concurred in his lordship's behaviour and then, when all failed, tried to kill me – all, I may say, for gain. The Falcon paid her well, and doubtless she expected Anna Cameron to reward her, had her evil plan come to fruition.'

'I am appalled,' Princess Augusta murmured faintly. 'I can scarcely believe such monstrous conduct.'

'Lady Falconer will doubtless wish to press charges,' Lord Bute began, but Analee held up her hand.

'I do not care to press charges or persecute a misguided woman who can live only on her wits. I merely make the proviso that she should withdraw her accusations against me in writing, to be lodged with Lord Bute, and then I hope she will never trouble me again.'

'But, Lady Falconer, if she tried to murder you . . .'

'I am prepared to destroy the evidence once I have the withdrawal from Lady McKeith. Only those here will know the real truth of the matter, and God alone will judge her.'

'Treachery, Lady Falconer,' the King said sadly, 'is something it is impossible to overlook. Whereas you have denied murder, and everyone believes you, you have admitted treachery.'

'Foolish conduct, Your Majesty.'

The King nodded his head and tried to stretch his foot. He was very old and tired and his sights were already fastened on the next world. The scandal that had rocked London concerning Lady Falconer and Lady McKeith had eventually come to his ears, but he had been urged to take action by his mistress who sat beside him now, as though she shared his throne.

'Very foolish, Lady Falconer, very, very foolish. Your husband may have done a lot of stupid, maybe wicked things in his time, but he was never a traitor.'

'Neither was *I*, Your Majesty.' Analee, nearly at the end of her tether, felt close to tears. She had known the scandal regarding Lady McKeith would not die down and it had not. Too much was known and those who had been privileged to witness the unique spectacle at Leicester House soon told everyone who had not. Before the week was out Lady McKeith, her withdrawal of her accusations safely lodged with Lord Bute, had fled the country vowing never to return. Some said she was lucky to escape so easily; some said she only left because she would have been arrested and tried, whatever Lady Falconer wished, and Lord Bute had urged her to go.

But the matter of the treasonable activities remained. Lady Falconer had conveyed a message from Prince Charles Edward to Leicester House and the King could not ignore it. The government urged him to take action in case anyone else should be tempted.

The King leaned forward and looked at her kindly. 'I believe you, my dear. You are a headstrong, impulsive woman and your warm generous nature would have ruled the wisdom of your head. I know that. We have known Catherine Walkinshaw for so many years as a good and loyal servant that there was no question of her ever being involved in a plot – but, if she were not loyal, and you did not know that . . .'

'I knew Your Majesty was never in danger, that your throne was secure. I did it as a favour . . . for an old friend. I knew the cause was hopeless, or I would not have acted as I did.'

'I hope it is your last favour for that particular friend,' the Countess of Yarmouth said, looking anxiously at the tired King. 'That friend is finished with, you must know that.'

'I do, Lady Yarmouth.' Analee bowed her head, her eyes stinging with tears.

'Lady Falconer,' the King said, 'I am not long for this world and my grandson George, a Briton born in Britain, will be your King. Until such time as he comes to the throne I propose to impose on you a sentence of banishment. You will return to your country estates and remain there until my death is announced and my grandson is King. In saying this I am depriving myself and my daughter-in-law of your delightful company. We shall miss you in London and at court, Lady Falconer. But justice must be seen to be done by the people; treasonable behaviour must not be condoned, however misguided and well-meant. I know you are no traitor, that you loved your husband who, although a great man, was not a particularly good one. I know that you have many, many virtues that outweigh your faults and I know, my dear Lady Falconer,' the old King bent down and touched her shoulder as she knelt before him, 'that this sentence I am imposing on you will not be too onerous for you to keep, neither is it like to last very long.'

The King gave her his hand to kiss and Analee, seizing it, held it to her face and bathed it with her tears.

Analee looked round at the furniture covered with sheets, the carpets rolled on the floor and stacked against the walls. The white outlines of the individual pieces of furniture reminded her of the silent shrouded form of the Falcon, of her vigil beside it in the chapel of Falcon's Keep the night before his funeral. She shuddered and felt the tears spring to her eyes; but they were for the Falcon, not for her banishment or because she was leaving Falconer House for the duration of this monarch's life. She had no regrets about that; none at all.

After one last look round she adjusted her hat in the mirror and began fastening her cloak when one of the servants entered and bowed.

'I will be ready in a moment, Robert. I . . .'

'There is a gentleman to see you, ma'am. A Mr Cameron.'

'Mr Cameron?' Analee glanced at herself in the mirror, set her hat and finished fastening her cloak. 'Pray tell him we are about to leave for the north; but he is welcome to a few minutes of my time.'

'I told him, ma'am. He is most anxious to have a word with your ladyship.'

A fire still burned in the grate; it was a bitterly cold December, and Analee stood warming her hands, glancing round as Mr Cameron was admitted. She felt she should be polite to him, but not gracious, and did not offer him her hand to kiss. After all, had he not falsely denounced her in public, in front of one of the premier earls in the country and the Princess of Wales herself?

'Pray come and warm youself, Mr Cameron. Two of our servants remain to clear up before the house is closed, so we still have a fire.'

Mr Cameron stood timidly by her side and nervously extended his hands to the blaze.

'I only came with great trepidation, Lady Falconer. I am about to embark for America, but I felt I had to see you before I left. I penned several drafts of a letter but cast them all onto the fire. I wanted to see you myself and . . . apologize.'

Analee straightened up and looked at him kindly. Her sympathetic heart always went out to a troubled soul however much she herself had been wronged, and poor Hector Cameron clearly was suffering. He had a film of sweat on his forehead and his upper lip, and kept anxiously tugging at a forelock of unpowdered red hair that had fallen over his brow. Anna had inherited her colouring from him, Analee thought, a good-looking man who had kept his figure, with a ruddy face and red hair, and bushy brows above clear blue eyes with the slight hint of turquoise that had been so strong in Anna.

'Would you had come to me first, sir, rather than listen to that tittle-tattle from Isobel McKeith. You might, thus, have spared us all.'

'Would that I had, ma'am. I meant to see you but, as Lady McKeith had spent so much time in the company of my . . . late daughter, I wanted to hear news at first hand from her, never dreaming of the accusations she would make. The woman was clearly deranged.'

'No, she was not deranged, Mr Cameron,' Analee said, enunciating very carefully. 'She was evil. The two states are quite separate. The person afflicted can do nothing about the one, but plenty about the other. They could pray to God for help to turn them from their wicked ways, but they are too close to their master, Satan. To have hatched such a plot which involved instilling thoughts of murder into your own daughter was infamous. Your daughter actually *wished* me dead; she told me.'

Hector Cameron bowed his head dejectedly and folded his hands to stop them trembling. ''Twas so unlike my Anna. She had the gentlest, kindest nature.'

'When I first knew her indeed she had. She was delightful and charmed everyone; unfortunately she charmed my susceptible husband too much and this mutual infatuation turned her head. She wanted to displace me as his wife, to assume my title and finally, when all had failed, deprive me of my life.' Analee straightened herself and regarded the rings on her fingers, twisting them around. 'However, having said that, Mr Cameron, I have the greatest regard for the memory of your daughter. In affliction and pain she was magnificent and she died nobly and well. I did all I could to save her. I never left her side. What happened to her could have happened to anyone, and those who say the medical care would have been better in London are wrong. Our doctor in Keswick has a very fine reputation for obstetric practice and has performed many difficult deliveries. The amazing thing was that your grand-daughter survived the trauma of her birth, for it had proved too much for the mother. We have buried her in Keswick churchyard, Mr Cameron, and it is my intention to raise a fine stone and keep her grave well-tended. I will honour your daughter's memory and it will live in that of your grand-child.'

Hector Cameron was now openly shedding tears and dabbed at his eyes with a large handkerchief.

'Which brings us to your grand-daughter,' Analee said, setting aside the covers of two chairs and sitting down in one, while indicating to Hector Cameron that he should take the other. 'She is now nearly six months old. She is a lovely child with your family colouring, fierce red hair and her mother's beautiful turquoise-coloured eyes. I already love her as my own, so gentle and sweet is her disposition. She is also the daughter of my late husband, whose memory I will always cherish and respect. I am quite willing to bring her up as my own, though of course she will never bear a title; this cannot be. It could never be thought she was my daughter because everyone knows the Falcon and I were separated for eighteen months before his death, and that when he did come home he was ready to die and in no condition to beget children; but I will bring her up as my child. I will adopt her unless it is your wish that she should be brought up by you and your wife in her mother's home. If you wish that, then I will willingly, though sadly, give her into your care.'

'Oh no, Lady Falconer!' Hector Cameron held up his hand and shook it from side to side. 'My daughter's shame must never become common knowledge. That I should bring up her bastard . . .'

Analee's lips curled. 'In that case, sir, I think you do well to leave her with me. I have no prejudice against children conceived out of wedlock. Indeed, I am one myself.'

'Oh nor I, ma'am, I assure you,' Hector Cameron protested cravenly. 'But in our society . . . it is so small and *narrow*, ma'am. I'm sure you understand.'

'But was it not thought your daughter was *married* to Lord Falconer?'

Mr Cameron grimaced. 'Well, yes it was; but too many people return to the old country for the truth to be concealed forever. It will come out one day and when it does it will be better – for her, you understand – that my daughter's child were not living with us. Her prospects for marriage would be negligible. But, of course, if your ladyship would be so kind, I would be glad enough of news from time to time of : . . what is her name?'

'I have called her after Stewart's wife, Elizabeth. I felt there should be some family connection. If you agree, she will be known as Miss Elizabeth Falconer.'

'Oh, that is capital, Lady Falconer! I am sure my daughter Elizabeth – she would be the least influenced by considerations of impropriety – will be highly gratified. She loved Anna. My eldest daughter, Perdita, would . . .' Hector Cameron made the same uneasy motion with his hands, 'not be so pleased.'

'I never thought to call her Perdita, sir. It would never have come to mind for I did not know how your eldest daughter was named. Now, sir, it is time to go. My servant will escort you to the door.'

Analee got up and pulled on her gloves. She was already tired and had a long journey before her. She had many things to think of and much to tell her children.

But more than anything else she had to write to Brent Delamain and tell him of her banishment and the unwisdom of their meeting for as long as it should last. She had saved him from implication in the supposed treachery; his name had never been mentioned as it was thought she had had direct contact with the Prince. As it was, he never came to London because it was understood that as long as this King lived he would never be received at court.

But in her heart she did not really wish to see Brent. She had buried the Falcon, but not her love for him and, for the forseeable future, she was content to embrace the long years of exile and widowhood.

17

Sir Brent Delamain put down his quill and gazed at the three girls playing in the garden – his nieces Mildred and Jessica, and his mother's ward Morella, who was the eldest by three years. They were playing with a ball and a wooden mallet, knocking the ball through hoops and every now and then the play was interrupted by gales of feminine laughter and one or other of the girls would be chased round the lawn by the others wielding their mallets like clubs.

'They get on so well,' Brent said, turning to his sister-in-law who sat sewing by the fire.

'Who, the girls?'

'Yes, they are like sisters.'

'Would my two had Morella's beauty.'

'They have nice dispositions. *That* is important, too.'

'But so has Morella. She is altogether a most exceptional child.'

Henrietta put down her sewing and came and stood by Brent.

'She is the light of mother's life,' Brent said. 'Sometimes, I think, of mine too.'

'Yes, you are very close.'

'I am inordinately fond of the child,' Brent sighed. 'Occasionally I feel that I have missed being a father.'

Henrietta put a hand on his shoulder. 'But it will not be too late for that, Brent! With men it is never too late! You could sire a child in your fifties or sixties and you are but thirty-seven years of age, is it not so? You were ten years younger than poor George.'

'Yes, poor George. I hope he would have approved of the way I have looked after his estate.'

'Oh, I am sure he would! You have been a model landowner and businessman. To tell you the truth, Brent, I never thought it was in you.'

Brent smiled and toyed with his pen again. He was writing a report on the potential for breeding pigs on one of the home farms where the soil was poor. 'You thought I was a scatterbrain. Well, I was. I never thought I would settle down to gentlemanly pursuits and the joys of cattle-rearing and pig-breeding!'

'All you need is a family of your own, Brent. A wife and . . .'

'Do not say it, Henrietta.' Brent's smile vanished and his face assumed that severity she was used to whenever she introduced this topic.

'But, Brent, you cannot remain forever in love with Lady Falconer! She will not even see you.'

'She has her reasons. It is not that she does not love me.'

'Are you sure?' Henrietta clasped his shoulder and looked into his eyes. He roughly brushed her hand away and got to his feet.

'Of course I am sure! She feels her banishment keenly. What she did was to protect me, so that my name should not be associated with hers in this disgrace. *That* shows she loves me.'

'But, Brent, that was two years ago, nearly three! The King could live forever.'

'I can wait. He cannot live forever and he is a great deal older than I am. Analee and I will be happy one day. I know it. Ask Reyora. She promised it.'

'Does she still?'

'I have not asked her, but I am sure she would say "yes".'

But he was afraid that she would say 'no'. That was why he avoided Reyora whenever she came to see his mother or Henrietta. It was a long time since her prophecy – nearly fourteen years. Besides, he had not told his sister-in-law everything. It was true that Analee had written about the banishment and her desire not to implicate him, but she also told him that, when her husband lay dying, she had discovered a renewal of her love for him. That to honour his memory she did not wish to see Brent.

How long could a memory last? And was it true that she loved him after the way he had treated her, leaving her with a natural child by his mistress to bring up? How much love could a woman have for someone like that? Or was it merely that, conscious of her dignity as Lady Falconer, she felt she owed it to the memory of a great lord to remain chaste?

They gazed for a while at the children playing, each wrapped in their thoughts. Henrietta was envious of Morella's beauty, the Delamain beauty – blond hair and deep blue eyes. But Morella was not a Delamain! She often thought that she was because in so many ways she seemed to resemble Brent and Emma, whereas her two children took very much after her side, the Dacre family, who tended to be dark and short, a rather cruel gift of nature – when it came to women, anyway. They were amiable, sweet-natured girls; but they would have to fight hard for husbands when they grew up, whereas Morella . . .

Morella, breathless with laughter, stopped playing and suddenly looked at the long window where the people whom she knew as aunt and uncle now stood. She waved at them and then she beckoned to them to come down.

'What does she want?' Henrietta asked Brent.

'She wants us to go down.'

'She wants *you* to go down. She adores you, Brent. You had best take care, with those devilish eyes . . .'

Brent again stopped smiling and looked at his sister-in-law severely. 'Henrietta, I am old enough to be her father! Indeed she regards me as the father she never had. I assure you there is nothing else in her simple affection for me.'

'Are you sure? She is uncommonly well-developed for fifteen, and with the mind of a woman, too. I declare the way she behaves with you is sometimes close to being flirtatious.'

'Oh come!' Brent protested. 'I would feel highly flattered if such a young girl should find me attractive; but it is not the case. I can assure you of that. However, let us go down and see what she wants.'

'You go,' Henrietta said, turning towards the fire. 'It is too chilly down there for me today.'

Whenever Morella beckoned, Brent went. It was true he was half in love with the girl though he could not, dared not, call it an adult passion. He liked to think of himself as a fond uncle; but he knew that he was attracted to her, that he felt a little better when he saw her, better still when he was with her, and altogether bereft when she was not there.

'I shall be glad of some air,' he said and walked swiftly along the huge stone corridors, down the central staircase and across the wide hall to the great front doors where Morella waited for him.

'I knew you would come,' she said, holding out her hand.

'You know I can't resist you,' he said laughing, 'you little minx!'

'I am no minx, Uncle Brent!'

'You are! You can twist me round your little finger. I was writing a report on pigs.'

'*Pigs*!' Morella exploded with laughter and put her fingers to her nose. 'Ooo, *Pigs*!'

'They are very useful animals. They are easy to feed and rear and their yield is prodigious. I am going to become one of the biggest pig-breeders in the north of England.'

Morella put her arm through his and drew him away from the lawn. He fell into stride alongside her in a companionable way and knew that she felt as he did: they wanted to be alone together. They enjoyed each other's company. They could talk so easily, whether it was about pigs or the progress of the war, or books, or Brent's adventures with the Prince whom Morella fervently admired. She could never hear enough of Prince Charles. But today she wanted to talk about something else, something she hardly ever touched upon and when she did she was always met by a wall of silence, whether she asked Brent or Henrietta or the woman she called Aunt Susan.

'Uncle Brent.' She stopped and looked into his eyes. Anyone seeing them then would have been astonished at the likeness, but as each only saw the other – and neither was given to gazing in the mirror – they were unaware of it. 'Uncle Brent, do you *really* not know who my mother was?'

He gazed back at her gravely. He knew it was something that disturbed her, as, in a way, it disturbed him; he wasn't quite sure why.

'No, I do not, my dear.'

'But it is said she was a gypsy. Do you think it is Reyora?'

'No, I don't. Why should Reyora not claim you if you were her child?'

'She is like a mother to me, so fond when she comes; but she will never speak of my mother. It is a subject she forbids me to mention. Maybe she thought I would be better reared in a castle than a gypsy camp. Uncle Brent, I wondered if, when she comes again, you would ask her for me. Would you, Uncle Brent? *Please*.'

Brent avoided Reyora, but for his own reasons. What a lot that unfathomable woman could tell if she wished. It was even rumoured that she had refused to save the Falcon; had hidden

874

when Analee sent messenger after messenger begging her to come.

'All right, I will speak to her,' he said, recommencing their walk. 'But I fear she does not tell you because the truth is quite simple.'

Morella gasped and again they stopped walking. 'And what is that?'

'I think she does not know. They were very painful days. It is difficult to imagine them now as you survey our peaceful land; but fifteen years ago much of the countryside was pillaged and plundered by bands of marauding soldiers crazed with hunger. Families were split up and separated; many went into exile and never saw one another again. I often think that you are the child of such a house, maybe a noble house such as ours, and that Reyora found you and took care of you – perhaps feeling later that she had done wrong. Maybe she wished to return you and could not. That is all that I suppose.'

'So my mother might not have been a gypsy?'

'I don't think she was. I never have.'

'I do,' Morella said gravely.

'Why?'

'I have a feeling she was. It is a very strange feeling. That is all I can say. I sometimes feel I can see into the future and that my mother is there, waiting for me.'

Brent squeezed her hand and said gently, 'I hope you are right, my dear. I know it means a lot to you, to find your mother. I . . .'

'Sir Brent, Sir Brent! Miss Morella!'

They both turned at the shouting that came from the direction of the dower house and a servant began to run towards them waving his arms in agitation. They were just about to descend the slope of the bank to the river and stopped abruptly. Brent started to climb up the way they had come.

'Oh, Sir Brent . . .'

'What is it? What is it?' Brent clasped the arm of the breathless man.

'Oh, it is your mother, sir. She has fallen and will not get up. Oh, Sir Brent, I think she is dead. Oh, Sir Brent . . .'

The man blubbered pathetically and Brent turned to Morella who was already clambering up the bank. He took her hand and they ran towards the house. Already a small crowd of servants awaited them at the door, anxiously huddled together. They stepped back as Brent and Morella ran inside and made their way to the small parlour where Susan liked to sit by the window and sew. She now lay on the floor as though she had simply fallen from her chair, the tapestry that she had been working on still clasped in her hand. Her eyes were open but she lay perfectly still.

Brent knelt by her side. 'Mother?'

She did not look at him or move. He felt her neck, and her pulse beat feebly. 'She is not dead. She has had a seizure. Morella, get two of the men to help me take her to her room.'

Although she was very slight and weighed hardly anything, it took a long time for the men, carrying her gently, to negotiate the winding corridors and staircases of the old house, some parts of it older than Delamain Castle. For some said it had once been a hunting lodge in the days of the Conqueror, and the castle had been built by one of the Marcher barons left by the Conqueror who used to hunt in the great wood which had stretched south from Penrith.

Susan Delamain lay on her bed, her eyes still staring in front of her, and Brent and Morella covered her with a blanket while one of the maids tried to light a fire. It was very cold in the room.

'What happened?' Morella asked.

'No one knows. She was apparently sitting on her own and they heard a bump.'

'I left her on her own, embroidering. She seemed perfectly well but tired.'

'She has been tired for a long time,' Brent said, the tears coming to his eyes. 'Someone must go for Emma.'

'Is she . . .'

'Shh, I do not know how much she can hear. The doctor will tell us more. He is on his way.'

Susan Delamain had had a paralytic seizure and the doctor could not tell how long she would live. Maybe for a few hours, maybe for years. All her senses were affected and she could not speak or move. The first twenty-four hours would be critical. So that they could all look after her, she was moved into the Castle and a member of the family sat by her bedside all the time. Emma arrived first with Hugo and then Sarah came, leaving her large family behind. The sister of her father, Jonathan Allonby, she had always been a favourite aunt – Susan Allonby who had married Guy Delamain.

Sarah took charge because Henrietta did not react well in a crisis; she immediately felt ill herself and was glad to take to her bed for hours at a time. Emma never left her mother's side, so Sarah took over. To her surprise she found her best helper was Morella, the orphan whom her aunt had so oddly decided to adopt. She was a wonderful help – calm and good humoured. She knew all the servants well, without being familiar, and knew where everything was to be found. She never flapped in a crisis or relaxed too much when things were smooth. She was alert and seemed to anticipate everything; her blonde head bobbed up all over the place accompanied by a willing smile.

'Let me do that, Aunt Sarah.'

Sarah smiled at the strange, beautiful girl. She didn't really know her well. Her duties kept her at home and Morella had only occasionally visited Cockermouth with Susan.

'You're a great help, Morella.'

'I like to be useful.' Morella smiled back and took the tray that Sarah was carrying to the large kitchen table before a footman took it upstairs. Sarah made all Susan's food herself, preparing the thin gruel and creamy custards which were all she could take. 'Do you think Aunt Susan will get well?'

Sarah looked at the glowing girl and shook her head sadly. 'I do not think so, Morella. I don't see how she can live on the little she is able to eat. She must surely fade away.'

'But Uncle Brent thought she was a little better. He says she can even recover completely.'

Morella arranged the things on the tray with a little bouquet of twigs and late flowers she had found in the garden.

'How long can you stay, Aunt Sarah?'

'Only a few more days. My own family will miss me.'

'Oh I wish I could see more of them!' Morella clasped her hands, her eyes shining.

Sarah looked surprised. 'Then you must come over more often. You must come and stay whenever you like.'

'It is because I do not have relations of my own. I feel that when Aunt Susan dies . . .' Morella faltered and gazed at the ground.

Sarah carefully placed the pot she was stirring on the hob and put her arm round Morella. 'You must not think you will be on your own, Morella. You *are* part of our family. We regard you as one of us, and we love you. All my children are your cousins and you must come over and stay whenever you wish. Why, Elia is only a year older than you and Henry is quite a young man! He will adore you. You must not think you will be alone. Besides, you have Brent.'

'Oh yes, Uncle Brent.' Morella brightened. 'Maybe I can move into the castle and live here with him?' Her eyes shone again and she went about her tasks with a spring in her step. Sarah gazed at her thoughtfully, a little apprehensive, before turning back to the stove.

Hugo Fitzgerald and Brent Delamain were uneasy in each other's company. They met from time to time because of their mutual business interests; but their memories were too long and they had little liking for each other. Hugo was chafing to get back to work.

'I think I shall leave Emma here,' he said, accepting the glass of whisky that Brent offered him. 'There is no saying how long your mother . . .'

Brent shook his head. 'None at all. The doctor said that if she didn't die soon she would probably live for a long time. Yes, leave Emma here, she is very welcome. But will not your children miss her?'

'Oh they are well taken care of, and the baby has a wet nurse.'

'I long to see the baby,' Brent said.

'You must come over.' Hugo's voice was indifferent. 'Thank God your mother saw him before this happened. Ah, here is Emma. I was saying I should get back to Whitehaven, my dear. Is there any news of your mother?'

Emma shook her head. She was pale and there were dark shadows under her eyes. 'There is neither good news nor bad news. She lies there quite calmly; sometimes I fancy I see a faint smile. And she *is* definitely trying to talk; she plucks at the sheets with the effort.'

Hugo stood up holding his glass, his right hand in the pocket of his waistcoat. His general air was one of impatience. It made everyone uneasy. 'I feel I must be getting home.'

'Of course; but I must stay here.'

'Shall I send the children to you? It might give your mother pleasure to see them.'

'Yes, I think she would be happy to see them. And so should I. I have never been parted from them since they were born.'

As she knew they would be, Emma's children – two boys, Connor and James, born within a year of each other – had been her main joy in her marriage. Her husband was, on the whole, a cold man and their relationship a loveless one except on rare occasions. However, he was a good father, and a careful and meticulous husband and provider. Their house was one of the finest in the district and they entertained all the local gentry, people of quality and those who had made their fortunes in business. Emma felt she had very little to complain about, except for the lack of that one, longed-for ingredient that had so far tragically eluded her in life – love.

'Then I shall be off after dinner,' Hugo said. 'I shall be home by nightfall if I ride over Honister.'

'Honister?' Brent said, looking up. 'Would you care to pass by Furness Grange and give to Lady Falconer the news of my mother's illness? She is so fond of her.'

'Lady Falconer?' Hugo hoped they didn't notice the tremor in his voice. 'Why, certainly.'

'I'll pen a letter for you.'

'Pray don't,' Hugo said. 'I am perfectly capable of explaining the matter.' He looked at his timepiece. 'Well, if I am to stop at Furness I had best be gone. I shan't even wait for dinner.'

Now that he was going he was in a fever of impatience. Emma noticed and was puzzled by it. But somehow she did not link it with the visit to the Enchantress.

So her banishment was over. Analee let the letter fall on to her lap, the stiff parchment that had arrived from London by special messenger telling her of the death of King George II. His young grandson was on the throne – a Briton born in Britain. Now she could go where she liked, do what she wished. But where did she wish to go? Nowhere. What did she wish to do? Nothing. Sometimes she felt half dead, that her life was over and what remained she lived only in her children.

Four months of the year, the winter months, she spent at Falcon's Keep so that her children would be aware of their ancestral home. The spring, summer and part of the autumn were at Furness. In October they returned to Falcon's Keep and it was just as she was packing up, preparing to move the household, that the letter from Lord Bute, a favourite of the new King, arrived.

Hugo Fitzgerald stood at the door looking at her, even before she knew he was there. He had left his horse in the wood by the house and walked round, thinking she might refuse to see him.

As he coughed she turned and looked at him with instant disapproval showing. Hesitantly he advanced into the room.

'I wonder you have the nerve to show yourself, Mr Fitzgerald,' Analee said haughtily. 'The last two occasions on which we met were not propitious ones.'

'Is that why you do not call on us in Whitehaven? I know Emma asks you to.'

'It could be the reason,' Analee said, standing up, the letter falling to the floor. She neither asked him to sit down nor gave him her hand to kiss. 'Could you state your business now?'

'Is there no forgiveness, Lady Falconer?' Hugo looked at her wistfully. If only she knew that he could only make love passionately to his wife when he thought of her.

'I think you have put yourself beyond the pale, sir. No doubt your attachment to me has dissolved with the years, but . . .'

'It has not.' Hugo came up to her and she backed away, alarmed by the fierce light in his eyes.

'Then you had best depart at once.' She went to the bellrope and made as if to pull it; but he got there before her.

'You haunt me, Analee. I am not a good husband because of you. When I make love to my wife I think it is you . . .'

'Oh, la!' Analee turned her head aside to hide her amusement. 'I am grateful that I do not suffer its effects.'

'It is true. That is why I work so hard, to put you out of my mind. You are the Enchantress and you have enchanted me. I feel I will never be free of your spell until I hold you in my arms, lie with you . . .'

'I assure you, Mr Fitzgerald, that is unlikely to occur.' Analee spoke sharply because he was a big man and he could easily overpower her. 'I must warn you that if you come an inch nearer I shall scream. My servants are never far away.'

'That will not be necessary,' Hugo said sulkily, stepping back. 'I came to bring you a message from Delamain Castle where I have recently been staying with my wife.'

'Oh?' Analee's hand flew to her heart in alarm.

'Mrs Delamain is near death. Sir Brent asked me to give you these tidings because he knows you are attached to the old woman.'

'I am indeed. What has happened?'

'She had a seizure a week ago. They do not know how long she can live.'

'I am very sad to hear it. We are leaving tomorrow for Falcon's Keep and I shall stop at the castle on my way to pay my respects.' Analee tugged sharply at the bellrope. 'Thank you for calling, Mr Fitzgerald, and conveying this message. I hope we do not meet again too soon.'

Analee stood with her two eldest children and kissed first Emma and then Henrietta. Behind them stood Brent. She gave him a sisterly embrace and realized it was the first time she had ever been so near him without an instant feeling of passion. She looked briefly into his eyes and then greeted the girls who stood shyly at the back of the room – two rather dumpy and plain and one extremely beautiful. Analee's heart skipped and Morella met her gaze.

'Do you remember me, Morella?'

'A little, Lady Falconer.'

'You are a very big girl now, so tall. I suppose I should say, a young woman.'

She glanced at Brent, who was staring at Morella with undisguised admiration. At Morella, not her. Analee felt a pang of disquiet as she followed his gaze and then bent to greet the two younger Delamain girls.

'I hope you did not mind us calling, Brent.' Analee ushered forward her two eldest children. 'I have sent the carriages with the staff and the younger members of my family on to Falcon's Keep; but I had to stop and enquire after your mother. May I introduce Lord Falconer – Duncan, my eldest boy?'

Duncan stepped forward and gravely took Brent's hand, shook it, and then politely kissed those of the ladies. He bowed to the girls and Analee saw his eyes linger on Morella.

'And this is my first-born, Clare.'

Clare was as dark as Morella was fair; but the two were of a similar height as they were close in age, separated only by two years. They also both possessed an unusual degree of beauty. Already, at thirteen, Clare was developing a womanly form but her breasts were tiny compared to those of Morella, who had the figure of a full-grown woman with a firm bustline that showed to advantage even above the high décolletage of her simple girlish dress. Clare had black curls cut about her head and dark eyes ringed by jet-black lashes. She had the regal, imperious gaze of the Falcon, whom she closely resembled. She was undeniably his daughter.

When the introductions were completed, Analee asked to be taken to Mrs Delamain. Emma came forward eagerly to escort her, whereas Analee perceived how Brent held back. Was their passion dead, then? Finally interred after all these years? She remembered the way he had looked at Morella. It was not a fatherly expression he bore in his eyes.

'I hear you have two lovely babies, Emma,' Analee said as she was escorted along the stone corridors of the castle.

'Two boys, Analee! I am so overjoyed to have them.'

'And is all *still* well?'

They turned to mount the final flight of stairs.

'He is a good husband. He has done well for himself and is someone people respect. He is a magistrate and commands the local militia. I wish he loved me, that is all.' Emma sighed as they stood outside her mother's door.

'Love often grows in marriage,' Analee said. 'I know that. In the end I came to love my husband in a different way from when we were first wed. That is why I still honour his memory. I hope it will come for you, too, but before it is too late.'

She entered the room quietly and Sarah, who had been sitting by her aunt's bed, stood up. Analee greeted her with a kiss and then bent low over Susan Delamain, looking into her eyes. She took her hand and pressed it.

'I have come to wish you better.'

There was no answering squeeze from the paralysed hand, but the eyes seemed to smile.

'They tell me you are not suffering and that you will slowly recover.'

The expression in the eyes looked sad and Susan seemed to be trying to speak. Her lips actually began to move and both Emma and Sarah exclaimed in astonishment.

'She is trying to talk. Her lips moved!'

Analee continued to gaze at the stricken woman and there was suddenly a noise in her throat.

'She is speaking. Oh, Mama!' Emma threw herself beside the bed and grasped her mother's hand. 'I knew Analee would make you well. Oh, Mama, you are going to get better.'

'Lady F . . . F . . .' Susan said slowly. 'Lady F . . . Fa . . .'

'Lady Falconer. She is speaking to you, Analee.'

'Yes, I know.' Analee bent nearer to her and continued to gaze into her eyes. 'Do you think if I were alone with her the struggle might be less agonizing?'

Sarah and Emma looked doubtfully at each other. Then Sarah nodded. 'We shall be within call,' she said and tucked her arm through Emma's. 'Come and show me the new Lord Falconer. I hear he is very handsome.'

'And Lady Clare is extremely pretty. Analee is indeed fortunate in her children.'

Analee listened to them as the door closed and their footsteps grew fainter. Then she sat by Susan Delamain's side and took her hand. 'You wish to say something to me, don't you?'

Susan nodded, her eyes pleading.

'It is about Morella?'

The rasp in the throat came again and, with difficulty, she mouthed the word 'yes'.

'You have known for a long time that she was my daughter?'

'Yes,' again the flattering word. Analee squeezed her hand.

'You know that I could not claim her; but I have always had her and her welfare close to my heart. I knew that with you, her grandmother, she was in good hands.'

Susan's eyes grew wide and Analee felt a faint return of pressure on her hand.

'Yes, her grandmother. I was the gypsy Brent lay with before we were separated by circumstances and the war. He never knew he was Morella's father, for shortly afterwards I was forcibly captured, taken to a gypsy camp and made to wed. When Morella was born Reyora assisted at her birth. It was at once clear, from her fair complexion, that she was not the daughter of two dark-skinned gypsies, such as my husband and I were. So I was urged to escape from the camp and Reyora promised to look after Morella until we could be reunited. Alas, we never were. I despaired of finding my daughter alive again because I knew what had happened to the Buckland gypsy camp and I was then loved and wooed by Lord Falconer. The rest you know.'

'And n . . . n . . . ow. A . . . f . . . ter my d . . . death?' Susan Delamain whispered.

'She will be well taken care of. Brent, after all, is her father.'

'T . . . e . . . ll him,' Susan said hoarsely. There was an agonizing look in her eyes. 'Very f . . . f . . . ond of Morella.'

Analee looked sharply at the stricken woman. 'He is very fond of her? Yes, I have already perceived that; but how could a man of his age have anything but paternal affection for such a young girl?'

But as she spoke Analee knew in her heart that it was perfectly possible, especially as Morella looked so much older than she was, like a young woman. Analee too had been well-developed at that age, and she herself was born when her own mother was only sixteen.

Analee laughed as lightly as she could and her grip on Susan's hand tightened. 'Why do we talk so gloomily? They tell me you are better every day. I pray to God that you will be with Morella for many years to come and that what we have spoken about will not be necessary.'

'Pr . . . o . . . mise me.' Susan Delamain's eyes were pleading.

Analee gazed at her solemnly. 'If you die I promise you I will see that Morella is well taken care of.'

The pressure of Susan's hand on hers increased and a distraught expression came into her tired eyes.

'P . . . ro . . . mise to t . . . e . . . ll Br . . . ent.'

Analee squeezed her hand reassuringly but said nothing. She knew that telling Brent of Morella's paternity would be the most agonizing thing she would ever have to do after all these years . . .

especially if his passion for her had cooled and he no longer loved her. And why should he? She had kept him waiting for so long, with no promise of future reward; why should he wait for her when she spurned him, telling him that she was in love with the memory of her husband? For how long could fidelity be expected of a man?

But as she walked slowly along the corridor towards the drawing room, Analee felt an emptiness in her heart, and she knew that, for many years, the knowledge that she was loved single-mindedly by one man had sustained her.

Susan Delamain did not die and indeed she did slowly begin to recover. Her speech was halting but understandable if attended to with patience, and she managed to take a few steps from her bed and sit in a chair by the fire or the window.

Sarah and Emma went back to their respective homes and the castle household returned to normal. Everyone said that Susan's recovery dated from the arrival of Analee. The spell of the Enchantress had worked once more.

Brent found that he went about his tasks much as he had always done but with a new awareness of Morella who, the following June, had her sixteenth birthday. England had done well in the war, in India, in America and on the Continent, and although Pitt had left the government, feelers were being put out for peace. England was now an increasingly prosperous, well-ruled country, Brent thought as he rode around his estates looking with satisfaction at the acres of rich land he owned, as far as the eye could see.

He had a sense of exhilaration and expectation. This was the night of Morella's sixteenth birthday. He intended to talk to his mother about her as soon as he could. Maybe she would tell him to wait a couple of years, for the sake of decency. After all he was twenty-two years older than she was. But he would. He had waited so long for one love; to wait a little while longer for another was, to one so accustomed to patience, no hardship.

But would she have him? Or was she only flirting? She had been over to Sarah for part of the summer and had returned full of talk about Henry Rigg who, at nineteen, was a tall solemn-looking young man, erudite and with impeccable manners. Brent was relieved to discern that the spirited Morella had really found him rather dull. She was only trying to tease him, and he had stifled his jealousy. But there was no doubt – from Sarah's letter – that young Rigg had fallen in love for the first time with his mysterious cousin. It was partly the reason why Sarah had sent her home earlier than had been expected. 'She is a little temptress,' Sarah had written, 'mature for so young a girl and too aware of her charm and her power.'

Power? It was a curious term to use; but Brent knew what she meant. Morella had power. She exercised a fascination over most people with whom she came in contact. They seemed immediately to admire her. The only woman he had ever known with this sort of attraction had been Analee. Yes, in a curious but unmistakable way, Analee and Morella were alike; not in looks – no two women could be more different – but in temperament. Morella too was a little enchantress.

He looked at the sun and turned his horse towards the castle. He had come a long way, partly for the pleasure of riding and partly to think on this warm day with the countryside at its rich, verdant best. He had not eaten since breakfast and he felt hungry. He turned by the side of the river and chose the path that ran up through dense woods to the castle. Suddenly, in a ray of sunlight that splashed through the trees, he caught sight of a bright dress, of a head of flaxen hair. He reined his horse and called out.

'Morella! Is it you? Morella!'

He set off to weave his way among the trees, taking care not to let his horse trip in the tangled undergrowth. Suddenly he saw the skirt again and then it disappeared. He heard a trill of laughter. She was playing with him! He got off his horse and tethered it to a branch then stole silently through the wood, a smile on his face.

'Here! Here!' A voice called and he turned to the left.

'Here!' It came again from another direction.

'Morella, I'll spank you when I find you! You have no right . . . you are too far from home.'

Unless she had followed him? His heart began to beat quickly with excited speculation. Suddenly he saw her head bob round the tree trunk in his path and his arms reached out and caught her. 'There, you monkey!'

Her face was very close, he felt her pliable, young body immediately yield to his. He grasped it, closing his eyes as his arm encircled her tiny waist. Thoughts of the most deliciously lewd nature rose up to torment him. He had not lain with a woman for so many years, he: Brent Delamain, who had once had such a reputation for women . . . before the Enchantress enslaved him. She had bewitched him, unmanned him. Now he felt his loins on fire. He opened his eyes and her own blue ones, almost the colour of his, were very close. She parted her mouth slightly and he bent his head.

She was sixteen. A maid! What was he doing? Abruptly he wrenched himself from her, and he saw the disappointment in her face. His heart hammered in his breast and his jaw worked furiously.

'Uncle Brent?' she said diffidently. 'Do you not like me?'

'Of course I like you dammit! But, my dear, I am your guardian. I am old enough to be your father.'

'So what does that matter?'

'You mean you like me . . . in that way?'

She tilted her pert chin at him, her eyes sparkling with merriment. 'In *what* way, pray?'

'You know, you minx!' he groaned.

He caught her again and this time he pressed his mouth down on her cool, chaste lips. Oh, the delicious thrill of the encounter! His hands roamed over her taut virginal breasts and he was overcome with such powerful desire that he felt he would be unable to restrain himself.

'I want it, too,' she whispered and looked at him. 'I am a woman, you know.'

'I know, I know,' he groaned again. 'Oh, how I know. You shall tempt me, my darling Morella; but not yet . . . not yet.'

'Now,' she said and moulded her young body to his again. 'I want you to do it. You.'

Once more he crushed her to him, an arm encircling her waist. Yes, he would take her here as she wished, as he, oh, so strongly wished, and then they would announce their betrothal at her birthday dinner party. They could be wed immediately, tomorrow. There would be no shame. What if he was a lot older? It was not uncommon. He was not yet forty and he had so much to give her.

He could make Delamain Castle her own. Lady Delamain. At last all his years of suffering and loneliness would be over. They would have the children he so longed for; many. A lifetime of happiness with the beautiful Morella suddenly seemed a possibility. And she wanted it! She wanted him, as urgently, it seemed, as he desired her.

And somehow now it seemed so right that the baby he had saved so long ago should become his wife. She would no longer be a foundling, but a lady of status with her own home and servants.

He lowered her gently to the ground so that they could rest comfortably on a green sward. Shortly he would see her beautiful nubile body that he had so often imagined in his dreams. She was panting and moaning now and held up her arms for him as he lay down beside her. The excitement was such that he fumbled clumsily at his clothes like a first-time lover. He drew a deep breath and tried to control himself as, held tightly in her encircling arms, he began to ease her skirt over her thighs, gently so as not to frighten her, murmuring tender endearments. Even the boldest maid usually felt some trepidation at her first encounter and indeed Morella had begun to tremble, the passionate expression in her eyes slightly tempered with fear.

'Do not worry, my darling. I will be so gentle with you. Oh, my love.' Just as he bent to kiss her, his hands about to explore further, a movement – he thought a tree bending in the wind – made him look up and there was Analee standing before him, her eyes severe, her full red mouth twisted in scorn. Suddenly he held not Morella in his arms but Analee, and they were again in that moonlit glade making love on the forest floor as he was about to do here.

'Do not do it,' Analee said, speaking clearly. 'Do not touch her.' He gazed up at Analee who wore a long blue cloak, her face partly obscured by a wide-brimmed hat. 'If you touch her you will regret it all your life,' she said, and held up a hand to him in admonition.

Brent sat up and, rubbing his eyes, looked at her again; but where she had stood was only the blackened half-trunk of a blasted tree. Analee had gone.

Brent stood up, shaking. He looked down at Morella and quickly drew her skirts over to her ankles. He felt unclean and all the excitement had gone from his limbs. Morella sat up, her eyes blazing with wrath, her slender form shaking.

'And *why* was that, pray?'

Brent put out a hand and helped her to her feet. 'I was too ashamed of what I was doing.'

'But I *wanted* it.'

She tried to come close to him again, but he backed away, standing against the tree where he had seen Analee so clearly. 'You are too young. It was a wretched thing for me to do, to deflower a maid who is my own ward. I cannot do it, Morella. Forgive me.'

'You have made a fool of me,' Morella said furiously. 'For I have shown you that I want you.'

'There is no shame in that, my dear,' Brent said tenderly, but the feeling of passion he had for her had evaporated. 'I am an older man, used to the world; you are well-developed for a maid. But I cannot take you here, or introduce you to the delights of love. I would never forgive myself.'

'But *why* . . . Brent?' It was the first time she had used his name alone.

Brent put a hand to his head. 'I cannot tell you. I was about to take you and then someone told me it was terribly wrong. That is all I can say.'

'*Someone*?' Morella said crossly, dusting down her pink dress put on with special thought to its effect on Uncle Brent, for she had come into the woods intent on seducing him.

'I mean some*thing*, of course,' Brent said desperately. 'Something inside me told me it was wrong. Now come, let us go home and prepare for your dinner party tonight.'

Brent went to his horse and untied it. He had meant to get her to ride behind him, but now he did not dare. What he had wanted was evil and unclean, and he did not know why. Many much older men married women half their ages. Why could he not? Why had Analee come to him at that time? Because he knew in his heart that she had. It was not a vision; it was her actual presence, the Enchantress once again at work.

The dinner party was a sober affair with Morella unusually quiet and Brent very formal and reserved. Mrs Delamain, of course, did not attend and, beside Henrietta and her daughters, there was a sprinkling of worthies from the locality. Everyone noticed Morella's unaccustomedly low spirits.

'It is because she is getting old,' Brent said with an attempt at levity, and he felt his face redden when Morella gave him a glance of scorn. The conversation at the table was dull and the evening seemed interminable. He would be glad when it was over and he could go to his room.

Morella avoided his eyes for the rest of the evening and he avoided hers. He knew that, whatever else happened, nothing could ever be between them as it was. She had thought he did not desire her and her pride was hurt. She would never understand.

He suddenly thought of his beautiful young bride, Mary, and how he had been unable to prove his manhood with her, so besotted was he by the memory of Analee. Was he, for all his life, to have her come between him and his desires?

Wrapped in his thoughts he hardly noticed the guests going and when he looked round only the family was still there and one or two stragglers who were reluctant to leave the good smuggled French brandy that Ambrose Rigg kept Brent supplied with.

'Brent, you are out of sorts tonight?' Henrietta said smilingly.

'I have a headache. I think I will go and say good night to mother. It is time these young girls went to bed anyway.'

He went over to Morella, who was simmering in a chair near the fire toying with a golden curl which hung over her eyes. She scowled at him as he bent down and kissed her chastely on the forehead. 'Good night, my dear ward. Do not stay up too late.'

Then he kissed Mildred and Jessica likewise, bowed to Henrietta, clapped the two remaining guests on their shoulders and went along the corridor and up the stairs to his mother's room.

A candle still burnt beside her bed, and a maid sat with bowed head by the embers of the fire. She was asleep. Brent tiptoed to his mother's side and knelt to kiss her. To his surprise her eyes were wide open and the hands that had scarcely been able to move clutched at him. He felt their strength and was astonished.

'Mother, you are recovered!'

'I am dying, my son, and God has given me this p . . . ower to sp . . . eak to you before I go.'

Her voice was so clear and strong; she hardly faltered at all. He sat by her side and grasped her hands.

'Mother, you are well! You are recovered.'

'Do not spe . . . ak and listen to wh . . . at I have to sa . . . ay.'

'Yes, Mother, I will.'

'B . . . end your h . . . ead in case that st . . . upid girl hears.'

'She is asleep.'

'D . . . do as I sa . . . ay.'

Brent smiled. His mother was not only better, but had recovered all her old powers of authority. He bent his head obediently. 'Yes, Mother.'

'It is about M . . . Morella.'

'Yes, Mother?' Brent's heart sank.

'I kn . . . ow you are f . . . ond of her.'

'Yes, Mother.'

'But not as a f . . . ather.'

So she had noticed too.

'It is wrong, Brent, because . . .' Susan was suddenly seized by a spasm and the hands that had grasped his so strongly seemed lifeless once more. She shut her eyes and her teeth bared grotesquely in the rictus of death. He grasped her shoulders.

'Mother! Mother!'

Susan Delamain half opened her eyes, and once more her breath came raspingly, painfully. There was a rattle in her throat. 'As . . . k A . . . An . . . alee,' she said and, before she could say more, her spirit left her and she remained as she was, her form inert, her half-opened eyes gazing unseeingly before her.

18

Analee received Brent in her private sitting room where none were admitted, not even her children, except with prior permission. She knew that here they would be able to converse quietly. The room overlooked part of the great fortress that was Falcon's Keep, but from a second window there was an aspect of the grounds of the castle and, in the distance, the Cheviot Hills that formed the border with Scotland.

Analee wore a comfortable morning dress of patterned silk without hoop or bodice. With her hair loose and hanging over her shoulders she almost looked the young woman Brent had first met sixteen years before. He bowed gravely and kissed her hand.

'It is good of you to receive me so soon, Analee.'

'Your message sounded urgent, Brent. Pray sit down.'

It was very formal for two people who, for so many years, had enjoyed reciprocal feelings of passion; for a man who had sworn that he would never marry another but her as long as he lived. But seventeen years was a long time and now a blonde, blue-eyed girl, very junior to Analee but with some of her qualities, had intervened.

'My mother is dead, Analee.'

Analee felt a catch in her throat and impulsively took his hand. 'Oh, Brent, I am so sorry.'

'She lived much longer than was expected and I think was not in pain. She was serene. She enjoyed her grandchildren, Henrietta's girls and Emma's boys – Emma is breeding yet again – and the company of . . . Morella.' Brent paused before saying the name and looked at Analee.

'Morella must be grief-stricken. She was so fond of your mother.'

Brent took the seat she had offered and crossed his legs. 'It is about Morella I have specifically come to see you. Hers was the last name my mother mentioned before she died. Hers, and yours.'

'Mine?' Analee felt her heart quicken uneasily. This was the moment she had tried to avoid for so long. Indeed at times she had thought it might be avoided altogether; that the truth of Morella's parentage need never be revealed; that the secret, so long hidden, might remain buried forever.

'My mother tried to tell me something about Morella. For an instant she gained an extraordinary strength, such was the urgency of the message she wished to impart. She seized my hand and spoke almost normally. But she never finished her message. She said I should ask you. Analee, what is the secret about Morella?'

Analee rose from her chair and began agitatedly to pace the room. Brent admired her as she swept past him, the faint trace of perfume, the delicious subtle body odours of one he knew so intimately, though the number of times he had lain in her arms could be counted on the fingers of one hand. A wave of longing, of nostalgia swept over him, momentarily obliterating from his mind the constant image of Morella.

'Brent, have you formed an attachment with this young girl?'

Brent nervously cleared his throat. 'I am very fond of her.'

'But is it, shall we say, the *normal* affection of an older man for a much younger girl?'

'Normal? I know not what you mean.'

'Is it *paternal*, Brent?' Analee's voice sank to a whisper.

'No.' Brent uttered the brief word and was silent.

'That is why your mother wished to tell you something. You should have been told long ago. I know it now, and I reproach myself bitterly.'

Brent sprang up and grasped her arms, pulling her towards him. 'What is it about Morella I must know?' he shouted. 'Why is it so important that *I* know it?'

Analee shook herself free and rubbed her wrists, red from his painful grasp. He was still towering over her breathing heavily, angrily, and for a moment she feared him. She took a few paces back so as to put some distance between them and then she lifted her chin and gazed at him.

'Morella is our daughter, Brent, yours and mine. She was conceived the night you first took me on the forest floor and born nine months later when I was the wife of Randal Buckland.'

'Then how do you know she is *my* daughter?' Brent spat. 'She is

893

more like the daughter of the *husband* you so perfidiously took. You have lied to me all your life, Analee, and you lie yet again.'

'I do not lie, Brent. My husband Randal Buckland was dark-skinned and black-haired, as I am, with eyes the colour of mine. A child of ours could not have had fair skin, blue eyes and blonde hair. Never. It was because Reyora saw this that she kept Morella while I fled so as to save me from the wrath of the tribe. As she was the *cohani* they would never dare to touch her or the baby; but they would have stoned me to death. That was when I ran away and found the Allonbys. For a long time I did not know what had happened to Morella because, as you know, I found the gypsy camp burnt and Randal dead. That was when I met Lord Falconer. I think you know the rest.'

'Then the baby I met with Reyora on the road was my own daughter?' Brent said incredulously. 'Why did she not say?'

'She did not know; later, maybe, she guessed. Your mother guessed. She saw how greatly Morella resembled you, as a child, and bit by bit pieced the story together.'

'But why did *you* not tell the truth, tell me when you found out about Morella? How did you find out?'

'Nelly saw Morella and Reyora at the castle. She then told me that Morella was safe and in good hands. She advised me to leave her there.'

'Because you wanted to marry a marquess, of course!' Brent hurled at her contemptuously. 'You would let your daughter be brought up by strangers so long as you . . .'

Analee put out a hand and wearily sat down. '*Please*, Brent. You must know that is not true. I did not think this would ever be pleasant, which is why I unwisely delayed telling you. I wanted to leave well alone. I had suffered so much. What could I offer Morella? When Nelly told me where she was it was my intention to stay on the road as a gypsy. I had run away from the Falcon to look for her. I did not intend to go back to him but unexpectedly I was sent for because he was dying. I knew that Morella was with her own grandmother who loved her, the best possible place for her to be.

'You know how the Falcon hated you. What would he have done to us all if he knew Morella was our child?'

'Our child.' Brent repeated the words as if he could not believe them. Then he put his face in his hands. 'If you knew how I longed to have children by you in those days when I still hoped . . .' He gazed at her.

'And you no longer hope?' Analee said quietly, her voice close to breaking. 'It is past?' Brent didn't reply and Analee continued: 'I asked too much of you, to wait. I realize now that I put myself first, myself and Lord Falconer. I thought you would wait forever. How stupid we are to take too much for granted.'

'Beautiful women usually do,' Brent said bitterly. 'Aye, you put me second always. Who, after all, was I? Not *Sir* Brent Delamain, owner of vast estates and a considerable fortune, but plain Brent Delamain, a homeless, penniless vagabond. Did I not even command a fishing wherry and pull in the haul with the men? Certainly not someone for *Lady Falconer* to consider . . .'

'Brent, you know that is not true. Wealth and position never mattered to me and still do not. Remember it was you who were first unfaithful to me. You fell in love with Mary Allonby . . .'

'Until I saw you again!'

'I did not know that. You had proved fickle once, why should you not again?'

'But from then on I was constant, my marriage shattered because of you. I wanted to take you away from him, to give you a new life – but no. You pretended to love that ogre!'

'I did love him,' Analee said solemnly. 'His mettle matched mine. I said I would venerate his memory and I do. I have been faithful to my marriage vows.'

'In a way *he* never was!'

'He was certainly not faithful. But he had a different understanding of the roles of men and women.'

'He thought of women as chattels!'

Analee bowed her head in agreement. 'In a way he did; yet he was so dependent on them! But he was the most remarkable man and I shall remember and honour him until I die.'

'You were not *exactly* true to your marriage vows either,' Brent said slyly. 'There was a time you took me in your arms . . .'

'I do not deny it. May one not love two men, Brent? Is it not possible? You know my affection for you went beyond mere friendship. I loved you and I love you still; but circumstances have always intervened. I felt I had to live a number of years as a widow out of respect to my late husband and in deference to his children; but after that . . .'

'You expected me to come running.'

'No. I hoped that . . . we might come together eventually, if it suited everyone concerned.'

'Oh, who is concerned beyond you and me?'

'The children,' Analee said simply. 'My son Duncan is the Marquess of Falconer. He is now twelve years of age, my daughter Clare fourteen. And then . . . there is Morella.'

'Morella,' Brent said bitterly. 'How she has longed to know her mother. It has tormented her. She even said to me once, "I feel my mother is there somewhere waiting for me".'

'Oh, she said that!' The tears ran down Analee's cheeks. 'Oh, I feel I have done such a wrong. The worst of it being that you imagined yourself in love with your own daughter.'

''Tis a monstrous crime!' Brent said savagely. 'But how did I know? How *was* I to know? My mother knew. Why did she not tell me?'

'She did not know for sure until last winter when she was like to die. I told her then to comfort her; why she did not tell you when she got better I cannot say. Maybe, like me, she was content to leave well alone.'

'But all was not well! My affection for Morella was deepening, couldn't she see that? Everyone else could. My sister Emma even said she thought Morella was a little young for me. I nearly made love to her, my own daughter! Imagine that! I lay on the ground with her, in a clearing as we once did, she urging me to take her and . . .' Brent, ashen-faced, stared at Analee. 'You appeared to me. It was physical. I could have touched you. It was no ghost. You bade me to have nothing to do with her or I should regret it for the rest of my life. My desire ebbed immediately and before any harm was done, thank God. To have ravished my own daughter!' Brent kept his hands over his face for a long time, his shoulders jerking with sobs.

Analee went over to him and touched him. 'Brent, you can never blame yourself, never. Yes, I know I appeared to you. I sometimes in the past have had the sensation that I am leaving my own body. I had it quite often in the war or when the Falcon was ill. He once saw me when he lay wounded after Falkirk, emphasizing, as you did now, that it was not a dream. A few weeks ago I was very disturbed in my mind and anxious about you. I kept on seeing you and Morella . . .'

'You wore a blue cloak and hat . . .'

'Yes, I was walking in the grounds here. You know at this time of the year we are usually at Furness, but Duncan had some studies to complete and Clare had been in London, so I waited here for them. It was a beautiful day and I was walking in my own rose garden when I had that sensation that I was elsewhere . . .'

'Well, you were watching me attempt to make love to my daughter!'

'Oh no. I could not see anything. I never can. It is just an odd sensation in my body. I do not feel normal. I cannot really explain it to you; but, yes, I know the day. I remember it. I was thinking of her, and you. I wore my blue cloak, and a large hat to shield my eyes against the sun. Morella's sixteenth birthday.'

'Yes,' Brent whispered.

'You would have taken her virginity then, would you? Fie on you!'

'She *begged* me to.'

Analee gave a bitter smile. 'I am glad she does not lack passion. In that, at least, she resembles her mother.'

'She resembles her mother in many ways,' Brent said. 'I know it now. She has your spirit, your temperament. Oh, Analee, what have we done?'

He gazed at her pitifully and her heart went out to him in love. Yes – love – not passion, but gentle, understanding love. She felt as a couple do when they have lived together for many years and raised children.

'It is more what I have done than what you have done,' she said gently. 'I should have spoken years ago. Your emotions would never have got the better of you then, and she would have known who her mother and father were. I was a coward. I confess it now.' She sighed and turned to the window. 'I have made many mistakes in this life, but this I feel is one of the greatest, one of the most important, with consequences that went far beyond my control. Morella is now in love with you. What will her reaction be when she finds out that the man she had desired, idolized maybe, is her own father? Who will she blame for denying her this knowledge?'

Analee paused and once more the tears came into her eyes. 'She will blame me, her mother, for you were as ignorant in this matter as she was. Will she hate me now?'

'We must find out,' Brent said, rising to his feet. 'We must go immediately and tell her.'

Henrietta Delamain paced anxiously backwards and forwards, gazing out of the window. The reason for Brent's sudden visit to Lady Falconer so shortly after the burial of his mother was unknown to her; but the messenger she had sent to bring him back had been told to ride without stopping and now it was twelve hours since he had left. Yet, even as she looked she saw the carriage drive through the gates in the far distance, the messenger she had sent riding alongside, and she fled down the stairs to await them in the porch, twisting her handkerchief in her hands, so great was her feeling of guilt and responsibility.

Brent was out of the carriage door almost before it had stopped and he ran round to the other side to open the door for Analee before her own postillion could get to it. They had met the messenger outside Penrith as they were on their way and, apart from the urgent summons from Lady Delamain, knew no further details.

When Henrietta saw Analee she ran down the steps, tripping over herself in her anxiety to welcome her distinguished guest. 'Oh, Lady Falconer! Pray what brings you here? Welcome, Analee.' She kissed her cheek but Analee noted the pallor of her face and clasped her hand as she said anxiously:

'You do not look well, Henrietta. What has happened?'

Henrietta looked from one to the other, her handkerchief by now a twisted rag. 'I know not how to tell Brent,' she said. 'Oh, I blame myself.'

'But what is it? What has happened?' The look Brent gave her was so menacing that she felt frightened. She lowered her eyes.

'Morella has gone. She has run away.'

'Morella? Gone?'

'Yes, without a note, without her maid or packing any clothes. She went in the night like some spirit and her bed was empty when her maid went to wake her the next morning. She has taken nothing with her. Oh, I only fear that out of grief for Susan, or for some other reason I know not, she might have killed herself.'

'But why should she kill herself?' Analee intervened. 'Was she not a happy girl?'

'She has been so depressed since Mrs Delamain died. She has scarce smiled or spoken a word. Then, the morning after Brent left, she had gone. I dread her body being dragged out of the river.'

Morella knew the gypsy camp was near, but not where. She made several false starts and sometimes came back to the point from which she had started. She knew Reyora came by the river and that the camp was on the river. But the first time she went in the wrong direction and could see the town of Penrith perched on a hill. She knew she had to go south, not north.

As night fell she grew afraid and she kept to the woods to be out of sight of wandering beggars or thieves. Once she saw some charcoal-burners in a clearing; but she did not dare approach them, despite the tempting smell of roasting meat.

At dawn she rose, thankful that it was the summer and she could sleep outside without freezing with cold. When she woke she looked around for berries and drank water from the stream. She found that such activities came naturally to her and that the life suited her.

The food in her belly and warmth on her back renewed her courage and during the day she was not afraid to approach strangers on the road and ask them where the Buckland gypsies were. Everyone commented on her fine clothes and the way she spoke; but no one molested her. Finally, in the late afternoon, she came to the spot she sought, the gypsy tents around the field, their horses tethered in the shade. In front of the tents were many fires and the men squatted around while the women prepared the evening meal. Groups of children played with sticks and hoops, or balls made of rags and wrapped round twigs and leaves.

They all had the black hair and brown faces of their race; they looked at her with curiosity as she timidly made her way past the tents, not quite knowing whom to ask or what to say.

'Can I help thee, lass?' A fine young man sprang up in front of her, his chest bare, his eyes gleaming in admiration.

'I'm looking for Reyora,' Morella said. 'Can you tell me where to find her?'

'Reyora will be in yonder tent.' The young man pointed and Morella glanced at him with approval, noting the fine hairs on his brown torso, the red gleam of his nipples. He looked virile and vibrant with life. 'I'll take you to her,' the young man said. 'What is your name?'

'Morella.'

Reyora squatted by her fire looking into the flames as one of her daughters prepared the meal. Although she was not old in years she sometimes felt old because of all the hardships she had been through, especially during the Rebellion when her tribe had been almost annihilated. But the Buckland tribe, with true gypsy vigour, had revived itself. It had intermarried and married into neighbouring tribes. It was now large and as vigorous as it was when Randal Buckland been captured a bride and brought her there and Rebecca, old Rebecca, was the *phuri-dai*, the wisest and cleverest woman in the tribe. Now Reyora had held that position unchallenged for many years.

Reyora felt she was seeing a vision as she glanced up and saw Morella, carefree and laughing, walking alongside the tall frame of Timothy Buckland – one of her many nephews. She got up and drew her shawl closer against the chill evening, but Morella trailed her cloak behind her and seemed quite happy in a thin muslin dress, the hem of which was very dirty and torn from her long walk.

Reyora went slowly towards her and when Morella saw her she paused in her chattering and ran to her. 'Oh, Reyora! I have found you.' She threw her arms around the older woman and kissed her.

'But, Morella, where have you been? Your clothes are dirty. Your face . . . Your hair.'

'I have been wandering, Reyora, like you told me the Buckland gypsies used to do. I left home yesterday and took the wrong road. I then had to sleep the night in the wood; but I covered myself with dry leaves and ate berries and drank the clear water from the stream. I've enjoyed it, Reyora. I feel at home in this life!'

'And do Sir Brent or Lady Henrietta know where you are?'

'No, I have run away for good. I have left home. I want to be a gypsy and live as you do. I like the life. I knew I would.'

900

Morella looked archly at the handsome Timothy Buckland, who hung on her every word.

'Be off with you now, Timothy,' Reyora said. 'I must talk to Miss Morella.'

'Oh not "Miss Morella"! Morella.' The blonde girl burst out laughing and Timothy felt dazzled by her beauty. He had never seen such a lovely creature in his life.

'Dance with me afterwards,' he whispered. 'When it has grown dark we sing and dance round the fire.'

'Be off with you. Shoo!' Reyora made a gesture with her hand, but to herself she was smiling, remembering all those years ago when Morella's mother, Analee, had bewitched the Buckland tribe by her skill as a dancer, had made all the women jealous with her striking looks. 'Now, Morella, come to my tent and tell me why you are here. I will have food sent in.'

Reyora drew Morella past the curious glances of her family into her large tent. She lit a candle and bade Morella sit on the pile of soft cushions on the floor where she used to squat to weave her spells or simply to meditate.

'Oh, I like it here!' Morella said mischievously. 'I feel at home. May I stay, Reyora?'

'First,' Reyora said, squatting opposite her, 'you must tell me why you are here.'

Morella faltered a little at first; but then the story came out. How she admired her Uncle Brent, how about a year ago she began to dream of him and weave fantasies around him. How she was convinced now that she was in love with him and he with her. How she had tried to tempt him in the wood but he had changed his mind at the last minute.

'He said "someone" stopped him. I then challenged him. "Someone?" I said. "Some*thing*," he corrected; but I think he meant *someone*. That night my Aunt Susan died and from then to the funeral Uncle Brent hardly ever looked at me. He never smiled and he ignored me. As soon as Aunt Susan was buried he left to visit Lady Falconer. I know not why. I decided to run away and become a gypsy like my mother.' Morella reached out and grasped the hand of her old friend. 'Reyora, my mother *was* a gypsy, was she not? Tell me the truth. Tell it now. In the past, whenever I have asked you, you have evaded it. Uncle Brent said he thought it was because you did not know; but I think you do. I want to know *now* about my mother, and I want to know why Uncle Brent has changed towards me and does not love me. Am I not attractive?'

'You are very attractive.' Reyora nodded and scratched on the floor of the tent with a twig she was holding. She wrote some magical gypsy letters, a kind of charm, to bring her luck in the difficult task ahead of her. 'That is part of the trouble. It was the trouble with your mother, too. Her beauty was of little advantage to her. It brought her so much sorrow.'

'You are going to tell me about my mother?' Morella clasped her hands together. 'Oh, Reyora, pray go on!'

'I am going to tell you about how it was long ago,' Reyora answered, 'when this land was very troubled. A beautiful dark gypsy girl of undoubtedly noble bearing, but a gypsy for all that, fell in love with a nobleman. He had to go to the war before he knew that this woman he loved was to bear his child. He was on the side of the Stuarts and you know what happened to those who supported the cause?'

Morella nodded gravely. 'They were defeated.'

'Defeated and stripped of their lands and rights. The man was sentenced to death but escaped and the beautiful gypsy, who also underwent many vicissitudes and had been forced into a loveless marriage, eventually gave birth to a blonde baby with fair skin and blue eyes who, it was known, could not possibly be the issue of herself and her dark-skinned gypsy husband.'

'That was me?' Morella gasped.

'Yes, I was present at your birth and helped to bring you into this world. Already I loved your mother, and I urged her to flee because otherwise she would be killed by her tribe for lying with a *gadjo*, a non-gypsy. I would look after you and restore you to her in time. Well, that was not to be. Our camp was invaded by the Jacobites and you know how I took you on the road and, on the way, I met a man who took pity on us and directed us to his mother.'

'*Uncle Brent?*'

'Yes, and your Aunt Susan.'

'And what happened to the gypsy?'

'Well, for a while she did not prosper. She had no home and no and sleeping under hedges or in caves. It was a bitter winter the year of the Rebellion, the year you were born, 1745. She had heard by chance that you were safe, in a good home with people who loved you. She wished to reclaim you, but was advised not to in your own interests, not hers. She did what she did for the best. She knew where you were and that you were happy. You must always believe this, Morella; what your mother did was what she thought was in your best interests. She never thought of herself. That I know.'

'You *know*? My mother is still alive? Oh, where is she? Can I see her? Is she here among the gypsy people? Pray take me to her, Reyora.'

'It is not all that easy, Morella.'

'But why not? Does she think I will be ashamed of her because she is poor? Of course I will not! I forgive her anything, just to see her.'

Reyora got up and looked out of the tent towards the camp. It was now dark and the fires blazed, lighting up the faces of those around.

'I will have to think what to do,' she said at last. 'I cannot be too hasty. Let us eat now.'

She had not imagined it would be easy, but it was proving more difficult than even she had thought.

The girl was dancing, her lithe body weaving intricately in and out of the assembled gypsies. To see her dance you would have thought she had done it all her life, that, from being a small girl, she had learned the steps and how to click her fingers above her head and sway her hips.

But Morella had learned it in two nights, ever since Timothy Buckland had taken her onto the grass after her talk with Reyora. For two hours they had spun and twirled until the whole camp had gathered to watch them and called to those who were inside to come out and see the blonde girl who must surely have gypsy blood to dance with such skill.

That night Morella had slept in Reyora's tent and the next day, dressed in a gypsy skirt and blouse, she had lived the way the gypsy women did, cooking and cleaning and chatting as they chewed their nuts, sitting apart from the men. Then in the afternoon she had ridden with Timothy bareback and once even standing on the horse fearlessly, her fair hair streaming in the wind, while Reyora had gone on a mysterious mission, promising to be back at night.

Now the assembled concourse clapped and one or two played gay cheerful gypsy tunes on their tin whistles, while the fiddler did his best to keep up with them.

The tears came into Analee's eyes as she watched her daughter and, but for the colouring, she could see herself as the girl she had been, dancing for her living in taverns, in the houses of the great, just as the Buckland gypsies still did.

'You can see she is your daughter,' Reyora murmured. 'She has your talent. It came to her naturally as one born to it. See, Analee, if you now went into the crowd you could dance as well as Morella. You still have your figure and your skill.'

Analee pulled her cloak about her feeling herself trembling in the chill breeze. She had ridden over, through the forest with Reyora, and she wore a riding skirt and high polished boots. Her feet tapped to the music, but she smiled ruefully at Reyora's words.

'I have borne five children since I danced, Reyora. Even my greatest admirers would not say the girth of my waist is what it was.' But she found it difficult to joke. She was too full of trepidation as to what Morella would say. She wished Reyora had spared her the task.

'Who is the boy she dances with?'

'He is my nephew Timothy Buckland. The son of my sister Rose.'

'He is a fine-looking boy.'

'He *is* a fine boy. He is nineteen.'

'He never stops looking at her.'

'Or she him. He is more her own age. Morella had to meet boys of her own age. If she had, she would not have fallen in love with her father.'

'He knows that now. In time they will both forget it ever happened.'

'And is he in love with you again?' Reyora looked at her slyly.

'No, not yet.' Analee glanced knowingly at Reyora. 'But I am using the last of my failing powers to try and ensure it will not be for long. I will never tease him again for, now that he does not want me, I find I passionately desire him.'

'Hush, they are stopping.' Reyora looked anxiously at Analee. 'Now you must tell her.'

But Morella had disappeared, and it was a long time before they found her at the back of the camp with Timothy Buckland listening to his stories of horse-trading and dancing in the fairs.

'Oh, I would love to come with you!' Morella's eyes shone. 'I would like to stay here forever. My mother was . . .' Morella looked up and saw Reyora and with her a lady in a long cloak with the hood pulled well down over her face. Something about her was familiar. Morella stopped talking and ran over to Reyora. 'Did you see me dancing? Where were you today? Why . . . ?'

The lady dropped her hood and smiled timidly at Morella who gasped with amazement. 'Lady Falconer! Whatever brings you here?'

'I have come to see you, Morella.'

'Me?' Morella looked at Reyora. 'Oh, you have come to take me home. Uncle Brent is too angry to come himself. He has sent *you.*'

'Yes, but I have also come to talk to you.' Analee took her arm and led her away from the crowd. The only light came from the flickering fires, some being dowsed down for the night.

'What did Uncle Brent wish you to say?' Morella enquired petutantly. 'That he did not dare come himself. Well, tell him I like it here. I want to stay. I hate the castle and the boring, stilted life.'

'It is true Sir Brent did not wish to come himself, but not because he did not dare. I wanted to talk to you and explain why it was that the gypsy let her baby go, the blonde baby who was found on the road sixteen years ago.'

'But why should you know that?' Morella said, her eyes already showing a glimmering of understanding.

'Because, my dear child, *I* was the gypsy and you are my daughter, Morella.'

Morella gazed at her mother, her mouth wide open with shock. She moved away from her and, for a moment, turned her back to hide her emotion. Analee braced herself, resigned to whatever would come. When Morella slowly turned to her again, tears were streaming down her face.

'But why did you not tell me before? I have seen you throughout the years. Were you so ashamed of me?'

'Oh, Morella,' Analee was weeping now, and she drew her daughter to her. 'I was proud, *proud* of you! It is of myself I am ashamed; but, you see, I felt you had made a new life and that if I came into it, it would only upset and disrupt you. Besides, there was Lord Falconer. Not at first, but later. I loved him, but he was a harsh man. I had other children and I thought that if he knew about you he might send me away; part me from them too. He never liked your father. He hated him. I admit I was afraid and I have always repented of this cowardice and always shall.'

'You preferred your other children to me?' Morella's lip was trembling.

'Of course I did not! I always loved you best, my first-born. I thought of you constantly. Did we not like to play together when I came to see you? Were you not attracted to me?'

'I thought you were beautiful. I wished my mother was like you. Now that I know . . . I am not so sure.'

'But why, Morella?' Analee's arm tightened around her.

'Because I think it is too late. I have grown up without the love of a mother, with my mother pretending to be someone else, a stranger. You see it is very hard for me.'

'It is hard for me too, Morella, to show you how much I love you and always have. Even if you reject me now I will always love you. Besides I gave a promise to your father.'

'My father? He is alive too?'

'This is the hardest part,' Analee said her voice choking. 'For the man I loved and lay with all those years ago, the man who met Reyora on the road and out of compassion, directed you to his mother – although he did not know who you were – was Brent Delamain, my lover and your father.'

Morella gave a scream and ran off into the dark. Reyora, who had been watching nearby, ran after her and Timothy, who had been standing with her, ran faster. As Morella tore across the field and into the forest Timothy reached her and grasped her, holding her tight as she struggled against him, beating his hard young body.

'Let me go! Let me go!'

She tried to bite his hand, but he held her until Reyora came and, at the sight of those wise eyes, Morella's struggles grew less frantic and she calmed down.

'Come with me,' Reyora said. 'I will give you something nice to drink. It will blot out all the unhappiness and when you wake you will feel better.'

'Tell *her* to go! I never want to see her again,' Morella muttered, her eyes blazing with rage and humiliation, pointing to where Analee stood in the shadows. 'I never want to see either of them again. Her or *him*, as long as I live.'

19

'Thus,' the Marquess of Falconer said, as though explaining something to a simpleton, 'the earth goes *round* the sun. 'Tis not the other way about.'

'I see,' Brent replied, 'that you would make a fine sailor.'

'Oh no, sir, I wish to be a scholar.'

'Not a soldier like your father?'

'No indeed!' Young Lord Falconer's aristocratic features wrinkled in horror at the very idea. 'That is the ambition of my brother Beyrick. He plays with toy soldiers all the time. My mother has to send for them to London. I don't enjoy warlike things. I wish this war was over.'

'They say it soon will be,' Brent observed, looking out of the window for a sight of Analee. 'But England has made splendid gains. Was there ever a year like 1759? Hardly ever in our history. We shall drive the French into the sea and capture the whole American continent. And India, too. Are you not proud of our country?'

'Of course I am proud,' Duncan said. 'But I do not wish to be in the military. I would like to serve her by peaceful means – in the cause of science if possible.'

Brent smiled and leaned against the window sill of Duncan's large room filled with apparatus and instruments. Analee complained that he studied too much, whereas Beyrick, completely different, gave vent to his aggressive nature by drilling his toy soldiers and ordering the servants about all day long. Brent felt rested and at home at Furness where the Falconer family had gone for their usual summer retreat. The nagging irritation about Morella seemed less intense here, the reason he ostensibly came to see Analee.

'Ah, there is your mother now,' he said, eagerly glancing for the fiftieth time out of the window.

'Are the girls with her?'

'Yes. Your sister Clare is a beauty. I hear she loves London.'

'She is too giddy,' Duncan said derisively. 'She can't wait until she is presented at court! She has no love of the country as Mama has.'

'Let us go down and greet them.'

'I would like to finish this experiment, Sir Brent. I will join you soon.'

Duncan bent his head to his piece of apparatus and Brent left the room and ran downstairs with a feeling of excitement he could not altogether explain in his heart.

Analee had stayed on the terrace where the servants brought out chairs and refreshment because of the warmth of the day. Little Elizabeth Falconer sat near her; she hardly ever left her side if she could help it, while Charlotte and Beyrick went to the water's edge and started playing with the boat that was at anchor there. Charlotte was a tomboy and copied everything her brother did.

Clare was a languid girl, not given to over-exerting herself unless it was at a dance or riding in Richmond or Marylebone fields or occasionally here on Manesty Moor. She had already the air of a grand lady and lay stretched out in her chair, one arm trailing on the ground, her eyes closed, panting slightly.

'Oh, I am puffed! The heat is too enervating.'

'You do not take enough exercise, Clare,' Analee said. 'You will get fat and . . .'

'Oh, Mama, do not say such a thing!' Clare looked at her in horror. 'You know I am so careful about what I eat. I *never* let a chocolate past my lips or . . .'

'No, darling, I was only teasing.' Analee leant over to her and took her hand. 'You are lazy by nature, but you will always care too much about the opinions of others to let yourself get fat. But, Clare, I do not wish you to grow up *too* soon. You are but fourteen. Enjoy your youth. Your head is full of dances and parties and . . . men.' Her mother leaned heavily on the last word.

'Mama, Lady Agnes Dulcimer is already wed and she is just fifteen!'

'She is too young,' Analee said primly. 'I do not want thoughts of marriage to enter your head until you are at *least* seventeen, and I would prefer it a good deal later. Ah, thank you, Nell.' Analee looked up as Nelly put a cushion behind her back. 'Now Nelly makes me feel like an old lady, always fussing about me. Nelly, did I see Sir Brent at the window of Duncan's room as we walked past?'

'Yes, ma'am. He rode over to see you.'

'He is always here, isn't he?' Clare said, glancing at her beautiful mother meaningfully. Though the two were deeply attached there was a slight air of rivalry between them. Analee ignored her remark, looking towards the door.

'And here I am,' Brent said, walking onto the terrace and extending his arms. 'What a beautiful day! I could not resist saddling my horse and coming to see you all.' He gave Clare a friendly smile, deliberately offhand. He knew Analee thought him too susceptible to young females.

'Is everything all right?' Analee glanced at him anxiously, Morella being a constant source of worry to them both.

'I would like to talk to you later alone, but there is nothing really wrong,' Brent said while Clare gazed at them both from beneath the long black lashes that tantalized all the beaux in London.

'We do see a *lot* of you, Sir Brent,' she said haughtily.

'I am a *very* old friend of your mother's,' Brent replied, 'and having no family of my own to speak of I am very fond of you all.'

'What do you mean "to speak of"? I thought you had no family of your own?'

'Well, I have my sister-in-law Henrietta and her daughters, my sister Emma and her sons and my ward Morella.'

'Ah, Morella,' Clare said with a laugh. 'Mama said she is living with gypsies! How outrageous!'

'Not "living" with them, Clare,' Analee said reprovingly. 'She is staying with our old and valued friend Reyora.'

Clare managed a grimace of distaste and shuddered. 'Oh I should hate it! Imagine in a tent, and all those common people . . .'

Analee's eyes glinted dangerously. She found Clare the most unlike her and the most difficult of all her children to cope with on account of her fine airs and graces, her exaggerated manners. But still, she was the daughter of a marquess, and Analee supposed that daughters of marquesses felt entitled to give themselves airs. Not having grown up as one of them she didn't know. She was perpetually correcting her daughter, which was why Clare spent such a lot of time under the chaperonage of a sister of the Falcon, Lady Amelia Duguid, in London.

'Take care, Clare, what you say. Remember I am one of those "common people" by birth.'

'Oh, Mama!' Clare scoffed, 'and your father an earl! Common person indeed.'

'Yes, Clare, but, as you know, he did not bring me up. I grew up among the gypsies and Morella is like . . . that.'

Analee finished just in time, having been on the verge of saying 'me'. None of her children had yet been let in on the secret of Morella's parentage.

'Well, how long will Morella stay with those "dear" people?' Clare looked at Brent, who shrugged, the expression in his eyes unfathomable.

'Forever, as far as I can see. She shows no desire to come home.'

'Oh you cannot allow it, Brent!' Analee expostulated. 'She cannot stay there forever! I shall have to go and talk to her.'

'But why you, Mama?' Clare enquired curiously.

'Because she listens to me, that is all. Or rather she listens to Reyora who listens to me. I must say I can make very little headway myself with that wilful young lady.' She glanced at Brent in despair. Their worry over Morella had brought them close, and he got on so well with her children. Duncan loved him and valued his comments on his work. Beyrick liked him because he had fought in the war and played soldiers with him, though always on the enemy side, Beyrick being a staunch Hanoverian. Charlotte was obviously fond of him; but his favourite was Elizabeth, beautiful fragile little Elizabeth, who had never known her father. Brent was especially tender with her and he was gazing at her now playing tranquilly by the side of the woman she called mother.

'Do you think we could have a word inside, Analee?'

'But you are not going back too soon, are you? Why not stay a few days with us?' She gazed at him and he felt sudden excitement, a quickening of the pulse as when he used to look at Analee in days of old. He thought she was looking at him in the same way, too. How well he recalled that expression; amorous without being too blatant, seductive with a pleasing hint of diffidence.

'I cannot do that just at the moment, but I would like to take it

911

up in a week or two,' he replied slowly. 'The thing is that with Morella it is beginning to be a little serious.'

Analee got out of her chair and took his hand as he helped her up.

'Serious? You must tell me at once. Clare, keep an eye on the children.' She put an arm through his and together they walked slowly into the house, Clare's eyes on them, not on her small charges.

'Now what is it about Morella?' Analee turned to Brent as soon as they were inside.

'Reyora came to see me yesterday. She feels she must no longer stay in the camp.'

'But why? Is she not happy there? I hoped she would grow out of it naturally and wish to come home!'

'Oh, not a bit of it,' Brent laughed and, taking off his coat, put it over a chair. 'I hope you do not mind, Analee, but I am very hot.'

'Of course not.' How handsome he looked in his shirt and breeches Analee thought, his unpowdered hair still thick and fair, his jawline firm, his figure that of a much younger man. She closed her eyes and thought sadly of what might have been; but now they were like two elderly parents anxious about their errant daughter, clucking rather than billing and cooing. 'Tell me about Morella.'

'Reyora fears she is in love.'

'In *love*?'

'With that scamp of a gypsy, her nephew Timothy.'

'Oh, my goodness! I am afraid that Morella will always be in love from now on. She is rather like Clare in her attraction to the opposite sex.'

'All they have in common, I fear. Clare is much too elegant for Morella. Reyora says that Morella has become the complete gypsy – wears gypsy clothes, her hair in a band, never washing. She is always slinking off with Timothy and Reyora has to keep a very close eye on her and is growing tired of it. She wishes that you would come and speak to her. Ask her to go home. Clearly, as she is in love with Timothy, she is no longer a danger to me.'

'And you? Are you a danger to her?' Analee gazed at him, her voice scarcely above a whisper.

'Of course not! That is long since gone. I . . .' he looked at Analee then lowered his eyes.

'Yes, Brent?'

'Well I . . . I come over here a lot, do I not?'

'Yes, you do,' she replied lightly. 'As Clare has noticed.'

'It is not just to see the children, fond as I am of them.'

'And they of you.'

'Duncan is a very fine boy. I feel he will enrich the scholarship of this land.'

'His tutor hopes so, too. He feels he can teach him no more and Duncan will shortly go to Oxford to study with new tutors there.'

'Oh, Analee, I am so glad!' Brent looked at her, his eyes shining. 'What a credit to his father.'

'A real credit to his father,' Analee said, gazing at Brent. 'Or should I say a credit to his real father?'

'But what do you mean?'

'I cannot tell you now, Brent, but I may some day.'

'You mean the Falcon was not Duncan's father?'

'It cannot be proved, but that is my suspicion. They are neither alike to look at nor in temperament.'

'Yes, I noticed that. Duncan is very different from the rest, who all have the Falcon's imperious expression, even little Elizabeth. Duncan is gentle . . . Analee,' he gazed at her, the feeling of excitement returning. 'Do you mean to tell me . . .'

'I can tell you nothing, Brent, not yet anyway.'

He came close to her and took her hand, drawing her to him. 'You tease, you Enchantress, you! So you did not keep your marital vows too well after all? That is *two* men, at least, you lay with while you were wed, for I don't suppose *I* am Duncan's father?'

'Most certainly not.'

'How many more?'

'Children or men?' Analee said provocatively.

'Oh you . . .' He crushed his mouth down upon hers, feeling her yield to him as she had in days gone by. His head swam with desire for her; she was so familiar, yet always strange, new. She put her arms round his neck and drew him to her.

'I would imprison you forever in my arms,' she murmured.

'Forever?' Brent's voice was hoarse. 'You *mean* forever?' She let him go and he stepped back panting, his eyes alight. 'Oh, Analee, if we . . .'

'I was afraid the magic had gone; but it has not.'

'It never did! I only saw you in Morella, I know that now.'

'And you are definitely *over* Morella?' she said slyly.

Brent threw up his hands and gazed at the ceiling, the veins on his forehead bulging. 'Oh, never bring that up again, that folly! It has ruined my relationship with my daughter, but it is not too late to repair it with her mother. Analee . . . will you?'

He knelt down and took her hand, bringing it to his lips.

'Really, Sir Brent, is this a formal proposal?'

'You know it is, my darling. A passionate proposal for you to become my wife – at last!'

'And I accept you, Brent, with great joy. Oh, how I feared I would never awaken desire in you again . . .'

'You need never fear that, my Enchantress . . .'

Analee put a hand on his head. 'No, Brent, the Enchantress is gone. It is Analee, the mother and wife I have become.'

'But when you appeared to me? What was that if not magic?'

'That was because I was a mother. I could not let you have carnal knowledge of your daughter. I was being a mother then, not an Enchantress.' She bent and kissed his head and, drawing him up, led him to a seat by the window. 'Now, my darling, we have to think what to do about Morella. My only interview since I told her I was her mother was unpleasant; she was rude and sullen. You have not seen her at all. She presents a real problem to us, but do you know what I think will suit our wayward young daughter?'

'No?' Brent looked at her, still not believing his good fortune.

'A spell in a convent.'

Brent threw back his head and roared with laughter. 'A convent! Morella in a convent?'

'Only for a short time. I did not suppose she would wish to take the veil; but yes, why not? I thought of Mary, who would gladly look after her, supervise her studies and maybe teach her a prayer or two.'

'But Morella does not like to study.'

'It will do her no harm, before she is ready to be presented.'

'You are serious about this, are you not?'

'Very.'

'And what do you suppose Morella will say?'

914

'Once she is confronted with the wishes of her *united* parents she will have very little say in the matter.'

'United? You mean we are to be wed, that soon?'

'As soon as I have the permission of my eldest son.' Analee kissed him once more and then she led him through the house and up the stairs.

Duncan was still in his room when they went to find him. A candle was alight under a jar in which liquid slowly bubbled and his head was bent over a book. When he saw his mother he stood up and took her hand and kissed it. Instinctively his manners were as exquisite as those of Prince Charles.

'Mama, how good of you to visit me!'

'Sir Brent told me of your conversation. He is most impressed with your knowledge, Duncan.'

'I am honoured, Mama.' He bent his head and smiled. He was an extraordinarily handsome boy with the dark hair of his mother, but with fair skin and the distinctive regal air of the Stuarts. Fortunately he had not inherited his father's rather weak chin; but bore closer resemblance to his great-uncle Charles II as a boy. He was very tall for his age and moved with unusual feline grace. When his mind was made up nothing could bend him, but he was thoughtful and tolerant. The only thing he could never stand was any mention of the Falcon. He would close his lips tight and his eyes remained fixed while the virtues of his supposed sire were extolled.

'Will you not come into the sun, Duncan? We have had so many miserable days this year. Much as I love my Lakeland, the climate . . .' Analee shuddered. 'I think when you go to Oxford I shall come to London for a while and then, when the war is over, I am going to visit my father in Spain.'

'Alone, Mama?'

She looked at him with surprise. 'Alone? Well, if you mean my servants and maybe Clare . . .'

Duncan folded his hands gravely in front of him, a slight colour to his cheeks. 'Mama, if I am speaking out of turn pray forgive me, and you, sir.' He bowed solemnly at Brent. 'But I have noticed how often Sir Brent is over here of late. I welcome his company, but I have reason to think he does not come to see me or my brother and sisters. It is you, Mama, he comes to see.'

915

Analee glanced at Brent, her expression half-hopeful, half-fearful. Brent was looking at Duncan, something of the same emotions showing on his own face. It seemed for a moment as though their future happiness was in the hands of this twelve-year-old, but very mature, boy.

'It is true I am excessively attached to your mama . . .' Brent began nervously.

'Then why do you not *marry* her, sir?'

For a moment there was silence accentuated by the sounds of laughter from the terrace below, the splash of water as the children played with the boat.

'You would *like* us to marry, Duncan?' Analee looked at her son through tears.

'I would like nothing better, Mama. You have been a widow too long, and I know you are lonely even though the best of mothers to us. Sir Brent seems like an excellent choice for you.'

'Oh, my darling, we are all of one mind,' she said, throwing her arms round his neck. 'It was your permission to do this very thing that we came to seek.'

'Then you have it, Mama, and my blessing,' Duncan said and he drew Brent also into his arms.

The only one who objected to her mother marrying again was Clare. She thought she was much too old to contemplate such a step, and Brent likewise she considered in his dotage. However, when they said that they would still like the opportunity to support each other in their senility, she grudgingly agreed.

The wedding, which was not long delayed, was a very quiet one in Keswick Church with only members of Analee's family and staff attending. Brent did not want any word of this to get to Delamain Castle before they had seen Morella.

He lay alongside her and she looked at him with wonder, his long lissom body with its fine hairs, the big tuft at his groin out of which that interesting appendage was slowly growing to an enormous size. Morella gazed at it with astonishment.

Although she was in no doubt about wishing to shed her virginity, she had undressed completely with some show of reluctance despite Timothy's eager help, especially when it came to exposing her breasts to those excited male eyes.

'Do it quickly,' Morella demanded urgently. 'Because I need you.' And, with unmaidenly enthusiasm as well as a natural instinct, she lay back and he positioned himself upon her.

Suddenly there was a violent slap on his back and Timothy's senses reeled. A further cuff came to his head and he felt dizzy and sick. The fierce beating of his heart from desire turned into panic, and he rolled off Morella and lay gasping on the ground.

Reyora stood over them with a large stick in her hand and behind her, peeping eagerly through the opening to the tent, was a giggling group of onlookers. The stick thudded on Timothy again and he tried to roll away from her.

'Reyora, please!' Morella cried. 'You will kill him!'

'Death is *too* good for him, that is what,' Reyora snarled, turning to the tent flap and brandishing her stick. 'Get away, all of you. Get away!' The crowd reluctantly retired from the interesting spectacle and Reyora turned threateningly to Timothy again, throwing him his breeches which lay on the floor by Morella's crumpled, hastily shed clothes.

'Well, did you penetrate her?'

'No, Reyora.'

'Do you swear it?'

'I swear,' Timothy gasped.

'Well, it seems that you were lucky,' she said, straightening up. 'Thank God I was in time, for if you had I would have called such a curse down upon you that your over-eager member would have withered and fallen off.' She shook a finger at him. 'And *that's* what will happen if you ever touch her again. I am here to look after her in place of her mother and father. What would they think of me if she was deflowered within my own tent!'

'We thought you were in Penrith, Reyora.'

'Well I changed my mind! Thank goodness I did or I would never have looked her parents in the eyes again, especially her mother whom I love so much. Now get up and get dressed, you shameless pair. And wait until I see your mother, Timothy. You'll get such a hiding, I'll guarantee that. Morella, you are sent for to go to Delamain Castle and I am to take you there whether you like it or not.'

'I won't go,' Morella said.

'Oh yes you will. You have been here too long. I wrote a month ago and told your father so; but he had other things on his mind it seems. Besides, it is nearly winter and you will find it very different from the hot summer we have had.'

'Oh, Reyora.' Morella threw herself into the older woman's arms. '*Please* do not send me back!'

'I have to, my dear,' Reyora said, her expression softening. 'After what I have seen I know your blood is too hot for you to remain here. There is too much temptation for Timothy – and for you! I have been anxious about you too often, and something made me turn back as I started on my way. After what I nearly saw . . .' Reyora put her hand over her eyes as though to banish the awful sight. 'How near you came. Oh, my God. Yes, I think your parents have in mind to send you somewhere to cool your blood, and high time, too.'

'Well, they *won't*!' Morella said, but she did as she was bid all the same and finished dressing while Timothy was given a fresh smack on the backside with Reyora's stick and sent on his way.

Brent chastely pecked his daughter on the cheek, his arms lightly on her shoulders. The cheek was very cold and she was pale beneath the tan she had acquired in the camp. She had not smiled at all as Reyora had ushered her into their presence, but had stared rebelliously at Brent and Analee who were discomforted enough themselves.

After Brent had kissed her he stepped back, and Analee went over to her, embracing her more warmly. 'You look well, Morella.'

'I am well. I did not want to come back!' She stamped her foot and Reyora looked at her severely, a warning gleam in her eyes. She had promised Morella that if she was rude to her mother and father she would tell them about the incident in the tent.

'But you cannot stay there forever, my dear,' Analee said nervously.

'Why not?'

'Because we do not wish it. We have something to tell you, Morella. I hope it will please you.' Morella looked at her sulkily and Analee met her eyes. 'Your father and I are married, Morella.

Last week in Keswick. He has thus legitimized you and made an honest woman of me, at last. You are now legally Morella Delamain and I Lady Delamain . . . still a lady,' Analee said with a smile, 'but no longer a marchioness.'

'But, my dear, you said it did not matter,' Brent protested.

'Of course it does not. I was joking, trying to introduce a little levity into this solemn proceeding.' Analee took his arm fondly. 'Well, Morella, I hope it pleases you. We would have liked you to come to our wedding, but we did not know what to do for the best. It is not easy to understand you.'

Morella sat down and stared at her parents open-mouthed. 'Married?' she said.

'Aye, wed. Legally before a parson and witnesses. Just a quiet ceremony. It is something we have long wanted. Not only for you, but for ourselves, too. My other children are happy, they love Brent and you will now have a whole family of brothers and sisters.'

Morella burst into tears. Brent and Analee looked anxiously at each other, then at Reyora. Analee went to her daughter and knelt by her, her rich silken gown rustling as she did.

'My dear, we do want you to be happy. We love you so much. You will have what you have always wanted, a large family, your own parents united. Is it too late to begin again, Morella, to undo the misunderstandings of the past?'

Morella leaned against Analee and sobbed more loudly. Analee held her head against her breast and stroked her hair, thinking this was the first time she had held her like this, mother and daughter knowing each other. She put her chin on Morella's head and murmured, 'Would you like us to be alone?'

Morella shook her head. 'No . . . no. I don't know why I am crying. I don't know whether I am happy or sad. You see . . . Mama,' she looked at Analee into whose eyes tears sprang at the word 'Mama' used by her for the first time, 'I am in love, too! I want to marry Timothy Buckland. Oh, Mama, do say "yes" and then I will be very nice to you and . . . Papa.' She looked at Brent, bestowing on him a calculating smile of great charm.

'Marry?' Analee said, staring hard at Reyora.

'We are so in love, Mama, and you who know all about love, you will understand. He says we can have a gypsy wedding in the

919

camp and there will be music and dancing and, oh, Mama, we are going to earn our living as you did, dancing in the taverns. We thought you might ask us to dance here at the Castle and perhaps at Falcon's Keep?' She looked hopefully at her parents one after the other while Brent, who had tried hard to control himself, burst out laughing.

'But, Morella, you are an heiress! You are my lawful child. You will inherit great wealth one day.'

'But it does not matter, Papa.' Morella stared at him thinking as she did how *old* he looked. The memory of the agile young body of Timothy Buckland haunted her, his rippling skin, his flat pink nipples. How could she ever have imagined this *old* man before her . . . inwardly she shuddered.

'It does not matter at all. I want to live as Mama did.'

'Well, you can't,' Brent said, aware of the expression in her eyes, and relieved to see it. He could now exercise his full parental authority. 'And that is all there is to be said.'

'But, Papa, I am in *love*.'

'You are also sixteen,' Brent said sternly, 'and a minor. I hope you will never want to marry a gypsy, but if you do you cannot until you are twenty-one, and that is final.'

Morella stuck her chin out at him, but Analee put a hand round her waist, still kneeling beside her. 'I see you two are too alike. Stubborn. Morella, seeing that this is intended to be a happy family occasion *I* have a plan. Now listen to me.' She held up a hand gleaming with the sapphires and diamonds that Brent had given her as a wedding present. She smelt warm and fragrant, Morella thought, and memories of old suddenly came back to her . . . the beautiful lady who had come to call, looked at her so tenderly and held her in her arms. Yes, she had always been her mother, she had always wanted her – the women she had dreamed about, whom she had instinctively known was waiting for her. She leaned a little nearer to her and Analee felt the gesture and her heart leapt with joy. Morella needed her; she was going to trust her.

'Listen to me, my darling. I am not saying you *cannot* ever marry Timothy, I am sure he is a fine young man; but not just *yet*. Your father and I would like you to spend a little time in Paris.'

'Paris?' Morella's expression froze. 'So far from Timothy?'

'In a convent.'

'A convent!' Morella leapt up and stared at her mother, her eyes blazing. 'A *convent*?'

'Not as a *nun*, my dear, but as a young lady learning good manners and how to embroider and such – an education for a lady that I missed myself. It is very common for daughters of the aristocracy to be finished on the Continent, and now that things are more peaceful we would like you to spend a year or two with your Aunt Mary, your father's first wife, who is related to you, as she was his first cousin.'

'I never knew I had an aunt who was a nun,' Morella grumbled, clearly not enchanted with the idea.

'Well you have. There are all sorts of relatives you don't know about and what a joy it will be discovering them. Now Paris will be such fun, Morella, after the war! I had a wonderful time there in 1748 with my late husband. We went to balls and met the King and Madame de Pompadour who was greatly taken with the Falcon and most kind to me. Although I understand her health is not good, I am sure she would be delighted to receive you, and she still has the favour of the King. Please, Morella, it is a good idea. It will give you time to make up your mind and learn a little about the world. You have been painfully cut off here. If, when you come back, you feel about Timothy as you do now, well I am sure your father can have no objection . . .'

Analee glanced at Brent who clearly would object very much, if his face was anything to go by. She quickly looked away again. She felt she was going to have a hard time in cementing relations between father and daughter who, now that their mutual infatuation had become a matter of repugnance to both of them, clearly did not see eye to eye. She could see that Brent would be a strict parent, and Morella . . . well, she was her mother's daughter after all.

'Well,' Morella said with a grimace, 'If that is what you want I will do it. I would *quite* like to see Paris, but I tell you I am quite determined to marry Timothy and lead the life of a gypsy just as soon as I can. I will wait for him all my life if need be.' She flung back her golden head and gazed defiantly at everyone in the room.

Mother Mary Gertrude could see at once that she was a spirited girl and doubtless she would have trouble with her, but she liked

921

her. She was the image of Brent. She smiled at her and took her hand.

'I think we shall get on,' she said.

'I think so too,' Morella said, quite surprised by this nice aunt who must have been pretty and still had a beautiful smile.

'It is not as quiet as you think. We have some very sweet girls here from the best families all over the Continent.'

'I intend to marry a gypsy when I go home,' Morella said. 'I am going to live in a gypsy camp and wear gypsy clothes, and have gypsy babies . . . eventually.'

'Well, doubtless the girls will be very intrigued to hear that, and perhaps a little envious.' Mary looked over her head and smiled at Morella's parents sitting nervously behind her. 'I am sure you will have a lot of them visiting you in your new home.'

Morella gazed suspiciously at her aunt. She was not quite sure whether she was mocking her or not.

Analee stood up. 'I can see you two will get on. I knew you would. We are to stay for a few weeks in Paris, Mary, to see old friends. Brent has taken a house for us near the Bois. So we shall see that Morella settles down. Mr Pitt, having learnt of our intended visit, has even asked Brent to engage in a little diplomacy while we are here. He is very anxious for the war to be over.'

'Are not we all?' Mary said piously. 'We have petitioned Heaven for so long. God must be deaf. But I should not say that. Now, my dear Morella, I am going to get one of the girls to show you to your room and unpack while I have a word with your dear mama and papa.'

Mary rang a little bell and a lay sister entered. 'Sister, would you take Miss Delamain to the Comtesse de Beauséjour? She is waiting for her in her room.'

'Yes, Mother.' The sister smiled, bobbed at Morella and took her arm. Morella glanced anxiously at her parents who smiled encouragingly.

'Do not worry,' Brent said. 'I shan't make you take the veil.'

Morella stuck her tongue out at him before turning her back and following the nun out of the room.

'She is a lovely girl,' Mary said. 'I knew about her from Emma.'

'But not that she was our daughter?'

'I knew there was *something* special about her. I have often

922

prayed for her. I know not why. But, Analee and Brent, I am so happy that at last what you have always wanted has come to pass. Believe me, I am overjoyed.'

'I do believe you, Mary.' Analee smiled gratefully. 'I think you are really happy in your vocation and am I wrong in thinking that you are advanced in the hierarchy of your order? *Mother* Mary Gertrude?'

'I am professed now,' Mary said. 'We have to serve many years as a novice. When we take our final vows we are given the title "mother". We are choir nuns and sing the Divine Office in the choir. I am also to be in charge of the novices, to instruct them in the duties of our faith and our holy Rule. But what is this about Morella and a *gypsy*?'

'Oh, Morella is always in love,' Analee said airily. 'Her father and I are hoping it will pass in two years. I, naturally, have nothing against gypsies myself, but Brent hopes for a more, er, suitable marriage . . . though he who takes Morella will need a strong head, firm hands and a warm heart. We hope she will meet a number of interesting young men in Paris to take her mind off Timothy. But have her carefully chaperoned, Mary. She is very . . . hot blooded.' Analee glanced at Brent, who averted his eyes.

'Oh I will take the greatest care of her, never fear. Most of our girls here are young puppies. Alas, very few of them feel called to serve God and take the veil. They are never allowed to see young men without the closest supervision.' Mary smiled and moved her chair closer. 'Now, my dears, I have some very particular news for you. We have here under our roof a very important Personage. I know you will want to see him.'

'Oh?' Brent and Analee looked at each other.

'His Royal Highness Prince Charles is sheltering here. You know that his common-law wife Mistress Clementina Walkinshaw left him last year with their six-year-old daughter Charlotte? He has since then scoured the country for her and seeks her in every convent.'

'But do you know where she is?'

'No I do not and I do not want to. It is some convent in Paris, but I know not which. She has very powerful patrons. Some say King James in Rome himself supports her. But His Royal Highness is *here*! We could not deny him refuge, poor man. Besides, our Reverend Mother is a member of a distinguished English family impoverished and exiled by long support of the Stuarts. A family like the Allonbys.'

'But how long will he remain?' Analee said incredulously.

'Until a safe way can be found for him to leave Paris. He has never ceased his intrigues, of course. He has grown rather fat and drinks copiously, which is why she left him. He treated her vilely – but I still have some love for him. Do you not?'

'Yes,' Analee whispered.

'No,' Brent declared, standing up. 'I do not; most decidedly I do not. I have no wish to see him. I too knew of the foul way he treated this woman of good family who bore him a child, who gave everything up for him. I stayed in their house in Switzerland and saw myself how he abused her. I have finished with the Prince. I have no desire to see him. I have made a new life.'

'But, Brent, for the sake of the past?' Analee's eyes were pleading.

'The past is finished, Analee. I have made my peace with the English King, who has been gracious enough to indicate he will receive us together at court when we return. Mr Pitt has charged me with very delicate diplomatic negotiations. Do you think I want it put about that I have consorted with the young Pretender in Paris? No I do not, and I forbid you likewise.'

Brent looked at her severely and Analee bowed her head, acknowledging once more the absolute rights of a husband over her very existence.

Mary greeted her at the side door and drew her in.

'Where is your carriage?'

'I came by cab.'

'It is *very* dangerous.'

'I am used to danger, Mary. My servant will wait outside and call another cab when I am ready.'

Mary held up her candle and gazed at Analee. 'Does he know?'

'Brent? Of course not. He is dining with the Duc de Choiseul. Do you know, Mary, he has developed a taste for politics? I believe he will foresake the life of a country gentleman as soon as he can. Every day, unfortunately, he gets more and more like the Falcon in some ways.'

'Oh?' Mary looked at her in surprise.

'I only mean in his liking for this kind of life,' Analee said quickly. 'In other ways no, I am glad to say. I believe him to be very faithful, as I am. His eyes never stray and I don't think they will. He gives me a security in love I never enjoyed before.'

'He always loved you,' Mary said with resignation, the scorned woman momentarily showing through the sombre habit of Mother Mary Gertrude.

'He is also a devoted family man,' Analee went on quickly. 'My children love him – well Clare is a *little* jealous perhaps. I think she considers me in my dotage and too old to marry again.'

'But you are still a young woman in your thirties!'

'Thirty-six, Mary. It seems a great age to a girl of fourteen.'

'I hope you and Brent will have children of your own, more children.'

'I think he would like it,' Analee agreed. 'It is not impossible, though doubtless my eldest daughters would be shocked by the idea. He *would* like an heir. It is understandable because there is still that distant cousin who stands to inherit Delamain Castle and all its wealth if Brent has no son.'

The thought of motherhood all over again was slightly daunting to Analee, whose youngest child, Beyrick, was now a sturdy eleven-year-old. But Brent *did* want a son and she wanted to give him one if only as an expression of their deep and profound love. Brent had proved to be right. Their passion was not spent and it renewed itself over and over again in endless manifestations of mutual love and regard.

She put a hand lightly on her belly, wondering if she had already detected signs of quickening life and gazed at Mary, who smiled.

'And you, you want a symbol of your love. It is understandable. I hope your womb will prove fruitful, Analee. I will pray for you. Now come. The Prince is eager to see you.'

'And I felt I *had* to see him.'

'He is not the man he was.' With a warning look Mary led her swiftly, silently along the corridors of the convent, dimly lit and smelling of beeswax and candle grease. The statues with their lamps in front of them loomed out of the dark like ghostly emanations, and several times Analee was surprised and rather frightened.

'It makes me quite nervous,' she said.

925

'It is not always as dark as this. It is on account of the hour. We go to bed very early because we get up before dawn. Now here is the Prince's room. I will wait for you outside.' Mary stopped and, shielding her candle, knocked quietly on the door before standing aside to allow Analee to go in.

The Prince was sitting by the fire. Analee hardly recognized him. He had grown very fat and his face had a debauched expression that had replaced the nobility she always associated with him.

She knelt before him and took his hand. 'Your Royal Highness.'

The Prince started up as though he had not heard her enter and gazed at her for a long while. 'Ah, it is Lady Falconer! Now, let me see . . . Paris, oh, about ten years ago, was it not?'

'1748, Your Royal Highness.'

'Ah yes, I remember it.' A lecherous look came into the Prince's rheumy eyes and he lowered his gaze fixedly to her bosom. 'Still as beautiful as ever, Lady Falconer. They called you the Enchantress. Indeed you were.'

'It is Lady Delamain now, sir. I married Sir Brent after he succeeded his brother.'

The Prince's expression grew petulant.'Oh, yes. Brent Delamain, once a loyal supporter, now a traitor like the rest.'

'He is no traitor, sir.'

'They are *all* traitors who left me. I am alone, Lady Falconer, alone in the world. Did you know that?'

'I had heard that good times still do not attend your Royal Highness. I am very sorry.'

'My mistress left me, Lady Falconer . . .'

'Delamain, sir, Analee Delamain.'

'Well I liked not *him* either; the Falcon, I mean. I was delighted to hear of his death. Good riddance.'

Analee lowered her eyes, blushing with anger. She was sorry she had come. This gross, inebriate man bore no resemblance to the hero of her memory – Duncan's father.

'You may get off your knees, Lady Delamain, and pour me some more whisky.' The Prince held out his glass. 'I am uncommonly fond of this stuff. It is all I have. It makes the world barely tolerable. Yes, she left me, craven whore. You know she gave herself to me without the marriage bond? What *lady* would do a thing like that? I ask you? She was forever bragging that she came from the Scottish nobility. She was always begging me to marry her; but no, I have my sights on a Princess of France. It will happen, you will see. Those old hags, the unmarried daughters of the King, will have anybody, and I am not *anybody*,' the Prince added hastily, swallowing his drink as if to blot out the memory of the King's unmarriageable daughters. 'You can be sure Lady . . . Analee, I will yet sit upon the throne of England; then see Sir Brent Delamain and others like him come running. I will put them all in the Tower, I can tell you. Aye, all of them. Never forget, my father was the *son* of the last Stuart King of England, James II. These Hanoverian Georges are mere upstarts.'

The Prince lifted the bottle by his side and poured a glassful of whisky. 'Ah yes, she took my daughter. I had a daughter, you know, Charlotte. I loved her. She took my daughter. I will never forgive her for that. Never!' He leaned back and closed his eyes, a tired man only just forty but prematurely aged. 'If only I had a son.' He opened his eyes and stared at her. 'Do you know I think if I had married properly and had a son it would have made all the difference to me, all the difference in the world.'

The tears came into Analee's eyes as she thought of beautiful young Duncan with all the world before him, and this pathetic hopeless man, his father. Yet he had once been a great man, a brave Prince. His only misfortune had been the times into which he had been born, the circumstances of his sad life. He carried the blood of the Stuarts in him and this blood flowed on in her son. How could she not be proud?

'God grant that you will wed as you wish, sir, maybe a Princess of France, and have sons.'

'Yes, King Louis wishes it, I know,' the Prince said, closing his eyes. 'By God, I am very tired, Lady Delamain. Your husband is not with you?'

'No, sir.'

'He did not wish to see me, I suppose. No one does. I have few friends. Will *you* be loyal, Lady Delamain?'

'Always, sir.' She knelt again and took his hands. 'I will always honour your memory and that of your Royal House.'

'God bless you, Lady Delamain.' The Prince yawned drunkenly and began to unbutton his coat. 'Thank you for coming. It is good to know I have some friends left.'

'Thank you, sir.' she whispered. 'Thank you for everything.'

But the Prince did not seem to hear her. He waved her away and began to shake off his boots, pressing the toe of one against the heel of the other. 'As you go out tell my valet to come in and put me to bed,' he said.

She rose and went slowly to the door. There were two empty bottles of whisky on the table together with some remnants of food. The nuns were good to him. He could only rely now on people's charity. But he still had his pride. She knew he had no valet, that he was here on his own. She stood by the door and looked at him before knocking on it to bid Mary unlock it.

Suddenly there arose before her a vision of Brent, her husband and lover, his blue eyes alight as he made love to her. She had a mental image of his vigorous, youthful body and the comparison between him and this sad dissolute man in front of her was almost grotesque. She yearned to get back to Brent's arms, to enfold him to her breast, to smother his face with her kisses. The Prince was the past and Brent was the present and the future. The future for as long as she could see. What was more it was a happy, secure future. Of that she had no doubt, something that she could never say of her relationship with the man she had also once loved – the Falcon.

Yes, the Prince was the past; the Falcon was the past, even though in herself and her children she retained something of him and always would. She caught her breath, anxious to be with Brent, to reassure herself and him that the past was indeed gone and the future only beautiful.

'Goodbye, Your Royal Highness,' she whispered urgently.

He suddenly looked at her sharply and sat up. 'I remember it now,' he said. 'I recall it well. Aye, Analee. I asked you to be my mistress. Well, you would have done a better job than the other one. I am sure you would have given me sons. I might have married *you*.' He leaned back again and waved his hand. 'Farewell, Analee. Farewell, Enchantress.' He kissed the tips of his shaking fingers and gave her a bleary smile as his hand flopped by his side.

Analee tapped on the door and asked to be let out. As it opened she glanced again at the Prince. But the last hope of the Royal House of Stuart was fast asleep.